More GREAT GHOST STORIES

D0715729

More GREAT GHOST STORIES

Edited by John Cann

CHANCELLOR
PRESS

First published in 1966 by Odhams Books

Previously published (1994) as *50 Great Ghost Stories* by
Chancellor Press, an imprint of Bounty Books,
a division of Octopus Publishing Group,
2-4 Heron Quays, London E14 4JP

Reprinted 2002, 2005, 2006 (twice)

ISBN-13: 978-0-753707-22-7
ISBN-10: 0-753707-22-5

A CIP catalogue record for this book is available
from the British Library

Printed in Great Britain by Mackays of Chatham

Contents

CONTENTS

CONTENTS

Editor's Note

In the process of sifting the material for a book such as this, one becomes aware inevitably of the amount of evidence there is in support of ghosts. (I use the word "ghosts" not only in its normally accepted meaning of the ethereal presentation of a dead person to the living, but in the wider sense of psychic manifestations generally —precognition, telepathy, astral wanderings, clairvoyance, clairaudience, the psychical propulsion of physical objects, etc.)

Scientific circles, for so long sceptical, have shown a greater tendency than ever before to believe that there may be at least a field here for investigation. The Society for Psychical Research in London made a start in 1882; the researches of J. B. Rhine at Duke University have been notable, whilst in Europe the work of Whately Carington and S. G. Soal has attracted attention; and the University of Utrecht has set up a laboratory for the study of parapsychological phenomena.

Distinguished men brought up in the disciplines of science, such as Sir Arthur Conan Doyle and Sir Oliver Lodge, have been among the whole-hearted believers in psychic phenomena and life beyond the grave. And in any event the orientation of science has changed to provide an atmosphere much more favourable to the existence of paranormal occurrences. The old Newtonian conception of a universe of three-dimensional space separated absolutely from time has given place in physics to a universe of space-time in which space and time are indissolubly linked.

Dunne in his absorbing study of precognition through dreams,* argues impressively for a four-dimensional "serial" universe in which the dreamer, freed from the waking habit of viewing time from moment to moment in a one-directional stream, slips into a four-dimensional space-time consciousness which allows him to travel freely about time both forwards and backwards. Such a consciousness extended occasionally into the waking state could account for such happenings as are recounted in some of the stories in this book—"The Ghosts of Versailles", " 'Steer Nor'West' ", "The Return of Richard Tarwell", and a number of others. (It is

**An Experiment with Time*, J. W. Dunne.

interesting to speculate about the changes in men's lives and attitudes if such a faculty were in the course of evolution to become as established in their mental structure as, say, rational thought.)

However, when all is said and done, this is a book intended neither to prove nor disprove anything but simply to entertain. And I hope the reader will feel that this is what it does.

JOHN CANNING

August, 1966

Ghosts of Ancient Egypt

The obsession which the ancient Egyptians had with the other world seems to have created powerful supernatural forces which have lasted for thousands of years. Some of the most sinister and potent ghostly activity reported in modern times stems from Ancient Egypt, whose ageless hauntings have spanned fifty centuries and more.

The Cult of the Dead, which originated in India, reached its apotheosis in Egypt. At first the Egyptians believed that only members of the royal family and certain chosen companions were privileged to enjoy eternal life. Later the hereafter became democratized and at first nobles and high officials, and finally all "good men" were permitted through the eternal gates.

It is strange that, for all their preoccupation with eternity, the Egyptians never evolved a sophisticated religion. They were not however alone in considering life on earth merely as a brief preparation for the great hereafter. Their chief god became Osiris, who ruled in the region of the dead and who was believed to have fathered all the Pharaohs. The Egyptians were so obsessed with this Cult of the Dead that they turned the teeming and fruitful valley of the Nile into a place devoted to the dead.

They believed that a soul could not enter the blessed region of Osiris unless his body remained intact in the place where he had lived on earth, and therefore very great importance was placed upon the preservation of the body and the inviolability of the tomb. To despoil a tomb and remove a mummy from its coffin was to the

Egyptians an act of terrible desecration. The awful and solemn ceremonies which took place at the entombment included the most terrible curses on the tomb-breakers, and these curses were inscribed upon the walls of the death chambers.

In view of the intensity of their feeling on this subject, it is not surprising that we hear stories of spirits disturbed in their eternal rest by the despoliation of their earthly tombs, perhaps many thousands of years after their burial, and returning to earth to seek vengeance.

The dread inscriptions on the tombs were supposed to have an especial potency owing to the deep belief the ancient Egyptians had in the magic of the written word. They believed that the very act of writing down the curses would ensure their effectiveness.

Such imprecations were made at the rich and splendid funeral of Tutenkhamen in the middle of the fourteenth century B.C. This unimportant sovereign was only eighteen at his death. He was the son-in-law and successor of Akhnaton, one of the most remarkable of the Pharaohs.

Both the splendour of Tutenkhamen's unspoiled tomb and his father-in-law's religious convictions, which shook Egypt to its foundations, had strange echoes in the twentieth century, with stories which suggested that those ancient Nile curses had a remarkable and far-reaching power.

Akhnaton forsook the ancient gods of Egypt—including the sacred Osiris—and worshipped the sun-god Aton. He abandoned Thebes, the magnificent city of the god Ammon, and transferred the country's religious centre to Al Amarna in the plain of Hermopolis, where he built splendid temples to Aton.

But the ancient religion was not readily abandoned by the ordinary superstitious Egyptians, and the old priesthood, though temporarily dispossessed and forced to remain silent, worked relentlessly in the background against the heretic Pharaoh.

Akhnaton is regarded by many as an enlightened prophet who foresaw the truth of monotheism, an inspired intellectual in an age of priest-ridden superstition. His Queen was the beautiful and famous Nefertiti. Akhnaton had no son, but six daughters who constantly appeared with him in the religious ceremonies at Amarna. Entirely wrapped up in his religious activities, Akhnaton neglected his country and lost his empire in Syria, which fell to the Hittite hordes, while Akhnaton wrote poems to Aton.

He had made many enemies in Egypt, where a dangerous situation was brewing. In an attempt to combat this, he married his eldest daughter to the young Tutenkhamen, one of his favourites, and whom he appointed co-regent with himself when the boy was merely twelve years of age.

Akhnaton was faced with family as well as national dissension. It seems certain that his Queen Nefertiti fell into disfavour, for it has been discovered that her name was removed from some of the family monuments at Amarna. The inference is that the family trouble was religious. This was reinforced by another more sensational story which was told later.

One of Akhnaton's daughters turned violently against her father over the religious question. Akhnaton is said to have treated her with shocking brutality and had her raped and killed. His priests then cut off her right hand and buried it secretly in the Valley of the Kings. As she had reverted to the old religion, this would effectively exclude her from entering the blessed region of Osiris as her body was not intact at her burial.

Akhnaton did not live for long, dying in 1358 B.C. in the seventeenth year of his reign, and at about the age of thirty. His son-in-law, Tutenkhamen, succeeded him and reigned for about six years and was consigned to his magnificent and famous tomb.

The hand of his sister-in-law remained buried in the secret place in the Valley of the Kings under a curse that it was never to be re-united to the body of the princess, who was thus excluded from paradise. For more than three thousand years apparently the princess awaited at the gates of Osiris, her inexhaustible vigil being finally rewarded in a remarkable, if incredible, manner.

The story was told by Count Louis Hamon, a well-known occultist of the day, that in the 1890s he was in Luxor where he became friendly with one of the local sheikhs. The sheikh caught malaria and Hamon was able to cure him. The sheikh expressed his gratitude by presenting to him a mummified hand which, he said, had belonged to a princess of Ancient Egypt, the daughter of Akhnaton, who had been killed and mutilated for opposing her father's heretical religious faith.

This curious gift did not in any way repulse Count Hamon, who had a great interest in the religion of ancient Egypt, the priests of which he believed possessed knowledge and power undreamed of by modern man. He thanked the grateful sheikh and added the mummified hand of the princess to his treasures and curiosities which he had collected during his world travels in search of the unknown and the unfathomable.

In the 1920s Hamon and his wife were living in England, and in

1922 he noticed that the hand which had been shrivelled and mummified for the last thirty-two centuries began to soften and to his amazement and incredulity blood appeared in the veins under the skin.

Hamon and his wife were not unnaturally disturbed at this miraculous development. The count was well acquainted with the workings of the occult, and he decided to bring the matter to a head by burning the hand on the night of Halloween. This is the night when witches and spirits are abroad, and the night, too, when according to some ancient tradition, the souls of the lost are released from their eternal bondage to return to the earth. Hamon knew the story of the daughter of Nefertiti and that according to her deeply-held religion she was one of the lost.

Hamon cast the hand on the fire and read over it prayers from the Egyptian Book of the Dead. Upon that very moment, he says, the doors burst open with a sudden uprising of wind and in the door-way stood the figure of the princess from Ancient Egypt.

Nefertiti's daughter made a splendid appearance in her ancient royal apparel, with the serpent of the House of the Pharaohs glittering on her head-dress. As she went over to the fire Hamon noticed that her right arm ended at the wrist, just as she had been mutilated those many centuries ago. The phantom bent over the fire, and then in a moment was gone. Instantly Hamon went to the fire and found that the mummified hand had also gone.

This was on the last day of October, 1922, and a few days later Hamon read that Lord Carnarvon's expedition had discovered the tomb of King Tutenkhamen in the Valley of the Kings.

Why did the princess's hand come to life at this particular moment during her eternal vigil outside the gates of Osiris? Count Hamon did not pretend to know the answer to this riddle, but he believed that the ancient Egyptians possessed strange and remarkable powers, and had the key to many mysteries unknown to modern man. He obviously connected this weird and fantastic story with the discovery by modern Egyptologists of the tomb of the princess's brother-in-law, Tutenkhamen.

Now this famous tomb had an unusual history. As everyone knows, the Egyptians had for centuries buried their kings in the pyramids, which were just huge shells of masonry built around the royal burial chamber. But they had been a singularly ineffective form of protection, for every pyramid had been plundered of its treasures by generations of tomb robbers, who thrived in Ancient Egypt undeterred by the awful curses laid by the priests upon those who disturb the holy sleep of the royal departed. The Pharaohs eventually abandoned pyramid burial and made their tombs in the cliffs of the Nile. Even so, the tomb plunderers sought them out, and at the time of the fall of the Egyptian Empire (1150 B.C.) not one royal tomb remained unplundered.

It was quite by accident that the burial place of Tutenkhamen remained undisturbed throughout the centuries. Shortly after his burial had taken place, tomb robbers broke into the splendid sepulchre, and were discovered in the act. The grim fate of the robbers can be left to the imagination. The loot was all replaced, with the exception of some of the gold vessels which apparently proved too much of a temptation for certain officials and mysteriously disappeared during the replacement of the treasures. After that the tomb remained undisturbed, and probably well guarded. Two hundred years later the excavations for the tomb of Rameses VI resulted in the tomb of Tutenkhamen being completely buried underneath tons of limestone rubble.

The actual discovery of the tomb on 4 November, 1922—four days after the princess retrieved the precious hand which would at long last gain her access to the realms of Osiris—was made by Howard Carter, a well-known Egyptologist whose expedition in the Nile Valley was financed by Lord Carnarvon. The richness and beauties of Tutenkhamen's tomb had long been told in legend. It was said that it had been filled with the most priceless treasures. A story had been told for centuries that Akhnaton had chosen Tutenkhamen to succeed him because he possessed some kind of supernatural powers, and that these powers had protected his sacred tomb throughout the ages. The opening of the tomb therefore was surrounded by foreboding from the start.

When he read of the imminent opening of Tutenkhamen's tomb Count Hamon wrote urgently to Lord Carnarvon recounting his fantastic experience with the hand of the dead Pharaoh's sister-in-law, and begged him not to defy the curse and enter the forbidden tomb, which he would do at the risk of his life.

"The ancient Egyptians possessed knowledge and powers of which we today have no comprehension," wrote Hamon. "Take care not to offend their spirits."

Carnarvon was at first so impressed by this warning that he decided not to open the tomb and tempt the ancient curse, but Carter would not listen. He had no intention of giving up years of labour on account of an ancient curse which was calculated to frighten the superstitious and the ignorant. Carter was so determined that Carnarvon gave in. After all, he had given his warning.

On 22 February, 1923, they entered the tomb, Carnarvon being first, followed by Carter (the order was apparently important), the event being accompanied by a blaze of world-wide publicity. This was the first and only time that such a tomb had been found intact, and even the archaeologists who knew more or less what to expect were astonished at the unparalleled magnificence of the tomb furnishings of the young Pharaoh.

It was a sombre moment when these artistic wonders and treasures of the ancient world were revealed once more to human eyes after their three-thousand-year entombment in the Nile cliffs. Tutenkhamen lay in a splendid sarcophagus of blue and gold. The outer coffin richly wrought in gold was uniquely beautiful. The mummy case, made in his likeness, was inlaid with gold and lapis lazuli.

For many long and devoted months Carter worked among these ancient and mysterious splendours, salvaging the magnificent treasure, most of which was put in the National Museum at Cairo. When he opened the mummy-case, he found that the consecration balm had through the centuries hardened into a pitchlike substance which had made the body adhere to the bottom of the golden coffin. The examination of the body showed that Tutenkhamen had been about eighteen years old, and no sign could be discovered that he had not met a natural death.

Carter immersed himself in these fascinating excavations which occupied him until 1924, completely undisturbed by the curse which was presumed to have descended upon him.

It is not to be supposed that such spirits as have an eternal vigil at these ancient places of burial are less perturbed when the plunder takes place in the interests of archaeology. Taking a mummy from its coffin was considered an act of the most appalling desecration, the perpetrator of which was threatened with swift and fearful retribution, whatever his motive might be.

During the excavation of Tutenkhamen's tomb Lord Carnarvon was bitten by a mosquito, and after several months of illness he died in Cairo on 5 April, 1923. A few years later his brother committed suicide and his stepmother died after another mysterious insect bite.

Naturally much was made of the ancient curse. But Carter, an inveterate tomb-opener, and who had done the real work of excavating Tutenkhamen's tomb, suffered no ill-effects and continued his work until 1939 when he died at the age of sixty-six.

But those who believe in the tomb curse say that it applies to the first man to enter the burial chamber, and Lord Carnarvon, whose expedition it was, claimed that honour himself and was swiftly struck down.

Nevertheless the fact remains that many tombs of the Pharaohs upon which the solemn curse was laid have been opened and plundered with apparent impunity throughout the ages. Carnarvon seems to have believed in the curse, and it has been observed that people who believe in curses are more likely to be struck down by them.

More effective was the curse laid upon those who handled the mummy-case of another princess of Ancient Egypt who had been a high-priestess in the Temple of Amon-Ra. She was supposed to have lived in Thebes in about 1600 B.C. The outside of the case bore her image worked in gold and enamel. It was in an unusually good state of preservation and was bought by the late Douglas Murray many years ago while on a visit to Egypt.

Murray knew nothing about the curse at the time, and though he confessed to a slight aversion of this object of ancient curiosity, he could not resist the temptation to acquire it, which he did and had it packed up and sent to London.

Much has been written about this particular mummy-case, and it has been said that nearly everyone who had anything to do with it suffered accident or misfortune. Certainly Douglas Murray came by a terrible accident when, a few days after he had bought it, he went on a shooting expedition up the Nile and the gun he was carrying exploded unaccountably in his hand. Murray lay in great agony while the boat was hastily turned round to return to Cairo for him to have urgent medical attention, but head-winds of unusual force persistently held them up and it was ten days before they reached Cairo, by which time gangrene had set in. Murray suffered weeks of agony in hospital and his arm had to be amputated above his elbow.

Disaster also befell his companions, both of whom died during the voyage back to England and were buried at sea. Two Egyptian servants who had handled the mummy-case also died within a year. When the ship arrived at Tilbury it was found that valuable Egyptian curiosities Murray had bought in Cairo had been stolen.

But the mummy-case was there awaiting him. Whatever he had lost, he had not lost that, and he said that when he had looked at the carved face of the priestess which was upon it, her eyes seemed to come to life and look at him with a malevolence that turned his blood cold. He promptly gave the fatal mummy-case away to a lady, upon whom disaster immediately befell. Her mother broke her leg and died after months of prolonged suffering. The lady lost her fiancé, who for no apparent reason declined to marry her. Her pets died and she became ill herself with an undiagnosable complaint which wasted her away so much that she feared death and instructed her lawyer to make her will.

The lawyer, hearing the story, agreed to make the will, but at the same time insisted on packing up the mummy-case and returning it to Douglas Murray. The lady thereupon recovered, but Murray, whose health was broken, wanted to have nothing more to do with the accursed relic, and presented it to the British Museum, which was presumably too impersonal and scientific an institution to be affected by such superstitions as ancient Egyptian curses.

But, it seems, everyone who had anything to do with this mummy-case encountered disaster in some shape or form. A photographer who took pictures of it, which when developed showed living, malevolent eyes in the carved face of the priestess, died mysteriously a few weeks later. Likewise an Egyptologist who looked after the exhibit while awaiting the Museum's decision to accept it, was shortly afterwards found dead in bed. The Museum finally accepted it and spent much time subsequently denying stories of strange and unaccountable things taking place in the Egyptian Section. Eventually they had it removed to the cellars.

Many other strange stories were told about this famous mummy-case. It was even said that the British Museum presented the unwanted thing to the New York Museum and sent it over on the ill-starred *Titanic*. But perhaps it is stretching things a little to blame the ancient Egyptians for that particular disaster.

Chased by a Prehistoric Horseman

Ghosts of pre-history are scarce. Most of them, one presumes, are so old that they have become worn out. The Devil is the exception who proves the rule.

I have never met a man who has seen a Druidic ghost under the standing stones of Stonehenge on a lonely night of moon and stars, but I know a strange, incredibly ancient grove of gnarled and witch-like oaks in an old park meadow at the back of a little manor-house on the edge of the Essex marshes. The church is tiny, forlorn and derelict. When I knew it first some of the window-panes were of horn. The nearby heronry is in a little wood surrounded by double moats. And in the park at the back of Hall and church where the lines of ancient oaks are planted as to pattern, there was, the legend says, once a Druid altar where blood ran.

I have had the shooting on that remote, marshland estate for many years. I have crossed that old, small park under the moon, in snow-mist, in bright sunlight and in the glimmer of dawn. It has an atmosphere like that of no other place I know. It literally smells of pre-history. But I have never seen a ghost of a Druid or of any man of Ancient Britain.

I know a pictish broch on a high moor above Donside in Aberdeenshire built like a great stone beehive. There dwelt the Little Men, the Picts, long before Scottish history was written. I would not care to sleep in that broch alone.

We may count the Pixies of Cornwall and Devon and the fairies of elsewhere not so much as prehistoric people since they belong to all time, but when one speaks of prehistoric ghosts one thinks of spectres of the Ancient Briton, the little Pict creeping through the heather, the dark Girvii of the Eastern fens and the rest of the tribesmen of pre-Roman days and the lower, more brutal types, of mankind who were their predecessors.

I know a lonely island called Vallay, across a wide, seaweed-strewn strand of sand and shining pools off the coast of North Uist in the Outer Hebrides. On that island stands a great empty house, alone with the winds and the booming surges. In the heart of the island is a hollow where you will see the ruined walls and downcast stones of beehive-shaped dwellings.

There I have shot curlew and golden plover, wild duck and the grey geese, and seen the raven hunt the tide-line and the golden eagle pass over, lordly in the high sun. Vallay is a rare place for wild birds and wild beauty. There are sheep upon it and cattle, wild-eyed as hawks. Once a rich man, something of a hermit, but a very good naturalist and a keen sportsman, lived in that great house which now stands empty. One day he was drowned and his body was cast up on the rocks. Since then no one has lived in the Great House.

A year or two back, when I was shooting on Vallay, I said to the gamekeeper and the ghillie with him:

"The tide's right. The geese will be in soon. There are thousands of duck out at sea waiting to come in to the lochan. We'll stay for the flight and go home by the moon."

They refused point-blank. Two strong Hebridean men who would round up a bull, climb a mountain, walk the bogs and moors all day, launch a boat in an Atlantic blow and think nothing of climbing up to an eagle's eyrie. But the thought of an hour of dusk, let alone full night, on Vallay terrified them. Not once, but several times, politely but firmly, they hustled me off the island and across the sands to North Uist long before the sun had set.

"Is it the ghost of the drowned laird?" I asked them. It was not. They confessed in the end that "the auld people, the wee men" came out of those ruined stone beehives under the moon. Not for a handful of five-pound notes would they stay a night on Vallay. The ghosts of pre-history walked there.

Here and there, particularly in downland country and in ancient woodlands, you will come across places which have more than a hint, more than a whisper, of Diana and her nymphs, of the ancient gods of Rome.

My lamented friend, the late Patrick Chalmers, that graceful poet of gun and rod who knew and loved the corners of forgotten England, wrote, in one of his enchanting verses, of the wind in the pine tops:

> Its song was of wayside altars (the pine-tops sighed like the surf),
> Of little shrines uplifted, of stone and scented turf,
> Of youths divine and immortal, of maids as white as the snow
> That glimmered among the thickets, a mort of years ago.
> All in the cool of dawn, all in the twilight grey,
> The gods they came from Italy along the Roman way.

But, alas, on ancient hills and in Druidic groves, on hill-top camps and moorland brochs, on Badbury Rings and Arbor Low, on Avebury Downs and by classic streams:

> The altar smoke it has drifted and faded afar on the hill;
> No wood-nymph haunts the hollows; the reedy pipes are still;
> No more the youth, Apollo, shall walk in the sunshine clear;
> No more the maid, Diana, shall follow the fallow-deer.

Nymphs and fairies, Picts and pixies survive as charming beliefs seen by few, immortalized by poets.

No one sings a song to the Ancient Briton, yet he was a triumph of survival. He lived in a land hideous with wolves. His only weapons were flint-tipped arrows, a flint axe or a bronze-shod spear. He was a master of the art of survival. Wolves, those grey forest skulkers, "the witches' horses", who galloped under the moon, were not his sole enemies. We cannot say, within a thousand years, when the Stone Age merged into the Bronze Age, but it is probable that the man of the Bronze Age had to fight not only the grey wolves of the forest who swept down upon his flocks, more terrible than the Assyrians in purple and gold, but against the brown bear, shambling from its cave. It is possible even that cave lions and sabre-toothed tigers made his life a private hell.

We do know that the Bronze Age man could tame and ride a horse, bare-backed and possibly without bit or bridle. Even more incredible, he tamed the giant aurochs, *bos primigenius*, that vast shaggy animal who dwarfed the American bison of today. That much we know from Lydekker.

During the Bronze Age, which according to Montelius lasted from 2000 B.C. to 800 B.C., three-quarters of England was dark with forests or drowned by swampy moors and misty fens, haunts of wolves and boars, brown bears and yellow fevers. The Ancient Briton not only had a job to live, but few places wherein he could live with comparative safety.

That is why so many of his barrows, tumuli, camps, weapons, cooking-pots, ornaments and pathetic household goods are found on the high chalk downs. Chalk meant few trees. Where there were few trees there were few wolves.

So the Ancient Briton built his huts, fortified his camp, tended his herds of sheep, swine and goats, trained his wild horses, knapped his flints and lived his life mainly on the bare chalk, the thymy downs. There the winds blew free. Larks sang. Harebells danced in the summer breeze, like fields of asphodel. Conies burrowed in the chalk and were there for the catching. The night dews filled the dew ponds with sweet water. His children gambolled on the short turf in the bright sun. His stockade of pointed stakes was a barrier by day against foes, even as his glinting fire, leaping in red and yellow tongues, was the terror of wolves by night.

Far below, in the valley or on the outflung green and sullen waves of the wealden plains, there lurked every sort of terror that could menace a man and his family. Up here on the downs, where a man might see for miles, ambush and sudden attack were not easy. Astride his fleet horse, bow in hand, dagger in belt, hound at heel, the Bronze Age man was, in his far-off, fustian way, a knightly fellow.

Now, although the chalk downs of Wiltshire and Gloucestershire, of Dorset and Hampshire and all those wide and windy miles of still-lovely England are studded with the burial mounds, the ancient camps and the shadows in the grass that mean their vanished homes, although Stonehenge still stands against the stars in ghastly grandeur and cromlech and dolemn tell the bloody tale of far-off sacrifices, ghosts and hauntings are few and far between.

Here and there the Romans left their spirits behind. I know of a centurion who still walks the Roman Strood between Mersea Island and the mainland, with ringing steps on moonlight nights, and I could take you to a mud-flat on the Thames where a Viking in winged helm wades ashore under the moon, in endless quest for his vanished longship. But although I have stood in Stonehenge by night, and walked the glimmering woodland aisles of that ancient wood of the Druids which they call Staverton Forest in East Suffolk, I have never met man or woman who had any true tale to tell of a ghost of Ancient Britain, of a haunting of pre-Saxon days, until there came a letter in the post in August, 1956. The writer was Mr R. C. C. Clay, who lives at the Manor House, Fovant, near Salisbury. Mr Clay is not only an extremely busy professional man with a practice which covers a wide extent of that country of chalk downs nd glimmering plains, but he is a Fellow of the Society of Antiquaries.

In his letter, Mr Clay said: "In response to your letter in the *Salisbury Journal* of 24 August, I am sending you an account of a personal encounter with a prehistoric horseman, just over the Dorset border. Three episodes with 'ghosts' in my own house, which were not witnessed by others, would not come within the scope of your inquiry and I have not included them."

Mr Clay then went on to give the following account of the appearance of a prehistoric horseman, probably of the Bronze Age. It is, I believe, unique in the annals of ghost-hunters. Here it is.

"In 1924, I was in charge of the excavations carried out by the Society of Antiquaries on the Late Bronze Urnfield at Pokesdown, near Bournemouth. Every afternoon I drove down to the site and returned at dusk.

"One evening I was motoring home along the straight road which cuts the open downland between Cranborne and Sixpenny Handley. I had reached the spot between the small clump of beeches on the east and the pine-wood on the west, where the road dips before rising to cross the Roman road from Badbury Rings to Old Sarum. I saw away to my right a horseman travelling on the downland towards Sixpenny Handley, that is to say, he was going in the same direction as I was going. Suddenly he turned his horse's head, and galloped as if to reach the road ahead of me, and to cut me off.

"I was so interested that I changed gear to slow down so that we should meet, and that I should be able to see who the man was. However, before I had drawn level with him, he turned his horse again to the north, and galloped along parallel to me and about fifty yards from the road.

"I could see that he was no ordinary horseman, for he had bare legs, and wore a long, loose cloak. His horse had a long mane and tail, but I could see neither bridle nor stirrup. His face was turned towards me, but I could not see his features. He seemed to be threatening me with some implement, which he waved in his right hand above his head.

"I now realized that he was a prehistoric man, and I did my best to identify the weapon so that I could date him. After travelling alongside my car for about one hundred yards, the rider and horse suddenly vanished. I noted the spot, and found next day, when I drove along the road in daylight, that it coincided with a low, round barrow which I had never noticed before.

"Many times afterwards at all hours of the day, when I was weary, and when I was alert, I tried to see my horseman again. I tried to find some bush or other object which my tired brain could have transformed into a horseman. I had no success.

"I made inquiries in the district, and after a few months, Mr Young, the well-known iron craftsman of Ebbesbourne Wake, told me that he had asked many of his friends in Sixpenny Handley if anyone had ever seen a ghost on the downs between the village and Cranborne, and that one old shepherd had replied:

" 'Do you mean the man on the horse that comes out of the opening in the pinewood?'

"A year or two later a friend of mine, a well-known archaeologist, wrote to me as follows:

" 'Your horseman has turned up again. Two girls, cycling from Handley to a dance at Cranborne one night lately, have complained to the police that a man on a horse had followed them over the downs and had frightened them.' "

This record is of the first importance. Not only is it vouched for by a highly qualified eye-witness, but it has the additional value of being corroborated by other witnesses. In short, it is probably the best and, possibly, the first example of a Stone Age or Bronze Age haunting in the country.

Two significant points emerge from the evidence. The first is that Mr Clay saw man and horse both suddenly vanish near "a low, round barrow". The second is that the old shepherd apparently knew the ghost well and had often seen it come "out of the opening in the pinewood. We may deduce from this, first, that the horseman had probably been mortally wounded whilst in the woodland —the eternal haunt and hiding-place of the enemies of his race and time—and secondly, that he lies buried, with his horse, "in the low, round barrow". Thus his spectral ride from the pinewood to the barrow probably signifies his last living journey on earth.

There is no doubt that men of the Bronze Age, probably chieftains, were often buried not only with their horses, but with a pig to give them pork, deer to give them venison and goats to give them milk in the life hereafter. Frequently they were incinerated before burial. When, for example, the Money Hill Barrow on Therfield Heath on the Cambridgeshire–Hertfordshire borders was excavated by Mr Beldam, the local squire, in 1861, he found a cist cut in the chalk, 2 feet long by 18 inches in depth and width, containing the cremated bones of a child aged about two years, placed in an elaborately decorated cinerary urn. The barrow, which was 15 feet high and 100 feet in diameter, was apparently a family "vault" of the Bronze Age, in which numerous people, presumably of a noble or chieftainly family, had been buried. When the diggers got down through successive layers of clay, charcoal, ashes and decayed turf, they found not only clear evidence of other human burials, but the bones of pig, horse, roe deer and goat. Similar evidences of domestic animals and deer, including horses, being buried in Bronze and Iron Age barrows are by no means uncommon. The chances are, therefore, that if Mr Clay's low, round barrow were excavated today we should discover the remains not only of the spectral horseman, but also of his horse.

Now comes a very different sort of haunting, but equally well authenticated, from more or less the same wide, bright country of chalk downs and fertile plains.

Nor far from the village of Langley Burrell, a few miles from Chippenham in Wiltshire, there stands on a hill a remarkable monument. It is a tall, stone column, toppped by the stone figure of a little old lady, with a basket of eggs and lace beside her. It is the visible memorial of Maud Heath, a village higgler, who died more than a century ago.

She walked each week to Chippenham market, sold her eggs and home-made lace, and walked home again, in winter dark and autumn rainstorms, to her cottage in the village street. More than once she waded waist-deep through swollen brooks. So towards the end of her days this indomitable old woman made a vow that, should she ever leave any money, it should be spent on making a good footpath from her village to Chippenham, so that other poor persons like herself might walk to market in winter in comfort.

Maud did, in fact, leave a small fortune. The footpath and the monument are the results.

Now comes the up-to-date story of this little old lady who died when the last century was very young. Mrs V. Carrington of Biddestone, near Chippenham, widow of the late Brigadier Carrington, D.S.O., O.B.E., has very kindly sent me a cutting of an article which she contributed to a local journal some little time ago. It concerns Maud Heath. Mrs Carrington wrote:

"Not so very long ago I returned from an excellent day's fox-hunting, and as the fox had been a good one, we had all enjoyed a splendid run—almost to the Wiltshire Downs.

"I was not one of the more fortunate ones who could telephone for my horse-box to bring me home, and I turned my weary horse towards Chippenham in which neighbourhood we then lived.

"Alas, my horse was very tired, to say nothing of its rider. Night coming on and it was getting darker and darker.

"Down the hill we almost stumbled, past Maud Heath on her monument and on along by her path.

"Soon the good and faithful friend who had carried me well got so tired he could only go at a walk, and I began to think we'd never get home.

"Suddenly, to my astonishment, he snorted and began prancing across the road.

"I thought this strange, knowing how very tired he had been only a few minutes before.

"Could it be a car coming up behind?—for there seemed a strange light shining on the very quaintest of old women walking a few yards ahead of us on the footpath. But no, there was no car in sight, neither could I hear one.

"On looking at the strange old lady, I wondered at her old-fashioned dress.

"Was it some eccentric old village woman walking with her basket to shop?

"The dress that I could see by the quite mauvish-yellow light on her was of a strange coarse material not made nowadays. Her headgear was unusual; her shawl . . . those odd little steps she took!

"But, above all, the basket at her side. I could see large, white eggs and thick, heavily-made lace hung out from the basket.

"After a good deal of cross words and rough handling I at last got my horse to trot.

"I tried to overtake the strange lady, but to my utter astonishment the figure in front kept exactly the same distance away.

"On coming into the high road, the old lady became one long, shining shadow, and disappeared over the hedge opposite.

"My horse, although in a 'muck sweat', as the grooms say, became again the weary animal he had been before, and the groom told me afterwards that the horse kept breaking out in a sweat all night.

"Had it been myself alone I might have thought I was mistaken, but my horse that night, I know, was convinced there was someone not human just in front of us.

"Had I seen the ghost of Maud Heath, or was this just one of those optical illusions sometimes experienced in certain conditions by tired persons?"

Hauntings Royal

Henry VIII's matrimonial reputation is not of the best. His dealings with his six wives, two of whom he did to death, have certainly put him, according to popular opinion, among the arch-villains of history.

When he died at the no great age of fifty-six, he was an enormous mass of flesh, so fat and diseased that he could hardly move. The royal corpse was taken from Westminster to Windsor, and the ponderous coffin was placed upon a trestle in Syon House. During the night so great was the weight of the contents that the coffin burst open and the dogs scrambled forward to lick the dead king's blood. Syon House had once been an Abbey. It had been appropriated by Henry during the Dissolution of the Monasteries, and many people thought that his body being thus dishonoured, as Ahab's had been, was of some dread significance.

Nevertheless Henry's spirit has apparently rested in peace. This has surprised some who thought that the ghost of such a man would surely return to haunt the scenes of his wrong-doings.

It is in fact the two wives he executed—Anne Boleyn and Catherine Howard—who have remained behind to haunt the world with their disturbed spirits, while the lord and master who put them to death sleeps peacefully in his royal tomb.

We should not be surprised at this apparent injustice. It is the wronged, rather than the wrong-doers, whose spirits are uneasy, and it is not for us to question this inequitable arrangement on the part of the eternal forces. Also, it should be remembered that neither of these young Queens of England could with all honesty maintain their innocence of the immorality with which they were charged. Resentful they undoubtedly were at the treatment Henry meted out to them, but their conduct during their lifetime was hardly befitting that of Queens of England. Whether this merited death is another matter and one we are not concerned with here.

Anne and Catherine were cousins. Neither had had the kind of sheltered upbringing which is usual for future Queens of England, though of course neither girl dreamed in her youth that she would become the King's Consort.

Anne's father was Sir Thomas Boleyn. Her mother was the daughter of Thomas Howard, the second Duke of Norfolk (who was also Catherine Howard's grandfather). At a tender age Anne went to the French Court and was exposed to the influence of an elegant and unmoral society. Her sister Mary became Henry's mistress, and when Henry cast his eyes desirously upon Anne, she thought she would go one better than Mary and become the King's wife. She had not been to Paris for nothing, and she succeeded in becoming Queen after playing a remarkable game of hard-to-get with this redoubtable seducer, which lasted six years. Of course she would never have become the Queen of England if Henry himself had not been desirous of taking another wife, Catherine of Aragon having failed to produce a male heir.

It certainly appeared at first that Anne had had a more glorious success than her sister. But though Mary lost her reputation, she at least kept her head on her shoulders. Poor Anne in the end lost both head and reputation. She was accused of the worst of crimes—incest and witchcraft as well as adultery.

Her true crime was the same as Catherine of Aragon's—the inability to produce the all-important male heir. Henry turned from her in disgust, not suspecting that the despised daughter she gave birth to would turn out to be England's finest Queen—a better monarch than he, and a child he certainly would have been proud that he fathered.

There has always been controversy over Anne's guilt, but of her instability of character there is general agreement. Becoming Queen went to her head. She became arrogant, overbearing, and caused endless trouble at Court by her jealousies and improprieties.

Anne Boleyn has not only become England's most famous ghost, but her name has been loaded with infamy these past four hundred years. She lived at a time when the dangers of withcraft and sorcery were looming large in men's minds. It was all started by Henry, who in his anxiety to rid himself of her said she had bewitched him and that he had been a victim of her devilish sorcery. The fact that she is said to have possessed a third nipple, and a sixth finger on her left hand, lent colour to the belief that she was a witch. They said that as a child she had a curious dislike of church-bells, an aversion common to witches apparently, which is not surprising considering that they are supposed to have entered into a pact with the Devil.

In order to marry Anne, Henry broke with Rome and thus brought Protestantism to England. Anne was never forgiven for her incidental part in bringing about the Reformation. Her character has been traduced by centuries of Roman Catholic writers. Unspeakable crimes were attributed to her. When Bishop Fisher was beheaded in 1536 for refusing to acknowledge Henry as head of the Church, they said she had his severed head brought to her on a dish so that she could stick a silver bodkin through the tongue. She was also accused of trying to poison Queen Catherine and the Princess Mary. The diplomatic gossips of the time freely branded "the concubine" as they called her, as a witch who was devoted to the foullest diabolism. These fantastic stories were put about by Papists who held her responsible for England breaking away from the true Church.

Whatever might be said against Anne Boleyn, she did not deserve these calumnies. She went to her death with a scornful courage which aroused great admiration. She wore a gay robe of damask over an underskirt of red and upon her wonderful black hair she had a pearl-embroidered hood. It was a clement May morning in 1536 as she stood there on the scaffold, her dark eyes shining, laughing in the very face of death, making a joke about her little neck and the skill of the executioner. Her bravery on the scaffold caused the Governor of the Tower, Sir William Kingston, to write: "I have seen many men and also women executed, and they all have been in great sorrow; and to my knowledge this lady has much joy and pleasure in death."

Of course this courage in the face of death was open to various interpretations by the superstitious minds of the age. There were some who thought that it merely proved that she was a witch, anxious to go to that other world to her true consort, the Prince of Darkness. A fanciful theory indeed.

But whatever be the truth of Anne Boleyn, her restless spirit has haunted the world ever since, and has been seen in various places, particularly at the several homes where she had lived. At Blickling

Hall in Norfolk her much-travelled ghost is said to make a spectacular appearance every year upon the anniversary of her death, driving up the avenue to the hall in a coach. She sits holding her head in her lap, and the coach is drawn by headless horses. The whole grisly equipage pulls up in front of Blickling Hall and then vanishes into the air. Phantom coaches and headless horses have by tradition been associated with witchcraft and devil worship.

She has also been seen driving furiously along the roads of Norfolk, headless in her spectral coach, followed by a strange blue light. Her ghost has also been reported in Kent, this time being driven up the avenue of Hever Castle at a furious pace in a funeral coach drawn by six black headless horses. Hever, a thirteenth-century castle near Edenbridge, was once her home. Here Henry wooed both Anne and her sister Mary. The great oak under which he courted Anne still stands, and they say that her ghost is seen there every Christmas-time.

The Rochford district of Essex is said to be haunted by the ghost of a headless witch, clad in a rich silken gown, and no one would go near the grounds of Rochford Hall for twelve nights after Christmas on account of a terrifying apparition in white which haunted the place. Witches were burnt as a rule, not beheaded, and they did not usually wear silken apparel. Anne Boleyn had lived at Rochford Hall when she was a girl, and this story may just have been put about by the superstitious countryfolk to add colour to the accusation that she was a witch.

But Anne's most persistent haunting is in the Tower where she met her death with such scornful courage. She was buried in the Church of St Peter ad Vincular, which is within the Tower itself. Many years later, it is said, her coffin was opened and she was identified by the remains of the famous—or infamous—sixth finger.

She is said to haunt this little church in particular when a death is imminent. A ghostly ritual is then held in the aisle.

This was witnessed by a nineteenth-century officer of the guard who noticed a light shining inside the church and asked the sentry outside the church what it was. The soldier said he did not know. Nor did he wish to investigate. Queer things took place inside that church, he said. The officer decided to investigate himself. He ordered the sentry to fetch a ladder. The officer mounted the ladder and peered into the window of the church.

The church was filled with an eerie glowing light, and the officer saw a procession of people dressed in Elizabethan costume moving along the aisle. At the head of the procession was a splendidly dressed and bejewelled woman whose face, the officer said, was like that of the portrait of Anne Boleyn. This phantom procession passed along the aisle, then suddenly vanished, together with the ghostly light by which it had been illuminated, leaving the little church in utter darkness.

It was noted that Anne was seen this time unmutilated, and as she had been at the height of her success and power. But her ghostly appearances as a rule are more horrific, and many soldiers on guard at the Tower have been terrified when they encountered her. In 1817 a sentry had a fatal heart attack after meeting her on a stairway, and in 1864 a soldier was court-martialled for being found asleep on duty. He claimed to have been in a swoon after encountering Anne Boleyn.

The story was told to an incredulous, half-amused court-martial. The man said he was at his post near the Lieutenant's Lodgings when he was suddenly confronted by a white figure. He made the usual challenge, but, receiving no reply, he made a thrust with his fixed bayonet, whereupon there was a "fiery flash" which ran up his rifle and gave him such a burning shock that he dropped the weapon. After that he remembered no more. Further questioned about the appearance of the figure in white, he said: "It was the figure of a woman wearing a queer-looking bonnet, but there wasn't no head inside the bonnet."

This description was greeted with laughter in court, but the amusement ceased when the offending soldier called evidence to corroborate what he said. Several witnesses told the court that they had seen a headless woman in white near the Lieutenant's Lodgings that night.

An officer gave sensational evidence to the effect that he was in his room in the Bloody Tower when he heard the challenge: "Who goes there?" He looked out of the window and saw the sentry confronted by a figure in white. He saw the sentry thrusting at the ghostly intruder with his bayonet. The figure, he said, not only walked through the bayonet, but through the sentry as well. He then saw the soldier collapse unconscious. The soldier was found in this position and accused of sleeping while on duty.

The court-martial found him not guilty and he was acquitted. Whether the court believed the story is not recorded, but they must have come to the conclusion that something inexplicable had been going on at the Tower that night.

Anne Boleyn's ghost apparently made another appearance at the Tower in 1933 when, according to newspaper reports, she walked straight into the bayonet of a guard and scared him so much that he dropped his rifle and fled from his post into the guardroom shouting for help.

Considering its grim history, there are relatively few ghosts at the Tower. One of them is said to be the unfortunate Margaret, Countess of Salisbury, another of Henry VIII's numerous victims. She was a niece of Edward IV, was the last of the Plantagenets, and had a better title to the throne of England than Henry himself, his father Henry VII having usurped it from its lawful inheritors.

The Countess of Salisbury's son, the famous Cardinal Pole, offended Henry by opposing his political religious policies. Henry determined to exterminate the whole family, and the Countess, who was sixty-eight, and certainly too near to the throne for Henry's comfort, was executed at the Tower in 1541.

It was perhaps the most macabre beheading on record. The venerable lady, who had done nothing to justify execution, was dragged, violently protesting, to the scaffold. Unlike most of Henry's victims she not only refused to make the usual hypocritical declaration of loyalty to the King, but she flatly refused to do any-thing which showed that she consented to her death. When she was told to lay her head on the block, she replied: "No, my head never committed treason. If you want it, you must take it as you can."

The executioner tried to grab her, but she darted round the block, tossing her head from side to side, while he struck at her with his axe, as did the guards with their weapons.

At last, brutally wounded, covered with blood, she was forcibly held down crying out:"Blessed are those who suffer persecution for righteousness's sake,"and the headsman hacked off her head.

There are those who claim to have seen this whole dreadful scene in a kind of spectral tableau at the Tower, a remarkable effort indeed on the part of the spirit world which would seem at times to have a decidedly theatrical bent.

Henry's vengeance fell upon the Boleyn family too, after he had executed Anne, but her father, Sir Thomas Boleyn, continued to live at Hever Castle after his daughter's death. He could not have had a very easy conscience about his craven behaviour, for he had publicly declared his belief in his daughter's guilt at the trial of her reputed lovers, as indeed did Anne's uncle, the Duke of Norfolk. Maybe they had to do this to save their own heads.

Anne's father has had no peace after his death apparently, for according to tradition he is doomed to ride the countryside pursued by hordes of screaming devils. After Henry had executed Anne's brother, Lord Rochford, it is said that his blood-bespattered, headless corpse was to be seen dragged across the countryside by four headless horses.

A few days after he had disposed of the unfortunate—but apparently not unhappy—Anne Boleyn, Henry married Jane Seymour, who died of puerperal fever in the following year (1537) after giving birth to the child who became Edward VI. It was said that her life was deliberately sacrificed by the performance of a Caesarean operation in order to ensure the safety of the precious boy heir.

It was said that Jane herself had an uneasy conscience concerning the circumstances in which she supplanted Anne, and that after her death her worried and anxious spirit remained earthbound seeking to make contact with the ghost of Anne. She is said to haunt the Silver Stick Gallery in Hampton Court Palace every year on the birthday of the baby prince whose birth had meant her death. Dressed in white, she carries a lighted candle in her hand, ascends the staircase leading to the Gallery, along which she is said to glide wreathed in a silvery light, to vanish from sight at the end of the gallery. All this, despite the fact that she had a most lavish funeral and 1,200 masses were paid for to ensure that her soul had the peace it was considered it deserved.

Unlike the formidable Anne Boleyn, Jane Seymour is an elusive ghost, and can be seen, it appears, only by those with extra-sensory perception.

In 1540 Henry was married briefly to Anne of Cleves, and in the following year he made Catherine Howard his Queen. She was Anne Boleyn's cousin, daughter of a younger son of the 2nd Duke of Norfolk, and was a lush attractive girl upon whom Henry doted. She was his "rose without a thorn", and he did not dream of the scandalous youth she had spent under the disorderly household of the ancient Duchess of Norfolk, where, unknown to her grace, Catherine indulged in fun and games with various young men of the household. Before Henry married her, she had been enjoyed by a variety of men from spinet-teachers to page-boys. Her reputation for immorality was the talk of the Court, and when she became Queen it could not be concealed from the King. Henry wept, but sent her to the block, together with her lovers, past and present. She had after all taken a lover after becoming his Queen and was thus guilty of treason.

Catherine, young and in love with her cousin Thomas Culpepper, did not want to die, and the story is told how when she was arrested at Hampton Court she broke away from the guards and ran along

a gallery to the chapel where Henry—"the professional widower"—
with a typical touch of Tudor hypocrisy, was on his knees praying
for her soul. She tried to get to him to make a last plea for her life,
but the guards seized her and dragged her screaming from the
chapel where Henry pretended not to notice the disturbance.

Shrieking and lamenting, Catherine was hurried from the royal
presence, into a barge and then down the Thames to the Tower, and,
on 13 February, 1542, to the block.

Many say that there was a Protestant conspiracy against Catherine
Howard, who came from a powerful Catholic family, the Norfolks.
Undoubtedly the Protestants feared any Romanist influence on the
King, and exploited Catherine's youthful indiscretions for their own
political ends. Unhappily for the foolish, amorous Catherine—a lovely
young girl married to a fat, diseased man twice her age—she provided her enemies with plenty of evidence with which to destroy her.

She went to her death bravely enough, but her young protesting
spirit soon returned to haunt Hampton Court Palace, where she
was seen time and time again running frantically along that same
gallery, pursued by spectral soldiers, her screams and shrieks chilling
the spines of those who heard them.

This Haunted Gallery was closed up as a consequence of this
formidable invasion by the other-worldly spirit of the hapless
Catherine, and for many years it was used as a lumber-room for
worn-out furniture and moth-eaten tapestries. For centuries the
rats and mice of that neglected part of Hampton Court seemed to
live happily with the unquiet spirit of Catherine, while the other
inhabitants of the old Palace retreated from the sound of her distressing screams.

In the twentieth century, however, the Office of Works, who
don't believe in ghosts, had the Haunted Gallery cleared out and
renovated, and it was opened to the public in April, 1918. Apparently
this assault on her old stomping-ground had the effect of laying
Catherine's noisy ghost, for she does not seem to have been seen or
heard since in the Haunted Gallery.

She has also been seen in more tranquil fashion flitting about the
famous Hampton Court gardens on sunny afternoons, re-living the
memories of more pleasant times before she was sent on her sad way
to the Tower.

Henry VIII, the arch-villain of all these beheadings—for apart
from her lovers past and present, some members of Catherine's
family lost their heads in the general mêlée of her execution—sleeps
peacefully in his grave. At least we have no reports to the contrary.

So does his son, born to Jane Seymour, the sickly, interesting, precociously clever Edward VI, who died of consumption in his sixteenth year. But there is an interesting ghost story connected with Edward VI's foster-mother.

It will be recalled that Edward's mother died as a consequence of his birth, being deliberately sacrificed, they said, in order to ensure the survival of the much more important heir to the throne. Henry appointed Mistress Sibell Penn as the child's foster-mother. Mrs Penn was an excellent woman in every respect, devoted to her charge, and respected by the King with whom she remained in high favour. When Edward himself came to the throne at the tender age of nine she became an important personage at Court, and when the young King died she mourned him as though he had been her own son. Afterwards she lived in a grace-and-favour residence at Hampton Court, dying in 1562 of smallpox and being buried in an imposing tomb in the old church of Hampton-on-Thames.

There the worthy soul rested in peace for a full two and a half centuries until in 1829 when the old church was demolished and the present church erected in its place. During the demolition, Mrs Penn's tomb was disturbed—some say rifled—and the stately monument which had been erected over it moved to another part of the church.

This disturbance of her tomb disturbed also, it seems, the soul of this excellent and respected matron who had been well rewarded on earth for her many virtues, and who had no reason to have her eternal peace disturbed. But disturbed it was.

Very soon after her grave had been so unceremoniously opened, Mrs Penn's ghost returned to her old rooms at Hampton Court. At first nothing but angry mutterings were heard and the sound of a spinning-wheel. These sounds were so persistent and mysterious that eventually the authorities made an investigation in the apartments were they seemed to be coming from. They discovered a secret door leading to a room which had been closed and forgotten for centuries, in which was found an ancient spinning-wheel together with a variety of sixteenth-century curiosities.

Investigation of the Hampton Court records showed that this room had been occupied by Mrs Penn who had often used a spinning-wheel. Indeed the old oak flooring in the forgotten room had been worn away by the treadle where it had touched the boards.

Mrs Penn's ghost has been seen several times since, and people sleeping in the Palace have been awoken by icy hands placed upon their faces, and over them bends Mrs Penn, a luminous figure clad in grey—a frightening experience.

The Phantoms of Littlecote

Littlecote is one of Wiltshire's most historic stately homes. It has had many owners, among them people distinguished by wealth or birth—or by sheer iniquity. The wicked and the famous have left their ghostly mark in those old rooms, corridors and staircases. Replete with legend, with whispers of satanic deeds and secret murders, Littlecote sits in its woodland splendour, oblivious to the passing years, haunted, they say, to the end of time by the wickedness of those who have lived there.

For two centuries or more Littlecote, which is near Hungerford, was owned by the Darrell family, and it was they who finally beghosted not only the house but also the neighbourhood—even as far as the Hungerford to Salisbury road.

Wild Will Darrell, an Elizabethan rake, is the villain of Littlecote. The Darrell family had acquired Littlecote early in the sixteenth century. Through Wild Will's crimes they lost it, and local legend has it that had it not been for him the Darrells would be living at Littlecote to this day. Latterly Littlecote was owned by the Wills family, Sir Ernest Wills dying there in 1958.

The Wills family were troubled by the ghost. When Major George Wills was staying there his dog began to bark in the middle of the night, awaking not only the Major, but the whole household. In vain the Major tried to pacify the dog. The animal stood in front of the closed bedroom door, its hair standing on end, quivering in terror.

The Major opened the door and saw the Littlecote phantom pass by—a woman in a shift, wringing her hands, appearing to be looking for someone.

The woman's spectral search had its quite horrible origin one night four hundred years previously. It began with a thunderous knocking upon the door of the cottage of a Mrs Barnes in the little Berkshire village of Great Shefford.

Now Mrs Barnes was known as the village gamp—a midwife of few scruples and even fewer qualifications. She was not unused to being aroused in the middle of the night to perform her doubtful services for the unwise as well as the under-privileged.

She opened her door to be confronted by two arrogant young men, warmly as well as expensively cloaked, while behind them a pair of furiously-driven horses steamed in the cold night air as they pawed the ground, straining at carriage traces.

Mrs Barnes did not like the look of her visitors. Moreover their request aroused Mrs Barnes's suspicions. She was required immediately to attend professionally upon a lady who lived not far from Great Shefford. But she must be taken there blindfolded and even permit herself to be conducted to the bedside blindfolded. When she asked who the lady might be, she was informed that it was Lady Knyvett.

Now it is not likely that Mrs Barnes believed this. She knew of Lady Knyvett, the wife of Sir Harry Knyvett, Bart., of Charlton. It was highly improbable that such a lady would call upon her services.

What finally made Mrs Barnes agree to the proposition was her natural cupidity. When gold was thrust into her hands, she agreed to attend upon the lady, whoever she might be, in the manner demanded of her.

A bandage was placed over her eyes and she was led to the carriage which was promptly driven off at a furious pace. She was unable to tell in which direction she was being taken. When the carriage finally stopped, she found herself being conducted into what was obviously a great mansion. She was led through rooms, through galleries and corridors, and up a staircase. Carefully the curious Mrs Barnes, now convinced that she was not at Lady Knyvett's, counted thirty-one steps.

Of all the great houses in the district, only Littlecote contained a staircase of thirty-one steps. Mrs Barnes did not know this at the time. Nor did she know the masked young lady lying in the four-poster in the bedroom where her bandage was finally removed.

Mrs Barnes only knew that the lady was unmarried, for no legitimate birth in a great house would take place in this manner.

She became aware that a man was awaiting in an ante-room, in the hearth of which a fierce fire was burning. Every now and then the impatient father—for who else could he be?—piled more fuel upon the roaring fire.

Quickly and unhygienically Mrs Barnes delivered the masked woman of her child. No sooner had this been done than the man strode in from the ante-room and seized the infant roughly from the midwife's hands.

He took it straight into the ante-room, placed the little body on the fire and crushed it into the burning coals with his foot. In a few moments the briefly-lived life was extinct, and in a little while more the small body was consumed by the flames.

Mrs Barnes was not a woman of great conscience or reputation, which was why she had been chosen, but she was not inhuman. She was outraged at this act of barbarity.

She screamed and to her screams were added those of the distracted and terrified mother. Their screams rang through stricken Littlecote, the inhabitants of which listened in fear, knowing that the master of the house was up to some fresh devilry.

Mrs Barnes did not know Wild Will Darrell. She described him as being tall and slender with a dark and angry face. This was a fair description and helped to confirm the tale she later told. Mrs Barnes did not even know that she was at Littlecote, though she must have had her suspicions, for the tales of what went on in that house were the talk of the countryside. She was certain only that she was not at Lady Knyvett's.

Having performed her duty, Mrs Barnes was then seized at Wild Will's command to be blindfolded once more. She was now terrified as well as angry. For all she knew, she might well be put to death herself as the witness of this outrage. Nevertheless she vowed that this child slayer should not go unpunished if it should ever be within her power to help bring him to justice.

There was little indeed that she could do. If she had an idea that she was at Littlecote she had no means of proving it. She did not know the face of the murderer, or of the men who had come for her, nor the identity of the now-stricken and appalled mother whose new-born had been so brutally destroyed practically before her eyes.

As they seized her, Mrs Barnes turned once more to the distracted mother, her hands clutching desperately at the chintz curtains of the four-poster on which the woman lay. The curtains had an unusual pattern, and with sudden inspiration Mrs Barnes snipped a piece out of them, surreptitiously and unobserved.

She was then blindfolded again and led back to the carriage, the piece of chintz clutched in her hand. Once again she counted the thirty-one steps of the staircase.

Then she was driven back to her cottage in Great Shefford where she was informed in a forcible manner of the dire consequences which would fall upon her if she spoke one word to a living soul of what had happened that night.

Thus intimidated, Mrs Barnes kept silent, no doubt considering herself fortunate in escaping with her life.

But she could not forget. The infamy of that night haunted her for the rest of her days. But it was not until she was on her deathbed, at last out of the reach of Wild Will, that she told the story to a magistrate named Bridges, who recorded it on paper.

Now Bridges was Wild Will Darrell's cousin, and in view of this family connexion it is not likely that he would have officially recorded Mrs Barnes's story had he not thought that there might be some truth in it. Her remembrance of a staircase of thirty-one steps, and the piece of the chintz curtain—found to fit exactly a hole in the curtains of a certain four-poster at Littlecote—bore out the sinister stories which had long been rumoured about Wild Will Darrell.

The Knyvetts now came into the story. Sir Harry Knyvett and Darrell were bad friends. Sir Harry had long complained about Darrell's wild behaviour at Littlecote.

There must have been great bitterness between the two families, which explains why Darrell slandered Lady Knyvett by trying to persuade the midwife that she was the masked lady who had been so inconveniently with child.

Sir Harry Knyvett wrote a letter to Sir John Thynne of Longleat, whose family took the title of the Marquess of Bath in 1789, and later became the Dukes of Bedford. This letter was found at Longleat in the 1870s and was written in 1578 about the time of the Barnes's deathbed confession. Its subject was the suspected crimes and wicked behaviour of Will Darrell which had scandalized the counties of Wiltshire and Berkshire.

In Sir John Thynne's household at Longleat was a man named Bonham, whose sister had become Darrell's mistress. The girl's treatment at Littlecote and the murder of at least one illegitimate child she had borne was widely known.

Was it not time, wrote Sir Harry Knyvett, that Mr Bonham

FIFTY GREAT GHOST STORIES

should be urged to do something about his sister's "usage at Will Darrell's, the birth of her children, how many there were, and what became of them, for that the report of the murder of one of them was increasing foully and would touch Will Darrell to the quick".

This letter seemed to substantiate the deathbed story of the Great Shefford gamp. Wild Will Darrell was brought to trial. But the evidence against him was pretty slender. The tragically used Miss Bonham was unwilling to give evidence against him, or had died, her restless spirit, they said, already haunting Littlecote in search of her murdered child.

Darrell escaped justice, mainly, it was thought, through bribery and corruption. Returning to Littlecote, he continued his wild and reckless life.

But he did not live for long, and was thrown from his horse while riding in Littlecote Park and killed instantly. It was said that his horse had seen the ghost of his victim and reared up in terror, throwing Darrell to his death.

Littlecote then passed out of the hands of the Darrell family, but Wild Will's phantom has never left the place of his crimes, orgies and misdeeds. He is said to haunt the ante-chamber where he burnt his unwanted child, and the infant's bloodstains have been reported to appear in some mysterious fashion every now and then upon the floor before the fireplace, shedding blood that was apparently never shed in life.

Wild Will has also been seen haunting the place where his horse threw him to his death at the sight of the infant its rider had murdered.

And in the long gallery of Littlecote walks the ghost of the inconsolable Miss Bonham in search of her child. The screams of mother and midwife on that terrible night have echoed through the rooms and galleries of Littlecote for centuries, and are heard to this day, if we are to believe numbers of persons over the intervening years who said that they have heard them.

Littlecote has exercised a strange supernatural fear over people who never see its ghosts. Its domestic staff have always been affected by the hauntings and have refused to go into certain rooms.

It is always difficult to keep staff in haunted houses, and there was once an order at Littlecote that on every sunny day each of its three hundred and sixty-five windows should be opened, and closed by nightfall. Only one maid could be persuaded to perform this duty as none of them would dare to go into the haunted rooms when it was getting dark. This particular maid confessed that these rooms filled her with an unaccountable fear.

In 1914 Princess Marie Louise had a strange experience at Littlecote which she told in her book, *My Memories of Six Reigns* (Evans Brothers).

Her lady-in-waiting, Mrs Evelyn Adams, was the cousin of Sir Ernest Wills, then the owner of Littlecote. The Princess had never been to the house, nor had she ever seen a drawing or a picture of it. Sir Ernest invited her to lunch.

The Princess motored over with Mrs Adams, and as they approached it she experienced that not-unknown sensation that she had been there before. Littlecote and its surroundings were quite new to her, or should have been, yet they were strikingly, disturbingly familiar. In some strange way she felt that she knew the place.

Luncheon was served in the great hall, in honour of the royal guest, who confessed both then and afterwards that every detail of the place was known to her.

Naturally talk reverted to the story of Wild Will Darrell and the tale told by the gamp of Great Shefford on her deathbed, and after lunch Sir Ernest offered to show the Princess over the house, an offer which the Princess eagerly accepted in view of her strange feeling of having been there before.

Finally they came to the long gallery where the ghost of the wretched Miss Bonham walks in search of her child. Lady Wills pointed to a door at the far end of the gallery and said that that was where Mrs Barnes came up.

"Oh no, you are quite mistaken," contradicted the Princess. "This is where she was brought up." She pointed to another door.

She now closed her eyes and walked along the gallery, warning Mrs Adams that there were two steps ahead of them, and that she must take care not to fall. Eyes still closed, the Princess opened a door and stepped into a small room.

"Here is the fireplace where Wild Will Darrell burnt the child," she exclaimed. Then she crossed the room, still with her eyes closed, and took hold of the chintz bed-curtains, pointing to the hole made in it by Mrs Barnes nearly four hundred years previously.

Then she opened her eyes. She was quite unable to explain how she could have known these things. She could only assume that she must have been Mrs Barnes in a previous existence—perhaps because of her being able to go there with her eyes closed, as Mrs Barnes had been taken there blindfolded.

Princess Marie Louise is now dead herself and may or may not know the answer to questions which arise out of her story.

It will be remembered that Mrs Barnes never saw the interior of

Littlecote, being blindfolded, and there is no reason to suppose that she ever saw the interior of it during her lifetime, so she could not have known what it looked like.

Yet it was all familiar to the Princess. Her assumption that she must have been the gamp in a previous existence was probably a false one.

It is more likely—if we are to believe in previous existences—that she had once been Miss Bonham, for Miss Bonham would know the things the Princess claimed to know about Littlecote, and the gamp would not. Miss Bonham would certainly know the interior of Littlecote, which Mrs Barnes had never seen.

If this was so, then perhaps some recompense was made to the tragic Miss Bonham by becoming a Princess in another life. But if this was the case, would her troubled spirit continue to haunt Littlecote? We shall never know the answer to such questions.

Phantom Lovers

Throughout the ages lovers have been victims of disapproving parents, and recalcitrant lovers have often been dealt with in a cruel and heartless manner. Acts of violence, even murder, have been committed against those who have put love before obedience to parental authority. These tragic victims of love, whose happiness was so brief in life, may seek and find each other in the spirit world, their unhappy souls haunting the place where they once had met and loved, and were warm flesh and blood, delighting in each other's embraces.

Just such a tragic love story was that of the Lady Dorothy, daughter of Sir John Southworth of Samlesbury Hall, Lancashire, and Robert, the handsome son of a noble family who owned a large estate near-by. One would have thought the match to be ideal, and that the most choosy of parents would have welcomed such a union, especially as the young pair were so much in love. But this was not the case with Sir John, one-time Sheriff of the County Palatine of Lancaster, who held high military commands in the service of Queen Elizabeth I. The trouble was that he was a strict Catholic and Robert's parents were Protestants.

In those days there was great bitterness between members of the old Roman faith and the reformed anti-Papist church which had supplanted it. The conflict was as much political as it was religious and was one which was to drag on for centuries. The fact that the diplomatic and clever Queen Elizabeth employed both Protestants and Catholics in her service did little to damp down the feeling in the country, and Sir John Southworth felt more strongly than most. He belonged to the old school and regarded the Protestants as heretics whose souls were destined for the eternal fires.

Imagine his consternation therefore when this young man from a staunch Protestant family called at Samlesbury asking for Dorothy's hand. When Sir John learned that his daughter had been freely associating with the young heretic and had fallen in love with him, he made no bones about the way he felt to the young suitor. Suppressed anger turned his ruddy complexion into purple, and his neat beard bristled and twitched above his starched white ruff. How dare a Protestant even enter his house—let alone approach him as a prospective son-in-law!

"You seem to be under a misapprehension, young sir. No daughter of mine would dream of forming an attachment for someone not of the true faith. You must know that the Southworths are devout Romanists. If my daughter Dorothy is known to you, she has never divulged her association to me, and as her father I would have forbidden such a friendship. As to marriage, that is absolutely out of the question. Marry a Protestant! I would rather see her dead."

Robert was taken aback by Sir John's outburst. He had not expected anything like this, though Dorothy had warned him that her father would object to a proposal from anyone who was not a Catholic. But he had been optimistic. After all, it wasn't as if he was a penniless nobody. Sir John was treating him as though he was the stable boy. But he was determined for Dorothy's sake to keep his own temper in check.

"But surely, sir, you do not refuse your sanction to your daughter's marriage solely because I am a Protestant? I love Dorothy, and she has given me to understand that she returns my love. We wish to become——"

"That is enough, sir! How dare you force your way into my house and confront me with such falsehoods! My daughter would never flout her father's wishes. And I say that she will marry a Papist, or she will not marry at all."

"Does not your daughter's happiness mean anything to you, sir? Since the English prayer-book has been revised, the Church embraces the Catholics as well as the Protestant-minded. Could you not be all-embracing, for your daughter's sake?" Robert was quite pale. He felt as though he was pleading for his very life.

"I am the best judge of where my daughter's happiness lies and it is not in the arms of a heretical Protestant. The revision of the English prayer-book has not been recognized by the Holy Father, so enough of your false reasoning, young man. I forbid you ever to see my daughter again. She will soon forget you. I shall make sure of that. And now you will oblige me by leaving my house, never to enter it again."

"I will leave now, sir, as you wish. But I beg you to reconsider. Think of Dorothy. We truly love each other, and we will not be parted for long."

Sir John's colour deepened once more. "Get out of my house, you insolent young dog," he exclaimed, "or I will have you thrown out. My daughter will never marry you, and you will not see her again."

The heartbroken Dorothy was confined to her room for several days after this by her irate parent, but somehow her loved one managed to smuggle a letter to her in which he suggested a secret meeting in the woods surrounding the Hall, which in the sixteenth century was situated in the midst of a great forest of oaks. (Today Samlesbury Hall stands beside the main road between Preston and Blackburn.) An obliging maid-servant, who was walking out with one of the neighbouring knight's footmen, delivered her young mistress's reply into the hands of her sweetheart, who passed it on to Robert, and thus a meeting between the parted lovers was arranged.

They met under a particular tree in the woods, far enough from the Hall so that it would be most unlikely for anyone to pass that way, and where they could find a little privacy surrounded by the broad sheltering trunks and enveloping branches of the friendly oak trees.

Sir John's opposition to their attachment made them even more determined to marry, and after two or three meetings they planned to elope. Sir John was going to be away for a few days on business of state, and the lovers made their plans accordingly.

But they reckoned without Dorothy's brother, as rigid a Romanist as his father, and totally opposed to his sister's marriage into a family which espoused the hated Protestant faith.

One evening the two lovers met in their usual secret place and planned the details of their elopement, unaware of the fact that the trees which sheltered them also concealed an eavesdropper— Dorothy's brother. Overhearing their plans to run away together, and well knowing of his father's objection to such a union, which he certainly shared himself, he decided that he must prevent the elopement at all costs. He knew that his father would commend him for doing so, for protecting the family honour in his absence. The brother laid his own plans accordingly.

Meanwhile Dorothy, blissfully unaware that her secret had been discovered, went about her own preparations with a light heart. By the time her father returned to Samlesbury she would be far away with the man she loved. She dressed in white, as befitted a bride, and ventured out of her room and along the broad corridors, choosing the right moment when both members of the family and the servants were otherwise occupied. Her wide-skirted dress with the fulness held out from a tight bodice by the fashionable farthingale, made her appear as though she was floating across the long gallery and down the wide staircase, so quickly did her dainty feet carry her, her heart beating fast with excitement, fearing every moment that she would be discovered and her happy plan frustrated.

But she met no one and let herself out quietly by a little used side door which she had chosen so that the nearby bushes would give as much concealment to her as possible. So she hurried across the park into the woods where her lover was awaiting her in the company of two trusted friends who were there to help them and to speed them on their way to happiness.

Alas, neither of the three young men was armed. But Dorothy's brother, watching from a vantage point, was. His sword was at the ready. He was an excellent and experienced swordsman, and the fact that he had three men to contend with did not deter him in the least. On the contrary, his triumphant fight for the Southworth honour would be the more glorious.

When Dorothy arrived and was greeting her lover, the waiting swordsman sprang out to the attack, and was upon them before they realized what was happening. The three unarmed men were defenceless before the flashing steel of the determined brother. Robert's two friends went down mortally wounded from well-aimed sword-thrusts. Robert's first thought was to protect his loved one, and he fell at her feet with her brother's sword plunged into his heart.

Dorothy knew nothing of what happened after that, for she swooned and when she recovered her senses she was back in her room at Samlesbury, crying out the name of her lover who would never again embrace her.

That night the bodies of the three men were secretly buried within the precincts of the domestic chapel attached to Samlesbury Hall.

Lady Dorothy never really recovered from the shock of witnessing her lover's death at the hands of her own brother. She was ill for a long time, a prisoner in her room. Her father's reaction to the tragedy and the part his over-zealous son played in it, is not on record; but he was a man of importance at the court of Queen Elizabeth, and could not afford a domestic scandal of this kind. The

Queen did not desire to widen the already wide breach between the Protestants and the adherents of the old religion.

Whatever Sir John might have thought of the violent and murderous manner in which his impetuous son dealt with the situation in his absence, it was not possible to do anything about it. He did not wish such a scandal in the delicate political balance which existed in England just then.

As for the unfortunate, broken-hearted Dorothy, there was only one thing to do, and her parents had no hesitation in doing it. She was bundled into a convent. It was the conventional solution for such circumstances in those days, though what Dorothy's parents must have thought at having to do it in these particular circumstances can well be imagined, for it must not be assumed that they were insensitive or without any feelings towards their wronged daughter.

They decided to send her abroad, where, it is said, she was kept under strict surveillance, for she was showing signs that her mind was breaking under her desperate grief. "The name of her murdered lover," said Harland in his *Lancashire Legends*, "was ever on her lips". Her great grief finally drove her right out of her mind, and she died, her lover's name being the last word she spoke.

According to legend, Lady Dorothy's ghost was seen in her old home and the surrounding woods immediately after her death, when her spirit returned to seek her lost love. On quiet, clear evenings—the same as that happy evening when she had tip-toed starry-eyed for that last meeting with her lover—many people have seen a white lady gliding down the corridors and the galleries of Samlesbury Hall, descending the staircase, floating across the entrance hall and through the door out into the grounds, where she is met by a handsome young knight who receives her on his bended knees, and then accompanies her on her ghostly walk.

She has been seen in the woods accompanied by this ghostly knight dressed in Elizabethan garb. Some have said that at the end of their walk together the two phantom lovers embrace and lie down in each other's arms under the great oak tree where they had met and embraced in their lifetime; and it is said that at this time the air is filled with mournful sighs of despair and sorrowful whisperings among the branches above, where they eventually disappear together, still clasped in each other's arms.

This very romantic and fanciful story received a certain confirmation about two hundred years later when Samlesbury Hall fell upon bad times and was neglected, eventually becoming a farmhouse. Later it was restored to its original condition, it being a unique example of the ancient type of Lancashire manor-house of the late fourteenth century. Workmen re-inforcing a wall near the old chapel came across a skeleton, and later two more skeletons were found. Local opinion considered the finding of the three skeletons to be ample confirmation of the basic facts of the tragedy of Dorothy Southworth and her unfortunate lover.

Another romantic haunting came about as the result of the unfortunate love affair between the Lady Arabella Stuart and Sir William Seymour, whose romance ended in imprisonment in the Tower and death from madness for the doomed Arabella, whose only crime was that she was born too near the throne.

Descended from Henry VII's eldest daughter, Margaret Stuart, the Countess of Lennox, Arabella was next in succession to James VI of Scotland (James I of England), and she became the subject of intrigues by those who would not accept James as Elizabeth's successor. When Arabella was only ten, Elizabeth paraded her at her court as the heir to the throne, mainly to provoke James, whom she regarded in the same odious light as she did Mary Queen of Scots, his mother.

Lady Arabella had many requests for her hand, but all her suits, commoners and royal princes alike, were repulsed by both Elizabeth and James whose policy was to keep her unmarried, because the child of such a union would be a claimant to the throne which would complicate the succession.

Arabella pretended that marriage did not interest her, for she was clever enough to realize that any other policy would land her in trouble, so she devoted herself to literature, poetry, and even theology, a subject more fashionable in those days than now, for theology was changing the face of England in a way which we find it difficult to imagine.

When, upon Elizabeth's death, James was safely in possession of the throne, he acted more liberally towards Arabella, allowing her apartments in the palace and settling an allowance upon her. James's Queen, Anne of Denmark, liked Arabella and enjoyed her lively and intelligent companionship, for Arabella was always ready to participate in the masques and pageants which the Queen liked so much, and she became very popular at Court where she met again an old childhood acquaintance, the handsome Sir William Seymour, son of Lord Beauchamp, and their renewed attachment quickly turned into something more serious. They were in love.

At first they managed to keep their affair secret, but an alarmed

James at length came to hear of it, and also the highly disturbing news that they were planning to get married. Such a marriage he saw as a threat to his own safety on the throne, for Sir William Seymour was also descended from Henry VII, and any offspring of such a marriage would be dangerous indeed.

James summoned each of the offending lovers before his Council, and they were told in no uncertain manner that such a marriage between them could not be countenanced unless the King gave his express permission. In order to disarm suspicion Arabella and Seymour agreed to part.

They well knew that James would never under any circumstances permit them to marry, and so they married secretly. Eventually this came to the ears of James, who, incensed at their duplicity, ordered their arrest. Seymour was sent to St Thomas's Tower and Arabella to Lambeth Palace under the guard of Sir Thomas Parry. This was in the summer of 1610.

There was a great deal of sympathy for the young couple, and it was made quite easy for them to meet secretly. All their friends were ready to help them, and Seymour did not have much difficulty in leaving the Tower to go to Lambeth. All he had to do was to bribe his jailer, who was then quite willing to turn a blind eye to the absence of his charge.

The two lovers often met in the gardens of Lambeth and sometimes in the Palace. These meetings were as happy as they could be under the circumstances, and during their walks together beside the banks of the Thames they talked of the day when they would be able to live a normal, happy life together. It seemed that the only solution was to escape to the Continent.

Meanwhile their friends at Court—even the Queen herself—were trying to intercede for them and to persuade James to adopt a more lenient attitude. But James, afraid for his throne, was adamant. It was inevitable that news of their stolen meetings should eventually come to his ears, and he ordered a stricter guard to be put on Seymour, and that Arabella should be moved to Durham under the surveillance of the Bishop, who was ordered to keep a firm watch upon her.

But Arabella, being of strong character, refused to be sent to the north of England where she would not be able to see her husband. When ordered to go, she flatly refused to get out of her bed. So her bed was carried out of Lambeth, with her in it, placed in a boat and rowed up the river.

Poor Arabella became extremely agitated at such forthright and demoralizing treatment and by the time they reached Barnet she appeared to be really ill with a high temperature. A doctor was called, diagnosed a fever, and pronounced her too ill to travel. James therefore arranged for her to be taken care of in the home of the Earl of Essex at Highgate, stating that he would allow her to remain there for only a month, after which time it was reckoned she would be strong enough to continue her journey to Durham.

This respite brought about a swift recovery in Arabella's health, and she instantly got in touch with her husband through their many friends, of whom James probably had much to fear, for he had proved a disappointing King to many people. Apart from being extremely unprepossessing and scandalous in his private life, he had broken many promises and made many enemies.

Sir William Seymour realized that he and Arabella must make their escape plans quickly. With the help of their friends they arranged both to escape at the same time and to meet at Blackwall where they would board a ship for France. The day chosen was one when the Bishop was to go to Durham to prepare for Lady Arabella's reception, and thus Arabella's escape was made much easier.

She disguised herself as a man, wearing a large black hat and a cloak. She wore also a peruque, doublet and hose and a sword, and passing very well as a young blade of the times, she set off with one retainer as an escort to an inn at Crompton where horses were waiting. They rode to Blackwall and arrived at the agreed time, but there was no sign of Seymour. After inquiring for him at the inn, they boarded the French ship which was to take them across the water. Arabella waited for her husband, anxiously scanning the riverside as the precious time went by, watching the tide go down, and praying desperately that her beloved would get there in time.

The French captain was concerned about other things than the tide. He was worried about the serious nature of his commission, and despite Arabella's entreaties he moved his ship further down river to the mouth of the Thames.

Meanwhile Sir William's escape from St Thomas's Tower had been planned with the help of a carter who delivered cartloads of faggots and hay. The carter had been bribed to exchange places with the prisoner on an outward journey. However, the switchover took longer than anticipated and the coast had to be quite clear before the carter would part with his smock and enveloping hat and hide himself under the hay. Seymour, dressed in the carter's clothing, and wearing a peruque and a black beard, walked out of the Tower with the empty cart without a hitch, though well behind the agreed time.

When he reached Blackwall, he was too late. The French barque with Arabella on board had sailed without him. He eventually managed to bribe the captain of a collier to take him to Ostend. It cost him forty pounds—a large sum in those days—and after many delays he finally landed on the Continent, and made his way to Calais where he reckoned his wife would be awaiting him.

But Arabella's luck had deserted her. Her inquiry for Seymour at the inn at Blackwall had come to the ears of Admiral Monson, to whom a courier had been dispatched telling him to be on the lookout for the Lady Arabella and Sir William, whose flight was already known to James and was causing him the greatest consternation, for he was certain that a new conspiracy against him was afoot. Couriers had in fact been sent in all directions in an effort to intercept the runaway couple.

The Admiral immediately ordered H.M.S. *Adventure* to pursue the French ship, which the swift naval frigate overhauled in midchannel and ordered it to heave-to. After some resistance the French ship was boarded and the unhappy Arabella was seized and brought back to London and lodged in the Bell Tower, where she was closely guarded.

At first her imprisonment did not bother her too much. At least her husband had escaped and she knew that he would leave no stone unturned until he could get her release, for he had influential friends. Arabella did not relax her efforts to appeal to James for her liberty and the Queen did her utmost to this end.

But James was adamant. He had been scared, quite certain that Arabella and her husband had been party to a conspiracy to seize the throne. It has been said that the fugitives were to have been received in the Netherlands by the Spanish commander, at the instigation of the King of Spain and the Papists, whose plan had been to bring them back to London at the head of a Catholic host. James was determined that nothing like that should happen if he could help it. While it is true that in the case of Arabella his fears on this score were groundless, it is just as true that his fears of a conspiracy against his throne in order to place a Roman Catholic monarch upon it were very real. There were several such conspiracies actively afoot, both in England and on the Continent.

At first Arabella bore her imprisonment well, but as time went by and James showed no sign of relenting and the Queen was unable to influence him, for he was convinced that Arabella's only wish was to take his place on the throne, all hope gradually left her, and she sank into the deepest melancholy. Of her husband she never heard again. He had to go into hiding on the Continent on account of the activities of James's agents, and he was unable to lift a finger to help her.

Arabella's end is wrapped in mystery. It is said that her splendid and sensitive mind eventually gave way and she became hopelessly insane. The only certainty is that she died on 27 September, 1615, after having been four years in the Tower, and she was buried in the tomb of Mary Queen of Scots in Henry VII's Chapel in Westminster Abbey.

Arabella Stuart's ghost has been seen several times since her death terminated her sad romance. Occasionally a lady in grey is seen at a certain window in the Bell Tower. She does not, however, often show herself, but doors are sometimes opened by unseen hands and the tapping of heels is heard along the corridors.

She is seen more often in Lambeth Palace where she roams the corridors and staircases in a rustling grey gown looking for her lost love. Sometimes the two lovers are seen in the Palace gardens as dusk gathers, walking hand in hand.

The White Lady of Berlin

At the end of the Unter den Linden in Berlin stands a huge, imposing quadrangular building known as the Old Palace. But the only palatial thing about it now is its appearance. After 1919 it was turned over to government offices, and later became a museum. But once it knew great splendours: Frederick, first King of Prussia, began to build it in 1699 with the aim of rivalling Versailles itself. Here lived the powerful race of Hohenzollerns, and here flourished their courts. They ruled by absolute authority—an authority that could proclaim to the nobles of the land: "I am king and lord, and will do what I wish! Holiness is God's, but all else must be mine!"

It is not surprising that in a place where passions ran strongly they should leave strong currents behind them. Frederick, its builder, was a wild, vicious and cruel man. In a tower of the Palace, known as the Tower of the Green Hat, he kept an Iron Maiden, that terrible instrument of torture and death shaped roughly like a woman and lined with steel spikes, which pierced and crushed its victims. These would often be innocent people against whom a court had not been able to find sufficient evidence. Beneath the Maiden a trap-door let down the torn remains of the Maiden's prey into the engulfing darkness of an oubliette.

But the phantom of the Old Palace, who is said to have come from the Tower of the Green Hat, was not one of these victims. The White Lady who has appeared to so many Berliners is said by some to be the model for the Iron Maiden, a beautiful woman whose likeness was used to make that horrid travesty of womanhood.

After her death, her mission was to visit the descendants of Frederick, her inventor, and warn them of their coming fate. According to some who saw her, she was dressed in the white robe and veil of the Virgin, because the statue had been so made, and the victim, as he was pressed into it, had been told to "Return thanks to our Holy Mother". So a profanation was punished.

There are other stories, however, of the White Lady's origin. Some say she was Anna Sidow, the lovely, low-born mistress of Elector Joachim II, a half-mad ruler of the sixteenth century, who squandered his people's gold on her. But the pious son who followed him had Anna imprisoned in Spandau, and she died miserably there. It may be that her spirit travelled from the royal dwelling on the outskirts of Berlin to the Palace built long after her time.

Also before the stones of the Old Palace rose was the wrong done that caused the third claimant to the White Lady's title to "walk". One of the early Hohenzollerns was Margrave Albert, known as the Beautiful, who fell in love with a young widow, the Countess d'Orlamunde, who had two children. Unthinkingly, he remarked to someone that he would gladly marry her, if he were not held back by the influence of *four eyes*. Hearing of this, the widow took it to refer to her children; and her way of disposing of these obstacles to her ennoblement was to kill them by running a gold pin into their heads. It was only after she had done this that she found out the Margrave's true meaning—he had been referring to his parents' opposition to the marriage. Nature had its way—Agnes d'Orlamunde went mad, and wanders without rest.

But whoever she may have been—artist's model, unhappy prisoner, or crazed mother—the White Lady has been seen by many, usually on occasions when tragedy threatened the Hohenzollern princes. The first recorded appearance was in 1619, in the reign of John Sigismund. A cheeky young page was sauntering down a corridor of the Old Palace when he turned a corner and came face to face with a silent white figure, gliding towards him with a fold of its veil drawn across its features. He knew instantly who—or what —it was; and knew that those who had seen her in the past had drawn aside, trembling, to let her pass. But the page did not see why he should be frightened by a mere white shadow. He stood in her way, checked her with a hand on her arm, and inquired briskly, "And where might you be going, madam?"

The White Lady lowered the hand with which she had been holding the veil over her face. She held in it a great key—the key that was said to unlock for her each one of the castle's six hundred doors—and she brought it down heavily upon the page's head. He fell to the ground, dead; just as two horrified fellow-servants appeared round the corner. They had more sense than the dead boy. They stood back as the White Lady flitted past them and disappeared.

On the next day, Elector John Sigismund died.

There is no story of the White Lady's appearance in the reign of Frederick William, the Great Elector, a strong ruler and a simple man. Nor did she visit his son and grandson, with their extravagances and eccentricities; nor Frederick the Great, perhaps because he was well known to be a sceptic.

Yet it seems that after death Frederick's scepticism must have been considerably modified. His nephew, Frederick William II, had invaded Champagne, during the French revolutionary period, with such success that he was able to announce his army's victorious arrival under the walls of Paris. He himself was staying at a Verdun inn. Dissatisfied with the wine that had been brought to him, he went down to the cellar of the inn to choose a better vintage; and there, to his horror, slowly materialized before him, against an unlikely background of bottles and barrels, the figure of his uncle, the Great Frederick.

"Unless you call off the Prussian army from Paris, nephew," said the spirit, "you may expect to see someone who will not be welcome to you."

The terrified Frederick William stammered that he did not know what was meant.

"I mean," replied Frederick, "the White Lady of the Old Palace, and I am sure you know what *her* visit implies." And he faded away into a cloudy shape less substantial than the cobwebs festooned from the cellar beams.

Frederick William took the warning seriously. He called off his troops, returned to Berlin, and lived another five years.

From this story, and that of the White Lady's next appearance, it would almost seem that she held some watching brief over France. For in the early autumn of 1806 she was seen several times. It was just before the Battle of Jena, when the Prussians were threatening to drive Napoleon's army "with whip-lashes" back to the Seine. At a party, Prince Louis of Prussia gaily asked a young girl to play on the pianoforte as many tunes as he would kill Frenchmen the next day. She played until dawn. The Prince, as he rode away, called: "Forward, gentlemen, to crush Napoleon!" The next night he lay dead at Saalfeld. Elector Frederick William III took the White Lady's hint, and fled from Berlin; and Napoleon himself moved into the Old Palace and stayed two months. The White Lady was quiet; perhaps French occupation pleased her.

When the White Lady was seen again in June, 1914, Kaiser William II may well have expected his own death to follow. But the victim this time was the Archduke Francis Ferdinand, heir to the throne of Austria. William lamented his friend, but kept on with his violently militarist policy, and in August, 1918, its results broke upon the world—war between Germany and England. The White Lady's prophesy of disaster had been more accurate than ever this time. Four years later the defeated William left his empty title and the Old Palace behind him for ever. It is not recorded whether the White Lady ever appeared again during his lifetime. Perhaps she had no need to, for the long exile at Doorn was as fantastically tragic an end to the rule of the Hohenzollerns as even she could have wished.

There is a story that on 29 April, 1945, as Berlin's death agony approached its end and the fires of Allied bombing blazed brightly, the White Lady walked once more in the no longer princely corridors of the Old Palace. Their glory was departed, like the glory of the Hohenzollerns, and the man who was to die ignominiously in the ruins of the Reich Chancellery was a low-born person of the name of Schickelgruber. It is hardly likely that she would have troubled to warn *him*. Perhaps this time she appeared in triumph, for the enemies of France and England and the true Germany were slain upon the high places.

School for Ghosts

It is no surprise that China, for many centuries so remote and isolated, should have developed a ghost lore different from the Western
world. Chinese ghosts are not usually the frightening apparitions so
familiar to us. European ghosts frequently appear in the guise of the
dead, with faces of the dead, clad sometimes in grave-clothes,
sometimes without their heads, and to the accompaniment of
terrifying noises.

But Chinese ghosts as a rule—for there are exceptions—are not
like this. They are often indistinguishable from the living. They are
frequently beautiful maidens who return from the other world, not
to frighten man, but to play with him, tease him, make love to him,
or even help him in the endless and burdensome examinations which
the men of Old China had to pass before they could reach any status
in their country.

Chinese ghosts are not the insubstantial wraiths of Western tradition. They are ghosts of flesh and blood, and they are often ghosts of
animals, particularly of foxes, for the Chinese believe that all creatures
have spirits.

A collection of these ghost stories was made by Pu Sung-ling,
who lived in the seventeenth century, and who recorded the
incidents from the people who reported them. The following two
stories, which I have broadly adapted from his collection, are
typical of these quaint and romantic tales of the supernatural.

When Yang Shien heard about the haunted house, once the home of a high official, but now empty and deserted, he decided that he would approach the owner to allow him to live there as a caretaker, for it was just the sort of home Yang had dreamed that one day he would own. Yang secured an interview with the owner of the house and put his proposition before him.

At first the high official would not hear of it. "Young man," he said, "no one has been able to live there for years. The spirits which occupy it are such that they bring trouble to anyone who stays in the house."

"I am prepared to risk that. It is a great pity that such a lovely house should be left to spirits who care nothing if it falls into ruins. I will look after it for you."

The older man shrugged his shoulders. "I have nothing to lose, young man. I have warned you, and seeing that you still insist, you can have the key. But at the first sign of trouble you must leave. Otherwise I would not want to be responsible for you."

Yang was jubilant and immediately moved his belongings into his new home. He had to make several journeys back and forth, carrying everything himself, for he could not afford to hire a cart, and it was past sunset when he returned with his last load.

Yang's books were his pride and joy, and he had carefully placed them upon a table which he had decided would be admirable for his studies, but when he returned with his last load they were no longer there. He hunted high and low, but they were not to be found in the house and there was no sign of anyone having broken in. When however he returned to the room where he had left the missing books, they were back on the table. Puzzled, but happier now at the return of his most precious possessions, he went to the kitchen to cook some rice for his supper, and when he returned to his room where he thought he would read a while before retiring, he found his books had again vanished. He then heard the patter of light footsteps and saw two beautiful young girls carrying his books in their arms. They were laughing together as they quietly replaced the books on the table.

They turned round and gazed straight at him, looking so human in the half-light of dusk that he could hardly believe they were ghosts at all; but knowing that they were, he turned his head away and would not return their saucy looks. Whereupon they laughed at him and came closer.

Yang's heart bumped against his ribs with fear, as he remembered the warning of the owner of the house. One of the girls prodded his body with her finger. The other one stroked his face, and they started walking around him trying to make him look at them, touching him and laughing as they did so.

Yang had now revised his disbelief in spirits, and if he had not seen them with his own eyes walk right through the door just now, he would not have believed they were ghosts. However, they seemed as harmless as little children and he decided to treat them as such.

"Get out of my sight, you silly ghosts," he exclaimed. "How dare you come here to disturb me?" He made his voice sound as cross and belligerent as he possibly could. All the same, he did not expect them to take fright and scuttle away as quickly as they did.

His confidence returned, Yang lit a lamp and began to read, but all the time he was aware of other presences in the room and conscious of flitting shadows in the dark corners. He tried to concentrate on his book, but could not quite ignore those now quiet but eerie spirits which were around him. He soon gave up trying to read and got ready for bed.

He was very tired after his busy day, but no sooner had he closed his eyes than he was disturbed by a tickling sensation on his nose. Many times he brushed away whatever was tickling him, but it always returned. Eventually he sneezed and in the darkness he heard sounds of suppressed laughter. He got up, lit a candle and went back to bed again, closing his eyes and listening.

Presently he heard a faint sound and he opened his eyes. One of the girls was coming towards him with a feather in her delicate little hand. Immediately he jumped out of bed and shouted at her, and she ran away. Eventually he managed to get off to sleep, only to be awakened by a tickling sensation, this time on his ear. And so it went on all night. He couldn't get any sleep for the wretched little ghosts, until cock-crow, and then all was peaceful, and he relapsed into a deep sleep, not waking until long past noon.

The rest of the day was quiet and normal and Yang did some cleaning, arranging everything to his liking. Then he settled down to study, realizing that he would probably be plagued again by his ghostly visitors after sunset. He was reading when he became aware of a presence, and looking up from his book he beheld his beautiful visitors of the previous night watching him. He ignored them and continued reading. Then suddenly one of them came up to him and closed his book.

He jumped up in anger. "Am I to have no peace in this house?" he shouted. "I have important work to do, so go away."

They ran off, but no sooner had he returned to his book when they returned. Yang held on to his book, determined to continue his reading, but one of them came up behind him and put her cool hands over his eyes. Again he jumped up in anger, but they only laughed at him. So he tried a different approach.

"I have work to do and must study to pass my examinations," he told them in a friendly manner. "So why don't you be good girls and leave me in peace? Go and do something useful."

This approach surprised them and they stopped laughing and looked at him in a contemplative way. One of them whispered in the other's ear and they both smiled sweetly at him and then left the room. Presently he heard sounds of activity in the kitchen and he went back to his work, thankful that he was getting a little peace at last.

About half an hour later the two pretty ghosts came back and started to lay out a meal on the low table. It all looked delicious, but even though Yang was hungry he was a little dubious about eating a meal cooked by ghosts. They might poison him! He thanked them and told them how clever he thought they were. "But I am not hungry", he said, going back to his book.

"If you do not trust us, how can you expect us to be good?' asked the one who seemed to be the elder of the two.

Yang looked up in surprise, for she had spoken in a sweet, tinkling voice. "Of course I trust you," he felt obliged to reply.

"Then if you trust us, you will eat the food we have laboured to prepare for you."

Yang thought that if he refused to eat, he would continue to be plagued by them and would be unable to stay there. He took up a bowl of rice and chop-sticks and tasted some of the food, and, feeling no ill effects, he pronounced it excellent and perfectly cooked, and the two little ghosts were delighted.

After he had finished his meal, they sat together and talked, but they would say little about themselves. He learned that the name of the older one was Ching-Yen and the younger one was Shai-Lu; but of their families they would tell him nothing, saying that as they were only spirits his interest in them could not be marriage—therefore why was he so curious?

"As I never thought to meet such charming spirits when I came here, it is natural that I am curious about you, especially as we are to live together in this house."

To this Ching-Yen replied: "Fortunately for you, the other spirits which occupied this house have been recalled to the world below by the Black Judge, while we await whatever fate is in store for us.

But if you wish to stay here, we will continue to serve you."

And so Yang was able to settle down and work, and the girls—for he could no longer think of them as ghosts—came every evening after sunset and cleaned and cooked for him, taking an interest in his work, disturbing him no longer, and he was very happy.

One day he had to go out and did not return until well after sunset. He found the younger girl, Shai-Lu, seated at his desk laboriously copying from the book which he had been transcribing. She showed him what she had been doing and he praised it. "But there is much room for improvement," he told her with a smile, "and if you like, I will teach you."

Shai-Lu was delighted at the suggestion and Yang, seating her on his knee, held her hand and showed her how to hold the brush correctly. Just then Ching-Yen came into the room and, on seeing them thus, her face flushed up to the roots of her shiny black hair as though she was jealous of the younger girl.

On seeing this, Yang set Shai-Lu on her feet again and offered his knee to Ching-Yen. "Let me see how well you can wield the brush, my dear," he said to her, and smilingly the girl wrote with Yang guiding her wrist.

Seeing that they were both very interested, Yang gave them a piece of paper each and told them to copy a verse, and while they laboured at their tasks he was able to continue with his own studies. When they had finished, they brought their work to him and he gave them marks. The younger girl's work got the higher marks and again Yang had to placate Ching-Yen with encouraging words, telling her that if she worked hard she would soon improve.

Thus Yang became the teacher to the two young ghosts, and when their writing improved he taught them how to read. They were apt pupils and once they had grasped anything they did not forget it.

One evening Ching-Yen brought her young brother, Song, a handsome youth of about sixteen years, but also, alas, like his attractive sister, a ghost, having departed this life at a tender age. Could Song also be Yang's pupil? Yang agreed, and Song proved to be a very intelligent boy. Before long he was reading the classics and writing poems.

Yang was delighted with the success of his school for ghosts. The lessons kept these naughty spirits occupied and out of mischief, and Yang was able to continue with his studies and also earn a little money writing poems of satire on current affairs, which became quite well known, but not always popular.

Eventually the day came when Yang had to leave to take his examinations, and say good-bye to his phantom pupils. He was gratified to find how badly they took his news. The girls wept and Song was full of forebodings, begging him not to go. "The Gods are not with you at this time," he said, "and if you go now some dreadful calamity will befall you."

But Yang would not listen and the next day left the house to keep his appointment with the examiner. When Yang arrived at the capital he learned that his works of satire had enraged a prefect of great influence in the district, and his examiner, far from being sympathetic, accused Yang of improper conduct. Yang was thrown into prison, and, penniless, without food, becoming weaker every day, he wished that he had taken heed of Song's warning.

One night he thought he was dreaming when he saw Ching-Yen, but when she gave him food he knew it was really her. She told him that his examiner had been bribed to accuse him of improper conduct and that her brother, Song, had gone to the court to plead for his release. She would return the next night to tell him how Song had fared.

When she had gone he ate the food which gave him new strength and hope. But Ching-Yen did not return the following night as she had promised. Neither did she come the next night or the next, and Yang became even weaker—all hope gone.

Then one night Shai-Lu came to him, but she was very sad and downcast. She told him that Song's request for Yang's release had fallen on deaf ears and he also had been taken into custody. Ill had also befallen Ching-Yen, who on her way back from visiting Yang had been accosted by the Black Judge and had been carried off to be his concubine, but, refusing to submit, she too had been imprisoned.

Yang, weak as he was, tried to console Shai-Lu, taking the blame upon himself. She gave him some money, so that he could buy food and then left him, saying that she must go back to watch over Song.

The next day Yang was brought before the Judge who asked him who was the young man called Song Tsai, who had pleaded for his release. Yang, not wanting to cause any more trouble for his spirit pupils, pretended that he did not know, whereupon the Judge told him that the young man had been brought before him to be beaten, but, throwing himself upon the ground, he had disappeared. Yang still kept silent, and the Judge, thinking that Song's disappearance was a sign to indicate Yang's innocence, told him he was free to go.

Yang could hardly believe his good fortune. He went back to his house as quickly as he could, arriving there just after dusk, but no one was there to greet him. When he went to bed that night he could hear the sound of weeping, but when he got up and lit his candle he could see no one.

Henceforth Yang often heard in the night the sound of quiet weeping, and it made him feel very sad and helpless. He was not visited by his little ghost maidens any more, and he missed them very much, and often thought of them when he sat alone at his studies in the evening. He thought of taking a wife, but how could he afford to do so when he had not yet passed his examinations? He began to work harder than ever, dreaming of the wife he would be able to have one day, and she always looked like either Ching-Yen or Shai-Lu.

One night the sound of weeping was louder than usual, but it came from outside the house. Yang got up and went to the door to investigate. A young girl was there. He asked her whence she came.

"I have travelled a long way and now I am so tired that I cannot walk another step. I was told that you would give me refuge."

Yang invited her inside and saw that she was very beautiful, with lovely eyes and teeth like pearls. "Who told you to come to me?" he asked, thinking how pale she looked and wondering if she was another ghost.

But the girl fell at his feet with exhaustion and he lifted her on to his bed. He watched over her all through the night and in the morning when she awoke he made gruel for her. He knew now that she was not a ghost, and yet she had talked in her sleep calling him by name and reciting verses which had been written by his spirit pupils and known only by him. He was mystified and could hardly wait to ask her again how she had come to him and from where.

"I only know that I was very ill, indeed near to death, when a girl came to me and told me of Yang and his teachings. She said that you needed me and that I must come to you. She seemed to enter into my body and give me the strength, and here I am."

Yang was amazed at what he heard and asked: "Did the girl who came to you tell you her name?"

"She told me her name was Shai-Lu. Do you know of her?"

"Yes, I know of her. Did she say anything else?"

The girl blushed and lowered her eyes. "She said that you would want to take me for your wife."

And Yang knew that nothing would make him happier. "But,"

he said to her regretfully, "your family would not want you to marry a poor man."

"I will not marry anyone but you," she told him.

And so a messenger was despatched to the girl's parents who soon came to fetch her away, but she would not go with them, and therefore they had to agree to the marriage, which took place the next day.

But one thing marred their happiness, and that was the sound of weeping which haunted the house every evening until they were blessed with their first child, and then the weeping ceased.

The child was a girl and she strongly resembled Ching-Yen.

*   *   *   *   *

Nui Chang was a personable young man of an age when he should have been thinking of marriage, but he seemed to have little interest in the opposite sex, apparently quite content to live alone reading and studying in the hope that he would pass his examinations and get his degree, thus attaining high office and honour in the state at an earlier age than most.

His neighbour who visited him occasionally was always telling him that he should take a wife, warning him that a student young and unmarried and living alone as he did might well be visited by ghosts or foxes. Nui told him that he was not afraid and laughed at his neighbour, who, thinking to teach him a lesson, arranged that a local singing girl should one night call on Nui and when he saw her she should pretend to be a ghost.

The girl came and knocked on his door asking to be let in, but Nui was wary and would not let her in no matter how much she entreated him. For, although he had laughed at his neighbour, he knew that foxes had the power to turn into beautiful girls, and he did not want to have anything to do with such creatures.

The next day the neighbour called to find out what had happened. Nui told him of his ghostly visitor and that he had been afraid to go to sleep that night. His neighbour was highly amused, and, laughing heartily, he spoke of the beauty of the singing girl who had called on him, and of the delights he might have enjoyed with her.

Several nights later Nui was visited by another girl, and thinking his neighbour was playing the same game upon him, he this time opened his door and invited her in. He was astounded at the beauty of this girl. Never in his wildest dreams had he expected to be confronted by so much loveliness. He asked her who she was and from whence she came.

"My name is Lien," she replied. "I am a singing girl from the district west of the town, and I have come to relieve your loneliness." Her eyes were bright and bewitching and her smile inviting.

Nui believed what she told him, thinking that his neighbour had not over-praised the girl's beauty in any way. She untied his robe and her touch was soft and warm and he was filled with desire. She extinguished the lantern and they retired to his bed. When she left him some hours later she promised that she would come to him again in a few days' time. She visited him three times during the next two weeks.

Nui always worked at his studies when Lien did not come, and one night he was immersed in his work when someone softly entered the house. Naturally he thought it was Lien, but the girl who stood before him was only about fifteen years of age, with loose flowing hair as befitted a virgin. He knew that she could not be a singing girl, and she looked so delicate and moved with such grace that he did not think she could be a fox. He asked her who she was.

"I come from an honourable family," said the girl in a voice of dulcet tones. "And my name is Ying. Having heard of your lonely diligence with your books, I have long admired and respected you and wished to know you. As it seemed impossible for us to meet, I have come to you without the knowledge of my parents. I am yours to command, for I already love you."

Nui was touched at such devotion and his blood quickened at the thought of embracing such a young and delicate maiden. He took her hand in his and remarked upon its coldness, and she reminded him that she had come through the chilly night air to be near him, and he could soon warm her with his love.

Overjoyed at his good fortune, Nui took her to his bed, and lay with her, drinking of her cool, sweet fragrance to his heart's content. Later, when she had to leave him, she gave him one of her dainty shoes and told him that he had only to hold it in his hands when he wanted her and she would know that he was thinking of her and would come to him. But only at night, she said, when her parents would not know that she was not in her own bed. "Does anyone else visit you?" she asked of him.

"Sometimes a singing girl comes to me, but not very often," Nui replied truthfully, for the wide-eyed innocence of her lovely eyes gazing into his own forbade him to tell her a lie. He need not have worried for she was quite unconcerned about his other visitor, but warned him that it would not do for the two ever to meet. "I must be careful not to come when she is here and you must keep my visits secret. I would not want to be classed with a singing girl."

Nui promised that he would honour her wishes and the next evening Lien did not come and so he took out Ying's dainty shoe and thinking of her stroked it lovingly, his fingers caressing its delicate curves as though it was Ying herself whom he was caressing. He wished that she would again honour him with her presence, and almost as soon as the thought had formulated in his mind she was there beside him. He marvelled at her swift and silent arrival.

Ying gave a tinkling laugh. "I knew that you would wish to see me again, and I have been waiting in case your singing girl should come. As she did not, here I am."

And so Ying again embraced her and he was enraptured by her delicacy and her beauty. They took pleasure in each other as on the previous night, and she came to him night after night. He had only to stroke her shoe and there she was.

Then one night Lien, the singing girl, came to him once more and when she set eyes on him she exclaimed in dismay: "Whatever have you been doing with yourself since I last saw you?" she cried. "Are you not sleeping well? You look quite ill."

Nui replied that perhaps he had not been eating as well as usual and every night he was deep in his studies, working into the small hours.

"It is obvious that you are not taking care of yourself. Since my mother is sick and I will not be able to see you again for at least a week, I want you to promise me that you will not work so hard and that you will have your meals regularly."

But when Lien saw him again she was shocked at his appearance, saying that he was even worse than before. "You are so frail and ill-looking, I am sure you have the spirit sickness. I think you have been playing the love game with someone else and that is why you have become so weak. Tell me truthfully if you have and who she is, and I can help you."

But Nui denied that he was seeing anyone else, for had he not promised Ying that he would keep her visits secret? In any case, how could anyone so delicate and fragile as she was be the cause of his sickness?

Lien did not believe him and the next night she waited hidden by a tree outside his window. She was determined to find out if Nui had lied to her and she did not have long to wait before she saw Nui take out Ying's shoe from its secret hiding place, and as he stroked it with his thin hand a truly beautiful girl appeared as if by magic and Lien knew that her worst fears had been realized. She made her presence known to them and immediately Ying took fright and left.

Lien told him: "She is a ghost. No wonder you have the spirit sickness. You are being slowly poisoned by contact with her, and you must give her up immediately. Fortunately the poison has not yet penetrated too deeply into your system and I can drive it out of your body with some special herbs. I will bring them to you tomorrow and will nurse you until you are well again. But you must promise me that you will not see your ghost maiden again."

Nui did not think that Ying would come to him again in any case, for she would be too frightened of being seen by Lien. He promised not to see her again, for he was too weak to do anything else. So Lien brought the herbs and nursed him back to health and in time he was quite better and eating well, his vigour returned as before. The day came when Lien said that she must return to her home and that she would not be seeing him for a few days. She warned him once more about the folly of associating with his ghost maiden.

But Nui did not believe that he had been suffering from the spirit sickness and still less did he believe that Ying was a ghost. He had to know if the shoe could still bring her to him. He took it from its hiding place once more and fondled it, thinking of the beauty of its owner, and Ying appeared as before.

As soon as Lien saw him again she knew that he had not kept his promise to her. "You must be besotted with love for this maid of the underworld, and you must want to die," she told him sorrowfully. "Before long you will again suffer from the spirit sickness and this time I will not be there to help you." And with that she left him.

Lien's words came true and some weeks later Nui was indeed very ill once more. He lay on his bed getting weaker and weaker, praying that Lien would come back to him and eventually she did, but only to tell him that his end was near. He begged her to save him and she told him that he had not heeded her warning and why should she nurse him back to health so that he could again go back to his ghost girl?

Nui told Lien about the shoe, saying that he would not summon Ying to him ever again, and Lien must take the shoe and burn it. Lien took the shoe and no sooner had she touched it than Ying appeared. Lien upbraided her, saying that she was the cause of Nui's illness and why did she not admit it?

"I do admit it," said Ying with tears in her lovely eyes, "and I have come only to beg you to save him. If you do, I promise that I will return to the underworld never to see him again, for I do not wish to be the cause of his death."

Lien, somewhat mollified by Ying's obvious distress, for she was now on her knees pleading to Lien to do what she could to save Nui, who was in great pain and having difficulty in breathing. Lien agreed to try to save Nui and together they worked, making herbal medicines, massaging his heart and lungs, but he still seemed unable to breathe properly.

Lien then put her mouth to his and forced her own breath into his lungs until she was exhausted, but she had given him the breath of life and he was now breathing more easily, and eventually he dozed off into a natural sleep.

Ying, seeing that Lien had indeed managed to save his life, told her that she must now go and never would return. "I thank you for your goodness," she said to Lien. "I had no idea that beings like yourself could be so forgiving and so clever in healing the sick.

Lien looked at Ying in surprised dismay, for the ghost girl obviously knew *her* secret, but she did not feel strong enough after her efforts on Nui's behalf to deny anything. "We are just the same when it comes to loving, and caring for the sick," she said.

Ying told her that she need have no fear. Nui would never know from her. She would keep her promise and would be happy knowing that Nui was in good hands.

Lien nursed Nui day and night, and as Nui regained his strength so Lien gradually lost hers, until eventually it was Nui who was nursing Lien. But nothing he did for her could save her and she became weaker and weaker.

Lien knew that she was dying and with her last breath she told him the truth about herself. And so it was that her now wasted body lying on the bed changed into that of a fox.

Vengeful Ghosts

One cannot generalize about ghosts any more than one can about the living, for spirits have various reasons for returning to haunt this earth, and some seem to have a definite purpose. The following story is of one who sought vengeance against a tardy lover who lived to regret deserting his sweetheart when he thought his own life was in danger.

Caisho Burroughes was said to be one of the most handsome men in the England of his day, extremely valiant, though proud and bloodthirsty. Even so, the ghost of his sweetheart was to reduce him to a trembling wreck of his former self. His father was Sir John Burroughes, Garter King of Arms during the reign of Charles I, and Keeper of the Records at the Tower of London. He was sent by King Charles to Germany as English Envoy to the Emperor.

Caisho was the eldest of two sons and two daughters, and Sir John was persuaded to take Caisho along with him, journeying by way of Italy, where he left the young man in Florence in order that he should learn the Italian language. If Sir John had had the slightest idea what was going to be the devastating effect of his son's hand-some looks upon a certain beautiful courtesan and the tragedy which would ensue, he might have had second thoughts about continuing his journey without him.

Caisho, with his good looks and proud family background, was soon received into the highest social circles, and made many in-fluential friends. He was entertained royally and his studies took second place, especially when he met the beautiful mistress of the

Grand Duke of Tuscany, with whom he soon became deeply involved, and who fell so passionately in love with him that she cast caution to the winds and was constantly to be seen in his company.

Their affair became so public that it inevitably came to the ears of the Grand Duke, an extremely proud and jealous man. He was something of a diplomat and had no desire to offend King Charles by taking direct measures against this inconvenient young English blade. The most discreet way out of the awkward situation would be for Caisho to encounter a fatal accident in one of the less reputable Florentine haunts which he was in the habit of frequenting.

Mutual friends came to hear of the Duke's plan to have Caisho murdered, and warned him that his life was in danger if he continued to stay in Florence. Caisho did not at first believe that the Duke would go to such lengths to stop his affair with his mistress; but on the very night of the warning he was innocently involved in a brawl and an attempt was made to stab him. Fortunately for him he had two men friends with him, and when the would-be assassin found himself outnumbered, he made off as fast as his legs could carry him. The three friends laughed at the sight, but Caisho was now in no doubt of the seriousness of his position. He did not wish to die just yet, in the full flower of his youth. Life was far too sweet and no woman was worth dying for—especially another man's mistress. Even though she had given him to understand that she was willing to give up everything for his sake, he was not in the position to keep a mistress. She would be a luxury he could not afford.

He left for England immediately.

Meanwhile his lady love waited and pined for him in vain. He had left Florence in such haste that he had not even said goodbye to her, nor sent her a message telling of his impending departure. As for her, she knew nothing of the Duke's design, and she waited as usual for her lover, miserable and unhappy because he did not come, for all her hopes and thoughts had been centred around the handsome young Caisho. She no longer cared for the Grand Duke, nor for her envied position as his mistress, for she loved Caisho as she had never loved anyone before.

It was the Grand Duke himself who informed her of her lover's flight. He had been disappointed that his prey had escaped him and he had been robbed of taking his revenge. He took it out on his mistress instead, deriding her for her treachery and faithlessness, and reproaching her for choosing so unworthy a young man—a coward who ran away at the slightest sign of danger, and who did not even wait to say goodbye to her.

The poor girl was heartbroken and bitterly disappointed at the way her lover had deserted her. She knew that the Grand Duke would never permit her to leave and follow Caisho to England—and life with the Duke after this would be unbearable. She might as well be dead. So in despair she took her own life, hopeful perhaps that in death she would find her lover again.

Meanwhile Caisho had returned to London and was sharing a room with a friend, a Colonel Remes, a member of Parliament. One night they were in bed together when the ghost of his Florentine sweetheart appeared before them.

At first Caisho thought it was really her, and he asked her how she had known where to find him and what was she doing in England? Whereupon the beautiful ghost solemnly told him that she had killed herself because he had deserted her and left her to the vengeance of the Grand Duke, who after he had found out about their love affair had treated her shamefully, making her life miserable. She had preferred to die than to face life without Caisho.

"You, too, will die soon," she told her now frightened gallant. "You will be killed in a duel. But until that time comes, I shall haunt you and you will regret having left me without so much as a word. Every day that is left to you, you will regret it." She thereupon vanished with her words of doom and foreboding echoing in the wretched Caisho's ears.

If Caisho had been alone he might have dismissed the incident from his mind, putting it down to a bad dream after over-indulgence in the taverns. But Colonel Remes had seen the apparition as well, and was very much affected by what they had both seen. They tried to make jokes about their visitor from the other world, saying the next time she came they would invite her to join them in bed, but neither of them could shake off the fear of the unknown which the visitation had given them.

In the morning they were more inclined to dismiss it as a temporary hallucination probably evoked by a sorceress, who perhaps had been paid to use her witchcraft on them by some of their devil-may-care friends, who were perhaps at this moment laughing themselves silly after hearing of their reaction to the bedside apparition. The following night Caisho made some inquiries among his friends, but it was obvious that they knew nothing about the incident, and he returned to his lodgings a little the worse for drink.

Colonel Remes was already asleep and Caisho fell into bed beside him, but he had hardly closed his eyes when he was vividly and frighteningly aware of a presence in the room. Blearily he opened his eyes and once more saw the ghost of the woman from Florence.

Terrified, he shrieked at her, waking his friend, and they both saw her sad and beautiful face, and heard again her words of denunciation and her forecast of death for Caisho.

Caisho, still in his cups, jumped out of bed as though to attack her, but when he reached out he grasped nothing, and felt only a breath of icy air upon his face as she vanished before his sight, her words echoing in his ears: "You, too, will soon die. You will be killed in a duel. But until that time comes, I will haunt you . . . haunt you . . . haunt you."

"If this sort of thing is going to happen every night," said Colonel Remes, in the morning, "I shall be looking for new lodgings." He was as good as his word, for the ghostly visitations continued, and Caisho was becoming more and more terror-stricken, crying out as soon as he saw her. He dared not sleep alone at night and after Remes left he persuaded his younger brother John to sleep with him, and he too saw and heard the vengeful ghost of Caisho's dead sweetheart.

Caisho was indeed regretting his callous desertion of her. Death in some dark alley in Florence would have been preferable to this continued assault from the spirit world which was gradually driving him out of his mind. He would cry out in anguish every time he saw her, his whole body shaking with fear. "Oh, God! Here she comes! Here she comes!"

The story of the haunting was now the talk of London. It even aroused the interest of King Charles. John Aubrey (1626–97) wrote in his book *Miscellanies upon Various Subjects*: "The story was so common that King Charles I sent for Caisho Burroughes's father, whom he examined as to the truth of the matter; who did (together with Colonel Remes) aver the matter of fact to be true, so that the King thought it worth his while to send to Florence to inquire at what time this unhappy lady killed herself; it was found to be the same minute that she first appeared to Caisho in bed with Colonel Remes. This relation I had from my worthy friend Mr Monson, who had it from Sir John's own mouth, brother of Caisho; he had also the same account from his own father, who was intimately acquainted with old Sir John Burroughes, and both his sons, and says, as often as Caisho related this, he wept bitterly."

Caisho went to pieces and spent the nights with the women of the town and drinking in the taverns, rather than go back to his lodgings to face his nightly visitor from the other world. One night he became involved in an argument with a stranger who challenged him to a duel, and on returning to his room in the early hours, hoping to get some rest, for he was in no fit shape to wield a sword just then, the ghost appeared again, this time telling him that his end was at hand and that he would die that very day.

Perhaps he did not wish to live, having been thoroughly demoralized by this terrible campaign of revenge, or perhaps his health did not permit him to fight with his usual sureness and precision; but whatever it was he appeared to be quite unable to protect himself from his opponent, whose sword soon found its mark deep in Caisho's heart.

As he died on the grass, the early morning mist seemed to gather around Caisho's body, and some who witnessed the sight said the mist was more of a wraith, a phantom form bending over him as he died, and it was believed that his ghost-sweetheart had come to claim in death what she had lost in life.

Ghosts would be legion if everyone who had suffered and died in consequence of a treacherous act inflicted by another came back from the nether world to haunt the guilty person. That a number do come back is generally accepted, for many wrong-doers have experienced terrifying ordeals which seem to prove that the dead can and do return to exact vengeance. Engine-driver Brierly was not at heart a dishonourable man, yet through him his best friend, Jim Robson, had killed his wife and child and then himself, returning from the spirit world to take a terrible revenge.

If anyone had ever told Brierly that he would become obsessed by another man's wife he would not have believed him, for his own wife was a good woman and he loved her and their little daughter very much indeed. Jim was his best friend and drove the Night Express regularly, and had got him a job in the same yard as himself as a driver on one of the local trains. John Brierly was a happy man and when Jim got married he was his best man. The Brierlys were the first friends to visit the happy couple when they went to live in a cottage on the main line.

It was Jim who first threw them together. The Robsons had been visiting the Brierlys and Jim asked John to see his wife home for him. Both men were going back on duty and John's train, being a local, made its first stop at the station near the Robsons' cottage, which was close enough to the station for John to see her safely to the door.

After that it became a habit for John to call on Jim's wife for a chat every time his local stopped at the station. At first there was nothing between them, and she did not encourage him, but Jim was away a lot, only seeing his wife two or three times a week, and she was lonely. Brierly saw her at every opportunity, and their friendship soon ripened into something more serious.

John Brierly continued to visit her even when she was expecting Jim's child, and inevitably there was gossip, which eventually came to the ears of the husband.

Jim was not a church-going man, but he was strict about morals and marital fidelity, and he could not believe that his wife was carrying on with his best friend.

But when Jim tackled Brierly, he could not deny that he had visited the cottage at every opportunity. Jim told him never to go there again. He was white to the lips, his grey eyes cold and hostile as he looked at the man he had thought was his friend.

"You must ask for a transfer, Brierly, or as God is my judge I shall have my revenge on you." He turned angrily on his heels and walked away.

The next morning John Brierly asked for the transfer, and was put on a train running to the Midlands and back on the same day. But he still had to pass the cottage every night and every morning. The cottage was situated on a bend in the line which necessitated slowing down the train to quarter speed as they approached, and John would blow the whistle and lean out of the cab for a glimpse of Jim's wife. She was always there standing in the doorway of the cottage waving to him as he passed by, and every night she put a light in the cottage window for him to see.

But it was torture for him having only a glimpse of her, and Brierly was not content with this state of affairs for long. He started to write to her, pouring out his heart in wild words of love, forgetting the danger, thinking only of the woman he was obsessed with, heedless of the fact that his letters might be found and read by her husband.

A premonition of disaster came one dark Saturday night when for the first time there was no light in the cottage window. Brierly pulled the whistle as he had always done, so that she might hear him coming, but there was still no welcoming gleam. The cottage was in pitch darkness.

He continued his journey with a feeling of dread and foreboding, and when he reached the terminus the first thing that caught his eyes was a news bill in big black letters which said: ENGINE DRIVER KILLS WIFE, CHILD AND SELF. He knew without reading the newspaper that it was Jim.

Of course he should have gone right away when Jim first found out about his affair with her. It was his own fault. He was to blame for his weakness in not being able to leave her alone. If only he had been strong enough this terrible tragedy would never have happened. She would still be alive, and so would the child and Jim.

As fate would have it Brierly was promoted to take his friend's place as driver of the Night Express and he was asked to take over immediately, on the very night after the tragedy. He did not funk taking over Jim's engine and having Jim's fireman on the footplate with him; but he felt dead inside, with no heart and feeling left.

He did the usual things before starting out on his first trip, automatically, feeling more like a machine than a man, for life now seemed to have lost its meaning. He alone was to blame for what had happened, and there was nothing he could do about it now. It was too late.

Under his hand the great locomotive moved forward as it pounded out of the station, the wheels quickly gathering momentum. Soon he was reducing speed as they approached the bend in the line, where the cottage stood, a dark blur, where no welcoming light would ever shine for him again from the window. Tears welled up in his eyes and he quickly wiped them away with the back of his hand, glancing at the fireman to see if he had noticed. But the fireman was standing cap in hand, also wiping away a tear as they passed. The two men self-consciously grasped each other's hands, and without a word went back to their respective jobs which ensured the safe arrival of the express at its destination.

Every night the express swept by the cottage, and after some weeks of uneventful monotony a frightening thing happened.

They were approaching the bend near the cottage one dark night, and as usual Brierly pulled back the lever to reduce speed. He still made a habit of leaning out of the cab as they went round the bend at quarter speed, staring at the cottage and thinking of Jim's wife, as though hoping to see her once more.

His thoughts were this time interrupted by the voice of the fireman shouting at him: "For God's sake, look at the lever!"

Brierly jerked back into the cab, for he had already felt the steam valves opening, and he could see to his horror that the regulator lever was being pulled open as if by an unseen hand. He leapt at the lever to close it, as the engine rapidly gained a speed much too high for the curve. Trying to close the lever was like pulling against an irresistible force. He slammed on the brakes, and the engine rounded the curve swaying from side to side and bucking dangerously, while the long train followed, rocking on its bogeys, brakes hissing and grinding.

Both men thought the engine was going off the rails. Brierly had to pull with all his might to shut off the steam against the force of the unseen hand, but they got round the bend without disaster with both men white to the lips. Never was a train crew more thankful to pull safely into the terminus at the other end of the run.

Brierly had more reason to be afraid than the fireman, because he knew that there was no natural cause for such a thing to have happened. He was certain that the unseen hand which had fought to open the regulator lever against him was Jim's, and he was equally certain that it would happen again. Would he always be able to hold it?

From that time he often had to fight against the unseen force which tried to gain control of the lever. He hung on like grim death every time they approached the bend near the cottage, and never took his hand off it on that particular stretch of the line. But he realized that each succeeding time it happened the force was stronger, and he knew that one day he would not be able to hold it.

He decided to quit and go up North. He should have done this long ago. It was the only way of avoiding disaster—a disaster which would involve not only him but a trainload of trusting passengers.

Soon he was going on his last journey driving the Night Express for the last time, and for the last time he would drive past the cottage with its memories and its horrors. His wife and little daughter were travelling with him and were seated in the first coach nearest to the engine, and they had it to themselves.

Brierly had kissed them both before climbing up into the monster of steel and settling himself behind the controls. The final whistle sounded and he put his hand on the lever, gripping it hard, for the feel of it made him shudder despite the intense heat which came from the roaring furnace being tended by the fireman. There was a great hiss of steam and then another before the mighty engine started to move and then, gaining momentum, pounded away into the night.

The train was travelling at sixty miles an hour when it approached the bend, and according to the fireman there was nothing either of them could do to close the regulator. They both hung on to it with all their might, but it opened full and they could not move it to shut the steam off. They were pushing helplessly against an irresistible force.

The engine and the first carriage jumped the track. The fireman was thrown clear, but John Brierly, his wife and child were killed. Though the train was derailed there were no other casualties.

Jim Robson had had his revenge.

Pearlin Jean

The great house of Allanbank, which for over a hundred years had been the seat of the Stuarts, a family of Scottish baronets, stood grim and imposing in the bright moonlight of a June night. A few lighted windows showed that the family had not yet retired; it was the hour of card-playing for the ladies, and of the enjoyment of a fine old port by the gentlemen. The children slept in the nurseries, and below stairs the servants chatted, their work over for the day.

Allanbank was blessed with extensive gardens, and beyond them lay a large orchard. On this beautiful night the moon "tipped with silver all the fruit-tree tops" and made shining ornaments of the ripening apples. It was a night for lovers' meetings, and young Thomas Blackadder, standing beneath a particularly large apple-tree, was hoping for just such an encounter. On the bark of the tree a ray of moonlight picked out the initials "J.M." and "T.B." surrounded by the outline of a heart. Thomas had carved them, and Thomas was waiting for his sweetheart, Jenny Mackie. Every night at this time, when Jenny's duties as a still-room maid at Allanbank permitted, they would meet here and stroll beneath the trees, talking of their coming wedding-day and of the small cottage which Thomas's master had promised them. Jenny was well known as being the prettiest girl in the district, and what with this and the cottage Thomas considered himself a lucky man.

Jenny was late tonight, however. Thomas had no watch and could not have told the time if he had possessed one. But he was a countryman, and by the place of the moon in the sky and the gradual silencing of even the latest-singing blackbird, he knew that he was being kept waiting. A sharp little breeze was rising, and Thomas's coat was thin; he shivered slightly.

Suddenly, through the trees, a white glimmer caught his eye— the glimmer of a dress. At last Jenny had come! "Here I am, my lass," he cried, and ran forward with open arms, eager to embrace her. She halted and stood waiting for him to reach her, a few yards away; then, just as he approached her, she vanished.

Thomas stood as if spellbound. One minute she had been there, the next she was gone. What was she playing at, and where was she? He began to run about among the trees, calling "Jenny! Jenny! Come oot, I ken ye're there!" But no Jenny replied, and Thomas began to be angry, and to think of the sharp things he would say to her when she chose to reappear. Just then he saw her again—a faint white figure at the far end of the orchard, almost half an acre off. How could she have run there in the time? He started towards her, calling her name, and all the time she stood motionless; but once again, when he was within ten or twelve yards of her, she melted into the darkness. There was nothing to be seen of her in a light that was almost as bright as day—neither shawled head nor white skirts— and the orchard was silent as death.

Thomas could not have told at what moment he was struck by a chill of horror that made him quite forget his anger with Jenny. But after a moment of contemplating the empty air where the white girl had stood, he turned on his heel and ran, never stopping until he reached the farmstead where he worked, a mile away through the village.

A few minutes after his abrupt flight, a white dress again gleamed out among the tree-trunks, and a hurried step rustled through the grass.

"Thomas! Where are ye? I'm sorry I'm late!"

But neither searching nor calling produced any sign of Thomas, and soon Jenny went home, puzzled and cross. Tomorrow, she decided, she would demand a full explanation.

But to her surprise she found Thomas reproachful instead of apologetic when they met on the following evening.

"Why did ye lead me on, lass, and then rin awa'? It was no' like ye to dae sic a thing," he complained.

"I never did! I never set eyes on ye, Thomas, and well you know it!"

They were anxious to believe the best of each other, and Jenny listened patiently to Thomas's account of his Vanishing Lady.

When he had finished telling her of the final disappearance, and of his flight, her face changed.

"Guid help us, Thomas! Ye saw Pearlin Jean!"

And so for the first time Thomas heard the story of the ghost of Allanbank. Jenny had never told him of it before, knowing him to be of a nervous, sensitive disposition, such as avoids graveyards at night-time. But she consoled herself with the thought that he would in any case have heard the tale sooner or later, for it was known to all the domestics at Allanbank and to most of the villagers.

Nearly a hundred years before, in the 1670s, young Mr Robert Stuart set out from his home, Allanbank, to finish his education as a gentleman, by making a tour of foreign cities. He was a gay, handsome young man, with bright dark eyes and a face of almost feminine beauty, well set off by the long curled wig of the time and the foppish clothes which had adorned men since the Restoration. There was not much life in Scotland for a rich and frivolous young man, and Mr Stuart was glad enough to escape to the Continent.

He had explored Italy to his own satisfaction, spending a very little time in its famous churches and a great deal in its fashionable salons, and had made his way to that Mecca of young men, Paris.

The brilliant Court of Versailles reckoned little of the wars with Spain and Holland that raged intermittently throughout those years. Luxurious living, witty conversation, and amorous intrigue were the main occupations of Louis XIV's courtiers, and the latter diversion, in particular, appealed to Mr Stuart. A strict Scottish upbringing had not been able to quench a strong natural enthusiasm for feminine beauty, and he was delighted to find the ladies of France a good deal more accommodating and accessible than those of his native country.

It was not, however, a court lady who made the sun of Paris shine most brightly for Mr Stuart. The windows of his lodgings in a tall, ancient house, once the home of a noble Parisian family, overlooked a long garden belonging to a neighbouring convent. Every morning and afternoon the nuns and novices walked there in sedate groups. As they walked, some read their breviaries, some meditated. But among those who had not yet taken their vows there were eyes that wandered—eyes as yet undimmed by the shadows of the cloister. One particular pair of eyes was often raised to Mr Stuart's windows, and the vision which frequently appeared there of a young man as handsome as any archangel—to eyes as unsophisticated as these. They were blue eyes, very large, and the hair that peeped beneath the severe hood was corn-yellow and curled softly into something suspiciously like modish ringlets. Altogether, Mlle Jeanne de la Salle was a most un-nun-like young lady. Deeply emotional and romantic, she had at the age of fourteen developed a wild attachment for one Soeur Thérèse, a teacher at the convent school which Jeanne attended. Nothing would do but that Jeanne must follow her into the cloister, and live a life of rapt piety, clad in radiant white and with her charming face surrounded by a highly becoming wimple.

But convent life, so far, had proved to be ever so slightly dull. Jeanne found her devotional rapture distinctly weak at the unheard-of hours at which a relentless bell summoned her to prayer. Perhaps she had made a mistake in thinking she had a vocation. When her eyes met the dark eyes of Mr Stuart, and held them, she was sure she had made a mistake.

Very soon a wordless rendezvous was kept every day between the young man at the window and the girl in the garden. Before two weeks had passed, a convent servant had been bribed to bring Mr Stuart a note telling him at what hour Mademoiselle would walk in the garden alone, and which garden gate would be left unlatched. On Monday of the third week, the little bell called Jeanne to prayer in vain. Her narrow bed was empty. But the more ample bed of Mr Stuart, hung with rosy curtains and watched by carven Cupids, was by no means empty.

Jeanne threw herself into the business of being Robert Stuart's mistress with the same concentrated devotion that she had at first given to her novitiate. To him, her simple sweetness and extravagant adoration brought more pleasure than had the easy favours of the Court beauties. He was as much in love as it was possible for him to be. He transferred his servants, his luggage, his lady and himself to a hotel discreetly far away from the convent, and for some two months the lovers led an idyllic life.

Ironically enough, it was the very simplicity and intensity which had attracted Robert Stuart to Jeanne which now began to repel him. He began to exchange glances with other young ladies, in public places. He invented important errands which kept him out in the evenings, while Jeanne sat in their lodgings, tapping her foot impatiently, adding a few stitches to her embroidery, then dropping her needle to sigh. Then he would come home to find her weeping and reproachful, and a quarrel would break out.

It was cowardly of Mr Stuart not to tell Jeanne that he was leaving her—that their affair was ended. He thought seriously of it one evening, when she had been more vehement than usual in her reproaches, protestations of love, and pleas for marriage.

"I left the convent for you—I broke my vows! And now, having led me into mortal sin, you won't keep your promise and marry me."

"I have told you a hundred times," said Mr Stuart patiently, "that I cannot marry you without my father's consent. He would be mortally offended, and I should lose my inheritance."

"Then take me back to Scotland with you! He will not refuse when he knows that I am a demoiselle of good family."

"I have told you I cannot. How would it seem if we travelled to Scotland together, unmarried? You must let me go back myself, while you remain here."

Jeanne wept and pleaded, but in vain. In the early hours of next morning, when it was still hardly light, a carriage drew up at the door of the hotel, and the muffled figure of Mr Stuart stepped into it. Just as the postilion was about to whip up the horses, another figure appeared in the hotel doorway. Jeanne, her face tear-streaked and her hair dishevelled, and still wearing the dress in which she had thrown herself down on the bed the night before, ran to the coach door and frantically shook the handle.

"Let me in! Take me with you! You are going to Scotland, I know it. Robert, don't leave me—don't leave me!"

But he held fast to the handle, and made wild signals to the bewildered postilion.

"You shan't go!" she shrieked. "I tell you this, Robert Stuart—if you marry any woman but me I shall come between you to the end of your days!" And she leapt on to the fore-wheel of the carriage, one foot on the hub, clinging to the top of the wheel with both hands.

"Drive on! Drive on!" cried Stuart. The postilion, half-dazed with sleep and surprise, obeyed him. As the wheels turned Jeanne fell—not to the side of the carriage, but directly in front of it. To the end of his life Robert Stuart heard her scream, as the wheel went over her forehead.

It was a dusky autumn evening, two or three weeks later, when another carriage bore him along a quiet, hilly road towards Allanbank. He was more quietly dressed than in his Paris days, but not a whit less jaunty. As a pretty shepherd lass herded her flock together to let the coach pass, he swept off his feathered hat to her and gave her a smile which irradiated her life for many a week. And why, after all, should he not smile? He was going home, after a highly instructive—and amusing—tour, marred only by one unfortunate incident of the sort which could happen to any man of the world, and which is best forgotten. His parents would be awaiting him with a warm welcome, there would be charming girls produced for his inspection. The spacious estates of Allanbank awaited him. As the coach turned a corner, the familiar arched gateway came in sight, and he leaned forward eagerly to see it.

Up the road rumbled the coach; then, thirty yards or so from the gateway, one of the horses gave a frightened neigh, and reared. A second later the other echoed it.

"Get on, ye daft cattle! What ails ye?" shouted the driver, lashing out with his whip. But both horses were as though riveted to the ground, their eyes rolling with fear.

"What is it? Are the horses mad?" Mr Stuart put his head out of the window. There was nothing to account for the animals' behaviour—no highwayman in the road, no flapping scarecrow. Suddenly his eye took in an unfamiliar object; something white and red on top of the gateway, that he had never seen there before. He stared, and stared again, and his face grew as pale as the rich lace skirts that moved softly in the breeze, as Jeanne stretched out her arms to him in welcome, and bent her terrible head, from which the blood streamed on to her white shoulders and her white bodice.

It is not recorded how Mr Stuart made his way home that night, but the celebrations for his return were not held; nor was he ever again the same confident young man who had driven up to the gateway of Allanbank.

Nor was Allanbank the same. It had been a placid house, where nothing more eventful than domestic births and deaths had ever taken place. Now it became a place to be feared at night. Unaccountable things happened. Doors opened and shut with a great noise, at midnight—a hideous scream was sometimes heard, enough to chill the blood—and the rustling of silks and pattering of high heels were heard in rooms and passages. For some time nothing was seen; then one night a maid, on her way to bed, met face to face an apparition which frightened her into shrieking hysterics. For hours she could say nothing but "The pearlin dress! The pearlin dress!" At last she managed to explain that the figure had been clad in a dress made of pearlin, or thread-lace.

The worst of the hauntings occurred when the master of Allanbank was at home. During his absences in Edinburgh or London the noises abated and the form of "Pearlin Jean", as she was now known, was seldom seen. But as soon as he returned the footsteps and rustlings began again, doors slammed, furniture moved—nobody could be sure of a good night's rest. The whole household suffered, and servants were hard to replace. But Robert Stuart suffered worst of all; he lived in constant fear of a glimpse of his dead love's lacy skirts, or of the whole dreadful figure appearing to him, as it sometimes did.

It was with a certain relief that he took to himself a wife. She was a young lady of excellent background, highly suited to become Lady Stuart—for in 1687 Robert Stuart had been created a baronet. Her temperament, fortunately, was calm, even phlegmatic. She had been told of the ghostly disturbances at Allanbank—indeed, it would have been hard to keep the information from her—but regarded them as something in the nature of a household nuisance, like jackdaws in the chimney. "Pearlin Jean" seemed furious at Lady Stuart's arrival, and redoubled her efforts to annoy; but the young lady of Allanbank refused to be put out even by a full-scale appearance of the ghost.

Sir Robert was pleased with his wife. He had her portrait, in satin and pearls, painted by a London artist, and hung with his own in the Long Gallery. On the day it went on the wall, all hell broke loose at Allanbank—objects were hurled about, tables and chairs moved of themselves, china ornaments fell and smashed—and the insistent angry footsteps paced rapidly from room to room, through halls and corridors, running down stairs and up stairs, only pausing to stamp on or kick whatever lay in their way.

Sir Robert became desperate. Finally he decided to resort to exorcism. Seven ministers of the Church of Scotland agreed to come to Allanbank and attempt, with solemn ceremonies, to send the spirit of Jeanne back to its Paris grave or to a better world. But all in vain: "they did no mickle guid," as Jenny the maid told Thomas Blackadder long after. The hauntings continued as though the reverend gentlemen had never been.

In desperation, Sir Robert sought about for another solution. The last words Jeanne had ever spoken came back to him: "If you marry any woman but me I shall come between you to the end of your days." Could she, perhaps, be pacified by appearing to "come between" himself and his wife—if only in paint? It was a strange, macabre idea, but worth trying. He nervously explained it to his wife, who with her usual calm good temper agreed that he must be prepared to try anything that would stop the nuisance. Accordingly, Sir Robert consulted a portrait-painter who was only too glad of a commission. No portrait of Jeanne was in Sir Robert's possession—

not surprisingly—but he gave the painter a full description of her as she had been, and in rough masculine fashion sketched out the style of her dress. (He had seen it often enough, Heaven knew!) Working on this, the artist produced a full-length painting, not the most accurate likeness of Jeanne, but sufficiently like, Sir Robert hoped, to please her. This he had hung in the Long Gallery between the portraits of himself and his wife.

The effect was immediate. The ghost became comparatively quiet. She made no appearances, and for the first time the Stuarts were able to go to bed with a reasonable expectation of sleeping through the night. This happy state of things continued so long that Sir Robert's confidence began to return. Now that Jeanne was pacified, he thought, might not the portrait be removed? After all, awkward questions were often asked about it, and now that his young family was growing up it was a little embarrassing for them to have the picture of a strange woman hung prominently between those of their mother and father. The picture was accordingly removed, and banished to an attic.

In the hour in which it was taken down, the hauntings returned. For some reason long forgotten, the picture was not restored to its place, and Allanbank continued to be a pestered house. If Jeanne did not actually succeed in coming between her false lover and his lady, she made their life extremely uncomfortable, and may even have hastened his death. Even after he was gone, Jeanne continued her perambulations. They extended to the grounds and gardens, as witness the teasing of young Thomas Blackadder,—though, to do her justice, she did not appear to him in her full horror.

Long after Thomas and his Jenny were man and wife—somewhere about the year 1790—two ladies paid a visit to Allanbank, which had now passed out of the Stuart family. No word of the ghost had been mentioned to them, but the night they spent there was made hideous by the constant pacing of someone unseen up and down their bedroom. In the nineteenth century the ghost was both seen and heard, but by now her power was failing and she was regarded almost affectionately. Time creeps like ivy over the memory of all wrongs—even the cruel one that had been done to poor "Pearlin Jean".

Child Ghosts

All ghosts frighten most people, but the ghosts of children, whose young lives have been tragically cut short, excite pity as well. There is always tragedy in the death of a child.

In olden times there were many of these young ghosts, but it is an interesting fact that the number of ghostly children has considerably decreased through the centuries, and the reasons for this are not hard to find.

Peoples of the ancient world did not care for their children in the way we do in modern times. It was not unusual to sacrifice a child to ensure protection from the gods and to ward off evil spirits. Children were used as foundation sacrifices and walled-up live in buildings, even in churches, and small skeletons have often been found in ancient walls as horrifying evidence of this pagan practice of long ago. The ghosts of these unfortunate children were relied upon to haunt the buildings in which they were immured and ward off the evil spirits. In some cases the haunting has gone on for centuries.

Relatives of the unwanted could be equally cruel to children in their charge, and everyone knows the legend of the Babes in the Wood, who were Norfolk children and whose rascally uncle paid two cut-throats to take them into Wayland Wood and murder them. However, their innocence and sweetness so touched the heart of one of the paid killers that he persuaded the other that instead of killing the children they should leave them to their fate. The children never found their way out of the wood, and ever after it was haunted by the two little ghosts wailing and bemoaning their fate.

Another well-known story is that of the little Princes in the Tower—twelve-year-old Edward V and his ten-year-old brother, Richard Duke of York—who were believed to have been murdered at the command of their uncle, Richard III. According to the narrative of Sir Thomas More, the Constable of the Tower, Sir Richard Brackenbury, had refused to have anything to do with Richard's plan to kill the Princes. The unsavoury task was said to have been undertaken by Sir James Tyrrell, one of whose ancestors was said to have murdered William Rufus. Tyrrell hired two ruffians, Miles Forest and John Dighton, who smothered the boys with their pillows as they slept. The Bloody Tower was haunted for centuries by these two pathetic boy ghosts. In 1674, during certain structural alterations at the Tower, a wooden chest was discovered inside which were found two small skeletons. It was presumed at the time that these were the remains of the two Princes, and Charles II had them buried in Henry VII's chapel, after which the Princes' ghosts were never seen again in the Bloody Tower.

The cessation of the haunting might have been considered reason enough to believe that the skeletons found in 1674 actually were those of young Edward V and his brother. But the authorities needed further proof apparently and the urn containing the skeletons was opened and examined in 1933. A celebrated anatomist concluded that the remains were those of two brothers of the age of the young Princes, and that the skull of the elder boy bore traces of death by suffocation. In December, 1964, the remains of eight-year-old Anne Mowbray, the child bride of the younger Prince, Richard, Duke of York, were found in a casket on a Stepney building site. It is not known how this unfortunate little girl met her death. Some think that she, too, may have been murdered, thus completing the circle of death which encompassed the innocent lives of these tragic royal children.

It is worth noting incidentally that the examination of the remains of the Princes in the Tower in 1933 was completed in five days. Three months after the discovery of the body of Anne Mowbray in 1964, the experts were still at work on the remains, despite protests by Lord Mowbray, Anne's descendant. But the authorities pleaded historical and scientific necessity.

In medieval times children were often given in marriage at a tender age for political and other reasons. Girls were considered to be grown up at fifteen and it is evident that they ripened more quickly in those days. Well-to-do families often sent their daughters away to be educated at a convent where they would learn to read and write, spin, embroider and sing.

Boys were also boarded at monasteries, or they might be sent away as pages to a nobleman's household, or taught at home by the chaplain. One boy who was sent to be a page at Hayne, in Devon, ended up haunting the Manor where he had worked and from where he had vanished together with a quantity of his master's silver.

When the master first started to see the ghost of his missing page boy he took no notice, thinking that he was dreaming, or that his imagination was playing tricks, as he had been considerably upset by the loss of his valuables. But the page-boy ghost was not to be ignored and appeared more and more persistently, always at the foot of his bed and beckoning to his old master as though asking him to follow him when he left the room.

Impatient at his continual loss of sleep, the man eventually got out of bed and followed the ghostly page-boy, who went ahead along the passage, down the stairs, across the hall and through the great front door, constantly turning back and beckoning, obviously anxious to lead his former master to some place. The man opened the front door and went out into the night to find the apparition awaiting him in the garden. The boy ghost beckoned again and continued on its way, always a little ahead of the man, whom he led into a nearby wood. Eventually the ghost stopped at the foot of a large hollow tree, and there he vanished.

Convinced now that the ghost of the page-boy was trying to tell him something, the man had the tree chopped down, and inside the hollow trunk were the remains of the page boy, who obviously had been murdered. Underneath the body was some of the missing silver, the recovery of which, with the help of the ghostly page boy, eventually led to the culprit—the butler, who had been taking the silver and hiding it in the hollow tree piece by piece until he could dispose of it. The page-boy had found out and the butler murdered him to silence him and put his body in the tree along with what was left of the stolen silver. The page-boy had returned from the dead to clear his name.

Some little ghosts are able to convey to the living what has happened to them, or what appears to worry them. Others are not able to do so, as in the case of the unhappy little girl who haunts St Helen's Church in Worcester. She is often to be seen wearing dark clothes, grovelling about on the floor of the aisle as though searching for something. She has been seen by several visitors to the church, most of whom do not realize that she is not of this world. Her white, unhappy little face as she searches the floor with tears in her eyes has brought many sympathetic words from visitors who want to know what the little girl has lost and whether they can help her to find it. Some have even offered her money, thinking that she looked ill and under-nourished, but any approach always sends her running off in the direction of the chancery where she disappears. But she returns again another day to begin her search all over again. No one knows who she is or what she is looking for.

Another sad little ghost is that of William Hoby, the boy who blotted his copybook. He was a son of Sir Thomas Hoby, whom Queen Elizabeth I appointed Ambassador to France, and Elizabeth, one of the five brilliant daughters of Sir Anthony Cooke of Essex, and who was tutor to the young and ailing King Edward VI.

The Hoby family lived at Bisham Abbey, near Marlow, Bucks, once owned by Henry VIII, who gave it to Anne of Cleves, from whom Sir Thomas Hoby acquired it.

Poor little William showed none of the brilliance of his parents, and he was so nervous when he was doing his lessons under the eagle eye of his clever mother that he always made ink blots on his copybook. Lady Hoby was a brilliant French scholar who could write verse in Latin and Greek, and the fact that her small son not only did not take after her intellectually, but could not even keep his work free from blots and inkstains, annoyed her beyond reason. One day she completely lost her temper with him, and beat him so hard and so long that the boy died.

Bisham Abbey is now haunted not only by the mournful William, but also by his mother, majestic and penitent in coif, weeds and a wimple. Lady Hoby glides through the corridors of the Abbey and along the banks of the river, for ever wringing her hands, as though trying to wash away the blood of her small son. Other reports say that she is washing her hands in blood.

In the nineteenth century a number of badly-blotted copy-books were found hidden behind the wainscoting in one of the rooms at the Abbey. One of the books had ink blots on almost every line, and it is thought that this is the one that belonged to William.

In 1946 Bisham Abbey was taken over by the Central Council for Physical Recreation, and it is used by athletes who go there for training. More alterations were being made to the Abbey in 1964-65 in order to build a gymnasium and hostel for students, when it was hoped that more papers would be discovered to throw additional light on this colourful legend.

Child ghosts are sometimes accompanied by the ghosts of older people, in many cases the mother. Watton Abbey in Yorkshire sheltered both monks and nuns in medieval times. Their vows of chastity were reinforced by a wall separating the two communities. The ghost of a headless nun, believed to be that of the beautiful Elfreda, who committed the unforgivable sin of getting over the forbidden wall, falling in love with a monk and having a child by him, still haunts the ruins of Watton Abbey. In the seventeenth century the Lady of Watton and her child were murdered by Roundheads, and their ghosts also haunt the ruins of the Abbey. It is not unusual for ghosts of different times to haunt the same place, and it would be interesting to know what, if anything, they think when they encounter each other.

Perhaps the best known of Yorkshire's many hauntings can be seen through a window in Holy Trinity Church, Micklegate, York. The window in question has four divisions of stained glass, and a strip of plain glass about two inches wide separates each division. Through this window, sometimes in broad daylight, a hooded robed figure, apparently female, has been seen passing from north to south, and then returning across the window again, this time with a child. The woman wears a long, trailing and transparent robe, and her approach is heralded by a bright light. When she is alone, she glides rapidly by the windows, but when she has the child with her she takes a little longer. They stop for a brief moment at the last pane but one and then vanish.

Many stories have been told to explain these ghosts, and one account recalls the plunder of the convent attached to the church by a party of soldiers during the reign of Henry VIII. Thomas Cromwell was the king's instrument in the dissolution of the monasteries and convents, which were a source of wealth to Henry, whose ego-mania had brought him inevitable money troubles. When Cromwell's men burst into the convent at Micklegate, they were faced bravely by the Abbess, who told them they would only enter her convent over her dead body, and that if they did kill her, she would haunt them for the rest of their lives and that her ghost would haunt the defiled convent until a new holy building took its place. Undeterred by her words, Cromwell's men slew her in brutal fashion. A terror-stricken child hiding in a corner witnessed the barbarous death of the Abbess, and was dealt with in similar manner.

Many believe the Abbess haunted the convent until it was demolished, and that she is the hooded figure who still haunts Holy Trinity Church accompanied by the ghost of the child who was killed so barbarously with her.

The ghosts of a woman and her babe in arms have long haunted the churchyard and mill-stream of Ebbw Vale in South Wales. People who have seen her say that she is clad in misty white and cradles her precious bundle in her arms, walking lightly but steadily along the path by the mill stream, looking neither to right nor to left. The stream bends near a bridge and here the phantoms disappear briefly, to reappear on the other side, the woman still clasping the ghostly child in her arms. Finally the ghostly pair come to the churchyard on the other side of the village, pass through the closed gates and walk a short distance up the path leading to the church, where they disappear.

A sad and truly Victorian legend is linked with this ghostly mother and her babe and their unsuccessful attempts to get to the altar of the church at Ebbw Vale.

They say she was a pretty Welsh country girl who had an affair with the son of a wealthy farmer. The young man's name was William, and at first he was quite serious and honourable in his intentions. The girl was much in love with William, but William's father had other plans for his son and wanted him to marry the daughter of a sea captain.

The young man's desire for the pretty dark-eyed Welsh girl was aroused and his intentions became debased to those of mere seduction. But the girl was virtuous and refused to give herself to the hot-blooded young man except in marriage. So intent was he on getting his way with her that William conceived a plan of going through a form of illegal marriage with her. This the innocent girl fell for under a pledge of secrecy, and thus William got what he wanted.

At first he visited the girl regularly at her home, much to the indignation of her father, whose reproaches she endured with fortitude, for she believed that she was William's wife in law and before the sight of God, and that the day was not far distant when she would be accepted as such.

Soon, as was only to be expected, William tired of her, and began to visit her less. His manner towards her changed, and he was cold, even cruel to her. In vain she pleaded with him to let the world know about their marriage, but he told her that his father would disinherit him if he found out. One day he told her that it was finished and that he did not want to see her again, and he left before she had been able to tell him that she was expecting his child.

When her child was born, her father threatened to turn her out of the house for the disgrace she had brought upon him. She was forced then to break her promise and tell him about the secret marriage.

Her father instantly went to William's father and told him the story. The farmer coldly assured the girl's father that there was no question of his son marrying the girl, who was beneath his station in life. Other plans had been made for William's marriage. William, summoned before the two men, admitted going through an illegal form of marriage in order to gain the girl's favours.

In vain the girl's father pleaded that William should be made to do the right thing by his ill-used daughter, but though the farmer undertook to deal with his erring son, there could be no question of him marrying beneath him. His marriage with the sea-captain's daughter was already arranged.

The girl's father solemnly laid a curse upon William, and his forthcoming marriage, and then returned home to tell his daughter how she had been so basely deceived, and to comfort her as best he could.

Just before William was to be married to the sea-captain's daughter the young abandoned mother went to see her false lover. Perhaps she thought even at that late hour that he might change his mind on seeing his own child, or perhaps she threatened to tell his future wife. What transpired was never known, but she was never seen again. The bodies of her and her child were found in the mill-stream near her home. It was never known whether the despairing girl committed suicide, or whether, as many believe, mother and child were murdered.

Poltergeists have been a source of trouble and terror throughout the ages, and when they attach themselves to places of business, such as inns, the trouble and embarrassment they cause are magnified a hundredfold.

An old inn called "The Jolly Collier" at Dudley, Worcestershire, was, according to legend, beset by such phenomena, causing visitors to be thrown out of their beds, objects hurled about the rooms, crockery broken, bells ringing unaccountably at all hours. It became so bad that no one would stay at the inn. The landlord's wife had died leaving him a young daughter.

It has been long believed that poltergeists are attracted towards children. In many cases they only operate when children are in the house. It certainly seemed to be so in the haunting at "The Jolly Collier".

Business was so bad that the distraught landlord got into debt, and eventually, threatened by bailiffs and debtors' prison, he killed his daughter and then took his own life. The poltergeists then left the inn which has ever since been haunted by a flaxen-haired girl and a man in a brown suit.

The mortality rate in Europe was very high right up to the end of the nineteenth century. The parish registers tell a frightful story of whole families of children dying one after the other from poverty and the diseases it brought. The Industrial Revolution which brought about a great increase in child labour made things worse than they had been in the previous century. The Napoleonic wars also caused great poverty all over Europe, particularly among the poorer classes. Children were always the first victims of the pestilences which followed in the wake of Napoleon's armies. The factories brought no prosperity to the working people, only hard and grinding work in conditions of labour and hours of work which their grandparents, let alone their descendants, would not have tolerated. This had such an effect upon a whole generation that people born in the eighteenth century were much stronger than either their children or their grandchildren. The cholera epidemic of 1832 took a dreadful toll, affecting the rich as well as the poor. The children went down like flies. Perhaps one or other of these circumstances might account for the grisly discovery in the following story.

A mother and her two daughters went to stay in a certain house in the north of England during the middle of the nineteenth century. The house was rather full and their hostess asked if the older girl, May, would mind sharing a room with her small sister. During the night May was awakened by feeling that a child's head was resting upon her shoulder. Thinking it was her younger sister, she asked why the child had come into her bed? Was she afraid as they were in a strange house? On getting no reply and not being able to feel her sister in bed with her, May lit her candle and saw that her sister was sleeping peacefully in the bed next to her. Thinking she had been dreaming, she put out her candle and went back to sleep, only to be awakened again by the same feeling of a child's head resting on her shoulder. She put out her hand, but there was no child there. She decided that it was all in her imagination and eventually went to sleep. But the next night the same thing happened. She kept waking up convinced that a child's head rested on her shoulder.

She had very little sleep that night and in the morning she told her hostess, who then moved her to another room where she slept soundly and undisturbed.

Some time later the house was pulled down and under the floor of the room where May had slept with her little sister were found the skeletons of five children.

The Club of Dead Men

Cambridge is full of ghosts. What else could one expect of that enchanting city of chiming bells and soaring spires, of echoing courts and oaken stairways. Cambridge will hold my heart for the rest of my days, even as it captured it when young. It is the city of eternal youth, of grace and beauty, dusty with age, bright beneath its blue East Anglian sky. It has a spirit and an atmosphere a world away from this drab, standardized modern world of birdcage architecture, mediocrity and hyena pop-singers.

You might expect, therefore, that its attitude towards ghosts is rather different. It was put, blandly, by a College "bedder" when I woke up one morning in a small room in the oldest part of Corpus. As she put my cup of tea down by the bed I remarked cheerfully: "There's a ghost on the next staircase, isn't there—the old man who looks out of a window?"

"Lord! Bless you, sir," said she cheerfully. "There's a ghost next door all right, but there ought to be one in that there very bed you're a-sleeping in! One of the gentlemen shot hisself in that bed on'y a few years ago. Sech a nice gennleman too. He left £5 to me and the other bedder with his apologies for the mess he made a-shootin hisself."

I have sat up in the ancient house of the Ghostly Squire and dozed in the room where a White Nun walks. I have heard chains rattle in a cellar as midnight struck from all the bells of Cambridge.

I know the ghastly tale of The Man Who Changed Into a Cat and I know a room in Scrope Terrace where extremely odd things happen. The most macabre of all the ghosts of Cambridge is The Club of Dead Men. I heard of it first on a bright May morning when I sat at the feet of the Sage of English Literature.

"Spend a night in Cow Lane if you want to write about ghosts," said "Q", with an amused twinkle. He pushed a Georgian decanter of Warre's '08 gently across the table. It reflected roses in a silver bowl. The year was 1920, so the wine was in its prime. "You'll see enough there to keep you busy writing about them for a year," he added, "if you come out alive!"

Through the windows, the sun lit that oaken-floored, panelled room of his in Jesus and made pools of light on the polished floor. The long refectory table bore, as always, its bright picture of roses in silver, and port wine winking in cut-glass.

The late Sir Arthur Quiller-Couch, that master of English literature, did not, I fancy, ever believe in ghosts, although in 1900 he wrote a book called *Old Fires and Profitable Ghosts*, when this scribe was at the thoughtful age of one year. Then came *Q's Mystery Stories* in 1937. Whether he believed in ghosts or not, he made them profitable. Perhaps not such money-spinners as *Troy Town*, *The Splendid Spur*, *The Golden Pomp*, *The Ship of Stars* and those others with shining titles. Nonetheless, ghosts to him were fun.

The man who held a Master of Arts degree at both Oxford and Cambridge and was a Doctor of Literature of the Universities of Bristol, Aberdeen and Edinburgh, as well as Professor of English Literature at Cambridge, and author of some fifty-three books and editor of the Oxford Book of Prose, never quite grew up.

That fact and his love of lordly language, his devotion to the beauty of simple English and his infinite wisdom, made him unforgettable. He had no peer. Such another will not soon arise.

I went off to look for Cow Lane. It is not, as you might suppose, a twisting alleyway of cobblestones, such as might have led once to a cattle-market or a buttercup meadow among the river willows, but a staircase. Neck-breakingly steep, it rises in headlong flight from the stone floor in the angle of the cloister next to the Hall of Jesus College at Cambridge. You could pass it by easily, without glance or thought. If you did glance it is unlikely that you would think of climbing that steep and sudden flight of stairs, which, half-way up, is crossed by a great beam so that you must duck your head or be brained.

Yet if you climb those stairs, as I did, rosy with port, ducking your head on the way, you will come to a massive oaken door on the right of the landing on the top floor. When I climbed it first, more than forty years ago, a great padlock on a chain closed the door like a prison. I stood, frustrated.

Then came footsteps climbing the steep stairs from below. A "gyp", swinging a key in his hand, whistling gently between his teeth, ducked his head beneath that murderous beam and, in a few steps, was on the landing and fitting the key into the padlock. He swung the door open.

"Ah!"I said."Just what I wanted! May I have a look in that room?"

"You may, sir," he chirruped cheerfully, for he was a bird-like little man, with a striped waistcoat which somehow made one think of a chaffinch. "Not at there's much to see, sir, 'cept jugs and basins, plates and bowls, cups and saucers—an' a few dozen domestic bedroom-ware—them what the young gennlemen likes to 'ang up of a dark night over the front door of the Senate House, the day before Degree Day, or 'oist to the pinnacles of King's Chapel. We keep our reserves of sich in 'ere."

A gloomy room with, if I remember rightly, a great stone fireplace, a lot of old oak and a window which was either walled up or heavily curtained. The bare oak floor was stacked with glimmering, ghostly piles of crockery, chinaware and those bulbous unmentionables in which the"gyp"seemed to take a personal pride.

"This 'ere is the Ghost Room,"he remarked brightly. "It's where the Everlastin' Club meets, once a year. They 'ave met 'ere for two 'undred years or more. 'Orrible goings on! When them ghostly gennlemen gather in this room, they kick up such a 'ell of a row that you'd think they was smashin' up all this 'ere china and cuttin' each other's throats. That's why it ain't used any longer as gennlemen's chambers but jest a storeroom.

"I 'ave 'eard," he went on, drawing in his breath between his teeth and sucking an invisible lollipop with ghastly relish, "as 'ow the last gennleman as 'kept' in these 'ere rooms was so 'orrified by the 'orrible crew of ghosts as met 'ere one midnight, when he wasn't expectin' of 'em, that 'e bolted out of this 'ere door, went down them stairs three at a time, bashed his blessed 'ead on that there beam, stunned 'isself cold and rolled over and over to the bottom of the stairs where 'e lay for dead. Pore gennleman! Never was right in the 'ead arter that lark."

He whistled brightly, obviously delighted with his own story, dusted a few dozen plates with lightning flicks of a napkin, balanced a monstrous pile of them on both hands, from his navel to his chin, and asking me to lock the door behind him trotted gaily down the stairs like a circus artiste. I slammed the door, turned the key in the padlock, descended those cliff-like stairs, taking care not to 'bash my 'ead', and joined the little man in the cloister.

"Sir Arthur says I ought to spend a night in those rooms," I remarked, conversationally. "But as I'm not a member of this College, I suppose I'd better get the Master's permission."

"Wot flowers would you like on your cawfin, Sir?" the little man inquired brightly. "Carnations, pinks, lilies or jest a bunch o' roses? I'd like to remember you, sir, when you passes over!"

He suddenly became serious. "I wouldn't sleep in that there room for all the tea in China, all the suvvereigns in the Bank o' England. No, sir! And don't you do it neither. Anyway, the Master wouldn't let yer."

That little chat took place more than forty years ago. Today, I believe, the rooms at the top of Cow Lane are occupied by an undergraduate, who, so far as I could find out on a visit to the College in 1955, slept well at night. He had not, in the year of 1955 at any rate, bashed out his brains in headlong midnight flight.

It was not always thus. As you will have gathered from the "gyp's" spirited description and Sir Arthur Quiller-Couch's quizzical suggestion, the rooms at the top of Cow Lane have a certain cachet.

Cachets, however, like cliches, wear thin with the passing of time. What is a fad in one decade is a bore in the next. Old gods are overthrown. New gods arise. Sometimes sheer atheism takes their place. It may be, therefore, that the ghosts of Cow Lane have given up the ghost. So let us unravel the tale before it is all forgotten.

It began in the days of George II, or of his successor, the third George; the days of brocade and powdered wigs, knee breeches, silk stockings and buckled shoes, clouded canes and curious clubs.

Cambridge University, like that other place somewhere on the upper reaches of the Thames, has always been a hot-bed of clubs. Literary Clubs, Debating Clubs—who remembers the Magpie and Stump nowadays?—Political Clubs, Dilettante Clubs, Wine Bibbing Clubs, Dining Clubs, Clubs for Fox-hunters and Beaglers, Clubs for Fossil Diggers and Bird Worriers, Card-playing Clubs, Highbrow Clubs for Pale Ineffectuals—any, and every, excuse is good enough to found a club.

So it was in the days of George II and his poor Queen Caroline, who, I am sure, often wished herself back in her father's Margravate of Brandenburg-Anspach. The Georgian undergraduates had their clubs for dining, wining, talking, gambling, reading, debating, dicing and dancing, in College rooms and inn-parlours, in raftered halls and the panelled rooms of pleasant private houses, new-risen in their Georgian red brick. They were all harmless enough—except the Everlasting Club. It was evil, a callow sort of evil.

It aped that other Hell Fire Club of Medmenham Abbey, not far from that other place on the upper reaches of the Thames. But this pale, Cambridge shadow of the gilded, gaudy evil spawned by that other place, boasted no Barrymore, no Dashwood, no orgiastic revels in the underground caverns of West Wycombe Park, or bawdy profanation of abbey cloisters. It merely met in the rooms at the top of the landing, on the right-hand side, as you go up the stairs called Cow Lane—without bumping your head. There were seven members only. They were all young and foolish, between twenty-two and thirty years of age. One was a Fellow of Jesus named Charles Bellasis, a sprig of that noble family which produced the Lords Bellasis, more than one of whom died on the point of a sword in riot and wine. Another was a young Cambridgeshire squire. The third member was a Fellow-Commoner of Trinity. The next two were Fellows of other colleges. The sixth was a young Cambridge doctor.

The Founder and President of this Club was the Honourable Alan Dermot, the son of an Irish peer, who had a nobleman's degree at the University, which meant that he wore a tuft in his "square"or academic cap. Hence the word "tuft-hunter", to describe those who fawned and fattened on noble undergraduates in the days when they were distinguished by dress and privilege from the common run. Dermot, an idle fellow, was vain, cruel and wicked. He learnt nothing but vice, lived for naught but folly, and died with a rapier in his stomach, coughing out his blood, in Paris in 1743. You may regard him as the evil genius of the other six members.

It was the duty of the secretary of this foolish, futile, but nonetheless Everlasting Club to keep a Minute Book. That book, detailing the Club's activities from the years 1738 to 1766 was, according to the late Arthur Gray, until recent years Master of Jesus College, "a stout duodecimo volume, bound in red leather and fastened with red, silken strings". There were forty pages of goosequill writing, in a plain, legible, educated hand. They ended abruptly with the date 2 November, 1766.

The first pages of this book set out the laws of the Club. Here they are:

"1. This Society consisted of seven Everlastings, who may be Corporeal or Incorporeal, as Destiny shall determine.

"2. The rules of the Society, as herein written, are immutable and Everlasting.

"3. None shall hereafter be chosen into the Society and none shall cease to be members.

"4. The Honourable Alan Dermot is the Everlasting President of the Society.

"5. The Senior Corporeal Everlasting, not being the President, shall be the Secretary of the Society, and in this Book of Minutes shall record its transactions, the date at which any Everlasting shall cease to be Corporeal, and all fines due to the Society. And when such Senior Everlasting shall cease to be Corporeal he shall, either in person or by some sure hand, deliver this Book of Minutes to him who shall be next Senior and at the time Corporeal, and he shall in like manner record the transactions therein and transmit it to the next Senior. The neglect of these provisions shall be visited by the President with fine or punishment according to his discretion.

"6. On the second day of November in every year, being the Feast of All Souls, at ten-o'clock post meridium, The Everlastings shall meet at supper in the place of residence of that Corporeal member of the Society to whom it shall fall in order of rotation to entertain them and they shall all subscribe in this Book of Minutes their names and present place of abode.

"7. It shall be the obligation of every Everlasting to be present at the yearly entertainment of the Society, and none shall allege for excuse that he has not been invited thereto. If any Everlasting shall fail to attend the yearly meeting, or in his turn shall fail to provide entertainment for the Society, he shall be mulcted at the discretion of the President.

"8. Nevertheless, if in any year, in the month of October and not less than seven days before the Feast of All Souls, the major part of the Society, that is to say, four at the least, shall meet and record in writing in these Minutes that it is their desire that no entertainment be given in that year, then, notwithstanding the two rules last rehearsed, there shall be no entertainment in that year, and no Everlasting shall be mulcted on the ground of his absence."

There are other rules, but they are either too impious or childish to be worth printing. They do show, however, the remarkable levity with which the Everlastings took on their fantastic obligations.

Morals were bad enough throughout England in the first half of the eighteenth century. The reflex in the University was equally bad. Nonetheless, the behaviour of the seven members of the Everlasting Club scandalized even that lax age. The College authorities came down heavily on them. Charles Bellasis was "sent down". Somehow he contrived to retain his Fellowship.

Other members were sent down by their various colleges as the years went on. Yet, each year, they met in the rooms of whoever might be Secretary at the time. There they drank and sang far into the night and scandalized the college and the stars alike with their riotous debaucheries.

The Minutes were kept religiously; perhaps one should say irreligiously, for not only is there a record of attendances, fines inflicted and the rest of the Club business, but each page carries obscene and irreverent remarks.

The first entry which begins to give a hint of the terrible end of the Club is that under the date of 2 November, 1743. That night the members dined in the house of the young Cambridge doctor. One member, Henry Davenport, a Fellow-Commoner of Trinity, was not there. He had been an officer in King George's army, and had been killed at the Battle of Dettingen, the last battle, incidentally, in which the British Army was led in person by the Monarch.

The members did not know, when they sat down to dine, that Davenport was dead. He was absent, so he had to be fined. And he was. The Minutes contained the simple entry: "Mulctatus propter absentiam per Presidentem, Hen. Davenport."

Did the ghost of the dead Davenport, now an Incorporeal Everlasting, sit down to dine that night, as he had sworn in life to do? It seems likely, for on the next page there is this entry: "Henry Davenport, by a Cannon-shot, became an Incorporeal Member; 3 November, 1743."

How, you may ask, could the members know of his death within a few hours of their dining that night, unless he, Davenport, appeared in spirit that night, at the dinner table, to tell them that he was either dead or about to die? He may, indeed, have been dead by the time the dinner was finished, since they went on well into the early hours of 3 November, when the second entry was written.

There was no telephone, no wireless, no railways, no aeroplanes, no means of communication save couriers, who took days on horseback and aboard sailing ships to bring such news so swiftly in so short a time.

So it seems likely enough that the six Everlastings, those still alive sat down to dine that night in the young Cambridge doctor's house with Dermot at the head of the table—and one empty chair. They dined and they drank wine. The "claretted and punched", topped up with black-strap and dosed themselves with brandy, sang their ribald songs and screamed their insults to God until the stars wheeled in their courses.

At some time, probably at the beginning of the dinner, the Secretary formally reported the absence of Henry Davenport, The President, equally formally, inflicted his fine. Then they drank their sherry and sat down to dinner.

One may imagine the decanter of claret or burgundy or Rhenish being pushed round the table in its Georgian silver coaster—until it came to the empty chair.

Then a ghostly hand, silvery, impermanent in the yellow candle-light, reached out, lifted the decanter, filled the empty glass—and raised it to the slowly-seen, grinning spectral lips of Henry Davenport. There he sat, gradually taking shape, in his tarnished regimentals, his powdered wig, sardonically smiling, the first Everlasting to become an Incorporeal Everlasting.

Consider the gasp which went round that suddenly chilled table. The blanched whiteness of six frightened faces. The stuttering attempts to recapture the old, profane defiance of God and Death.

Then, perhaps, Davenport spoke. Probably he called them, poked fun at them, reminded them that they had all sworn to turn up each year at the dinner, *dead or alive*.

And so, said he, here am I, Henry Davenport, one-time Fellow-Commoner of Trinity, for all time the first Incorporeal Everlasting come to honour my pledge—*as you must all do*—dead or alive, each year throughout eternity.

If that were not horrible enough to contemplate, what does one make of that other entry in the book, on the same date, 2 November in the same year, 1743, for there, boldly written, in his own unmistakable handwriting at the top of the list, is the signature of "Alan Dermot, President at the Court of His Royal Highness".

Now it is an historical fact that the Honourable Alan Dermot was at the Court of Prince Charles Edward Stuart, the Young Pretender, in Paris, in October, 1743. It is equally a fact that he was killed in a duel in Paris on 28 October—*five days before the Club met*. The news of his death cannot have reached the Club on the night on which it met and dined, 2 November, for, under the date 10 November appears this entry: "This day was reported that the President was become an Incorporeal by the hands of a French chevalier." It was followed by a sudden written gasp from the Secretary, for, in his goose-quill handwriting, he slapped down the unexpected prayer: "The Good God shield us from ill."

Yet how came the President's handwriting, unmistakably his own, to appear at the top of the list, when the entries of attendance were written down at that dinner of 2 November? In short, the

President must have been there, *although dead*, in his normal, earthly, human form and semblance of being. He must have eaten and drunk with them, cracked his wicked jokes, uttered his profanities, cursed his God and generally behaved as the man whom they all knew—leaving them to find out later that they had dined not with a living man but with *a ghost*. That is the sort of ghastly joke one would expect from Dermot.

The news that they had dined with a dead man, who seemed in every sense to be a live man, shattered the Club. The five remaining members were paralysed with fear. They left Cambridge. They buried themselves on their distant country estates—for most of them were landed men. The Cambridge doctor tried to banish from his mind the memory of the dead man sitting at the head of his table, leering and laughing as though alive. Better, far, the pale, half-seen, ethereal wisp in the empty chair that might, or might not have been, Henry Davenport. He, at any rate, had not signed *his* name in the book. Had he seemed to have been there, it might so well have been a mere trick of the wine. Yet no matter how the doctor might seek to forget these things by dedicating himself to his patients and his medical researches; no matter how the other four members might hunt the fox, shoot their pheasants with long, single-barrelled muzzle-loaders, play cards at night with their neighbours, devote themselves to their home farms or to the bottle, each man knew that unless he wished once more to face the hateful, leering presence of the President, at the Annual Dinner on 2 November, he and the others must not fail to turn up and record their objections to the dinner being held each year "in the month of October and not less than seven days before the Feast of All Souls".

So for five years, five wretched men met annually in October, lodged their formal objection to the holding of the dinner and the Secretary duly recorded it in the Minute Book. Then another member died and, like the little nigger boys, "then there were four".

For eighteen years after, the four haunted, wretched survivors continued to meet each October and record their protests. Among them was Charles Bellasis. He had become middle-aged and respectable. Jesus College had once more admitted its one-time renegade Fellow to its ancient bosom. He was a model of decorum. He lived in the rooms at the top of Cow Lane.

Finally, we come to the year 1766. Under the date of 27 January appears this entry in the Minute Book:

"Jan. 27th. On this day, Francis Witherington, Secretary, became an Incorporeal Member. The same day this Book was delivered to me, James Harvey." Harvey died a month later. On 7 March is another entry, which tells us that William Catherston is the new Secretary. He lived little more than two months. For, on 18 May, Charles Bellasis sets down the fact that Catherston had died on that date and that he, Bellasis, was now the last Corporeal of the Club and therefore the Secretary.

Now you will remember that under Rule 8 it was laid down, hard and fast, that an objection to the holding of the annual Dinner could only be lodged by "the major part of the Society, that is to say four at least." So long as four of them were alive, they were safe. When Francis Witherington died on 27 January in that year of 1766, it left only Harvey, Catherston and Bellasis. Harvey and Catherston, by now middle-aged, were probably so terrified out of their wits at having to face the ghastly banquet in November that they died of heart failure or sheer terror—perhaps by their own hands.

Bellasis was a tougher type. He determined to live. Moreover, he determined to defy the rules of the Club. He was now a respected, honoured and more or less welcome Fellow of Jesus. The young generation knew nothing of his past. The older ones had either forgotten or forgiven him.

What happened behind the heavy oaken door at the top of those steep stairs in Cow Lane in that dark panelled room on the night of 2 November will never be known. One would have thought, to begin with, that Bellasis would either have left College that night altogether and stayed elsewhere with a friend in a house full of lively people or, at the least, would have slept that night in the rooms of another Don or Fellow of the College. He was not that sort. It may be that the spark of his old youthful spirit of devil-may-care still flickered bravely. At any rate he stayed in his rooms and "sported his oak".

At ten o'clock, precisely, pandemonium broke out. Shouts and yells, oaths and bawdy songs, blasphemies against God, the crashing of glass and the breaking of furniture horrified the night.

Dons shivered in the Senior Common Room. Undergraduates quaked in their beds. The Master fumed in his Lodge. The porters and other college servants trembled in their shoes. None dare climb the steep stairs of Cow Lane, to discover what unholy visitors were revelling in the rooms of Charles Bellasis, Fellow of the College. Dead on midnight, the uproar stopped. The College slept uneasily the rest of that night.

When dawn came the Master and braver Dons, with some sturdy

workmen, crept up the steep staircase. They listened outside the stout, low, oak door of Bellasis's rooms. Not a sound. Quiet as the grave. They knocked. No answer. They rattled loudly on the door. There came no reply.

"Break the door down," the Master ordered.

A sledge-hammer splintered the lock. Crowbars sent the bolts starting from their sockets. The door splintered and swung open.

There, at the top of the long oaken table, sat Charles Bellasis. Dead. His head was bent low; his folded arms shielded his eyes. He had died in fear of the dreadful sight, whatever it may have been, which he had seen.

About the table were six other chairs, drawn up as though at a dinner. Some were turned upside down. Some were smashed. Broken glass glittered in the thin light of dawn. Smashed china littered the floor. The terrible smell of death was in the cold air.

On the table lay the red, leather-bound Minute Book, in front of Bellasis. Goose-quill pen, a silver ink-pot and a sand-sprinkler were beside it. On the last page, dated 2 November, were written, for the first time since 1742, the full names of the seven members of the Everlasting Club. None had given his address. In the bold hand of the President, Alan Dermot, was written these words:

"Mulctatus per Presidentem propter neglectum obsonii, Car. Bellasis."

That was the end of the Everlasting Club. From that day until at least 1920, and possibly twenty years after that, the rooms remained tenantless. They were used, as I have said, for storage. The legend persisted that, annually on the night of 2 November, "sounds of unholy revelry" were heard from Bellasis's chamber. That, I believe, is a fiction. No one has been able to pin down any witness who can swear that he heard any sounds from the room on the night of any 2 November. Indeed, if one reads the Minute Book, it is quite clear that no provision was made for the holding of the Annual Dinner after the last Everlasting had become an Incorporeal. As for the Minute Book itself, Arthur Gray says:

"The Minute Book was secured by the Master of the College, and I believe that he alone was acquainted with the nature of its contents. The scandal reflected on the College by the circumstances revealed in it caused him to keep the knowledge rigidly to himself."

He addes: "And though, so far as I am aware, it is no longer extant, I have before me a transcript of it which, though it is in a recent handwriting, presents in a bald shape such a singular array of facts that I must ask you to accept them as veracious."

For myself, having known and loved Cambridge for more than half a century, I can affirm that this tale is a living legend. It endures to this day. Not one, but many members of Jesus College and of its staff have assured me that the rooms at the head of Cow Lane, the last meeting place on earth of the Everlasting Club, are not the rooms in which they would choose to sleep. Why else were they left untenanted for nearly two hundred years?

A Piece of Black Velvet

Why I tie about thy wrist
Julia, this silken twist
'Tis to show thee how in part
Thou my pretty captive art,

quoted Sir Tristram Beresford, looking admiringly across the breakfast-table at his young wife. Even at this time in the morning, and clad in a simple loose sacque, she was appealingly beautiful. But a little pale and distrait today, thought Sir Tristram; perhaps she had slept badly. As he spoke she gave a little start.

"I was not attending; what did you say?" she asked.

"I was only quoting Herrick, my dear—as being relevant to your new ornament." His eyes went to her wrist, about which was tightly bound a piece of black velvet ribbon, hiding the white skin for some two inches. Lady Beresford's pale face flushed, then paled again.

"I——" she began, then bit her lip, and seemed unable to go on. Sir Tristram waited patiently. She rose from the table, walked to the window, and stood looking out unseeingly. Then she turned to face her husband.

"Tristram," she said, "I have something to ask of you. Never inquire of me why I wear this ribbon. I shall wear it always—you will never see me without it—but I cannot tell you why—I *cannot*."

Sir Tristram was a kindly man, much in love with his wife, and prepared to make every allowance for women's fancies. When their two daughters had been born Nicola had had strange whims—it was all part of the fascinating panorama of femininity. He went to her and patted her shoulder affectionately.

"What you do not wish to tell me I shall not ask, now or at any time, my love," he said. "Now pray do sit down and finish your breakfast."

Lady Beresford obeyed him, though without much appetite. After a few mouthfuls she laid down her knife.

"Has the post come yet?" she asked nervously.

"Not yet, my dear."

"Oh. I thought, as I was up so late, it would have been here by now." Sir Tristram was not unduly curious about his wife's interest in the post. They were on a visit, this October of 1693, to Lady Beresford's sister, Lady Macgill, at Gill Hall, in the County Down, southern Ireland. It was natural that she should want letters from home, where their two children had remained in the charge of nurses.

Lady Beresford sipped her chocolate abstractedly, then laid down her cup and rang the handbell which was beside her on the table. In a moment her maid appeared.

"Have the letters come yet, Bridget?" she asked.

"No, my lady, not yet."

"Bring them to me as soon as they arrive."

When the girl had left the room Sir Tristram looked humorously at his wife.

"Really, my love, I shall begin to think you are expecting a communication from some gallant, if you continue to show this anxiety," he said.

"Don't joke!" she flashed at him. "If you knew——"

"If I knew what?" he asked gently. "Won't you tell me, my dear? What is it you expect to hear in a letter today?"

His wife's head drooped, and her fingers strayed to the black-bound wrist.

"I expect," she said in a low voice, "I expect to hear of Lord Tyrone's death."

"Of Tyrone's death? Your old playfellow? But, my dear Nicola, why should you anticipate his death? Surely he is only the same age as yourself. You have always told me you were brought up by the same guardian as if you had been twins."

"We were born in the same year," she replied. "Nevertheless, I know that he is dead. And that he died on Tuesday."

Sir Tristram came round the table and sat by his wife's side, with his arm about her shoulders.

"My sweet Nicola, this is not like you. You have never been superstitious—in fact I think our good chaplain believes you to be rather too worldly for your soul's welfare."

"Yes," she answered tonelessly, "I have never been a true churchwoman. I was brought up to think freely of spiritual matters. But now you will see, I shall be different."

"You've been dreaming, my love. That is all. Get dressed now, and we'll go for a ride in the Park. The exercise will restore you."

At this moment the door opened, and Sir Tristram, seeing his servant, said: "Oh, Patrick, see that the horses are brought round in half an hour, will you?"

"Yes, sir. The letters have arrived, sir."

He laid them on the table, and Lady Beresford eagerly snatched at them. Among them was one sealed with black wax.

"It is the Tyrone crest!" she cried hysterically. "You'll see, he is dead. Open it, Tristram, for I cannot!"

Sir Tristram did as she asked. As he read the letter, his face changed. He laid down the letter and looked at her gravely.

"God knows how you knew, my dear; but it is true. Tyrone's steward writes that he died in Dublin on Tuesday, at four in the afternoon."

"I knew it! I knew it!" she cried, and burst into tempestuous weeping. As Sir Tristram tried to console her, his mind was busy. Strange things had been known in this fairy-haunted land of Ireland, and strange prophecies had been made in dreams. It was not for him to deride his wife's premonition. Young Tyrone and she had been brought up together, and had had for each other the deepest affection—as deep as though they had been truly sister and brother. The fact that their guardian had reared them in the principles of Deism, and not in the Christian faith, had only bound them closer together, making them allies in a world that condemned them. There must, Sir Tristram reflected, be a strong soul-tie between them, and it was quite possible that in a vivid dream the news of Tyrone's death had been conveyed to the woman who had been his "sister Nicola".

Lady Beresford had become calmer. Drying her tears, she assured her husband that she felt relieved now that she knew the worst. "And I have something else to tell you," she added with a rainbow smile, "something that will please you."

"What's that, my dear?"

"I am with child," she replied. "And it will be a boy."

Her husband was almost speechless with delight and amazement.

If her premonition of death had been true, why should not this happier premonition of birth? At last perhaps he would have the son he longed for. He rang the bell for the servant.

"The horses may go back to the stables," he said. "My lady will not ride today."

Soon afterwards they left Gill Hall for their own home in Derry. In the following July, true to her prophecy, Lady Beresford bore a son, Marcus. Six years later Sir Tristram died.

Only thirty-four years old, and still beautiful, Lady Beresford might have been expected to make an early second marriage. But it seemed to her friends that she wished to avoid even the possibility of it. Even when the period of mourning was over she refused invitations to social gatherings, dressed in black, and lived as quietly as possible in the company of her three children. Close friends found that she did not relish their society any longer; and her only intimates were now a Mr and Mrs Jackson, of Coleraine. Mr Jackson, a clergyman, was one of the town's leading citizens, and was related to the late Sir Tristram on his mother's side. His wife had a brother, Colonel Richard Gorges, a young man who had risen rapidly in his Army career. He was handsome, charming, slightly dissolute, and a good many years younger than the pretty widow; but it soon became obvious that he was paying court to her. One day Mrs Jackson and Lady Beresford were sitting together at tea when Lady Beresford, who had been very silent for some minutes, rose from her chair and seated herself on the sofa by her friend.

"Jane," she said, "I have some news for you. I think you will not find it hard to guess."

Mrs Jackson looked at her apprehensively.

"Nicola, it is not—Richard?"

"Yes. We are to be married."

"But, my dear, have you thought? He is so much younger—and so—though he is my own relative, I cannot think he will make you a good husband. Pray do consider this carefully!"

"I have considered it," said Lady Beresford. "I have given it earnest thought and prayer." (For some years now she had been a devout member of the Church.) "It is my conviction that Richard and I are destined to be husband and wife, and that our mutual love will compensate for the difference in our ages."

"Will you not at least wait another year—six months?" urged Mrs Jackson. Lady Beresford shook her head.

"The marriage is to be in six weeks. I have quite made up my mind."

Mrs Jackson sighed. She knew her brother only too well.

Her fears, and those of Lady Beresford's other friends, were justified. For a short time after their marriage in 1704 the ill-assorted couple seemed happy enough; it was apparent that the former Lady Beresford was infatuated with her young husband, and in order to get control of her money and possessions it suited him to please her for a time. But soon, in spite of the birth of two daughters, they began to drift apart. Colonel Gorges treated her cruelly and contemptuously, laughing at her tears and reproaches when some fresh evidence of his infidelity came to her ears. The children were brought into contact with his roistering companions, who came to stay at the house and behaved shamefully there. At last, goaded into action, Nicola Gorges insisted on a separation.

Their parting lasted for several years, during which Mrs Gorges reverted to her former quiet life. But her infatuation for the unworthy man she had married never quite died. He had now risen to the rank of General, and his way of life seemed to have steadied somewhat. When he came to her and fell on his knees, begging her to forgive his past faults and take him back, and promising most solemnly to be a reformed character and a model husband in the future, she at first wavered and then relented. In 1715 they once more lived together as man and wife; and a year later Nicola Gorges, though now middle-aged, became the mother of a second son. All was joy. General Gorges appeared pleased, and treated his wife with particular affection. The Jacksons said to each other that perhaps they had been wrong, after all, since this apparently ill-fated marriage had been blessed so late and so unexpectedly.

Mrs Gorges was happy beyond expression, and particularly so because her fiftieth birthday, that milestone in a woman's life, was past, and here was she restored to youth by the gift of a baby son to her arms. She kept her bed for three weeks, as was the custom of ladies in that age, but a month to the day after her son's birth she felt so well that she decided to hold a small celebration. A party was planned, to include her son Sir Marcus Beresford—now twenty-two—and her married daughter, Lady Riverston. Also invited was Dr King, the Archbishop of Dublin, who had become a great friend of Mrs Gorges since her conversion to the church; and of course the Jacksons could not be left out.

About noon on the day of the party Mr Jackson called to inquire after the hostess's health. He found her up and dressed, blooming and youthful in a white satin dress laced with pink, the only sombre note in her costume the black ribbon which still bound her wrist. Mrs

Gorges rang for Madeira and biscuits to be served, and a nurse was summoned to exhibit the baby for Mr Jackson's admiration.

"My dear madam," said the clergyman. "This is indeed a happy day."

"Indeed it is," replied the beaming mother. "And what is more, it is my birthday."

"Of course—I had forgotten. But Jane no doubt has remembered and will bring you a gift this afternoon."

"I want no gift but my son," she said, looking fondly down at the occupant of the cradle. "Tell me, do you think I look my age? Has he not waved the wand of youth over me?"

"Whatever age you are, madam," replied Mr Jackson gallantly, "I can assure you that you do not look it."

"Well then," she said, smiling, "I am fifty-one years old."

Mr Jackson's eyebrows rose. "Fifty-one? I had not thought—let me see, I had a discussion with your mother, many years ago, upon this very point. What was the issue, now? She declared that you had been born in 1665."

"That is so. Lord Tyrone and I were almost twins."

"But I assured her that it was not so" said Mr Jackson. "Indeed, I confirmed it by consulting the baptismal register, in which it was clearly stated that you were born in 1666. I remember it well, because it was about the time we had news of the great Fire raging in London."

Mrs Gorges paled, and her youthful radiance seemed to fade in a moment. "Then," she said tremblingly, "I am not fifty-one years old, but only fifty."

"That is the case, madam. Are you not glad to find yourself a year younger than you imagined?"

Nicola Gorges rose and walked slowly to the window. She stood looking out at the pleasant garden and the pearly clouds sweeping above the trees, as though she had never seen them before. After a few moments she turned, and said in a calm voice:

"You have signed my death-warrant, Mr Jackson. I have not much longer to live. No,"—cutting short his anxious exclamations—"there is nothing you can do to help me, except to send my son and daughter here to me as soon as you can. And send word to the Archbishop that I shall not be able to entertain him today."

Puzzled and alarmed, Mr Jackson obeyed her orders. The two young people were soon at their mother's side, distressed to see such a change in her since earlier in the morning. She kissed her baby, bade the nurse take it away, and, telling her son and daughter to sit down, solemnly addressed them.

"I have something most important to tell you, my dears, before I die."

"Die, Mamma!" exclaimed young Sir Marcus. "Pray don't jest with us.'

"It is no jest, my son. Be patient, and listen to me. You know that as a child I was brought up with Lord Tyrone like sister and brother —indeed, I doubt if you two, fond though you are, are as attached as we were. Our guardian was a free-thinking man who held that the beliefs of the Church were all superstition, and that only a materialistic view of existence could be held by sensible people. Now, a great many of our friends were shocked by his views, and lost no opportunity of putting their own to us. Poor confused children that we were, we did not know what to believe; particularly as regarded a future life. One day, after talking for a long time, we made a pact, as young people will. Whichever of us died first would, if permitted, appear to the other and tell him or her what were the real great truths.

"Years passed. We grew up, and I married your father, Sir Tristram. John—that is, Lord Tyrone—and I saw little of each other, though we kept up our friendship by letters.

"Now comes the strange and dreadful part of my tale. One night, in October, 1693, your father and I were on a visit to your Aunt Arabella at Gill Hall. We had gone to bed as usual, and were sleeping soundly, when I suddenly awoke with the consciousness that somebody else was in the room with us. I sat up—and saw Lord Tyrone, sitting by the side of the bed. I did not know what to think, but I was very frightened, and screamed out. Your father did not stir, and even shaking his shoulder could not wake him. Then Lord Tyrone, bending on me a solemn look, said:

"'It is myself and no other, Nicola.'

"'But why are you here at this time of night, John?' I asked, trembling.

"'Have you forgotten our youthful promise to each other? I died on Tuesday, at four o'clock. I have been permitted to appear to you thus to let you know that the Church's religion is the true and only one by which we can be saved. And I am allowed to tell you something else. You are with child, and will bear a son, who will marry my daughter.'

"'But——' interrupted Sir Marcus.

"'Peace, son. You will see it will come true.' Then Lord Tyrone told me that Sir Tristram would not long survive after the child's birth, and that in the course of time I should marry again, and die as a result of childbirth in my fiftieth year. 'Good Heavens,' I said, 'cannot I prevent this?' 'Of course you can,' he replied, 'you are a free agent and may resist any temptation to a second marriage, but your passions are strong.' 'Oh, tell me——' I began; but he held up his hand (which was perfectly solid, and could not be seen through) and said: 'More I cannot tell you, but one thing— that if you persist in your present opinions your fate in the next world will be miserable indeed.' 'Are you happy yourself, John?' I asked. He smiled. 'Had it been otherwise I would not have been permitted to appear to you.'

" 'But now,' I said, 'when morning comes, shall I be convinced that your appearance has been real, and not a mere phantasm of my imagination?' 'Will not the news of my death be sufficient to convince you?' he asked. 'No,' I replied. 'I might have had such a dream, and that dream might accidentally have come to pass. I want some stronger proof of your presence.' 'You shall have it,' he said. He waved his hand, and the crimson velvet bed-curtains were instantly drawn through a large iron hook by which the oval tester of the bed was suspended. 'Now you cannot be mistaken,' he said. 'No mortal arm could have done that.' 'True,' I replied, 'but in sleep we are often far stronger than in waking. Awake, I could not have done it—asleep, I might—and therefore I shall still doubt.' Then he said: 'You have a pocket-book here in which I shall write. You know my handwriting?' 'Yes,' I said. He then wrote his signature on one of the leaves. 'Still,' I objected, 'in the morning I may doubt. When I am awake I cannot imitate your handwriting, but asleep it's possible that I might.' 'You are hard to convince,' he said with a smile. 'I might—but I must not touch you, for that would mark you for life.' 'I don't mind a small blemish,' I replied. 'You are a brave woman, Nicola,' he said, 'hold out your hand.' I did so. He touched my wrist lightly with his hand, which was as cold as marble, and in a moment the sinews shrank up and the nerves withered. 'Now,' he cautioned me, 'let no mortal eye see that wrist, while you live.' I looked down at my injured wrist, then back to him—but he had vanished.

"While he was with me I was perfectly calm and collected, but the moment he was gone I felt chilled with horror and dismay. A cold sweat came over me, and again I tried to wake your father; but he would not stir. For a time I lay awake, weeping, and at last fell asleep.

"In the morning your father awoke and dressed himself without waking me—he apparently found nothing unusual about the bedcurtains. When I awoke they were still as Lord Tyrone had left them. I went into the gallery adjoining our bedroom, and found there a large cornice-broom, with the help of which I unhooked the curtains, fearing that their position might cause inquiry. Then I found a length of black velvet ribbon, and tied up my wrist with it before going down to breakfast.

"You, Marcus, came into the world exactly as Lord Tyrone told me you would, and your father died, as he had prophesied. Remembering his other warning, I tried to avoid society and not mingle again with the world, hoping to avoid the dreadful fate a second marriage would involve. But alas! At the house of my only real friends I met a man I found deeply attractive, and in a fatal moment—for my own peace—I married him. Then his conduct drove me to demand a separation, and again I hoped to escape the prophecy. I thought today that I *had* escaped it. But Mr Jackson has just told me that I am only fifty today, not fifty-one—all this time I have been mistaken about my age. I know, therefore, that I am about to die."

Sir Marcus and Lady Riverston wept, and protested that their mother must be mistaken. But she held to her story, and seemed now quite calm and resigned. One thing only she asked them.

"When I am dead, my dears, I want you, and you alone, to unbind this black ribbon from my wrist, and see what it covers."

Sadly, they promised, and left her alone to rest, as she requested; but at Lady Riverston's earnest plea she agreed to let a maidservant with with her in case she should need anything.

An hour after they had left her, the bell in her room rang violently. The brother and sister ran upstairs, to meet the frantic maid standing outside the door of Mrs Gorges's room and crying:"Oh, she is dead! My mistress is dead!"

Before Mrs Gorges's body was committed to the grave, Sir Marcus and Lady Riverston knelt alone beside it, and, as she had wished, unwound the black ribbon. There, in proof of her story, were the shrunken and withered sinews.

The last of Lord Tyrone's ghostly prophecies soon came true— his daughter married young Sir Marcus, and their daughter, Lady Betty Cobbe, allowed her grandmother's strange story to be known in 1806. It aroused widespread interest, and impressed Sir Walter

Scott sufficiently for him to base a poem on it, in which the verses occur:

> He laid his left palm on an oaken beam,
>   His right upon her hand—
> The lady shrunk, and fainting sunk,
>   For it scorched like a fiery brand.
>
> The sable score of fingers four
>   Remains on that board impressed;
> And for evermore that lady wore
>   A covering on her wrist.

The Ghost in Two Halves

At the physical heart of Scotland lies the county of Perth, and almost bisecting the county laterally is Glen Lyon, the largest of all the Scottish glens, whose cold clear stream, rising on the borders of Argyllshire, swells as it tumbles its way down eastwards, until it meets the River Tay as a considerable tributary just north of the northern tip of Loch Tay.

Even among the barbaric romanticism which characterizes so rawly the glens and their inhabitants, Glen Lyon's history has a special glow all its own. Originally the property of the Clan Macgregor, it was taken from them in the late sixteenth century, when, as a punishment for opposition to the throne, "letters of fire and sword" were issued against them, and those who escaped death were deprived of their patrimony, and dispersed. About a century later, some of the Highland chiefs took a deep dislike to the new regime of William and Mary. One of them, Alexander Macdonald of Glencoe, was so slow in taking the oath of allegiance to the monarchs that the government resolved to punish him and his men as technical traitors.

The Master of Stair, Sir John Dalrymple, the official responsible for ordering and organizing the Macdonalds' punishment, probably recalled the "letters of fire and sword" issued against the Macgregors, for he gave orders for the destruction of the clan. He bestowed the commission upon Captain Campbell of Glen Lyon, who went about his task with such devotion that he cheerfully resorted to treachery. Though the majority of the Macdonalds escaped with their families to the hills, when Captain Campbell had finished forty Macdonalds were dead, and the Massacre of Glencoe remained a permanent blot on the already violent history of Scotland.

On his way to the homes and mountains of the Macdonalds, Captain Campbell had stayed the night at Meggernie Castle, which lies roughly half-way up Glen Lyon. The oldest parts of the castle date from the fifteenth century, and are characterized by walls of immense thickness. But additions were made later when Scots architects were under the influence of their counterparts among their French allies. For example, the square baronial tower, with its high-pointed roof and battlemented parapet, might well have graced a rather solid château.

Since Meggernie Castle was taken from the Macgregors it has passed through various hands, and in 1862 it was owned by a Mr Herbert Wood. Wood was an hospitable man, and enjoyed nothing so much as having a castle full of guests.

To one such party he invited a friend, E. J. Simons, who lived at Ullesthorpe, in Leicestershire. Simons was late in arriving, and by the time he reached Meggernie all the guest rooms had been allocated, with the exception of a large room in the tower.

"I hope you won't mind being tucked away up there," Wood said to his guest. "You won't be alone. In the adjoining room I've put a very good friend of mine, Beaumont Fetherstone."

"I don't mind at all," Simons assured Wood. "The tower is the oldest part of Meggernie, if I'm not mistaken. I shall find it most interesting."

"It is quite pleasant up there," Wood admitted. "There are fine views of the glen, and I'm sure you'll find Fetherstone a congenial sort of chap."

Shown to his room, Simons discovered that his host had, in fact, been too modest in describing the prospect it provided. From the north window he looked out on the hills at whose base the castle stood, and which sheltered it from the cold northerly blasts. From the south window was a view of the rich meadows and majestic park, with a swift silent stretch of the River Lyon beyond, at no farther distance than a long stone's throw. Across the river lay the heather-carpeted moors.

In the drawing-room before dinner, Simon found his fellow guest in the tower to be as agreeable, in his own way, as the room. Beaumont Fetherstone was a man of about his own age—in the early forties—good-looking, good-humoured, with a gay laugh and lively eyes, giving an overall impression of levelheadedness. "A man after my own heart," Simons told himself.

It had been a long and tiring journey from the railhead at Perth to the castle, and not long after dinner Simons excused himself, saying that he would like a good night's rest to refresh for the stalk which had been arranged for the following day. Beaumont Fetherstone overheard him making his apologies and said that it was a good idea, and one that he himself would follow.

Together the two men made their way to their rooms in the tower, pausing outside Simons's to wish one another good night. In his room, Simons closed his door, and as he turned into the room his attention was caught by another door which he had not noticed earlier and which looked as though it should connect with Fetherstone's room next door.

Crossing to it, Simons discovered that it had been securely fastened and that even its keyhole had been blocked up. He knocked on it to attract his neighbour's attention, and when Fetherstone called out, asked, "Does this door lead into your room?"

"Well, yes and no!" Fetherstone replied. "It leads into a small cupboard which looks as if it might have been used as a powder closet. I tried it before you arrived, but it's securely screwed up on my side. Would you mind if I came and had a look at it from your side?"

"Certainly," Simons told him, and for the next twenty minutes or so the two men inspected door and cupboard, surmising this and that reason for its being securely walled up. Then once more they bade one another goodnight and prepared for bed.

How long Simons had actually been asleep he could never say, but in the early hours he was awakened by what felt like the light touch of a branding-iron on his cheek. The sensation was nevertheless so fierce that he believed that the flesh had been seared through to the bone.

It brought him to his senses with such force, however, that not fully realizing what he was doing, he leapt out of bed. And as he did so he saw distinctly the upper half of a woman's body drifting across the room towards the sealed-up door, through which it disappeared.

Simons rushed to the door, expecting to find it open. But it was as securely fastened as it had been when he and Fetherstone had carefully inspected it a few hours earlier.

He was, however, a man of cool courage, recognizing no misapprehension of phenomena for which at first sight there appeared to be no rational explanation. At least that is the kind of man he seems to have been from his immediately subsequent behaviour.

For he did not call out, nor do anything to rouse his fellow guest next door, but having first lit his candle he went to the mirror above the dressing-table to examine his still smarting cheek, expecting to find some sign of the cause of the pain. To his complete surprise he found not the slightest mark.

At last it began to occur to him that what had happened seemed to have in it elements of the supernatural. This his cool-headedness could not accept, so taking up his candle he left the room and began to search the passages and staircases of the tower for some sign which would provide an acceptable explanation of the apparition.

When he had searched every corner of the tower and found nothing, he returned to his bed and passed the remaining hours till dawn sleepless and perplexed.

As soon as he heard Beaumont Fetherstone moving, he called out to him, "Fetherstone, I've had a terrible night!"

"What did you say?" Fetherstone called back through the sealed-up door.

Simons repeated that he had had a terrible night.

"That's what I thought you said, Fetherstone replied. "May I come round?"

"Of course," Simons told him.

A minute or two later Fetherstone came into the room, a splendid morning figure in a rich brocade dressing-gown which swept the floor. For the moment Simons forgot the reason for the visit.

"How very splendid!" he commented.

But clearly Fetherstone was less interested in his dressing-gown than in the experiences of the night. "Passed on by an ancient uncle," he said lightly and briefly, going on quickly, "Did your terrible night include a ghost?"

"I suppose you could call it that," Simons admitted. "But I've always thought of myself as a rational man, and ghosts are not submissive to reason."

"A woman would you say?" Fetherstone asked.

"Well, part . . ." Simons began.

Fetherstone held up his hand. "Don't say another word, old chap. I have an idea. We'll each tell our stories separately to Herbert Wood, and see what happens. Do you agree?"

"Certainly," Simons replied. "It will be interesting, but I don't mind telling you that I am still disinclined to believe in ghosts."

"Then we're both in the same boat," Fetherstone said. "I didn't.

Reason tells me now not to. But . . . well, I'll go and dress. See you at breakfast."

Mrs Wood was already at the table when Simons went into the dining-room. Indicating a vacant place on her left, she said: "Herbert and Beaumont have gone to the library. They won't be long. I understand you had a disturbed night."

"I'm afraid so," Simons agreed, and was on the point of telling her when she put her hand on his arm. "Later, Mr Simons, please!" Then in a whisper, "The servants are very superstitious."

Presently their host and Fetherstone came to the table. Wood was somewhat withdrawn, but Fetherstone seemed in the best of spirits.

At the conclusion of the meal, Wood reminded his men guests that the stalk would assemble at the main entrance of the castle in half an hour's time. Then looking towards Simon, he said: "Edward, Beaumont tells me you would like to speak to me in the library."

"If you can spare a moment," Simons replied, now rather wishing that he had not agreed to Fetherstone's plan.

"Perhaps you will come too, my dear," Wood suggested to his wife. "You, of course, Beaumont."

In the library Wood said: "It was as I thought, my dear, our guests have had a disturbed night. Beaumont has told me his story. Edward will tell us his now. I thought it would interest you to hear it, my dear, in view of what the servants have been claiming recently."

Succinctly, but careful to leave out no detail, Simons related his experiences, and as he did so he noticed that Fetherstone was becoming more and more excited, though he did not interrupt; while Mrs Wood regarded the speaker with increasing bewilderment. When he had finished, Fetherstone exclaimed, "There, Herbert, the same in every detail!"

"In *almost* every detail," Wood corrected him.

"In every essential detail," Fetherstone persisted.

"What exactly happened to you?" Wood asked.

"Well, it was round about two o'clock," Fetherstone began. "I had been asleep for quite a time, when suddenly I woke up and realized that the room was faintly illuminated by a suffused pink light. At first I thought one of the out-houses had caught fire and the light was coming from the flames via the windows, until I remembered that I had not drawn back the curtains, which were still closed when I looked at them.

"It was as I turned from looking at the windows that my glance caught the figure of a woman standing at the foot of the bed. At first I thought it might be the housekeeper . . ."

"Mrs Menzies in a guest's room in the middle of the night!" Mrs Wood exclaimed. "My dear Beaumont, please never let her have the faintest whisper of your suspicions. She would be outraged!"

"I had no ill opinion of her motives, I assure you," Fetherstone exclaimed. "It struck me that she might be sleep-walking."

"I'm sorry, Beaumont," Mrs Wood smiled. "I'll not interrupt you again."

"As I was wondering what I might do for the best, for I have heard or read somewhere that it can be dangerous to waken a sleep-walker," Fetherstone went on, "she began to come round the side of the bed and as she came level with me started to incline towards me.

"A little alarmed by what I thought she intended to do, I sat up fully, the better to ward her off; and as I did so, she backed away and then turned and went hurriedly across the room towards the old powder closet. It was as she passed through the door into the closet that I realized I could not see her legs. In fact, she seemed to be walking on invisible legs."

Like Simons, however, though shaken, he lit his candle and when the lady did not emerge from the closet and not a sound came from that direction, he got out of bed and quietly made his way across the room. Though, under his night-shirt his flesh was covered with goose-pimples, he compelled himself to enter the little room.

"There was no one there!" he said. "The hip-bath and the clothes-horse were there, untouched, just as you saw them, Edward, and as you know there is no window; no opening, in fact, except the door into my room, the sealed-up door into Edward's room and the two long narrow loop-holes in the outside wall, which in any case are so narrow that not even the domestic cat could squeeze through them."

Mystified, and still not realizing that he had perhaps seen an apparition, he thought that while his attention was directed towards lighting the candle, the lady might have slipped out of the closet and concealed herself in the bedroom. So, before getting back into bed, he had made a thorough search of his room, even to the extent of looking under his bed. But all without result.

"She must have come to me after she had visited you," Simons remarked, "otherwise I should have heard you moving about. At least she spared you her burning kiss."

"I'm certain she intended it," Fetherstone said. "I seemed to have frightened her when I sat up in bed . . . Well, there you are, Herbert! Your castle is haunted by half a female ghost!"

"Exactly!" Wood replied. "The question is—which half?

Both the men looked at him sharply.

"Which half?" exclaimed Simons. "What do you mean? Fetherstone and I both saw the top half."

Wood glanced across to his wife with a faint smile. "You'd better tell them your story, my dear," he said.

"Why, have you seen her, too?" Fetherstone asked Mrs Wood.

"No, I have been spared that so far," Mrs Wood answered, "But one day last week one of the young housemaids ran screaming on the verge of hysterics into the still-room, where I was, crying out that she had seen a ghost."

"What time of day was it?" Fetherstone asked.

"Mid-morning," Mrs Wood replied. "It was a bright morning, too, full daylight, and I thought the simple girl had been frightened by a shadow, but when I had calmed her down she declared that what she had seen had been the *lower* part of a woman; that is to say, from the waist downwards, moving at speed along the north corridor leading from the tower. The lower part of the gown which covered the legs, she said, was covered with blood at the waist, or where the waist ought to have been.

"Somehow I managed to persuade her that she had been the victim of her imagination. I say persuaded her, but I don't think I did, really, for she gave in her notice before the day was out.

"Naturally, it was impossible to keep this sort of thing from the ears of the other servants, and I decided to warn my housekeeper what might be in store. She told me then that this was the first time the apparition had made its appearance for some years, but that, on the other hand, there were several among the older servants and people who live in the glen who claim that they have seen these ghostly legs not only wandering about the castle, but in the avenue of limes and in the graveyard. I must say it is a slight relief to know that there is an upper half also."

"Until this latest manifestation," Herbert Wood put in, "I had no idea at all that the castle was supposed to be haunted."

"The housemaid's experience," Mrs Wood went on, "has, as I am sure you will appreciate, unsettled the servants, and I'm afraid some may leave us. That was why I stopped you when you seemed on the point of telling me what had happened to you during the night, Edward."

"But you've lived here for five years now, Herbert," Fetherstone commented. "Had you really heard nothing until now?"

"Not a whisper?" Wood told him.

"I suppose you've made inquiries, Herbert," Simons said.

"No, I haven't," Wood answered. "I thought it best to leave well alone. You know what the folk up here are like. Start asking questions, and you'll let them know at once that something has happened. Tongues will begin to wag, and before long the servants will be frightened off. Situated as we are, we should never be able to replace them."

He looked at his watch.

"Well, it's time for us to be moving off. I can rely on you both I know, not to talk to any of the others about what has happened, and we must hope that the lady, whoever she is, will keep her top half and her bottom half well out of the way."

"Of course we'll say nothing," both men agreed.

"Fortunately," Mrs Wood said, the "Hawthornes are leaving today, so you will not have to spend another night in the tower."

Simons and Fetherstone protested that it was not necessary to move them, but Mrs Wood believed she detected a certain half-heartedness in their protests, and insisted.

"For my own peace of mind," she said, "I'll have your things brought down while you are out."

In the next few days Fetherstone's visit came to an end, but Simons stayed on for a week or two. Before he left the castle, he was to have yet another encounter with the legless ghost.

It was late at night and the other guests and their hosts had already gone to bed. Simons, however, wished to catch the next day's post, and went into the library to write his letters.

As he bent over the writing-table, presently he became aware that the atmosphere in the room had become so cold that he was beginning to shiver a little. Yet when he glanced towards the grate, a large log was blazing on a deep bed of glowing embers. And he became aware, too, that there was beginning to envelop him, some of the sensations of terror that had made him so uncomfortable during the night he had spent in the tower.

He glanced round the room, half-expecting to see the upper half of his former visitor. She was not there, but his attention was attracted and held to the heavy studded door to the library which was slowly and noiselessly opening.

As he stared at the door, unable to take his eyes from it, he saw pass down the corridor outside the upper half of a woman's body go gliding by. With a tremendous effort of will, he put down his pen, picked up the lamp by whose light he was writing, and frozen to the marrow he forced himself to set out for his bedroom, with the intention of taking refuge there.

To get to the room, however, he had to pass down a long flagged passage on the ground floor. The passage was lit by a single window, and as he passed it he saw peering in through the glass a woman's beautiful face, upon which was an expression of infinite sadness.

He recognized it at once as the face he and Beaumont Fetherstone had seen on the night they had spent in the tower. It brought him to a stop, but even the full beam of his lamp, which fell fully upon it, did not seem to disturb it, for it remained looking in through the window long enough for him to take a long look at its features. Then suddenly it was gone.

When he reported his experience to Herbert Wood next morning he begged him to let him make discreet inquiries to try to discover whether any local tradition existed which might provide an explanation for the haunting of the castle. Wood gave his permission on condition that Simons would be really careful not to say or do anything which might increase the superstitious misgivings with which, if the servants were a true guide, the inhabitants of Glen Lyon regarded Meggernie Castle.

It took Simons many days of skilful and cunning interrogation before he finally pieced together the story which clearly formed the basis of the haunting. It was, indeed, a gruesome tale.

In the days when Meggernie Castle formed part of the estates of the Clan Menzies, the then chief of the clan had a very beautiful wife. Though utterly innocent and completely modest, the lady attracted the attention of all the local gentlemen, who paid her gallant court.

Instead of taking this universal admiration as the compliment it was to himself as much as to his wife, the Menzies was constantly creating scenes which showed that his jealousy bordered on insanity. One of these scenes, in which he reached new heights of invective and accusation of infidelity, took place one day when the couple were in the room which Beaumont Fetherstone had occupied in the tower on his and Simons's first night at the castle.

On this occasion, the Menzies's jealousy roused him to a pitch of violence which surpassed all his previous attacks, and culminated in his striking his wife. She fell and caught her head, as she did so, against one of the bed posts.

Immediately his rage evaporated, and he ran to her and knelt beside her, imploring her to open her eyes and try to find it in her heart to forgive him. It was some minutes before he was sufficiently calm to realize that she was dead.

Jealousy was not the only flaw in his character, for now he began

to search for means by which he might be able to escape the consequences of what he had done. After some thought he formulated
his plan.

In the powder closet, he knew, was a large chest-of-drawers; the
same which still stood in the tiny room when Beaumont Fetherstone and Edward Simons inspected it that night. He dragged his
wife's body across the room with the intention of concealing it in
one of the drawers. But though his wife had been slightly built
none of the drawers of the chest was large enough to take her.

The Menzies was now beside himself, and reacted with the stark
ruthlessness which characterized so many of his contemporary
countrymen. He fetched a saw, and sawed the body in two at the
waist. One half he then put in one drawer; the other in the drawer
above.

This gruesome task finished, he then nailed up the door leading
from the closet to Simons's room, locked the door leading into
Fetherstone's room, then left the bedroom, fastening its door securely
behind him.

Going downstairs he ordered one of the grooms to bring round
his wife's carriage, saying that she wished to visit a relative who
lived farther up the glen. He told the groom that he would drive
the carriage himself.

None of the servants saw the carriage go, and when the Menzies
returned alone in it shortly before dinner time no one was surprised,
either by the absence of Mistress Menzies, or by his further orders.
These were to the effect that he and the mistress had decided to go
on a visit abroad, that her maid was to pack a suitable selection of
clothes, and that the carriage was to be ready shortly after dawn.
Once more he announced that he would drive it himself, and added
that as the visit would probably keep them away for several months,
the servants were to be sent home on board-wages, and the castle
shut up.

Early next morning the servants watched him drive away in the
carriage. Seven months passed before they saw him again, and heard
from him the sad news that the mistress had been drowned in a
boating accident in Italy.

There was no reason why they should not believe him, and soon
the glens-folk and neighbours were calling to offer the Menzies
their condolences. The Menzies played the part of bereaved husband
convincingly.

When life had settled down once more into the normal run, he
decided that he must no longer delay in disposing permanently of

the evidence of his crime. So, one night, taking a dark lantern and a spade, after the servants were safely in bed, he went to the nearby kirkyard and prepared a shallow hole.

He then returned to the castle, and made his way to the tower. The room was still locked, as he had left it, and so was the closet, he noted with satisfaction. But some of his composure left him when he let himself into the closet and, on opening the lower drawer, smelt and saw the putrefaction of the limbs it contained.

It took some minutes for him to steel himself to lift the decaying flesh into a sheet. By the time he had deposited it in the grave in the kirkyard and covered it over, he had had more than he could stomach for one night, and decided that the second part of his task must be left for another occasion.

But he did not dare to put off the task too long, for the stench from the closet would undoubtedly betray its contents if it were not soon disposed of. So next night, fortifying himself well with whisky, he forced himself to prepare a second grave in the kirkyard.

Before going up to the tower, he went to the library where he poured himself another glass of whisky, which he swallowed at one gulp. He was so intent upon what he had to do that he was completely unaware of the dark shape which followed him silently, concealing itself in the shadows.

Despite the false courage which he had hoped the whisky would have given him, when he reached the powder closet and opened the drawer the state of what he found there was too much for him.

"I can't do it!" he muttered to himself. "But it can't stay here! What is to be done with it?"

As he spoke, he staggered back into the bedroom, and in doing so he stood on a loose floor-board. With a whimper of awesome joy, he pulled back the carpet and inspected the board. It was a half-section, newer than the rest of the floor, and whoever had been responsible for laying it, he had not nailed it down, for when the Menzies tried he found that he could prise it up with the point of his dirk.

Below was a deep cavity whose floor was the ceiling of the room beneath.

Hurrying to the closet, not daring to think of what he was doing, he dragged the stinking remains of his wife's torso from the drawer, thrust it between the joists, replaced the board, and drew back the carpet.

It was as he turned to take up the candle with which he had lighted his way that he saw the tall figure standing in the doorway.

Who the figure was, tradition does not say. It is clear, however, that the Menzies realized that he had been watched, and that his secret was no longer safe. He rushed at the figure, dirk in hand; but the figure was too quick for him. The servants, searching for him next morning found him dead in the already drying pool of blood which had seeped from the wound in his heart.

Thus the top half of the murdered Mistress Menzies lay beneath the floor-boards of the room in which she had been killed, while her lower half lay buried in the kirkyard. This, so tradition had it, was why the Meggernie ghost haunted the rooms of the tower, while the lower half wandered about the ground-floor corridors and the avenue of limes.

After the experience of Fetherstone and Simons, Mistress Menzies remained quiet for some time. But there are records of more recent manifestations, the most recent being to a local doctor who was called to the castle late one night in 1928, and accepted an invitation to stay the night.

He was put in a room in the tower below the one in which Fetherstone had slept. The doctor fell asleep, and after an hour or two suddenly awoke, and believed that he heard footsteps approaching his door. He expected that he was being summoned to his patient, but as he waited for the knock on his door which did not come he had the impression that someone had entered the room.

As he glanced about the dark room he saw, illuminated in a kind of aureole of pink light, a woman's head and shoulders gliding round the walls of the room, high up near the ceiling. As he watched it, suddenly it disappeared.

In more recent times there has been no sighting of the apparition, but successive occupants of the castle have heard occasional inexplicable rappings and knockings.

The Ghost of Nance

In the days when the fastest traffic on the Great North Road were the mail-coaches, one of the coachmen, Tom Driffield, was engaged to marry Nance, the daughter of a farmer at Sheriff Hutton in Yorkshire. The day was fixed for the third Sunday in May; the farmer had contracted with the local builder to build them a cottage in one of his fields standing back from the road, and Nance and her mother and sister were spending every spare minute sewing her trousseau.

Nance was some fifteen years younger than her husband-to-be, but she had no doubts on that score. He was handsome and strong, and no driver of the mails could match him in skill between Edinburgh and London. But it was neither his looks nor his strength nor his skill which had won the heart of Nance. It was the warm kindness that shone from his great brown eyes, the quiet kindness of his deep soft voice and the gentle kindness in the caresses of his broad hands.

The banns were to be called for the first time on the last Sunday in April.

"It's a pity you can't be at the church to hear them," Nance had said when Tom had told her that on that day he would be carrying the mails from York to London. "But I'll go and I'll think of you all the time, dear Tom."

She had arrived at the church for matins that Sunday morning with her father and mother, brothers and sisters, with few other thoughts besides those she had of Tom. But as the five-minute-bell began to toll, there came striding down the aisle a young stranger. His jet black hair, shining with pommard, was drawn tightly down over his head into a queue in the nape of his slender neck, held in place by a splendid bow of crimson velvet. His coat sat with elegance upon his well-formed body; the calves encased in flashing white stockings were perfectly proportioned with swelling thighs and tapering ankles; his feet in their leather pumps glistening with silver buckles were the neatest to be seen on any man; the frills at his wrists, and the jabot at his throat, were of finest Brussels lace; while on the long slender index-finger of his right hand scintillated a diamond the size of a hedge-sparrow's egg, the only piece o jewellery about him.

The beadle, taking him to be gentry, conducted him to pews reserved for distinguished strangers, on the left side of the chancel steps which looked inwards and faced the squire's pews. He bowed to the beadle, who closed the door of the pew after him, then placing his black tricorne he was carrying on the seat, he knelt with his face in his hands for some seconds, before sitting back and allowing his gaze to wander over the congregation.

Presently his eyes came to rest on Nance, who had been regarding him frankly since the moment of his appearance. He held her gaze for a time, until a nudge from her younger sister brought her to her senses.

"You're staring, Nance," Prue scolded. "It's not polite."

"Who is he?" Nance whispered, lowering her eyes.

"Some London gentleman," Prue told her. "Been staying at the inn since Thursday."

(Prue was being courted by Dick Driver, son of the inn-keeper, and was always the first of the Tucker family to learn any news.)

The organ struck up, the choir emerged from the vestry, and soon matins were in full swing. Nance, staring hard at her prayer-book, did her best to concentrate on versicles, psalms and responses, but every so often she felt her gaze going across the aisle, and each time she looked up she saw that his eyes were on her. Only when she heard the Rector call Tom's name with hers as he read the banns did she remember to think of her future spouse, and she felt a spasm of shame. It was short-lived, however, for when she looked up, blushing, the young gentleman's eyes were still on her.

When the service was over, many of their neighbours in the village had waited by the porch to give her their good wishes for her happiness. She thanked them demurely, leaving her mother to do the talking. And while they stood there, he came out of the church.

Seeing her he smiled, and in great trepidation she watched him coming towards her. His tricorne pressed lightly to his chest, he leaned forward in a bow.

"Ma'am," he said. "I believe I have the honour and great pleasure of addressing the fortunate young lady whose banns were called for the first time this morning?"

"Sir," she said, bobbing a curtsy. Then turning to Mrs Tucker, she went on, "My mother, sir."

He bowed again, and Mrs Tucker curtsied.

"Ma'am," he said, "may a stranger offer one of the prettiest girls he's ever set eyes on his most cordial wishes. Your future husband is the most fortunate of men."

"You are kind, sir," replied Mrs Tucker. "My daughter thanks you."

Once more he inclined towards her, smiled broadly at Nance, put on his tricorne and strode off down the path back to the inn.

"Fine manners these gentlemen have!" Mrs Tucker sniffed, "if many of them have little else besides."

"You saw his great diamond, mother?" Nance exclaimed.

"Glass, if the truth was known," said Mrs Tucker tersely.

But here she was wrong. It was a genuine stone, only lately come into the gentleman's possession.

Three days later Sheriff Hutton was thrown into an uproar. Jill Thornton, who helped Mrs Tucker in the kitchen, had come scurrying down to her mother's cottage with the incredible news that during the night Nance Tucker had eloped with the fine stranger at the inn, who had decamped, incidentally, without settling his account. She had left behind a note telling her parents so, and a note for Tom Driffield, begging his forgiveness, but saying that she had lost her heart utterly.

On Sunday evening, Jill went on, Jane Croft, a maid at the inn, and a friend of hers, had come to the farm on the pretext of visiting her. At the first moment they were alone together, Jane had produced from her blouse a note which she begged Jill to give to Nance secretly as soon as possible.

"He's sent you this," Jane said, pressing into Jill's hand a silver crown piece.

Jill entered excitedly into the plot, and contrived an early opportunity to pass the note to Nance. After supper, when her work in the kitchen was finished, and she had gone up to her bedroom, as she was drawing the curtains she had seen a woman in a long hooded black cloak glide quickly across the farmyard, making for the field behind the long barn.

When Tom Driffield learned that his Nance had forsaken him, he seemed to be broken. But there was in him a vein of stoicism and presently he told himself that nothing happens without good reason. So he continued to drive his coach from Edinburgh to London with the care and skill that he had always employed, maintaining his reputation as the fastest mail on the Great North Road, and in December he married a Thirsk girl, and made a home for her there.

Nothing was heard of Nance in Sheriff Hutton; no word came from her to her parents. It was as if she had vanished from the face of the earth.

Then one wet and miserable day in the following March, as Tom was driving his coach south and was a few miles from York, he saw a woman standing by the roadside with a baby in her arms. Though illness and exhaustion had much changed her appearance, he recognized her at once, and reined in his horses.

"Why, Nance," he exclaimed, jumping down. "You are ill. There's room in the coach. Get up and I'll take you to York to a doctor."

She was almost too weak to speak, but as he lifted her and her baby into the coach she whispered, "Dear Tom."

In York, when he had set down his passengers for the night, he took Nance and her child to the York Tavern, where the proprietress was a friend of his. While Nance was being put to bed, he fetched a physician, who, after examining her, took him seriously aside and told him that neither she nor the child could live long.

That evening he sat by her bedside, hoping to comfort her. He could not reproach her, and he asked her no questions. If she wished him to know how she had come to this plight she would be telling him, and this it seemed she wanted to do.

It was a pitiable story. The fine gentleman had proved to be a highwayman; but what was worse, after they had gone through a marriage ceremony at Northallerton and the child was already coming she had discovered that he was married already, and she had left him. Since then she had been working in service with a family in Oswaldkirk, over by Helmsley, but when the baby was born they had turned her out. Scarcely knowing what she was doing, she had wandered over the moors, and had reached the main road shortly before he had come along.

"If ever I set eyes on the scoundrel," he promised her, "I'll flog him within an inch of his life."

She took his hand and smiled at him wanly.

"Dear Tom," she said, "if you don't catch him, sooner or later the law will."

Throughout the night he dozed by her bed, and she was sleeping still when he had to leave her. Handing a sovereign to the landlady, he said: "Look after her well. Whatever more you spend, I will repay you when I return."

When he came again to York going north, and called at the Tavern, it was to be told that Nance and her baby had died three days after he had gone.

"Before she died she said to me," the landlady told him, " 'Dear Tom, he never uttered a word of reproach. Tell him that to repay his kindness, if ever he, or his son, or his grandson, are ever in any need of help, I will come back to help them.' "

Tom smiled.

"She'll keep her promise," the landlady said sharply, seeing him smile. "You see if her words don't come true."

During the next two years nothing happened, and then one day, as sometimes happened, Tom was given a special commisssion. He was to take a carriage to Durham and there pick up four very important passengers and drive them to York.

When he arrived at the Royal County Hotel in Durham, where his passengers were waiting for him, he found them very impatient to get to their destination as quickly as possible.

"How much will your charge be for the journey?" one of them asked.

"Four guineas, sir," Tom replied.

"Get us there by eight o'clock this evening and you shall have twenty!" the man declared.

It was a tall order, but it was a challenge. If the weather held, Tom might just do it, though no other driver on the Road could. So they set out, and Tom whipped up the horses, and all went well until at half-past six, when they were only seven miles from York, they ran into a thick fog.

Stopping the carriage, Tom got down and opening the door said to the passengers, "I'm sorry, gentlemen, unless the fog clears in the next quarter of an hour it will be impossible to reach York by eight o'clock."

"But you are going on, coachman?" the spokesman asked. "The fog may lift after a mile or so."

"We still shouldn't make it, sir. In normal circumstances I would wait here until the fog cleared. It's impossible to see more than a yard or two ahead, and it really is folly to go on . . ."

"You must try, we beg you. It is a matter of life and death. You shall have thirty guineas."

"It's not a matter of money, sir; that wouldn't be much good to me if I were to be killed, would it? However, since you are so urgent, I will go on."

He closed the door, and climbed back on to the box. But through the mist he saw that someone else was already sitting there and had taken up the reins.

"Why, Nance," he said. "So you've kept your promise!"

She smiled at him, shook the reins and the horses broke at once into a gallop. For the next seven miles, through the swirling mist they kept up their mad pace.

From time to time Tom could hear the cries of alarm coming from inside the carriage as it swayed from side to side on the uneven road. But he grinned to himself, feeling no fear, having absolute faith in the driver who sat beside him.

There was even thicker fog enveloping York, but the horses abated their speed not one bit as they writhed and turned through the narrow cobbled streets of the ancient city, until they pulled up at last before the Black Swan Inn in Coney Lane.

Smiling at Tom again, Nance passed him the reins and vanished. When he went to the carriage, he found his passengers still almost speechless with fright.

"You asked for it, gentlemen," he laughed. "But come, cheer up. It is five minutes to eight. I have kept my bargain, and it is all over now."

"We never thought," said the spokesman, "that when we urged you to go on you would drive through thick fog at such breakneck speed. I'll wager no other gentlemen in the North or South of England has ever had such an experience."

"No other gentlemen in the North or South of England," Tom replied, "have ever had such a coachman."

This was but the first of many appearances that Nance made to Tom before he retired, always coming when he stood in special need. When he handed over the private business he had acquired when he grew too old for the long journeys with the mail-coaches, he told his son the story of Nance.

"She has come to my aid many a time," he said. "She promised to come to your aid, too, and to the aid of your son. Whenever she comes, you must do exactly as she tells you. Even if she wishes to take the reins, you must let her."

There is no record that Nance ever appeared to Tom's son, but there is one account of an appearance she made to his grandson.

Peter Jackson and his brother John one day took the coach, driven by Robert Driffield, from Pickering to York. As it was a fine night, the brothers took seats outside. Before they had set off from Pickering, Robert Driffield, who knew the Jackson brothers, had taken them privately on one side.

"I'm a bit anxious," he told them. "I've got a feeling about the man who's sitting beside me on the box. I don't know anything mind, but it won't surprise me if he's up to no good. So be ready for anything that happens."

Nothing happened, however, until as they were approaching Malton the horses suddenly swerved to avoid a woman standing in the middle of the roadway. Although it was bright moonlight, it was clear from their exclamations that none of the passengers had seen her but the Jackson brothers.

Driffield stopped the coach, and getting down made an inspection of the wheels and axles. While he was doing so, Peter Jackson went to him and said quietly, "Is anything wrong, Bob?"

"With the coach? No," Driffield replied. "But I've been warned."

"You mean the woman?"

"You saw her?"

"Yes. So did John. Where is she now?"

"I'll tell you about her presently," Driffield promised. "But now I'm going to drive back to the village on the excuse that something is wrong with the springs. Play up with me."

So he turned about, and when they came back to the village inn, he made another inspection, and then announced to the passengers that he regretted that they would have to pass the night at the inn as there was damage to the coach, and it would be dangerous to go on until it was put right.

All agreed that this was wise, except the man who had been riding on the box. He protested loudly that he must go on, as he had very important business in York early the next morning. He did not protest for long, however, for the Jackson brothers seized him, and the innkeeper, who had previously been taken into Driffield's confidence, showed them to one of the attics of the inn, where they locked their prisoner in.

When the passengers had gone to their rooms, Driffield, with the innkeeper's help once more, rounded up a party of stout villagers, and presently the coach, with the Jackson brothers the only outside passengers, set out again for York.

As they reached the spot where the horses had swerved they saw the woman still there. This time, however, she was at the roadside, and made no attempt to stop them, but waved them on.

"But who is she?" Peter Jackson begged Driffield to tell them.

"Do you believe in ghosts?" he asked.

"No, of course not," John Jackson replied shortly.

"Well, you've just seen one," Driffield laughed, and told them the story of Nance.

As he came to the end of his account they were approaching Barton Corner.

"Watch out here!" Driffield warned them, and had scarcely spoken when three masked men rode out of the trees and barred the road.

As one of them pointed his pistol at the men outside his two companions opened the carriage doors.

"Is he in there?" the leader called, but his question went unanswered, for before they knew what was happening the labourers concealed inside the coach had leapt out and overpowered them. Putting his spurs to his horse, their leader was clearly intending to leave them to their fate, when Peter Jackson drew the pistol he had been holding under his cloak and took aim.

"He's out of range!" his brother exclaimed. "You're too slow."

Nevertheless, Peter fired, the fleeing horse stumbled, throwing his rider over his head, and leaving him lying motionless on the ground, galloped on.

"I hit him!" Peter Jackson cried triumphantly.

"No, you scared him," his brother corrected.

"Or Nance did," Driffield remarked. "Didn't you see her there, under the trees?"

The Haunting of Itchells Manor

Itchells Manor, in Hampshire, was a small but pleasant country mansion, standing in an estate of several hundred acres of park-land and farm-land.

Towards the very end of the seventeenth century, the lord of the manor of Itchells was a certain Squire Bathurst. The Bathursts had been squires of Itchells for several generations, but though they had been good husbandmen they had not laid up for themselves great treasure. This is not to say that they were not comfortably off, but they could not comport themselves so lavishly as many of the other county gentry could, and, in particular, their neighbours, the Bushnells.

All preceding Bathurst squires had chosen their wives carefully from among the Englishwomen of their acquaintance, so it came as something of a shock to the county when the father of our Squire Bathurst returned to Itchells from a tour of the continent, bringing with him an Italian wife who, besides possessing a small fortune, bore also the high-ranking title of Marchesa.

These were not the only attributes which set the new Mrs Bathurst apart from the usual run of Itchells chatelaines. She was dark, whereas the predominant colouring of the family was brunette or fair; she was exceptionally beautiful, rivalling in this respect the contemporary Countess of Southampton, who was one of the outstanding beauties of the times; and though she could be, and often was, the source or centre of laughter and merriment, there was in her composition an instability of temper and a broad streak of morose-ness which she could not or would not control when thwarted in any degree.

Within a year of her arrival at Itchells she gave birth to a son, who was eventually to become our Squire Bathurst. In the two succeeding years, she presented her Squire with two daughters; and these three children represented her contribution to the family. Since nature seems to delight in contrariness, the boy was dark, selfish and uneven tempered like his mother; the girls had the fair colouring and sunny disposition of their father. It was not strange, therefore, when the mother made the son her favourite, though it was unfortunate, for she encouraged him to be more like herself than a Bathurst, and urged him to seek his friends among those of a more elevated station and wealth.

It was in this way that he first made the acquaintance of and then became on intimate terms with the Bushnell family, the birth of whose heir had almost coincided with his own. Robert Bushnell was not unlike Alexander Bathurst in many ways. At fifteen he was outgrowing his strength, which made him inordinately slim and pale, and kept him in a constant state of lassitude, so that he languished rather than lived. Though the physicians assured his parents that this was merely a passing phase, they did impress upon Sir George and Lady Bushnell the necessity for his being cosseted for the time-being.

Under the influence of this cosseting and from the effects of his general lack of stamina, the youth became spoiled and selfish. Soon he seemed to be enjoying his poor health, for he discovered that it was a formidable weapon for getting his own way. He used it first chiefly against his tutor, a poor timid wretch who was a distant cousin and who depended entirely on the largesse of his wealthy kinsman for his very existence.

Robert's campaign of tutor-baiting presently reached such a pitch that the young man felt that starvation would be the lesser of two evils and took his complaints to his employer. Sir George, the fourth baronet, was distressed, and talked seriously to his wife.

"The poor boy's bored, naturally," said Lady Bushnell, and suggested that Robert's two brothers should be brought home from Eton to keep him company. But Sir George would not hear of it.

Then Lady Bushnell had an inspiration. She ordered her carriage and called upon Mrs Bathurst, and at the end of a short conversation the two ladies had agreed that Alexander Bathurst should share Robert Bushnell's tutor in the hope that they would become friends.

By good fortune the two strange boys, so strange as to be almost

changelings to their respective families, took an immediate liking
to one another, and were so absorbed in this new relationship that
they had no time to devote to bullying their tutor; for it was a
relationship of a kind neither of them had experienced before, but
for which clearly both had been unconsciously yearning. In addition, Alexander Bathurst had a natural leaning towards learning,
and fired Robert Bushnell with a new, if restrained, enthusiasm, so
that the tutor found his task of instructing them no longer a chore,
but a pleasure.

The initial arrangement was that Alexander should live with the
Bushnells from Monday to Friday. Within a short time, however,
the boys found that the deprivation of each other's company, even
for two days out of seven, more than they could bear, so it was
agreed that Alexander should remain permanently in what was
quickly becoming his real home.

The two mothers were delighted. Only Sir George growled,
"Don't be over-confident, Lady Bushnell. My view is that it is too
good to last."

In holding this view, however, he was holding an erroneous one.
The longer the relationship extended, the more inseparable did the
boys become. To each other they were quite different from what
they were towards others, though even in this respect they had
changed. They never quarrelled, they did not behave selfishly, and
they supported one another in every way.

It must be revealed, nevertheless, that Robert Bushnell was the
dominant character, and of the two it was Alexander Bathurst who
paved the way for harmony, by being prepared to give in and thus
avoid any clash between them. But he was quite content with
this role, for though his affection for Robert was genuine, he had
good, if entirely private and secret, reasons for doing nothing which
might lead to a breach between them.

His motive was a simple one. The Bushnells lived on a far more
lavish scale than the Bathurst income would allow. There was no
stinting of money, as there was intermittently at Itchells Manor when
crops were bad, live-stock less productive or rents not forthcoming.
Even the Marchesa's fortune was not sufficient to off-set these
temporary set-backs, and when they occurred, not only the whole
family, but the entire household were required to contribute to the
general economies.

But what Mrs Bathurst called "these times of poverty" were not
the main reason, though they were a tributary one, for her son's
attitude towards his friends' family circumstances. It was the whole

atmosphere of comfort and well-being which enveloped the Bushnells. There was, for example, a large army of servants who were
always on hand whenever one needed them. The furnishings were
not shabby through generations of use and lack of funds to keep
them in good shape, as were those at Itchells. The food was always
exciting—the Bushnells' Swiss chef, brought back by Sir George on
his return from a diplomatic mission to Berne, saw to that—and its
service was impeccable. Finally, there was the ever-full purse of
Robert himself, who at sixteen received an allowance of fifty
pounds, which his mother privately doubled. Whatever his friend
had a whim for, he could buy without humiliating application to his
father.

The effect of all this on any perceptive boy must have been marked.
On a boy brought up as the Marchesa had brought up her son, to
believe his home surroundings to be unworthy of his aesthetic
needs, they had an impact that was never to be eradicated. He learned
the lesson that money not only spells power, but makes possible the
kind of comfort he found he required not merely for his physical
but for his mental well-being also. It was now that he determined
that he would employ every means to avoid the cheese-paring which
differentiated the Bathurst way of life from the way of life of the
real aristocracy.

As the years went by the boys grew into young men, and when
they were twenty, as the Bushnell dower-house was unoccupied,
with Sir George's consent they moved into it and set up their own
establishment, the bill for which was entirely footed by Robert.
Though Alexander had to accept it—or part with his friend—he did
so; but how much it irked him not to be able to pay his way, only
he knew. It was no use Robert trying to persuade him that since
they were more than friends, mundane considerations should never
be allowed to enter their relationship; Alexander felt the
indignity of living on Bushnell wealth more than he cared to admit
to himself, and became all the more determined to put an end to
this false position in which his comparative poverty confined him.
Once he became squire of Itchells there would be changes.

Though his rank was not superior, the Bushnell wealth made
Robert, at twenty-one, one of the most eligible bachelors in the
county. To the chagrin of mothers of eligible daughters, he kept
himself aloof from all female company. Balls and receptions were
seldom honoured by his presence, he declined invitations to stay and
he made it quite clear, if he did appear, that it was useless for mothers
to hope that their daughters might find favour with him. Had they

asked him why, he would have told them, "So long as Alex and I have one another, we have no need of anyone else!" But mothers of daughters are particularly obstinate, and despite the warnings of their wiser husbands that they were tilting at a windmill, they continued to hope.

Their hopes, however, were destined to be short-lived. A year after they had moved into the dower-house, the two young men decided to embark on the Grand Tour. They went, they saw, they were conquered, particularly by Italy, and especially by Florence; and there they decided to stay until the spirit moved them.

Unfortunately, after they had been there for several months, Robert Bushnell was accidentally drowned in a boating accident. Devastated by the loss of his friend, for a time it seemed that Alexander Bathurst was in danger of going out of his mind. He was preserved from this fate, however, but was faced not only with loneliness, but with returning to Itchells and to the state of penury from which he had been protected for the last ten years. But there was nothing else he could do; it was a prospect which would have daunted many a more normal young man.

On his return to Itchells he found his sisters married, and the squire and Mrs Bathurst existing in a state of fragile armistice which inevitably infected the whole atmosphere of the manor. The chief cause of their estrangement was Mrs Bathurst's insistence on keeping up with the aristocratic Joneses and running into debt to do so. The death of Robert Bushnell exacerbated this unhappy situation, for the Marchesa foresaw that with her son's usefulness to the Bushnells terminated, her own relationship with the family might be changed, and she increased her social efforts to prevent this.

The reappearance of his son also affected the squire, who, robust countryman that he was, found exceptionally distasteful the widespread reputation Alexander had acquired as a result of his friendship with Robert Bushnell. While they had been boys, it could be ignored; while they were abroad and out of sight, it could be successfully put out of mind; but to have the dark, handsome young man in his foppish clothes sulking about the place, his white hands a constant reminder that he was not fitted to be a country squire who had the practical oversight of his estates, produced in him a profound irritation and incipient feelings of hatred, which he was too constitutionally ingenuous to be able to dissimulate. To comfort himself he increased his drinking.

Since this bibulousness can be traced directly to the man his heir had become, it can be said that Alexander Bathurst was responsible for the deaths of his father and mother. For, a little less than a year and a half after Alexander's return to Itchells, one night the drunkard squire insisted on driving home from dinner with a nearby neighbour. He could hold his liquor as befits a gentleman, and though his companions knew that he had imbibed unwisely, they made no attempt to dissuade him from getting up on to the box himself, since he was only slightly uncertain in speech and gait. But as soon as he laid hold on the reins a devil seemed to possess him, and he whipped up the horses, which, surprised and frightened, leapt down the drive at tremendous pace. The groom beside the squire tried to seize the reins from his master's hands, and for his pains was flung from the box, broke his back and died. As the swaying carriage charged through the ornamental gateway guarding the exit to the drive a wheel struck a pillar, the squire was catapulted from the box and broke his neck in his fall, while Mrs Bathurst, inside the carriage, received head injuries which led to a haemorrhage of the brain, and after lying in a coma for several weeks she also died.

As soon as he had recovered from the shock, not of his parents' deaths, but from his unexpected elevation to the lordship of the manor of Itchells, Alexander Bathurst immediately set about implementing the plans which he had formulated secretly over the years against the time when he would be in control of whatever revenue the estates brought in. His main object was to increase his personal income until it would provide him with the standard of living which his friendship with Robert Bushnell had made possible for him. He realized that this he could never achieve by the working of the estates alone. He would have to invest, and for this he would need capital.

To raise the capital, he sold several hundred acres, raised the rents of his tenants, bought inferior grain and stock, and by this means acquired some thousands of pounds. With them he went to London and, to begin with, invested them in the East India Company. These investments secured him very reasonable returns, but even so he realized that it would take him a long time to acquire the fortune he needed.

By this time the South Sea Company had been started, but Squire Bathurst had had his doubts about the soundness of its transactions. However, when, in 1719, the company gained further concessions from the government, he allowed himself to be caught up in the speculation mania, which was now quickly approaching its peak, and he invested £8,000.

As everyone knows, the population of England went mad during the first six months of 1720. Rich and poor alike scraped together every available penny to buy South Sea stock at any price, and by mid-summer £1100 was being offered for every £100 of the company's stock. Prime Minister Walpole did his best to warn the speculators of the risk they were running, but few took heed.

Though he could never afterwards explain why he disposed of his holdings when the stock was at its peak price, that was precisely what he did. Now worth some £90,000, he invested two-thirds of it in East India Company stock, and took himself to Florence with the sole intention of impressing the friends he and Robert Bushnell had made there, with his own financial status.

It took some time for news of the bursting of the South Sea Bubble to reach him, but when at last it did once again he suffered a profound shock. Wasting no time, accompanied by his young Italian valet, he returned to England. When he learned in London of the narrowness of his escape from absolute ruin, the first shock, instead of subsiding, increased, and had the effect of implanting in him an absolute distrust of all commercial ventures. Withdrawing all his investments from the East India Company, and converting it into gold coin, he withdrew to Itchells Manor.

Now that he had wealth enough and more, to surround himself with the luxuries he had learned to desire so ardently, his recent experiences seemed to have wrought such a change in his character as to turn him into a miser of classic mould. He dismissed his domestic staff with the exception of the Italian valet, and kept open only one room for himself, the kitchen and a room for the valet. He sold his horses and carriages, again keeping only one. To save the expense of a groom he looked after the horse himself, and he required the valet to cook and do such other duties about the house that would prevent it from becoming, in the complete absence of other servants, a veritable pig-sty. He never went out into society, and, in fact, very rarely emerged from the manor, certainly never leaving the estate.

As time went by, it became obvious to the valet that his master had become mad. There were constant quarrels over the cost of the simple foodstuffs which the valet insisted were essential to sustain life. When the valet asked for replacements of clothes, he narrowly escaped being horsewhipped.

It was inevitable, therefore, that sooner or later the valet would forsake his master, and presently this he planned to do. But he planned something else besides.

He had been aware of the arrival of heavy chests, iron-bound and securely bolted, shortly after all the servants had been dismissed, and guessed that they contained valuables, for Squire Bathurst kept them in the room which served him as bedroom, study and dining-room. This room he was never allowed to enter except in the presence of his master. Its door was kept locked whenever the squire was not in it.

It did not take him long, either, to discover what the chests contained, for squire Bathurst formed the habit of counting the contents of one chest each night before he retired to bed. One evening, wishing to speak to the squire, the valet had knocked on the door, and receiving no answer had tried the door-handle, and found the door to be locked.

At first fearing that something might have happened to the squire, whom he believed to be in the room, since a light shone under the door, he bent down and put an eye to the keyhole. He could see nothing, because the key was in the lock, but on listening for any sound which might tell him that the squire was not unconscious, he heard the clinking of metal and Bathurst's murmured counting.

It was this discovery which set the valet thinking. No one came to the manor except the tenants with their rents. The master never left the estate and rarely the house. He himeslf went only to the village once a week to get supplies of food. If he gave it out that the squire had decided to go to London, and if he drove the carriage which would contain the money chests and a dummy made of the squire's clothes, only in case they were seen by a poacher as they passed through the countryside, he could be safely back in Italy long before anyone began to think that the squire was making a protracted stay in London. Of course, he would have to make certain that the squire's body was hidden in a place where it would never be found, and it was to this end that he spent much of his time during the next week on opening up the chimney-piece in one of the upstairs bedrooms.

His practical plans completed, on the chosen night shortly before eleven o'clock he went to the squire's room. In case the squire should be awake, he took with him a posset which he would beg his master to take, saying that he was worried about his health, which had indeed become generally undermined by lack of food. He expected that the door would be unlocked, because it invariably was when he took in the squire's so-called breakfast, and when, more often than not, the squire would still be asleep.

He opened the door with some difficulty, since he had to hold the tankard containing the posset, and the candle-stick with which he had to light his way, in one hand. As he moved towards the bed, the squire made no move; but as he set down the posset and candle on the bedside table, and put up a hand to draw back the curtain, Alexander Bathurst awoke with a start, and with surprising agility sprang from the bed.

"Who is it? What do you want?" he shouted.

"It's Giuseppe, master. Quietly, quietly!" the valet soothed him.

"Oh God!" the squire exclaimed shakily. "I thought you were an intruder. What do you want?"

"You are looking ill, master, and I am anxious for your health," the valet told him. "I've brought you a posset which I beg you to drink."

"Who told you to make a posset?" Bathurst demanded. "Such things are luxuries I cannot afford!"

"A few pence, master, for the ale!" the valet remonstrated.

"You are not to make such things without my orders."

"No, master. But please, drink it. You will not have it waste?"

"Oh, very well," Bathurst grumbled.

"Get back into bed, master, and I will give it to you."

"No, no! You have unsettled me. Bring it to the table and I will sit there and drink it," the squire told him, as wrapping a coverlet from the bed about him, he went to the table and sat down.

The valet carried the tankard and the candle-stick to the table and seemed to be waiting.

"You needn't wait," Bathurst said, wanting the man to go so that he might check his chests.

But the last word had barely come from his tongue when he felt himself seized by the hair, his head jerked back and a momentarily sharp pain strike across his throat, as the valet drew the razor's edge across it.

In his nervous determination, for he had not intended to kill the madman thus—he had planned to smother him with a pillow, and had brought the razor only as a safeguard—the man had employed too great strength, so that the head was half-severed from the body. But his viciousness served the squire well, for he choked once, blood spurted from his mouth across the table, and he fell forward into the pool of it, dead.

With precise cold-blooded movements the valet went about his business. Binding a cover from the bed about the dead squire's neck and head, he hoisted the emaciated body of Alexander Bathurst over one shoulder, and with ease carried it upstairs to the hiding-place he had prepared for it. He worked quickly and deftly, and within half an hour the hole he had made in the chimney-piece was bricked in.

This done, he hurried down to the coach-house and harnessed the horse to the carriage, which he drove round to the main entrance. Returning to the squire's room, which had formerly been the large drawing-room, he began to carry the chests out to the carriage. They were heavier than he had imagined they would be, and by the time he had taken four of them he was feeling the strain of his exertions. He was also aware that the weight of them was pressing down alarmingly on the springs of the dilapidated carriage, and reluctantly he decided that he must be content with them, though it pained him to have to leave two chests behind.

He returned to the squire's room, cleaned up the blood on the table to his satisfaction, made the bed and carried the candle and tankard to the kitchen, having locked the door of the room behind him. In the kitchen he put on his own great-coat and hat, took the dummy-figure he had already prepared from its hiding-place in a cupboard, and went out to the carriage.

As he went back to close and lock the entrance door, he was seized with a desire to make certain that he had left no trace of his work behind him in the bedroom. It was fortunate that he did so, for he discovered that he had forgotten to extinguish the candle by which he had worked, and that its wick was bent over, carrying the flame perilously near to some silk hangings. In another few minutes it must have fallen on to them and set them ablaze, and the manor with it. Hastily he extinguished it, and finding his way across the room by a bright beam of moonlight falling through a window he made for the door.

He was but a yard or two from the door when he was startled by loud bangs behind him, and he heard Squire Bathurst's voice calling out, "Let me out! Let me out!"

He slammed-to the door behind him, and with heart pounding and cold sweat breaking on his brow, he rushed, half-falling, down the staircase, locked the door and flung himself on to the carriage.

Across the park, on the brittle frosty air came the bells of the church clock striking the hour—midnight.

Urging the half-starved horse with whip and words, he drove the carriage down the drive. But neither horse nor carriage were equal to what was demanded of them, and less than a mile on the other side of the village the horse gave a sigh, stumbled and collapsed between the shafts, dead, like its master; and as the carriage stopped suddenly thus, with slow, sharp-sounding rending noises, the floorboards gave way under the weight of the chests.

Frightened out of his wits by the predicament he was now in, the valet wrenched open the lid of one of the chests, filled his pockets with gold coins, and drastically changing his plans set out on foot for Southampton.

The carriage and its contents were discovered not long after dawn by a farmer, who rode post-haste to the magistrate, Sir George Bushnell, who hurried to the spot. Examining the dummy found with the chests, he believed he knew at once what had happened, and rode straight to Itchells Manor. Having ordered an entrance to be gained to the house, and finding neither the squire nor his valet, as he had expected, he gave instructions for a "Hue and Cry" to be raised throughout the county, with special attention to be paid to the London and Southampton roads—the quarry, the valet.

Giuseppe Mancini was arrested in Southampton docks as he was trying to find a ship to carry him to France. Before his trial at Winchester assizes he made a full confession. The sentence of death he accepted with resignation.

"It is the just retribution of Squire Bathurst's spirit," he told the chaplain to whom he made his last confession.

Alexander Bathurst's assets now passed to his two sisters. Since both had married well and had households established in their husbands' family homes, an arrangement was reached whereby it was agreed that when the second son of Chloë Bathurst, Lady Foxendean, came of age, he should take over Itchells, live in the manor and manage the estate. This involved some complicated apportioning of the late squire's possessions, so that the sisters should receive a fair division after the arrangement had been taken into consideration, but all was done amicably and caused not the slightest dissension.

As Martin Foxendean was still a young boy, the house at Itchells was left unoccupied for several years. However, a couple were installed as caretakers, whose duty it was to keep all in order. A bailiff was put in to oversee the management of the estate, and after several years of hard work Itchells at last reverted to its original good shape.

The choice of Martin Foxendean as lord of Itchells Manor proved a wise one. From the time that he took occupation of the estate in 1735, for the next eighty years or so, he and his descendants gave it the attention which former generations of Bathursts had lavished upon it. There was one great difference, however: the endowment of the estate with a portion of Squire Alexander's South Sea hoard obviated the intermittent financial difficulties which had bedevilled the Bathurst squires.

There can be but little doubt but that the Foxendeans would have continued as lords of Itchells Manor had not misfortune overtaken them in the early years of the nineteenth century. The then owner, Charles Foxendean, like his seventeenth-century forebear, fathered only one son among the bevy of daughters. This caused the family no anxiety, for the boy was strong and healthy and had every prospect of reaching maturity and marrying. At nineteen he was a robust and lively young man, restless, for ever seeking some diversion with which to satisfy his passion for physical activity. He was quickly absorbing the intricacies of estate management, but Itchells was too small to accommodate two strong-charactered Foxendeans, and hoping thereby to provide him with an interest for a year or two until maturity calmed his son down a little, Charles Foxendean proposed that he should embark upon the Grand Tour. To this the young man agreed, and in the spring of 1814 he crossed to the Continent.

The following year Richard Foxendean was in Austria when the news arrived of Napoleon Bonaparte's escape from Elba, and his arrival in France. Immediately young Foxendean set out for Belgium and there applied for, and was granted, a commission in the Duke of Wellington's army. On 18 June, 1815, he went into action at Waterloo, and shortly before six o'clock in the evening was killed defending the farm-house at La Haye Sainte.

Charles Foxendean never recovered from the shock of his son's death, and in the spring of 1818 he died. His widow, having no inclination to be burdened with the management of the estate, decided to dispose of it, and it was acquired by a family called Lefroy. For some reason or other which the records do not disclose, the Lefroys left the manor-house in the charge of caretakers for five years, and did not enter into occupation themselves until 1823.

They were the first "outsiders" to occupy Itchells for nearly three hundred years, and perhaps the fact that they were not of Bathurst stock has some bearing on their experiences throughout the greater part of the century. For until they acquired the place there is no record of the haunting of the house, which began within a month or two of their moving in.

Among their domestic staff was a young housemaid called

Margaret Smilie. Meg's parents lived in the village, and her father and brothers were employed on the estate, as previous Smilies had been for several generations. She was a happy-natured, level-headed girl of eighteen, physically sturdy and bright mentally. As Mrs Lefroy later said of her, "Meg Smilie had both feet firmly planted on the ground, and was the last person to succumb to imaginings."

Proud of their new possession, the Lefroys were naturally anxious to show it off to friends and relatives, so about Eastertide, 1823, they arranged a house-party for a dozen guests. This number meant that every bedroom in the house would be occupied.

Though the spring had come with bright sunshine and dry days that year, by evening the temperature dropped and there were several nights of sharp ground frost. The house, having been empty for so long, had not yet warmed itself, so to prevent her guests from suffering discomfort Mrs Lefroy had given orders for fires to be lit in all rooms from four o'clock.

It was the duty of the housemaids to bank up the fires for the night shortly before the guests retired, and they began their rounds for this purpose between half-past ten and quarter to eleven. So it was that Meg Smilie came into one of the bedrooms allotted to her shortly before eleven o'clock.

The fire had burned rather low, and she realized that if she made it up with dust in the condition it was in she would stand a good chance of putting it out altogether. So kneeling down before the hearth, she put on a log and began to blow some life into the embers with a pair of bellows. She was tired and would be glad to get to bed; nevertheless, as she blew on the fire, she hummed a tune to herself.

Presently her efforts were rewarded; the log burst into flame and was soon burning merrily. Carefully she arranged round it some smallish pieces of coal, and on these blew also, until they had caught.

It was as she was gingerly covering the whole conflagration with coal-dust that the banging began. At first she thought it must be Jess Richards making up the fire in the room below, but when the knocks continued in groups of three or four, now slow and measured, now quick and imperious, that she realized it could not be Jess, for no one in their right mind would treat a fire so. Besides, the sounds now seemed to be coming from too nearby for them to originate downstairs.

Puzzled, she surveyed the massive chimney-piece. (Only one other room in the house had a similar "piece", and that was the room above.) As she did so, another series of knockings began, and there could be no doubt that they were coming from the left-hand side of the fire-place, just above her head.

Cool and level-headed though Meg was, she felt the blood in her veins beginning to run cold, the skin tightening across her skull, ice forming in her cheeks and her hands begin to tremble. For one or two terrible moments she imagined that she had been rooted to the spot, for she wished to get to her feet, yet her limbs would not obey the commands of her will.

The sounds of someone breathing heavily near to her were so loud and close that she thought for a brief second that she could feel the rush of air on the nape of her neck. Momentarily she was on the verge of panic, from which reason saved her as she realized that what she was hearing was the sound of her own breathing.

"Silly girl!" she told herself aloud, with a shamefaced laugh. "Pull yourself together, do!"

Taking a deep breath to quiet the pounding of her heart, she began to get up from her knees. As she did so, the heel of her shoe caught in the hem of her dress, and to save herself from stumbling headlong into the fire she put out a hand to the side of the chimney-piece, and steadied herself. But while her hand still pressed the brickwork, the knockings began again, and she felt distinctly the bricks under her hand tremble.

She drew back her hand as if she had been burned, and now all her fear returned, she stooped to pick up her pail and began to hurry from the room. Before she was half-way to the door, a man's voice called to her from the fire-place, "Let me out! Let me out!"

It was too much! With a cry, she dropped the pail and fire-irons and ran from the room, pulling the door shut after her with a bang, which only served to heighten her fear. Though normally she would have taken the back-stairs, the main staircase was nearer, and throwing obedience to her mistress's orders to the wind, she scurried down the carpeted stairs.

The noise of the falling pail and irons, and her shriek, had been heard throughout the house, and as she came to the last leg of the staircase she saw that all the guests were crowding from the drawing-room into the hall, and that some of the other servants had joined them from their quarters.

The sight of the anxious faces, and the sound of Mr Lefroy's voice calling up to her, asking what was amiss, restored her courage a little. But as she steadied herself by the bannister, suddenly she seemed to be pushed aside roughly, and as she began to stumble down the remaining steps, she heard a avoice saying, "Oh, my God! Oh, my God!"

By the time that James Lefroy, one of the sons of the house, who had hurried forward to help her, caught her in his arms, she was in a dead faint. As he picked her up and began to carry her towards the drawing-room, the heavy front door blew open. An icy blast of night air swept in, and as the startled guests turned to see what had happened the door swung too with a loud bang, as quickly as it had opened.

A silence had fallen on the still company, and everyone there afterwards declared that they had heard a carriage moving off down the drive. Certainly Mr Lefroy heard it and he jumped towards the door to see who it could be. But when he tried to pull open the door he found that it had jammed, and that all his strength could not move it.

He rushed from the door to the drawing-room, and pulled back the curtains at one of the windows from which the whole length of the drive could be seen. Outside, under the bright moonlight, not a twig or bush or tree stirred, and the drive was completely empty.

Bewildered he returned to the hall, where Jevons, the butler, had gone to the door and was trying to open it.

"It will need tools," Mr Lefroy told him. "It's jammed fast."

"Yes, sir," Jevons agreed quietly. "May I have a private word with you, sir?"

As he went towards the servants' quarters, Mr Lefroy followed him, even more puzzled. When they reached the butler's pantry, Jevons closed the door behind him.

"What is it, Jevons?" Mr Lefroy asked, impressed by his butler's solemnity.

"I thought it best not to say so before the guests, sir," Jevons replied. "They are perturbed enough already. But the door is not jammed, sir. The key is turned in the lock."

"Are you sure, Jevons?"

"Perfectly, sir."

"But how can that be? Did any of the others go near the door after I went into the drawing-room?"

"No, sir."

"But I did not turn the lock, Jevons, I swear."

"No, sir. You couldn't, the key is still hanging on its hook to the right of the door, sir, where I keep it during the day."

"Are you quite sure you are not mistaken, Jevons?"

"I am quite certain, sir." He opened a drawer and took out a large key. "Here is the spare key, sir. I suggest that I take tools and feign unjamming the door, and under cover of my activities, sir, do you put this key in the lock and turn it. You will see that I am right."

And so he proved to be.

By this time Meg had been carried to a sofa in the drawing-room and restored to her senses. At first she could not speak for weeping, and though she was still trembling Lefroy asked her if she could walk to his study. She nodded, and Mrs Lefroy, supporting the girl, helped her from the room.

"I am sorry," Lefroy apologized to his guests. "The girl has obviously had a fright, and we must discover the cause of it. Will you forgive us if we desert you for a few moments?"

Above the murmur of assent, one of the men asked, "Whose carriage was it, Tom?"

"I didn't recognize it," Lefroy lied.

"Are you sure you saw a carriage, Tom?" someone else asked.

"I couldn't be sure. I thought so. Let's not frighten the ladies any more, gentlemen. Excuse me."

By the time he reached his study Mrs Lefroy had been able to coax Meg into talking. When the girl had finished her story, Mrs Lefroy said: "I'll have Mrs Smart make you a posset, and bring it to you in bed. Jessie sleeps with you, doesn't she, so you won't be alone. If anyone asks what frightened you, say you thought you saw a large rat."

When the butler had taken the girl away, Mrs Lefroy turned to her husband.

"Well, Tom, what do you make of it?" she asked.

"I don't know, my dear. Have you ever heard that the house is haunted?"

"Never. If it had been any of the other girls I would have said they were imagining things. But Meg has both feet firmly on the ground, and would be the last to succumb to imaginings."

"The rat was a good idea, Bess," Mr Lefroy said. "We will tell the others that that is what it was."

Though the guests pretended to be satisfied with this explanation, secretly they were not convinced, for it did not explain the sounds of the carriage moving down the drive, which all said they had heard. But so that their hosts should not be embarrassed, they did not refer to it when the Lefroys did not. But there was not one of them who was sorry when their visit came to an end.

The effect on Meg had been deeper than Mrs Lefroy had believed it would be, and next morning the girl was all for giving in her notice. Fearing the effect this might have on the rest of her staff, Mrs Lefroy pleaded and coaxed, until at last Meg told her, "Very well, ma'am, I will stay so long as I never have to set foot in that room again.

"That I promise you," Mrs Lefroy replied. "Miss Nightingale leaves us today, and we will close up the room and not use it again."

As it turned out, the closing of the room had a not entirely satisfactory result, for knockings were heard in other parts of the house for several years, and on account of them many of the maid-servants left hurriedly. Then there seems to have followed a period of quiescence for Alexander Bathurst's ghost, for it is not until 1840 that there are further reports of it.

It would seem also that Meg's experience had not been remembered after nearly twenty years, for William Lefroy, now squire, had not been at home on the night of that occurrence, and if he was ever told, he had forgotten, for when a Captain Anstey arrived to stay he found the family in a state of upset.

"I hope you will be comfortable, John," his host greeted him. "But the truth is, we seem to have a ghost, and we cannot get servants to stay with us. So, please, overlook any shortcomings there may appear to be in our hospitality."

The mention of the ghost aroused the Captain's curiosity, and he insisted that William Lefroy should tell him all about it.

"I'd like to hear him," he said at last. "I hope you have put me in his room."

"Of course not," replied Lefroy.

"Then please do so."

"Nothing would make me, John. But what I will agree to, if you are game, is that we should both keep watch and try to find out what really happens, for to tell the truth none of us have heard it."

So the two men kept watch in the room. For three nights nothing happened, but on the fourth, about eleven o'clock, the bangings began.

"They come from the room downstairs," Anstey said when they had inspected the fire-place. "There must be some shaft which carries up the sound."

They listened for a time, and the knockings came again, slowly sometimes, urgently at others.

"Let's go downstairs and investigate," Anstey suggested. "And if we find nothing there, I'll wager that a bird has built its nest in the chimney-stack."

So saying he made for the door, followed by William Lefroy. As Anstey reached out his hand to the door-knob, both men were brought up suddenly by a voice demanding, "Let me out! Let me out!"

Though he had turned round, Anstey had kept his hand on the knob, and as he stood looking in bewilderment at his friend he felt himself being roughly pushed on one side, and the door was pulled open by some unseen hand, and then swung-to with a bang.

"God in heaven! he exclaimed. "No birds, William. You are haunted!"

"Listen!" Lefroy said sharply.

From the drive below them came the sounds of a carriage being driven away. They ran to the window and peered down—but the drive was empty.

The Brown Lady of Raynham

One of England's most celebrated ghosts is the wraith of a lady whose portrait used to hang in a room at Raynham Hall, Norfolk, the seat of the Marquesses of Townshend. According to the best authorities, she was Lady Dorothy Townshend, and her ghost which has haunted this particular stately home for nearly two hundred and fifty years once caused considerable affright to George IV, was shot at by the author Frederick Marryat, and later successfully photographed.

The lady, who has achieved such success on the spectral plane, had, according to her portrait, large and shining eyes, and was dressed in brown with yellow trimmings and a ruff around her throat. A harmless enough looking lady of the early eighteenth century, except when seen by candlelight, when a strange almost evil expression was seen upon her face. It was also said that when the candlelight was thrown upon the portrait from some angles the flesh appeared to shrink from the face and the eyes to disappear giving it almost the semblance of a skull.

This portrait was sold among the Townshend heirlooms at Christies in 1904 and was called "The Brown Lady—Dorothy Walpole, wife of the second and most famous Marquess of Townshend".

Dorothy Walpole was the daughter of Robert Walpole, Member of Parliament for Houghton in Norfolk. Her brother was the great Sir Robert Walpole, who was England's first Prime Minister, though the office was not recognized in those days.

When Dorothy was a young girl her father became the guardian to Viscount Charles Townshend, whose father died when the boy was thirteen. In the Walpole home two future statesmen were growing up and maturing, for young Charles Townshend achieved greatness in the political sphere as well.

There was also the beginning of a rather sad romance. Dorothy fell in love with Charles, but her father, so the legend went, forbade the match, for he did not want it to be thought that he was trying to gain a family advantage by marrying his daughter to his ward. Lord Townshend married a daughter of Baron Pelham of Laughton, but she died in 1711. A year or so later he married Dorothy Walpole, his first love.

But Dorothy in her disappointment had apparently gone off the rails. Unknown to Lord Townshend, already a rising young statesman, his mind fully occupied with such matters of high state as the negotiation of the Treaty of Utrecht, Dorothy had not apparently conducted herself as a young unmarried Georgian lady should. She had in fact acquired a somewhat tarnished reputation, having been, it was said, the mistress of a well-known profligate by the name of Lord Wharton, who had the doubtful distinction of being bitingly satirized by Pope. Wharton later fled the country, and his creditors, and lived in eccentric and disreputable exile, throwing in his lot with the Old Pretender.

Dorothy Walpole was twenty-six when she married Lord Townshend. The legend adds substance to the rumours of her reputation, for according to it there was an estrangement between her and her husband, who, having belatedly discovered about the Wharton episode, kept her locked in her apartments at Raynham Hall and treated her so badly that in 1726 she died of a broken heart. According to another story it was a broken neck, which she acquired by falling down the grand staircase at Raynham. A contemporary record, however, says she died of smallpox.

At that time her husband and her brother were ruling England between them, so she was a lady of some importance, and if her death had been, to say the least, inconvenient for someone, it is possible that the actual cause of it was concealed. The bewailing of her ghost ever since would suggest that this was so.

In 1730, after differences with his boyhood friend and brother-in-law, Walpole, Townshend retired to Raynham and devoted the rest of his life to agriculture.

We may never know whether Lady Dorothy Townshend died of smallpox, of a broken heart, or by falling—or being pushed—down

Raynham's grand staircase. Whatever unsettled her spirit for all time is something of a mystery. But, however she met her death, her ghost soon became the terror of the visitors and servants at the Hall. She has been seen by a number of persons for the better part of two and a half centuries, and is in fact an extremely well-established ghost—one of the few who have been tackled by both firearms and camera.

It is no use trying to shoot a ghost, of course. The celebrated author who tried to do so should have known better. But the photographer was more successful and achieved one of the rare ghost pictures which all the experts agreed had not been faked.

For her photograph the Brown Lady seems to have appeared in her bridal dress, though on the occasion of the foolish and rather ungallant attempt to shoot her she was dressed in brown as in her portrait.

The Townshends became marquesses in 1786, and their seat at Raynham Park, which is about four miles to the south-west of Fakenham, was one of the country's great houses, where royalty as well as the aristocracy were lavishly entertained. There George IV visited the Townshends when he was Regent, and the Brown Lady frightened him out of his wits.

His Royal Highness awoke Raynham in the middle of the night, saying that a lady dressed in brown "with dishevelled hair and a face of ashy paleness" had appeared at his bedside in the State bedroom. "I will not pass another hour in this accursed house," he declared to the accompaniment of many vigorous Regency oaths. "For tonight I have seen that which I hope to God I may never see again."

The Brown Lady, it was becoming clear, was no social asset. In those days of princely hospitality and great house parties it was a serious business for the family ghost to frighten away the First Gentleman of Europe.

They told a story of how some gentlemen of the household sat up for three nights in the corridors where the Brown Lady had been seen. They had gamekeepers stationed at the doors and played écarté to pass the time. On the third night they saw her.

She appeared to be coming through the wall at them. One of the gentlemen and the gamekeepers were petrified with terror, but the other gallant, bolder than the rest, stood resolutely in the path of the Brown Lady as she approached, but she passed right through him in a puff of icy smoke and disappeared through the wall beyond, leaving her bold challenger utterly devastated by his uncanny experience.

The Brown Lady made another appearance in 1835. It was appropriately enough at Christmas-time and there was a large house-party at Raynham Hall.

Among the guests of Lord and Lady Charles Townshend were Colonel and Mrs Loftus. Colonel Loftus was Lord Townshend's cousin and was also the brother of Lady Townshend. It was the practice of the aristocracy in those days to marry within narrow circles, and marriage between cousins was very common.

Loftus and another guest named Hawkins lingered late one night over a protracted game of chess and finally went upstairs. They saw the Brown Lady standing outside the door of Lady Townshend's room. The apparition turned and walked along the corridor, pursued by Loftus, but the old warrior had to give up, and the Brown Lady soon melted from his sight.

This night Loftus saw it only dimly, but the following night he came face to face with it on the grand staircase—a stately lady, he said, in rich brocade with a coif on her hair. "Although her features were clearly defined, where her eyes should have been were nothing but dark hollows.

During that spooky Christmas at Raynham the host himself reluctantly admitted to having seen the ghost. "I am forced to believe in it," he told one of the house guests, "for she ushered me to my room last night."

But the ghost caused great alarm among the servants, some of whom had seen it, and were horror-stricken at the sight of her face, which consisted of dark hollows and was truly macabre. The servants were all for leaving.

Normally there was no servant problem in those days, but a really frightening supernatural apparition could cause one. His lordship in desperation had all the locks changed at Raynham and even employed policemen disguised as manservants in case the ghost turned out to be a practical joker, though Townshend had little hope that this was the case. Certainly no practical joker was found and the Brown Lady continued to haunt.

Townshend then summoned the assistance of Captain Frederick Marryat, a local celebrity, who had recently settled in Norfolk at Langham Manor. Marryat, who had spent years at sea, had become famous for his sea stories and books for boys, such as *Mr Midshipman Easy* and *The Children of the New Forest*.

Captain Marryat, by no means the superstitious sailor, did not believe in ghosts. He thought some sort of trick was being played upon the Townshend family. He had a theory that it was connected

with the smugglers and poachers who abounded in that part of
Norfolk in those days, and who were, he thought, using some old
ruined buildings near the Hall for their hiding places. He was sure
that there were ruffians lurking around who would have much to
gain by frightening the Townshend family away from the Hall.

The story was later told in Marryat's biography, written by his
daughter, Florence Marryat, herself a novelist with a keen interest
in psychic phenomena.

Marryat was invited to stay at Raynham and he insisted upon
sleeping in the room where hung the portrait of the Brown Lady—
a splendid bedroom panelled in cedarwood.

How serious the celebrated author was about his theory that the
apparitions were caused by some cunning trick of desperate
smugglers anxious to frighten the Townshends away is open to
question. The Townshend family had lived at Raynham for well
over a century and the Brown Lady was part of the Townshend
legend. She had even scared George IV out of the house in the middle
of the night. It was not likely that anyone would believe that the
Townshends, having endured the ghost for so long, would be
scared away from their historic country seat by a few smugglers.
It is not seriously to be supposed that Captain Marryat, that professional romancer, was foolish enough to entertain such improbable
fancies.

Anyway, he got his coveted invitation to the Hall and ghost-
hunting was good fun, so he enjoyed himself.

One night, after he had retired to his room and undressed except
for his trousers and singlet, Lord Charles Townshend's two young
nephews knocked on his door and asked him if he would go into
their room and give an opinion about a new gun which one of them
had just acquired.

During the evening there had been much talking and joking
about the Brown Lady, and as he left his room Marryat picked up
his loaded pistol, saying laughingly to the two young men: "In
case we meet the Brown Lady."

After the Captain had inspected the gun, the two young men
offered, in the same joking mood, to escort him safely back to his
room— "in case you are kidnapped by the Brown Lady."

It was a long, dark corridor, and the lights had been extinguished,
and as the three men walked along it they saw a woman approaching
them carrying a lamp. They were in that part of the house reserved
for the men guests, and the sight of the approaching woman caused
them a little unease, especially Marryat in his vest and trousers. But

the Hall was full and it was possible that a lady had lost her way in the labyrinthine corridors and staircases of Raynham.

There was only one thing to do, consistent with modesty and gentlemanly behaviour, and that was to hide. The three of them stepped quickly into the open doorway of an empty room and stood there in the darkness waiting for the lady to pass by.

But the lady did not pass by. She stopped at the doorway, and when the three men saw the manner in which she was dressed they had no doubt at all as to who she was. Her resemblance to the portrait in Captain Marryat's bedroom was unmistakable—"the waxy countenance, the large shining eyes and the noiseless step". There was no reference this time to the hollows in the face. The spectral lady was plainly not in her macabre mood that night.

The Brown Lady held the lighted lamp before her face and then, said Marryat, looked straight into his eye and smiled at him. But it was a diabolical, a wicked smile, which so alarmed Marryat that he stepped into the corridor, pistol in hand, and discharged it point blank at her.

As the bullet passed through her insubstantial form, still evilly and mysteriously smiling, she disappeared, leaving nothing but a wisp of smoke, and a bullet-hole in the door behind her.

After that Captain Marryat entertained no doubts at all about the reality of the ghost at Raynham Hall. But the Brown Lady herself must have been affronted by such ungallant behaviour, tor she did not return to her old haunts for many a long year after Marryat himself had joined her in the shades, which he did in 1848.

What should Captain Marryat have done? To shoot at a ghost is pointless. It has been said in his defence that he genuinely thought it was someone playing a prank, but if he had thought that his action was no more pardonable. One doesn't shoot people who play pranks, not even when they are played upon the aristocracy.

It is far more probable that Marryat was scared out of his wits and panicked, believing he was seeing the famous ghost and that his theories about the desperate smuggling characters had been wrong.

At all events, the Brown Lady of Raynham Hall, after her encounter with Captain Marryat in the 1830s, remained sulking on the eternal shores for the rest of the century and more before she troubled the haunted staircases and galleries of Raynham again.

It was in November, 1926, when she was next reported. The then Marquis Townshend, a boy at the time, encountered her on the famous staircase. With the Marquis was another boy, who also saw the phantom. The Brown Lady's return caused something of a newspaper sensation. Both boys were carefully questioned. Neither had heard of the ghost story, or seen the picture, the family legend presumably having been all but forgotten. Their description of the Brown Lady was apparently the traditional one. It was not considered a boyish prank.

Ten years later the Brown Lady provided an even greater sensation by getting herself photographed.

Lady Townshend wanted a series of pictures taken of the interior of Raynham Hall and she commissioned Mr Indre Shira, a professional photographer, to take them. On the afternoon of 19 September, 1936, he and a Mr Provand were taking flash-light pictures of the grand staircase. Mr Provand was wielding the camera while Mr Shira was standing a little behind him, casting his professional eye upon the splendid staircase.

Provand took a picture and was putting in another plate and re-setting the camera and flash equipment, when Shira, looking up the first flight of the staircase, saw what he described as a vapoury form gradually assuming the appearance of a woman draped and veiled in some diaphanous material.

Down the staircase the figure glided with floating steps, and the excited Shira told his companion to aim his camera and get a shot quickly. Here was something which would make a sensational picture.

Provand had not seen the apparition, owing perhaps to the effect of the photo-flash, and wondered what had got Shira so excited. Nevertheless he aimed his camera at the required spot and took another picture. After the flash the spectre presumably disappeared.

Provand then asked Shira what all the fuss was about, and when Shira told him that he had seen a ghost descending the staircase, Provand pooh-poohed the idea. It must have been an optical illusion, he said, the effect of the flash, or perhaps even someone playing a mirror trick from the gallery above. Shira thereupon bet Provand five pounds that the ghost would appear on the plate.

Shira won his bet and the Brown Lady came out on the plate. This time she was not in her traditional brown brocade, but appeared, though only in outline, as a bride in white, enveloped in a clinging veil.

This photograph was reproduced in the magazine *Countrylife*, dated 16 December, 1936. It naturally aroused considerable controversy. A number of experts examined the plate, and all agreed that there was no fake about it. The figure—whatever it was—had been photographed all right, or at least it appeared on the exposed plate. There was a suggestion that the ghost photograph had been caused by some freak of light or perhaps a flaw in the negative, which of course might be considered a possibility. But to accept this you would have to assume that Mr Shira made up the story, which is an assumption both unwarrantable and improbable, for he would have no reason to do such a thing.

The Brown Lady of Raynham, however, might well consider herself sufficiently well established and attested not to require photographic proof.

The fact that she would have appeared to have put on her wedding gown to pose before Mr Shira and his companion might be said to lend a little colour to one legend about her—that she had been a young and beautiful girl of the eighteenth century and forced to marry an old roué against her will and to endure a horrifying wedding night with him.

It cannot be said for certain that this photograph, if it is of a ghost, is that of the Brown Lady. While ghosts have been known to change their habits, they do not as a rule change their clothes.

The Return of Richard Tarwell

In the first half of the eighteenth century the well-known family of Harris of Heyne made their permanent headquarters at their ancient seat in Devon, not far from the borders of Cornwall. Though not ennobled, the Harrisses were a wealthy family and their broad acres stretched for several miles on every side of the mansion. They occupied a prominent place among the West Country gentry and were greatly respected by the discerning inhabitants of Devon and the neighbouring shires.

At this time, the head of the family, Mr George Harris, held an appointment at the Court of King George II, which obliged him to spend a part of the year in his town house in Sloane Square. When his attendance at Court was required, it was Mr Harris's custom to move the greater part of his establishment to London, leaving only a few servants behind in Devon in the charge of Richard Morris, who had been butler to the family for many years.

While in London to perform his duties in 1730, Mr Harris found among his post one day a letter from Richard Morris. Since he had instructed his butler that he need not bother to communicate except on a matter of urgency, Mr Harris broke the seals with some slight degree of trepidation and with a strong premonition that the butler's letter could only contain bad news. His premonition proved right. The news was of a kind which made him summon his carriage and hurry to the office of the Lord Great Chamberlain, whom he begged to act as his intercessor with His Majesty for permission to absent himself from Court for two or three weeks as he had totally

163

unexpected personal affairs to attend to at his home in Devon.

When the Lord Great Chamberlain heard the nature of this business, he agreed at once to seek an audience of the King, and having sent in his request, was informed that His Majesty would receive him at once. The King, too, was sympathetic to his petitioner's request, and early next morning Mr Harris set out for Devon, and arrived at his home five days later.

As soon as he had refreshed himself after his journey, he summoned the half-dozen servants, headed by Morris, to him in his study.

Now, Morris," he said, when the two footmen, the cook and two housemaids were drawn up before him. "Tell me what happened."

"One night some three weeks ago, sir," the butler began, "I was wakened in the night by noises which I was sure were coming from my pantry, which I do not need to tell you is below the room in which I sleep. At first I thought I must be mistaken, for immediately before I had retired for the night I had made my rounds of the house, as I always do, and checked that every window and door were secured. However, when the noises continued and it was certain that someone was in the room below, thinking it must be one of the servants who had no business to be there, I decided to go down to see what was afoot.

"When I came to the passage outside my pantry, it was clear to me that I had not been mistaken, for a light in the pantry was shining under the door. I also heard men's voices talking quietly, and was convinced that Eames and Barnwell, the two footmen, were going about some act, which I believed to be nefarious because of the time of night, the fact that no one is allowed in the pantry without first having asked my permission, and because of other sounds issuing from the room."

"What sounds?" Mr Harris interrupted him.

"Sounds which seemed to indicate to me, sir," the butler continued, "that one of the strong-boxes in which the silver plate is stowed was being broken into."

"Did you really suspect that the voices you heard were those of the footmen?" Harris again interrupted him.

"There were two men's voices, sir, and they were talking low so that I could not recognize them, but I fear that the thought came at once into my mind that it must be the footmen, because I could not imagine who else it could be. I am sorry now that I should have harboured such suspicions, since I realize that in thinking so I slandered their good names. I have apologized again and again, sir, but both of them have insisted on handing in their notices."

"Is that so?"Harris asked the two young men sternly. They looked embarrassed and nodded. "Then you are being very foolish. Morris has apologized, but you must admit that it was a justifiable mistake in the circumstances."

"With respect, sir, I do not think so,"Eames replied. "Mr Morris, by his suspicions, has virtually accused us of being thieves, or at least of being capable of dishonesty and of treachery to you and the family."

"What have you to say to that, Barnwell?"

"I agree, sir, with every word. We have been in your service now, myself for two years and Eames for nearly five,"Barnwell replied. "Mr Morris should know us well enough by this time to realize that our loyalty to the family, sir, is no less than his own, for all he has served you upwards of thirty years."

"I still think it was a justifiable mistake,"Harris told them. "Will you reconsider your decision if I add my apologies to his? I do so abominate having to engage new servants. Well?"

"I don't know, sir,"Eames said stubbornly.

"Well think about it, and we will talk of it again later. Continue, Morris."

The butler went on to explain that because he had (wrongly) supposed that the men in the pantry were the footmen, that it had not occurred to him to go for help. He was the only other male in the house, and the maidservants would have been too frightened to be of any assistance.

"But you must have known that whoever was in the pantry doing what you were sure they were doing—namely, breaking into the strong-boxes—would physically attack you or anyone else who interrupted them?"Harris commented.

The butler replied that that had occurred to him in the light of day, but that at the time he thought only of protecting his master's property.

"What you should have done was to arouse two of the maids and sent them post-haste to the village to fetch the constables, while you kept watch to see what the intruders did or where they went."

"Yes, sir, I realize that now,"the butler agreed, a tone of anguish in his voice.

"Mr Morris is wrong in saying that we were the only males in the house, sir," Barnwell said. "The boy was in the cubby-hole opposite Mr Morris's own room, so far as he knew then."

"The boy?"Harris asked.

"I engaged a young lad of fourteen, sir, a day or two after you had gone, to help me in the pantry with the silver," the butler explained. "He came to the house one day with his father, whom I knew of slightly by reputation as a sound and honest man, to ask whether there was an opening for the lad. The other boy, Franklin, left to join the household of Mr Soames, the day you departed for London, so I offered this boy, Richard Tarwell, the position."

"Where is he now?" Harris asked. "Why isn't he here?"

"He's disappeared, sir," Morris replied.

"That night, sir," Barnwell added.

Seeing that he was in danger of confusing the butler with his interruptions, Harris determined to wait until the man had finished his relation before he asked more questions and told the man so.

Morris then described how he had approached the door of the pantry quietly, and then flung it open to take them, he hoped, by surprise. To his amazement, however, the two men he found there were not the two footmen, but men he had never seen before; and with them was the boy, Richard Tarwell.

Before he had had time to recover, one of the intruders had jumped on him brandishing an iron bar, and had struck him so hard about the head as to render him unconscious. When he had regained his senses, he found himself securely bound to a chair, and a gag tightly fixed in his mouth. Two of the strong-boxes had had their lids burst open, and he could see that their contents, or at least most of them, had gone.

"Did no one else hear any noise in the night?" Harris asked.

The footmen and the servants shook their heads.

"No, sir," said Mrs Coombes, the cook. "We heard nothing. I got up at seven and called Mary and Joan, as I always do, and went down to the kitchen to prepare breakfast for half-past seven. The two maids came down at about twenty minutes after the hour and busied themselves with some chore or other, and five minutes later the footmen came in. I think it was Eames who remarked, 'Isn't Mr Morris down yet?' and when I said no, he laughed and said, 'Escaped again!'."

"What do you think he meant by that?" Harris probed.

"Mr Morris is very strict about punctuality at meals, sir," the cook told him. "He always comes into the servants' hall, or the kitchen when the family is in London, five minutes before the appointed time, by when all the other servants must be assembled. Once or twice recently in the mornings, the footmen had cut it fine, sir, as they had this particular morning. Or I should say, would have cut it fine if Mr Morris had come in at his usual time.

"Still, I didn't think much about it as I was busy at the stove, until Eames said, 'What's happened to the old man? Has the miracle happened and he's overlain?'

"'He'll be here presently,' I said. 'You'd best not draw up until he comes. He dislikes it if he does not sit down first.' So we waited and when ten minutes had gone by I did begin to wonder, so I asked Eames to go up and knock on Mr Morris's door and tell him politely what the time was."

Harris looked at Eames, who took up the tale.

"I went up to Mr Morris's room and knocked on the door, and when after two or three knockings I got no answer, I opened the door and looked in. He was not there, but I noticed that his bed had been slept in. When I came out of the room, I noticed that the boy's cubby-hole was empty, too, and recalling that the boy had not been in the kitchen waiting with us, as he usually was, I thought that perhaps Mr Morris and Tarwell had risen early and were working in the butler's pantry and had overlooked the time. So, I went downstairs to the pantry and found Mr Morris gagged and bound to the chair as he has told you, sir."

"The next thing we knew," Mrs Coombes said, "was Eames's voice shouting something that sounded like *Help*! Barnwell rushed out of the kitchen first and the girls and I followed hard on his heels. When we got to the pantry, Eames had released Mr Morris and was just loosening the gag. Mr Morris's first words were, 'We've been robbed! Go for the constables!'

"'You go,' Eames said to Barnwell, and when Barnwell had run out, he helped Mr Morris to his feet. Mr Morris was very upset, and when he saw the strong-boxes were quite empty, I thought he was going to collapse."

"Did the constables come quickly?" Harris asked.

"Within the half-hour, sir. I told them what had happened, and what was missing, and that the boy, too, appeared to be gone. They began to make inquiries at once, but up to now they've uncovered no trace, sir."

"And what of the boy?"

"No trace of Tarwell either, sir. His father protests that his son is no thief. But I saw the boy in the pantry with the robbers, sir, with my own eyes."

"How had the thieves gained entry to the house?" Harris asked. "Was a window broken?"

"No, sir. Through the side door, which was unlocked. The boy must have known they were coming and let them in," Morris said.

"And what did they take?"

"The four great silver candle-sticks with the birds," Morris began to enumerate, "three entrée dishes of silver, two silver sauce-boats, the salt-bowls that were presented to Mr Joseph Harris by Her Majesty, Queen Anne . . ."

When he had come to the end of the list, Harris considered briefly. "I suppose it could have been worse," he said. "But it is bad enough. I regret the candle-sticks and the salt-bowls particularly."

"Perhaps they will be recovered," Mrs Coombes suggested.

Harris smiled for the first time. "Perhaps, Mrs Coombes," he replied. "We must hope for the best."

"I blame myself for taking the boy on without making more searching inquiries about his family and his character," the butler said. "But the father seemed honest enough."

"You mustn't blame yourself. God bless my soul, we are not the first family to be burgled, and I dare say we shall not be the last. Well, thank you. I will dine, Mrs Coombes, as soon as you are ready, and I warn you, I am famished. The rest of you may go. I would like Eames and Barnwell to remain."

When the other servants had gone, he looked at the two young men.

"Look here," he said. "I want you to change your minds about your notices. Morris is growing old, and he takes upon himself great responsibilities when I and the family are absent. You must do your best to excuse him."

"He at once thought we were the thieves," Eames reminded him. "It's that that sticks in my gullet, sir."

"Yes, I know. I add my apologies to his yet again. Would it make any difference if I also added a guinea to your year's wages?"

There was a brief silence, then Eames said with a smile, "Yes, sir".

"And you Barnwell?"

"Well yes, sir."

"Right. Then that's settled! I do so abominate having new servants about me, especially footmen. You may go now."

As they walked across to the door, he called after them, "Did the boy strike you that he might be a thief or a person likely to be in league with thieves?"

"No, sir," Eames turned and said. "He seemed a good, honest, simple boy, eager to please."

"He was happy enough, too, sir," Barnwell added. "He'd only been here a few weeks, but he was not backward in playing harmless jokes on Eames and me."

After two days of making his own inquiries, which revealed nothing, Mr Harris returned to London and completed his tour of duty at Court. Four months later, he and his family and household returned to Devon, there to learn that the authorities had lost all interest in the case and that they must resign themselves to the loss of their property.

Since they were tired after their long journey, Mr Harris suggested that he should pass the night on the bed that was always kept made up in his dressing-room, leaving to his wife the exclusive comfort of the four-poster. Mrs Harris, who was even more exhausted, had no objection, and shortly after dinner announced that she was going to retire.

"I'll go the rounds with Morris," Mr Harris told her, "and follow you up."

As the two men went round the house, Harris noted the meticulous care with which his butler examined every window-latch and shutter, and the lock on every outside door, even going to the extent of locking some of the inner doors as well. They spoke little, according to their usual custom while performing their nightly ritual, for it was at the end of the day and both were anxious to get to their beds. He supposed it must be one of the effects of the robbery that made him this evening take more notice of the butler's routine than he ever remembered doing before; for he found himself becoming more and more surprised by the butler's care.

"Have you always gone to these lengths, Morris?" he asked.

"Oh, most certainly, sir."

"Even to the extent of locking the inner doors?"

"Why, yes, sir!" The butler seemed surprised now. "Braunton, your father's butler, always made me do it, sir, for it was upon the late Mr Harris's instructions that the inner doors were locked—after another robbery, sir—and they have been every night for, I suppose, the last forty, or fifty years."

"God bless my soul!" Harris exclaimed. "It shows how much I trust you, Morris, for tonight is the first time I have observed you locking the inner doors. Which ones do you lock?"

"Of the inner doors, sir? Those from the ball-room, those from the conservatory into the large drawing-room, those of the large drawing-room into the hall, the door to the servants' quarters, and the door to my pantry, sir."

"Indeed!" remarked Harris.

By this time they had returned to the hall, and saying good night to Morris, Mr Harris began to mount the stairs. As he went, he heard Morris turning the key in the door closing off the corridor leading to the servants' quarters from the hall.

Mrs Harris was already in bed and had dismissed her maid when he went in to say good night to her.

"Do you know," he remarked as he perched himself on the edge o the great bed, "I've been going round locking up with Morris every night—at least while we're here—for the past thirty years, and I discovered for the first time this evening that besides checking every window and outer door downstairs he actually locks a number of the inner doors?"

"But I could have told you that, my dear," Mrs Harris yawned.

"Yes," he mused, preoccupied with his own thoughts, "even the door to his pantry! Good heavens, I must ask him about that in the morning!" he exclaimed.

"About what, my dear?" his dutiful wife asked.

"Where he keeps the key of the pantry at night after he has locked the door."

"Is it important, dear?"

"Very important!"

"Then I'll remind you in the morning. Kiss me and say good night, and get you to bed. You look as though you have need of some repose."

"Yes, you're right, my dear," he confessed, performed his connubial duties, drew the bed-curtain and went to the dressing-room. Within a quarter of an hour he was himself in bed and on the verge of sleep. Five minutes later, had Mrs Harris herself still been conscious, she would have heard the undeniable sounds of her spouse's unconcern for the problems of the world.

Rarely had Mr Harris slept so soundly; yet in the middle of the night he suddenly awoke. Relating the incident later, he declared that he was in an instant thoroughly wide-awake, though how or why he could never explain.

And by the light of a small lamp he had kept burning, he saw a young lad standing at the foot of his bed.

"Though I had never seen him before," he would say, "I knew at once that he was the boy, Richard Tarwell, who had disappeared on the night of the robbery four or five months previously."

Mr Harris's amazement was extreme, and the thought passed through his mind that the boy must have evaded capture with great cunning by hiding somewhere in the house, the last place anyone would ever think of looking for a fugitive from justice—the very site of his crime.

But he was puzzled, too, by the lad's coming to him now. If he had been an accomplice of the thieves, as Morris swore he had been, his master would surely be the last person he would come to.

Sitting up in bed he demanded, "What do you want with me at this time of night?"

The boy made no reply, but merely beckoned with his finger.

"Are you mute?" Mr Harris demanded now. "Tell me, why have you come to me at this hour?"

Again the boy did not speak, but beckoned once more and then turned and pointed to the door.

Thinking that perhaps the boy had suffered some fright that had deprived him of his speech, and understanding from the signs he made that he wished his master to follow him, Harris, with some feelings of exasperation, got out of bed, partly dressed himself, and taking his sword under his arm, followed the boy, still beckoning and pointing with his arm out of the room.

As he heard his own footsteps padding on the carpet covering the floor of the corridor, he became aware that the boy was moving without any sound whatsoever, despite the fact that he appeared to be wearing boots; and it was now that Harris suddenly began to wonder whether or not the boy was alive or an apparition.

"I felt no fear," he said afterwards, "for the boy, whether alive or spirit seemed to me a gentle creature. My strongest desire was to see where he would lead me and for what purpose."

With the boy leading several paces before him, the two went down the staircase, along a short passage to a side door, which to Harris's still mounting amazement was unlocked and open, though only a short while ago he had watched Morris lock it. So they passed into the park.

The boy led the way for about a hundred yards making for a very large oak, the trunk of which was surrounded and almost hidden by low shrubs and bushes, which had been allowed to grow wild there for time out of mind. At the tree the boy stopped, pointed to the ground with his forefinger, and still having spoken not a word seemed to pass round to the other side of the tree.

It was a bright starlit night, and Harris had been able to see his way without any difficulty since they had left the house. When, however, he followed the boy round the tree he had vanished.

"Richard Tarwell," Harris called out softly. "Where are you? Do you hear me?"

No answer came, nor when he called again. If the boy were alive it would be impossible for him to move through the tangle of undergrowth without being heard; but though Harris listened intently, he heard no sound at all. He told himself then that it was an apparition he had seen.

Now he must discover what the boy's intention had been in bringing him here, but as there was nothing he could do at this hour, he returned to the house, locking the side door after him when he had gone in. Back in his bed, he did not sleep, but turned over in his mind the best course he should take.

As the first light of dawn began to penetrate the room by the window, whose curtains he had drawn back before getting into bed, he got up and dressed. Going quietly, he found his way to the room where the two footmen, Eames and Barnwell, slept.

When he had reassured them that they had nothing to fear, he said, "I want you to get up and come with me. Go very quietly, for I do not wish to rouse anyone else in the house".

When they joined him at the side door, he had already fetched two spades from the gardener's sheds.

"Take these," he said, "and follow me."

He led them to the oak to which only a short time before the ghost of Richard Tarwell had led him, and pointing to the spot to which the boy had pointed before he had vanished he said, "I want you to dig there".

Though they were puzzled, they asked no questions, but set to with the spades. Within a few minutes Barnwell exclaimed, "There is something buried here!"

"Ah!" Harris exclaimed quietly. "Go carefully, then. I fear you will be shocked as well as surprised by what you will find."

"There is clothing here!" Eames next remarked. Putting aside their spades, the two men knelt down and began to scoop the earth from the shallow hole, uncovering with each handful more and more of the clothing.

"Good God!" they both exclaimed together, as they recognized the coat which, though soiled and mildewed, could now be plainly seen; and Eames explained, "This is the boy's coat."

"And if I am not mistaken," Harris said, "his body will be in it."

Realizing what thoughts must be passing through their minds, as they worked Mr Harris told them briefly what had made him bring them here. "I fear," he said, "that we have been grossly deceived. For many years I have trusted Morris without question. Had anyone come to me and suggested however slightly that he was a dishonest man, I should have told them that they were no longer any friends of mine."

"But I found him tied up, upon my honour, sir!" Eames protested.

"I am not doubting you for a moment," Harris assured him. "What I believe happened was this. Morris had accomplices whom he let into the house. While they were robbing the strong-boxes, the boy came upon them. Naturally, they had to silence him to protect their own skins. Which of them did the terrible deed does not matter, since before the law they are all guilty. You will recall that when I questioned you Morris made no mention of the boy's bed being empty when he left his room, yet he must have noticed it. But he claimed to have been surprised when he found the boy in the pantry. You also corrected him when he said there was no other male in the house. Do you know where he keeps the key of his pantry after he has locked it for the night?"

"Always in the drawer of the commode by his bed," Eames replied.

"Then that fact will convict him more than any other," Harris commented, "because, for anyone to gain access to the pantry with the key, he must have got it from the drawer without disturbing Morris as he slept, a thing which it would be very difficult for an inexperienced boy to perform.

"Say nothing to any of the servants, and particularly to Morris, of what we have discovered. As soon as you have breakfasted, Eames, go at once to the village and bring the constables."

When the constables arrived and Morris was summoned to them and accused, he at first denied the accusation. But when they led him out to the oak, he broke down and confessed. It had happened as Harris had deduced. He had had two accomplices, whom he had let into the house by the side door; the boy had disturbed them and one of the men had attacked him and killed him; all three of them had buried the body under the oak. When they had done this, they talked for a time about what they should do now, and hit upon the plan of gagging Morris and binding him to the chair.

They were to have taken the silver to Plymouth and there disposed of it, sending the butler his share of the proceeds. But they had crossed him; he had heard no word from them.

Morris was found guilty at the next Exeter assizes, sentenced to death and hanged. His accomplices were never found, however, nor any trace discovered of the stolen property.

Every detail of this story is based on the transcript of Morris's trial, at which Harris gave evidence, avowing most solemnly his belief that Richard Tarwell had returned to avenge his own death.

Ghosts of Old France

La Clairon was one of the most famous actresses on the French stage during the reign of Louis XV. She acted in all the great roles of classical tragedy, created many parts in the plays of Voltaire, Marmontel and Saurin, and her talents were praised by Goldsmith and Garrick. She was for many years the toast of Paris theatre-lovers. Rich and elegant gallants from the Court of Versailles patronized her salons. She lived until the ripe age of eighty, and in 1798, a few years before her death, she wrote her memoirs in which she told a remarkable ghost story.

She was born Claire Leris in 1723 in the little town of Condé, near the Belgian frontier of France, the illegitimate daughter of a sergeant of King Louis's army. She made her first stage appearance at the Comédie Italienne when she was thirteen. For some years she lived the life of a demi-mondaine, as a consequence of which she had some difficulty in getting the title role in Racine's tragedy *Phèdre* at the Comédie Française in 1743.

La Clairon was singularly beautiful, and had, said Goldsmith, the most perfect female figure he had ever seen on any stage. She was, as can be imagined, much sought after by the voluptuaries of that luxurious and licentious age. But her ambition was set firmly upon a stage career. She was well aware of her talents in that direction.

It was in the year of her début at the Comédie Française at the age of twenty, when she was in the full bloom of her youthful beauty, that she was very ardently pursued by a young man whom she calls discreetly M. de S—— in her *Memoires d'Hippolyte Clairon*.

Now La Clairon had hosts of admirers. She could have become the mistress of many a rich aristocrat, and no doubt she had been. But her ambition lay in another profession, respectable as well as ancient; and, besides, she confesses, there was something about M. de S—— which quite turned her against him.

He was ashamed of his humble beginnings. His father was a prosperous merchant in Brittany, and M. de S—— had come to Paris to pose as a person of birth and quality, as apparently he was able to, for he had both the education and the manners to enable him to be accepted in the Parisian society of the day. He had realized all his assets and had come to Paris to climb the social ladder. He made a show of lavish living in order to be taken for someone who came from a higher class.

All this he confessed to the forthright Mademoiselle Clairon, without realizing that it was quite the wrong thing to say to her, for she had never troubled to conceal her own even more humble beginnings and wasn't ashamed of them. People took her for what she was, and the fact that she was a lovely and brilliantly talented girl who was taking Paris by storm meant that all society was at her feet. She did not have to indulge in the pretences of M. de S——.

It is likely that M. de S——'s method was the only means by which a man of humble birth could have been accepted in the snobbish society of eighteenth-century Paris. At all events, La Clairon could hardly be blamed for considering his ambition rather ignoble, even though her own mode of life was open to much criticism.

M. de S—— had other disadvantages which repelled the volatile, sought-after young actress. He wanted to have her completely to himself, and take her into the country away from her admirers, so that he could enjoy her by himself. It was not that he was a fascinating and entertaining person, or that his passion for her was romantically exciting. He was not an amusing or sophisticated companion. He was in fact often morose, and his obsession for her had made him more so.

La Clairon, who had no intention of entering into such a relationship with anyone at that particular time in her life, then began to discourage him. The affair had dragged on for a long time. She had known him for more than two years, and it was not that she had been ungenerous with her favours, but his passion for her grew and grew until it was the all-consuming thing of his life, and he was causing her both distress and embarrassment with his terrible jealousy and impossible demands.

Gradually, and with what tact as she could, she took steps to end the association. She refused his invitations, saw less of him, and devoted herself more ardently to her stage career, at which she was having her first great success at this time.

The rejected lover took it very badly indeed. His passion for her completely dominated his life. Without her, he was nothing. He became desperately ill. On top of this, he got into financial troubles. He had entrusted part of his money to his brother-in-law who failed to respond to his urgent requests for funds. M. de S—— would have starved on his sick-bed but for his former mistress, who with a warmness and generosity one would expect from such a girl immediately came to his aid and gave him money to help him out of his difficulties, though she was adamant in her refusal to resume the affair and would not even accept the letters he wrote to her.

She did not realize that her former lover was dying, and on the evening he sent a last pathetic message to her begging her to come round to see him for the last time, just for a few minutes so that he could look upon her once more, she was entertaining friends to a supper party at her house. She would have gone to him, but her friends stopped her, and, not liking to desert her guests, she did not insist.

M. de S——'s only companion as he lay dying was an elderly lady who had befriended him. He died at eleven o'clock, and just at that time La Clairon had been entertaining her guests with some of her delightful singing.

She had finished her song and bowed to the enthusiastic applause, and as the handclaps died away the clock on the mantel struck the hour of eleven. On the final stroke a loud and terrible cry echoed throughout the whole house. The cry seemed to come from the room itself and was one of such appalling, heart-broken anguish that it chilled the blood of all who heard it.

La Clairon herself fainted, having no doubt at all in her mind that her old lover had died and that the cry had in some way come from him and was intended for her to hear. Terrified and not wishing to be alone that night, she persuaded several of her friends to stay with her until morning.

Her friends were perhaps more puzzled at that dreadful cry than she, and when it was heard the following night at the same hour, and the night after, it became the talk of Paris. At first it was thought someone was playing a practical joke, because the cry could be heard not only in the house, but in the street where, night after night, it now was heard not only by her friends and her neighbours, but also the police, who sought in vain for the person who uttered it. So great was the interest aroused by the strange cries that crowds gathered every night to hear them.

La Clairon had no doubt at all that she was being haunted, and she bitterly regretted that she had not responded to M. de S——'s dying appeal to pay him that last visit. One night she had been out to supper after the theatre, and as her escort was bidding her good-night at her doorway, she said that the terrible cry suddenly exploded between them. Her companion was as terrified as she, though he knew the story, as did all Paris, and he had to be assisted to his carriage in a state of collapse.

On another occasion she was driving to a friend's house near the Porte Sainte-Denis with one of her admirers, a young aristocrat who mocked at the supernatural and who was wittily sceptical about her ghost voice, challenging her to produce it for his benefit, before he would believe in it.

Half seriously, she accepted his challenge and the next instant the carriage was filled with the most appalling and pitiful screams. The coachman had difficulty in preventing the horses from bolting, and when they arrived at their destination Mlle Clairon said that she and her companion were found lying senseless in the carriage.

For some time after that the ghost voice left her in peace, and she heard it next, and for the last time, some months later at Versailles where she and the company of the Comédie Française had been commanded by Louis XV to give a performance on the occasion of the marriage of the Dauphin. They had to stay three nights at Versailles, and the town was overcrowded for the festivities. La Clairon had to share her room with one of the other actresses and her bed with her maid. She was joking about their cramped, un-comfortable quarters, and the weather being so foul. "I doubt if my ghost would ever find me here at the end of the world," she laughed.

Immediately, she says, the fearful cry once more burst upon their ears, and the whole house was in uproar, for everyone heard it, and none of them, she says, slept a wink that night.

When she returned to Paris, her ghost began the second phase of its vengeful campaign against her. Upon the first stroke of eleven one evening a week later when she was sitting in her house enter-taining some friends, there was the sound of a musket being dis-charged outside her window. Everyone in the room not only heard the shot but saw the flash, and the men rushed gallantly to the protection of the idol of the Paris stage, thinking an attempt was being made upon her life. But there was no bullet-hole in the window and outside was no sign of an assailant.

The police were immediately summoned by her alarmed companions, and though they made a rigorous investigation and questioned all the residents of the road, they could discover no explanation for the shot. Every night now at eleven o'clock the shot rang out and the flash was seen outside the window; and although the police were constantly on duty, they were unable to solve the mystery. They had no means of stopping the noise or of detecting its origin. Mlle Clairon declared in her memoirs that this continued every night for three months, and the proof of it is to be found in the records of the Paris Police of 1744.

She became so used to the phantom shot that eventually she looked upon it as something of a joke, and she recalls an incident which happened when she and a man friend were on the balcony of the haunted window at the appointed time making jokes about it. The shot rang out as the clock struck the hour, but the explosion this time was so great that they were both thrown back into the room and each felt a sharp blow on the side of the head which seemed to have been dealt them by a human hand. This brusque reprimand for their unseemly levity did not have the desired effect, for they both burst out laughing.

La Clairon was troubled by the phantom shot for the last time two nights later when passing in her carriage the very house where her former lover had died a couple of years previously. As she pointed out the house to her companion, the shot rang out once again, and the coachman, believing they were being ambushed by armed robbers, whipped the horses into a gallop.

The haunting continued for several months, but she heard no more shooting, only mysterious hand-clapping and the singing of a strange and curious song which was truly haunting, for it was an air which was both tantalizing and fascinating, and which she could never fully recall afterwards. This ghostly song ended the haunting which had begun two and a half years previously and to which its victim had now become thoroughly accustomed.

During this time La Clairon's success on the stage had brought her both wealth and fame, and she moved to a more luxurious house in a fashionable part of Paris. She decided to let her old home. A number of people came to look at the famous residence of La Clairon where the strange haunting had taken place, and it was not surprising that among the viewers were some who had no intention of renting the place.

With most of these her servants had no difficulty in dealing, but there was one lady of advancing years who was unusually persistent and seemed to be in a state of some agitation, demanding to see Mlle Clairon, saying she had been a friend of M. de S——. The young actress immediately saw her.

The lady told La Clairon that she had nursed and looked after her former lover during the last few weeks of his life and was with him when he died. She knew all about his affair with La Clairon and his hopeless love for her, and she had done her best to make him accept the inevitable and forget her, but in vain. On the contrary, he said he would never forget her in this life or in the next, and that he would return from the grave to haunt her.

But why? asked La Clairon, puzzled as well as distressed at what her visitor had told her.

The woman replied that if La Clairon had complied with the dying man's request to go and see him for the last time, he would have passed away in peace and he would have left her in peace too. When she refused his request, he declared with his dying breath that he would come back to haunt her and do so in a way which would alarm and frighten her. He would haunt her, he said, for the same length of time as he had been held enslaved under her spell.

As La Clairon recollected, his passion for her had lasted two and a half years, when it was terminated by his death, after which his spirit had terrorized her for another two and a half years before finally releasing her from its ghostly attentions.

Her experience had no effect upon her great success on the Paris stage during its golden years in the reign of Louis XV, when she herself reigned at the Comédie Française for twenty-two years. She retired in 1766 and opened a dramatic school in Paris which flourished for many years. La Clairon outlived the Revolution and died in the year 1803.

Eighteenth-century France was the setting for another interesting ghost story in which an English family was involved.

During the reign of Louis XV a young man inherited some property in and around Lille. He was placed under the guardianship of his uncle, who turned out to be a villain of the blackest hue, prepared to go to any lengths to rob his nephew of his inheritance, which included two imposing houses in Lille and an estate in the country.

The young heir was a weakling and was somewhat under the influence of his guardian, who tried to make him sign documents to transfer the property, but the nephew was not such a fool as all that. The uncle then proceeded to sterner more ruthless measures. In the garret room of their house in the Place du Lion d'Or at Lille he installed one of those fearsome iron cages sometimes used in those days to confine human beings. This hideous contraption was eight feet high and four feet square and contained an iron collar attached to a chain. The whole apparatus was riveted to the wall. The wicked uncle then put his nephew in this cage and kept him in it, it is supposed, until he died.

Afterwards the murderer sold up all the property and disappeared. Such was the state of affairs in the *ancien régime* that he took little trouble to conceal his crime, which became the talk of Lille. The wretch did not even dismantle the iron cage in which he had killed his nephew. Nor in fact did the man who bought the house in the Place du Lion d'Or from him.

For many years the house was empty. No tenant would stay in it for more than a few days on account of the *revenant*. The house passed from father to son and vain attempts were made to let it. Its evil reputation lingered on through the century.

Then in the autumn of the year 1786 a wealthy and aristocratic English family came to Lille. They were Sir William and Lady Court and four of their children. They arrived in style in their coach with a retinue of six servants—coachman, groom, footman and three maids. Their object in coming to France was for the children to learn French, an accomplishment as desirable in Georgian times as it is today. In pursuit of this laudable object they were to remain there for the winter in the charge of Lady Court, while Sir William went elsewhere on business of his own.

The arrival of this cavalcade of English wealth and quality in the ancient town of Lille was a matter of some interest. They were looking for a house suitable for their needs and appropriate to their station, and the large and well-built residence in the Place du Lion d'Or seemed to meet both requirements. It was offered to Sir William at what seemed a ridiculously low rental. He took it and moved his family and servants into it without delay.

Having settled his family at Lille, Sir William furnished his wife with letters-of-credit which she could cash at the local bankers in order to meet her expenses, and then betook himself elsewhere. He may have returned to England on business, or he may have gone to enjoy the pleasures of Paris; but what he did is of no further importance to this story.

No sooner had the Courts settled themselves in the house than they began to hear mysterious noises at night—particularly the sound of a slow, measured tread in the room above the large chamber which Lady Court shared with one of her daughters, Elizabeth. They may have been reduced to sleeping together in this way on account of the fact that they had so many servants to accommodate. Six domestics were not enough for their requirements, for they engaged in addition a cook, a butler, a footman and a house-boy, all of whom were French. The footsteps above therefore had not unduly disturbed Lady Court and her daughter, as they thought it was one of the man-servants walking about.

After they had been installed there for a short while, Lady Court and Elizabeth went to the bank to cash a letter-of-credit. The money was paid in six-franc pieces, the bulky coinage of the day, and the banker offered to send the money round to the house. When Lady Court told him that she lived in the Place du Lion d'Or he looked surprised, and said that the only house in that thoroughfare suitable for her ladyship's occupation was haunted and as a consequence had been impossible to let for many years.

Neither Lady Court nor her daughter believed in ghosts, and they greeted this piece of information with well-bred laughter, bordering on derision. They implored the banker to order his clerk to say nothing about the *revenant* to their servants, who being ignorant people were probably superstitious. On the way back Lady Court jokingly said to Elizabeth: "I suppose it must have been the ghost walking about over our heads that kept us awake."

They dismissed the matter as not really being worthy of their attention, though of course the footsteps which they heard again in the night above them brought it back to the mind of Lady Court, who was of a somewhat nervous disposition.

"Who sleeps in the room over us?" she demanded of Cresswell, her personal maid.

Cresswell looked at her in surprise. "No one, my lady. Above your room is a large garret which is quite empty."

Within a week the story of the ghost was the talk of the household and all the French servants were for leaving. It was then that Cresswell enlightened her ladyship about the story of the man in the iron cage, adding the thrilling information that the very cage itself was in the garret above her ladyship's head.

The children, of course, rushed upstairs to see this fascinating object of horror and Lady Court was not far behind them. The English sceptics gazed enraptured upon the rusty old iron cage which reminded them of a place in which beasts were kept. The very thought that a human being had been imprisoned in it filled them with creepy horror.

But they did not believe that the house was haunted. Educated and intelligent people in the eighteenth century did not believe in ghosts. The Courts had a theory that the footsteps heard in the empty garret were made by someone who, for some reason, wished to keep the house untenanted—though why there should be such a human conspiracy against them they could not imagine. Nevertheless the Court family were convinced of it, and it was the thought that someone other than themselves and their gaggle of servants having access to the house, that made Lady Court decide to move elsewhere. But another house was difficult to find and she decided to stay where she was until she was successful.

Cresswell shared a room with a Mrs Marsh, who was Elizabeth's personal maid—for the favoured Court children each had a servant of their own—and a couple of nights after the discovery of the iron cage both the servants were woken in the middle of the night by the appearance of a tall, thin man in their room. He walked towards the door and disappeared through it. The terrified women hid under their bedclothes shivering with fright until morning.

When Cresswell recounted this story to Lady Court the next day, Elizabeth, who was there, burst out laughing, and this made Cresswell cry and say she could never sleep in that room again. Both mother and daughter comforted her and told her she could sleep in the little room next to theirs, and that they would soon be moving into a new house.

The door which opened into the room which had been occupied by Cresswell and the other maid was in a recess leading from a wide staircase which led to a passage where the main bedrooms were.

A night or two later Lady Court asked Elizabeth and her son Charles to go to her bedroom and bring down her large embroidery frame. It was dark, and as brother and sister started up the wide staircase they saw, by the light of the lamp fixed in the hall, a tall, thin man ascending the stairs in front of them. According to Elizabeth, the figure was wearing a powdering gown and wore his hair long at the back in the style of the mid-eighteenth century.

Neither of the young people believed it was a ghost. They thought it was Hannah, one of their maids, playing a trick on them. They called out:"It's no good, Hannah. You can't frighten us like that."

The ghost thereupon turned into the recess leading to the doorway of the room Cresswell had occupied, then melted into the door and disappeared.

Elizabeth and Charles continued on their way not disconcerted, still thinking it was one of Hannah's little jokes which had been brought off rather successfully in the uncertain light of the lamp at the foot of the stairs. When they returned with the embroidery frame they told their mother of the trick they imagined Hannah had played upon them, but Lady Court informed them that Hannah had gone to bed some time ago with a sick headache.

Elizabeth and Charles at once went to Hannah's room where they found another of the maids, Alice, with Hannah who was fast asleep, and had been so, Alice assured them, for more than an hour. Later they told Cresswell of the incident, and described the figure they had seen ascending the stairs. Cresswell went white and said that was exactly the same figure she had seen in her bedroom that night.

Brother Harry, who was Head Boy at Westminster School, now came to spend ten days with the family at Lille. After his first night in the house in the Place du Lion d'Or the youth appeared at breakfast in a state of high indignation, accusing his mother of sending "some Frenchy" to spy upon him and see that he put his candle out at the proper time. Harry had heard the footsteps in the passage, jumped out of bed and opened the door to see the figure in the loose gown. If he'd had any clothes on, he said, he would have gone after him and taught him a lesson. His mother assured him that she had sent no one to spy upon him.

A young English couple named Atkyns, who lived near Lille, visited them and upon hearing of the ghost, Mrs Atkyns recklessly offered to sleep in the room where Cresswell had been frightened. Lady Court agreed and Mrs Atkyns spent an extremely restless night, accompanied by her pet terrier, who was reduced to a state of terror, as was Mrs Atkyns, by the sinister movements and footsteps which were heard in the room during the night.

"Perhaps you dreamed it all," said her husband unsympathetically the next morning, and Lady Court was just as disbelieving, despite everything, and despite the fact also that she confessed that she would be terrified if there really was a ghost in the house. By now she had arranged to take over the house of a nobleman who was going to spend a few years in Italy, and during their last night in the house in the Place du Lion d'Or, Elizabeth saw the ghost in the bedroom she shared with her mother.

The ghost was standing with one arm resting upon the chest-of-drawers, and with its face turned towards Elizabeth as she sat bolt upright in her four-poster, eyes staring at it with terror. She saw that it was the face of a young man, ghastly pale, and thin, with hollow cheeks and with an expression of infinite suffering and unhappiness—a ravaged and terrible face which made her think of that dreadful iron cage in the room above her head, in which he had been chained like an animal with the metal collar around his neck. The face of this wretched and unhappy ghost haunted Elizabeth for years.

But just then, though frightened out of her wits, she would have been even more frightened to have awoken her mother who, she was sure, would have had hysterics at the sight of the phantom standing by the chest-of-drawers—a melancholy but terrifying thing from that other world.

Elizabeth heard the clock strike four, and then, copying Cresswell, she suddenly slid down and lay under the bedclothes, shivering with terror. She lay like that for nearly an hour and when at last she ventured her head above the clothes and looked once more to the chest-of-drawers she saw nothing. Nor had she heard a sound. The bedroom door had not opened or closed. And then she heard the clock strike five.

She did not sleep that night, trying to persuade herself that what she had seen had been something human, and that she had omitted to lock their bedroom door, which was always done in that house.

In fact when Cresswell came in as usual to rouse them in the morning, she called out to the maid that she must have forgotten to lock the door, and so there was no need for her (Elizabeth) to get out of bed. But she had not forgotten. The door was locked and the key was in its usual place. It was impossible to get in from the outside.

When she heard about her daughter's experience during the night, Lady Court was most grateful that Elizabeth had not awoken her, for she believed the shock of witnessing such a sight would have killed her.

Elizabeth, still reluctant to believe in the supernatural, made a thorough search of the room with the help of Cresswell, to see if there was any concealed or secret way of getting into it, but they found nothing.

That day Lady Court with her children and domestics left the house for the more comfortable and certainly less sinister home of the nobleman who had gone to Italy.

Then followed the French Revolution and the Napoleonic Wars, but by this time the Court family were safely back in England, and these "disturbances", as they termed those momentous events, made them forget their *revenant* at Lille, and it was not until some years later that the story was recalled, and was told in various forms, garbled and otherwise, during the ghost-conscious nineteenth century. A form of the story was told by the author S. Baring-Gould in a long-forgotten number of the *Cornhill Magazine*.

But in Lille, it was impossible to ignore the ghost. It will be recalled that in the case of a similar haunting at Hinton Ampner (q.v.) the owner pulled the place down when its spectral residents made the place uninhabitable for human beings. The French, however, are more practical people. They turned the haunted house in the Place du Lion d'Or at Lille into a hotel, and it remained so for many years during the nineteenth century. Of course the ghost still walked, although the sinister iron cage was removed. Doubtless a number of guests were thoroughly frightened by the spectral goings-on, but a haunted hotel is not necessarily bad for business. Many have thrived upon such a reputation.

The scene of the Court family's *revenant* now became the Hotel du Lion d'Or, and a small party of English people stayed there in the 1880s and described it as an old-fashioned, unpretentious hostelry. In those days the landlord was reticent about the ghost and kept the haunted room locked. The English guests noticed that it was approached by a recess, now full of the brooms and pails used by the housemaids.

In the night they were disturbed by the footsteps, slow and dragging. They had been assured that they were the only guests in that part of the hotel, and each of the men thought it was the other restlessly pacing his room unable to sleep. When they consulted each other in the middle of the night, they found that it was not so, and came to the conclusion that the footsteps were in the room above.

They went to sleep, lulled by that "stealthy dragging step" above them, not knowing until they later heard the story of the Court family, that their sleep had been troubled by the ghost of the man in the iron cage.

The Spirit of Sergeant Davies

When a war is over and won, the true reckoning begins. The Jacobite Rebellion of 1745 ended in total failure for the Stuart cause. Prince Charlie had fled back to France, leaving his faithful Highlanders to suffer unspeakable wrongs at the hands of the English victors, under their cruel leader "Butcher" Cumberland. Murder, rape, house-burning were the order of the day, and nothing was left undone that might break the spirit of the brave Clans. They might no longer wear their traditional tartans, nor carry swords—officially. But Highland blood is high, and the heaths and mountains hid as many broken and outlawed men as they did rabbits and foxes; each with some vestige of a knife or rusted gun, and each with hatred in his heart for the conquering Sassenach.

There is the tale of one Donald Ban and his wife, who were visited one night by a ghost, and sorely frightened. But the woman retained enough self-possession to beg the ghost to answer one question for her: "Will our Prince come again?" The phantom replied in the following lines:

> The wind has left me bare indeed,
> And blawn my bonnet off my heid,
> But something's hid in Hieland brae—
> The wind's no' blawn my sword away!

But this poetic spirit is not the ghost of our story.

By 1749, three years after the Rising was quelled, the English government was still uneasy about the Highlands. The feeling that "something's hid in Hieland brae" was only too strong upon them, and an Army of Occupation still kept a sharp watch on the territory. It was as popular as Armies of Occupation usually are.

But an exception to the general label of "bluidy redcoat" was Sergeant Arthur Davies, of Guise's regiment, who in the summer of 1749 was posted from Aberdeen to Dubrach in Braemar, eight miles away from the nearest guard-station at Glenshee. Between the two places stretched a wild waste of bog and mountain, rock and river. Sergeant Davies was not perturbed by the difference between this savage land and his own gentle countryside, and soon settled down. He was quickly accepted, for he was one of those men born to be liked by their fellow-men—kindly, honest, fair in his dealings, and in his private life devoted to his young wife and fond of children. This last must have been a remarkable attribute in a country where a second Slaughter of the Innocents had just taken place. His wife later testified that "he and she lived together in as great amity and love as any couple could do, and he never was in use to stay away a night from her".

The sergeant, who was comfortably off in England, and of saving disposition, must have appeared very wealthy to hungry Highland eyes. He wore a silver watch, and two gold rings—one with a peculiar knob on it. His brogues had silver buckles, and, like Bobbie Shafto, he wore "silver buckles at his knee". On his striped lute-string waistcoat were two dozen silver buttons; his coat was a cheerful bright blue, his hat, with his initials cut into the felt was silver-laced, and his dark brown hair was gathered into a silk ribbon. He had saved fifteen guineas and a half—a huge sum for those days—and was in the habit of carrying it in a green silk purse and innocently displaying it to those interested. He carried a gun—an envied possession in those parts. Such was Sergeant Davies, "a pretty man", every detail of his appearance and attire noted by those who saw him leave his lodgings at Michael Farquharson's in Dubrach on 28 September, early in the morning. His wife, in her cap and bed-gown, came down to kiss him good-bye at the door. Did her arms hold more tightly and long around him than usual? Or did she watch him out of sight, with the uneasy feeling that this was the beginning of a very long journey? Probably not; she was an English-woman, not a Highland lass with "the sight". "Good-bye, Arthur—take good care of yourself," was more than likely to be all she said, before shutting the door and beginning her household tasks.

Sergeant Davies briskly collected four men, and set out towards Glenshee to meet the patrol which was coming from there. On the way he met a man called John Growar, and noticed that Growar was wearing a tartan coat—a thing forbidden by law. Instead of arresting him, as most English officers would have done, Davies kindly advised him to take it off and not to wear it again, and then let him go on his way. Davies was by this time alone, having left his men temporarily because he thought he would like to cross the hill and try to get a stag—he fancied himself as a sportsman. He promised to rejoin the men later on their way to the rendezvous with the patrol.

But when they met with the patrol, Sergeant Davies had not rejoined them. They gave him an hour or two, then went back and searched the route. They called, they shouted, but no voice answered, only the frightened moorland birds. The sun of a late summer was hot on their heads, and by the end of the day they gave up, exhausted.

For three days it was expected that Sergeant Davies would return of his own accord; on the fourth day a band of soldiers from the combined forces of Dubrach and Glenshee went out on an intensive search for him. But no trace of him was found; the substantial Sergeant Davies had vanished as if the fairies had taken him. Some simple folk believed they had; others had darker ideas.

The weeks passed, and the months. It was June, 1750, and the rooms where Sergeant Davies had lodged were occupied by his replacement. Poor Mrs Davies had gone home to England; after waiting for months in Scotland for her lost husband to return, she had given up hope. Michael Farquharson's son, Donald, was at home when the servant came to tell him that there was a visitor asking for his father, one Alexander Macpherson. His father being away on business, Donald offered to see the man himself.

Alexander Macpherson was a middle-aged man who had so far stayed out of trouble with the English, and was living humbly but peacefully enough in a shepherd's hut among the hills. The story he had to tell was a strange one. He had, he said, been visited repeatedly at night by the ghost of Sergeant Davies, looking exactly as he had done in life but with an anxious, troubled expression. The ghost had begged Macpherson to go and look for his bones, which were buried in a peat moss, about half a mile from the road taken by the patrols. Macpherson, afraid, refused to do this. "Bury my bones! bury my bones!" repeated the ghost over and over, despairingly. "I will not—I am afraid," returned Macpherson. "Then you will find one who will. Go to Michael and Donald Farquharson at my old lodgings, and tell them to bury my bones—bury my bones!"

Donald Farquharson listened to this recital incredulously. He was a level-headed person, and had heard many wild tales from his fellow-Highlanders. Frankly, he did not believe Macpherson, and said so.

"But at least come with me and see if the bones are there!" Macpherson pleaded. "If you could have seen and heard the ghost you would have believed!"

His insistence finally succeeded with Farquharson, who agreed to go with him. The next morning they set out, and within an hour or two arrived at the spot described by the ghost. They had brought spades, and now used them. Not far below the surface they turned up a shred of blue cloth. Deeper still they dug, until the peat yielded what the ghost had promised—the pathetic bones of Sergeant Davies, the brown hair still clinging to the skull, but the silk ribbon gone; the silk waistcoat almost intact, but without its silver buttons, and the buckles vanished from the bones of knee and foot. His murderers had torn the silver lacing from his hat and thrown the hat down beside him. There it lay, rotting, the initials "A.D." still clear.

Reverently, Farquharson and Macpherson dug a neat grave away from the peat moss, and it in they laid the poor bones, saying over them a service of prayer and committal; for they were both devout men. The rags and relics of clothing they collected and took back with them to Dubrach, as evidence of the murder that had been done.

A trial was held, and Alexander Macpherson was called upon to give evidence. His testimony differed substantially from the story he had told Donald Farquharson. According to what he now said, he had been visited late in May by a vision of a man clothed in blue, who said "I am Sergeant Davies!" At first he thought the figure was a real living man—a brother of Donald Farquharson's. He rose and followed the shape to the door, where it told him that its bones lay in a spot the direction of which it pointed out, and said that it wished them to be decently buried, and that Donald Farquharson would help to do this.

Next day Macpherson went out and found the bones, afterwards covering them up again. On his way back to his hut he met Growar, the man of the tartan coat whom Davies had encountered on his last day on earth. Growar said that if Macpherson did not keep quiet about the discovery, he himself would impeach Macpherson to Shaw of Daldownie, a magistrate. Macpherson, taking the wise course, went to Shaw himself and told his story; but Shaw told him to keep his mouth shut about the whole affair, and not give the district a bad name for harbouring rebels. Macpherson went home with a disturbed mind. That night the ghost again appeared to him, reproaching him, and once again commanding him to get Donald Farquharson to bury the bones. He also—and this caused a sensation in the court—revealed the names of the two men who had murdered him, Duncan Clerk and Alexander Bain Macdonald.

At this point the magistrate interrupted to ask in what language the ghost had spoken to Macpherson.

"In the Gaelic," Macpherson replied. The magistrate wrote down his answer.

Then came an uncanny piece of evidence from Mistress Isobel MacHardie, for whom Macpherson worked as a shepherd. One night in June, 1750, she said, she had been sleeping in the sheiling (a hut for the use of shepherds) while Macpherson slept at the other end; a double watch was kept on the sheep. While she lay awake "she saw something naked come in at the door, which frighted her so much that she drew the clothes over her head. When it appeared it came in in a bowing posture, and next morning she asked Macpherson what it was that had troubled them in the night. He answered that she might be easy, for it would not trouble them any more".

Incredible as it may seem, no further inquiry was made into the doings of the men Clerk and Macdonald; the whole matter was suspended. Then, three years later, in September, 1753, they were suddenly arrested—on charges of rebellious behaviour, such as wearing the kilt! They were kept in Edinburgh's Tolbooth Prison until June, 1754, and then tried. At the trial it emerged that Clerk's wife wore Sergeant Davies's ring—the one with the characteristic knob—and that Clerk, after the murder, had suddenly become prosperous and had taken a farm. Witnesses came forward to swear that Clerk and Macdonald, armed, were on a hill in the neighbourhood of the murder on 28 September, 1749. And one Angus Cameron swore that he saw the murder committed, while he and another Cameron, now dead, had been hiding in a little hill-hollow all day, waiting for Donald Cameron, *who was afterwards hanged*, together with some of Donald's companions from Lochaber. The implication is that some underground Jacobite business was afoot. The watchers had seen Clerk and Macdonald strike and shoot a man in a blue coat and silver-laced hat, and then had run away.

Their evidence impressed the court greatly. But, 142 years later, it was contradicted by the story told by a very old lady, a descendant of one of the witnesses at the trial. She said that her ancestor had been out stag-shooting on 28 September, 1749, with gun and deerhound. He saw Clerk and Macdonald on the hill, and, thinking they had got a stag, went towards them, his dog running in front of him. As he drew nearer, he saw *what it was they had*. He called to the dog, and began to run away, but they fired a shot after him and the dog was wounded. Then he ran home as fast as he could.

Between the story of 1754 and that of 1896 it seems more than likely that Clerk and Macdonald were guilty. Their lawyers were certainly convinced of their guilt. And yet, when the jury of Edinburgh tradesmen returned to give their verdict, it was that of— Not Guilty. The reason for their acquittal was that the ghost had spoken to Alexander Macpherson in Gaelic, *a language it did not know in life.*

And so the unfortunate Sergeant Davies, who had struggled back through the gates of death to beg for Christian burial and to denounce his murderers, had made his journey in vain; for his bones were never interred in a kirkyard, and Clerk and Macdonald went free. They lived in prosperity, for those times, on the proceeds of the sergeant's guineas, watch and rings, and the silver buckles and buttons for which they had killed him. Small wonder if his forlorn blue-coated spirit walks the Braemar hills to this day.

The Haunting at Hinton Ampner

The strange events which took place at the old manor house of
Hinton Ampner between the years 1767 and 1771 constitute one of
the best observed and most carefully checked ghost stories on record.
After studying the reports of the various independent witnesses,
there can be little doubt that something took place at Hinton
Ampner Manor which cannot be accounted for by natural events—
a haunting which has its echoes right down to the present century,
even though the old beghosted manor, being long destroyed, is no
more.

The fact that these events took place during the eighteenth century
should not deter us, or make us think we can doubt the
reliability of the accounts which have come down to us. On the
contrary, the period of the story should make us take it more
seriously than if it had taken place in almost any other century.

The eighteenth century was the Age of Reason. People were
superficially religious, and certainly not superstitious. Materialism
was the creed of most educated people. There was less belief in
ghosts then than there is now.

The Georgian lady who set down the chronicle of this strange
haunting at first steadfastly refused to accept that she was living in a
haunted house. She plainly did not believe in ghosts, and when her
servants came to her with weird stories of the eerie goings on in her
house, she scornfully dismissed them as the superstitions and fears
"to which the vulgar minds of the lower classes of people are so
prone".

She was to learn very differently, and finally to be driven from the house by the terror of the unknown forces she at first despised and disbelieved in.

Hinton Ampner is a tiny Hampshire village which lies just off the main road between Winchester and Petersfield. The old manor-house was built in the 1620s during the reign of James I by Sir Thomas Stewkeley, Bart. It was a comfortable though not a large manor-house by the standards of the day, and the Stewkeleys lived there for about a century.

In 1719 Miss Mary Stewkeley, the eldest daughter of Sir Hugh Stewkeley, married Edward Stawell, the younger brother of Lord Stawell. As the latter had no children, Edward was the heir presumptive to the title.

On her father's death, Mary inherited the property. Her younger sister, Honoria, came to live with them at Hinton, and after Mary's death in 1740 the attachment was such between Honoria and her widowed brother-in-law that she stayed on at Hinton, thus causing a great scandal.

Stories told by the servants at the manor spread throughout the district. They told not only of an immoral relationship between Stawell and his sister-in-law—incest no less, as the law did not permit them to marry—but also that a child had been born in consequence of their criminal affair. Worse, it was even whispered that the body of the child had been "done away with".

No one knows for sure whether there was any truth in this story, which spread like wildfire through the gossiping countryside, and which had a remarkable echo half a century later. It certainly seemed that the sad and disturbed spirits of the two lovers remained behind after their deaths to haunt the scene of some tragic and terrible happening.

In 1742 Edward Stawell's brother died and he inherited the title. He continued to live at Hinton Ampner with Honoria, who died in 1754. The following year Lord Stawell died of a stroke. He was fifty-six and the date was 2 April, 1755.

Shortly after his death his ghost was reported to be seen in the house "dressed in a drab coat".

Hinton Ampner Manor and the estate now passed into the hands of the Hon. Henry Bilson Legge, presumably as part of a marriage settlement, for he had married Lord Stawell's only daughter, Stawell's only son having died at Westminster School at the age of sixteen.

The Legges came to Hinton Ampner for only a few weeks every

year for the shooting season, and the place was looked after by three old family retainers, who lived there, and who had indeed lived there all their lives. They were Thomas Parfait and his wife Sarah, who had been coachman and housekeeper respectively to Lord Stawell, and had been with the family for forty years, and Elizabeth Banks, a housemaid, also an old family servant.

Legge died in 1764. His widow later married the Earl of Hillsborough, who apparently did not want Hinton Ampner as part of the price of marrying the lady. Nor did he desire to use the place, so she decided to let it furnished.

It is here where the heroine of this haunting comes into the story. She was Mary Jervis, a well-born young lady whose father was Swynfen Jervis, Solicitor to the Admiralty and treasurer of Greenwich Hospital, a man of some importance in London. Her brother, Captain John Jervis, R.N., who also had an encounter with the Hinton Ampner ghosts, was the brilliant naval officer who became the Earl St. Vincent—one of the most illustrious names of the British Navy. As Admiral Jervis, he led the Fleet to the great victory of the Battle of St. Vincent, at which Nelson served under him.

Mary Jervis married William Henry Ricketts, of Longwood, Hampshire, in 1757. He was a wealthy merchant whose affairs frequently took him to the West Indies. Mr and Mrs Ricketts had three children, and in January, 1765, they rented Hinton Ampner from Lady Hillsborough through the Hillsborough steward, a man named Sainsbury.

Mary Ricketts was then twenty-eight, an educated young lady who had been brought up in the sophisticated society of Georgian London—the London of Dr Johnson, Addison and Steele, Burke and Fielding. She had never been a country-girl, and she had the Londoner's contempt for countryfolk, their ways and their superstitious beliefs. In London she had mixed in an elegant, informed and reasoning society, which considered that it knew practically the sum total of knowledge about life and all that lay beyond—for was not Sir William Herschel already mapping the very shape of the Universe? Mary Ricketts was a product of this sophisticated and unhurried age. She scorned the very idea of ghosts, "knowing", as she put it, "how exploded such opinions were".

Not even after her devastating experience would she admit the supernatural. To her it was just "unexplained".

This is the great value of her testimony. Her one concern at all times was to tell the truth. Even before these events she had a widely recognized reputation for veracity.

The documentation of this story consists of letters from Mary Ricketts to her husband, to the Rector of Hinton Ampner and letters from her brother, John Jervis, to her husband in Jamaica, and also a "Narration" she wrote for posterity.

But as so often happens in such cases, posterity did not get it until a hundred years later. There were two copies of the "Narration" and they were jealously kept away from the public by the family until a garbled version appeared in 1870 in the biography of Richard Harris Barham, author of *The Ingoldsby Legends*. Mrs Ricketts's descendants then gave the complete "Narration" to *The Gentleman's Magazine* which published it in 1872.

It is the "Narration" which is the main source of this account.

When the Ricketts family took possession of Hinton Ampner Manor in January, 1765, Thomas Parfait, Lord Stawell's old coachman, was lying dead in his bed. It was not the best of omens. People these days, not even the eccentric aristocracy, are scarcely in the habit of letting furnished houses with dead bodies lying in the beds.

But the Ricketts were undeterred. The first thing they did was to get the old man buried and to pension off his widow Sarah, and also Elizabeth Banks, the ancient retainers who had lived in the manor all their lives and considered it their home, as was the custom of the times in such houses.

Shortly after their arrival at Hinton, Mary and her husband both heard noises in the night, particularly that of doors being slammed. This happened frequently and the master of the house got out of bed and searched, imagining robbers had broken in, or that irregularities were taking place in the servants' quarters. But he found no sign of intruders, and the servants were all in bed, and in their proper rooms.

When the noises continued Mary believed that some of the villagers had somehow acquired keys to the house and were coming in to make mischief, perhaps some sort of revenge for the importation of "foreign" servants. So they had all the locks in the house changed. But the strange noises continued nevertheless. They had to get used to them.

In the summer of 1765 the ghost of Lord Stawell again made its appearance in his old haunts of alleged incestuousness and infanticide.

He was seen first by Elizabeth Brelsford, the nurse to the Ricketts's eight-month-old son Henry. She was sitting by his cot in the nursery, the open door of which faced the yellow bedchamber used by the mistress of the house. It was a bright summer's evening and she plainly saw a man in "a drab coloured suit of clothes" go into the yellow room.

The nurse was not really surprised, imagining there was some strange visitor in the house, but when she and a fellow servant who assured her there was no stranger in the house, searched the yellow room immediately after the apparition had gone into it, they found no trace of the man in the drab-coloured suit.

A few months later George Turner, a groom, encountered the ghost while crossing the great hall to go to bed. He mistook his drab clothes for those worn by the butler while off duty, and thought indeed it was the butler. But when Turner got upstairs he found all the man servants, including the butler, were in their beds.

In the July of 1767 several of the servants were sitting in the kitchen when they heard a woman's footsteps come down the stairs towards the kitchen. It could not be one of the servants because they all heard the rustling of clothes which must have been made of the stiffest silk.

They looked to the door and all of them plainly saw a strange woman pass by. She was tall and she wore dark clothes. She went in the direction of the yard and the street. Almost immediately afterwards a man came through the door from the yard and could not have avoided seeing her, if she had been a live person. But he declared that he had seen no one.

The servants heard other eerie noises—dismal groans, and strange rustlings at night around their beds.

When they recounted these experiences to their mistress, Mary Ricketts treated the whole thing with ridicule. Ignorant, lower-class people were full of these stupid fears and superstitions.

In 1769 her husband went to Jamaica on one of his protracted business trips, and she remained alone at Hinton with her three young children and eight servants, all of whom were trusted and reliable, and none of whom came from the neighbourhood. Mary makes a great point of establishing the trustworthiness of her servants, as she long suspected that she was being made the victim of some kind of trickery, in which case her servants would be the first to be suspected.

Mary herself now began to hear the spectral noises in a way which thoroughly disturbed her. She heard people walking about in rooms which were subsequently found to be empty, and the rustling of those silken clothes was so pronounced and so loud that it often awakened her from sleep. As so many other people have found, locked and bolted doors could not keep out intruders of this nature.

During the winter of 1769-70 an old man came from the poor-house at West Meon, knocked upon the door of Hinton Ampner

Manor and desired to speak to the lady of the house upon a matter of importance touching upon the mysterious happenings at Hinton which had been the talk and the wonder of the countryside for miles around.

Mary, herself disturbed, though still suspecting she was the victim of some kind of conspiracy, condescended to see the old man, who then told her that he could not rest in his mind until he had acquainted her with something his late wife had once told him.

In her younger days, the old man said, his wife had known a carpenter who told her that Sir Hugh Stewkeley—the father of Honoria, whose ghost the servants in the kitchen had seen—had employed him to take up some floorboards in the dining room, and that Sir Hugh had concealed something underneath, after which the carpenter had been ordered to replace the floorboards. The carpenter imagined it was some kind of treasure which was hidden.

Mary's reaction to this piece of information was to write to the Mr Sainsbury, who was Lord Hillsborough's attorney, telling him what the old man had said, and suggesting that he might think it worth while to take up the floorboards and see whether there was any truth in the story. But neither Sainsbury nor the landlady herself seemed sufficiently interested in what they no doubt considered an idle tale.

Nor did Mary or her staff make any investigation, for she would certainly have recorded in her "Narrative" the finding of the thing that really was there under the floorboards all the time, and the cause—who knows?—of the terrifying haunting which then followed.

One night in the summer of 1770 Mary had just gone to bed in the yellow room and was wide awake, when she heard the heavy plodding footsteps of a man walking towards the end of her bed. She rushed from her room in terror into the nursery opposite, where the nursemaid, Hanna Streeter, was with the children.

Accompanied by Hannah and candles, she returned to the yellow room, but there was no one there. Nor was there any way by which an intruder could have got out of the yellow room unseen. This alarmed and perplexed her very much, as she had heard the footsteps so distinctly, being perfectly wide awake and her mind composed and collected at the time.

Nevertheless Mary refused to be frightened out of her yellow bedchamber, and even though she could easily have had one of her domestics to sleep in the room with her, she determined to go to bed there alone. She heard nothing more that summer.

When the chills of winter came to Hinton Ampner, she moved into the chintz bedroom which was over the hall and was a warmer room. In this room she heard sounds of music, and one night three distinct and violent knocks, as though someone was hitting a door with a club.

During this winter she became aware of a strange and hollow murmuring which seemed to fill the whole house. This was not a wind, for it was heard on the calmest of nights. It was a sound, she said, such as she had never heard before, so eerie that she was unable to find words to describe it.

On the 2nd of April of that year—the sixteenth anniversary of Lord Stawell's fatal seizure—Mary was awakened at two o'clock in the morning by the sound of people walking about in the adjoining lobby. She got out of bed and listened at the door for twenty minutes or so, during which she heard distinctly the sound of walking and a noise like someone pushing up against the door. Only when she was certain that her senses were not being deceived did she ring the bell for her maid. Elizabeth Godin came in immediately.

Mary continues the story thus: "Thoroughly convinced there were persons in the lobby before I opened my door, I asked her if she saw no one there. On her replying in the negative, I went out to her, examined the window which was shut, looked under the couch, the only furniture of concealment there; the chimney board was fastened, and when removed all was clear behind it. She found the door into the lobby shut, as it was every night. After this examination, I stood in the middle of the room, pondering with astonishment, when suddenly the door that opens into the little recess leading to the yellow apartment sounded as if played to and fro by a person standing behind it. This was more than I could bear unmoved. I ran into the nursery and rang the bell there that goes into the men's apartment."

Mary was still sceptical that the phenomenon was being caused by a supernatural agency, for when her coachman, young Robert Camis, a big, stolid farmer's son, answered her ring, she informed him that she was sure someone had broken in. It should be noted that the landing door, to which Robert came in answer to her ring, was also locked and barred, so it was impossible for anyone to get into her apartments, except by way of the windows, which were all shut and locked.

She let Robert in, armed him with a light and a stout stick and told him to go and investigate. But there was no one there. The yellow bedroom, from which the disturbance seemed to be coming, was bolted and locked as usual. Everything was in order. There was no intruder, and no place where one could have hidden. After dismissing Robert, she went to bed, but still heard the mysterious knocks. Other members of the household heard these noises.

Throughout the spring and summer of that year, the noises continued and increased, and were heard by several members of the household.

With midsummer, the noises became well-nigh intolerable. The great humming which Mary had noted before now seemed to be evolving into human sounds, articulate sounds, and both she and Elizabeth Godin were soon distinguishing human voices. There were three voices, one female and shrill and the other two male.

These three voices were conducting a conversation quite close to Mary and her maid, but neither of them could distinguish any of the words which were said—an incomprehensible, impassioned conversation, plucked from the past, and in some unfathomable way caught, imprisoned in that house in a kind of unending echo. These strange noises went on often all night, and continued until after daylight in the morning.

At night Mary's bed curtains rustled and it sounded as though some person was walking up against them, and yet no one was there. "I had taken every method to investigate the cause," she wrote. "And could not discover the least appearance of a trick. On the contrary, I became convinced it was beyond the power of any mortal agent to perform, but knowing how exploded such opinions are, I kept them in my own bosom, and hoped my resolution would enable me to support whatever might befall."

Her brother, Captain John Jervis, had just returned with his ship from the Mediterranean. Though eight years older than his sister, there had always been a very strong bond between them, but when he came to see her at Hinton she could not bring herself to tell him about the weird things which were taking place in the house, even though the noises continued while he was with her. But apparently he did not hear them on that occasion.

As light dawned on the day after he had returned to Portsmouth, even more violent sounds began at Hinton. "The most loud, deep, tremendous noise which seemed to rush and fall with infinite velocity and force upon the lobby door adjoining to my room." This was heard by both Mary and Elizabeth, who was too terrified to speak.

This extraordinary whirlpool of sound ended with a piercing scream which was repeated several times, growing fainter and fainter and seeming to sink into the floor.

The whole household was now in such a state of fear and alarm that Mary determined to tell her brother, who was expected back at Hinton within a week, what had happened.

This she did. With Captain Jervis was Captain Luttrell, a mutual friend, and when Mary told them the story they resolved to stay watch all night. They were armed, and with John Jervis was his personal servant John Bolton. Before they settled down to watch that night, the men searched every nook and cranny in the house.

The strange rustlings and noises took place that night, the same as before, and were heard and attested to by both Jervis and Luttrell as well as Bolton. Doors were slammed and banged unaccountably and John Jervis heard the most fearful groans as well as other weird and strange noises.

The gallant Captain sat up every night for a week to protect his sister from these unknown forces. During one of the nights she heard a pistol shot, followed by groans of agony, but no one had been shot at Hinton that night. One afternoon the Captain heard a tremendous noise as though some great weight had fallen through the ceiling into the room where he sat.

The man who was to rout the Spanish fleet off the Cape of St Vincent and thus establish British naval supremacy for a hundred years and more, retreated before the spectral hosts of Hinton Ampner, and urgently pressed his sister to leave the place.

This she did in the August of 1771. The story of course was the talk of the countryside.

With tenants unobtainable, Lady Hillsborough gave up the struggle with the supernatural forces and ordered Hinton Ampner Manor to be pulled down. During the demolition the housebreakers found a small skull under the floor of one of the rooms. It was said to be that of a monkey. But it was never professionally examined. Nor was any inquiry made into the circumstances and nature of the find.

It was said to have been found in a box, and near it were papers which had apparently been hidden under the floor during the Civil War.

The answer to the mystery of the skull of Hinton Ampner will never be known. One can only guess. The skull of a newly born baby could have been mistaken for that of a monkey by the ignorant workmen, and this might fully explain why the restless spirits of the guilty parents haunted the place. Was that awful scream which so frightened Mary and Elizabeth the unwanted infant's first cry smothered in death?

At the end of the eighteenth century a new Hinton Ampner House was built about fifty yards from the old site. But in the new house strange noises were heard—and are still heard—usually about dawn. It seems that the restless spirits of Lord Stawell and the sad Honoria are still abroad at Hinton Ampner.

The Drunk who Lost his Way

Half-way between the west and east coasts of the western claw of Cornwall, a few miles south of the line St Just–Penzance, lies the little village of Sancreed. In 1783 undoubtedly the best-known inhabitant of Sancreed, then known as San Crete, was John Thomas.

Thomas was a man of sixty-four, tough and vigorous, which was surprising when one considers that for more than two-thirds of his life he had been one of the most notorious drunkards in the whole Duchy of Cornwall, a region renowned for its hard-drinking men. It was the reputation which lifted his fame head and shoulders above all the other villagers.

Thomas at this time had been a widower for approaching fifteen years, and he had not yet accustomed himself to the loneliness which the death of his wife had brought into his life. For despite his drunkenness she had loved him deeply and he had worshipped the ground she trod. There were some among the more sympathetic who would excuse his failing by claiming that it was the loss of Mary, at an age when she could have anticipated another quarter of a century of life, that had increased his indulgence of ale and rough cider when un-Customed brandy and armagnac were not to be come by, and anything else he could lay hands on, maintaining that it was only during the last decade and a half that he had taken no measures to curb his weakness for strong drink. Their toleration did them credit; unfortunately it led them into some error; for there were those who had known John Thomas as a young man who remembered the villagers running into their houses and securing their doors as soon as it was known that the handsome, sturdy smallholder was roaring his way home.

The true facts were that from the first moment he had broached the keg of cognac which he had found washed up on the beach in Whitesand Bay after the wreck of a French merchantman on her way to Dublin, he had formed a passion for hard liquor. Before he was thirty his outbreaks of tipsiness had become part of the canon of local legend, and since then he had done nothing which might have helped the legend to fade.

Before Mary had died she had given him two sons and two daughters, all of whom, in 1783, were married with families of their own. His children having grown up with his excesses, had become accustomed to them, and, having watched their mother patiently drive the devil out, had had no fear of him when he was in his rampageous cups. Sons-in-law and daughters-in-law had come to share wives' and husbands' tolerance, and when he was left alone all of them had encouraged him to make his home with them, for all were aware of the profound, if somewhat strangely based, relationship that had existed between him and their mother, and knew that he would be lonely.

Their invitations had warmed him, but he had declined them.

"You know I can't keep off the drink," he told them, "and you know what I get like then. You've all young children, and it would not be right for them to see the degradation into which a man can fall when he's plagued with the thirst I have."

"What harm did it do us?" they asked.

"You were my flesh and blood, and hers," he said. "Besides, times are changing and, with them, people."

"You're changing, too, by all accounts," they pointed out. "Now, instead of getting drunk every night, you get drunk once a week."

"I told you people were changing," he grinned.

But they could not persuade him. The fact was that his talk of his drinking was an excuse. The real reason for his refusal was that he could not bear to leave the cottage where he and Mary had lived all their married lives, where every article had been found a place and put in it by her, where her spirit still seemed to hover with kindly protection, as in life she had always surrounded him with the guard of her understanding and love.

Once every other year, however, he visited his children and stayed a week, or two or three, as the fancy took him, at Easter and at Christmas. This Christmas it was the turn of his son Frank to have him for the festival.

"Come over on the Sunday before," Frank's wife had told him. "Maybe then you'll get here safely. If you wait for Christmas Eve those well-meaning friends of yours at Sancreed will want to drink with you, and like as not you'll spend the holiday in a stupor and we'll never see you. Besides, there'll be a wreck, I shouldn't wonder, and it would be useful to have an extra hand."

He saw the point of her argument about the drink, but it was her hint of the wreck that decided him.

"I'll come in the morning of Sunday," he answered her. "If I leave Sancreed at mid-morning, I'll be in St Just in time for dinner."

"And don't call at the inn on the way!" she warned him.

"I promise solemnly," he said.

They were right when they had said he had changed, and not only in the frequency of his bouts, but in the effects he exhibited after them. He no longer became pugnacious, wreaking his vengeance on anything or anyone that got in his way. And he seemed to have soaked up so much strong drink in the past that as much as he drank now, though he might sway and reel, he did not lose consciousness of what he was doing or must do. It was only when he reached the cottage, kicked off his boots and dropped into a chair, that he would sink into a sleep from which he might not wake from Saturday night to Monday morning.

From Monday morning to Saturday night he pottered about his garden patch or his little house, passing the time with odd jobs, gathering kindling and chopping logs and being in every sense a good neighbour. This was why it was that he only got drunk on Saturday nights, for, appreciative of the many good turns he did them, the inhabitants of Sancreed were always willing to pay all their indebtedness to him at the inn. Otherwise he could not have afforded to drink enough to get drunk.

They were surprised therefore when he had not appeared in the taproom on the eve of the Sunday before Christmas by the time the evening was nearly spent.

"Do you think the old man's ill?" someone asked.

"He wasn't just before dusk," he was told. "I came by his cottage and he'd lit his lamp and was sawing wood in the kitchen."

"Then why hasn't he come?"

"I seem to have heard someone say that he's spending Christmas with Frank at St Just, and has agreed to go over tomorrow. Maybe he intends to stay sober tonight so as to keep his promise tomorrow."

"Ah, that'll be it," it was agreed.

"Dang it, I owe him a drink," a man sitting on the settle before the fire remarked. "He brought the missus two sacks of logs on Thursday. Well, I suppose it will wait until the New Year."

"If you don't forget," he was chaffed.

Meanwhile in his cottage the old man was waging a struggle with an appalling thirst. But Beth, Frank's wife, was his favourite. There was something in her manner that reminded him of Mary. He intended to keep his promise to her, no matter how much it cost him in suffering. So he tried to tell himself that it was not Saturday night and sat down in his chair and busied himself in putting the finishing touches to the head of a fox he was carving on a briar root, which he intended as a Christmas gift for one of his grandsons.

When he began to nod over his patient work, and he realized that he was ready for bed, he was surprised at the ease with which he had prevented himself from going down to the inn. Next morning he awoke earlier than usual and, wondering why, he presently recognized the craving which denoted his special thirst.

"I'll hang on now till I get to St Just," he told himself, and when he said the words he meant them in all sincerity.

He got out of bed, pulled on his breeches and boots, blew on the black embers on the hearth until they were red again, went to the pail he had drawn the previous afternoon from the well, took a hammer and chipped off lumps of ice into a black pot, which he hung over the flames.

When he had eaten, he pottered about the cottage until the gold time-piece, which he had taken from the body of a Spanish nobleman washed up on the shore of Mount's Bay, opposite Mousehole, more than thirty-five years ago, told him that it was time to set out. So he tied up his bundle of odds and ends he was taking with him for Frank's family, took his stick from the corner, and left the cottage.

It was unfortunate that the road that was to take him to St Just should bring him past the inn. It was more unfortunate still that at the moment of his passing a neighbour who owed him a drink should be entering the inn and caught sight of him.

"Well met!" the man called to him. "Come in and let me get out of your debt."

"That's kindly said," Thomas called back. "But I'm on my way to St Just. I'll see you when I come back."

"I'll have forgotten by then."

"Then I'll remind you," Thomas laughed.

"Come in and have just one," the neighbour urged. "It'll set you up. It'll be a cold walk if you're aiming to go over the dunes."

"No thanks," Thomas insisted. "I promised Beth . . ."

"Oh, come in! Just one drink! That won't harm you."

While they had been talking, the craving which had roused him had returned. It was true what the man said; it would be a cold walk; a drink would set him up. Well, he would have one! But only one!

"Only one then!" he cried to the neighbour. "Then I must be on my way."

But there were other neighbours in the inn, and yet others came in after them. Some called up drinks for him without asking him; some insisted on paying debts; some that he should drink with them for Christmas's sake, since he would not be there.

No one was more surprised than he when he found on next looking at his time-piece that it was three o'clock. He knew that he was drunk, for he read the swaying time only with difficulty. But he was not so drunk as to have forgotten that he must get to St Just.

"I must go," he shouted to the company. "Where are my bundle and stick? I said I'd be there for dinner. Beth will flay me for this. A happy feast to you, neighbours!"

They gave him his bundle and his stick, clapped him on the back and wished him well in return, and went with him to the door to put him on his way. It did not occur to any one of them that he could not now reach St Just before dark.

With the approach of night it had become colder. As he passed out into the fresh air, it rushed at him with a staggering blow. He steadied himself and strode out uncertainly, the frost striking him a fresh blow with every stride he took.

When he had come outside the village, his brain had become so befuddled that he sat down by the side of the track to rest, so that he might get some easement.

"Old fool!" he muttered. "Whatever happens you must get to St Just!"

He awoke to the brittle twinkling of stars, and scrambled to his feet with an oath. He searched the heavens for The Plough and when he found it muttered, "Half-way to midnight! But I must get to St Just!" and he strode off, steadier now, along the track.

But his head burned like a thunder-bolt must burn, and for minutes at a time he was only half-conscious of what he was doing for the pain of it.

When he had been walking about an hour, he suddenly realized that the landmarks about him were strange, and in a sobering moment he knew that he had left the track. He stopped and looked about him, but could see nothing that he recognized.

Turning about, he began to retrace his steps, hoping that they would bring him back to the right track. What he did not know was that there was no path beneath his feet, that he was going off at a tangent and that when he looked up at the Pole star he was already more than a mile too far to the south.

In his anxiety at the thought that he would not now reach St Just by midnight, he began to panic a little. He plunged forward, not knowing where he was going, telling himself again and again that he must get to St Just come what may.

Then suddenly there was no ground at all beneath his feet. He was falling and falling until it never seemed as if he would stop, his cries deafening him with the fright. At last the ground struck him. It shook every bone in his body and he lay while the pain of it receded and his shaken brain cleared.

Gingerly he put out a hand and felt about him. There was solid earth beneath his hands, but what they touched were mostly stones. He knew then that he had fallen into one of the pits that the Romans had dug in their search for tin. It might be any one of half a dozen such pits, but not one of them was within a mile or more of the track over the dunes from Sancreed to St Just.

He put his weight on his hands to pull himself up, but as he tried to gather his legs under him, frightful pains burned their way through every limb, making red and green lights shudder before his eyes and his brain recoil. He sank down again with a groan.

The pain having eased a little, he tried again. This time the effects were more terrible than before, and he lost consciousness. When he came round he told himself that one or both of his legs were broken, and that he would not be able to move till help came.

The non-arrival of his father on Sunday, as he had promised, neither surprised nor worried Frank Thomas or his wife. He was not even perturbed when he had not arrived by bed-time on Monday.

"He'll not have been able to stay away from the inn on Saturday night," Frank remarked to Beth. "He'll be sleeping himself sober."

"I suppose you'll be right," Beth agreed. "But he did promise me solemnly, and this is the first time he has ever broken his promise to me."

"It is Christmas, you know," Frank reminded her. "They will have got him as drunk as a lord."

But when her father-in-law had not arrived by dinner-time on Tuesday, Beth did become anxious, and before the meal was over she had persuaded her husband to take a lantern and go to Sancreed to see what was amiss.

"I feel it in my bones something has happened to him," she insisted.

At his father's cottage, Frank found all in darkness. From the general tidiness of the place, however, he surmised that his father had not been there that day, or had set out for St Just. But if the latter were the case, they must have met.

Puzzled, Frank went down to the inn. There he learned that his father had left at three o'clock on the Sunday afternoon. Certainly he had been drinking, but he knew what he was about; and if he was a bit unsteady in his gait, he knew the direction he must take.

"Then he must have gone off the track," Frank told them, "because there was no sign of him as I came over."

It was too late to do anything that night, but early next morning, as soon as it was light, the men and boys of Sancreed met at the inn, divided themselves into parties and set off in all directions. They returned at dusk, all to report failure. No sign of John Thomas had been found.

A similar search next day having similar results, they concluded that whatever had happened to the old man he must now be dead. All they could do was to wait until some wanderer stumbled on his skeleton.

The following Sunday, James Trethewy, one of John Thomas's neighbours, set out from Sancreed to visit his sister in St Buryon. Like the old man, he decided to cross the dunes.

Not far from the track which he was following there were two or three of the ancient workings, one of which he had to pass by quite close.

As he approached this pit, though was still some distance away, he saw a stranger sitting on the bank which had been thrown up round the edge of the pit on the track side, as a protection for travellers like himself. On his coming nearer, the man stood up and walked round to the other side of the pit, and disappeared behind a bush.

Thinking to warn him of the danger he was running, Trethewy left the track and hurried round the edge of the pit, but when he came to the place where he had last seen the man there was no ne there, and though he went carefully round the edge of the pit, searching behind every bush, and looking in every direction, he could find no one, nor any indication that anyone had been there.

Bewildered, but wishing to be in St Buryon before darkness fell, Trethewy went on. He stayed the night with his sister, and in the middle of Monday morning, set off back to Sancreed, following the way by which he had come.

It was a bright, sunny day, though the sun was low in the heavens, and the rays of it pale and feeble. Still, it was a practical day for practical people. On such a winter day there could be no possibility of seeing strange sights or hearing strange sounds, as could often be heard over the dunes when the skies were black and lowering, and heavy banks of clouds scudded over sea and land.

During his short stay with his sister, Trethewy had forgotten about the man who had been by the pit as he had come over the day before. But as he started to cross the dunes the scene brought the incident back to him, and as he went along whistling quietly to himself, stepping out with the exhilaration of the autumn borrowed day, he pondered upon who the stranger might be and where he had gone. Cornishmen, even today, do not take kindly to those they do not know or cannot identify as having legitimate business among them. In the times of which we are writing, when the smugglers and the wreckers were at the peak of their activities, they disliked even more anyone who might be an excise spy.

"It was obvious that he didn't want to speak to me, or to let me get a close look at him," Trethewy mused. "But what I can't make out is, how did he manage to disappear so completely? I've never heard of there being caves in or nearby the pits. This will keep Tom Blower happy for hour after hour."

Blower was the Sancreed parson's clerk, who, because he could read, write and cipher, believed himself to be, among his illiterate fellow-villagers, the fountain of all knowledge.

And so Trethewy went along, now creasing his forehead with answered questions, now smiling as he heard Blower from the chimney settle in the inn begin, "Well, my ignorant friends, it is like this, as you would know if any two of you had an A and a B between you ..."

He was perhaps half a mile from the pit, when his eye caught something which made him stop in his tracks, and utter an oath.

"By St Michael! That's him again!"

There was no mistaking the man, who, despite the cold of the last days of December, wore no hat, a point about him which Trethewy had unconsciously taken note of the day before.

"What's he doing here? He must be an excise agent. I've heard that some of the Boskenna men have a hide-out hereabouts. If he is an excise man, they must be warned. I'll catch up with him and see what he has to say for himself."

So he began to walk more quickly, but the faster he went so the man walking before him seemed to go. He put his hands about his mouth and called out as loudly as his lungs would give, "Holla, there! Wait for me, and we can walk together."

But if the man heard he did not turn his head or stop, but hurried on.

Angry at the man's refusal, and more suspicious now than ever, and determined to come up with the man and have a look at him, Trethewy broke into a run. But though the man did not appear to be running himself, he came no nearer.

As the bank edging the pit came in sight, the man left the track and began to move round the top of the pit, exactly as he had done yesterday.

Trethewy swore aloud.

"He must have a hide-out there somewhere, and he's making for it," he said aloud between pants, for he was not so young as he had been. "I'll watch carefully where he goes."

So he slowed up to a walk, and moved from the track himself, keeping his eyes always on the man, who was now nearing the bush behind which he had seemed to disappear on that first occasion. But this time, when he reached the bush, he did not go behind it, but stood on the edge of the pit looking down, his back still turned to his pursuer.

Now at last Trethewy was coming up with him.

"Hi," he called. "Stand back from the edge. It's dangerous, man. If it breaks away, you'll be done for."

Still the man ignored him.

Trethewy had come within a dozen yards of him, and again he called out a warning.

Now the man turned, and Trethewy stopped dead in his tracks. He knew the man after all. But this was not as he was now, but as he had been thirty or more years ago.

"John Thomas!" he gasped. "You!"

While these words were being forced from his throat, the figure raised its right arm and pointed with its finger over the edge of the pit.

"What is it then, lad?" Trethewy asked, and found himself approaching against his will. He was near enough to touch the figure now. "What is it?" he asked again.

Gesturing with what seemed to be impatience, the figure looked him full in the face, its eyes shining, its brow creased with an expression of anger; and even as Trethewy peered back at it, slowly it began to dissolve and disappear, until only the hand with the finger pointing downwards remained, disembodied. Then it, too, vanished.

If Trethewy lacked the learning of Tom Blower, he was not entirely devoid of commonsense. Throwing himself down at full length, he worked his way carefully towards the crumbling edge of the pit, but when he could see the bottom there was nothing but stones and clumps of coarse grass.

He was never able afterwards to explain why he called out, "Hallo, is there anyone down there?"

And then he received another shock, for faintly there came up to him a cry, "Help! It's me, John Thomas of Sancreed. Help!"

Trethewy pushed himself a little farther out, and now he could see, right up under the wall of the pit's side, the figure of a man lying, and what was more he recognized him as his neighbour, John Thomas, not as he was thirty years ago, but as he had last seen him in Sancreed inn nine days back.

"It's me, James Trethewy," he called down. "I'm going to fetch help. We'll be back in no time."

He scrambled to his feet and despite his paunch, he ran all the two miles to Sancreed. He had some difficulty in persuading his neighbours that he had spoken to John Thomas, but they could not deny that he had seen him at the bottom of the pit.

"We can't leave his corpse there," they said, "otherwise the old man will haunt us for the rest of our lives."

So they fetched ropes, and marched out to the pit. There they lowered two men with ropes, and when they heard the voices of the men excitedly calling up to them, "He's alive! James was right! He's alive!" no one could have been more surprised.

William Moore of Redruth gave the first account of this strange event in a letter to the *Arminian Magazine*, which was published within a month of its taking place, on 22 January, 1784. Mr Moore had taken the trouble to travel to Sancreed to interview Thomas and his friends before he wrote his description. He concluded his letter:

"As Thomas had been there in the pit more than eight days, he was very low when he was got out; but is now in a fair way to do well, his legs mending amazingly for so old a gentleman. In the bottom of the pit, near to where he fell, he found a small current of water; which he drank freely of. This, in all likelihood, was the means of keeping him alive."

There were few in Sancreed, however, who would credit this. "He has pickled himself over the years," they said. "That s what kept him alive."

Radiant Boys

Radiant Boys are a particular kind of ghost. They are the spirits of children murdered by their mothers, and their usual function is to warn those to whom they appear that a violent end threatens to overtake them.

Though far more numerous in German spirit-lore—where they are described as *Kindermorderinn*—English spirit-lore does contain a number of outstanding examples. It has been suggested that their presence in England has its origin in the Scandinavian and North-European settlers who came here in the ninth and tenth centuries, bringing their folk-lore with them.

This explanation can certainly be acceptable for one of the most famous of all English Radiant Boys, the one which, until the early years of the last century, haunted Corby Castle, which stands above the densely wooded banks of the River Eden, in Cumberland.

The Howard family have for many years been the owners of Corby. Nowadays the castle has the appearance of being the typical eighteenth-century country mansion that it chiefly is; but the site on which it stands has been the site of numerous ancient buildings, whose remains have been incorporated in successive ones. The first of these ancient buildings was a tower built by the Romans as part of their defensive system against marauding Picts and Scots. This tower was extended in Norman times into a castle, but when the Norman extensions fell into decay it remained and, with its massive walls, from eight to ten feet thick, and its spiral stone staircase, still forms part of the present so-called castle.

The room frequented by the Radiant Boy of Corby was in the older part of the castle adjoining the Roman tower. Its windows looked out on the inner courtyard. It was, therefore, neither remote nor solitary, but surrounded on all sides by rooms which were in constant use.

Reached by a passage cut through an eight-foot-thick wall, it measured twenty-one feet by eighteen. At the beginning of the nineteenth century it was used as a bedroom, but later as a study. When it took over the latter function, the current owner removed the bed and replaced some of the more ancient heavy dark furniture with modern pieces. Apart from this, however, the room remained as it had been for many years.

One wall of the room was hung with tapestry, the others with old family pictures and some pieces of embroidery thought to have been worked by nuns. Over a press, which had doors of Venetian glass, was a wooden carving of an ancient figure, with a battle-axe in his hand. This figure had been one of a number which the burgesses of Carlisle had placed on the walls of their city to give the impression to would-be invaders that the border-town was well guarded.

The owner had hoped that by taking away the bed and replacing some of the furniture he would remove "a certain air of gloom which I thought might have given rise to the unaccountable reports of apparitions and extraordinary noises which were constantly reaching us. But I regret that I did not succeed in banishing the nocturnal visitor."

The last authenticated appearance of the Radiant Boy was early in September, 1803. In this case, however, the Boy seems to have been behaving wilfully, for no calamity overtook the man who saw him. In fact, twenty years later, this man was still dining out on the strength of his experience.

A house-party had been invited to the castle, and among the guests were the Rector of Greystoke, near Penrith, and his wife. It was a large party and all the bedrooms of the castle had to be used. In her allocation of the rooms, Mrs Howard assigned that overlooking the courtyard to the parson and his wife. She did so without any deliberate intention, for her mind was completely void of any thoughts of the Boy.

On the morning after their arrival, the guests were at breakfast with their hosts in the dining-room when suddenly their attention was attracted by a commotion in the drive outside. A chaise-and-four was dashing up to the door at such speed that the driver seemed to have difficulty in controlling the horses, for the carriage knocked down part of the fence protecting the flower-beds from the drive.

"Who on earth can it be arriving at this early hour?" Mr Howard remarked. "It would seem from the coachman's emulation of Jehu that he is the bearer of important tidings. Not ill, I hope," he concluded, smiling at his guests.

As he looked round the table, he noticed that the Rector of Greystoke had become very agitated. For a moment the parson could not speak, but as the chaise drew up on the gravel outside the windows he managed to stammer out: "I cannot expect you to forgive me, sir, but it is my chaise. I sent for it as soon as it was light. I fear we must leave at once. Come, my dear."

"But, Rector!" Mr Howard exclaimed. "Have you had bad news? Is there anything one might do to help you?"

"Nothing, sir," replied the Rector. "Except that you will not try to detain us."

"But something must be wrong, Mr A ..." Mrs Howard said. "Have we offended you in any way? If so, we are extremely sorry and will do all we can to make amends."

"No, no," the Rector told her with increasing embarrassment, since all the guests were looking at him and his wife in silent bewilderment. "No, madam, you have been more than kind."

"Then why must you go?" asked Howard. "We were looking forward to your company for some days. Besides Colonel and Mrs S ... are dining this evening especially to meet you. Pray, change your mind, there's a good fellow, and send the chaise away."

"I am truly sorry, sir," the Rector replied. "We realize that we are risking your friendship and kindness in responding to your hospitality in this way, but I implore you not to press us further, but to let us go."

"How can we do that unless you tell us what is wrong, for something so clearly is?" Howard persisted.

The Rector had already risen to his feet, and his wife, silent and weeping, followed his example.

"Forgive us," the Rector said, his voice catching a little, and left the table.

Mrs Howard, moved by Mrs A ...'s obvious distress, followed and tried to comfort her. "If only you would tell us," she said.

Mrs A . . looked at her husband, but he shook his head. "Later, perhaps," he said, "but not now."

The Corby servants and the Rector's groom had already loaded the visitors' bags into the chaise, and holding out his hand to Mr

Howard, Mr A... attempted one last regret, but articulation failed him, and he turned abruptly, with a bow to Mrs Howard, and hurried to the carriage, where he helped his wife to mount. A moment later the chaise was hurtling down the drive.

Mr and Mrs Howard, perplexed and a little hurt, returned to their guests, whom they found discussing the strange occurrence among themselves.

As Howard sat down, one of the men asked, "Did he say anything to you out there?"

Howard shook his head. "Not a word," he said. "The Rector tried to assure us that nothing we had done was the cause of their sudden departure. But I am not so sure."

As he confided later to his diary, "They departed, leaving us in consternation to conjecture what could possibly have occasioned so sudden an alteration in their arrangements. I really felt quite uneasy lest anything should have given them offence; and we reviewed all the occurrences of the preceding evening in order to discover, if offence there was, whence it had arisen. But all our pains were vain; and after talking a great deal about it for some days, other circumstances banished the matter from our minds."

The "other circumstances" to which he referred was the entertainment of his guests, and when all had finally departed he discovered that he was still exercised in his mind by the Rector's hasty departure. For a day or two he tried to dismiss it from his thoughts, but eventually had to confess that he would know no peace of mind until he had learned the truth. So he decided that he must visit Greystoke and try to persuade the A...'s to be frank with him.

At Greystoke he was surprised and his bewilderment greatly increased by the warmth of the A...s reception.

"You will surmise why I have come," he said, as Mrs A... led the way to the drawing-room.

"Of course," the Rector told him. "Perhaps now we can set your mind at rest by proving that it was no default of your kind self which caused us to leave the castle so precipitously. I am sorry that we left as we did, but we had both been so much shaken by the experience—an experience which, I may say, both my reason and my profession ought to have rejected out of hand . . ."

As he heard these words, Howard understood at last what had happened.

"You saw the Radiant Boy!" he exclaimed, and was at a loss to imagine why this explanation had not occurred to him before, except that he had not known which room the A . . .'s had been allotted.

"You mean you know that the castle is haunted by what you have so exactly described as a Radiant Boy, sir?" the Rector exclaimed.

"There is some sort of tradition at Corby that such an apparition does from time to time manifest itself," Howard confessed, "but we—the family, that is—have always been somewhat sceptical about it, as it has never appeared to any Howard, but only to guests visiting the castle. He has not appeared for many years now, and I fear he did not cross my mind as a possible reason for your curtailing your visit so abruptly. I am sure, too, that Mrs Howard is equally innocent."

"My dear sir!" the Rector expostulated. "I do assure you that neither Mrs A . . . nor I have ever entertained the thought that you deliberately set out to frighten us."

"Could you bear to tell me now what happened?" Howard asked.

"I am happy to say that we have long since recovered from the shock we had," replied the Rector. "But I hesitate to relate what occurred because as a man of intelligence and education, and more particularly as a priest, I feel I ought to reject the whole matter as a figment of the imagination."

"I feel much the same as you do," Howard told him. "On the other hand, I find it very difficult to dismiss as chimera the serious pro-testations of sensible men, and I do assure you that in the records of the Radiant Boy's manifestations, among the men and women who have declared they have seen him, are those whose level-headedness as well as their intellectual talents are beyond reproach or dispute. I will give you my solemn word that if you will tell me what you saw, I will breathe not a word of it to any living soul. My interest is purely in relating your account to previous ones."

The Rector, perceiving that it would be boorish of him not to comply with his visitor's request, agreed to accept Howard's assurances.

"Very well, sir," he said. "On those terms I will tell you. Soon after we went to bed, we fell asleep. It might be one or two in the morning when I awoke. I observed that the fire was totally extin-guished; but although that was the case, and we had no light, I saw a glimmer in the middle of the room, which suddenly increased to a bright flame.

"I looked out, apprehending that something had caught fire; when to my amazement I beheld a beautiful boy clothed in white, with bright locks resembling gold, standing by my bedside. He remained in this position some minutes, fixing his eyes upon me with a mild and benevolent expression.

"He then glided gently towards the side of the chimney, where it is obvious there is no possible egress, and entirely disappeared. I found myself again in total darkness, and all remained quiet until the usual hour of rising.

"As soon as he had disappeared, I seemed to come suddenly to my senses. The vision was so real that at the time I could have reached out and touched him. It was the realization that it was no dream, that I had actually seen the Boy, as you call him, when I was in a state of complete awareness, which made my heart fail. I began to tremble and was so violent in my trembling that my wife awoke, and inquired what was wrong with me."

"I believed he had been struck with an ague," Mrs A . . . interpolated. "He was shaking uncontrollably. When he assured me that he was not ill, I became alarmed and pressed him to explain what had caused his trembling. For some minutes he refused."

"But I could not keep it to myself," the Rector went on. "I had to tell my wife, though I knew it would disturb her. Like me, she slept no more that night. I was in such a state that I could not risk a second experience by staying another night in the room, But we knew that all your other rooms must be occupied, so as soon as dawn broke I went down and dispatched one of your servants to summon my chaise.

"I had imagined that my groom could not possibly reach Corby until well after breakfast. His sudden and spectacular arrival while we were still at table frustrated our intention of slipping away quietly without disturbing you or your guests. I apologize sincerely for the embarrassment we caused you by leaving as we did, and for our refusal to give the reason. But as I have said, I was sure we should become laughing-stocks if I attempted an explanation. I fear I preferred to be thought impolite than to be the butt of jokes."

"I understand perfectly," Howard assured him. "Thank you for being so forthcoming now. You must pay us another visit at Corby and we will see that you do not occupy the Boy's room again."

Howard kept his word, and put the Rector's experience on record only in his personal journal. Whether the parson eventually decided that perhaps after all he had been too sensitive to the possible reactions of his neighbours, or his wife proved garrulous, not long after his revelations to Mr Howard he is found recounting his experiences in all kinds of company. As we have said, as late as 1824 he was still dining out on the story.

As for the Boy, throughout the next half-century he is recorded as having appeared to a variety of people, some of whom died in violent circumstances, but many of whom, like the Rector of Greystoke, found his manifestation a benevolent experience. Since the middle of the last century the Corby Boy seems to have deserted the castle altogether.

The origin of the Boy is explained neither in record nor in tradition. The same applies to the Radiant Boy who appeared to Lord Castlereagh many years before he cut his throat at North Cray Place, in 1822.

At the time, Castlereagh was still Captain Robert Stewart, second son of the Marquis of Londonderry, and was quartered in Ireland. He was fond of sport, and one day while out shooting he went so far into unfamiliar country that he lost his way. The weather, by the time he realized he was lost, had deteriorated, and this prompted him to seek shelter at a country house.

He sent in his card, with a request for shelter for the night, and Irish hospitality being what it is the master of the house received him warmly, though he pointed out that he already had many guests, and could not make Captain Stewart so comfortable as he would have wished. However, to such accommodation as he could give the Captain was heartily welcome.

"You are very kind, sir," Castlereagh assured him. "I shall be more than grateful for shelter, warmth and somewhere where I may stretch out."

"I am sure there must be a bed," his host replied, and rang for his butler, to whom he gave instructions to do his best for Captain Stewart.

As his host had said, the house was crammed, but the guests, some of whom were casual refugees from the weather like himself, made a good party. Over dinner, when his host asked him if he had to return to his regiment the next day, and learned that he had still three days of his leave left, he agreed with alacrity to accept the invitation to stay as long as he could, for he was promised some good shooting.

After an agreeable evening, the party at last went to bed, and the butler showed Stewart to his room. It was a large room, empty of furniture except for a couple of chairs and a press. In the wide grate, however, a magnificent peat fire was burning, and before it a mattress and a heterogeneous collection of cloaks and other covers had been made up. Rough though it was, to the weary Captain Stewart it was as inviting as the most comfortable of beds.

It seemed to him that the fire was blazing up the chimney in a rather alarming manner, so he removed some of the peat, and then stretched out on the mattress and was quickly asleep. He had slept about two hours, when he awoke suddenly and was startled by such a vivid light in the room that, like the Rector of Greystoke at Corby, he thought at first it must be the fire. But when he turned and looked at the grate he saw that the fire was quite dead.

As the light gradually grew brighter, he sat up, hoping to discover where it was coming from; and as he watched he saw that by degrees it was forming itself into a human form, which presently revealed itself as a very beautiful naked boy, surrounded by a cloud of light of the most dazzling radiance. The Boy gazed at him intently, and as the Captain gazed back, slowly the apparition began to fade until eventually it quite disappeared.

Stewart's first reaction was that his host and the other guests were amusing themselves at his expense, and were trying to frighten him. Naturally, he felt very indignant, and when he went down to breakfast next morning he showed by his demeanour that he was still displeased.

His host was puzzled by this change in his guest, who, the previous evening, had been the most genial member of the party; but when Stewart told him that he was leaving as soon as he had eaten, he realized that something was wrong.

"But, Captain Stewart!" he exclaimed. "You promised that you would join the party for two or three days!"

"I have changed my mind, sir," Stewart replied, and so coldly that his host took him on one side and pressed him to tell him what had offended him.

All Stewart would say, however, was that he had been the victim of a practical joke, and that in his view this was quite unwarrantable treatment of one who was not only a guest, but also a stranger.

"By God, sir, you are right!" exclaimed his host. "Some of these young devils are quite thoughtless, and I apologize. If I make them present their apologies also, will you overlook the incident and continue to give us the pleasure of your company? I beg you to be so far generous. The shooting, I assure you, has never been excelled."

Stewart's fondness for sport persuaded him to be magnanimous. But when they returned to the breakfast room, and the host sternly demanded that those who had been responsible for the practical joke played on their distinguished fellow-guest during the night should apologize immediately, all the young men roundly protested their innocence.

Suddenly a thought struck the host, and clapping a hand to his forehead with a muttered imprecation he summoned the butler.

"Hamilton," he said to the servant, "where did Captain Stewart sleep last night?"

"Well, sir," the butler said, "you know the house was full. Some of the gentlemen were lying on the floor, three or four to a room. So I gave him the Boy's room. But," he went on hurriedly, "I lit a blazing fire, to keep him from coming out."

"But you know," his master told him angrily, "I have forbidden you to put anyone in the Boy's room. Why do you think I had all the furniture removed? If you do this again, Hamilton, we shall part company. Be good enough to come to my study, sir," he said to Stewart.

There he said, "Sir, I must offer you ten thousand apologies. You should not have been put in that room!"

"What's this about 'the Boy'?" Stewart asked.

"Forgive me, Captain, I would rather not go into particulars. Let us say that you saw the family ghost."

Stewart burst out laughing. "Come, sir, this really will not do," he said. "He was the prettiest ghost I am sure anyone ever saw."

"So others have deposed, sir," said his host. "When he took to haunting us, the family must have been on better days, for I am told that his golden suit . . ."

"Last night he was completely naked," Stewart interrupted him.

"Naked? That I have never heard before."

"Who is he?"

"He was the son of an ancestor, sir," his host explained. "Unhappily, his mother lost her reason, and in one of her most violent moods strangled the Boy, who was her youngest and favourite child, while he was asleep in the room where you passed the night. He was only nine or ten years old."

"And now he haunts the room. Does he trouble you?" Stewart asked, interested.

"He troubles us only if someone sees him," his host replied.

"Why only then?"

Once more his host seemed reluctant to answer him, and only when Stewart said that he would be offended if he would not satisfy his curiosity did the man acquiesce.

"Please remember that you have insisted. The tradition is that the Boy portends good and bad news. Whoever the Boy shows himself to experiences a period of the greatest prosperity. He will rise to the summit of power, but at the very climax of his rise he will meet a violent death."

This reply seemed to sober Stewart. He was silent for some minutes, then he smiled, and said, "Well, sir, we've all to die sooner or later, and it does not seem to me to matter how death comes. If my period of prosperity makes life pleasant for me, then the end should be worth it. For you must know, sir, that I am only my father's second son, and my prospects are no better than any second son's. Indeed, at the moment it would appear that I shall spend the rest of my active career as a soldier. I am no great shakes at soldiering. A colonelcy is the most I can hope for."

Within a few years of the Boy's appearance, however, Captain Stewart's fortunes suddenly and spectacularly changed. His elder brother, the heir to the Marquisate of Londonderry, was drowned in a boating accident, and Stewart succeeded him, taking the courtesy title of Viscount Castlereagh.

The change in status brought a change in responsibilities, too, and soon the new Lord Castlereagh found himself occupying a prominent position in Irish affairs. The part he played in the political manoeuvres which resulted in 1800 in the Act of Union between England and Ireland was merely the opening of a brilliant career.

He now discovered that he possessed abilities of which he had been previously ignorant. These led him onward until he won a commanding position in successive English administrations. In 1805 he was appointed Secretary of War, and again in 1807; while from 1812 onwards, as Foreign Secretary, he conducted the country's foreign policy during one of the most important periods of its history.

Unfortunately, he developed into a man of cold, even actively antagonistic, manner, which caused him to be not merely unpopular, but cordially hated, even by the members of his own party. Yet he was not merely a strong man, such as the times demanded, but also successful in most of his schemes as a Minister for the welfare of the nation.

In 1821, on the death of his father, he became Marquess of Londonderry, though he remains best known as Castlereagh. There are two accounts as to the cause of his death. One states that towards the end of his life he suffered greatly from gout, and the continued anxieties of a long and trying public career began noticeably to tell upon him. His manner grew strange, and, on the suggestion of the Duke of Wellington, he sought medical advice, which did nothing to relieve his condition.

It was then seen that he appeared to be in imminent danger of losing his reason, and so serious did his condition become that he had to be confined to his country house, North Cray Place. As a precautionary measure, his razors were removed. This proved unavailing, however, and on 12 August, 1822, he cut his throat with a pen-knife.

The other version is less kind. It is purported by some social historians that he was a homosexual, and that he committed suicide as the result of blackmail. If this is true, the fact that the Radiant Boy appeared to him, alone of all its victims, naked adds a footnote which the psychiatrists will no doubt find interesting.

The third most famous manifestation of a Radiant Boy is recounted in connexion with Thomas, second Baron Lyttleton, known even during his life-time as The Bad Lord Lyttleton, on account of his dissipation, which he made no attempt to conceal. His affairs and his gambling were a scandal of the times, and the times—the latter half of the eighteenth century—were scandalous enough.

After an extremely colourful period on the continent—where his family had more or less banished him in an attempt to protect the good name of the Lyttletons—he returned to England and married a wealthy widow, named Apphia Peach, who possessed a fortune of £20,000. He refused to let her see her solicitor so that her money might be "tied up" in her favour, and under the laws of the times the £20,000 became legally his the moment he put the ring on Mrs Peach's finger. Within three months he had got through it all, and had so outraged his wife that she died shortly after.

The final curtain came down on this dissolute man in November, 1779. He had staying with him at his London home, Hill House, a Mrs Amphlett and her three young daughters, Elizabeth, who was nineteen, Christina, seventeen, and Margaret, fifteen.

Mrs Amphlett was more likely than not unhappy at the close proximity of her three pretty girls to the Wicked Lord. At all events, she cast such a wet blanket over the party that while she was lying down in her room, Lyttleton summoned his carriage, bundled in the three girls and hurried them down to his country house, Pit Place, not far from Epsom.

Just before midnight Lyttleton retired to bed. What happened next has been recounted by a friend, who was also staying in the house.

"He had been asleep only a short time," this account states, "when he was awakened, by his own account, by a noise like the fluttering of a bird, outside the bed-curtains. He drew them back, and saw a figure dressed in white.

"Shocked, he demanded 'What do you want?' To which the apparition replied, 'Prepare to die. I am here to warn you that you have very little time left.' 'How long?' his lordship demanded in return. 'Weeks, months, perhaps a year?' 'You will die within three days,' the figure replied.

"His lordship was much alarmed, and called to a servant in a closet adjoining, who found him much agitated and in a profuse perspiration. The circumstance had a considerable effect all the next day upon his lordship's spirits. On the third day, which was a Saturday, his lordship was at breakfast with his guests, and was observed to have grown very thoughtful, but attempted to carry it off by the transparent ruse of accusing the others at table of unusual gravity. 'Why do you look so grave?' he asked. 'Are you thinking of the ghost? I am as well as ever I was in my life.'

"Later on he remarked, 'If I live over tonight, I shall have jockeyed the ghost, for this is the third day'.

"Early in the afternoon, his lordship experienced one of the suffocating fits which had troubled him during the preceding month. After a short interval he recovered, dined at five o'clock, and went to bed at eleven. When his servant was about to give him a dose of rhubarb and mint-water, his lordship, perceiving him stirring it with a tooth-pick, called him a slovenly dog, and bade him go and fetch a teaspoon.

"On the man's return, he found his master in a fit, and, the pillow being placed high, his chin bore hard upon his neck; when the servant, instead of relieving his lordship on the instant from his perilous situation, ran, in his fright, and called out for help; but on his return he found his lordship dead."

So, he did not "jockey the ghost", as he expressed it and as he might reasonably have hoped to do, for he was only thirty-five.

Another strange incident is told in connexion with his death. It would seem that Lord Lyttleton had proposed visiting an intimate friend, Miles Peter Andrews, who lived at Dartford, on the day of his death. His spirits were so low, however, that he did not feel equal to the occasion; he also failed to send an explanation for his absence.

During the evening Andrews was taken ill and retired to bed early. He had not yet fallen asleep when the curtains of his bed were suddenly drawn back, and he saw Lord Lyttleton standing there, wearing the distinctive dressing-gown which he kept at his friend's house.

The surprised Andrews believed that Lyttleton had made a belated arrival, and probably intended some practical joke. So he called out to the figure, "You are up to some of your tricks. Go to bed, or I'll throw something at you". But the figure merely gazed at him seriously, and said, "It's all over with me, Andrews".

Andrews, who still believed that it was his friend who stood before him, reached down, picked up a slipper and threw it; whereupon the figure moved silently into the dressing-room. Having been a previous victim of Lyttleton's practical joking, Andrews got from his bed and followed the figure into the dressing-room. But when he tried both the door of the dressing-room and the door of his own bedroom, he found that both were bolted.

Mystified, but still suspecting nothing but a trick, he rang for the servants, and asked them where Lord Lyttleton was. They replied that so far as they knew, he was not in the house.

"Well," said Andrews, "if he does come, tell him that all the beds are occupied, and that he must seek a room in one of the inns at Dartford."

It was not until late on the following day that Andrews heard of his friend's death. He fell into a deep faint, and "was not his own man again for three years".

Alarm at Wellington Barracks

George Jones was nineteen, a private in the Coldstream Guards. Like any other soldier in His Majesty's Army, even at the best of times he did not find sentry-go at the Recruit House, as Wellington Barracks was known in 1804, one of the more attractive of the military duties he was called upon to perform. But there was no getting out of it. Every man in the regiment had to take a turn at it some time or other, though to some, among them George, it seemed to come round more often than it did to others more fortunate.

The trouble with George was that he missed the Welsh valley which he had deserted at the same time that he had deserted Geronwy Williams, who would so firmly claim that the brief, and to him disappointing, incident that had happened "up the mountain" had yet been long enough, so she insisted, to make a father of him. If Geronwy had been less like her mother he would have "done right by her" while hoping for the best; but he saw the force of his own mother's remark when he had confided in her that Gwyneth Williams for mother-in-law would make life hell for any man, while the combination of Geronwy as wife would undoubtedly be the death of him.

"If you wanted to go up the mountain," his mother had gone on, "why didn't you take a nice sensible girl like Gladys Evans the Butcher? She would have played fair by you, because she isn't like Geronwy who knows that her chances of getting a husband while her mother continues in the land of the living are very slim. If anything had happened with Gladys you could have married her and had a good wife. Sometimes, George bach, I wonder why the good Lord has given me such innocents for children. This valley is no Garden of Eden, I tell you, even if all you young fellows imagine yourselves to be Adam. There are more serpents here than in a hundred Edens, and they don't walk on their bellies, but upright on their feet—and they're all female."

"Geronwy says she'll let the whole valley know I took her up the mountain against her will—dragged her up by the hair, she said —if I don't marry her. But you're right, mam, her mam would be the death of me. What shall I do?"

"If it was any other girl, I'd say defy her, stay and brazen it out," his mother told him. "But that won't work with Geronwy Williams in league with her mother. They'll have you in the church before you can say coal-mine. There's only one thing you can do, George— leave the valley while the going is good; and that means before first-light tomorrow.'

"Leave the valley, mam!" The very idea made him go cold all over. "But, mam, where shall I go?"

"Go to London, like David Rees and Alun Griffiths, and apply for fat George s pence," Mrs Jones advised briskly. "They've joined the Coldstream Guards, so you'd have friends there. It's a pity the Welch aren't in London, but you can't have everything. Once you're in the King's uniform, she can't touch you. But if you stay here, I'll guarantee she's Mrs George Jones within three months."

"I suppose you're right, mam," her son agreed. "Oh God! What's me dad going to say?"

"You leave him to me!" his mother promised. "Say nothing."

It all happened so suddenly that almost before he knew where he was he was in London and asking the way to the Recruit House, and before he could say *coal-mine*, he was donning the King's uniform, and pocketing the King's pence.

That had all taken place some eight months ago. He had settled down reasonably well, and was in the process of being transformed into a fair specimen of a fighting-man. He was happiest when taking orders—which was mostly all that was required of him— and both he and his NCOs appreciated the fact that he was unlikely for reasons of intellectual quality to rise above the rank of private.

To begin with he had found London a bewildering place. There were so many people, and the press of carriages in all the main thoroughfares made a clatter which would have sent the people of the valley mad. He was also disappointed when he found there were no mountains one might go up, until David and Alun showed him that mountains were not necessary. But even so, there were times when he longed for the peace and quiet of the valley, a longing accentuated by a letter he received from his mother three or four months after his arrival at the Recruit House, telling him in effect that his flight had been unnecessary, since time had proved that Geronwy Williams had suffered no effect, either good or ill, from going up the mountain with him.

He was thinking about the valley now, and musing on the immoral designings of females, as he stood at ease in his box at half-past one in the morning of 3 January, 1804. All was quiet, and the quietness was made more acute by the thick carpet of snow which blanketed the streets and dwellings of London.

It was piled in long low ridges along the edges of the parade ground, the result of hours of shovelling by his fellow privates. He supposed that there was some advantage in being on guard at times like this, since while his companions had laboured, he had been snugly asleep in his bunk; though it would have been good to have a shovel in one's hands again.

Peering surreptitiously round the edge of his box to make certain that no snooping NCO or orderly officer was making his rounds, George cradled his rifle in the crotch of his left arm and banged his gloved hands together. It was a cold night, though not so cold as he had known it in the valley.

As he tried to increase the feeling in his numbed fingers, he stared across the square at the trees in the park. Under the silver light of the lately risen moon they looked like sugar-coated pyramids. "Pretty, they are," he muttered half-aloud. "Mam would like to see them."

The sound of heels being clicked dully two hundred yards on his left brought him to his duty. Shouldering his rifle, he stepped smartly out of his hut, jerked himself round so that he faced his left, and counting to himself, with right arm swinging in the approved fashion, he set off at measured pace to meet the figure he could plainly see approaching him with the same gait.

It was David Rees, who, as he drew nearer, called softly to George, "Hellish quiet, ain't it, bach?"

"As quiet as the valley," George agreed. "The trees in the park are pretty."

The two soldiers came together face to face, halted with muffled thuds of their feet, and slowly began to turn about.

"Saw your Polly tonight," David said between closed teeth, as he performed his motions. "She asked where you were. Said you'd missed a treat tonight. Where were you?"

"Cleaning the colonel's copper scuttles, worse luck!" George explained. "That was the greatest mistake I made."

"What was?"

"Tell you next time," George said over his shoulder, for they were now standing back to back. "Was Polly peevish I wasn't there?"

"You're right. She said tell you to be there tomorrow or she'll look around. You're seldom there, she said, when the time's most right."

Though they spoke no word aloud, both men stepped smartly off, making back to their boxes with unhurried tread.

"I'll be there!" George told himself. Somehow he would have to arrange it that the colonel's lady called for someone else to clean her scuttles the next time she thought it necessary.

The short walk had done a little towards restoring his circulation, and he settled back into his box, the valley forgotten, what he had missed put out of his mind by the anticipatory warmth of his meeting with Polly tomorrow. The pleasure he was experiencing, however, was not so all-embracing as to prevent him from ruminating on the dictatorial propensities of womankind. For in her way, Poll was little different from Geronwy Williams, or Gladys Evans, or Blodwen Richards, when it came to the point. Nevertheless, of the half-dozen or so girls whom he had known in the way that he had known Polly, she was the one with whom he felt most safe; safe enough to marry, later on perhaps—if he could get out of cleaning copper scuttles at unpropitious moments.

Once more the quietness all around made itself known to him. Once more he looked across at the trees in St James's Park, and remarked to himself how pretty they were. Odd though it might seem, he found himself sighing with contentment.

Suddenly, however, his peace with the world was shattered, the pretty trees in the park sent scurrying from his thoughts, and all his limbs were seized with a cramping coldness that had nothing to do with the snow or the frost. Had some emergency arisen now, he could not have dealt with it, for he was clamped to the spot, unable to move even those muscles which would have allowed him to cry for help, while his eyes were rooted to a spot on the ground before him from which the cause of his terror slowly rose.

From the hard and gravelled surface of the parade-ground, at a spot where no manhole cover was, not four feet away from him, with slightly swaying motion, ascended a figure of a woman. In the moonlight George could clearly discern the pattern of her gown; it was of cream satin with broad red stripes, and between the stripes were vertical rows of red spots. When she had emerged to the height of her waist, a curiously phosphorescent mist gradually began to form about her, and as more of her appeared, until at last the hem of her gown swept the ground, so it enveloped her, and yet did not envelop her, but swirled about her in a kind of eddying frame.

Her very appearance, as George was later to confess, would have been enough to throw him off balance; but there was one specific feature of her that was the real cause of his terror.

She had no head!

The stump of her neck, jagged and torn and raw, rose up out of a lace ruffled collar. It swayed a little towards him two or three times, as if, had there been a head, its owner were addressing herself to him.

Completely paralysed though he was, George knew that he ought to challenge the apparition, but when he tried to speak he could force no sound from tongue or lips.

For fully two minutes, he afterwards deposed, the apparition stood there facing him. Then slowly it turned about and began to walk with slow stately stride across the parade-ground towards the park. When it was some fifty yards from him, it disappeared from his sight.

Only when it had gone did George regain the power of movement. So well had his drill sergeants done their work, however, that without any outward panic he stepped out of the box, and marched to the half-way point between his box and that of David Rees. There he paused.

"David! David!" he called quietly. "Come here, quick!"

"Don't be a damn fool!" he heard David call back. "Do you want us both in the guard-house?"

"David, please come here!" George called again. "I'm not fooling. I've seen something."

"I'll knock the daylight out of you," David replied, "if you are fooling." But he had detected an unwonted urgency in George's voice, and swung out of the box and marched smartly to him.

When George had told him what had happened, David replied that it must have been a trick of the moonlight on the snow.

"It wasn't, I tell you!" George insisted. "It was a woman, and she had no head. She stood there for fully two minutes, before she turned and walked off across the square. If it had been a trick of the moonlight it wouldn't have lasted so long. What do you think I ought to do?"

"You'll have to tell the orderly officer and the sergeant of the guard who are just coming up behind you,"his friend told him.

"What do you think you two men are doing?" the sergeant asked sharply when he came up. "Don't you realize that you both risk a charge for leaving your post while on guard duty?"

"Jones says he's just seen a ghost, sir."

"That's likely!"snapped the disbelieving sergeant.

"Well," said George. "It can't have been a living person, because it had no head."

"There are no ghosts in the Recruit House,"affirmed the sergeant. "I'll deal with you when you're relieved. Come to me in the guardhouse as soon as you've handed in your weapon."

"Sergeant!"George replied smartly.

"Get back to your posts, both of you."

As the sergeant and orderly officer walked away, the sergeant quite forgetting that the Ensign's name was ap Rice, said, "Bloody Welsh! They're as bad as the Scots when it comes to seeing things."

"I would suggest that you might be mistaken,"replied the recently-joined young Ensign diffidently.

"I beg pardon, sir," the sergeant apologized. "But your countrymen are . . ."

"Shall we say more sensitive than you very practical Englishmen? the Ensign suggested.

"By all means, sir,"agreed the sergeant, silently telling himself that this young gentleman would go far. "Perhaps you would care to question Jones when he comes off duty."

"No, sergeant. I'll leave that to you. But perhaps I might be present."

When half an hour later, in response to the sergeant's invitation to give a full account of what he thought he had seen, George did so exactly, and refused to be persuaded that the whole incident could be rationally explained. His stubbornness puzzled the sergeant. If the Ensign had not been present, he would undoubtedly have put George on extra duties, but since he was anxious to show Mr ap Rice that Englishmen are not the irrational beings he and his countrymen were he dismissed George with a warning.

"Well what do you think?" the Ensign asked when George had gone.

"A trick of the moonlight, sir,"the sergeant said.

"You don't think the man was lying?"

"No, sir, I don't. But no more do I believe in ghosts."

"Don't you, sergeant? Don't you?" Smiling, the Ensign left the guardroom.

After a moment's cogitation, the sergeant drew the incidence-book towards him, and wrote, "Private Jones, G., reported that while on sentry duty on No. 3 point, at about half after one in the morning, he saw the ghost of a headless woman on the parade ground".

When the adjutant inspected the book the following morning and read the sergeant's laconic entry, he smiled. One could always trust the Welsh to be diverting, he told himself.

The incident might have been quite forgotten had not another sentry, three nights later, on guard at No. 3 point, been found by the orderly officer and sergeant of the guard in a dead faint in his box. When he came to, he told much the same story as George had told.

At his later interrogation, it was suggested to him that he had allowed George's story play too much on his imagination. On the face of it this seemed unlikely, because the man was a guardsman with some years' service, during which he had proved himself to be an eminently practical soldier. In any case, he told his interrogators, he had not heard George's story.

This turned out to be quite true, because when George had had some sleep, and came to think over what had happened, in the cold light of day it seemed too fantastic. So he had decided to keep quiet about it, and made David Rees promise to do the same.

The Englishman was then recalled, and was instructed on pain of court martial on a charge of disobeying a lawful order to keep absolutely mum.

When, however, the following week yet another veteran guardsman reported an identical experience, it became virtually impossible for the story not to get around the regiment, with somewhat unsteadying results.

Nor was this all. The headless lady was soon found not to be the only ghost haunting the environments of Recruit House. Another sentry, one Richard Donkin, while on duty behind the Armoury House, had an unsettling experience which he reported not only to his superiors, but to all who would listen to him.

The matter had now reached such a pitch that the Colonel realized that unless something were done the effect on the regiment could be extremely detrimental.

"Somehow we must show these stories to have no basis in fact whatsoever," he wrote to the Secretary for War. "I therefore intend, subject to no veto emanating from you, sir, to ask Sir Richard Ford, one of the Westminster magistrates, to undertake an inquiry, and to take from all those who claim to have had these experiences statements under oath, with all the consequences for the committal of perjury attached thereto."

So Sir Richard Ford set up his court of inquiry in the barracks, and took statements from all concerned, beginning with George. The one point which immediately struck him on comparing the various statements was the similarity of the facts set out by the witnesses. The apparition rose from the ground, the aura of light was bright enough for the pattern of the gown to be seen even on a moonless night, and every man deposed that the figure was headless. Then, too, it always turned away, and began to walk towards the canal which (at that time) ran through St James's Park.

Now Sir Richard was an old inhabitant of Westminster, and going back over the history of the Foot Guards he recalled that some twenty years before there had been some scandal attaching to the Coldstreams; something to do with murder. On looking up the records, he discovered that his memory was sound. A sergeant in the Guards had killed his wife, and in an attempt to make it difficult to identify the body, had hacked off the head before throwing the remainder of the corpse in the canal in the park, from which it was eventually recovered. His gruesome attempt to escape the consequences of his crime failed, because five witnesses came forward who were able to show that the gown—of cream satin with red stripes and red spots between the stripes—in which the body was clothed when taken from the canal, was the same that the sergeant's former wife had once possessed.

This, contrary to the hopes of the colonel, provided a basis of possibility for the headless lady, though it did not explain why she had not decided to "walk" before, for there was no record of her having been seen by anyone before she appeared to George Jones. With Richard Donkin's ghost, Sir Richard Ford had less success.

Donkin's signed statement, which he made to the magistrate, reads thus:

"At about twelve o'clock at night, I was on sentry duty behind the Armoury House, when I heard a loud noise coming from an empty house near my post.

"At the same time I heard a voice cry out, 'Bring a light! Bring me a light!' The last word was uttered in so feeble and changeable a tone of voice that I concluded that some person was ill, and consequently offered them my assistance. I could, however, obtain no answer to my proposal, although I repeated it several times, and as often the voice used the same terms.

"I endeavoured to see the person who called out, but in vain. On a sudden the violent noise was renewed, which appeared to me to resemble sashes of windows lifted hastily up and down, but that they were moved in quick succession and in different parts of the house, nearly at the same time, so it seems to me impossible that one person could accomplish the whole business.

"I heard several of my regiment say they have heard similar noises and proceedings, but I have never heard the calls accounted for. I would not have reported this occurrence had it not been for the incidents relating to the headless lady."

The house was identified and searched. It had been empty for a number of years, but except for deterioration natural to being so long unoccupied, nothing was found which would account for the sounds of the opening and closing of windows. The records were also searched, but nothing came to light to suggest a possible reason, whether rational or irrational, for the ghostly voice, or the other sounds.

With regard to the headless lady, to restore confidence among the men the sentry points at the Recruit House were re-sited, so that no box stood near to the spot where she always appeared. This reorganization soon proved to have been unnecessary, however, for a clergyman, having asked permission to spend the night at former No. 3 point, and having passed the whole of his watch reciting prayers for the souls of the faithful departed, she was never seen again.

The Ghost of Garpsdal

Iceland is a country famous for ghosts and supernatural manifestations of all kinds. One of its most impressive stories concerns a minister of the Church, and has been set down and witnessed by another.

In the year 1807 there was living at a house called Garpsdal a young minister, Mr Saemund, and his wife and child. Mr Saemund was a man of some fortune, and Garpsdal was by way of being a small estate, something between manor-house and farmstead. There were sheep and cows in the Saemund pastures, Saemund boats on the sea-shore close by, servants and farm-workers "living in" at Garpsdal. It was a comfortable and peaceful household, which made the disturbances of Autumn, 1807, all the more strange.

It all began one September night when three of Mr Saemund's servants were sleeping in the room they shared. Outside a harvest moon shone on quiet fields, a few white still forms that were recumbent sheep, and a silver sea beyond. Suddenly, a shattering noise broke the silence—the door of the servants' bedroom cracked and splintered as though an axe had been driven through it. The three started up—Thorsteinn Gudmundsson, the eldest, reaching for his staff, which always lay beside him at night—Magnus Jonsson, the young shepherd, rubbing his eyes, while the boy Thorstein ran behind him for shelter.

"Stand by to fight him, lads!" shouted Gudmundsson.

But no one entered. When they unlatched the broken door, there was no one on the landing outside, nor had anyone else in the house been disturbed. Baffled, they all went back to bed.

Next day another alarming thing occurred. Mr Saemund was sitting in his garden-house, making notes for a sermon; it was a fine, warm day. His peace was broken by the sound of loud, furious hammering and the splintering of wood. He looked up; there was nothing to be seen, and he concluded that the noise was coming from the direction of the seashore. He put down his notebook and hurried through the home-meadow and out by the gate that led to the shore. All the way he could hear the steady sounds of chopping, hammering and breaking. He arrived on the beach, and stopped in consternation. His finest fishing-boat, the *Sigrid*, lay ruined on the sand—her timbers shattered, her mast broken, her sails torn off and flung into the sea. Deliberate violence of the most savage kind had destroyed her. But whose violence? As far as the eye could see, the beach was deserted. Other boats lay quiet and empty. Nobody could have run away in the short time since the sounds had ceased— which had been about the time Mr Saemund passed through the meadow-gate to the shore. No bobbing head revealed a fugitive swimming out to sea. There was nothing to account for the *Sigrid*'s wanton destruction.

Mr Saemund afterwards said that at this moment it did not occur to him that there might be a supernatural explanation. Somebody had done the damage and got away. How they had done so was another matter.

He was in church, marrying two of his parishioners, when the next outrage occurred. Nobody saw it, for most of his household were also at the ceremony. When they returned, they found the doors of four sheep-houses chopped to matchwood. "Aha!" said the minister, "this time the villain has been clever; he has picked a time when we were all away. Magnus, you must keep a sharp watch on the place tonight." He knew Magnus Jonsson for a smart, intelligent youth who would not be slow to strike down and capture the enemy.

But the stranger Magnus encountered that evening was not at all of the kind he expected. His dog, Glam, had rounded up the sheep and got them into the sheep-houses, and Magnus was going from one sheep-house to another making sure that the broken doors, which he had temporarily boarded up, were secure. He returned to the first one, and stopped in his tracks. All the ewes but one were huddled in a corner, as if in fear; the exception lay on its side on the ground, kicking and struggling as if held by an invisible attacker. Beside it, but not touching it, stood a young woman. Magnus's impression was of a tallish, thin figure, fair hair dressed in two long braids, after the fashion of unmarried girls, and a blue or grey dress over which was a large apron. The face he could not describe except to say that it was "sharpish".

"What are you doing here?" he asked. "And what have you done to my ewe? She's dying!"

"I have not touched her," replied the woman. "I came to ask you to sell me a ewe for roasting, and thought I would choose one for myself. But since the creature is dying you may as well give her to me."

"We'll see what my master has to say about that!" replied Magnus angrily, and called out (though he knew his master was nowhere near), "Mr Saemund, come quickly! we've got a thief here!"

"He will not hear you," said the stranger with a cold smile. "The sheep is mine; see, it is almost dead."

At that moment there arrived on the scene an old woman servant, Gudrun Jonsdottir, who had lived at Garpsdal all her life. She was known for something of a Wise Woman, and had a wonderful way with animals.

"Come here, Gudrun!" called Magnus. "Here's one of my ewes been hurt by this woman here—see what you can do with it!"

Old Gudrun bustled in and knelt down creakily by the writhing animal, ignoring the woman who still stood motionless by it.

"Why, the poor thing—it's in a convulsion!" she exclaimed. "What has given it such a turn? There, there, be easy, lamb, be easy." And she handled, stroked, and patted it as if it had been a sick child. Magnus watched in astonishment as its struggles lessened and its panting breaths grew slower. After a moment or two it began to try to get up, and Gudrun gently helped it to its feet. It trotted quietly to join its sisters in the corner, while Magnus stared and Gudrun smiled contentedly.

"Gudrun can cure all the sick ones, you see," she said. "But what brought the poor thing into such a case?"

"Why, *she* did!" Magnus pointed to the strange woman—— she stood immovable, her face expressionless. "Get out, will you?" he said to her. "I'll set the dogs on you if you don't."

He moved to the door and opened it. As he did so, a beam in the ceiling broke as if a rending blow had been delivered to it, and the broken pieces of timber were flung with violent impetus in Magnus's face, by no visible agency. He threw up his hands to protect his eyes from the flying splinters; when he lowered them, the strange woman had vanished, though he had not felt her pass him. A moment later, Mr Saemund's horses, which were stabled in the yard outside, began to whinny, neigh, and kick their stalls as if badly frightened. Magnus went out to them, but they were in too frenzied a state to approach; even Gudrun's soothing words had no effect.

Two days later a fearful outbreak of smashing and breaking occurred all over Garpsdal; panels were ruined, doors broken in, upstairs and downstairs the havoc was wrought. Half-crazed, Mr Saemund collected the servants and told them to stay in the hall while his great Bible was fetched. Then, as the bangs and crashes rang through the house, he held a short service of exorcism, and opened the house door, commanding the evil spirit to leave. Suddenly Magnus cried out: "There she goes!"

"Where? Where? Did you see her leave the house?

"No, she has gone into the sitting-room."

None of the others had seen this, but to Magnus's eyes the figure of the girl from the sheep-house had been clear. He ran into the sitting-room, Mr Saemund and some of the braver servants behind him. There she stood by the window, her dress now a clear grey and her hair lighter than it had looked before. Magnus pointed her out to his master.

"I see nobody!" said Mr Saemund in a puzzled tone. As he spoke, a pane of glass in the window shattered into small pieces.

"She has gone through the window!" cried Magnus; but could not explain how she could have done so—he merely knew that her figure had disintegrated and that he had seen something flit like a bird through the gaping hole in the glass.

That night, and for a week after, the sitting-room resounded with bangs and thumps, making it impossible to talk quietly or read without disturbance. Mr Saemund repeated the service of exorcism more elaborately, but without effect. Poor Magnus, the only one to have seen the spirit who was causing all the disturbances, came under some suspicion from his fellow-servants, who thought that he was in some way responsible and was playing some kind of trick on them. Magnus indignantly denied this, and Mr Saemund absolved him of blame, having stood beside him in the hall and sitting-room when the damage was being done.

On 28 September the troubles reached their height. That evening Magnus and two women servants were out in the barn; Mr Saemund and his wife were in the sitting-room. The evening had been fairly quiet after the noise of the previous week; but about eight o'clock a great blow was struck on the sitting-room ceiling, bringing down some plaster on to the carpet. At the same moment, the wooden partition between the sitting-room and the weaving-shop was broken down. As the minister's wife rushed to her husband for protection, three windows smashed simultaneously—one above the bed where Mr Saemund occasionally slept after working late on sermons or parish duties, another above his writing-desk, and a third in front of the cupboard door. Glass littered the floor and papers blew wildly about—then, through one broken window came flying a piece of wood that seemed to be part of a table, and through another came a garden spade. Mr Saemund and his wife rushed out of the room, into a hall full of terrified servants.

"Come on—into the loft!" cried one, and others followed him like driven sheep. Magnus and Gudrun, however, stayed with their master and mistress; and as Gudrun moved to Mrs Saemund's side, a great tub of washing, which had been standing in the kitchen, came hurtling at Gudrun's head, knocking the old woman over and submerging her with dirty linen. It was hardly noticed in the confusion—for now everything that was at all loose was flying about in the air, amid the screams and cries of the servants. The minister opened a cloak-room door, intending to take refuge, but a sledge-hammer came whirling out at him from the interior, hitting him sharply on the side and the hip. He fled back to the sitting-room, and the others followed him and huddled there in a terrified group, with nightmare around them. Everything was dancing—ornaments, books, chairs—and a volley of deal splinters from the broken partition rained into faces and stuck like burrs in hair and clothes. Mrs Saemund fainted with terror, and several of the women were in hysterics.

"Come," said Mr Saemund, "I am taking my family to shelter away from here, and those of you who wish must come with us. My neighbour at Muli Farm will take us in, I know." And picking up his unconscious wife he carried her out of the dreadful room, while Gudrun followed with the baby, who—after the way of babies—had slept peacefully through all the din.

That night Garpsdal was deserted, and its dwellers slept at Muli, an exhausted terror-haunted sleep. But next day Mr Saemund returned, declaring that he would get the better of this demon, and that it should not drive him away from his home. He found Garpsdal in a fearful state of disorder, but quiet; and gradually the servants returned to it, though Mrs Saemund and the baby remained at Muli

For some weeks there was peace, though there were those who declared that the ghost had not finished with Garpsdal. The men worked hard; glass was replaced, new doors and panels fitted, until the house began to look almost like its old self. Then, one morning, the troubles began again.

It was Sunday, and the household was almost ready to go to church. Everyone, from the small boot-boy upwards, was dressed in sober Sunday best, and Garpsdal was a place of peaceful bustle. Mr Saemund, sermon-notes in hand, paused at the front door as one of the maids called him back.

"Sir, sir, it's started again! It's hammering in the pantry!"

His mouth grimly set, the minister shut the door and hurried towards the kitchens. His staff followed him, cowed and whispering. As they neared the pantry the familiar, dreaded sounds grew louder. Mr Saemund flung open the door.

"There she is!" cried Magnus. The girl was standing with her back to them, pulling at the pantry shelves with her bare hands. She seemed to use little effort, yet the strong wood broke at her touch and the shelves and their contents crashed to the ground. There was a terrifying, slow, wanton destructiveness about her method that struck Magnus with horror.

"I cannot see her," said Mr Saemund. "Speak to her, Magnus."

Magnus stepped forward. He noticed for the first time that the figure was by no means transparent—he could not see the portion of the shelves before which she was standing. But yet he knew her for no human being.

"Stop, in God's name!" he called out to her.

She lowered her arms, which had been reaching to the upper shelf, and turned round. For the first time he had a clear and close view of her face. The sharpness that he had noted before was the sharpness of bone, and the eyes were cold because they were quite hollow; the cold smile was a lipless one. It was the face of a skull that confronted Magnus. With a cry of horror, he stepped back and fell on his knees, praying.

"You do well to pray, Magnus," said Mr Saemund. "On your knees, the rest of you, while I wrestle with this fearful thing." Though he could not see the ghost, he sensed vividly its malevolent presence.

"This is a duel between you and me, Spirit," he said. "I have bidden you away before with bell, book and candle, according to the rites of the Church. Now I say to you in my own person—get back to the Hell you came from, and leave this Christian house! You have done your worst to it, and you may assault the bodies of those who live in it, but our souls you cannot touch, for they are God's and not the Devil's. Look to yourself, Spirit, for the Church too can curse! Begone, I say—begone!"

FIFTY GREAT GHOST STORIES

Magnus raised his head from his hands to see how Mr Saemund's words affected the visitant. He could hardly believe what he saw. "She's going, sir—fading through the wall!"

He ran to the window. "Yes, there she is, outside in the byre-lane. I'm going to chase her away!"

Mr Saemund tried to pull him back, but Magnus was out of the room and out of the house before anyone could stop him. Gudrun, who had a particular fondness for the boy, hobbled out after him, calling that he was a foolhardy lad. As she reached the lane, she saw Magnus stop in his tracks as a shower of mud and dirt rose up from the road to envelop him. He shook himself and ran on—only to be stopped again by the impact of a huge stone which struck him full in the chest. He fell, and Gudrun, hurrying to his side, received a violent blow on the arm. So badly hurt was the old woman that for three weeks afterwards she kept to her bed.

Here the hauntings might have ended, but for the folly of Magnus's cousin, the shepherd Einar Jonsson, a brave and hard-headed young man who had not shared in the general terror. For the most part of the time he had been out in the fields or the sheep-houses, tending his flock, and so had not witnessed the doing of the damage, or heard much of the noise. One night, after a Christmas revel, Einar and some of his mates were discussing the ghost.

"I don't believe she existed at all," said Einar. "You were always making up stories, Magnus, even as a lad."

"I *did* see her," replied Magnus. "I wish I had not; I shall never forget it."

"I tell you what—I'll command her to appear to me—then I shall see for myself. She seems a forthcoming lass—she won't refuse a personable man like me!" Einar was laughing, and laughed more at the protests of Magnus and the others that he would be committing the wildest and wickedest folly if he did any such thing. The subject was changed, the cup passed round again, and before long the party retired to bed.

Einar slept in his hut near the sheep-houses, for some of his ewes were due to lamb, and he had to be within sound of them. He lay down on his pallet the worse—or the better—for wine, and thought of his joking threat. *Should* he summon the ghost—and tomorrow tell the others some fantastic story of the result? Perhaps then they would realize how credulous they had been to believe Magnus's story at all.

He sat up, clapped his hands three times, and called out: "Ghost of Garpsdal, I command you to appear to me!"

It was the anxious bleating of the sheep that brought lanterns bobbing through the yard to the sheep-hut, an hour or so after midnight. Within the hut Magnus and the others could hear a noise as of something frantically throwing itself from side to side, and strange muffled cries. They opened the door. Within was a wild thing in torn clothing, bleeding from self-inflicted wounds, and raving incoherently as it repeatedly dashed its head against the walls. Two hours before it had been the gay, daring Einar Jonsson.

It seemed for some time as though Einar's brain would be permanently affected; but slowly he regained his senses, though he was never to be the same man again, and had aged ten years in looks during his illness. When asked what had happened in the hut, he could only say: "The girl appeared over my head and attacked me." No questioning could extract more than this. When he was as recovered as he was ever likely to be, Einar left Garpsdal and went to work on a farm many miles away.

Only one more piece of evil was worked on the Garpsdal household; during Einar's illness Mr Saemund rode over to Muli Farm one day, and spent the night there. When next morning he went to collect his horse from the stable, he found it dead from no apparent cause, its body black and swollen. She who had been baulked of a sheep had claimed a horse.

Seeing that the evil influence could even reach to Muli, Mr Saemund brought his family back to Garpsdal. Every night and morning special prayers against daemonic power were held; with effect, for the hauntings ceased. Some months later, on 28 May, 1808, Mr Saemund solemnly recounted to his friend Gisli Olafsson, another minister, and to two other witnesses, everything that had happened since the outbreak began; and his wife and servants confirmed his story.

Magnus lived to be an old man—he was still alive in 1862—but there is no evidence that he ever again saw the Ghost of Garpsdal.

Mischief Among the Dead

A poltergeist, said the late Harry Price, is an "alleged ghost", with "certain unpleasant characteristics". The ordinary ghost, though often inconsiderate, clumsy, noisy and frightening, is generally considered to be inoffensive, and even friendly and well disposed to the living persons who occupy its place of haunting.

But the poltergeist has none of these supposed feelings of friendship to those of us on this side of the grave. Its reported activities would suggest that it is animated by a destructiveness and spite which seems to be without purpose. It is a vindictive agency which has a nuisance value the ordinary ghost does not have. A poltergeist is said to infest, rather than haunt a place.

Poltergeists have been reported in many places, among them, not surprisingly, churchyards.

They are not to be confused with the many harmless ghosts reported to haunt countless churchyards—such as the pathetic child victims of Mary Cotton, hanged in 1873 for the murder of her four children, and suspected on good evidence of having murdered twelve more, at West Auckland, Durham.

These children haunted the churchyard and rectory where their bodies had been buried, exhumed and dissected. One disconsolate little ghost girl, clad in her pathetic burial shroud, they said, followed the terrified village postman home one evening, and then went into the room where his child lay asleep. This poor little ghost was finally consoled and sent back on her eternal journey by an old woman who lived in a haunted house and was used to ghosts, and who said afterwards: "It was lonely and cold in the dark churchyard. I did my best to comfort it. It won't trouble you again."

She was right. That little ghost was not seen again. In a previous century the kindly old soul who was not afraid of it would no doubt have been burnt alive as a witch in league with the devil.

Poltergeists cause a different sort of trouble to those sad phantoms whose sudden appearance among the gravestones is calculated to make the bravest heart quail. In certain churchyards they have been known to get into family vaults and play havoc with the coffins.

The following occurrence was reported from the village of Stanton in Suffolk in the year 1815:

"On opening the vault some years since, several *leaden* coffins with wooded cases that had been fixed on biers were found displaced, to the great astonishment of many inhabitants of the village. The coffins were placed as before and properly closed; when some time ago, another of the family dying, they were a second time found displaced, and two years after they were not only found all off the biers, but one coffin, as heavy as to require eight men to raise it, was found on the fourth step that leads into the vault. Whence arose this operation in which it is certain no one had a hand?"

There was a suggestion that the displacement of the coffins might have been caused by underground water, but there was no sign of this on the different occasions when the vault was opened, and it would be surely impossible for lead coffins to be displaced by even a sudden inrush of water.

The classic case of this, and certainly the best authenticated, comes from Barbados in the West Indies. The events took place in the little churchyard attached to Christ Church which is near the lighthouse on the southernmost point of the island, about a half-hour's drive out of Bridgetown.

The vault was a hundred feet above sea level and hewn into the solid rock. It had a stone floor and walls, and was sealed with a great slab of blue Devonshire marble, so heavy that it took several men to lift it.

The vault had belonged to several old Barbados families. Originally it had been built for the Walronds. Then it passed to the Elliotts, who married into the Walrond family. These families were members of the King's Council, rulers of the island, plantation and slave owners, people of wealth and position.

In the year 1724 the Honourable James Elliott, a member of Barbados Council, died at the age of thirty-four, and his sorrowful widow, Elizabeth, daughter of Thomas Walrond, put her husband's remains in her family vault, upon the tombstone of which she caused an inscription to be carved, saying he was "brave, hospitable and courteous, of great integrity in his actions, and conspicuous for his judgement, and vivacity in conversation". He was "snatched away from us on the 14th of May" in that year, "and died lamented by all who knew him".

It is not recorded what other coffins the vault contained in 1724, but it fell into disuse for the better part of a century. In July, 1807, an application was made to the Rector of Christ Church to permit the remains of Mrs Thomasina Goddard, who was a relative of the Elliotts, to be buried in the vault. Permission was granted.

Workmen accordingly broke the seals which were found to be intact. Negro slaves moved aside the massive marble slab to open the tomb, and it was discovered to everyone's surprise that the vault was empty. There was no sign of the remains of any of the Elliotts or of the Walronds. The burial, however, was proceeded with and Mrs Goddard was laid to rest in the tomb on 31 July, 1807.

The vault then came into the hands of the Chases, a wealthy, influential family in the island, plantation and slave-owners as were all Europeans of substance in the West Indies in those days. The Chase family coat-of-arms was carved upon a tablet over the entrance of the vault and can be seen there today.

The first Chase to be buried there was Mary Anna Maria, the infant daughter of the Honourable Thomas Chase, who died in February, 1808. The child was put in a lead coffin and brought to the vault, which, when it was opened, was found to be in order, the wooden coffin of Mrs Goddard being in its proper place.

On 6 July, 1812, the vault was opened again to receive the body of another daughter of Thomas Chase—Dorcas Chase. This time the burial party found the vault in a state of confusion. The lead coffin containing the body of the infant Anna Maria was found standing nearly upright, head downwards on the opposite side of the vault to which it had been originally placed. The large wood coffin of Mrs Goddard had also been moved out of its place.

The surprised burial party put the coffins in their right places, laid the lead coffin of Dorcas Chase upon the floor of the vault, replaced the massive slab of marble across the mouth of the vault where it was cemented in the presence of the rector and other persons and sealed with the mason's seal.

The tomb was apparently opened again that year for the burial of the Honourable Thomas Chase, upon which occasion no disorder was reported in the vault. The vault was not opened again until

25 September, 1816 for the burial of an infant, Samuel Brewster Ames, when it was observed that the lead coffins were in a state of disorder. Once again the vault was tidied up and resealed.

During that year there had been one of the many revolts among the slaves who had become so numerous in the West Indies that their white masters had difficulty in keeping them under. Among the white people murdered by the slaves was Samuel Brewster, a relative of the Chase family, and when the vault at Christ Church was opened to receive his body they found the place once more in a state of great confusion, the heavy lead coffins being toppled from their places and apparently hurled across the floor of the vault.

On 9 July, 1819, the body of Miss Thomasina Clarke was brought to the vault for burial, and once more the same confusion was found. The Rector, Dr T. H. Orderson, D.D., was greatly concerned. He noticed particularly that the disorder was confined to the lead coffins. Coffins of wood had not been moved.

Negroes were brought in to tidy up the mess. It was observed that the wood coffin of Mrs Goddard, buried there in 1807, had fallen to pieces. This was "tied up in a small bundle", as Dr Orderson put in his report, "and placed between Miss Clarke's coffin and the wall."

So disturbed were the good rector and the Chase family at the strange and apparently unnatural happenings in the vault that they brought the matter before Lord Combermere, the Governor of Barbados.

Combermere had served in the Peninsular War, when he had commanded the cavalry under Wellington and had fought with some distinction at Salamanca. He was an honest-to-goodness soldier and he decided to make a practical test of these strange stories. No doubt he thought the Negroes were up to some of their black devilry, but he had to be sure that it was not just a case of tomb-breaking. He took the matter into his own hands and went to the churchyard himself with his ADC, the Hon. Major Finch.

Under their supervision and in the presence of Dr Orderson the coffins were replaced and Major Finch made a drawing of their exact positions, which has been preserved. Fine sand was then sprinkled over the floor of the vault, the heavy marble slab was cemented in position and the masons and the officials put various secret seals and marks in the soft cement.

The original intention of Lord Combermere was to wait until another death in the Chase family would occasion the re-opening of the vault. Nine months went by, but the Chases did not oblige with a death. Then Combermere decided to open the vault.

There was a meeting on 18 April, 1820, at Eldridge's Plantation, which was next to the church. According to one report the meeting was brought about by a story that a great noise had been heard coming from the interior of the vault. Others said that his lordship had merely become impatient, and indeed curiosity was burning hotly in the minds of all those who knew about the strange happenings inside the Chase vault.

The Governor had with him on the momentous morning of 18 April the Hon. Nathan Lucas (who later made a careful and factual report of the affair), Major Finch, the Rector (Dr Orderson), and two other gentlemen who had an interest in the matter—Robert Bowcher Clarke and Rowland Cotton.

First of all a careful examination was made of the various seals and secret marks made at the entrance of the vault on the previous July. All these were found to be intact. Despite the careful scrutiny which was made, there was no sign that anyone had tampered with the entrance of the tomb. Combermere and his companions satisfied themselves that it was impossible for anyone to have entered the vault. "Not a blade of grass or stone was touched", wrote Nathan Lucas. "Indeed collusion or deception was impossible."

It was noon and the negro slaves of the adjoining plantation were coming in from their whip-driven labour in the fields. Eight or ten of them were taken into the graveyard to undertake the heavy labour of opening the vault.

The place was found to be in the uttermost confusion—the great lead coffins, some of which would take a half a dozen men to handle, had been hurled across the vault and tumbled against the stone wall, some upside down, one standing on its head. But the wooden coffins were in their original positions. The tied-up bundle of Mrs Goddard's coffin had not been moved. Major Finch made a drawing of the positions of the coffins, which remains part of the documentation of this interesting case.

The vault was then thoroughly examined. There were no imprints or marks of any kind in the sand which had been sprinkled on the floor when the vault was closed and sealed the previous July. Lucas himself examined every part of the walls and the arch of the vault. Every square inch of the walls was struck by a mason in his presence and found to be solid rock. There was no water in the vault, or marks where it had been.

Someone suggested that it had been caused by an earthquake,

but an earthquake which would topple immense lead coffins from their places and hurl them about the vault would have been a very severe one and it would have levelled every building in the neighbourhood, if not in the whole island. This theory was discounted, as was the suggestion that it had been caused by flooding. The rock vault was tinder dry on 18 April, 1820, and was in a level churchyard where there could not possibly be a flow of water. In any case, it would require the force of a hurricane wave to throw immense lead coffins around. Water would certainly have made the wooden coffins float, and yet these had not been moved.

Nathan Lucas confessed himself at a loss to account for the strange thing which he had witnessed in company with other persons of unimpeachable integrity, who were equally puzzled.

"Thieves certainly had no hand in it," Lucas wrote, "and as for the negroes having anything to do with it, their superstitious fear of the dead and everything belonging to them precluded any idea of the kind. All I know is that it happened, and that I was an eye-witness of the fact."

Lord Combermere's investigation at the Chase vault, and the conclusions drawn from it, caused a great stir in Barbados where an official report on the matter was published.

At the request of the Chase family, all the coffins were taken from the vault and buried in separate graves, and the vault was abandoned. The Governor ordered that it be left permanently open, and thus it has remained ever since.

Although the affair caused a great stir in the island neighbourhood at the time, no mention of it was made in the newspapers of the day, nor was any comment made about it in the contemporary burial register at Christ Church, the entries of which were made by Dr Orderson. The story has been told many times and has several sources, though none so documented and reliable as that of Nathan Lucas.

A similar occurrence was reported to have taken place in the cemetery of Arensburg on the island of Oesel in the Baltic. This was in the year 1844. The details of this coffin disturbance were almost identical to those of the Barbados incidents, and there is some doubt that they ever took place.

The subject of coffin disturbance took a Gothic turn in a story emanating from Lincolnshire in the mid-eighteenth century, which though undocumented and improbable to a degree is worth the telling.

A squire's lady fell out with her husband's brother who lived with them, and for years they lived in a state of bitter hatred and quarrelsomeness which continued without respite or forgiveness until the day of their respective deaths. The squire's lady died first and was put in the family vault. On his deathbed the brother-in-law begged not to be buried in the same tomb "with that accursed woman", for their mutual hatred was such that it would endure into the other world. His request was not taken seriously and he was accordingly put into the family vault. Thereupon a mighty uproar was heard within the sealed vault. So great was the noise of human and material conflict issuing from within the tomb that it was forthwith opened. The great coffins had not only been hurled about the vault, but were even thrown together in positions suggesting they were in mortal combat. When they were replaced and the vault closed, the same thing happened again. The wise old squire who had survived his quarrelsome relatives and was living at last in peace in the manor-house, solved the problem by building a dividing wall inside the vault with the coffins of his wife and brother on either side of it. Whereafter peace and quiet was restored in the embattled graveyard.

A pretty story, but not to be taken as seriously as the Barbados coffin mystery, which was so thoroughly investigated and tested at the time. These events cannot be dismissed as having been caused by earthquakes or flooding. The reader may prefer one of several explanations, but the poltergeist theory is the only one which seems to fit the facts.

The negroes believed that an evil spirit called a Jumbie caused the disturbances among the coffins, and this is still believed today among the natives. Jumbies apparently originated from Zombies, the walking dead. They are mischief-making spirits who wander about at night causing the kind of pointless disturbances which took place in the Chase vault.

The Whiskered Sailor of Portsmouth

Not many years after the *Victory* had sailed from Portsmouth, bearing Nelson towards Trafalgar and death, a certain Mr Hamilton arrived in that town. He was on his way to join a ship, in which he was to proceed abroad. As his chaise rolled through the narrow, twisting streets, he saw, with some dismay, that Portsmouth was fuller than he had ever seen it.

It was at all times a bustling town, with its sailors home on leave and waiting to join their ships, the wives and families who were lodging with them, and the townspeople to whom the Fleet meant daily bread and butter. Blue jackets, shiny hard hats, and the gay scarves and vests beloved of sailors were everywhere. On the arms of their pigtailed wearers hung ladies as bright as parakeets in the finery of the Regency. Muslin dresses outlined their figures; their white-stockinged feet twinkled in black sandals, their high-dressed curls sprouted coloured feathers. Jewish clothes-dealers lurked outside slop-shops heaped with gaudy garments, while above their heads swung the sinister black doll that was the sign of their trade. Here and there a tar overcome with Portsmouth ale was being removed from the gutter by officers of the Watch, and outside every inn an uproarious group was drinking and commenting, not always printably, on passers-by.

Today, Mr Hamilton noticed unusual figures in the crowds. Well-dressed folk who could only be Hampshire gentry, and others who were patently farmers in from the country districts, were almost as numerous as the sailors. Mr Hamilton, who did not rejoice in the company of large numbers of his fellow-men, turned his mouth down in disapproval.

His face lengthened still further when, after disembarking from the chaise at the door of the George, his usual hostelry, he inquired for a room and was told there was none available.

"Everything taken, sir. I've even had to put two gentlemen in the loft over the stables."

"But this is ridiculous!" exclaimed Mr Hamilton impatiently. "You've always had a room for me before. Well, I shall take myself somewhere else."

"You'll be lucky if you do, sir," returned the landlord. "It's the same all over the town, not a bed to be had."

"Why, what's the matter with the place?"

"The matter? Why, just about everything. There's a county election on, and all the folk have come crowding in from round about. Then there's this pesky wind, that won't let the Fleet sail."

"But my ship leaves tomorrow!" said Mr Hamilton.

"I'll be surprised if it does, sir. Not a vessel's left Portsmouth since last Friday, and the place is choc-a-bloc with tars and passengers bound for foreign ports."

Mr Hamilton sighed. "Then can you recommend me to any place at all where I might get a bed for as long as I have to stay here?"

"Sorry, sir—no idea. Your best plan would be to hire a horse and get out to Cosham or Bedhampton—you might get a room out there."

Mr Hamilton thanked him, without any great enthusiasm for the suggestion, and turned away, after arranging that his valise and a heavy carpet-bag might be left at the George until he was ready to sail. Then he set out to wander the Portsmouth streets. Traipse out to Bedhampton? Ridiculous. As like as not there'd be nothing there but some dark hole of a room in a one-eyed country inn with a piggery under the window. A man with profound confidence in his own exemption from the misfortunes to which others were liable, Mr Hamilton felt sure that somewhere in Portsmouth he could find a respectable lodging.

It was a fine day, with a sharp breeze blowing, which, if the enemy of the Fleet, was still refreshing to a man who had just endured a coach journey from London. He briskly negotiated knots of strollers who swarmed across his path like shoals of fish, skirted the unofficial public meetings that were taking place wherever a reasonably open space presented itself, beneath banners bearing the legend: "Bloggs for Prosperity!" or alternatively "Snooks for King George and Old England!"

Once, while threading his way through a particularly close press of people, Mr Hamilton was conscious of a groping tug in the region of his waistcoat. Spinning round, he found himself looking down at a small, bright-eyed, extremely dirty young woman resplendent in an orange dress with green flounces. So close were they pressed together that she could barely withdraw the hand that had been seeking his fob-watch and purse of guineas. Mr Hamilton raked her with a cold naval eye, and she vanished as though the earth had swallowed her, beneath the arm of a bulky farmhand at her side. Mr Hamilton walked on, shaking his head. There were some shady characters in Portsmouth.

The landlord of the George had not erred on the side of pessimism. Every inn Mr Hamilton tried was full to overflowing. At one he was graciously invited to share a bed with two other men; an offer which he hurriedly declined. At another, he was approached by a furtive-looking person of Lascar features who offered to conduct him to a "prime billet" kept by a "decent woman". Hastily pulling his sleeve away from the filthy hand that clutched it, Mr Hamilton moved sharply away and began to traverse yet another street. Suddenly a brilliant thought struck him—he would go down to the dockyard and request a berth in the ship in which he was to sail. Why had he not thought of such a thing earlier? Quickening his step, he made his way back to the swarming environs of the dockyard, and accosted the sentry at the gate.

"*Euryalus*, sir? She's not come round from the Downs yet."

Mr Hamilton muttered an imprecation. "Well, when do you expect her?"

"Not today, unless the wind changes."

Further inquiries revealed that such ships as lay in port were filled to capacity with officers who had got there first; no quarters for Mr Hamilton could be found.

He returned to his wanderings, by now in a very bad humour. He was hot, tired, and footsore. The sun was going down and an autumn dusk was spreading. Time pressed, for any honest citizen who tramped the Portsmouth streets after dark ran the risk of anything from minor robbery to murder. By this time Mr Hamilton felt he was wandering in a maze, as he recognized places and objects he had passed before. There was the very same dead cat he had noticed in the gutter as his chaise drove into the town; and here was the milliner's window containing a very fetching rose-pink bonnet that he had considered buying for his wife. He determined to find a new direction, and struck off north-east of the town, where the streets were quieter.

His enterprise was almost immediately rewarded. Turning a corner, he found himself in a short street of which the principal feature was an inn, announcing itself to be the *Admiral Collingwood* and bearing an unflattering likeness of that gentleman on its swinging sign. With the boldness of despair, Mr Hamilton charged the door and found himself in a reasonably clean hall-way, with a tap-room opening off it and a door which he imagined led to the kitchens at the end. A smart double rap brought immediate response in the shape of the landlady.

"Yes? What were you wanting?"

She was sharp-featured, even vinegary, with steely grey eyes and a rat-trap of a mouth. But at least she was not sluttish; and after a day in Portsmouth Mr Hamilton was a connoisseur of sluts. He asked her if she had a room to let.

"Why, yes, Captain, if you've no objection to a double-bedded one."

"I don't wish to share a room, if you mean that."

She shrugged bony shoulders. "Take it or leave it, Captain."

Mr Hamilton thought of the falling dusk, and the hardness of the streets, and the guineas in his purse.

"I'll take it—if you'll let me pay to keep the other bed empty."

The landlady eyed him suspiciously. "Pay double for one bed? Got some prize-money to spend, eh, Captain?"

"My money's my concern, and I am not a captain. You heard my offer."

"Very well. It's all the same to me, if you're that fond of your own company, so long as the bed's paid for. I'll show you the room."

She stumped up the stairs in front of him to a door on the first landing. "Here it is, and there's not a finer in Portsmouth."

Mr Hamilton rather doubted this, but had to concede that the room was large, airy and clean so far as he could see, though the bed-curtains were shabby and the furniture sparse and poor. However, beggars could not be choosers. He paid her the five shillings she demanded as a surety of his good faith, and ordered a meal—for by now he was extremely hungry and thirsty. After a refreshing wash (it was an agreeable surprise to find the basin uncracked and the ewer full) he descended, and found his meal set out in a small private room. Anything in the way of food would have been welcome to him, and he enjoyed every mouthful of his supper—a brace of roast pigeons, a dish of sweetbreads, and the best part of an apple pie, washed down with draughts of excellent beer. Having smoked a pipe or two, to allow the food to digest, and read a copy of the local paper which was lying in the bar, he decided to make an early night of it.

The bright moonlight which streamed in through the windows made the room less shabby and more attractive altogether; the bed in particular looked inviting, and examination revealed the mattress to be free from lumps. Mr Hamilton undressed; gazed from the window for a few moments at the garden outside, in which a few tired small trees and rambling plants surrounded a plot of earth which had been recently dug. Perhaps they were going to grow vegetables there, he reflected sleepily; or possibly the digging was done by cats. He hoped the cats would not make their presence obvious later. As it was, things were pretty quiet. The noise in the tap-room had died down before he came upstairs, and in any case was hardly audible from this room. He locked the door—one could not be too careful—got into bed, and was asleep in a moment.

It seemed hours later that a noise woke him. He looked at his watch on the bedside chair, and found that he had only been asleep a little over an hour. Cursing, he subsided and turned over, preparing himself for sleep again. Then he hastily sat up. In turning, he brought himself to face the other bed; and the other bed, to his astonishment and indignation, was occupied.

The brilliant moon showed him the occupant clearly. He was a young man, obviously a sailor, naked to the waist but wearing full-bottomed trousers and what seemed to be the type of red spotted handkerchief known as a "Belcher" about his head. He half sat, half lay, on top of the bedclothes, and seemed to be in a deep sleep.

Mr Hamilton was furious. He thought of the sum he had promised the landlady to ensure privacy, and of the money he had already paid her. How dared she cheat him like this? Well, he would soon put a stop to it. He swung his legs out of bed—and then paused. The night was cold—too cold to spend in altercation with a power-fully built young tar, particularly when one was only clad in a shirt oneself. The man seemed quiet enough—he was not even snoring. With luck, he would lie there till morning, and Mr Hamilton would enjoy a peaceful night. He got back into bed, and though ruffled soon fell asleep again.

It was broad daylight when he awoke, and the moonlight had been replaced by equally brilliant sunlight. The sleeping sailor still lay in the same position, as if he had never stirred all night. Mr Hamilton looked curiously at the handsome, composed face—really rather distinguished, for a common seaman—and reflected that the Polls and Sues of Portsmouth must admire beyond expression the fine pair of black side-whiskers that sprouted from the jaw. He bent nearer to examine the handkerchief round the man's head —and saw, with a slight start, that what he had taken for a red-and-white spotted band was really a white bandage heavily soaked with blood, a smear of which had trickled down the man's left cheek and marked the pillow.

Before he had had time to reflect on this, another thought struck him. How had the man got in at all? He remembered clearly locking the door before going to bed—and in fact it was still firmly locked, as he found when he tried it. The door was in the centre of one side of the room, nearly half-way between the two bed-heads; and as Mr Hamilton stood by it, a bed-curtain hid the stranger from his view. He turned back, determined to shake the man awake and demand an explanation. Then he stopped short, his mouth open in amazement. The man had vanished! Scarcely an instant before he had been there—now he was gone. Silently and with the speed of light he must have slipped out.

Mr Hamilton began a frantic reconnaissance of the room. There must, of course, be another door. He felt round the walls. There was no panelling, only shabby and peeling wallpaper beneath which the outline of a hidden door would have been perfectly obvious. No tall cupboard or press was in the room. The window-curtains were too skimpy to hide even a small child, and there was no one under either bed.

Mr Hamilton was baffled, to say the least of it. He dressed, unlocked the door, and went downstairs. It appeared that he was the first person stirring, but there soon appeared a slipshod, dirty maid-of-all-work, armed with coals to lay the tap-room fire. Mr Hamilton inquired of her whether she had seen his companion anywhere in the house.

"Sailor? I ain't seen no sailors. They don't come in not as early as this."

"But this man spent the night here—you must have seen him! Look, the front door is still bolted. Have you let him out at the back?"

The maid looked at Mr Hamilton as if she doubted his sanity.

"I dunno nothing of it, I tell yer," she said, gathering up her bucket and departing.

Mr Hamilton paced an imaginary deck until the arrival of the landlady on the scene. He had been preparing a little speech for her.

"Good morning, madam."

"Morning to you, sir."

"May I have my bill, please? I am leaving immediately.

"Your bill? Why, won't you be requiring breakfast? You can have it as soon as you like."

"I shall certainly not take breakfast, nor anything else in this house, madam, after your unpardonable breach of faith in respect of my sleeping arrangements."

"Here—what are you talking about? What do you mean?"

"What do I mean? I paid for the sole occupation of the room."

"Well," she flashed back, "and you had it, didn't you? And though I say it, there ain't a more comfortable room in all Portsmouth. Why, I might have let that spare bed five times over last night, and just because of your fancy I didn't do it. Call yourself a gentleman, trying to bilk an honest woman!"

Mr Hamilton took a deep breath. The lady had sharp, untended nails, and he imagined them preparing for an attack on his cheeks. He laid a guinea on the bar.

"Far from trying to bilk you, madam, I am quite prepared to pay you the money you asked. I suffered no actual inconvenience from the presence of my fellow-lodger—only, having agreed to pay double for the indulgence of my fancy, as you call it, I did expect the conditions to be kept on your side."

"Why, and so they were!" she retorted.

"If you say so of course I must take your word for it. I suppose, then, that one of your servants introduced the man into my room without your knowledge."

"*What* man? There was nobody in your room, unless you let him in yourself. You had the key, hadn't you? Why, I heard you lock the door, as I was going to bed."

"Yes, that's true," conceded Mr Hamilton. "But be that as it may, there was a man—a sailor—in my room last night; though I know no more how he got in or out than I do where he got his broken head or his remarkable whiskers."

Mr Hamilton delivered this parting shot from the door, and glanced back to see how his opponent had taken it. To his surprise, her face had lost its angry flush and had turned very pale. For a moment she struggled to speak, and then managed to breathe out one word.

"Whiskers!" she gasped.

FIFTY GREAT GHOST STORIES

"Yes, whiskers. I never saw such a splendid pair in my life."

"And a broken head—oh, come back, sir, for heaven's sake come back, and tell me truly what you saw last night!"

"Why, no one, madam, but this sailor. I suppose he took refuge in my room from some drunken party, to sleep off the effects of the liquor."

"What was he like? You must tell me!"

Mr Hamilton described the man, his dress, and the bandaged head; after which the landlady threw herself into a chair, flung her apron over her head, and sat rocking herself to and fro in an agony of distress.

"God have mercy on me!" she cried. "It's all true, then, and the house is ruined for ever!"

Mr Hamilton, concerned, sat down beside her. "Pray compose yourself, madam. There is some strange story here—won't you tell me what it is, and satisfy my mind?"

After a burst of sobbing, and a restorative draught from one of her own brandy-bottles, the landlady became quiet enough to give her explanation.

"Truly, sir, it was not murder!"

"Murder!"

"Three nights before you came, it happened. This party of young sailors was drinking here quietly enough, when in come some marines as had been at the bottle elsewhere. One of these gin-shops, I shouldn't wonder—nasty places, as I wouldn't lower myself to keep. Well, a quarrel broke out between the two lots, and the noise brought me running from the kitchen. You understand, sir, I could do little, being a widow with no man behind me, but I did what I could to quiet them. When I saw it was no use I drew away for fear of being hurt myself. Then as I watched from behind the hatch, there I saw one of the marines throw a pewter pot into the party of sailors. and I saw it hit the tallest of them on the head. He fell straight to the ground senseless, and oh! the blood! Blood everywhere. Well, I feared the worst for him, poor lad, and indeed I was right to do so, for though they carried him upstairs and placed him on the bed, in a few minutes he was dead."

"But why did you not call the watch?" demanded Mr Hamilton.

"Because of bringing a bad name upon the house, sir. Some of his mates were for making trouble and said that the marine who threw the pot should hang, but others persuaded them out of it, and some went away as quick as they could. At last I agreed to let the marines bring him down and bury him in the garden at the back."

Mr Hamilton remembered his vision of excavatory cats, and shuddered slightly. Then he said:

"I can't understand why this man was not sought after to rejoin his ship."

"He had just been discharged, his mates said, and no one would inquire after him. So I thought it was all hushed up. But now I see it was of no use, sir, and a punishment on me for trying to hide a bad deed. I shall never dare to put anybody into your room again, for it was there they laid him. They took off his jacket and waistcoat, and tied up his wound with a handkerchief, but they never could stop the bleeding till—all was over. And as sure as you stand there a living man, he's come back to trouble us, for if he'd sat to you for his picture you could not have described him better than you have done."

Mr Hamilton thanked the landlady courteously for her story, and promised that he would not add to her troubles by spreading it about in Portsmouth. Then, having strangely little appetite for breakfast, he bade farewell to her and walked down to the Point, where he found that his ship was expected hourly. That afternoon she appeared and he immediately went on board. The next morning he set sail for the Mediterranean, and did not set foot again in Portsmouth for eighteen years.

After all this time, he was once more on his way to the Dockyard; this time to take up a shore appointment there. He was sharing a chaise with Captain Hastings, R.N., and Mrs Hastings, who noticed, as they approached the centre of the town, that Mr Hamilton's face became increasingly grave. Mrs Hastings, a lively, inquisitive lady, demanded the reason.

"I was thinking of events called up by the sight of that lane we have just passed," he replied. "I have never told any living soul of it before, but to old friends like you, and after such a lapse of time, I think I may now repeat it." And when they reached their lodgings, he recounted to them the whole strange story.

Nothing would satisfy Mrs Hastings but that next day they should go and reconnoitre the haunted inn. They walked through the busy streets to the turn of the lane; but no *Admiral Collingwood* could they see. A building something like what Mr Hamilton remembered of it certainly stood there, but it now housed a greengrocer's shop, and behind it rose the pinnacles of a Methodist chapel which had certainly not been there before. They called at the shop, bought some apples, and led the conversation round to the vanished inn; but could learn nothing from the shopkeeper except that it had been converted into a shop some five years before. Then, at Mrs Hastings's insistence, they strolled round to the Chapel which backed on to the building, and accosted a lady helper who happened to be arranging flowers in the choir. The most cunning of questions, involving such matters as burials and consecrations, failed to extract any information from her; and they were obliged to leave the scene without knowing whether any skeleton had been turned up when the place was built. Mrs Hastings would have pursued the matter, but Mr Hamilton felt it inadvisable to push it any farther.

It remained long in Mrs Hastings' mind. One day she told it to her friend Mrs Hughes, grandmother of the author of *Tom Brown's Schooldays*; and Mrs Hughes in turn told it to the Reverend R. H. Barham, author of *The Ingoldsby Legends*. Mr Barham wrote it down at her dictation, but, sad to say, never retold it in one of his immortal poems; and the Whiskered Sailor of Portsmouth lies in a nameless grave, forgotten by all but a few who have read Mr Hamilton's story.

The Reverend John Jones
and the Ghostly Horseman

At the beginning of the last century, the Reverend John Jones was minister of Bala, in Merionethshire. He was a clergyman of high principle and unblemished character, and was famed throughout the whole Principality for the zeal and fervour with which he preached the Gospel.

Because of his gift of oratory, he was much in demand at religious meetings, and having appreciated that his eloquence had been bestowed upon him by the Almighty so that he might use it as an instrument to bring souls to salvation, he never refused a request to speak, no matter how far he would have to travel from his own parish. In the summer of 1820 he had received such an invitation to attend a religious meeting at Machynlleth, in the neighbouring county of Montgomery.

He left his house in Bala about two o'clock in the afternoon, travelling on horseback and alone. It was a hot day, and when he reached the village of Llan̂wchllyn he stopped at the inn to water his horse and refresh himself with a stoup of ale. As he sat on the bench outside the inn, tasting his ale and watching his beast drink deeply at the trough, he noticed a man reclining in the shade of a tree. By the man's side was a sickle sheathed in straw, and from this, and from the man's appearance, Mr Jones judged that he was an itinerant reaper in search of employment.

When the minister had finished his ale, he put down the mug on the bench beside him, and took from his pocket his heavy silver watch, flicked open the front and saw that if he were to reach Machynlleth in time he must delay no longer. As he put his watch back into his pocket he happened to glance across at the man, and saw that he was now sitting up and was watching him.

Mr Jones remounted his horse, and set off. The next part of his journey lay through a wild and desolate region, almost completely uninhabited.

When he had ridden for about an hour, and was on the point of emerging from a wood at the top of a long and steep slope, he saw a man coming towards him on foot. As the man drew nearer, Mr Jones recognized him as the man who had been resting near the inn in Llanwchllyn. On coming up, the man touched his hat, and said, "Good day to you, Minister, is it possible that you can tell me what hour it is?"

"Why certainly," the parson replied, feeling in his pocket for his watch. "It is a few minutes past a quarter after four."

"I am obliged to you, sir," the man said, touching his hat again. "Good journey to you."

"And good day to you, my good man," replied Mr Jones, and urged his horse on once more.

The track down the hill was bordered on both sides by tall hedge-rows, and at the foot of the hill was a gate which gave access to a field through which the next part of the track ran. When he was about half-way down the hill, Jones's attention was attracted by something moving on the other side of the hedge on his left, and going in the same direction as himself.

At first he thought it must be an animal of one kind or another, but when he came to a place in the hedge where the bushes were lower than the rest and not so thick, he saw that it was a man bent double and that over his shoulder he carried a sickle sheathed in straw.

Made curious by the man's strange behaviour, the parson watched him for some time wondering what he could be about. But when he saw the man stop, kneel on one knee and begin to unsheathe his sickle, he felt a shudder of fear pass through him. For he recalled that the man had seen his watch, which was a valuable one, and now seemed to be preparing to attack him as he reached the gate, in order to rob him of it, since, while Jones watched, he had run on to the gate and was crouched down behind a bush beside it.

Though he was at this time in his early thirties, and was sturdy and strong, the minister was totally unarmed, and would be at a grave disadvantage in warding off any attack from a man armed with a sharp sickle. He reined in his horse, and looked about him in all directions, hoping to see someone he could tell his fears to and for whose help he might plead. But there was not a person in sight.

His fear mounting as each minute passed, he considered that discretion would be the better part of valour, and had actually half-turned his horse, intending to make his way home again, when he realized that his craven alarm was about to make him temporarily forsake the Lord. What he was doing, and from the same motives, was what Peter had done when he had denied Jesus thrice before cock-crow.

The meeting which he was on his way to attend was a very important one. Many would attend it seeking the Lord, and he had been asked especially to speak to them so that his inspired words might show them the way. If he did not go, he told himself, how many might be lost that day who but for his cowardice would have been saved. As long as there existed the faintest possibility of his getting there, he must go on.

Right though this decision might be, however, it did not change the situation in which he found himself. Only a few hundred yards away from him was an armed man waiting to spring on him while he was at a disadvantage. For in order to continue he must pause at the gate, open it, pass through and close it behind him.

What could he do to make the attack fail? Should he put his heels to his horse, urge her at the gate, hoping that she would leap over it? But she was aged and docile, and in the four or five years that he had owned her she had never once been put into a gallop, and certainly had never leapt over anything, let alone a five-barred gate. If only the gate had been open!

He then looked about him, wondering whether he could leave the track and make his way across the fields. But this was not possible either. Where the hedges were not too high, they were too thick with brambles for the horse to pass through; and even where, on his right, there were open gaps in the hedges, these gaps were protected by sheer rocky banks which only a beast far more nimble than his mount could hope to negotiate with success.

He could not go back, and ever again be at peace with his conscience; an alternative route was denied him; and to go forward he must risk a personal encounter with his potential armed assailant, the outcome of which, unless a miracle happened, must certainly mean his injury, if not his death.

Once again he pulled himself together. For a minister of God he was exhibiting an unforgivable lack of trust and confidence in Divine protection.

"I am a weak and sinful man, O Lord!" he groaned. "Please show me what I must do!"

For several moments he bowed his head in silent prayer. As he confessed later: "For all my self-abasement, I prayed rather in despair than in a spirit of humble trust and confidence. Yet, when I had said my Amen, my prayers seemed to have had a soothing effect on my mind, so that, refreshed and invigorated, I proceeded anew to consider the difficulties of my position."

Aged and slow though his mare might be, by this time she had grown impatient at the delay, and of her own accord began to move off down the slope. Jones had allowed the reins to fall on her neck while he had been pondering what to do, and her unexpected movement made him clutch at them. He pulled on them to check her, but as he did so his eyes fell upon an object close to him, and he saw to his utter astonishment that he was no longer alone.

There by his side was another horseman. He was dressed in a black suit and hat, which contrasted sharply with the whiteness of his mount. Jones's surprise at seeing him there was so intense that for several moments he was unable to speak.

"He had appeared," the minister recounted, "as suddenly as if he had sprung from the earth. He must have been riding behind me and overtaken me. And yet I had not heard the slightest sound. It was mysterious and inexplicable!"

Now his situation was completely changed, for no assailant, however desperate, would attempt to attack two opponents. Overjoyed by his release from his perilous position, Jones soon overcame his feelings of wonder, and he began to speak to his companion.

"Have you seen a man since you came out of the wood?" he asked.

Having waited for some seconds for an answer and not receiving one, he went on: "Hiding down there by the gate is a man with a sickle. He has designs upon my silver watch, and possibly upon the few coins I have on me. Did you see him?"

Still the man did not reply, and becoming embarrassed the minister said: "I cannot tell you how happy your coming has made me. I have desperately been considering what to do. I am on my way to Machynlleth to address an evangelist meeting there. I had thought of turning back, may the good God forgive me, but then I thought of the souls I might save from damnation with my humble words, and knew I must go on. But I could see no way of avoiding an encounter with the villain yonder. Now that you have come, I have no longer any fear. Shall we go on?"

He turned and looked at his companion, and realized that the man had been giving him only the slightest attention, but was gazing intently in the direction of the gate at the bottom of the hill. His embarrassment increased, particularly as the horseman seemed deliberately disdaining to reply to him. So he decided to keep his peace, and looked in the direction of the gate.

And now he received yet another surprise. For as he watched he saw the reaper come out of his hiding place and begin to run across the field to the left, re-sheathing his sickle as he went.

"There he goes!" he pointed excitedly. "Perhaps you thought I had been imagining the man. But now you can see him."

His companion nodded, but still did not speak.

Almost overwhelmed with relief at the passing of the danger, Jones urged his mare forward, and the horseman rode by his side towards the gate. The relief had made the minister even more garrulous, and as they went he continued to address the man in black, though he was both surprised and not a little hurt by the traveller's continued and, as it seemed to him, mysterious silence.

As they reached the gate the figure of the reaper was disappearing over the brow of a neighbouring hill.

"He has gone!" the minister sighed. Then to the horseman, "Can it be doubted for a moment that my prayer for help was heard, and that you were sent for my deliverance by the Lord!"

It was at this point that the minister realized that, having from his appearance judged the horseman to be English, he had spoken in the English tongue ever since he had been in his company. He is a Welshman, he told himself, who does not or will not speak English, and he repeated his last question in Welsh.

To his joy the man at once replied, with a single word, *Amen*.

As he rode forward to examine the fastening of the gate, Jones continued to ply his companion with questions in the Welsh.

"Have you come far, sir? Are you going far? I am going to a religious gathering at Machynlleth; are you going in that direction? If you are, perhaps you will give me the honour and extreme pleasure of your company? Or is your destination Llangollen; or are you perhaps going south? It is deserted countryside hereabouts . . ."

While he was speaking, he was pulling at the latch of the gate with his stick. It was proving a difficult operation, and for a moment he thought he would have to dismount; but at last the latch came up and the gate swung slowly into the field.

Jones pulled his horse to one side, and as he turned towards where he expected to find the horseman waiting he said, "Do you go on . . ."

He did not finish the sentence, for the horseman had disappeared.

Dumbfounded, the minister looked up the slope, the whole of which he could see. The horseman was not in sight, and yet if he had returned by the way he had come he could not have had time to reach the wood.

"What could have become of him?" I asked myself, the minister recorded in an account of his experiences which were later included in a memoir published in a number of the Welsh quarterly periodical *The Essayist*, in commemoration of his recent death in 1853. "He could not have gone through the gate, nor have made his horse leap the high hedges which on both sides shut in the road.

"Where was he? Had I been dreaming? Was it an apparition, a spectre which had been riding by my side for the last ten minutes? Could it be possible that I had seen no man or horse at all, and that the vision was but a creature of my imagination?

"I tried hard to convince myself that this was the case, but in vain; for unless someone had been with me, why had the reaper resheathed his murderous-looking weapon and fled? Surely, no; this mysterious horseman was no creation of my brain. I had seen him; who could he have been?

"I asked myself this question again and again; and then a feeling of profound awe began to creep over my soul. I remembered the singular way of his first appearance—his long silence—and then again the single word to which he had given utterance; I called to mind that this reply had been elicited from him by my mentioning in our own tongue the name of the Lord, and that this was the single occasion on which I had done so.

"What could I then believe?—but one thing, and that was that my prayer had indeed been heard, and that help had been given me from on high at a time of great danger.

"Full of this thought I dismounted, and throwing myself on my knees I offered up a prayer of thankfulness to Him who had heard my cry, and found help for me in time of need.

"I then mounted my horse and continued my journey. But through the long years that have elapsed since that memorable summer's day I have never for a moment wavered in my belief that in the mysterious horseman I had a special interference of Providence, by which means I was delivered from a position of extreme danger."

"Steer Nor'West"

Captain John S. Clarke, master of the schooner *Julia Hallock*, trading between New York and Cuba, put down his glass, and looking his companion straight in the eyes said firmly: "I'm telling you in all seriousness, sir, that though I've never had personal experience of one myself, I am utterly convinced of the existence of apparitions which can give warning of future events."

Mr Robert Owen, formerly United States minister to Naples and now enjoying a well-earned retirement in Cuba's sunshine, returned the gaze and shook his head.

"You surprise me, sir," he remarked. "You are a tough old sea-dog, if you will forgive the expression, an eminently practical and rational man, huh?"

"Right, sir."

"Then how can you, in this year of Our Lord eighteen hundred and fifty-nine, possibly believe in spirits? The idea that they exist and are capable of manifesting themselves to human beings goes against every concept of rational thinking. For consider, sir, the predicament we should be in if it were true. Let me try to put it concretely. Supposing you had been happily married for some time and your dear wife died. In your bereavement you would at first ridicule every suggestion that you should find a replacement for your dear departed. However, as time passed, you discovered that the loneliness of your single state was more than you could bear and presently you realized that a certain lady of your acquaintance was of such character that you felt you could make a happy life together.

"The more you thought about it, the more you became certain of the feasibility of the idea, and one day you plucked up courage and asked her to become Mrs John S. Clarke, and she consented. Once the nuptials were performed, they would have to be consummated. Right?"

"Right," agreed Captain Clarke.

"But supposing, when you took your new spouse in your arms, you recalled that your former spouse was a spirit, capable of watching every move you made, even if she did not actually manifest herself to you? You get my meaning?"

"Perfectly, sir," said the Captain. "But that is not the point. In my view there are certain spirits to whom the gift of revealing themselves to those left behind is given."

"You mean only some spirits have special gifts, so to speak, bestowed upon them? But, sir, the Good Book tells us, that however class-ridden we may be in this life, in the life hereafter all are equal."

"I was thinking," replied the Captain, "of the generally accepted principle of spirit-lore that, for example, the spirits of suicides or the victims of murder are deprived of eternal rest, and roam the world earth-bound, because of the sin they have committed in taking their own lives, or because of the violence with which they have been deprived of life."

"I have heard of that conception, sir, but again I must reject it for the simple reason that it, too, goes against all the teaching of Holy Writ. Would the Almighty in His great mercy further punish those who had been so unfortunate as to be incapable of tolerating life here below to such a degree that they robbed themselves of His most precious gift, or, in the case of those murdered, had this precious gift taken from them—would God, I say, further deprive these unhappy people of the delights of Paradise? Surely, if anyone were to receive special treatment in Heaven, it would be these unfortunates."

"I can follow your arguments, sir, and I must admit that the logic of them does not escape me," Captain Clarke replied. "At the same time, however, I find myself very much in the position of an eminent French lady I once read of.

"As I recall, her name was Madame du Deffand. Perhaps you have heard of her, sir?"

"Certainly," replied the former Minister. "The Marquise Marie-Anne de Vichy-Chamrond du Deffand. She was a great *salonière* and renowned for her letters. She had a great if cynical wit, and her later fame rested on an outstanding talent for the analysis of character.

She was a great friend of Voltaire, Montesquieu, Fontenelle, D'Alembert and her other great contemporaries. In her later life she formed a close, but entirely moral relationship with the eminent English writer, Horace Walpole. I have read the published volume of her correspondence."

"I did not know she was so famous a lady," Captain Clarke admitted. "But if she was all you say, then her comment gives much greater force to my argument."

"And that comment was?"

"A gentleman asked her one day, 'Do you believe in ghosts, Madame?' to which she replied, 'No, sir, but I am afraid of them.' "

Mr Owen laughed.

"Without meaning to make fun of you in any way, sir," he said, "I think you have not fully appreciated Madame du Deffand's incapacity for foregoing the coining of an epigram whenever the opportunity was afforded her."

"That's as may be, sir," retorted the Captain. "But on the other hand, I submit that while apparitions have not yet been scientifically accounted for, the many authenticated ghost-stories told for many centuries, and very widely believed, in my view, sir, forbid any thinking person from declaring that there is nothing in it when haunted houses and the return of disembodied spirits are being discussed. I mean no offence, Mr Owen."

"I take none, sir."

"I have travelled widely about the world, sir," the Captain went on, "and I have found a belief in ghosts to be as widely distributed as the Religious Idea itself. Even in the remotest islands of distant seas, and among the most unlettered savages, religion has been found and as invariably the belief in ghosts."

"The unlettered are always more susceptible to suggestion, Captain, than those who have been trained to think," Owen said. "With savages, whatever their religion is, it is more than nine-tenths superstition—and so is the belief in ghosts."

"Maybe, sir, maybe. But it is also true that there cannot be smoke without fire. I am convinced that if I were capable of discoursing on the philosophy of religion and of the supernatural, I could show that a belief in religion, even in the Christian religion—did not an angel or spirit release Peter from Herod's prison?—I would go so far as to say, necessitates a belief in ghosts. I can't do that, because I haven't the learning; but can I tell you a story that I had at first hand, which, more than anything else, has confirmed my belief in apparitions?"

"Certainly you may," Owen replied. "I shall listen attentively.

*   *   *   *   *

In 1836 and 1837 (Captain Clarke began) I sailed in the same ship with a certain Robert Bruce, who was first mate. Bruce was an Englishman, a Devon man, despite his name. He had been born in the last years of the last century at Torquay when that now famous watering-place was just a village, consisting of a few straggling cottages on a shingly beach. Like his father before him, he was reared to the seafaring life, and by the time he was thirty had become the first mate of a ship sailing between Liverpool and St John's, New Brunswick.

I joined the *Evening Star* as second mate, and this threw us a good deal together. It is some time since I heard of him; indeed, I don't know if he is still alive. I did hear of him for some years after I left the *Star*, the last news being that he was master of the brig *Comet*, and back on his old Liverpool to New Brunswick run.

Robert Bruce was as truthful and straightforward a man as ever I met in my life. We were as intimate as brothers; and two men can't be together, shut up for nearly two years in the same ship, without getting to know whether they can trust one another's word or not.

He always spoke of the circumstances of the incident I am about to relate in terms of reverence, as of an occurrence that seemed to bring him nearer to God and to another world than anything that had ever happened to him in his life before. I'd stake my life upon it, that he was speaking the truth, the whole truth and nothing but the truth, in the very extraordinary account which I shall now deliver to you.

Robert Bruce was such a good seaman that he became a first mate by the time he was thirty. At the time of the incident, the ship he was in was on her way from Liverpool to New Brunswick. They had been about six weeks at sea, and were near the banks of Newfoundland.

After sunset one day, the captain and his first mate, Robert Bruce, after having taken an observation, went below to calculate their day's work. For some reason or other, Bruce's calculations did not answer to his expectations, and he became so absorbed in the problem before him that he did not notice that the Captain had quitted the cabin.

Presently he found that he had made a simple error in his reckonings, and as soon as he had finished the calculations he called out, supposedly to the captain, but without looking round, "I make the latitude so and so, and the longitude so and so. Can that be right? What do you make them?"

When he received no reply, he repeated the question, and this time glanced over his shoulder, and seeing a man, whom he took to be the captain, bent over the latter's writing table, he expected an answer. But when there was still no reply, he got up and began to cross to the captain's table.

As he did so, the figure at the table raised its head, and to his utter astonishment Robert Bruce saw that it was not the captain, but an utter stranger!

Like his great namesake, Bruce was no coward, but as he met that fixed gaze looking silently at him, and became conscious that it was not the face of anyone that he had ever seen before, he was overcome with apprehension. Instead of stopping to question the apparent intruder, he rushed up on deck in such evident alarm that he alarmed the captain whom he found back on the bridge.

"Why, Mr Bruce," exclaimed the master, "whatever is the matter? You look as if you'd seen a ghost."

The discovery of the captain on the bridge astonished the mate even more.

"I did not see you leave the cabin, sir," he exclaimed. "How long have you been here?"

"Oh, five or ten minutes, Mr Bruce. Why do you ask?"

"Then who is it, sir, sitting at your desk?"

"Sitting at my desk?" the captain said sharply, in his turn becoming more astonished by the all-too-apparent trepidation of his customarily cool-headed senior officer. "Mr Bruce, have you taken leave of your senses?"

"No, sir, I assure you. There is someone sitting at your desk in the cabin. Who is it, sir?"

"No one I know of," the master told him. "You must be suffering from hallucinations, Mr Mate."

"But I tell you I'm not, sir. I plainly saw a stranger sitting at your desk."

"But there's no stranger aboard the ship, Mr Bruce. We've been six weeks at sea, so how could a stranger come aboard? You must have seen the steward there, or the second mate; who else would go down without orders?"

"Sir, I know the steward and the second mate as well as I know you," Bruce retorted. "I swear it was neither of them. It was someone I had never seen before, sitting in your armchair, writing on your slate. I did not know you had left the cabin, and when I had finished my calculations I asked you what you had made yours. When no one replied, I turned round and saw you sitting at your desk, still writing, so I began to cross the cabin, and when I was about halfway across you looked up, only it wasn't you, but this complete stranger. Sir, I can't be mistaken, because he looked me full in the face, and if ever I saw a man plainly and distinctly in this world, I saw him."

The captain now realized that Bruce was absolutely convinced of the truth of what he was saying.

"But who can it be?" he said, half to himself.

"God knows, sir, I don't," Bruce replied. "All I know is, I saw a man, and I had never seen him before in all my life."

Sure that Bruce was allowing his imagination to run away with him, the captain said sternly: "You must be crazy, Mr Mate. I repeat, how could a stranger come aboard when we're six weeks at sea without our knowing!"

"I realize that, sir," Bruce replied. "Yet I am prepared to swear on the Bible that I saw a stranger sitting in your arm-chair.

The captain regarded the mate for some seconds in silence, then with a shrug of his shoulders he said: "All right, Mr Bruce. Go down and ask him to be good enough to step up here on the bridge and we'll ask him how he came aboard and what it is he wants."

The mate hesitated, and this the captain knew to be unlike him.

"Come now, Mr Mate!" he said. "I've given you an order which I wish to be obeyed."

"The truth is, sir," Bruce replied with a good deal of embarrassment, "I'd rather not go down alone."

Now the captain's anger was rising swiftly.

"Mr Bruce, pray go down at once, and don't make a fool of yourself before the crew," he said quietly, yet sternly, for he had noticed that one or two sailors engaged on their duties nearby, as well as the helmsman, were regarding the mate in some alarm.

"I hope, sir," Bruce replied obstinately, "that you've always found me willing to do my duty, but could you not come down with me, sir?"

Not wishing to provoke more of a scene before the crew, and beginning to realize that his thoroughly reliable first mate was the last man to make such a fuss without good cause, with a grunt he left the bridge followed by Bruce.

When they reached the cabin they found it empty, as the captain had suspected they would.

"Well, Mr Bruce," he exclaimed, "didn't I tell you you had been dreaming?"

"It is all very well, sir, to say so; but if I didn't see that man writing on your slate, may I never see my home again."

"Ah! Writing on the slate!" the captain said. "If he was writing on the slate, the writing should still be there; provided of course that *he* was ever here and ever wrote."

As he said this, the captain strode across the cabin to his desk, and picked up the slate.

"Good God!" he exclaimed. "There's something here, sure enough. Is that your writing, Mr Bruce?"

The mate took the slate, and there in plain, legible characters were the words, "Steer to the nor'west".

"Is this your idea of a joke, Mr Bruce?" the captain thundered.

"On my word as a man and a sailor, sir," the puzzled Bruce replied, "it would not be my idea of a joke either. I have told you the exact truth, sir. I know no more of this writing than you do, sir."

The captain sat down at his desk, and was silent for several minutes, while Bruce stood by more apprehensive than ever. At last the master turned over the slate, and pushing it towards the mate said: "Write the words, *Steer to the nor'west*".

When Bruce had obeyed, the captain closely compared the two specimens of handwriting, for some moments. Then he said: "Mr Bruce, be good enough to tell the second mate to come here immediately."

When Bruce returned with the second mate, without any explanation the captain said to the younger man: "Please write on Mr Bruce's slate the words *Steer to the nor'west*."

With a slightly puzzled air, as though he believed the captain might be becoming somewhat eccentric, the second mate complied. Once more the captain compared the two examples of handwriting, and now bewilderment began to crease his forehead.

Dismissing the second mate, he turned to Bruce, saying: "Someone must have written these words, and I intend to find out who it is, who is trying to make fools of us. Every man who can write shall come here and write the words. In that way we shall soon find out who the ruffian is. We'll begin with the steward. Call him up, Mr Bruce. God help the man who thinks he can play this dangerous kind of joke with me."

So the steward came and wrote the words, and the handwriting on the captain's slate was clearly not his. He was followed by the nine men of the crew able to write, and within a comparatively short time, the captain realized that he still had not solved the mystery.

"Sir," Bruce suggested. "Could anyone have stowed away before we left Liverpool?"

"I don't see how, Mr Bruce, without his being discovered long before now," the Captain said. "But we will find out. The ship must be searched. Order up all hands, Mr Mate."

By this time, something of the incident had circulated among the crew, who believed that a stranger had come aboard in some mysterious manner and had to be found. They did not need the captain's order to search every nook and cranny of the ship, and went about their task thoroughly and with eager curiosity. Two hours later, Bruce had to report to the captain that no strange person had been found, nor was there any sign at all that a stowaway had been on board.

"I must admit I am strangely puzzled, Mr Bruce," the captain confessed. "What can it mean? That's what I would like to know. What can it mean, if it does mean anything?"

"I can't say, sir, I'm sure," Bruce replied. "I saw the man write; you see the writing. It must mean something."

The captain paced the cabin, while Bruce stood patiently by until a decision had been made.

"Do you believe in ghosts?" the captain asked him presently.

"Why, no, sir," Bruce told him. "Though I have met some who do."

"Neither do I believe in ghosts or apparitions or call them what you will," said the captain, "but do you know what, Mr Bruce?"

"No, sir."

"We have the wind free, and I have a great mind to keep her away and see what will come of it. Just by way of experiment, Mr Mate, if you understand. What would you say to that?"

"In your place, sir, I surely would," Bruce agreed. "At the worst, we shall only lose a few hours."

"I'm glad to have that answer, Mr Bruce. Well, be it so. Go and give the course *Nor'west*; and, Mr Bruce, have a good look-out aloft, and let it be a hand you can depend on thoroughly. I am sorry that I should have ever doubted your word, Mr Mate."

"I would have done the same, sir, situated similarly." Bruce smiled his gratitude for the apology.

So the necessary orders were given, and about three o'clock on the following afternoon the look-out reported an iceberg nearly ahead.

As the captain and the mate trained their glasses in the direction given by the look-out, the latter's excited voice informed them

that he could now see what looked like a vessel of some sort close
to it.

"Can it be true?" the captain said quietly to the mate. "Do you
imagine, Mr Bruce, that Providence has sent us this way to assist
an unfortunate ship that has run foul of an iceberg?"

"If that man sitting at your desk, sir, was Providence, or sent by
Providence," Bruce replied, "then I should say yes."

On coming nearer to the iceberg, both men could begin to make
out a vessel, somewhat dismantled, apparently frozen in the ice,
and from the movement on her decks it seemed that she still had
a good many human beings on board. And so it turned out.

As soon as they had communicated their distress, the captain
sent out boats to the stranded vessel, to bring those still living on
board his ship. She proved to be a schooner from Quebec bound for
Liverpool, with between fifty and sixty passengers aboard. She had
run into pack ice and had finally been frozen in fast. She had been in
this situation, which was now most critical, for several weeks. She
was stove in, her decks swept—in fact, she was a wreck. All her
provisions and almost all her water had gone, and her crew and
passengers had given up all thoughts of being rescued. It was no
wonder that their gratitude for their unexpected deliverance was
proportionately great.

All were physically in a weak condition, but the crew of the
rescue ship quickly devised all kinds of tackle, and with great tender-
ness for the hardened, rough men they were, they lost no time in
transferring the victims from the wreck to the warmth and shelter
of their own vessel.

As Mr Bruce stood at the side of his ship supervising the taking
on of the guests, one of them, more vigorous than most, hauled
himself up the ladder which had been lowered over the side. But
even he was almost exhausted when he reached the deck, and Bruce
hurried forward to support him.

It was when the man lifted up his head to thank the mate that
the latter almost started back, letting the man fall. His consternation
now equalled the bewilderment he had experienced when he had
seen the man sitting in the captain's arm-chair. For the face that he
now gazed into was the face of the stranger whom he had seen
writing on the captain's slate, "Steer to the nor'west".

At first he tried to persuade himself it must be his fancy playing
him tricks, but the more he examined the man the more sure he
felt he was right. It was not only the face; the man's build and even
his dress corresponded exactly.

As soon as the exhausted crew and starving passengers had been cared for, and the ship was back on course again, Bruce went to his captain and asked him to go down to the privacy of the cabin with him, as he had something of importance to tell him.

When they reached the cabin, the captain exclaimed with a laugh, "Not another ghost, I hope, Mr Mate!"

"On the contrary, sir," the mate replied. "It seems that it was not a ghost which I saw this morning, for I swear that man is alive and now aboard this ship."

The captain strode to his chair and sat down in it heavily before he said with a feigned tone of weariness: 'I beg you, Mr Bruce, let us have no more mysteries. Explain what you mean. Who is alive?'

"Why, sir, Bruce told him, "it is a mystery, but the same one. One of the passengers we have just saved is, I am convinced, the very man I saw writing on your slate yesterday. Indeed, I'd swear to it in any court of justice."

"Upon my word!" the captain exclaimed. "This gets more and more singular. But since you proved right on that other occasion, I cannot reject what you say now. Have the goodness to show me this man."

So going below, they found the man talking to the captain of the wrecked ship. On their coming up, both the captain and the passenger expressed their gratitude for having been saved in the warmest terms.

"It was a terrible fate you have preserved us from," the passenger said. "For I cannot conceive a worse way to die than by slow death from exposure and starvation."

"Sir," replied the captain, "we have only done our duty, and I am sure your captain would have done the same for us had our roles been reversed. Gentlemen, I wonder if I may trespass upon your indulgence, and ask you to step up into my cabin for a few moments?"

Both men gave their ready agreement, and when they were in the cabin with the door closed, and the captain had put generous tots of rum before them, he said: "I hope, sir, you will not think that my mate and me are trifling with you if I ask you to write a few words on my slate."

Plainly surprised by this somewhat strange request, the passenger laughed, and taking the slate and pencil he asked: "How can I refuse to do anything you request, no matter how strange the request may seem at this moment? What shall I write, sir?"

"A few words are all I want," the captain told him. "Suppose you write, *Steer to the nor'west*?"

Still smiling, the passenger complied, and when he had done handed the slate back to the captain. In silence, though inwardly excited, the captain took the slate to his desk and getting the slate on which the words had been so mysteriously written the day before out of the drawer in which he had carefully placed it, put the two side by side on his desk.

After but a quick glance, he let out an exclamation and called Mr Bruce to his side.

"I knew it, sir," the mate said, his voice trembling a little.

Turning to the passenger, the captain handed him the two slates.

"Would you," he asked, "say that both of these specimens are in your handwriting?"

"You know one of them is," the passenger replied, "for you saw me write it. And . . . and this I could also swear to, though I know I did not write it. Sir, what is the meaning of this? Who wrote the other?"

"Ah, that, sir, is more than I can tell you. My mate here, Mr Bruce, told me that he saw you sitting writing it at this very desk shortly after dusk yesterday evening."

On hearing this, the captain of the wreck and the passenger exchanged what seemed to be glances of intelligence and surprise, and then the captain asked, "Did you dream that you wrote on this slate, Mr . . . ?"

"Not that I remember," replied the passenger.

"You speak of dreaming," said Bruce. "May I ask what this gentleman was doing say about half after five yesterday evening?"

"Mr Mate," said the captain, "the whole thing is quite mysterious, and I had intended to speak to you about it as soon as we got a little quiet.

"This gentleman, here, was so exhausted by yesterday afternoon as to be at the end of his tether. We had already lost three passengers, and I hoped, though I feared it, that we should not add a fourth to that number. In mid-afternoon, however, he fell into a deep sleep, and he slept so for two hours and more. In fact, he awoke shortly after six o'clock.

"I was by his side when he came to again, and on seeing me he said, "Captain, we shall be rescued, and that very soon; by sunset tomorrow at the latest." I thought at first that he was still light-headed, as he had been some time before he slept, but then I realized that he was quite rational, so I asked him his reason for making such a statement.

"He then told me that he had dreamed he had been on board a

vessel, and that she was coming to our rescue. He described the vessel's appearance and outward rig, and to our utter astonishment, when your ship hove in sight, she corresponded exactly to his description.

"To be honest, I had not put much faith in what he had said, yet still I hoped there might be something in it, for drowning men you know, captain, will catch at straws. As it has turned out, I cannot doubt it was all arranged in some incomprehensible way by an overruling Providence, so that we might be saved."

After a pause, the other captain said: "Well, gentlemen, there cannot be a doubt that the writing on the slate, let it have come there as it may, saved all your lives. I was steering at the time considerably south of west, and altered my course to the nor'west, and had a look-out aloft to see what might come of it. But you say, sir, you did not dream of writing on a slate?"

"No, sir, I have no recollection whatever of doing so. I got the impression that the ship I saw in my dream was coming to rescue us, but how that impression came I cannot tell. There is another very strange thing about it," he added. "Everything here on board seems to me quite familiar, yet I am certain I was never in your vessel before. It is all a puzzle to me. But what did your mate see?

Bruce then told them the story exactly as I have told it out here, Mr Owen, and I must say, as I said earlier, sir, that knowing Bruce as I did, and knowing that he would not lie even to save his life, I fully agree with their conclusion—that it was certainly a special interposition of Providence which saved them from what seemed a certain death.

"It is certainly a most impressive relation, Captain Clarke," replied Owen. "You almost have me converted, but when you began our discussion you spoke of ghosts. This man was still alive."

"But it was his spirit or ghost that Bruce clearly saw," Clarke insisted.

"But was it, was it, Captain?" Owen asked. "I would be the first to admit that your friend Bruce did see the likeness of the passenger sitting in the captain's arm-chair; but in that case, if the man was alive, as indeed he was, it might have been that somehow he projected his plea to be saved so strongly that in some quite incomprehensible fashion his thoughts went out across the ocean to the nearest vessel ... To be quite frank, Captain, I can't explain it, any more than you can."

"But you still don't believe in ghosts, sir?" Captain Clarke asked.

"To misquote Madame du Deffand, Captain, 'No, but I own they do exist'."

The Haunted House at Hydesville

The hamlet of Hydesville, New York State, was in 1848 a very humble place. It was a cluster of small wooden houses, in one of which lived a farmer named John Fox, his wife, and their two little girls—Margaretta, aged about thirteen, and Catherine, about nine. There were other children out in the world, and one had died in infancy.

The Foxes were a highly respectable family, devout Methodists, and until March, 1848, had led a very normal life. They believed, no doubt, in the Devil, but John Fox was not deterred from taking the little house by rumours that it was "queer". Rapping noises had been heard in it, which had gained it a certain reputation for unpleasantness. After three months of living in it, the Foxes began to hear these raps themselves. Sometimes there was merely a light knocking, but at other times the sounds were louder, and gave the impression of furniture being moved. Margaretta and Katie were very frightened—they insisted on their bed being moved into the bedroom of their parents—but when it was placed there both beds were rocked and shaken by the heavy rain of knockings that broke out.

"I'll find the cause of this, if I have to take the house to pieces," said John to his wife. And they searched every nook and cranny—renewing their efforts when they noticed that the sounds were much stronger at night than by day. But no concealed trickster could be found. Then, on the night of 31 March, there was a new development. The noises had been getting louder and louder, and on the night of 30 March the family had had very little sleep. On the 31st they therefore went to bed early—Mrs Fox "almost sick with tiredness". Hardly had they lain down when the noises began. The elder Foxes groaned; but little Katie, emboldened by the presence of her parents, called out to the unseen presence—whom she obviously imagined as a cloven-hoofed Devil—"Mr. Splitfoot, do as I do!" and she clapped her hands several times. The sound instantly echoed her with a similar number of raps. When she stopped, it stopped. Then Margaretta said: "Now, do just as I do—count one, two, three, four," clapping as she spoke. The rappings echoed her. Then Katie thought of an explanation. "Oh, Mother, I know what it is. Tomorrow is April-Fool day, and it's somebody trying to fool us."

Mrs Fox thought of a test. She asked the unseen rapper to rap out her children's ages, successively. Instantly it obliged, leaving a pause before recording the age of her three-year-old child who had died.

"Is this a human being that answers my questions so correctly? she asked. There was no answer. "Is it a spirit? If it is, make two raps. Two raps smartly followed. Then Mrs Fox's questions elicited the information that the rapper was the spirit of a man who had at the age of thirty-one been murdered in the house, and that his remains were buried in the cellar. He added some details about his family, and said that his murderer would never be brought to justice.

"Will you continue to rap if I call my neighbours?" asked Mrs Fox. The raps indicated that the entity was willing. Accordingly, Mr Fox called in several neighbours, who came to scoff and remained to marvel. One of them, a Mr Duesler, interrogated the spirit, by whom he was told that the murder had taken place in a bedroom about five years before—that it had been committed with a butcher's knife—that the body had been taken on the night after the murder down the cellar stairs and buried ten feet below ground. The victim had been murdered for five hundred dollars, he said.

The awe-struck circle who heard this strange story called in other friends and neighbours, until the house was full. But Mrs Fox, alarmed, took her children away, leaving her husband on guard, while more and more curious neighbours piled in to listen to the noises. They were simple, superstitious people, the folk of Hydesville; the spirit's story was widely believed. It was decided to try to prove it by digging for the remains, and John Fox led a working party to the cellar.

But alas! Although they dug and dug until they came to water and had to stop, nothing came to light. Sceptical glances were cast at the Fox family. Both husband and wife made affidavits, to protect their own reputation. The neighbours, behaving with great good sense, formed themselves into a committee of investigation, recording and collating the facts, and even having the evidence printed within a month. *A Report of the Mysterious Noises Heard in the House of Mr John D. Fox* was published at Canandaigua, New York.

In the summer, when the ground was dry, digging operations began again. This time they were not quite fruitless. There was evidence of *something* having been buried—a plank, some traces of charcoal and quicklime, and some strands of hair and pieces of bone, which a doctor thought came from a human skull. But nothing more evidential was found.

Then another piece of testimony was produced. Four years before, the house had been occupied by a Mr and Mrs Bell, whose hired help had been a girl called Lucretia Pulver. She now came forward and told her story. One day, she said, a travelling pedlar had come to the door—a man of about thirty, wearing a black frock-coat and light-coloured trousers. Lucretia heard him talking to Mrs Bell about his family, and Mrs Bell told her he was an old acquaintance. Soon after he arrived Lucretia was surprised to be dismissed by Mrs Bell, who gave the excuse that she could not afford to keep her. Before going, Lucretia told the pedlar that she would like to buy some things from him, but had no money with her; and he agreed to call at her house with them the next morning. But next morning came without a sign of him, nor did Lucretia ever see him again. Three days afterwards, she was astonished to be asked to return to the Bells' home. A job was a job, however, and she went back to work for them. She noticed, without thinking much of it, that Mrs Bell was re-making some coats, which she said were too large to fit Mr Bell; and that several articles from the pedlar's pack were lying about the house. One evening Mrs Bell sent Lucretia down to the cellar to shut the outer door. In crossing the floor, the girl fell near the centre of it, and landed on uneven, loose earth. Her scream brought Mrs Bell, who laughed at her servant's fright, and said rats must have been busy in the ground. Soon afterwards Mr Bell went to work to fill in the "rat-holes".

There were other strange things about the house—rappings, and the footsteps of somebody who seemed to be walking about but was never seen. Mrs Pulver called and reproached Mrs Bell for letting her daughter be terrorized. Mr and Mrs Bell were not any too comfortable themselves, and after some weeks they left.

After them, a family called Weekman moved in. They too heard the noises and footsteps, and doors opened of themselves. Then a Mrs Lafe, who shared the house, saw a strange man in the bedroom next to the kitchen. She had been in the kitchen for a long time, and had seen nobody pass her. The stranger, she said, was a man in a black frock coat, a black cap, and light pantaloons. "I know of no one like him," she added.

Lucretia's story immediately drew suspicion on Mr Bell, who was by now living at Lyon, New York. Affronted at the rumours, he sent a statement of his personal integrity signed by forty-four people; there was no evidence against him, and the rumours ceased.

But, whoever might be his murderer, the ghost became more active than ever. Poor Mrs Fox's dark hair turned white in a week. As the hauntings were more noticeable when Margaretta and Katie were at home, they were sent away—Margaretta to a brother, David Fox, and Katie to her sister at Rochester, Mrs Fish. The noises followed them. Mrs Fish, a music-teacher, was unable to continue her work. In vain the family prayed with their Methodist friends for divine help and relief. Where the girls went, the spirit went too. Other people, including Leah Fish, began to develop gifts of what was later to be called mediumship, and spirit messages began to be received from other departed people than the original communicator. Hydesville had, in fact, become the birthplace of modern Spiritualism. But that is another story.

It is sad to record that the fame which came to the two Fox sisters, as they grew up, eventually brought ruin to Margaretta, who towards the end of her life became an alcoholic. She confessed publicly that the famous rappings had all been trickery, produced by herself and her sister by means of cracking their toe-joints. But although on her death-bed Margaretta was unable to move hand or foot, a woman doctor who attended her distinctly heard strange, unaccountable knockings.

Many years passed, and the famous haunting of Hydesville was forgotten by all but a few. Both sisters were dead, and the truth or untruth of Margaretta's confession died with them. Or so it seemed, until a news item appeared in the *Boston Journal* for 23 November, 1904.

Some children had been playing in the cellar of an old house at Hydesville—known as "Spook House" from local tales of what had happened there. Suddenly one of the walls had crumbled and fallen, partly burying one child. The rest, terrified, ran for help. Mr William Hyde, the house's owner, came to the rescue and brought other men with him. When they rescued the child from the heap of stones and rubble in which it lay, they found that the collapsed wall was a false one, and had a space between it and the original cellar foundation. In it lay—the headless skeleton of a man, and beside it a pedlar's tin box.

The discovery completely exonerated the Fox sisters of trickery, and corroborated the statement of Lucretia Pulver and the doctor's diagnosis of the bone fragments as being those of a skull. Bell—for the murderer can have been no other—must have cut off his victim's head, attempted to burn it, and then clumsily buried it in quicklime, under the loose earth which Lucretia had noticed. Then, after Lucretia's tumble, he had reburied it and the rest of the body under the false wall.

So, after fifty-six years, the story told by the pedlar's wandering ghost was proved true in every detail; and, as he had prophesied, his murderer was never brought to justice.

The Guardian Ghost

In 1850 there lived in the village of Ringstead, in Northampton-
shire, a butcher with the somewhat outlandish name of Weekly
Ball. He was in his later forties, married with several children.
Broad-shouldered and thick-set, with the florid complexion of the
chronic drinker and misshapen with an incipient paunch, even on
sight he was not, one would have thought, physically attractive.
Add to his uncomeliness a generally known ill-temper, and he was the
last person a young girl would be likely to risk her reputation for.

But the female psychological structure is for ever providing
surprises and even some shocks; and there was one girl at least
who provided both for the worldly-wise inhabitants of Ringstead.
Perhaps if her father had still been alive he would have made her
see sense or so impressed her with his paternal authority that she
would have forgone the consummation of her attraction to the
butcher, though even this is problematical, since her nature was
derived entirely from her father. Her mother was a faded, retiring
woman, worn out before her time by the strain of her late husband's
conjugal demands and the shame of his infidelities, and she had
neither the personality nor the urge to attempt to curb her husband's
traits so blatantly obvious in his daughter.

On the other hand, it would be unfair to attach too great blame
to Mrs Atley for her daughter's amatory non-conformism. Lydia
Atley was in service at the hall. When Weekly Ball first impinged
on her consciousness, she had already been a member of the squire's
household for six years, and at eighteen she had graduated from

maid-of-all-work to second housemaid. She shared a room with the third housemaid, and since her duties kept her occupied from half-past five in the morning until after dinner, except for one afternoon a week and one Sunday in three, she had little opportunity for visiting her mother. Mrs Atley, therefore, was not in a position to bring any great degree of influence to bear on her daughter's development into womanhood, even had she had any great inclination in that direction.

Lydia was a comely girl. Her hair was raven black, which often, as the light caught it, shone with a rich green sheen. Her face was oval, a shape accentuated by the highly set, faintly prominent cheek bones and tapering chin. In the nun's coif, with downcast mien, she would have given the appearance of genuine asceticism, an effect which would have been immediately dispelled when she raised her head and revealed a full moist mouth and large dark eyes which smiled even when she was out of humour. As for the rest of her, it was only too evident, despite the swinging fullness of her mid-Victorian print and her starched apron, that her bosom was ripely firm and her hips roundly supple.

She was not quite eighteen when Weekly Ball first set eyes on her. It had been a chance occurrence. One of his roundsmen had been laid up, and the other had been delayed by an accident to his trap, and it was three o'clock in the afternoon when he realized that the saddle of mutton for the squire's dinner was still hanging from its hook at the back of the shop.

Calling to his happy-go-lucky but submissive wife to keep a look-out for any customer who might come along, he saddled his mare, wrapped up the mutton in a cloth, and mounting with it before him as though he were riding pillion to it, he trotted up to the hall. It was his first visit to the hall for several years. Orders were either given to the roundsman, or a servant with business in the village would call at the shop with them. Regularly on the first of each month the squire's lady would draw up in her carriage, he would go out to her with the account already drawn up, she would scrutinize it, and, always satisfied, since she had "a poor head for figures" and the squire was generous, she would tell her companion to count out into Weekly Ball's hand the sum due. And it was to Weekly Ball's credit that though he could have done so with impunity, he never once attempted nor was tempted to overcharge the hall.

Dismounting at the kitchen door, he knocked. The face of Mrs Knowls, the cook, appeared at the window.

"Come in, Mr Ball," he heard her call faintly to him through the glass.

The kitchen was a large and spacious room. Down the centre stood a vast white scrubbed deal table, and along one of the long walls stretched a dresser on which countless plates and moulds and pans were set out. Practically the whole of the opposite wall was taken up by an immense kitchen range, with ovens on either side.

On one half of the table, on wire trays, lay batches of newly baked scones and cakes. They were still steaming from the oven, and the smell of them filled the kitchen with a heady aroma.

"I was just beginning to be anxious, Mr Ball," Mrs Knowls said. "I thought the impossible had happened at last and you had forgotten. You're only just in time, you know."

The butcher explained, with apologies, the reason for the late delivery, but while he was addressing the cook his gaze was held by one of the two girls who were cleaning numerous brass fire-irons at the far end of the table. They were there by the kindness of the cook, who appreciated their complaints that they could not do their work properly in their own pantry which, having no fire, was today as cold as a tomb.

"Well, no harm's done now you've come," the cook said. "Would you take a glass of elderberry wine, Mr Ball?"

"That's civil of you, Mrs Knowls," he accepted. "Thank you kindly."

"It will keep out the cold, Mr Ball. It's a long time since it's been as cold as this so early in October. Lydia, put the poker in the coals, there's a good girl."

The girl, who had attracted the butcher's attention, left the table and went to the grate, her movement supple and subtly suggestive, at least to a man of Ball's sensitivity to such things. The cook was fetching the wine from the larder, and going over to the range and pretending to warm himself Ball said quietly to the girl, "I don't think I've seen you before. Are you from the village or hereabouts?"

"Yes, Mr Ball. Tom Atley's girl."

"Then I know your mother. She's a customer of mine."

"If spending a few pence weekly makes her that, I suppose she is," the girl agreed pertly.

"How is it I haven't seen you in the village then?"

"Because I don't come down much. My mother lives this side, and I don't get much time off."

"When do you get time off?"

"One afternoon a week. Wednesdays mostly."

"Then you'll be off tomorrow. I'm planning to pick my pippins tomorrow before the hard frost gets them. You know my orchard. If you stop by, I'll give you a basket for your mother."

The girl looked him straight in the eyes, her own eyes shining with amusement and excitement. Mrs Knowls's footsteps could be heard crossing the flagstones of the larder.

"Will you come?" Ball whispered urgently.

With a slight toss of the head and a broad smile, the girl said, "You work fast, Mr Ball . . . Yes, I'll come!"

"Lydie!" the girl at the table exclaimed, but could say no more as Mrs Knowls emerged into the kitchen weighed down by a large unopened flagon of elderberry wine.

"Sorry to have kept you waiting, Mr Ball," the cook said. "I thought—in fact, I'm sure—I had a flagon opened, but like as not Tom Fletcher's finished it off. I'll have a word with him. He'll never make a butler if he can't keep off the liquor."

"You shouldn't make such good wine, Mrs Knowls," Ball remarked with buoyant gallantry.

"Tom Fletcher would drink anything. Besides, I made the wine for all the servants' hall, not just for him," the cook said.

She went to the dresser and took down a pewter tankard from its hook. Having dusted it with her apron, she uncorked the flagon and filled the tankard two-thirds full with blood-red elderberry wine.

"Is that poker ready, Lydia?" she asked.

The girl drew the poker from the fire.

"It's got the glowingest red tip you ever saw, Mrs Knowls," she said, smiling at Ball.

"Bring it here, then, quick. Come along girl, before it goes dull. You know what to do with it? Plunge it straight into the tankard, but be sure it doesn't touch the glass at the bottom."

With a firm, unhesitating movement, the girl followed the cook's instructions. Even when the contact of the red-hot iron with the liquid made a sudden sizzling and sent up a cloud of steam, she did not flinch. The watching butcher noted every action she made, and became aware of an inner tension rising in him.

The girl withdrew the poker from the tankard, and passing so near to him that he caught the special aroma of her, put the iron back on its hook.

"There you are, then, Mr Ball," the cook said. "Mulled elderberry wine will keep the dampness out of any bones."

Ball took up the tankard, and with a graceful bow for one so sturdily built, said, "Your good health, Mrs Knowls . . . ladies!" He took a draught and smacked his lips. "Finer than any other I've ever tasted, Mrs Knowls!" he complimented her. "No wonder Tom Fletcher can't keep away from it."

"Thank you, Mr Ball," the cook beamed with pleasure. "It is my speciality."

As he slowly quaffed from the tankard, though he addressed his inconsequential gossip to the cook, he kept his eyes on the girl who had returned to her work with renewed vigour. From time to time she glanced up at him, her eyes still shining, a faint smile playing about her lips.

When he could no longer reasonably prolong his visit, he took his leave.

Within a short time of his going, the girls, having finished their chore, went up to the room they shared at the top of the house. As they went, they did not speak, but as soon as they were in their room the younger girl burst out, "Lydie, you're not serious about going to old Ball's orchard, are you?"

"Of course I am!" Lydia Atley replied firmly, throwing herself down on her bed. "Why not? My mam could do with some apples."

"It's more than apples he'll be giving you, if you don't watch out. My dad says he's as las . . . lascivious as a young ram."

"Betsy!" Lydia Atley exclaimed in mock horror. "How could you bring yourself to say such a thing. A girl of your age."

"I'm nearly as old as you are, Lydie," the girl protested, "and when you've got six brothers like I have, you have to be as simple as Silly Tommy Hodge not to know what's what."

"Tommy Hodge isn't all that simple by what Mabel Penrose says," Lydia replied.

"Don't change the subject!" the younger girl snapped. "Promise me you won't go."

"I'll certainly promise no such thing!"

"Then let me go with you."

"How can you when your afternoon's Thursday?

"I'll slip out."

"And get caught and lose your place!" Lydia swung her legs off the bed and began to unpin her apron. "Don't worry about me, Betsy dear. I can look after myself."

"You'll get caught, like you thought Ben Ridgeway had caught you a couple of months since."

"I've learned a thing or two since then."

"So you think! Besides, how can you ever think of letting an old man like Weekly Ball even lay a finger on you?"

"He's not old ... not all that old." Lydia's voice changed, and she seemed to be musing to herself. "I know he's not handsome; anything but. But there's something about him. Like and like, I reckon." She stood up, and unbuttoning her dress shrugged it off her shoulders and let it fall about her feet. "Anyhow, I'm tired of wasting my time with fumbling boys who've got no idea what a girl wants. Weekly Ball will know, I'll be bound."

"Please, Lydie, for the last time!" Betsy pleaded.

"Sorry, Betsy dear!" her friend told her. "If you were made like me, you'd know."

So, Lydia Atley met Weekly Ball in his orchard the next afternoon. It was the first of many meetings, not only on Wednesday afternoons, but in the dark winter evenings and the gloaming of summer ones. From time to time, Betsy would try to remonstrate, but to no avail, and presently she became engrossed in her own affair with Lydia's late boy, Ben Ridgeway, the nineteen-year-old son of the head groom.

But then there came a time when Betsy noticed that a change had come over her friend. She no longer chattered, no longer smiled and joked; instead she went about her work in a kind of automatic daze.

Betsy said nothing, though she was sure she knew the reason for the change. She had no desire to taunt her friend; she could only feel pity for her. If the same thing should overtake her, at least Ben Ridgeway could marry her—not that it was likely to happen, because she was keeping Ben at his proper distance, the better to keep him attached—but Weekly Ball was married already, with a slatternly wife and a brood of seven, soon to be eight, to prove it. So she kept her counsel, knowing that if Lydia wanted to tell her what was in her mind she would in her own good time.

So it happened a night or two later, when Betsy went to their room and found Lydia already in bed and sobbing her heart out. Betsy tried to cheer her friend up, still hesitating to reveal that she had guessed. Eventually, when Lydia's sobs only increased the more comfort she received, Betsy did blurt out, "You're in the family way, aren't you?"

Lydia at once stopped weeping and sat up, exclaiming, "How did you know?"

Betsy smiled, "I guessed. It wasn't difficult. It's about the only thing that would lower your spirits."

"He promised me it wouldn't happen. He said he'd see to that. But it has, Betsy. There's no doubt of it."

"Have you told him?"

"No."

"But whyever not? I know he can't marry you, but he's well off. He can afford to help you."

"He won't like it. Not a little bit. He's mean and he's selfish, and ever since he became a churchwarden he's been scared someone will find out about him and me."

"Well, then, I don't know what you're worrying about. Tell him if he won't help you, you'll ask the squire to. Squire'll soon put him in his place. Promise me you'll tell him. Even if he says no, and you don't tell squire, you won't be any worse off than if you keep it to yourself. Anyhow, you won't be able to keep it to yourself much longer, and as soon as it shows the missus won't keep you on. Promise, now."

"You're right, Betsy dear. Sensible as always," Lydia replied. "I promise."

Next evening, Betsy was in bed with the candle still burning, waiting for her friend, when Lydia came quietly in. She could see at once from the change in Lydia's spirits that she had kept her promise.

"What did he say?" she asked.

"He didn't like it," Lydia told her, "but he's promised to give me some money so that I can go away. We've got it all planned. I'm going to give in my notice tomorrow, and next week he'll give me the money."

"What excuse are you going to give for your notice, Lydie?" the practical Betsy asked.

"I'm needed to look after a sick aunt in Northampton, I'll go there and take a room, and he'll come and visit me. He has a friend, a butcher there, who'll give me a job when the baby's come."

So Lydia Atley gave a week's notice, and the night after she left the hall she kept a rendezvous with Weekly Ball at their customary meeting-place—a hut in the butcher's orchard.

It so happened that one of the villagers, Robert Hickens, was taking a short cut down a little-frequented track that ran beside the orchard. He later deposed that as he was passing the hut he heard a woman's voice which he recognized to be Lydia Atley's, saying: "I don't believe you mean to give me any money at all. I've a feeling you mean to kill me, Weekly Ball." Asked why he had said nothing when Lydia Atley disappeared from the village, an embarrassed

Hickens mumbled that he had always been of the opinion that it is best to keep out of other people's business.

After that night, Lydia Atley was never seen alive again. When her mother was asked where her daughter was, she replied that Lydia had left the cottage that evening, her few possessions packed in a wicker basket, saying that she was going to Northampton. She was tired of country life, she had said, and wanted to live in a town. Since this came from her mother, everyone was prepared to accept it as the explanation of Lydia's disappearance from the village.

All might have been put out of mind had not Betsy, in the early weeks of the following spring, allowed herself to be lured to the secluded spot near the butcher's orchard by Ben Ridgeway. There, after a while, Ben began to press his attentions, but as usual, when in Betsy's view he started to be too importunate, she told him that she was not prepared to grant him any further favours until they were married.

"But we're going to be married in June!" Ben exclaimed. "That's only two months away, so why plague ourselves by waiting?"

"Something could happen," Betsy replied firmly.

"But we'd be married before it began to show!" the young man pointed out. "Supposing I say I can't wait? It's not just the birds and the sheep, and the cattle and foxes that get extra lively in the spring, Bet."

"I'm beginning to know that!" Betsy retorted.

Ben changed his approach. Stroking her hair, he said quietly, "Look, my dear, when you've said 'No' before, I've always stopped haven't I? But I needn't have; I'm a good sight stronger than you. Then why do you think I stopped? I've done that to show you I love you."

"I know that, Ben."

"Do you think I'd ask you now if I didn't love you?"

Betsy sighed, and when she did not reply he increased the ardour of his caresses, pleading in whispers that made him sound as if he were moaning with pain, as indeed he was. And suddenly Betsy became aware that she was beginning to suffer, too, and that her resolve was weakening. "It can't matter much now, like he says," she found she was telling herself. "He does love me, and I love him, and we are getting wed in June." Then she had no strength, no desire, to resist him any more; and he knew she had stopped resisting.

All the weeks of longing pent up seemed to burst the banks of his respect for the chasteness of the girl whose arms were about his neck, and whose breath brushed his cheek in encouraging searing waves.

Suddenly, however, his excitement was cut off in mid-course. Taken by surprise by the strength of Betsy's unexpected action, he saw her sit up, and heard her crying out, "Lydie! Lydie!" Then she jumped to her feet and began to run down the track, still calling her friend's name.

He scrambled to his feet, perplexed, and began to hurry after her, but before he came up with her she had stopped, and having looked round as though searching for something or someone, she turned and ran towards him, and when she threw herself into the protection of his arms he found her trembling from head to foot.

"What's up, old girl?" he asked, holding her tightly to him.

"I saw her," the girl wept. "I saw her, Ben! Lydie Atley! She was looking down at me and moving her finger backwards and forwards as though to warn me. When I sat up, she turned away and began to walk down the path; then, just as I was catching her up, she disappeared. Where has she gone?

"You were seeing things, sweetheart!" the young man tried to comfort her. "I didn't see anyone."

"But I saw her! I tell you I saw her! She was warning me I was doing wrong."

"If she'd been walking down the path, I would have seen her, too," Ben Ridgeway insisted, "and I tell you there was no one. Besides, if she'd been there, she would have stopped when you called her. She was your best friend, wasn't she?"

"I tell you I saw her?" the girl persisted. "I'm scared, Ben, please take me back to the hall."

It took several days for Betsy to recover from the experience. She had implored Ben to say nothing to anyone about what had happened, and he had agreed, attributing the whole incident to the inscrutable ways of womenfolk. However, when they met a week later, she saw at once that he was more than ordinarily serious.

"What is it, dear?" she asked.

"There's a tale going round the village," he said. "Vicky Easton's putting it out. She and Charlie Baynes were in the glebe meadow last night, when Vicky cried out and said there was Lydia Atley watching them. I went and had a quiet word with Charlie, and he told me they were going to do what we were doing when it happened. You haven't said anything to anyone, and Vicky's heard, have you, Bet?"

"I haven't told a soul," she assured him.

He scratched his head, puzzled. "Well, I don't know," he said. "Charlie says keep it quiet, because he didn't see anything, like me.

But Vicky says Lydia was standing there, wagging her finger at them, like you said." He laughed and shook his head. "Poor old Charlie's fed up, too,"he grinned,"because that was the end of that, and Vicky says he'll have to wait now until they're wed."

"And so will you, Ben Ridgeway!"Betsy told him firmly.

In May another story was heard in the village of yet another couple in similar circumstances being interrupted by Lydia Atley. Again the man had seen nothing, but the girl had watched the figure walk as far as the churchyard gate, look in for a time and then, on turning away, had disappeared.

By this time there was no point in Betsy and Ben Ridgeway keeping silent, and when yet a fourth couple added their story, it would have been strange indeed if the people of Ringstead had not begun to attribute the otherwise unseen Lydia's appearances to supernatural causes. Though Robert Hickens still kept his counsel, soon everyone was certain that the girl had met an untimely end; and in the secret conversations of the village, the butcher Weekly Ball was being named as Lydia's murderer.

There was no evidence, however. Only Betsy knew of the liaison between Lydia and Ball, and uncorroborated evidence was not enough, while the absence of a body made a direct accusation impossible. .

If Ball knew of the stories which were circulating in the village, he gave no sign of it. Stories of his promiscuity continued to make the rounds, but every Sunday he bore his staff before the Rector, who had chosen him for his warden, at Matins and Evensong.

So fifteen years went by, during which time the legend of Lydia was kept green by her occasional appearances to couples who were in train to cool the intolerable heat of their blood. She appeared only in the light evenings of spring and summer, and sometimes on a Sunday afternoon in winter. But for her obvious preference for the daylight, Ringstead might have become the most chaste village in England.

Then one day in the spring of 1865, Daniel Hobson was hedging and ditching in the lane that ran by Weekly Ball's orchard. The previous winter, a nearby stream had overflowed its course and had tumbled into the ditch which skirted one side of the lane. It had never happened before, and when the ditch had carried the water into the churchyard, so that two or three vaults near the gate had been flooded, the rector had consulted the squire, and the latter had given instructions that next hedging-and-ditching time the ditch was to be dug out and deepened, so that if the stream overflowed again the ditch would contain the surplus.

The task of doing this had been allotted to Daniel Hobson, and it was while he was engaged upon it, not far from the hut in Weekly Ball's orchard, that he uncovered the skeleton of a woman. In the natural order of things, an inquest was ordered, and at it Dr James, who was also the coroner, informed the jury that the skeleton was that of a young woman, not yet fully mature, and that the lower jaw had two teeth missing.

Betsy was not the only acquaintance of Lydia Atley who knew that she had had two teeth missing. Several members of the jury did also, and despite all attempts of the coroner to deter them by pointing out that the evidence was too slight, they found the skeleton to be that of Lydia Atley, that she had been murdered and that the man who had murdered her was Weekly Ball, the butcher. Nothing Dr James could say to them could make them bring in the open verdict he advised, or withdraw the name of Weekly Ball, and he had no alternative but to register their findings officially, and automatically inform the authorities.

The sheriff's officers were equally required to make an investigation, and to every lawyer's surprise they decided that the evidence, though circumstantial, warranted the arrest of the butcher on a charge of murder. So he was committed by the magistrates, the squire and the rector, to the next Northampton assizes.

Weekly Ball took the matter seriously enough to engage one of the most astute lawyers in the county town, who in turn engaged the services of one of the best pleaders on the circuit.

Both these lawyers comforted their client with their opinion: "You have no cause for fear, Mr Ball. The Grand Jury are bound to throw out the indictment."

To these gentlemen's surprise, and to the surprise of many others, however, the Grand Jury returned a True Bill, and it was just as well that Weekly Ball had spared no expense for his defence. After a hearing lasting two days, at which Betsy Ridgeway, now a matron with five children who proved that their father had eventually assuaged his particular thirst, and Robert Hickens, were the principal witnesses, the butcher was acquitted. The chief factor in his acquittal was the discovery by his counsel that not far from the spot where the skeleton had been found there had formerly been a traditional gipsy burial ground, and he successfully argued that there was nothing to prove that the bones turned up by Daniel Hobson were not those of a gipsy girl who had died of natural causes and been buried there by her tribe.

The people of Ringstead, convinced of the rightness of their own convictions, could not accept this verdict. Though they might not be able to avenge the life of the girl with the life of the butcher, they could refuse to have him any longer among them. Weekly Ball recognized the power of their opinion, and wisely sold up and left the county.

As for Lydia Atley, the burial of her bones in the consecrated ground of the churchyard with the full honours of the church was not sufficient to calm her spirit. For several years thereafter she prevented, by materialization at the crucial moment, the conception of many a potential inhabitant of Ringstead on the wrong side of the blanket.

But as the years went by, her appearances became fewer and fewer. The last time she was seen was in 1874, when, with poetic justice, she interrupted the midsummer-eve celebrations of Isaac Ridgeway, Betsy's eldest.

Charles Kean's Ghost Story: "Nurse Black"

Charles Kean and his wife Ellen were the leading lights of the English stage in the 1850s—London's most eminent actor-managers. Both were enthusiastic antiquarians, and it must have been gratifying to them when an authentic ghost-story occurred in their own family circle. For years after the actual happening, the Keans would tell it, with great dramatic effect, and every assurance to their listeners of its absolute truth.

Mrs Kean's sister, Ann Tree, had married John Kemble Chapman, ex-theatre manager and a well-known London publisher. Their family was large—eleven children—and finding London unhealthy for the younger ones they decided to move out to the country.

The house they chose was in Cheshunt, Hertfordshire. Owned by Sir Henry Meux, it was let to them furnished. The number of rooms was ample, even for their many children and servants—for a comfortable household in those days included a staff of at least eight. There were good grounds, extensive lawns, and stout trees for the more adventurous children to climb. Altogether Mrs Chapman, surveying her new home, was very pleased with it.

Like her sister, she appreciated picturesque antiquity, and of this there was plenty. The house was about two hundred years old, built some time in the early seventeenth century. Ancient oak beams supported its ceilings, the fireplaces in the best rooms were carved with elaborate and fantastic designs. Not only was there a fine, broad, central staircase, but two others, spiral and break-neck, for the use of servants. The original diamond-paned windows remained, some scratched with the initials of previous owners; and a wealth of sound panelling kept the house snug and draught-free. A complete nursery suite was available for the children and their staff, a head nurse and two assistants, and the children were delighted to discover above it a range of attic rooms, in which they could play games, dress up and revel noisily to their hearts' content.

As with many fortunate country dwellers, John Chapman found himself inundated with friends in need of a weekend rest and the benefit of country air. Both he and his wife were social, hospitable characters, and it was well known among their London friends that they could always be counted on for hospitality and cheerful entertainment. Particularly so, as John Chapman spent several nights a week in London, in order to attend to his business, and liked his wife to have the pleasure of lively company as often as possible, to off-set the evenings she spent with no one to talk to but her elder children. Rooms were always kept ready for guests, and Ann Chapman never complained when they arrived unexpectedly. She was a practical, well-balanced woman, capable and sensible; and John frequently congratulated himself that he had not married a specimen of the feeble and helpless femininity so much in fashion at that time.

Ann did not employ a housekeeper, preferring to see to household details herself. Always, when guests were expected, she supervised the preparations, and undertook a last-minute inspection of the rooms to be occupied. The best of these, reserved for her husband's more important business acquaintances, was known as the Oak Bedroom—so called from its richly-carved oak panelling, and from the large four-poster bed, also made of oak, with hanging curtains embroidered with a design of oak-leaves and acorns. The room was dark and possibly a little forbidding, but was certainly impressive, and Ann insisted that it should always be kept in perfect order.

One autumn evening, as dusk was coming on, she went up to the Oak Bedroom with a pile of aired linen. John was bringing home an author friend, whose work he wanted to discuss in the peace of his own home rather than in the bustle of a Fleet Street office. The maid responsible for the linen stores was new, and Ann did not trust her to make the bed up as it should be made.

The lock on the Oak Bedroom door was old and strained, and Ann had some difficulty in turning the handle, cumbered as she was with an armful of sheets and pillow-cases. Once in the room, she put down her bundle and looked round for a candle to light. In this dark room it was hardly possible to make the bed as neatly as it should be made.

But as she stretched out her hand for the match-holder, she stopped short. She was not alone in the room. By the far window stood a woman. Ann took in at a glance that she was young and slender, with long dark hair down her back. She was dressed in what seemed to be a white shawl or wrapper over a silk petticoat—Ann particularly noticed how the fading light from the window caught the shine of the silk. The girl was leaning forward eagerly, looking through the window, as if at someone in the garden below.

Almost without conscious thought, Ann remembered that the servants were all at tea and the children in the nursery. It could not be any of them. There remained the possibility that a stranger had somehow got into the house and wandered upstairs; but, without knowing why, Ann dismissed this idea at once. She felt, as she afterwards put it, that she was seeing something she ought not to have seen—something that ought not to have been there—and with a sudden shudder of horror, she covered her eyes with her hands. When she uncovered them, the figure had vanished.

By this time her skin was cold with panic. But she was not the kind of woman to let fear stop her from carrying out a task. With shaking hands, she unfolded the linen, stripped back the bed coverings, and made up the bed ready for the night, turning in corners and smoothing down pillows as though nothing out of the ordinary had happened.

She said nothing to anyone about her experience, even to her husband when he came home that night. Next morning she looked up anxiously as their guest entered the breakfast-room, wondering what he might have to say—or even whether he might sharply ask for a carriage to take him back to London at once. But he seemed calm and cheerful, and congratulated his hostess on the comfort of his bed and the peace of his room. Ann told herself that she had suffered from an optical illusion. Of course there had been no figure there. How could there have been?

It was all the more of a shock to her when, some days later, a young nursery-maid, Kitty Brocket, came to her shaking and crying, with a tale of having seen something awful. It was difficult to get sense out of the girl, but with patient questioning Ann got her to say what the trouble was. She had been going down the lobby in the kitchen quarters, taking the nursery rubbish to the back door, when she had seen a face at the small window which gave on to the yard outside. Kitty found it difficult to explain in what way the face frightened her; but Ann gathered from her confused account that it was the face of an old woman, hideously ugly, with some kind of old-fashioned cap on the hair and an expression of awful malignance.

Ann had no wish to encourage the girl's fears. It must have been a gipsy, she said—there were plenty in that part of the country. In that case, Kitty pointed out, how could she have got into the yard at all? There was no way into it except through the kitchen, and Cook would never have let a gipsy past her. Ann had to admit that this was true. To satisfy Kitty, she went down with her, and together they looked through the small window where the face had been seen. The yard was empty. Flagstones, a pair of clothes-props, and a pump were all that was to be seen in it. They visited Cook, who confirmed that she had had no callers that morning, and would never have let such people in. Ann hastily agreed with her that young girls were very fanciful—Kitty must have been deceived by some trick of the light.

Two nights later, another tale was brought to Ann. The house-parlour-maid had been disturbed in the night by loud noises, like someone beating with an iron bar on the pump in the yard, which her bedroom overlooked. The children's nurse confirmed that she had heard the same sound on the previous night, when she had gone down to the kitchen to heat some milk.

The next story came from the nursery. Little Maria, who was not usually a nervous or imaginative child, complained that when she had been lying awake a very ugly lady had looked at her round the edge of the nursery door. Her mother assured her that it was a dream. If only she could have believed herself that it had been!

All this week John Chapman had spent in London. Ann was more than relieved to think that he would be home for the weekend on Friday night. The strain was beginning to tell on her of keeping a cheerful face in front of the family and the servants, for fear of spreading panic. Superstitious country girls were only too ready to entertain tales of haunting, and Ann might very well find herself faced with a staff determined to give notice in a body. Besides, there might be some reasonable explanation for the manifestations. In a final attempt to clear up the mystery, she called the servants together and told them, as casually as possible, that gipsies were rumoured to be in the neighbourhood and that it would be as well to search the house thoroughly, in case one had concealed himself somewhere in order to carry out a robbery. Dutifully, if apprehensively, they dispersed—opening every cupboard, tapping every panel, exploring every outhouse and the darkest corners of the cellars. But no trace was found of any gipsy—not greatly to Ann's surprise.

When John Chapman arrived home she was waiting, prepared to tell him everything that had happened. But he was not alone; a Mr Hall, a member of the publishing firm, had returned with him for the weekend. Ann welcomed the visitor, and after making sure that he would be happily occupied in her husband's study, went upstairs to prepare the Oak Bedroom.

In the bustle of her husband's homecoming her preoccupation with the "hauntings" had temporarily been banished. She thought of nothing beyond sheets and warming-pans as she tripped up the broad staircase, and when she heard footsteps behind her turned to see who it might be.

But there was nothing, nobody; only an empty staircase, and the shadowy hallway below.

Panic seized her, as she hurried downstairs again, and took refuge in the cheerful, noisy day nursery until it was time to go down to supper. The meal proceeded pleasantly enough, and the gentlemen retired to the study with port and cigars, while Ann occupied herself with her needlework. A few moments later there was a tap at the door. The house-parlour-maid, a middle-aged woman called Mrs Tewin, entered, pale-faced and shaken out of her usual calm. She, too, had a story of footsteps—footsteps which had followed her all the way upstairs to the Oak Bedroom, and into it. When she stopped by the fireplace, and put down the warming-pan she was carrying, the steps also stopped. Mrs Tewin, who had been the first person to hear the strange knockings some nights before, was thoroughly frightened, and wished to give her notice.

Ann soothed her, and told her to reconsider her decision in the morning, when she had slept on it, and Mrs Tewin, fortified by a little brandy-and-water, took herself nervously to bed.

That night, Ann told her husband everything. Many men would have laughed and told her not to be ridiculous. But John Chapman came of a theatrical family, and like all in the world of the theatre he was prepared to believe in the supernatural. To Ann's great relief, he promised to arrange his work so that he could stay at home during the following week, and investigate the mystery for himself.

He was not disappointed. Within the next few days the footsteps were heard again, by several of the servants and two of the elder children—soft, steady, infinitely menacing. They were heard not only on the staircase and in the Oak Bedroom, but in other parts of the house. Lying in bed one night, Ann heard them coming up to the door—she leapt out of bed, threw open the door—to find the landing completely empty. The next night John saw her putting something under her pillow as they were retiring to bed. He asked what it might be, and Ann silently produced a loaded pistol. Her husband was horrified, and pointed out that though she showed a brave spirit in arming herself against the intrusions, she would make no impression upon a ghostly visitant with a bullet, and might very well shoot some harmless passer-by of flesh and blood. Ann saw the sense of this, but insisted on keeping the pistol within reach.

By now she had ceased to pretend in front of the servants that nothing unexplainable was happening. A spirit of dread had crept through the house, and the servants took to moving about the house in droves, like wild animals herding together against a common enemy. The children caught the infection of fear, especially the two older girls, Patty and Maria; and the younger children began to be nervous and fretful, particularly after the ugly old woman was seen again in the dark night nursery. As the servants sat at dinner one day the latch of the door lifted, and the door slowly opened—to admit Nobody—and then quietly closed itself again, at which one of the maids fainted and the girl Kitty Brocket went into violent hysterics.

John Chapman, hearing of this, determined to share the servants' dinner next day in case the phenomenon repeated itself. Exactly the same thing occurred, and though he ran at once to the door and examined it, there was nothing to explain the silent opening and shutting.

That afternoon he was reluctantly obliged to return to town, first making his wife promise that she would have one of the maids to share her bedroom. Willingly enough, she chose Mrs Tewin, who was to sleep in a single bed in the corner of the Chapmans' bedroom.

About one o'clock in the morning Ann was roused by agonized muttering from the other bed: "Wake me! Wake me!" Mrs Tewin was saying, her eyes tight shut and her face working with agitation. Ann leapt from her own bed and shook the woman awake. Mrs Tewin thanked her earnestly for rousing her from a dreadful dream she had had, in which she was conscious of having been asleep, but quite unable to wake herself.

She had dreamt, she said, that she was in the Oak Bedroom, in bed. By the window a young woman was standing, pale and dishevelled, with long dark hair, and dressed in an old-fashioned white robe. She had her back against the wall and was staring across the room at another woman, who stood over on the fireplace side of the bed. The sight of this woman, said Mrs Tewin, filled her with indescribable fear—not merely because of her extreme ugliness but because of a dreadful malignancy in her expression. Mrs Tewin noticed that she too was dressed in old-fashioned clothes, with a frilled cap on her scanty grey hair.

"What have you done with the child, Emily? What have you done with the child?" she asked the young woman, in a mocking tone.

"Oh, I did *not* kill it!" replied the girl. "He was preserved, and grew up, and joined the —— Regiment, and went to India."

Then the young woman drew nearer to the bed and spoke to the sleeper directly. "I have never spoken to mortal before," she said, "but I will tell you all. My name is Miss Black, and this old woman is Nurse Black. Black is not her name, but we call her so because she has been so long in the family."

Here the old woman interrupted the speaker by coming up and laying her hand on the dreaming Mrs Tewin's shoulder, saying something which she could not afterwards remember—for, feeling a burning pain in her shoulder where the phantom hand touched her, she had been aroused enough to know that she was dreaming, and had called out to her mistress to waken her.

Next morning Ann lost no time in making inquiries in Cheshunt for anything that might be known about the house and its history. At last, an old inhabitant was able to tell her that seventy or eighty years before, about 1775, the house had been tenanted by a Mrs Ravenhall, who had a niece named Miss Black living with her. Nothing else was recalled about them.

It says much for Ann Chapman's courage that she voluntarily spent a night alone in the Oak Bedroom, after hearing this. Again she saw the young woman in white—this time standing in one corner of the room, weeping and wringing her hands, and looking down mournfully at the floorboards. Next day a carpenter was called in to take up the boards; but whatever had lain underneath them had been taken away.

As time went by, the disturbances began to grow less, and finally died away altogether, to the relief of the Chapmans. But one more strange thing was to happen. Some years after the manifestations, John Chapman was compelled by reasons of business to leave Cheshunt and remove his family back to London. A few days before they were due to leave Ann awoke one morning to see standing at the foot of her bed a dark-faced man in a workman's clothes, with a fustian jacket and a red scarf round his neck. As she looked at him, he vanished. John Chapman lay beside her asleep, and saw nothing, and she did not tell him of the incident.

A few days later it was found that the supply of coals had run out, and that more were needed to keep the family warm until the removal. John Chapman said that he would order them that day on his way to London. Next morning, Ann congratulated him on having remembered the commission; but he replied, with surprise, that it had entirely slipped his memory. None of the servants had ordered the coals, and Ann, thoroughly puzzled, decided to go into the village and make inquiries herself. The coal-merchant told her that he had indeed sent the coals, in response to an order given by a dark man, wearing a fustian jacket and a red scarf, whom he did not know but took for a new servant of the Chapmans.

It was with immense relief that John and Ann drove away finally from the haunted house of Cheshunt, and not until they arrived at their new home did John tell his wife that he had heard of several previous tenants who had been driven out by the uneasy spirits of the unhappy young mother and the evil Nurse Black.

Ghosts of the Mutiny

The Indian Mutiny, that great revolt of the Bengal native army in 1857, was a bloody and treacherous business undertaken by violent men, and involving the brutal murder of many harmless civilians. So many women and children were horribly slaughtered that the reputation of Herod pales beside that of some of the mutineers.

It is not surprising—especially in a country noted for legends and mysticism—that supernatural echoes of the Mutiny were heard for long after it was over. Nearly all involved violent haunting. Such was the case of the Haunted Palace, visited about 1890 by a government official, Mr Gerard, and his wife. The Gerards had reached the town of Hissar, where, on behalf of the Government, they exchanged hospitality with the Europeans living there.

Their visit coincided with Christmas. On Christmas Day they were invited to dinner by Colonel Robinson, an officer holding a staff appointment. The party was small—the Gerards, Colonel and Mrs Robinson, their elder and younger sons, and the Civil Surgeon of the station. The Palace, where the Robinsons lived, had once been the residence of the Rajahs of Hissar; but after the Mutiny the then Rajah was removed and the Palace taken over by the British Government.

Mr and Mrs Gerard were struck by the strange approach to the Robinson's apartments, which were in the upper part of the Palace. The huge doors on the ground-floor level were boarded up and had obviously not been used for a very long time. An iron staircase like a fire-escape, attached to the outside wall, led up to a long, high hall, running along the front of the building, and containing many high windows. Parallel with this was a similar room, used by the Robinsons as a dining room. Next to this came the drawing-room, and at the far end of it a door led into the bedroom, and another from the bedroom into the bathroom.

Dinner was a pleasant, informal affair, and Mrs Gerard remarked to her host that they must have an excellent cook. She was surprised when he replied that this treasure was shortly leaving them, in spite of raised wages and other inducements. A new one, he sighed, would have to be recruited from somewhere outside the district.

This struck Mrs Gerard as very odd, and she inquired why a local servant would not do. "Because nobody for miles around would take service here," answered Colonel Robinson. "We were told so when we came, but we didn't believe it." Mrs Gerard expressed great surprise that such a pleasant couple could not keep their servants. The Colonel, smiling, told her that it was not their employers the servants did not like—it was the Palace. "It's haunted, you see," he explained.

Mrs Gerard raised her eyebrows, and replied that it was just like superstitious native servants to believe such nonsense. *She* didn't believe in such things, and she hoped Colonel Robinson did not, either. He raised his eyebrows and smiled at her; and Mrs Gerard, slightly annoyed, called across the table to Mrs Robinson that the Colonel was teasing her with a stupid ghost-story.

Mrs Robinson, who had been chatting away gaily enough to the Surgeon, immediately stopped, and looked nervously at her little boy, who, at the mention of ghost-stories, had become all eyes and attention.

"It's true enough, unfortunately," she said, "but I'll tell you about it later, if you don't mind."

Mrs Gerard instantly turned to Colonel Robinson and apologized for mistaking his intention. "It would not be the first time I've been disbelieved!" he told her.

After dinner, Mrs Robinson and Mrs Gerard, the only ladies of the party, moved into the drawing-room, while the gentlemen remained to smoke and drink their port. Mrs Robinson's small son was taken to bed by his ayah, though he would obviously have preferred to stay and listen to whatever fascinating story his mother was going to tell. As soon as the ladies were seated by the drawing-room fire, Mrs Robinson offered to tell her guest the truth about the manifestations that made it impossible for her to keep servants; and Mrs Gerard, sipping her coffee, listened attentively.

The Robinsons had moved to Hissar fifteen years before. They were pleased with the appointment, but less pleased to find that no arrangements had been made about quarters for them. At last they decided to move into part of the old Palace, now shut up and deserted. It was well-built and weather-tight, and only wanted thoroughly cleaning and airing. The Robinsons could make themselves a splendid flat from the four large parallel rooms, and the smaller ones would easily adapt into bedroom and bathroom.

So far so good. The cleaning and refurbishing of their apartments proceeded, and they were able to move in very speedily. But, they were told, they would never keep servants—the place was badly haunted—"wicked things had been done there"—and nobody who knew the Palace would work in it. Like most Europeans of their day and age, Colonel and Mrs Robinson were not prepared to take this seriously. They imagined that somebody wanted them to stay away from the Palace—perhaps somebody who wanted to use it as a headquarters for some nefarious undertaking. So they laughed, and moved in.

Rumour proved all too true. No native of Hissar would agree to join their staff; and the old servants they had brought with them soon left, with feeble excuses. Undefeated, and still healthily sceptical, the Robinsons recruited servants from other districts, and paid them well. The household at the old Palace settled down into a well-organized routine, and the Robinsons were very content with their dwelling. "You see, dear, it's all nonsense about this haunting," said the Colonel to his wife.

Then came an unpleasant surprise. One night Mrs Robinson had gone to bed as usual, and was just hovering between waking and sleep when she heard what she thought to be her husband fumbling about with her bunch of keys at the locked wardrobe. She remembered, sleepily, that she had put her keys and watch under her pillow before going to bed, as she always did—her husband must have got up and removed them while she was dozing. Hardly bothering to open her eyes, she called to ask him what he was doing.

There was no answer; the rattling noise continued. Mrs Robinson roused herself and sat up—to see her husband, not at the wardrobe, but beside her in bed, staring at her. He, too, had heard the noise, and had thought it was his wife, rattling her keys. To prove that he had been wrong, she put her hand under the pillow, and withdrew the keys. The Robinsons stared blankly at each other.

Meanwhile, the sound grew louder. It seemed to them now more like the rattling of chains than of keys. Nor did they hear it alone—their two great dogs, who always slept in their room, had stirred, risen, and were now growling in their corner. The noise was certainly alarming, for to the rattling was now added a dragging sound, like metal trailing on stone, and a heavy, ominous thudding like gigantic footsteps.

"What on earth can it be?" said Colonel Robinson. "Someone's playing tricks—that's it. I told you they wanted to keep us out of this place. Well, I'm getting up to find out."

Slipping out of bed, he turned up the lamp, put on his dressing-gown and placed his loaded revolver in the pocket of it. His wife began to reach for her dressing-gown.

"I must come with you! Don't leave me alone in here, George!"

Gently he pushed her back, telling her that if there was going to be a physical struggle, and perhaps shooting, she would be better out of it. She remained sitting on the edge of the bed, trembling violently, and watching her husband as he took up his hurricane-lamp and opened the door, calling the dogs to come with him. But there was no need. As soon as the door was opened they rushed past him and out of the room, growling deeply. Then Mrs Robinson was alone in the room.

It seemed to her that she had been there for hours, though in fact it was not more than a few minutes, when a remarkable thing happened—the strange sounds stopped, suddenly, after drawing so near and growing so loud that Mrs Robinson felt she would be deafened by them. There was absolute silence, and she felt this to be as frightening as the previous noises.

Then, through the open door, came the dogs; not the bold creatures that had rushed out ahead of the Colonel, but beaten, crawling things, dragging themselves along, their eyes rolling and their bodies shaking with fear. Mrs Robinson had never seen them look like this before. They appeared to have had a terrible shock, which had sent them almost out of their minds. She approached them and tried to comfort them; but they crawled out of her reach and hid under the bed, where they crouched, whining. Then Colonel Robinson returned.

"Whatever has happened?" asked his wife. "What have you seen?"

"These two poor dogs have seen something," he replied, "but I haven't. I can't understand it. As I walked from room to room the sounds seemed to come nearer and nearer——"

"Just as they did in here," she put in.

"——until when I came to the dining-room they stopped, all in a moment. Before I got to it I met the dogs coming back—as you see them now, poor things. I don't know what all this means, Mary, but I intend to find out."

And he lost no time in calling up the servants to make a thorough search of the Palace. All night the Robinsons and the staff tramped up and down with lanterns, through great empty rooms, up and down winding staircases, into cellars and dungeons. Not one trace of the night's activity rewarded them—not a single footprint in the dust. Eventually they gave up the search and went, exhausted, to bed.

When they woke next morning, hardly believing in the strange events of the night, a dreadful confirmation met their eyes. Under their bed lay the two beautiful dogs, cold and dead. They had died of sheer fright.

The Robinsons' distress was great. They had hardly taken in the tragedy when the first of their servants gave notice. After him came another, and another—all with excuses involving sick parents or family troubles. By the end of the day not one was left.

Now that the Robinsons were alone in the Palace, the noises of the night returned with a regularity that amounted to persecution. Always they were the same—beginning softly, with a light metallic rattling, and increasing to a dreadful clashing and tramping. It seemed to occur always on a festival or holiday, whether native or English. The Robinsons became partly resigned to it, though they never ceased to cling to each other in apprehension when the terrible crescendo began. One night, Mrs Robinson, who had been lying with the bedclothes over her head, trying to shut out the sound, suddenly sat up and clutched her husband's arm.

"Elephants!" she exclaimed. "George, it's elephants!"

Her husband stared. "How on earth can it be elephants? Where?"

"How do I know where? Phantom ones, I suppose. But it *is* elephants, dragging chains and tramping. Can't you hear it?"

He listened, and finally agreed.

It was not long before Mrs Robinson's guess was confirmed. A native who was not too frightened to talk to them told them the dreadful legend of the man who had been Rajah of Hissar at the time of the Mutiny. An inhumanly cruel man, in the tradition of the terrible Indian rulers of the eighteenth century, he had elephants specially trained to destroy people. If any of his many wives angered him, he would have them shut into the underground dungeons of the Palace; then the elephants were admitted to them, and either trampled them to death or caught them up and dashed out their brains against the dungeon walls.

When the Mutiny broke out, the Rajah prepared to treat the hated British as he had treated his own people. As the rebellious troops swept in from Delhi, many Europeans fled. But those who were unable to escape were seven men and their wives, with fifteen small children and two Eurasian native servants.

Desperate, they risked the Rajah's evil reputation and begged him for help. He would give it, he said; they should be safe. Let them only take refuge with him in the Palace and nobody should touch them. Thankfully they came, the pathetic little band, babies in arms, small children led by the hand, expectant mothers and anxious husbands. They were brought up to the apartments later used by the Robinsons, and shut into the room at the end—the Robinsons' future bathroom. Then the Rajah's soldiers burst in and hacked them to pieces, leaving not a single one alive.

The British relief troops, when they arrived, found the room ankle-deep in blood, corpses heaped on top of one another, the walls sticky with brains and blood; and—almost worst of all—sixteen of the corpses were headless, and the heads, in a graded line, were placed mockingly on the mantelpiece of the room to be used by the Robinsons as a drawing-room.

Mrs Robinson ended her story. Her guest, who had been listening in appalled silence, looked up at the mantelpiece, now cheerful with flowers and family photographs.

"And do you still hear the sounds now?" she asked.

"No. It seemed as though, having got us on our own and nearly frightening us to death, they had served their purpose. But none of the servants will believe that, of course."

"I wonder why it was only the elephants you heard, and not—the other sounds?"

"We don't know. But I thank God we were spared those."

Mrs Gerard remembered the great barred doors that had led to the basement—and the dungeons—glanced up again at the mantel-piece, and shuddered deeply. The door opened, and she looked towards it in fear; but it was only the gentlemen who entered, rosy and good-tempered from their port.

*　　*　　*　　*　　*

Another strange story of the Mutiny concerned Mrs Torrens, widow of General Torrens. In 1856 she was living at Southsea, Hampshire. Her daughter had married a Captain Hayes and gone out to India with him. Mrs Torrens naturally regretted that she was so far away, but knew her to be happy and had no fears for her future.

One night, however, her attitude was abruptly changed. She dreamed, vividly, that she was in India, in the town where her daughter's husband was stationed. There seemed to be something like a revolution in progress. Dark-faced natives were surging in the streets, shouting and waving guns and other weapons—some of which, Mrs Torrens noticed with horror, had blood on them.

As is the way of dreams, she was not particularly surprised that nobody seemed to notice her presence or to offer to molest her in any way. Nor did it seem strange to her that she knew by instinct how to get to Captain Hayes's barracks, though the situation had never been described to her. In a few minutes she was there. The building was encircled by a mass of yelling natives, all apparently bent on murdering those within. And yet Mrs Torrens passed unharmed through them, entered the building, and found herself guided to the quarters of Captain Hayes.

To her intense horror, she found the Captain and her daughter had already been attacked by the insurgents, and were struggling wildly in the grasp of five or six savage-looking Sepoys. Now came the most terrible part of her dream. She found herself quite helpless to move, to call out, or to make any sort of impression on the attackers or the attacked. She could only stand there, paralysed by her dream-state, and watch the indescribably horrible death of her daughter and son-in-law. So ghastly was it that she awoke, trembling and in a cold sweat.

So dreadfully vivid had been the dream that she could not feel the usual relief of a sleeper waking from nightmare. The terrible impression remained with her, and prompted her to sit down and write to her daughter, urging her to come home at once. Posts in those days were slow, and it was some weeks before the reply came. To her disappointment, it was to say that Mrs Hayes felt she could not leave her husband in India on such slight grounds; but she took her mother's warning seriously enough to promise to send her children to England. Before very long they arrived, and Mrs Torrens's mind was relieved on their account, at least, although she had not seen them in her dream.

1857 came, and with it the outbreak of the Indian Mutiny. When Captain Hayes and his young wife were reported to have been brutally murdered, Mrs Torrens's distress held no quality of shock, for she already knew too well the manner of their death. The supernatural warning had been true in every particular.

*   *   *   *   *

Presumably the dream of Mrs Torrens had been sent to her by the forces responsible with kindly intentions. An equally good spirit operated in the case of a Captain's wife whose fate was happier than that of Mrs Hayes. She had been warned, at her husband's quarters in Meerut, of the approach of the mutineers, and was packing, ready for flight. Suddenly the door of her bedroom flew open, and there entered a terrible figure—a huge, wild-faced Sepoy, waving a blood-stained axe. Mrs X, like Mrs Torrens in her dream, was rooted to the spot; but with fear, not with the helpless immobility of the dreamer. She managed to pray, however, for the habit of prayer was strong in her and she knew that she stood more in need of help now than ever before.

Time was suspended as they faced each other—the giant Sepoy, a dreadful genie-figure drunk with blood-lust, and the small Englishwoman, half-dressed, her pathetic possessions strewn at her feet. Then an extraordinary thing happened. The floor-board beneath her shook and creaked, as though somebody tremendously heavy had stepped in front of her, and she felt something brush against the front of her skirt. The Sepoy's grinning face changed. If it were possible for a brown face to turn pale, his paled in an instant, and his eyes widened with horror. For a moment he faced his ghostly antagonist; then turned and fled from the room.

Mrs X fell on her knees and prayed once more. But this time it was a prayer of deep thankfulness.

The Artist's Ghost Story

Charles Dickens was fascinated by ghost stories, and never lost the chance of telling one in print. In the magazine *All the Year Round*, which he edited, he published one told to him by an acquaintance. Some time later he received another version of it, much fuller and more circumstantial, from a Mr Heaphy, an artist, saying that this was the true story and he was prepared to vouch personally for all its details. Dickens questioned him closely, and was satisfied with his answers. He reprinted it, as told by Mr Heaphy, and described it as "so very extraordinary, so very far beyond the version I have published, that all other like stories turn pale before it".

This is the story Mr Heaphy told:

I am an artist. One morning, a few years ago, I was at work in my studio when a military acquaintance of mine dropped in for a chat. I was not sorry to be interrupted, and pressed him to stay to luncheon, which he did willingly. While we were still sitting over our sherry, a young model arrived for a sitting which I had booked with her; but I was in no mood for work, and told her to go away and come back the following day—I would, of course, recompense her for loss of time. She left, but in a few moments was back, to ask hesitantly whether I could possibly manage to pay her at least a part of her money then and there, as she was rather short that day. Of course, I was only too pleased to do this, and she went away happily. My friend and I resumed our chat, but again there was an interruption. This time my visitors were strangers.

They introduced themselves as a Mr and Mrs Kirkbeck, of

Yorkshire, and were an agreeable and obviously well-to-do middle-aged couple. I inquired how they had found me, and they answered that they had heard of me previously but had forgotten my address, which had just been given to them by my model, whom they had met in the street. They had seen a portrait of mine, and admired it—would I be prepared to come to their country home, and paint themselves and their family? Naturally, I was delighted at the chance of such a commission—they made no objection to the fairly steep price I named, and asked if they could look round the studio and choose the style of picture they would prefer. My military friend, something of a wag, took it upon himself to show them round and dilate on my artistic merits in a way that I would have been ashamed to do myself—but the Kirkbecks, simple souls, listened reverently and seemed deeply impressed. The commission was mine. All that remained was to settle the date of my visit to them, and we found a mutually convenient one in the first week of September. Mr Kirkbeck then gave me his card, and he and his wife left the studio, followed soon after by my friend.

Left alone, I looked at Mr Kirkbeck's card, and was surprised and disappointed to find that it contained only his name—no address. I looked in the Court Guide, of which I happened to have a copy, but the name did not appear in that. Well, I thought, the Kirkbecks would no doubt realize soon enough what had happened, and get in touch with me. I put the card in my desk and forgot the whole affair for the time being.

When September came, I had heard nothing more from the Kirkbecks, and left London to carry out a series of painting engagements in the north of England. Towards the end of the month, I was dining at a country-house on the edge of Yorkshire and Lincolnshire—not, I must add, with people I already knew, but because the friend with whom I was staying had been invited, and had asked if I might go with him. Out of the chatter over dinner a name came to my ears—that of Kirkbeck. I enquired whether anyone of that name lived locally. No, was the reply—but the Kirkbecks did live at the town of A, at the other end of the county.

Naturally, I followed up this coincidence by writing to Mr Kirkbeck explaining what had happened. I was pleased to get an almost immediate reply, saying that he was very glad to have heard from me after his ridiculous mistake in neglecting to give me his address, and suggesting that I should call on my way south. Accordingly, I arranged to go to see him the following Saturday, stay the week-end, return to London to attend to business, and come back to Lincolnshire a fortnight later to carry out my commission.

On the Saturday morning I boarded the York–London train, from which I proposed to change at Retford junction. It was a wet, foggy, thoroughly nasty October day, hardly worth looking out at. I was quite glad at the prospect of company when at Doncaster a lady joined me in the carriage, which had so far been empty except for myself. I was sitting next to the door, with my back to the engine, and this seat I offered her; but she graciously refused it, and took the corner opposite, remarking that she liked to feel the air on her face. Then she began to settle herself comfortably in her seat— spreading her cloak beneath her, arranging her skirts, and putting back her veil over her hat. Now that her face was revealed, I could see that she was about twenty-two. Her hair was auburn, and in sharp contrast to it her eyes and rather thick eyebrows were almost black. Her eyes were large, expressive and beautiful, and her mouth generous and firm. Her complexion was of that healthy, transparent pallor which sets off so well such dark eyes. Altogether, although she was not strictly a beauty according to the taste of our times, her face pleased me more than if she had been.

When she had settled herself to her satisfaction, she borrowed my Bradshaw, and asked me to help her to look up the London–York trains. From this, we passed to more general topics, and I was surprised to find that we were soon talking with the ease of old friends. There was in her manner something that one does not usually find when chatting to a perfect stranger, though there was nothing in the least forward about it; and she even seemed to know things about me that I could not possibly have told her. It was all very odd, but a most agreeable way of passing a long, dull, journey.

When I prepared to get out at Retford, and rose to say goodbye, she offered me her hand, and I shook it. "I dare say we shall meet again," she said, and I replied, with truth, "I hope we shall, indeed". And so we parted.

I arrived safely at the Kirkbeck's house, unpacked, dressed for dinner, and went down to the drawing-room some time before seven, at which hour the butler had told me we should dine. The lamps were not lit, but a good blazing fire threw its cheerful light into every corner of the room, and illuminated the figure of a lady who was standing by the mantelpiece, warming a very handsome foot on the edge of the fender. I noticed that she was dressed in black, but did not at first see her face, which was turned away from me. Imagine my astonishment when she turned to face me, and I saw that she was none other than my lady of the railway-carriage! She showed no surprise herself, but smiled and said, "I told you we should meet again".

I was completely without words. I had left her in the London train, and had seen it start when I got out of it. The only way in which she could have reached this place was by going on to Peterborough, and then returning by a branch line, a circuit of about ninety miles. When I did recover my voice, I said I wished I had come by the same conveyance as she had done.

"That would have been rather difficult," she answered.

At this moment the servant came with the lamps, and said that Mr Kirkbeck would be down in a few minutes. The lady strolled to an occasional table and, picking up a book of engravings, handed it to me, open at a portrait of Lady A., and asked me to look at it and tell her whether I thought it like her. I was looking at it when Mr and Mrs Kirkbeck appeared, and I was requested to take Mrs Kirkbeck in to dinner. She took my arm, but I hesitated a moment to allow Mr Kirkbeck to precede us with the lady in black. Mrs Kirkbeck, however, did not seem to understand what I meant, and we passed on at once.

The dinner-party consisted only of us four—Mr and Mrs Kirkbeck at the top and bottom of the table, the lady and I on each side. I, feeling my position as guest, addressed myself mostly, if not entirely, to my host and hostess, and I cannot remember that I or anyone else addressed the lady opposite to me. Remembering a slight want of attention to her in the drawing-room, I concluded that she must be the governess. I noticed, however, that she made a splendid diner—she seemed to enjoy both the roast beef and the tart that followed, and to drink her claret with a connoisseur's appreciation. Probably the journey had given her an appetite.

Dinner over, the ladies retired. Mr Kirkbeck and I remained over port for a few minutes, and then joined the ladies in the drawing-room. By this time a large party had collected. Brothers and sisters-in-law were introduced to me, and several children, together with Miss Hardwick, their governess. So my mysterious lady was not the governess, after all. Once more I found myself talking to her, and she led the conversation round to portrait-painting, and asked me if I thought I could paint her portrait. I replied that I thought I could, if I had the chance. She then asked me to look at her carefully.

"Do you think you could remember my face?"

"I'm sure I could never forget it," I answered.

"Well, of course, I would have expected you to say that—but do you seriously think you could paint me from memory?"

I could try, I said, but I would much prefer sittings. She replied firmly that that would be impossible; she could not promise me even one sitting. Before I could argue further, she declared that she was rather tired, shook me by the hand, and left me. I need hardly say that it was some time before I slept that night, so many were the problems she had presented me with. But at last I told myself that it would all wait until breakfast-time, when no doubt some of my puzzlement would be resolved.

However, breakfast came, but no lady in black appeared. We went to church, we returned to luncheon, and so the day passed, but still no lady—and what was even more curious, no reference to her. She must be some relative, I thought, who had gone away early in the morning to visit another member of the family. But at least I was entitled to find out. When the servant came in to draw my curtains the next morning, I asked him the name of the lady who had dined with us on Saturday evening.

"A lady, sir?" he replied. "No lady, only Mrs Kirkbeck, sir."

"Yes—the lady who sat opposite me, dressed in black?"

"Perhaps Miss Hardwick, sir?"

"No, she came down afterwards. Come, come, you must remember—the lady dressed in black who was in the drawing-room when I came down to dinner on Saturday."

The man looked at me as if I were mad, and said:

"I never see any lady, sir."

I decided to ask my hosts to solve the mystery for me. You may imagine my feelings when they assured me, most positively, that no fourth person had dined at the table on Saturday evening. They remembered it clearly, as they had discussed whether they should ask Miss Hardwick to take the fourth place, but had decided against it. They could not even think of anyone they knew answering to my description of the lady.

Weeks passed. I re-visited the Kirkbecks, and returned to London. One afternoon, near Christmas, I was sitting at my table, writing a letter, with my back towards the folding-doors of my waiting-room. Suddenly I became aware that someone had come through the doors, and was standing behind me. I turned—it was my lady of the railway-carriage, my lady in black.

I suppose my face must have given away my astonishment, for she apologized for entering so quietly, and disturbing me. Her manner had subtly changed since we had last met—it was not exactly grave, but somehow more mature and composed than it had been. She asked whether I had made any attempt at a portrait of her, and I said I had not. She was sorry about that, she said, for she wanted one for her father. Then she produced an engraving—not the one she had shown me at the Kirkbeck's, but a different one—which she thought would help me because of its likeness to her. Then she laid her hand on my arm very earnestly, saying:

"I really would be most thankful and grateful if you would do this for me—and believe me, *much depends on it.*"

I snatched up my pencil and a sketch-book, and by the dim light that remained in the room began to make a rapid sketch of her. But when she saw what I was doing, she turned away, and instead of helping me by standing still, began to wander about the room looking at pictures. In this difficult way I made two hurried but rather expressive sketches of her, and shut my book, for I could see she was preparing to leave. This time she took my hand in hers, and held it firmly instead of shaking it. "Goodbye," she said; and I remembered she had not said this to me before. I saw her out, and on the other side of the folding doors it seemed to me that she faded into the darkness like a shadow. But I took this to be something thrown up by my imagination.

I rang for my maid, and asked why she had not announced the visitor properly. She was not aware there had been one, she replied; anyone who had been in must have come in when she left the street door open about half an hour before, while she had slipped out to the shops.

Shortly after Christmas I set out on my travels again, and by a long train of accidents and delays found myself at Lichfield, with no train to Stafford, my destination, that evening. It was a most annoying situation, and I had no choice but to accept it and put up at the Swan Hotel for the night. I particularly dislike passing an evening at an hotel in a country town. I never take dinner at such places, preferring to go without rather than eat the sort of meal they give one—books are never available, the local newspapers are uninteresting, and I have always read *The Times* from cover to cover during my journey. So when forced to stay at such places I usually occupy myself with writing letters.

This was the first time I had been in Lichfield; but I remembered, while waiting for tea to be brought, that I had twice recently been on the point of visiting it, once for a commission, and another time to get material for a picture. "How strange!" I thought to myself. "Here I am at Lichfield by accident, when I have twice been prevented from coming here on purpose." I remembered that I had an acquaintance in Lichfield, and thought I might as well ask him to come round and pass an hour or two with me. Accordingly, I rang for a waitress, and asked her if, as I recollected, Mr Lute lived in the Cathedral close. He did, she replied, and she would see that a note was taken round to him. I wrote my note, despatched it, and sat down to wait for my friend.

About twenty minutes later there was shown in to me—not my friend, but a gentleman in late middle age, carrying my note in his hand. He imagined, he said, that I had sent it in error, as he did not know my name.

"I am so sorry," I said. "There is obviously another Mr Lute living in Lichfield."

"No," he replied. "I am the only one of that name."

"Well, this is very strange. My friend must have given me the right address, for I've written to him there. He was—how can I describe him?—a fair young man—he came into an estate after his uncle had been killed hunting with the Quorn—and he married a Miss Fairbairn about two years ago."

"Yes, indeed, I know who you mean," replied the stranger, "you're speaking of Mr Clyme. He did live in the Close, but left it recently."

I was completely taken aback. My friend's name *was* Clyme—how could I possibly have thought it was Lute and how could I have unconsciously guessed that a Mr Lute *did* live in the Close? I began to stammer out some of this to my visitor, who interrupted me quietly.

"There's no need to apologize. As it happens, you are the very person I most want to see."

"I am——?"

"Yes, because you are a painter, and I want you to paint a portrait of my daughter. Will you come to my house with me, and do so?"

I hardly knew what to answer, but he pressed me so hard to come with him, and offered to put me up at his house, that I decided without much reluctance to leave the unappetizing Swan and accept his invitation. I packed, cancelled my reservation for the night, and accompanied Mr Lute to the Cathedral Close.

On our arrival at his house we were greeted by his daughter Maria, a fair-haired, distinctly handsome girl of about fifteen. She had a self-possessed, composed manner older than her years, such as is often seen in girls who have been left motherless or otherwise thrown upon their own resources. Her father introduced us (saying nothing of the reason for my being there) and asked her to prepare a room for me; he then went upstairs. His daughter left me to give directions to the servants, then returned, to tell me that I should not be seeing her father again that evening, as he was unwell and had retired for the night. I could either sit with her in the drawing-room, or in the housekeeper's room, where there was a fire and I could have a smoke and a drink. The doctor would be in soon to see her father, and no doubt he would join me in a little refreshment.

As she seemed to be recommending this course, I followed her suggestion with some little private amusement. She joined me by the fire and chatted away, intelligently and with a remarkable command of language for her age. She was obviously inquisitive about my reason for coming to stay with them; and I told her that it was to paint her portrait.

At this she became silent and thoughtful. Then she spoke, in a different tone.

"It is not my portrait that Father wishes you to paint, but my sister's."

"Then I shall look forward to meeting her," I said.

"You cannot do that; my sister is dead—she died some months ago. My father has never recovered from the shock of her death, and his one wish is to have a portrait of her—something he does not possess. I think, if he could have one, his health would improve—for as you see, he is not . . ."

Here she hesitated, stammered, and burst into tears. When she could speak, she continued:

"It is no use hiding anything from you. Papa is insane—he has been so ever since dear Caroline died. He says he is always *seeing* Caroline. The doctor cannot tell how much worse he may be getting, but we have to keep everything dangerous out of his reach—knives and scissors, and such things. I hope he will be well enough to talk to you tomorrow."

I asked whether they had any likeness of the dead girl for me to work from—any photograph, or sketch. No, nothing, Maria replied. Could she describe her sister clearly? She thought she could—and there was a print somewhere that was very much like her.

It was not much to go on, and I did not expect any portrait I might produce under these conditions to be particularly good. I *had* painted portraits before merely from descriptions, but always from very detailed ones; and even so the results were not what I would call satisfactory.

The doctor came to attend to Mr Lute, but I did not see him, and retired early, seeing how much my little hostess had to attend to. Next morning I was glad to hear that Mr Lute was decidedly better, and that he hoped nothing would prevent my attempting the portrait. Directly after breakfast I set to work, on a foundation of such description as Maria could give me. I tried again and again, but without a hope of success, it seemed. The features were separately like Caroline's, Maria said, but the expression was not. I worked on for the best part of the day with no better result. The different studies I made were taken up to Mr Lute, but always the same answer came down—no resemblance. I was fairly worn out by the end of the day—a fact not unnoticed by kindly little Maria, who said earnestly how grateful she was to me for the trouble I was taking, and how sorry she was that her powers of description were so poor. And it was *so* provoking—she had a print, a lady's portrait, that was so like Caroline—but it was missing from her book—she had not seen it for three weeks or so. I asked if she could tell me who the print was of, as I might be able to get one in London. She answered, Lady Mary A. Immediately she said this a number of things began to make fantastic sense in my mind. I ran upstairs and came down with my sketch-book, in which were the two pencil sketches of my lady in black, and the print she had given me, glued in. Silently, I placed them before Maria Lute. She looked at me for a moment, then at the sketches and the print; then, turning her eyes full on me, with fear in them, asked: "Where did you get these? Let me take them to Father, instantly."

She was away ten minutes or more. When she returned, her father was with her. He seemed a different creature from the man I had seen the night before. Without preamble, he said:

"I was right all the time. It *was* you I saw with her, and these sketches are from her, and from no one else. I value them more than all my possessions, except this dear child," and he put an arm round Maria's shoulders. Maria, delighted but deeply puzzled, declared that the print in my sketch-book must be the one taken from her book about three weeks before—and as proof she pointed out the gum marks at the back, which exactly matched those left on the blank leaf.

I immediately began an oil painting based on the sketches, Mr Lute sitting by me hour after hour, chatting away sensibly and cheerfully. He avoided direct reference to what Maria had termed his delusions; but next day, after he had been to church for the first time since his bereavement, he asked me to go for a walk with him, and approached the subject directly. His extraordinary statement is best told in his own words.

"Your writing to me from the inn at Lichfield was one of the most inexplicable things imaginable. As soon as I set eyes on you, I knew you. When Maria and the doctor and others have thought me raving mad, it was only because I saw things that they did not. And I saw my dear Caroline. Since her death, I know, with a certainty nothing will ever disturb, that at different times I have been in her actual, visible presence. I saw her once, distinctly, in a railway carriage, speaking to a person opposite her, whose face I could not see. Then I saw her at a dinner-table, with others, of whom *you* were one. (This time, I learnt afterwards, I was thought to be in one of my longest and most violent paroxysms, for I saw her continuously with you, and in a large group of people, for some hours.) Then again I saw her, standing by your side, while you were either writing or drawing. I did not see you again until we met face to face in the inn parlour."

I have often visited Mr Lute since the day when he told me this strange story. His health is perfect, and he seems entirely to have recovered from the grief of his bereavement. The portrait now hangs in his bedroom, with the print and the two sketches by the side, and written beneath is: "C.L., 13th September 1858, aged 22."

Phantoms of the East

India, with its long history of violence, mystery and bloodshed, must have a million ghosts. Many of them are the sad spirits of English men, women and children who were murdered during the Mutiny of 1857. Towns which had once held military cantonments still had their ghosts many years afterwards, and in the country around many a bungalow is haunted by the restless ghost of a woman who had been murdered and mutilated while trying to escape from the inflamed mutineers. Some servicemen on learning the horrible fate of their families committed suicide in despair, thus adding to India's already prolific hauntings.

In Lansdowne, a small cantonment town in the foothills of Garhwal, a ghostly rider on a pale grey horse, wearing a white mess dress uniform, was sometimes seen riding slowly in the moonlight, head well down, along a bridle path under overhanging trees. He had been seen and followed many times, but no one had ever succeeded in getting near enough to him to see his face. Even the most venturesome of the young officers who had followed him on horse-back found that however fast they rode, the ghostly rider rode faster. Swift and silent he galloped ahead, always keeping his distance, until eventually he would dissolve and vanish into nothing.

Many a traveller coming into Lansdowne had reported seeing him and believed that he had appeared in order to warn them of danger either from marauders who would have robbed them, or from choosing unwise camping sites which might be inhabited by snakes. He would lead them to a more congenial spot and then vanish.

No one had ever seen his face, until one night in 1937. The native sergeant commanding the quarter-guard of a Frontier Force battalion was informed by the sentry that an officer had arrived to take Grand Rounds. He was not the field officer of the week, but he had answered the sentry's challenge correctly and the sergeant thought that he must have been instructed to take the Grand Rounds in place of the field officer of the week. Everything went off quite normally, and the time was noted in the log—Grand Rounds taken at 2.20 a.m.

The field officer had been ill, but no one knew until the next night when he saw the entry in the log. He questioned the native sergeant who told him that he had turned out to an officer wearing white dress uniform with a pale face and side whiskers. According to the sentry he had ridden up on a grey horse and had not said a word except to answer the sentry's challenge with the usual "Grand Rounds".

The Lansdowne ghost appeared every ten years, but he had not taken Grand Rounds before. It was said that he was an officer who shot himself in 1858, a year after his wife and children were murdered by the mutineers.

The way in which they had met their deaths was discovered from another source. One of the officers then stationed at Lansdowne had lived for a while in one of the old pre-Mutiny bungalows, a few of which were still inhabited, though most of them were derelict, empty and neglected, overgrown by creepers and left to the bats and the cobras.

This officer related how one hot June night he had been awakened by an irregular flickering light which played on the wall of his bedroom, and which looked as though it was reflecting a big fire burning outside. He could hear no sound of a fire, and when he got up to look he found that there was no fire. He could see nothing to account for the reflected flames which continued to crawl across the wall for about ten minutes before they died away.

This happened for three nights and on the fourth night the flames appeared to be stronger than ever. He could get no sleep in that airless, oppressive and eerie room, so he went on to the balcony to have a smoke. As he stood there he saw two shadowy figures moving across the parched grass of the lawn. He went down to see who they were, but they vanished. He did notice, however, that they were armed and that their dress was strange to him.

On making inquiries he found that there had been another bungalow in the big garden beside his own, and that on a June night in 1857, when the Bengal Native Cavalry then occupied the lines, two of the troopers came to give the signal for the beginning of the Mutiny there. They had been instructed to murder the adjutant in his bed, and afterwards to set fire to some of the surrounding bungalows. One of those bungalows had been the funeral pyre of the wife and two children of a certain officer who after a year's solitary brooding had committed suicide. He was believed to be the Lansdowne ghost.

India is a country of Black Magic where spells, charms and curses often bring disaster and sometimes death to the unfortunate person involved. Kattadiyas make charms which can harm enemies. They have the power to charm anyone, and it is believed that with the help of the devil they can kill. Much money can be made by a Kattadiya. Then there is the Light Teller, who can tell the victim of a charm what is wrong and how to counteract the charm and break it. The spirits evoked at practices of Black Magic are accountable for some of the worst kinds of hauntings, for they are evil and malignant, and dangerous to the mind as well as the body.

Just such an evil spirit attached itself to the wife of General Beresford of the Indian Army, who while out driving one day in the late 1870s with her husband became distressed at the sight of an ayah, dressed in rather grubby white robes, acting in a dangerous manner. She was walking rapidly and kept crossing the road in front of their horses, keeping so close to the carriage that Mrs Beresford entreated her husband to be careful or they would run over the foolish ayah.

"What ayah?" growled the General. "I don't see any ayah."

"But she's right in front of you in the middle of the road. For God's sake, Henry, stop. I am sure you have run her down."

The General could still see nothing, and had felt no sign of an impact, but his wife appeared to be so upset that he pulled up and, throwing the reins to her, jumped down into the road to look. As he expected, there was no sign of an ayah, and he told his wife she must be dreaming.

But Mrs Beresford was still convinced that she had seen the ayah, and when her husband remounted the box, she got down herself to make quite sure, for she was certain that she had seen the ayah as plainly as she had seen her husband. But the road was empty and there was no one under the wheels of the carriage. Puzzled, she took her place once more beside the General and they continued on their way without further mishap. She had to agree with the General that the ayah must have been a delusion brought on by the heat and fatigue.

But from that day poor Mrs Beresford was haunted by the tall white swathed figure of the ayah, who would suddenly appear in all parts of the house. Grinning evilly, it would glide noiselessly past her, leaving Mrs Beresford frightened and full of foreboding. But no one else saw it; nor did any other member of the household experience any of the horror and anguish which beset Mrs Beresford every time the apparition appeared to her.

She began to doubt her sanity and was fearful of the consequences, for the ayah's appearances were constant and usually when she was alone. But sometimes the fiendish-looking thing in the dirty white robes appeared to her when she was with her husband, but he never saw the apparition, and was disturbed by the sight of her state of fear, as with pale face and staring eyes she pointed a trembling anger at the non-existent apparition.

Something would have to be done, for he could see that his wife's health was deteriorating and she was becoming a nervous wreck. He contacted a doctor friend of his and explained her hallucinations, as he called them. His friend asked if the dear lady had not perhaps been attending spiritualist meetings, but the General assured him that his wife was not the type of woman to participate in such things, for she abhorred anything which was not quite "nice".

"In that case," said the doctor, "perhaps you should get leave of absence and take your wife home for a spell. It seems to me that her mental condition necessitates a complete change of environment.

"But we have only just got back from the Old Country. I can't ask for more leave already."

"Well, all I can suggest is that she should see a doctor who specializes in nervous complaints."

But Mrs Beresford would not hear of going to such a doctor. She had another, rather more pleasant, idea. She said that if only her daughter could be with her to keep her company, then she would be all right.

The General at first would not hear of it, for their daughter was still at school in England, and, being only sixteen, had to complete her education. But nothing else would satisfy Mrs Beresford, and eventually the General had to agree. Barbara would be sent for.

Mrs Beresford threw herself both physically and mentally into making preparations for her daughter's arrival, and though the terrible ayah still appeared to her, she managed enough strength of will not to let it upset her quite so much as it had done previously.

Perhaps she was getting used to its fiendish grin, and as it had never attempted to harm her physically her confidence increased, and by the time Barbara came she seemed a little better. Her daughter was with her a lot, and whenever the ayah appeared Mrs Beresford was able to ignore it to a certain extent.

At first she had wondered if Barbara might also see the fearsome ayah, but like her father the girl was unaware of its appearance. Barbara put down her mother's occasional nervous reactions, when her face paled slightly and her eyes held fear, to a neurotic state. She was having another of her hallucinations.

Then one night Mrs Beresford was awakened from sleep by the feel of a bony hand on her shoulder. Its touch was icy, and it seemed to bite into her warm flesh as the hideous, spine-chilling touch gripped her and shook her. Mrs Beresford screamed, for she knew that the bony hand which held her was that of the ayah, and as she opened her eyes she could see its shape bending over her. She was petrified. Her husband, sleeping in the bed next to her, jumped up in alarm and lit the lamp.

"What in the name of thunder is going on?" he asked his almost hysterical wife.

The ayah had vanished as the lamp was lit and between frightened sobs his wife told him what had happened, and how the awful apparition had gripped her shoulder. But the General dismissed the idea as ridiculous, saying that if his wife was going to start this sort of thing in the middle of the night he would have to sleep alone. He was not going to have his nights disturbed by such fancies.

By this time the servants and Barbara had arrived on the scene, and Mrs Beresford, though still frightened, told them that she had had a nightmare, and she was sorry to have disturbed everybody.

It was not until they had all gone back to bed that she was conscious of the pain in her shoulder. Just before the General turned out the lamp, she slipped her nightdress down from her shoulder and there she saw five distinct red marks, small and narrow, the marks of fingernails. Mrs Beresford dared not ask her husband to light the lamp again, and so she lay there sleepless and afraid until the light of morning seeped through the shutters. Not till then did she sleep, and then only fitfully until it was time to get up, by which time the marks on her shoulder had disappeared, and she had no proof to show of her story of the terrible ayah's attack.

But she was convinced that the ayah would come again, with the result that she was unable to sleep, and her restlessness disturbed her husband's nights as well. The General took refuge in another room and Mrs Beresford begged her daughter to sleep in the room with her. Barbara said she would do so if her mother would see a doctor about her nervous condition.

And so together they went to see a different doctor, one who had spent all his life in India and knew and understood the country. He listened to Mrs Beresford's story with both interest and understanding, and encouraged her to tell him everything. For the first time she was able to talk about it freely with an understanding person who did not even suggest that she was suffering from some kind of mental affliction. The ayah was something real and frightening, and the doctor seemed to understand that. She wished that she had gone to him before. The consultation impressed Barbara too, especially when he told them that he had other patients who had complained of similar persecutions.

"In this part of India," he said, "Black Magic is practised extensively and some strange cult may have evoked an evil entity. It is not unusual for such spirits to attach themselves to someone who has the misfortune to contact them. This ayah seems to have attached itself to you, Mrs Beresford."

"But what must I do?"

"If it appears again, you must speak to it. No matter how frightened you are, you must ask its purpose in the name of God. I believe that is the only way you will be rid of it. It has worked in other cases."

Mrs Beresford went away much relieved at having at last found someone who understood, and who assured her that she was not going mad after all. The fact that the apparition was still to be dealt with seemed of secondary importance now. But if she had known all, she would not have thought of it as secondary, for the doctor had neglected to tell her that spirits like the evil ayah could seriously injure their victims, and were quite capable of actually killing them.

However, Barbara was not now so disbelieving of her mother's story, nor was she so complacent about it. The thought that her mother's fearsome apparition was real and not just a figment of her nervous state was to her something much more frightening and distressing, and as the day wore on Barbara began to get afraid of the coming night. She would much rather have slept in her own room, but she did not want to be thought a coward by her parents. She noticed that her father had not offered to go back to sharing his wife's room, making the excuse that he had a busy time ahead and needed a good night's rest. So there was nothing for it. Barbara had to sleep in her mother's room, and the next two nights she was

FIFTY GREAT GHOST STORIES

miserable and nervous and slept very little. But the terrible ayah did not come.

On the third night Barbara slept from sheer exhaustion, and was suddenly and frighteningly awakened by a suppressed scream of terror from the other bed and the sound of struggling.

She sat up quickly, her eyes fixed on her mother's bed, and there in the feeble light of a flickering candle she saw it—the fearsome ayah with the horrible, grinning, ugly face, just as her mother had described it. It was bending over her mother and its long bony fingers had her by the throat. Frantically Mrs Beresford was trying to pull the hands away, but the ayah was tall and strong, and she was intent on killing her victim.

For a moment Barbara was paralysed with fear, and then she screamed at the top of her voice, knowing that the rest of the household would hear and come to their assistance.

The ayah released Mrs Beresford and turned its glaring, venomous eyes on Barbara, who felt herself engulfed in a feeling of hatred. She wanted to get out of bed and run as far away as possible, but she could not move a muscle.

Then Mrs Beresford, with an effort of will which took every particle of her remaining strength, managed to speak in a croaking voice which she hardly recognized as her own.

"In the name of God," she moaned, "go away! Leave me alone!"

As she spoke the long bony hands were lifting her bodily from the bed, and then she lost consciousness.

Barbara gazed in fascinated horror as the fearful apparition lifted the inert body of her mother, who was by no means a small woman, as though she had been a child. The ayah lifted Mrs Beresford right up and then flung her on to the floor, as though in disgust, and then, as the door of the bedroom burst open to admit the General, it vanished into nothingness, leaving behind a coldness which in the hot and humid night struck the General as remarkable as he bent over his unconscious wife.

While smelling salts were administered to Mrs Beresford, Barbara told her father what had happened. The doctor was contacted and he arrived early the next morning to find Mrs Beresford suffering from shock and somewhat bruised, but otherwise unhurt. He told the General that if his wife had been unable to speak to the evil spirit it would probably have killed her.

"But what I can't understand," said the General, still incredulous of the whole thing, "is why did the wretched thing attach itself to my wife in the first place? I was the one who ran it down. I never saw the damned thing of course. Still can't believe it myself."

"These things are difficult to explain, but I assure you, General, they do exist. It may have chosen your wife because she was obviously more vulnerable. On the other hand, it may have done so in order to punish you the more by attacking the one you love."

"And what if it turns up again?" asked the General, now somewhat subdued.

"I don't think it will. I have never heard of one returning after being spoken to. Most people are too terrified to speak to ghosts, of course. But if they do, it usually makes all the difference."

The doctor was right. The fearsome ayah was never heard of again.

The Fur-Trader's Corpse
and The Gold-Miners' Vengeance

What power has a body after death? Many people will ridicule the
idea that a corpse is anything more than an agglomeration of dead
matter. So how can it have any power? Indeed this is what reason
tells us.

But when considering some well-authenticated stories of very
strange happenings it is as well perhaps to suspend judgment
about what happens when death intervenes.

Here are two quite remarkable stories—the first one an eerie
experience which befell a party of fur-traders who were transporting
a body across the ice in the haunted Arctic wastes of North-West
Canada; the second a truly gruesome tale of ghostly horror from the
pioneer days of Australia.

There are many tales in legend and folk-lore of the body of a
dead person exercising a supernatural power. It is an accepted thing
in some primitive societies that a life of some kind lingers in the
corpse. Many stories have been told which suggest there may be
something in this.

In the wild places of the world strange things can happen, things
which are beyond reason. The tellers of both of these stories went to
some lengths to establish that the facts they told were true and that
these happenings really did take place.

Who knows what truth lies behind these strange events? The
reader can only use his own judgment and form his own conclusion.

The Arctic story concerned the body of a hardy fur-trader named Peers who managed the Hudson Bay Company's post at Fort McPherson, which is on the Peel River, a tributary of the Mackenzie River. This is in the farthest north, less than a hundred miles from the Arctic Ocean.

Peers was an Anglo-Irishman who went to the Far North in the 1840s. For two or three years he was at the Hudson Bay Company's Mackenzie District headquarters at Fort Simpson. He was then moved to Fort Norman, and finally to Fort McPherson, the company's most northerly station, five hundred miles nearer the Pole than Fort Simpson.

Peers was good at his job, well thought of by his friends, and popular among the Eskimos in the Peel River Preserve.

In 1849 he married one of those hardy women who went north with their menfolk to endure the rigours of the Arctic in the pioneer days when there were few modern comforts to soften the severity of that terrible climate. They had two children.

But Peers was not happy at Fort McPherson, though there is some evidence that his wife was, for she stayed on there after his death and remarried. The true story of Peers's unhappiness in this place was never revealed. It might have been a very human one—to do with his marriage, the fact that his wife was practically the only woman in this isolated outpost beyond the Arctic Circle, and may well have been sought by other men.

Although only thirty-three years old, Peers began to have premonitions of death and his mind dwelt rather morbidly upon his place of burial. He expressed the wish very strongly that he did not want to be buried at Fort McPherson, where he had not been happy. Nor did he wish to be buried at Fort Norman.

He died suddenly and unexpectedly on 15 March, 1853, and was buried, at least temporarily, at Fort McPherson.

The man who succeeded him as manager of the post was Alexander Mackenzie, and in 1855 Mackenzie married Peers's widow.

Peers's body was still lying in the permafrost of his temporary grave on the banks of the Peel River. With the temperature always well below freezing point, the body was in a state of perfect preservation, the flesh as fresh as on the day Peers died.

Finally in 1859 at the request of his widow, now Mrs Mackenzie, it was decided to transfer Peers's body to Fort Simpson and re-inter him there. Whether during the six years when he lay in this place where he did not wish to be buried, his restless spirit was troubling his good lady who had now married his successor, we do not know. But both Mrs Mckenzie and her husband were determined that the body had to go, and there is good reason to suppose that the late Augustus Peers, wherever he was, was eager for his refrigerated remains to make the arduous journey five hundred miles along the frozen floes of the great Mackenzie River to Fort Simpson.

So they exhumed Peers, finding him not unexpectedly looking exactly the same as when he was buried six years previously. It was decided to send the body south to Fort Simpson by dog-sledge during the winter months.

The body was placed in a new and large coffin, lashed on a sledge and the party set off in the early months of 1860, the coffin drawn by a team of three dogs. On the second sledge was bedding and provisions.

Despite the unwieldiness of the coffin, the first part of the journey was accomplished without incident. Above Fort Norman the body had to be removed from the coffin and secured in its grave wrappings on to the sledge, as the route lay across great masses of tumbled ice on the Mackenzie River, and to have carried the body in the cumbersome coffin would have been impossible.

On 15 March, the seventh anniversary of Peers's death, the party were encamping for the night by the river-bank. It was a fine day, unusually warm for the time of the year. The flesh of the body on the sledge began to thaw out, and the hungry dogs for the first time scented it. To them it was fresh meat—and it was feeding time. This explains why the journey was made during the winter. Temperatures well above freezing are usual in the summer months in the Far North, and the body would swiftly decompose during the long and difficult journey south. There was a furious and ravenous barking around the silent corpse while the party were preparing camp—the time when the dogs were always waiting impatiently to be fed.

As the party turned to investigate the disturbance, they all distinctly heard the word "Marche!" shouted in a loud voice. The dogs immediately quietened.

Not one of the party had spoken and there was no other living soul within hundreds of miles of them.

One member of the party who had known Peers said that it sounded exactly and uncannily like his voice.

"Marche is a French word universally used in the North-West to make dogs move or to drive them away. The familiar "Mush" now used is a corruption of the word, and is apparently the way the Indians and Eskimos pronounced it.

Three days later the call "Marche" was heard loudly once more while they were making camp. This time the temperature was well below freezing and there was no question of the dogs scenting the body again. But the party were attracted by the mysterious calls, and decided for some reason to move the body train from the place where they had left it to one nearer the camp.

In the morning they found tracks of a wolverine at the spot where they had originally left the body train. The wolverine would undoubtedly have torn the body to pieces.

On 21 March, 1860, the remains of Augustus Richard Peers finally arrived at Fort Simpson safely and intact and were buried in the graveyard there two days later.

The party were much concerned about their experience during this strange journey, and each of their accounts agreed with the other. They all heard the mysterious voice, coming on both occasions from the direction of the sledge on which the body lay, and at a time when no living person was anywhere near it. The voice sounded just like that of the dead man.

Roderick Macfarlane, who led the party, was convinced that, owing to the strong feeling Peers had about where his body should be buried, his spirit watched over that tortuous winter journey along the frozen Mackenzie River, that it knew the hungry dogs had scented his body on that unusually warm March evening, and knew also of the presence of the wolverine, a vicious and destructive animal which would certainly have made havoc of his remains.

*   *   *   *   *

The story of the life and death of George Woodfall is one of the strangest to come from the continent of Australia. The details were pieced together from Woodfall's own statement, and the accounts of the men who found his body in the strangest and apparently most unnatural circumstances.

George Woodfall was an Englishman of good family who emigrated to Australia about 1850 to seek his fortune, after losing all his money in the Old Country.

In February, 1851, a Californian gold-miner named Hargraves discovered gold at Summerhill Creek, which is a hundred miles or so to the north-west of Sydney. Woodfall was among the first of the immigrants in the great gold rush that followed when rich finds were also made in Victoria.

Woodfall joined up with two men—Harper and Freeth—rough characters both. Harper had come out years previously on a convict ship. But neither he nor Freeth were really bad characters. Living the pioneer life brings out the best as well as the worst in men.

Gold prospecting, however, is more likely to bring out the worst. Certainly it brought thousands of undesirables to Australia, to the great concern of the authorities.

No one, certainly not Woodfall, pretended that Harper and Freeth were blackguards of the deepest dye, and they did not deserve the treatment meted out to them by Woodfall—an educated man and an English gentleman.

Neither Harper nor Freeth could write their own names, yet they were good mates to Woodfall, welcoming him when he arrived at the diggings, and sharing, as Woodfall admitted, fair and square in everything.

The three teamed up together and struck gold. Between them they did well enough, travelling about in the mountains, prospecting, carrying with them their loads of gold dust and nuggets, already worth a considerable fortune. Indeed they had enough each to make themselves comfortable for life. But prospectors are never satisfied. Gold creates in them a fever which cannot be satisfied. They want more and more of it.

They were talking about going to Sydney and cashing up when they discovered a wondrous cave in what looked like a gold-bearing mountain, from which leaped a spectacular waterfall. The cave was difficult to get into. They found the entrance after some arduous climbing. It was a vertical shaft in the face of the mountain, and to descend it they had to drive wooden stakes into the soft rock.

When they got down they found a vast, cathedral-like cavern which reverberated to the distant thunder of the mighty waterfall. Their torches illuminated great stalactites and stalagmites, and glittered on multi-coloured prisms of rock. Most exciting of all to them, they saw quartz in the great pillars which supported the roof of the cave.

But this splendid and awe-inspiring place yielded little in the way of gold. The quartz, though exquisite in appearance, was poor in gold.

To get it they had to break into a rock formation which was like one of those great exquisitely carved altar-pieces in a cathedral. Behind this, they found a smaller cave.

After searching in vain for gold in this strange and splendid place, they decided to pass the night in the small cave, before resuming their journey to Sydney.

The talk that night was of their plans for the return to civilization

They each calculated the value of their gold, and came to the conclusion that they hadn't done too badly. Each said it would be the soft life for them in the future. They had had enough of roughing it, and wanted to enjoy the sweets of civilization, which their gold would enable them to do.

As the talk drifted to yarns about Sydney and the wild times of the old days, George Woodfall fell unusually quiet. His thoughts ran on very different lines to those of his companions. For them their share of the gold was enough, but not for him. He had come to Australia to rebuild his fortune, and he would not be satisfied with the kind of money that these simple diggers considered riches. The total amount of their gold represented a respectable sum of money. With that for his capital, Woodfall was convinced he could really make money.

But there was little chance of robbing his two companions and making away with the gold. He would be a marked man. That sort of thing would not be forgiven or forgotten.

There was only one solution—to kill them.

Harper and Freeth soon fell into a heavy sleep. Woodfall lay awake planning their murder. It would have to be done very swiftly, and before the fire they had lit in the cave burnt out.

Woodfall waited until the fire was low and then he struck silently and suddenly with his razor-sharp knife. First Freeth, who was closer to him. He got him with one blow right through the heart.

But though Freeth was dispatched so quickly and suddenly, Harper was instantly awake, that sixth sense which men often acquire while living in the wilds suddenly alerted.

Harper stumbled to his feet and launched himself straight at Woodfall. But Harper was still half-asleep, and Woodfall had not much difficult in dealing with him. He grasped him by the throat and tore at his gullet. They fell over, fighting madly. Woodfall's knife was dropped in the desperate struggle, but he retained his hold on Harper's throat, and Harper went down in a state of semi-consciousness.

Woodfall turned and picked up his knife, then came for his comrade once more to finish him off. Harper struggled up into a sitting position, his face livid, eyes protruding, mouth open and gasping. He was unable to speak, for he had been all but strangled by Woodfall. He looked up desperately at Woodfall, and put his hands together, praying for mercy.

But this Woodfall did not give. He had gone too far anyway. He plunged his knife deep into Harper's chest. Harper died with a harsh and terrible cry which echoed and re-echoed through the great vaults of the cathedral-like cave nearby.

Woodfall decided to leave the place at once, even though it was night-time. He collected the gold from his companions' packs, but the sight of his comrades lying there slain so treacherously by his own hand was too much for his conscience, and he decided to bury them. It would be the best way of hiding the crime, anyway.

But he found digging in the hard soil extremely difficult. It was more a case of hewing than digging. After he had dug a shallow pit, he gave up the idea of burying them. After all, it was unlikely that anyone would ever discover this cave in this lovely and remote spot. And if they did there would be nothing to connect him with the bodies of Freeth and Harper.

So he laid their bodies in the shallow pit he had excavated, and covered them with some loose stones. And thus he left them and went to Sydney.

The date was 20 September. The year 1852 or 1853.

No one knew him at Sydney, which in those days was a city with a population of 100,000, compared with two million today. It was a large enough place for George Woodfall to remain comparatively unknown. He told everyone he had lately arrived from England with a modest amount of capital he wished to invest.

When the occasion arose Woodfall took a chance, in the same way as he had taken a chance in the cave when he robbed and murdered his two comrades. He invested nearly all of his capital in the Benambra Mine. A week later the shares rocketed and he was a very rich man.

Woodfall was so pleased with his success that he forgot his crime and enjoyed himself. He bought a fine house on Pott's Point, where he entertained at first lavishly and not wisely.

September came around again, and one evening about the middle of the month he was sitting alone by the open window of his house gazing across the dark waters of Port Jackson to the harbour lights at the Heads, when he fell into a fit of bitter remorse over what he had done. He would have given all his wealth to have washed the blood from his hands. In that mood he had a strong impulse to rush to the police and confess his crime.

Momentarily the mood passed and he turned away from the window with the reflection that dead men could surely tell no tales.

As he turned into the room, he heard a voice distinctly say: "It is time. Let us begin."

Thinking at first that burglars were about, he got out his revolver and made a search. But there were no intruders around his house—no intruders from this world, that is.

Woodfall put out the lights and prepared to go to bed. He picked up the candle and started for the door.

He had hardly taken a step, he says, when suddenly something like a heavy body fell with a thud at his feet. As he stumbled back in alarm he began to hear sounds—sounds that had haunted him for months, but now they burst terrifyingly upon his ears.

There was the waterfall reverberating in the background, and then, splitting his eardrums, came Harper's last terrible cry as he died with Woodfall's knife deep in his chest. There were other noises, too, terrifying, indescribable, unspeakable noises which shook and echoed around the house.

He sank into a chair, covering his ears with his hands to try and shut out the spectral sounds, but was unable to do so. He was back in the cave now, in that awful night, in a living nightmare that appalled his senses.

At any moment he expected his servants to be aroused by the terrible, frightening noises which rose every now and then in a crescendo to Harper's unforgettable scream of death.

But no one in the house stirred, and he soon became aware that he was the only one who could hear these sounds—this devil's concert, as Woodfall called it.

When this thought was brought home to him, the sounds suddenly ceased. Then, as plain as if he was standing next to him, he heard Harper's voice.

"You are growing forgetful, George. In a week's time it will be September the twentieth. We are here to remind you."

George Woodfall was now in a state of the uttermost terror. He was convinced of the presence not only of Harper but of Freeth in the room. But it was Harper who spoke, Harper whose death cry was a living echo in his brain.

"Your time has not come yet, George, but before it does we will teach you to remember. We will expect you in the cave on the twentieth. Don't forget to come. That is the only way you will escape us."

"Yes, I will come," muttered Woodfall, and then his consciousness ceased.

A dream? A waking nightmare prompted by his tormenting conscience?

At all events Woodfall went to the cave and there he spent, he said, "a night of such agonizing horror that I wondered afterwards how I came to retain either life or reason after it".

What took place in that cave can only be imagined. But it is not likely that Woodfall could have brought himself to touch the bodies of the two men he had murdered and placed in that shallow pit. This is an important point, in view of what happened later.

Every year now he made this terrible pilgrimage to the cave, and spent a whole night in a kind of hellish communion with his victims, whose bodies lay rotting in the shallow pit. Each year they became more decayed, more skeletal, and yet in some unnatural way more alive.

But only by going there each year did they give him peace. After the fourth year, he tried not going. But there was no evading his grim pilgrimage. Harper and Freeth came and haunted him at Pott's Point—came after him and drove him to the cave for his grim annual ritual.

This experience had one beneficial effect upon Woodfall. It changed his whole life. He gave up all forms of gaiety and enjoyment, and tried to make amends by good deeds. He gave to charity. He went to church regularly, and became one of Sydney's most respected citizens.

No one dreamed he was a murderer, for he kept his terrible secret locked up inside him. For some reason, he could not confess to what he had done. He was quite unable to. If he did, would Harper and Freeth leave him alone in peace at last?

And after twenty miserable, haunted years, and after nineteen visits to the unspeakable cave, he finally decided to make his confession.

One night he wrote it out, and finished it by saying that he would make one more pilgrimage to the cave, because this, he felt, he must do. Then he would return and give himself up.

And so he went on his last pilgrimage, but he never returned.

Sydney mourned an upright and benevolent citizen, whose disappearance was both a sensation and a mystery. No foul play was suspected. His affairs were found to be in perfect order. He was greatly missed, and later they put up a monument to him.

The mystery remained unsolved for five years.

In the late 1870s two men, William Rowley, an engineer who had planned and made many canals in New South Wales, and the Rev. Charles Power, of St Chrysostom Church, Redfern, Sydney, were spending one of those energetic holidays typical of the nineteenth century, camping and travelling in the wilds of the Blue mountains, and living off the land by eating such meat as could be shot by Rowley's gun. The Rev. Power employed his energies more suitably catching butterflies for his large Australasian collection.

Both of them knew George Woodfall by reputation and by sight.

It was on 20 September when they came upon the mountain from which leaped the spectacular waterfall. Here they camped for the night, enchanted by the wildly beautiful scenery, fascinated by the waterfall, and totally unaware that the day marked the anniversary of a certain grim event.

After supper, while they were yarning over their pipes by the camp fire, there was a great thunderstorm, during which, by some strange trick of the eyesight perhaps, a blood-red glare settled over the waterfall, so that it appeared to them like a torrent of blood.

They regarded it as a strange natural phenomenon, but when the storm passed off the red glare was still above the waterfall and right in the midst of the water, it seemed, a man appeared.

They started forward, stumbling in the darkness, then stopped, transfixed to the spot, for they saw that the man had a face that was long dead, with the flesh shrunken and dried and in some places rotted away. It was a mere skeleton, a thing, they thought, from the outer darkness. It seemed suspended there in a blaze of crimson light, alternately beckoning to them and then writhing in anguish.

It took them an hour and a half to climb to the spot where they had seen the ghost, and another hour to reach the summit where the waterfall leaped down the chasm. The precipice was sheer and the mountain towered above them in the night.

Climbing higher, they saw a fallen ironbark tree which had been blazed with an axe and an arrow pointing directly downwards.

Close by they found the entrance to the cave, now overgrown with shrubs. Rowley cut a sapling and beat away the undergrowth, revealing the mouth of the cave which led vertically downwards.

The wooden stakes made by Woodfall and his two companions twenty-five years previously were still there and just as secure. Lighting their bull's-eye lantern, Rowley and Power descended.

Some minutes later they stood in wonder and astonishment in the great cathedral-like cavern. The huge rock formation made like an altar-piece particularly impressed and interested Power, and while he was admiring it Rowley went through past the broken quartz rock into the smaller cave beyond.

His exclamation of horror brought Power hurrying after him.

"What's the matter?" asked the clergyman.

"Come, let's go back," said Rowley, obviously shaken. "This is no place for us."

"For heaven's sake—what is it?" demanded Power.

Rowley illuminated the scene with the bull's-eye lantern.

In front of them was the shallow open grave. The earth which had been dug up to make it and piled at the side had been hardened almost to stone by the endless drip of water from above. Even the tools with which the grave had been dug were still lying there.

But what took their horrified attention was the skeleton of a man, bush shirt and trousers rotted to tatters, half sitting at the side of the grave, peering into it, grinning in a way in which only a skull can grin.

In the grave itself lay two more bodies, one on top of the other. The topmost was a skeleton similar to the one sitting at the graveside. Underneath it was the body of a man in the last stages of decay, though he had not been dead for anything like the time which the other two had been.

There was something weirdly familiar about him to the two horrified men who peered down into the grave, and when Rowley reached down with his sapling and brushed aside the upmost skeleton, they could see that the man underneath was the man who had appeared to them above the waterfall just after the thunderstorm.

Both men were mystified as well as appalled by their discovery. There was something weird, unnatural, about the whole thing—in the very attitudes of the two corpses in the pit, quite apart from the apparition by the blood-red waterfall.

The fact that two of the bodies had obviously been dead for many years longer than the third puzzled Rowley and Power. And how was it possible that the man who had plainly been the last to die was found lying *underneath* a man who had died many years before him?

To the Reverend Charles Power there was something devilish about the whole thing—something that smelt of the very pit of hell.

They looked around the cave and found an old coat, fast falling to pieces with age, but which was obviously well tailored and of good cloth. It had the label of Schuylen, one of Sydney's best tailors. In the coat they found a flat metal box containing the inscription: "George Woodfall, Pott's Point, Sydney", and they had the answer to the mystery, for inside was his confession of how he had killed Harper and Freeth for their gold, and then been made to return to this place every year by some hideous force he was unable to resist.

The answer to the mystery? It was only part of the answer.

In his confession Woodfall said he would go to the cave for the last and twentieth time after writing his confession, and then give himself up. But he did not return from the cave. How then was he killed?

Originally he had laid the bodies of Harper and Freeth in the grave. There they lay for nineteen years and more, and thus he found them on each wretched visit he made to this place of hideous memory. On the twentieth pilgrimage, after he had made his confession, *did he arrive there to find them sitting on the edge of the grave awaiting him, knowing that he had finally delivered himself into their power?*

Rowley and Power buried the three bodies in the cave, and Power read the burial service over them.

The clergyman never understood why Woodfall, having finally confessed to his crime, was then delivered into the power of the spirits of darkness. But he firmly believed that his and Rowley's footsteps had been guided to the cave to find Woodfall's confession, and to give the three bodies a Christian burial, so that their long-tormented spirits should rest in peace at last.

Over their remains he and Rowley piled a cairn of gold-bearing quartz.

The Coach Calls for George Mace

The village of Watton lies almost at the centre of the triangle formed by Thetford, Wymondham and Swaffham, in Norfolk. Today it has fewer than four thousand inhabitants; a century ago it had more than a thousand less, and one of them was George Mace.

By day Mace worked as stockman for a farmer at Ovington, a couple of miles or so north and slightly east of Watton. By night, he was the leader of one of the most successful gangs of poachers ever to operate in the county.

The country over which George worked under the stars has changed remarkably little compared with the changes which have generally overtaken the rural countryside of Britain. Here and there, there has been some ribbon development and the villages have tended to sprawl a bit. But there are still wide-open spaces devoted to the production of barley, wheat and oats, broken up by woods, coppices and spinneys, just as there were in George's days.

At the time of which we are writing, George was in his middle thirties. For a Norfolk countryman born and bred, he had an unusually lively mind. About five foot ten tall, he had the broad shoulders, fair hair and pale blue eyes of his Saxon forebears, and in his customary gait could still be observed traces of the Saxon lope. His ruddy, weather-beaten features had been given a handsome turn, too. When the older people talked of him, sooner or later they would hint at the story which had followed his mother from Breckles, where, before she had married her late husband, she had been in service at the hall; according to which she was already pregnant when Jos Mace had led her to the altar, that the Squire of Breckles had given Jos a marriage gift that was noticeably larger than was customary, and that he had once ridden over to the Watton cottage not long after the birth of Flo Mace's first-born, George. Certainly, none of her other children, whom she had produced annually until the day Jos drank too deeply at Swaffham market, fell into the Wissey on his way home and remembered too late that he could not swim. When they had fished him out of the mill-race by Hilborough and had filled in his grave in Watton churchyard, Flo decided that she had had sufficient connubial bliss to last her the rest of her life, and had settled down to bringing up the departed Jos's brood and George—if we are inclined to give credence to the local tradition.

George had been eight when Jos had so suddenly removed himself from the family circle, and he had immediately gone to work for the farmer at Ovington who had employed his father. In spring and early summer his duties were to keep the birds from attacking the seeds after sowing and the young shoots after sprouting, by wielding a noisy rattle. At harvest time he took his place with the sheavers, following the scythe-men; in autumn and winter he helped the stockmen.

It was during this apprenticeship to the land, and particularly during the long spring and summer days of bird-scaring, that he laid the foundations of his vast store of the lore of the countryside. He began leaving the cottage at night, after his brothers and sister were asleep, and though he invariably went out empty-handed, just as invariably he returned shortly before dawn with a rabbit or a hare, a pheasant or a brace of partridge stuffed inside his shirt. His mother, anxious to raise him well, never failed to scold him, just as she never forgot to wink as she took the booty from him, with silent but heartfelt thanks that today the stew-pot and her children's bellies would not be empty.

By the time there was down on his chin, George had impressed his employer with the way he had with animals, and his employer's youngest daughter with his knowledge of the ways of men. The stockmen of the neighbourhood respected his advice, and the more generally knowledgeable nodded sagely and murmured something about "a chip off the old block", and were not referring to Jos. But there also comes a time when recognition of professional skill cannot be invoked to overlook the visible results of personal concupiscence. Two small Georges had already been born to as many mothers, when the maternal grandfather of the third little George, egged on by his wife, arrived at Flo's cottage to declare that her George, at not quite eighteen, was nevertheless old enough to shoulder his responsibilities.

George, however, thought otherwise, though he did not say so. He was too young yet to be tied down; he had not yet had time to discover which of the wenches in the neighbourhood would suit him best.

However, he said, "Name the day, gaffer; that's all you've to do," and the man, relieved, had turned to Flo and said, "In that case, Mrs Mace, you'd best put your head together with my missus."

When they were alone, Flo had burst out laughing.

Surprised, George had asked, "Why're you laughing, mam? Aren't you going to scold me?"

"What? For something you can't help. It's born in you. Besides, I know you well enough, my boy, to know that you've no intention of marrying the girl."

Taken somewhat aback by this unexpected understanding, George laughed too.

"You're right, mam," he said. "I haven't—at least not until . . ."

"It'll be best if you get away for a bit," Flo said. "If you stay around here, one night we shall find our thatch alight. Out of sight, out of mind. Where do you plan to go?"

"In the army," George told her, "then I shan't have to worry where my next meal's to come from, or about a roof over my head. Besides, I'll get about a bit, see other men, go to other places. You never know, I may even get to India."

"Well, mind you come back, son."

"I'll promise you that. But are you sure you'll be all right if I go? There's my pittance from old Thrower, and there won't be so many rabbits for the pot. I don't know what's wrong with those boys, but neither Frank nor Bert have got it in them to be good poachers. I've done my best with 'em, but it's no good."

"Don't worry about me, son. We'll be all right," his mother assured him. "You might even get a commission. They do sometimes award commissions on the field."

"I doubt it, mam. You've got to have more education than I've got, and more breeding, to be an officer."

"More education maybe," Flo Mace agreed cryptically. "But you can read and write and figure. When will you go?"

"The end of the week. I'll walk over to Norwich and see the recruiting sergeant there. You'd best see Nan's mam tomorrow."

"You can leave that to me. I'm glad you'll be here a few days yet. But take care, George, don't whisper a word in front of the young ones."

Well, George joined the army on the following Sunday, and did not return to Watton for fifteen years. He saw India and he came through the shambles of the Crimea; he did not become an officer, but he did rise to be sergeant.

By the time he came home again, the youth of eighteen now a man of thirty-three, he found little changed. There were differences, naturally. Except for his youngest sister, who was in service to the widow of a late Canon of Norwich, and looked set fair to be an old maid, all his brothers and sisters were married and in their own cottages; the mothers of the three little Georges had also taken husbands, and the little Georges were all beginning to have down on their chins; the two eldest were even shaving once a week.

He had come from London by the Great Eastern Railway's line to Thetford, and there he had caught the carrier to Swaffham. The ancient man did not recognize him, which was no wonder, for the still developing youth had matured into a broad-shouldered man.

A mile or so from the village he had stopped the cart, and, thanking the old man, had got down. Hitching his pack on to his shoulder, he had watched the cart trundle away, then he had struck out across the fields. It felt strange to be among the old familiar sights again; but they were all there, and the air smelt as it always did, free and bold and strong, different from the air in any other place he had been in on this side and the other side of the world.

The strangeness had begun to come over him as soon as the carrier's cart had emerged from Thetford and turned into the Watton road, and as the familiar sights had begun to multiply the strangeness had turned to embarrassment. It was on account of his embarrassment that he had stopped the cart and got down.

As he trudged his way through the fields, the sun set, but it would not be dark yet for another hour. He had a mile or so still to go, so sitting down under the lee of a hay-rick he took his almost empty bundle of food from his pack and ate a little. And as he looked about him, presently two rabbits sped across the field to their warren on the edge of the spinney nearby.

He smiled to himself. He knew the place well.

Feeling in his pockets, he found a length of cord, and crossing to the spinney he carefully selected a twig, cut it and shaped it with his knife, fashioned a loop in the cord, and attaching the running end to the twig, which he stuck firmly into the ground above the entrance to the burrow he had chosen, he arranged the loop round the edge of the hole. This any poacher could have done; but what he did next, few could do.

Stretching himself flat on the ground so that he lay above the burrow with his head above the hole, he made intermittent, small, special sounds with his lips. Five minutes, perhaps, he waited, then below his face, and only inches from it, appeared the twitching muzzle of a rabbit. He made his sound a little more loudly, and suddenly a furry body was writhing violently, attempting to free itself from the loop about its neck, which drew tighter with every movement it made.

With a grunt of satisfaction, he put down a hand and seized the struggling animal by the nape of its neck. Pulling up the twig, he stood up, took hold of the rabbit by its hind legs with his left hand and brought down the outer edge of his rigid right hand on the back of its head. It quivered once, and was still. Again George Mace grunted with satisfaction.

Re-setting the snare, he repeated his ritual, and within another five minutes the still warm body of a second rabbit lay beside the first. Gathering two large dock leaves, he made masks of them, which he fitted over the rabbits' snouts, tying them in place with strands of long coarse grass. This done, he put the rabbits into his pack, certain that any blood that might trickle from their nostils would not soil anything with which they came into contact.

By the time he had done this the dusk was rapidly changing into night. He still had a short walk before he reached home, but before he came to the village it would be dark—as he had planned.

A light was burning in the kitchen window of the cottage. When he peered through it, he saw his mother sitting by the hearth, her hands busy with some sewing. Momentarily he was shocked to see that the jet black hair he remembered was now mostly white, until he recalled that his mother, too, had aged and must be now in her middle-fifties.

Moving quietly to the cottage door, he felt silently for the latch. His finger closed on it, and patiently he lifted it. When he felt it free of the catch, he pushed open the door and placed himself in the doorway.

For a moment his mother did not see what had happened. Then some little movement he made distracted her attention from her needle, and she looked up. During all of five seconds, she gazed at him; then with a cry, she sprang up, scattering her sewing, and flung herself into his arms.

"George!" she cried. "You've come home!"

"Yes, mam, I've come home," he said.

"Come to the light and let me look at you!" She looked at him hard and long. "Yes . . . yes . . ." she said at last. Then moving again into his arms, she asked, "Will you stay long, son?"

"I'm home for good, mam," he told her.

"For good?" she asked, disbelieving.

"For good," he repeated.

"You'll be hungry," she said, at once practical, "and I've little in the larder. I'll go and ask Mrs Utting if she can lend us a piece of bacon."

"No need, mam," he laughed, and pulled the rabbits from his pack.

She laughed, shaking her head as she took them, and remembered to wink.

As they ate together when the food was cooked, she asked, "What will you do, George?"

"Look round for a farmer who wants a stockman."

"Maybe Farmer Thrower will take you back. Then you could live here with me."

"I'll do that, mam, in any case. But I'll go and see Thrower first thing in the morning.

The farmer was doubtful at first. For fifteen years George had had no dealings with stock. Eventually, however, at George's suggestion, he took him on a month's trial.

At the end of a week he told George he could stay as long as he liked.

George Mace's return was a nine-days' wonder in the village. There were some, whose memories were long, who warned certain parents, "Lock up your daughters now George Mace is back!" But as time went by he proved them wrong. Not a girl in the village received his special attentions, though there were some who tried to attract them; each Saturday afternoon he walked the ten miles to Swaffham; on Sunday night he walked the ten miles back. What he did in between made him and the village happy.

There were even more who said that he would not be staying long. After the excitements of all that soldiering, Watton would be too quiet for him. He proved them almost as wrong; but not quite.

It would have been strange if he had settled down entirely to the slow tempo of the countryside. To begin with, however, he welcomed the change, and so great was his interest in animals that he became absorbed in his job. What excitement he felt he needed he tried to find in poaching, and for a time he did achieve it in pitting his wits against those of the gamekeepers. But he did not like killing for killing's sake, and now that there were only two of them at the cottage it was difficult to dispose of his catches. Admittedly some could be passed on to trusted neighbours, but in these days, when a man could be transported for fourteen years for stealing a rabbit or two, should the poacher be caught and the landowner invoke the letter of the law, it was too dangerous to be too prodigal with illicit gifts.

There was one other point, too. George was a born leader, as his attainment of non-commissioned rank had proved. Had he lived on the coast of Kent or Sussex or Cornwall he would have undoubtedly made a great reputation as a leader of smugglers. Here in the depths of the Norfolk countryside such an outlet was denied him. Or so he thought, until without warning one or two of the landowners decided to intensify their war with the poachers.

Within a space of four weeks, two men from Watton, one from Soham Toney and one from Ashill, fell into gamekeepers' traps, and on being brought before the magistrates, who were also the squires, instead of being dealt with summarily, were committed to Norwich assizes, where they were sentenced to transportation for periods ranging between twelve and thirty years.

Such a thing had never happened before within living memory. A fine of a shilling or two, or if the offender were young, a sound birching, had always been deemed sufficient punishment. The good people of Norfolk were scandalized; but they were also cowed; and one result was that the children of a number of families now often went hungry.

The landowners were led by the new squire of Holme Hale. He was a youngish man who had started out as a lawyer in London, and was not making much of a go of it, when he unexpectedly inherited his uncle's estate. He was an unpleasant character, in any case; but he added to this an ignorance of the Norfolk countryside and its people, while deceiving himself that they were like any other rogues. Somehow he managed to persuade one or two of his neighbours to join him in his anti-poaching campaign, and then when the men were brought before the Swaffham bench he dragooned his fellow magistrates into a committal to assizes.

This declaration of war was a godsend to George Mace. He accepted it as a personal challenge. When the two Watton men were caught he was sorry, but not wholly sympathetic, because he believed that if they had been poachers worth their salt they would have avoided any trap. But when the two others were also seized, he realized that the standard of poaching efficiency was inferior to the efficiency of the gamekeepers, and that this could lead, in a very short time, to a discontinuance of the art altogether. In his view, this would have been a calamity of the first order; first, because the poacher is an integral part of the English country lore; second, because it would mean victory for the squires, and particularly for the hateful squire of Holme Hale. This he perceived as his duty not to permit.

After some thought, he decided to band the poachers of Watton's immediate environs into a gang under his leadership. He would raise their standard of performance by tuition, and then they would operate on a military basis. If all went as he was certain it would they could have the gamekeepers with their backs to the wall in no time.

Personally, all he asked of the plan was the success of his gang's operations. He realized, however, that this would not satisfy his men, who would come in, not for the excitement or the satisfaction of defeating the enemy, but for the tangible rewards. But on the scale he planned, these rewards would be too large for local distribution, so he worked on a scheme for supplying the hotels of the district with cheap game, the proceeds from which would be evenly shared among the gang.

Within six months he was ready to begin operations. Under him he had a dozen men, who, though still not the expert he was himself, were, nevertheless, the cream of the poachers of East Anglia. From them he demanded and received unquestioning obedience.

For a time the gamekeepers were bewildered, until they learned, as they were bound to since the trees and the grass in the countryside have tongues, of the existence of the Mace gang. But knowledge without evidence is not sufficient to allow justice to be seen to be done.

To acquire evidence, they countered by forming an organization of their own. But still they had no success, for George conducted his operations with a strategy and tactics which would have gladdened the heart of old Wellington, had he still been alive to learn of it. He had his intelligence corps and his agents who planted false information, and by this combination he let loose his men in one section of the region while the gamekeepers waited miles away to pounce on poachers who were supposed to walk into their traps, but never did.

For a little over a year George and his gang operated with immense success. He lost not a single man, and every one of them was richer by five shillings a week from the proceeds of the sale of their booty after they had filled the bellies of their families and their neighbours.

George was well pleased, though he was wise enough not to underestimate his opponents; and it was in this frame of mind that in October, 1867, he planned his fiftieth operation. The territory chosen was to be five square miles due south of Watton, in the triangle of Thompson–Tottington–Breckles. Working in groups of three—two to operate, one to keep look-out—they were to begin on the Thompson–Tottington line and converge on Breckles, where at half-past three in the morning they were to meet at a hut which stood in a spinney edging one side of the drive leading up to Breckles Hall. George would fulfil his usual role of scout-out-ahead and liaison between the groups, for though his agents had filtered the information that the gang proposed working the Holme Hale estate, the property of the man who was primarily responsible for it all, he judged it wiser to avoid whatever independently working gamekeepers there might be in his area.

As the men had now come to expect, the operation went without a hitch, and shortly after three o'clock the groups began to arrive at the Breckles hut. While waiting, they laid out their haul, which was a particularly good one, and chatted in whispers about the experiences of the night.

Sometimes George would already be waiting at the rendezvous when the first group arrived. At others, he would come a quarter of an hour before time. Sometimes, though not often, he would arrive after all the rest.

As half-past three approached, and he had not come, a silence fell upon the men. He always had a good word for them, and did not stint his praise if the bag was a good one. And the simple countrymen, whose admiration for their leader was boundless, derived a great personal satisfaction from his approval.

"George is late tonight," one of the men murmured as the clock on the Breckles coach-house chimed the half-hour.

"He'll come!" he was assured.

Ten minutes later, he said again, "George has never been as late as this."

"He'll come, I tell you!" insisted his companion.

But as the minutes sped by and still Mace did not appear they began to be apprehensive.

"Something must have happened to him!" exclaimed the man who had spoken first, his voice unsteady with rising fear.

"Not to George," he was told, but this time with less conviction.

When four o'clock had struck, and there was still no sign of him, all the men were alarmed, and some were becoming angry. There were some who condemned the leader for exposing them to such risks; the hut was far too close to the house, they said.

"If we're to get home before light," one of them grumbled, "we can't wait much longer."

"We'll give him until the clock chimes the quarter," said Jim Harris, whom George had appointed his lieutenant. "If he hasn't come then, we'll hide the bag in Boulter's spinney. He'll have a good reason for not coming, you may be bound."

They crouched on their haunches, leaning their backs against the wall of the hut, straining their eyes at the grey darkness of the spinney, and their ears for the least sound which would tell them someone was approaching. They crouched in silence, stifling their individual emotions, tensed and puzzled.

The clock chimed the quarter.

"Right," said Jim Harris. "You, Dick, and you, Bert, you'll come with me to Boulter's spinney. The rest of you make your ways home separately."

But before any of them could move, sounds reached them which froze them where they squatted.

"A coach!" exclaimed Dick Utting. "At this time of night!"

"George said the squire's away in London," Jim Harris whispered. "This'll be him coming home. No one move till it's gone."

But fascinated by the sounds, no one obeyed him, and all edged their way to the end of the hut, from where they could see the drive.

Presently the coach came into view. Its lamps were brighter than usual and appeared in some strange way to envelop with their light the whole of the equipage.

As Jim Harris watched it come rolling up the drive, and heard the clop of the horses' hooves on the gravel and the scrunch of the wheels, he felt the skin of his scalp tightening and a river of ice course down his spine. For there was something truly strange about the coach—though the reins were clearly being held, there was no coachman sitting on the box!

Nor, apparently, was Jim the only one who had noted this lack of a driver, for from several tight throats about him came exclamations of "My God!"

There was not one of them who would not have jumped to his feet and fled had he been able. But although the desire filled them, limbs would not respond.

And all the time the coach was coming nearer, until presently it drew level with the hut.

Then they saw the reins pulled taut. They saw the horses halt.

Then, after a pause, they saw the door of the coach open and the steps let down.

Again there was a pause, then the steps were put up and the door closed.

But not one of the twelve had seen anyone step down.

The coach swayed a little, as though someone were re-mounting the box. The reins were shaken, and the horses moved forward.

But no sooner had they done so than the coach vanished!

The silence which followed was broken only by the expletives of men and the noise they made as they crashed their way through the spinney intent only upon escape.

Two or three hours later, one of the grooms who lived in the lodge cottage walked up the drive towards the Hall to begin another day's work in the stables. As he came to the hut, he saw lying in the driveway, at the very spot where the poachers had seen the coach stop, the still body of a man. He ran to it, and turned it over, thinking it must be one of his companions who had come home the evening before the worse for drink. But he did not recognize the man; and he was not drunk, but quite dead. Whoever he was, he had died peacefully, for his parted lips were curved in a happy smile. There was something familiar about the features, nevertheless, and for a time the groom was puzzled. But he had worked at Breckles all his life, and at last it came to him.

"The old squire!" he exclaimed, and rising to his feet began to hurry towards the Hall shouting as he went.

Later in the day the body was identified as that of George Mace of Watton, whose mother thirty-five years ago had been a housemaid at the Hall. From the heap of rabbits, hare and other game found behind the hut, it was clear that the poacher had had an otherwise successful night.

Dr Jessop, the local chronicler, who records these events in his book *Frivola*, has written: "There was nothing to show what had killed him. There were no marks of violence on the body nor any signs of sudden illness. His time had come, and he had been fetched away by a Power which even the boldest poacher cannot hope to defy."

Flo Mace's verdict was different. Through her weeping she murmured, "He went home at last!"

Shades of Murder

What causes a haunting we shall never know this side of the grave. The number of people whose deaths have been intermingled with tragedy, sadness or intolerable pain and anguish is infinitely greater than the number of reported hauntings. It is well known that some people see ghosts where others do not, and it may be that in places like Belsen and the battlefields of the First World War there is a haunting on a scale and on a plane of which mortals are not aware; for if hauntings do take place at all, and there is good evidence that they do, then the pattern must make sense, and there must be reasons why some hauntings come through to us and others do not, why relatively unimportant events cause a haunting and quite appalling tragedies apparently do not. And why do the romantic kind of hauntings seem to outnumber the other sort?

For centuries it has been believed that a haunting can be caused by a young life being cruelly and suddenly terminated. This creates an angry and vengeful spirit.

This belief was common among the priests of the early civilizations, who marked the burial of their monarchs by slaughtering young human victims and immuring them in the royal tomb. The idea was to create young and virile spirits to guard and protect the King on his journey into eternity. This rite was practised by many early peoples, including the Bronze Age Shang Dynasty, the Mycenaean Greeks, the Sumerians and the Aztecs, and was a world-wide part of religious practice. It has come down with the passing millenia into comparatively modern times when young victims were bricked up live into the foundation walls of buildings, their pathetic skeletons being discovered even today.

The theory of truncated lives creating angry ghosts seems to be borne out by the number of hauntings connected with crime, particularly murder. Murder has been a mere drop in the ocean of human suffering, if one does not term as murder the quasi-official slaughter which has gone on under various oligarchies since time began.

The numbers of children and young people who have been murder victims will never be told, for many murders have not been discovered, and murderers of course have been known to escape justice, even though they were tried for their crime.

Such a case was that of the murder of Jane Clouson in the parish of Kidbrooke, London, in 1871. Jane was a servant in the house of a Greenwich printer named Ebeneezer Pook. She was seventeen and a pretty girl and was seduced by Pook's young son, Edmund, who was twenty. It was more than just an isolated seduction. They had quite an affair, lasting several months, with the result that Jane became pregnant.

Mr and Mrs Pook found out what had been going on under their respectable, God-fearing roof, and sacked Jane on the spot, though they later denied that this was why she was dismissed. Jane, not unreasonably, turned to Edmund for support, for he had made the girl all sorts of false promises in order to secure her favours. But Edmund was neither willing nor able to support her and certainly had no thought of marrying her. His brother had already brought down the parental wrath by marrying beneath his station and he had no intention of provoking his formidable father in the same way. But Jane was insistent that he should do the right thing by her in one way or another, and the poor child was indeed desperate in the hard, Victorian world, with no parents to turn to.

Edmund, full of promises he did not intend to keep, arranged to meet her at Blackheath on the evening of 26 April, 1871. Early the following morning she was found battered nearly to death in Kidbrooke Lane, a haunt of lovers in those days. She died in Guys Hospital without recovering consciousness. Edmund was tried for her murder, but as the Judge ruled that all the statements Jane had made before her death which incriminated him were hearsay and inadmissible as evidence, he was found not guilty and discharged.

The verdict caused an uproar and there were disturbances in Greenwich. There were disturbances also in the astral plane apparently.

But it was not until Edmund had been found not guilty and been released that Jane's ghost returned to the scene of the crime and began to haunt Kidbrooke Lane. It should be remembered that this part of London, S.W.3, has been entirely rebuilt since the 'seventies, and the Kidbrooke Lane which Jane haunted no longer exists, having been completely built over. Then it was a stretch of open country between Kidbrooke and Eltham which was largely under cultivation.

Kidbrooke Lane was, as mentioned, a popular resort for the courting couples of the neighbourhood. It was narrow, shaded by trees and tall hedges and crossed by a small stream named Kid. The lane ran through cornfields and farmland and offered plenty of sheltered privacy for dalliance.

On the night of the murder it had been patrolled at regular intervals by P.C. Gunn. Jane was murdered about 8.30 and left lying by the side of the lane past which the constable patrolled twice during the night without seeing her. Towards dawn she partly recovered consciousness and crawled into the centre of the lane as the constable came by the third time, moaning "Oh, my head! My head!" Her face and head had been terribly battered with a lathing hammer later found. This was a long-handled tool with an axe opposite the hammer head and made a very vicious weapon. Lovers in the lane that night had heard her screams, but no one troubled to investigate.

Jane's spectral screams were heard again and again by courting couples in Kidbrooke Lane and her ghost was seen more than once by the patrolling policemen. She appeared in a white dress, her face running with blood.

Her dreadful cries were heard for some years until Kidbrooke Lane finally disappeared, as all the open land between Eltham and Shooters Hill Road was gradually built on. Rochester Way was built right across the old lane which was completely swallowed up in bricks and mortar. Only then did Jane's reproachful ghost desert the now unrecognizable place where her wretched lover battered her to death.

The only champion Jane had on this earth was a man named Newton Crosland, who wrote a deliberately libellous pamphlet after Edmund Pooke's acquittal. He was taken to court, but Edmund got only nominal damages, for Crosland's counsel, the redoubtable Sergeant Parry, put up a formidable case for justification on the grounds that Pook was guilty of Jane's murder, and would have been convicted but for the Judge's ruling about the hearsay evidence.

But a man cannot be tried twice for the same murder—at least not in this world. It would be satisfying to think that in his encounter with Jane in the next world he got his deserts. The Pook Case did not enjoy the fame of the story of Maria Marten and the Red Barn. Here was another wronged girl murdered, but this time it was the murderer who paid the penalty and who remained earthbound to haunt the place of his misdeeds.

Compared with Jane Clouson, Maria Marten was a rather more tarnished maiden when William Corder foully murdered her in the now immortal Red Barn. She had already had an illegitimate child by Corder's elder brother Thomas, and another by a man named Matthews. She was the belle of the Suffolk village of Polstead, and was certainly free with her favours. The countryfolk of Suffolk had a reputation for immorality during the nineteenth century, as was observed during the Peasenhall Case (1902). Whether it was deserved or not is another matter.

William and Maria had an illegitimate child which died a mysterious death, and Maria's ageing father pressed William, now relatively well off following the deaths of his father and brother, to make his erring daughter into a respectable woman. The reluctant Corder eventually appeared to agree, conditional upon the would-be bride going away secretly with him. She got no farther than the Red Barn, where he gave her both barrels and buried her beneath the earthen floor.

William Corder was not a clever murderer and he incriminated himself by writing letters about Maria which aroused the suspicion of her family—particularly her mother-in-law, old Marten's young wife, who dreamed twice, she declared, that Corder had shot Maria and buried her under the floor of the Red Barn.

The floor was dug and Mrs Anne Marten's remarkable dream prophecy turned out to be true. Corder meanwhile had married a school-teacher he met through a matrimonial advertisement in the *Sunday Times* in the year 1827, and was living in London. The case against him was overwhelming and he was publicly hanged outside the gates of Bury St Edmunds gaol on 11 August, 1828. All the workmen in the town went on strike that morning in order to go to the hanging.

The remarkable dreams of Anne Marten which had led to Corder's undoing were given a more natural explanation by the villagers of Polstead who knew the participants of this famous drama and who believed that Maria was hated by her stepmother, who it was, they said, who put the idea into William's head to lure

Maria into the Red Barn and kill her and bury her there. William agreed and promised to send Anne Marten money regularly as a sweetener to keep her quiet about what she knew. But he stopped sending her the money after a while and so she betrayed him—merely for the sake of a few pounds. At his trial he could not accuse her of being his accomplice, for his defence was a denial of the deed.

Another rather more picturesque theory told in Polstead after the murder was that William Corder was having an affair with Anne Marten, a young and attractive woman, just a year or two older than Maria. According to this theory, Anne planned the murder of her step-daughter to get her out of the way so that she could run off with William Corder.

Both of these theories support the view held by many people in Polstead at the time that Anne Marten invented the dreams in order to avenge herself on Corder for letting her down.

A haunting was fully expected as a consequence of this foul deed. Just after the discovery of Maria's body a false alarm about the raising of her ghost came about in the following manner.

Morbid sightseers gathered at the Red Barn, though perhaps in less numbers than they would have done today, for in the 1820s there were the full horrors of a public hanging and a dissection for those so inclined. One man arrived at the Red Barn and finding it empty went inside and looked into the empty grave, from which Maria's remains had been recently dug. Some singularly morbid impulse made him lie down in the grave. Just then a lady and gentleman, prompted by the same species of curiosity, entered the barn, and the man got up hurriedly from the trench. The transfixed couple thought, in the semi-darkness, that it was Maria's ghost rising from her uneasy grave. The lady screamed and fainted on the spot.

But apparently Maria's ghost did not walk, despite the fact that her poor remains were buried and dug up three times. The haunting arose from the manner in which her murderer's body was disposed of after his hanging.

After he had cut down the corpse, the hangman secured the remarkable price of a guinea an inch for pieces of the rope from the tumultuous crowd which thronged the scaffold. The rope was supposed to have acquired magical properties after the hanging.

The corpse was then taken to the Shirehall, Bury St Edmunds, for the dissection, an astonishing public performance on the part of the authorities of the day. The body was cut open from throat to abdomen and the skin folded back to display what was beneath. The remains were laid upon a table and then 5,000 people were admitted to view this gruesome exhibition of human butchery, shuffling past in a gaping endless stream the whole day long. At six p.m. the room was closed in the faces of thousands more hard-stomached wretches clamouring to see the sight.

Inside the hall two artists, with the assistance of a fourteen-year-old boy who held the bloodstained corpse, made various death masks of the hanged man. These, which are still preserved, bear little resemblance to William Corder, for hanging not only stretches the neck but completely distorts the features.

The following day Corder's body was taken to the West Suffolk General Hospital and completely dissected for the learning and information of the medical students there, who at least had some legitimate interest in such a proceeding. Corder's skeleton has been kept at the hospital and is used to this day for the teaching of anatomy—it being complete with the significant exception of the skull.

Several surgeons got busy on the grisly remains. Part of the scalp was dried and preserved and still exists. A book giving an account of the trial was bound in Corder's tanned skin, and this still graces the shelves at Moyse's Hall Museum, Bury St Edmunds.

The spirit of the guilty man might not have been too much disturbed at his body being used in this manner, but it is what happened to the skull which caused the haunting.

This was stolen from the skeleton in the hospital by a Dr Kilner, who substituted for it a spare skull he happened to possess. Dr Kilner took Corder's skull home, and for some reason best known to himself polished it and mounted it in an ebony box. This was about fifty years after the hanging.

Thereafter there was no peace in the good doctor's house. Skulls, as has been observed in many a strange story of haunting, seem to have an extraordinary power to create unaccountable mischief and disturbance. This is thought to be because the seat of the mind and thoughts is considered to be of great importance by the spirit which has left it.

Corder's ghost, it appeared, was considerably annoyed at Dr Kilner's action and proceeded to haunt him in the most nerve-racking manner. Candles blew out, doors slammed, a strange man in ancient clothes msyteriously appeared and just as mysteriously vanished.

The doctor soon found the haunting by the man whose skull he had tampered with merely to satisfy a personal whim rather more than he could bear, even though he did not believe in ghosts. Everywhere he went he heard footsteps behind him and heavy breathing over his shoulder. At night the doors of the house were opened and slammed violently, and his terrified household heard frantic hammering and sounds of sobbing issuing from the drawing-room where the skull was kept in its ebony box.

Dr Kilner, despite his disbelief in ghosts, knew very well by this time that his theft of Corder's skull was the cause of all the trouble, which soon held his whole household in the grip of terror. It looked as though he would have to get rid of the thing. It was out of the question to return it to its proper place in the hospital. It was highly polished and looked almost like tortoiseshell, quite different from the rest of Corder's skeleton. Too many questions would be asked.

In vain he hoped that Corder's disturbed ghost would settle down. One night he was awoken by one of the spectral noises and went on to the landing with a candle to see the door of the drawing-room being turned by a ghostly white hand. As the door was opened by the phantom hand, Kilner was stunned by a tremendous explosion like the report of a gun.

He ran downstairs and into the drawing-room where he was met by a gust of icy wind. The box which had contained the skull was lying in fragments on the floor. The skull itself was undamaged and was upon one of the shelves of the cabinet.

After that Kilner lost no time in getting rid of his ill-acquired trophy. He gave it to a friend of his, Mr F. C. Hopkins, a retired official of the Commissioners of Prisons who had bought old Bury St Edmunds gaol where Corder had been hanged, and was living in the governor's house.

Somewhat reluctantly, the retired prison official accepted the unwelcome gift and took it home wrapped in a silk handkerchief. On the way home he fell and sprained his ankle, and the skull rolled, grinning evilly, in front of a lady who fainted on the spot.

This was only the beginning of disasters for Hopkins too. Illness, family troubles, financial misfortunes, quickly overtook him.

He did the wisest thing and took the unwanted relic to a country graveyard where he bribed a grave-digger to give it a Christian burial.

Thus Corder's skull got its ardently desired peace, and thereafter, we are told, both the Hopkins and the Kilners flourished.

It will be seen that these hauntings resulting from murder do not run to pattern. In the case of William Corder, he returned from the shades fifty years after his crime and expiation, not because he was a troubled, uneasy spirit, but because he was, presumably, annoyed at the use to which his precious skull had been put. This is a widely observed characteristic of ghosts. They are very touchy about the skulls belonging to their mortal and long-discarded remains, and a skull can create a most remarkable haunting.

Jane Clouson's ghost hovered in Kidbrooke Lane in reproachful protest because her murderer never paid for his crime. The victims of Landru, however, the French mass-murderer, are said to haunt the Forest of Rambouillet, which is not far from his infamous Villa Ermitage where he used to lure women and murder them for their few paltry possessions. Landru was condemned and executed on 25 February, 1922.

Perhaps it was the sheer quantity of Landru's victims which caused the restless spirits of Rambouillet. He was condemned for the murder of eleven women, though he is believed to have killed many more. The French police at one time put the figure as high as three hundred. The eerie wailings and sobbings of the Forest of Rambouillet have been heard by a number of people.

For several years after the execution of Landru, bodies of murdered people were found in the forest, and the mystery of these deaths has never been solved.

Local legend has it that Landru himself—who went to the guillotine protesting his innocence to the last in face of incontrovertible evidence—returned to the scene of his former crimes as an evil spirit and entered into the bodies of innocent people and made them commit these murders. This at least would explain why the murders remain a mystery, for motiveless crimes are the most difficult to solve.

The celebrated Dick Turpin was in reality a coarse and vicious thug, despite the rather more romantic legends which have gathered around his name. He beat up and tortured his victims with pitiless brutality.

Once he fractured the skull of an old farmer and then poured boiling water over his head, while taking it in turns with his companions to rape the maid. On another occasion, when he met with an old woman's refusal to reveal the whereabouts of her valuables, he exclaimed:"God damn your blood, you old bitch! If you won't tell us, I'll set your arse on the grate." And he and his thugs sat the poor old lady in the fire until she finally had to tell where her money was.

Turpin was hanged at York in 1739, jumping off the ladder in order to secure for himself a quick end. Despite his brutalities, he was a very popular criminal of his day, and was hanged amid the ecstatic plaudits of the mob. But he doesn't seem to be having it so good in the other world, for his tormented ghost has been seen riding on horseback at Loughton in Essex with the ghost of the old woman he had tortured in the fire, clinging to his back.

Jack the Ripper caused the greatest murder sensation of the nineteenth century, and his horrific deeds of death naturally attracted people of a psychic turn of mind. The year was 1888.

Stories of hauntings naturally followed these memorable murders. A headless woman was seen night after night sitting on a wall in Hanbury Street, Spitalfields, near the spot where 47-year-old Anne Chapman was murdered and savagely mutilated by Jack the Ripper, who had cut her head right off and then tied it in place with a handkerchief.

Millers Court, where the Ripper killed his last known victim, Mary Kelly, echoed with her ghostly screams for long afterwards.

Some people suggested that Jack the Ripper's crimes were connected with witchcraft, and that his murders were a species of black magic. He certainly seemed to employ some strange ritual in the way he arranged not only the belongings of the women he murdered, but also the organs he took out of their bodies. This was particularly noticed in the case of Mary Kelly, the only murder he committed in the comparative safety of a room. It was thought by some people that in this murder he was obsessed by ideas of human sacrifice and obscene magical rites.

Be that as it may, he was never caught and the psychologists, rather than the occultists, have a more plausible explanation of his actions.

Black Shuck—the Dog of Death

The moon rose, red and round, over the wild, wet levels of Wicken Fen. There the swamps and pools, reed-beds and waterways are still much as they were nine hundred years ago when Hereward the Wake threw back the Norman knights and men-at-arms in the reeds on Aldreth Causeway. There was until recent years an inn on the river bank which bore the enchanting name of "Five Miles From Anywhere—No Hurry".

A rough crew of turf-diggers, sedge-cutters, and dyke-dydlers sat by the turf fire in the sanded, red-curtained parlour. I said casually: "Well, who's coming home by the bank?" The short cut by the bank would save a mile on the road home.

"That owd Shuck Dog run there o' nights, master," said Jake Barton, spitting into the white ash of the turf fire. "Do ye goo, he'll hev ye as sure as harvest. I 'ouldn't walk that owd bank, not if I had to goo to Hanover."

"Ne me yet nayther," chimed in two or three. "Yew recollect what happened to one young woman. She up and died arter that owd Dog runned her!"

"Well, I'm going," says I. "Are you coming, Fred? Your way lies my way, and it'll save you half a mile."

Fred shied like a horse.

"No, sir! No, sir! Yew 'on't ketch me on that there bank at night. I 'ouldn't goo theer not for the King o' England! Ah! Yew may hev your gret owd duck gun but if we'd got machine guns, I 'ouldn't goo. An' ef yew goo, the owd Dog'll heve ye, sure as harvest."

I have known Fred since boyhood. He was my constant companion on shooting days in the Fen. He could jump a dyke like a greyhound, walk any man off his legs, drink a quart, fight anyone. That night he was scared—and admitted it.

"What are you scared of, Fred? Do you think we'll find a dead monk in the water like the one Jake thought he saw that night he was netting the dyke for fish?" I asked.

"No, I ain't skeered of no monkses. That's the Dog. He run that bank o' nights, big as a calf, Master Wentworth, black as tar, wi' eyes like bike lamps! Do[1] he see you, you'll up and die! There ain't a man what can see that owd Dog and live. Do he does, he'll goo scatty."

"But my father shot on the bank scores of nights after duck, Fred. He said the best flight was by the old black mill."

"I dessay, but he niver seed the Dog. Do he'd ha' been a dead 'un."

Fred told me that a few years before his sister, who went to meet her sweetheart by moonlight tryst at the black draining mill, had seen the Dog.

"The Dog, sir, cum along that bank quiet as death. Jest padded along head down, gret olde ars flappin'. That worn't more'n twenty yards off when that raised that's head and glouted (glared) at her—eyes red as blood. My heart! She shruk[2] like an owd owl and runned along that there bank like a hare. Run, sir! Nuthin' could ha' ketched her. I reckon if we'd ha' sent her to Newmarket she'd ha' won the Town Plate for us! She come bustin' along that bank like a racehoss, right slap into her young man. He collared hold of her and she went off in a dead faint!"

"Did her young man see anything, Fred?

"Nit nothin'!"

"Well, she's still alive, Fred. The Dog didn't kill her. It won't kill us either."

"Ha! Take more'n an owd Dog to kill her. She's as tough as hog leather. But that wholly laid her up for a week and she've bin a 'clan-janderin' about it ever since."

So Fred did not walk with me by Spinney Bank that night. The presence of a double eight-bore and the promise of a quart of beer failed to shake the prestige of the Dog. And when I told him next day that I had walked home alone that night by the bank he answered: "More fule yew! But then, happen the owd Dog don't hut the gentry!"

[1] Do—if.
[2] Shruk—shrieked.

This legend of a ghostly dog persists all over East Anglia. A very dear friend, the late Lady Walsingham, about whom there was "no nonsense, my dear", believed in it implicitly. She had seen it!

One night at Leiston in Suffolk, on the coast, where the Dog is known as "The Galleytrot", she and the then Lady Rendlesham sat up in the churchyard to watch. At twelve precisely a slinking, sable shadow slipped among the gravestones like a wraith, leaped the low churchyard wall and slid down the dark lane towards the sandhills like an evil whisper. Neither of these self-possessed ladies drank, sat up late or had ever heard of Hannen Swaffer.

Now this Black Dog is the same mythological animal as Black Shuck, the enormous ghostly hound of the Norfolk coast who is said to pad along the cliff-top path between Cromer and Sheringham.

On the high coast road that goes dipping down through woods and over heathy commons where the sea-wind blows, between Cromer and Sheringham, there are villages whose inhabitants will not walk the windy miles of that lonely road at night if you were to offer them ten pounds and a cask of beer.

They are scared, these hardbitten Norfolk fishermen and ploughmen.

W. A. Dutt, in his book, *The Norfolk Broadland*, says:

"One of the most impressive phantoms, and one of the best known in Norfolk, is Old Shuck (from the Anglo-Saxon, Scucca or Sceocca, the early native word for Satan), a demon dog, as big as a fair-sized calf, that pads along noiselessly under the shadow of the hedgerows, tracking the steps of lonely wayfarers, and terrifying them with the wicked glare of his yellow eyes. To meet him means death within the year to the unhappy beholder. As Shuck sometimes leaves his head at home, though his eyes are always seen as big as saucers, he is, as Mr Rye says, 'an animal more avoided than respected'. One of his chief haunts is Neatishead Lane, near Barton Broad; but he also favours Coltishall Bridge, over which he always ambles without his head; and a very special promenade of his is from Beeston, near Sheringham, to Overstrand, after which his course is uncertain.

A curious variation of this ghostly hound is said to haunt an overgrown and little-used lane called Slough Hill in the parish of West Wratting on the Suffolk borders of Cambridgeshire. Police Constable A. Taylor, of The Tiled House, Panton Street, Cambridge, tells me that, in his youth, this lane, which is on the road from West Wratting to Balsham, was haunted by an extraordinary thing called

"The Shug Monkey". It was, he says, "a cross between a big rough-coated dog and a monkey with big shining eyes. Sometimes it would shuffle along on its hind legs and at other times it would whizz past on all-fours. You can guess that we children gave the place a wide berth after dark !"

He adds that Spanneys Gate into West Wratting Park was haunted by a White Lady.

Another believer in the Black Dog is Mrs Sophia Wilson, a native of Hempnall, near Norwich. Mrs Wilson writes to me:

"There is a stretch of road from Hempnall called 'Market Hole' and when I first lived at Hempnall sixty-one years ago, my husband told me that there was something to be seen and had been seen by different residents.

"Well, my dear husband passed on and I never really thought anything more about the incident until one night my son who was then about twenty-four came in from Norwich looking white and scared. I said, 'Whatever is the matter? Are you ill?' and he said, 'No. Coming down Market Hole I had a bad turn. I saw what appeared to be a big Dog about to cross in front of my bike and I thought I should be thrown off, but it just vanished. When I got off my bike and looked round, there was nothing to be seen, and I felt awful.' "

Another version of Black Shuck is said to haunt villages in the Waveney Valley round about Geldeston. It is known as "The Hateful Thing" or "The Churchyard or Hellbeast", and although usually seen in the form of a huge dog, it has been known to take the shape of a "Swooning Shadow", whatever that may be. It is a sign that some un-usually horrible wickedness has just been committed or is about to be.

An old village woman claimed that she saw it when walking home at night from Gillingham to Geldeston. She tells the story in the following words:

"It was after I had been promised to Josh and before we were married that I saw the 'Hateful Thing'. It must have been close upon the time that we were to be married for I remember we had got as far as 'waisting' it.

"It was between eight and nine and we were in a lane near Geldeston when we met Mrs S., and she started to walk with us, when I heard something behind us, like the sound of a dog running. I thought it was some farmer's dog, and paid little attention to it, but it kept on just at the back of us, pit-pat-pit-pat-pit-pat ! 'I wonder what that dog wants', I said to Mrs S. 'What dog do you mean?' she said, looking all round.

" 'Why, can't you hear it?' I said. 'It has been following us for the last five minutes or more! You can hear it, can't you, Josh?' I said. 'Nonsense, old mawther,' said Josh, 'just you lug hold of my arm and come along.' I was walking between Josh and Mrs S. and I lay hold of Mrs S's arm and she says, 'I can hear it now; it's in front of us; look, there it be!' and sure enough just in front of us was what looked like a big, black dog; but it wasn't a dog at all; it was the 'Hateful Thing' that had been seen hereabouts before and it betokened some great misfortune.

"It kept in front of us until it came to the churchyard, when it went right through the wall and we saw it no more."

She said that many people in the district had seen it and that its favourite haunt was the "Gelders", which was a local name for a clump of trees by the wayside on the Beccles Road. Mr Morley Adams adds:

"I found from conversation with other folk in the neighbourhood that her words were quite true; but apart from this woman, I found no one who had actually seen the beast, but they all knew someone who had. I gained the following further information about this weird wraith: At times it is seen as a large black dog, with eyes of fire and foaming mouth. If no fear is shown, he will walk just behind you, but his paws make no sound upon the ground. The person who sees him should not attempt to turn back or the beast will growl and snarl like a mad dog. He has been known to drag children along the road by their clothes, and dire disaster overtakes the individual who persists in running away from him.

"The people who are most likely to see the 'Hell-hound' are those born under the chime hours, or towards the small hours of a Friday night."

The same Dog runs in Essex along the lonely coast road from Peldon to Tolleshunt D'Arcy. William Fell, gamekeeper of D'Arcy, swore to me that he had seen it twice on Wigborough Hill.

The Black Dog is one with the Ghostly Hound of Dartmoor who haunts the moor and hunts terrified humans to their death in the quaking bogs. The Hound of the Baskervilles is a Dorsetshire version. All have their roots in the Hound of Odin, the mighty dog of war, whose legend came to Britain a thousand years ago when the long-ships grounded in the surf, the ravens flew at their mast-heads, there was battle and the clang of swords in the swirling mists, and "all around the shouts of war and the cries of sea-raiders beaching their ships".

In a letter dated 29 August, 1956, Mrs Barbara Carbonnell, who is deeply interested in folklore and church architecture in Devon, offered to send me various notes connected with the widespread legend of the Black Dog "together with some well-authenticated instances of its appearance in the County of Devon".

It will be noted that her hauntings all seem to occur in the vicinity of an "old straight road", precisely the same sort of road as the Peddar's Way in Norfolk and Suffolk. Mrs Carbonnell writes:

"These notes cover a period of roughly six to seven years. I began to interest myself in the legend of the Black Dog about 1923, and from then until 1931, followed every tale I heard, visiting the places concerned and talking to people of all classes, getting in touch with others who had left the neighbourhood and generally checking all information.

"About 1925, I became aware that there were a remarkable number of legends about it occurring on one particular stretch of road, and that this particular piece of road had the remains of a far earlier road forming part of its ditch.

"I had recently interested myself in the theory put forward by Alfred Watkins in his book *The Old Straight Track*, and it occurred to me to try if a straight line plotted on the map between the two points, Copplestone and Torrington, where legend said the Black Dog 'ran', would give me any clue as to where further legends of his appearance would emerge.

"It must be remembered that, in the first instance, I was only told by a man, at that time our gardener, that his father had several times seen 'the Black Dog of Torrington' that haunts the road by Stopgate, on the way to Copplestone, when, on his rounds as van man to a firm of millers, he came along that road at night. It was only after confirming this with the man himself, and learning from others that the dog had been seen near Stopgate, that I decided to 'plot' my line from Torrington to Copplestone (with extensions to the edges of the maps). I found instances of Black Dog hauntings in places through which the line passed, which otherwise it would not have occurred to me to visit.

"The whole distance, across country, from Copplestone westwards to the coast is no more than twenty-six to twenty-seven miles, and since I got no evidence of any 'Haunting' in the last five miles, the distance where such evidence did occur would be about twenty-one miles.

"In these twenty-one miles I was well rewarded by the stories I got from the country people, stories which had a certain similarity but which were told me without any prompting from me. I was well known in that part of the country, and it was my habit to go off either alone or with my husband, and get into conversation with farm folk and villagers asking for old tales of the countryside. I did not deliberately start asking questions about the Black Dog. It was known that I was engaged in getting notes for Parish history, that I was engaged in transcribing Parish Registers, and that any 'old tale' about olden days would be well received. In this way ghost stories were bound to crop up, and this was how those of the Black Dog emerged.

"I have given the accounts of what I was told briefly, confining myself to what my informants said, using as far as possible their own wording from my notes written at the time.

"A van driver, who first told me of his experience at Stopgate, was a man then between sixty-five and seventy, a most respected and respectable man, a Plymouth Brother and strict teetotaller, who for nearly forty years had driven the miller's wagon between Copplestone Mills and Torrington.

"His work kept him out to all hours; two heavy horses and a load of sacks, doing that journey sometimes three times a week in all weathers, meant long hours, and often it was not before the early morning that he got back to Copplestone.

"When asked about the Black Dog, he was quite willing to tell me of his experiences. He seemed to consider it nothing unusual to see 'they sort of things', while admitting that he was 'scairt' the first time, hastily getting under the shelter of the van hood (his van was, of course, a heavy four-wheel one with a stretched canvas hood) when the Dog 'appeared' the first time. Rather than remain seated on the side of the shaft, as was his custom, he said that as the years went on and he became familiar with the Dog's appearance, he did not trouble to do so, often walking at the head of his team regardless of the 'gurt Hound' running beside him, 'so big as a calf' were his words.

" 'But', he added, 'I durstn't touch him, nor speak when he were by.'

"I found no legend of such haunting to the east of Copplestone, on extending the line in that direction; and taking into consideration the fact that all my informants spoke of it as the Black Dog of Torrington, and of its 'running between there and Copplestone', I made little search on that side, concentrating on the NW line, but probing beyond Torrington towards the coast, with some success.

"The results of these years of search are small, but certainly give

some idea of the strong hold such legends have and how the apparitions, as described to me, have a definite likeness.

"In the years when I was following up these clues, motor transport
in the out-of-the-way parts of Devon was by no means so common
as today. Though a number of farmers, even then, had cars, very
few villagers had a motor-bus service connecting them; and even
now, thirty years later, there is only a small proportion of the
places named which have.

"There was, and still is, a very definite 'cliqueyness' about Devon
villagers, which not even modern conditions has really broken
down. Their own parish, their own church (even if they don't
attend it very regularly), their own customs, and, very strongly,
their own legends, are strictly their *own*, not to be confused with
those of other villages, and in getting these stories I seldom found
anyone willing to admit that the haunting known by them could
have any connexion with that in any other neighbourhood.

"Numbers of people, living in and near Copplestone, spoke of the
Black Dog of Torrington that comes to Copplestone Cross, but,
except for the van driver, none of them spoke of seeing it, and, as
will appear, his experience of the spectre was at a point some three
to four miles farther west.

"At Down St Mary, a hilltop village, with an ancient Saxon church
with tympanum, said to be pre-Domesday foundation, numbers of
villagers spoke of hearing the Torrington Dog baying and 'rushing'
up this lane on dark nights. It was said to be specially noisy as he
'tore by' the Smithy, and I was told that the old smith (dead before
I began my search) had often seen it. From the top of the Lane, the
Black Dog crossed the road and went rushing between the Church
and Schoolhouse, 'knocking down the corner of the Schoolhouse'
as he headed for the lane beyond. He reached the Schoolhouse
always about midnight.

"When I asked how it was that the corner of the Schoolhouse
showed no signs of damage, the old man who had told me this
shook his head and replied:

" 'Well, there 'tis, he do knock'n down. I've a-heard the stones
fall as he goes rorin' by, and I've heard the same from my father and
grandfather time and again. It's true, right enough.'

"Another man told me how, when he was a lad, he and several
others of the same age were going home after a choir supper at
Christmas. Their way lay down the lane towards Copplestone and,
as they passed the smithy, they all heard the Black Dog of Torrington coming up the lane. They ran into a field and saw a great dog

'as big as a calf', quite black, with shining eyes, pass the smithy and go towards the Schoolhouse. It was baying as it ran, and, as it passed the Schoolhouse, they heard a crash 'like stones falling in a quarry'. They did not venture out into the lane until they heard the sound of baying growing fainter and there was nothing to be seen. 'Us ran for it, to git back home,' he added.

"I heard this sort of story from others in the village.

"Following the lane from the Church at Down St Mary, the line goes through the farm called Thorne, and passes through the cross-roads of Stopgate, Blackaditch (so called, though the modern sign-post omits the second 'a') and Aller. It was along this stretch of road, which for some 32 miles has a deep ditch where the earlier road ran, that the Line conforms closely, and it was on this stretch that the van driver so frequently saw the spectre of the Black Dog of Torrington. From Aller Bridge the Line diverges from the main road through Holm (farm).

"In Wembworthy there were vague tales of 'something' that haunted the road by Smithen; there is nothing more definite, but the name Smithen is suggestive.

"At Wyke or Week Hill, St Giles-in-the-Wood, as at Hollocombe, the country folk were not inclined to speak of legends, and when, tentatively, the Black Dog of Torrington was mentioned, I noticed a secretive look (called in Devon 'looking sideways') as they shook their heads.

"The Line I had plotted ran here parallel with, and close alongside, a steep hill road to the SW of the village, called Wyke or Week Hill (spelt both ways locally), with a farm called Allens Week at the top. Having found the St Giles's search unrewarding, I should have given up hope of any tales hereabouts, but, on my return home, I remembered that the woman who kept the village shop in our village of Bow came from St Giles's, and that her father still lived there. Next day I went down to the shop. She had from time to time told me many trifles of local history, and was well aware of the interest such things had for me. I told her I had been to St. Giles's and asked: 'Did you ever hear of the Black Dog of Torrington?'

"As I spoke, two village women came through the door, and, to my surprise, Mrs Jewell, usually so friendly and forthcoming, snapped, 'No, never', and transferred her attention to the two who had come in, most pointedly bidding me good morning.

"Puzzled by her manner, I left the shop and went on down the village. Half an hour later, as I passed the shop again, Mrs Jewell came to the door, caught me by the arm and said:

" 'Come back, do. I've a lot to tell you,' and pulled me into her parlour behind the shop.

" 'What did you want to know about the Black Dog of Torrington?' she asked. I told her I wanted to hear any tales of it that I could and particularly if there were any stories of it having been see in St. Giles-in-the-Wood.

" 'It's always about there. Everyone knows of it,' was her reply, but she added: 'it's bad luck to speak of it there', and—hesitantly—'I'm not sure if it's a good thing for me to tell you of it now, but I've seen it myself several times when I was a child living there, again when I was a young maid, and, once again, years later.'

" 'Where, in St Giles's, did you see the Black Dog?' I asked. Her answer came: 'On Week Hill. He's all about in St Giles's Parish. but mostly he runs on Week Hill. That's where I first saw the old thing.'

"In great detail she told me her experiences, sending her daughter-in-law into the shop, and speaking in a low tone, for she said, 'if doesn't do to talk loud about such things, and I wouldn't want people here to know what is seen in St. Giles'.

"This is what she told me:

"When about ten years old, roughly in the early 1870s, she was walking back with her father after Harvest Festival supper in the village round about 11 p.m. Their way lay up Week Hill, where they lived in a cottage near Allen's Week. 'It was a moonlight night and suddenly a sound of something panting came from behind us, and a great black dog "as big as a calf" with great shining eyes came alongside us. I caught at Father's hand and cried out. Father said, 'tis the Black Dog! Hold my hand, don't speak, walk along quiet and don't cry out.' "

"For the most part of a quarter of a mile the dog kept beside them. She described how huge it seemed, how its tongue hung out 'like a great piece of red flannel', and how when she and her father turned off the road to their cottage the dog kept on past the gate 'and then disappeared'. Her father told her he'd seen it 'many a time', and it didn't do any harm, but, she added, she was shaking with fright and could not sleep for thinking of it.

"She did not see the spectre again until she was about fourteen, when, with two other girls, she was returning from one of the farms. Again the Dog was on Week Hill; the girls were crossing a field path leading to it. All three saw it running with its nose to the ground and baying 'as loud as a pack of hounds'. On another occasion, just before she got to her home, it passed her, 'appearing right in front of me and rushing by and gone in a flash as though it had never been there when I jumped out of its way.'

"Many years later, after she married, she and her father were driving home from Torrington market and between Great Torrington and Allen's Week, the Dog suddenly came from the ditch and made the pony shy and bolt. She assured me that even recently (this would be between 1925–30) the Dog has been seen in St Giles's, but that no one would be willing to speak of it.

"From a friend who, at that time, lived at Little Silver, a mile or so NE of Allen's Week I learned that the road near there was said by the country people to be 'haunted', but he was very vague as to what the haunting was.

"At Frithelstock, on the hill above the River Torridge, stand the ruins of a Priory adjoining the east end of the Parish Church. The Priory was built in the seventeenth century; there are several references to it in the Bishop's Registers (Exeter) and in the fourteenth century the Bishop found that the monks had badly fallen away from Christianity, had built themselves an altar to Diana, in the woods above the river, where they worshipped. Accordingly, he visited the Priory, forced the monks to destroy the Altar, 'and with their own hands, drag the stones away', removing all traces of it.

"The road on which the following incident occurred is a new road, cut out of the hillside along the bank of the River Torridge in the middle of the nineteenth century, the old road from Torrington to the west going up through the village of Frithelstock and passing between the Smithy and the Church and Priory.

"At the point where the incident recorded took place, the road, for half a mile, has sheer rock to a height of twenty feet on one side, with the river, bounded by a wall, immediately below, and at this point wide and swift flowing. My plotted Line extended from Torrington, across the Torridge in the Parish of Weare Gifford. The distance from the point on the road, as the crow flies, is one mile.

"The incident occurred on the road below Frithelstock Priory in January, 1932.

"In 1932, we were living two miles out of Bideford at a vicarage, where my married daughter and her husband were spending part of the latter's leave with us. He was in the Administration in Tanganyika Territory. One night in January, 1932, while staying with us, they went over to dine with a relative living at Winkleigh, and returned home soon after midnight.

"Their route to and from Winkleigh lay through Torrington from Bideford. I did not see them on their return, but at breakfast next morning my daughter asked in a casual way did I know of any instances of the Black Dog legend occurring between Bideford and Winkleigh.

"My reply was to tell her a little of the instances I had at Stopgate, Down St Mary, and St Giles-in-the-Wood.

" 'Nothing on the Torrington–Bideford road?'

" 'No,' I replied.

" 'Well, listen to this,' she said, and told me the following.

"She and her husband, returning from Winkleigh, passed through Torrington soon after 11 p.m. It was not a dark night. Though sometimes cloudy, there was a small moon.

"As they drove along the road beside the Torridge below Frithelstock, there suddenly appeared in the headlights what she described as 'the most enormous black dog I've ever seen', so suddenly, and so near, that her husband who was driving braked so hard as to stall the engine, to avoid hitting it. They both saw the dog, and both felt sure the front of the car must hit it. When the car stopped, the dog was nowhere to be seen.

"I fetched my map, and she and her husband identified the spot where this had happened. There was nowhere the creature could have gone other than up the sheer cliff on one side or over the wall into the river on the other, and there was no sign of him on the straight piece of road ahead or behind. He had, in fact, completely disappeared.

"My daughter described the incident as 'most uncanny'. Asked by me how big the dog was, she replied, 'bigger than any dog I've ever seen, quite black.'

"My son-in-law, who had always been strongly sceptical of such legends, and who had often expressed belief that those things were always capable of a normal explanation, agreed with the facts she had told me: indeed, he stressed the way in which the creature seemed to appear without any sign of where it came from, and the equally sudden way in which it disappeared without a trace.

"Later, on checking my Torrington to Copplestone Line, I found that the place on the road where this happened lay one mile from the Line across the river Torridge.

"Mr Freeman, some time Rector of the Parish, then a man of nearly eighty, told me in 1923 that the legend of the Black Dog had been current in Thorverton in his day.

"There is (or was, forty years ago) an Inn standing at the corner of a lane on the outskirts of Lyme Regis called the Black Dog Inn, and lending its name to the lane where there was the legend that the spectral Black Dog ran nightly, and at midnight 'knocked down the corner of the Inn'.

"Near Thelbridge there is an area called Black Dog, which thirty years ago was not even a hamlet, only an inn of this name, and a smithy there. It lies on a crossroad a mile or so south of Thelbridge.

"There is some legend of a Black Dog haunting in the neighbourhood of Tiverton, but the details I cannot give you. I was told of it by a man of the name of Blackmore, an exceedingly well-educated, superior type of man, who was gardener to a friend of mine who, in 1926, was living at West Hill, Ottery St Mary, Devon.

"He told me he and his father had both seen the Black Dog, that he knew many people in the Tiverton area who were quite certain that it appeared from time to time, adding that he knew of several other places where people he knew had seen it, but only in his own area had he had any experience of it."

Mrs Carbonnell's researches add more to the general knowledge of the Black Dog legends in Devon than any previous individual researches have contributed.

The Strange Haunting at Ballechin

The ghosts of Ballechin House, Perthshire, did not acquire anything like the fame of their spectral counterparts at Borley Rectory. Yet this Scottish haunting is in many ways a better one. It was perhaps more accurately observed and authenticated than the Borley haunt, and though it was enlivened by controversy, it is not tainted with the kind of suspicion which fell upon the great Borley haunting after the death of its sponsor, Harry Price.

The Ballechin haunting is relatively unknown, despite the fact that it has everything that a good haunting should have—house guests freezing with cold and fear in a lonely Highland mansion, ghostly nuns weeping by a frozen burn, spectral tattoos of a fearsome nature, the disembodied paws of a dog, to mention only a few of the unexplained phenomena which chilled the spines of the people who stayed at Ballechin.

The furious controversy which arose over the haunting and which raged in the stately columns of *The Times* during the year of Queen Victoria's Diamond Jubilee, was merely over the propriety of whether the matter should have been investigated by members of the Society for Psychical Research without the permission of the owners of the property.

This raises an interesting point as to whether the ownership of a house gives one any rights in respect to the ghosts which might be haunting it. This is not a matter which is ever likely to engage the attentions of a court of law, and need not detain us, for what happened at Ballechin during those haunted 'eighties and 'nineties is much more interesting and exciting.

Ballechin House is in a splendid Highland setting, a few miles from Logierait, overlooking the valley of the River Tay before it is joined by the Tummel below Pitlochry. Not far away at Dunkeld is a famous distillery which produces spirits of a different order.

The Steuart family owned the estate since the sixteenth century. The Steuarts were the lineal descendants of King Robert II of Scotland. Ballechin House was built in 1806 to replace the ancient manor-house which was then demolished and which stood on a different site.

The Steuart who apparently caused the haunting was Robert, who was born in the year of the building of Ballechin House. In 1825, at the age of nineteen, he went to India and became an officer in the army of the East India Company. Twenty-five years later he retired with the rank of Major. He had inherited Ballechin in 1834 on the death of his father. When he arrived home from India in 1850 he found his house occupied by tenants, and he built himself a small house in the grounds, called Ballechin Cottage, where he lived until the tenancy expired, when he moved into the big house.

Major Steuart had a pronounced limp, presumably acquired during his service, active or otherwise, in India. He was unmarried, but kept a young housekeeper. He had two brothers and six sisters. One of these sisters, Isabella, became a nun, assuming the name of Frances Helen, later to become a key figure in the haunting. She died in her nunnery on 23 February, 1880.

Old Major Steuart, who died in 1876, was a great eccentric. In India he had made a study of the supernatural, and he firmly believed in transmigration and of spirit return after death. During the quarter of a century he lived at Ballechin he acquired a reputation in the district for being a very queer bird.

He filled the house with dogs, his favourite being a large black spaniel, whose body he proposed to occupy after his death. Why the old Major should have expressed preference for a dog's life in the other world we do not know, and there is no intention here to speculate upon the workings of his eccentric mind. But people who prefer the company of dogs to that of humans are not uncommon. Presumably the next stage is the desire to become a dog.

However, the "mad Major's" intention to enter the body of his black spaniel was taken seriously enough by his heirs and relatives, who upon his death promptly had all his dogs shot, thus forestalling, as they imagined, the Major's post-mortem intentions. Obviously his spiritual society on a canine level, or indeed on any other level, was not desired by his relatives.

Under a will made in 1853 the Major left Ballechin to the children of his married sister Mary. There were five children of this marriage. The eldest son died in 1867 without issue, and the following year Major Steuart added a codicil which excluded the three younger children from any benefit under his will. This left John, the second son, who inherited Ballechin on his uncle's death in 1876, and who immediately changed his name to Steuart, in order presumably to maintain the family tradition, if not the direct family line.

This John Steuart was a Roman Catholic, as was his aunt Isabella, still secluded in her convent. The old Major had been a Protestant, and was buried in the churchyard at Logierait beside the grave of his previously mentioned 27-year-old housekeeper, Sarah, who had died suddenly and mysteriously in 1873.

Whether their lying side by side in Logierait churchyard paralleled in any sense their relationship during their life time at Ballechin House is a matter upon which there was much interesting speculation, though it was too delicate a matter to be touched upon by the Victorian ladies and gentlemen who investigated the old Major's post-mortem activities twenty years after his death.

But it was well noted that Sarah died in the main bedroom at Ballechin, which became the most haunted room in the house. The ghost of the old Major was often heard limping around the bed in which she breathed her last.

John Steuart enjoyed the amenities of Ballechin and the income that went with the estate for twenty-one years. He was a married man with several children. His eldest son went into the army, his youngest became a Jesuit priest. During John Steuart's lifetime Ballechin Cottage, the small house his uncle had built in the grounds when he returned from India in 1850, was used as a retreat for nuns. The Steuarts were a devout Catholic family.

It was during this time that the haunting started. Not long after the old Major's death, Mrs Steuart was doing her household accounts in the room which used to be the old man's study when suddenly the room began to smell overpoweringly of dogs. She remembered that this was how the place smelt at the old Major's death when they had all the dogs destroyed. As she sat at her little desk smelling the doggy aroma, she felt herself being pushed against by an invisible dog. It seemed that the execution of the Major's unfortunate dogs had not been sufficient to frustrate the intentions of their late master's disembodied spirit.

Ever since the Major's death Ballechin had been troubled by knockings and mysterious sounds, like explosions, and the sound of people quarrelling came suddenly from nowhere into the middle of a room in the most eerie fashion.

Servants would not stay. The strange goings on at Ballechin became the talk of the neighbourhood and it gained the reputation of being the most haunted house in Scotland.

In the late 1870s the governess of the Steuart children became alarmed at the queer noises in the house and left. Many other people complained of the noises. A Jesuit Priest, Father Hayden, who was staying in the house, said that the noises seemed to come from between his bed and the ceiling and sounded like continuous explosions of petards, so that he could not hear himself speak.

Father Hayden, who was at Ballechin for the purpose of giving spiritual ministrations to the nuns staying at Ballechin Cottage, complained to his host about the noises. John Steuart thought they were caused by the old Major, who was perhaps trying to attract Father Hayden's attention in order that prayers might be offered for the repose of his soul.

The good Jesuit priest was alarmed by other things, particularly by the sound of a large animal, such as a dog, throwing itself up against the bottom part of his door on the outside. There was no dog there to cause such a noise. Father Hayden also heard taps and knockings and something which sounded like a scream.

The Steuart family were very reticent about the haunting, and would have nothing to do with any investigation of it, but John Steuart himself is reported to have seen a procession of monks and nuns from a window, and there was corroboration from a totally independent source of Father Hayden's report of the curious noise overheard between the bed and the ceiling, from a married couple who later occupied the same room as he did.

Evidence that the haunting was assuming frightening proportions was seen in the fact that in 1883 a new wing was built at Ballechin House for the express purpose of providing rooms for the children of the family outside the haunted area.

This gave Ballechin House a total of twelve bedrooms, eight of them on the first floor in the main part of the house. On the ground floor was a spacious hall and three large reception rooms. In the basement, apart from the kitchens, and pantry, were a smoking-room and a large billiards-room. Servants were accommodated in the attics. One bathroom served the needs of the whole house, the front elevation of which was in Georgian style broken by a bold central bow, which gave the house a certain character, if not distinction.

There seems little substance in reports that Ballechin was haunted before the death of Major Steuart in 1876. Its ghostly reputation was acquired in the two decades which followed the demise of the eccentric old psychic, whose peculiar beliefs seemed to spark off some unaccountable happenings.

John Steuart, after, it can safely be assumed, having led an exemplary life devoted to the interests of the Roman Church, was gathered to his fathers in the January of 1895 in sudden and tragic fashion, the event being preceded by a startling omen on the morning of his departure for London on some family business. He was talking to his agent in the study when their conversation was interrupted by three knocks so loud and violent that the two men had to interrupt their conversation. Later that day the master of Ballechin left for London to meet a sudden death in the busy streets where he was run over and killed by a cab.

The next Steuart of Ballechin was a Captain in the Army, who had had enough of the haunted family house on the lonely Scottish hillside and had no desire to live there. It had 4,400 acres of shooting and he had no difficulty in letting it for the 1896 grouse season to a wealthy family whose identity was cloaked behind the description of their being "of Spanish origin".

Captain Stewart did not tell his tenants that Ballechin was haunted. They took it for a year, paying the rent in advance, and hurriedly evacuated the house after seven weeks of nightly terror and intolerable uproar for which they could find no physical cause.

The daughter of the house, terrified at the sound of a man limping around her bed, called in her brother, who then slept on the sofa. The limping began again and he heard it as well and agreed that someone was limping around his sister's bed, but neither of them saw anything. This was the room and presumably the bed in which Sarah, Major Steuart's young housekeeper, had died in 1873. The brother later claimed to have seen the ghost twice—once in the shape of an indeterminate mist and once in the shape of a man who came in by the door and vanished in the wall.

One lady who was a guest at Ballechin during that haunted September of 1896 wrote of the alarm caused by the violent knockings, shrieks and groans heard every night. Guests were awakened by blows upon their doors so violent that they expected the panels to burst in. When they opened their doors there was no one there.

There was one room, she said, into which even the dogs could not be coaxed.

The tenants did not return to Ballechin House, thus forfeiting the greater part of the year's rent which they had paid in advance.

The haunting was the subject of an article in *The Times* of 8 June, 1897, which made light of the whole affair. This was followed by a letter from a Harold Sanders, who was the family butler at Ballechin House during the haunted tenancy of the previous autumn. Sanders described the fearful uproar which disturbed everyone in the house, including the servants, and eventually drove them away. Parties of gentlemen, he said, sat up at night, armed with sticks and revolvers, vowing vengeance upon the disturbers of their sleep.

This redoubtable haunting had already received the attention of that band of devoted ghost hunters, the Society for Psychical Research, which had been formed in the 1880s. Following the flight of the 1896 tenants, several members of the S.P.R. decided to rent the place and investigate the haunting themselves.

The 3rd Marquess of Bute, who had been interested in the haunting since 1892 when Father Hayden had told him of his strange experiences at Ballechin during the lifetime of John Steuart, was the leading light in this most interesting investigation. Bute was himself a Scot. His family name was Crichton-Stuart. He was deeply interested in psychic matters, but he was unable to undertake the investigation himself, so he delegated it to Colonel Lemesurier Taylor and Miss A. Goodrich-Freer, both well-known psychical researchers of the 'nineties. Colonel Taylor took the lease in his name and the Marquess footed all the expenses.

Colonel Taylor was well known for his investigations of haunted houses, both in England and in America, and when he took on the lease of Ballechin House, Captain Steuart's agents in Edinburgh, Messrs Speedy, merely expressed the hope that the new tenant would not make the haunting a subject for complaint, as the last tenant had done. Taylor gave this undertaking, saying he was well aware of what had happened during the previous tenancy.

Bute and his investigators planned to invite guests to Ballechin who had knowledge of psychic phenomena, or who were open-minded and objective on the subject. None of them knew the history of Ballechin.

A hostess was therefore necessary, Colonel Taylor being a widower and without a daughter. Bute asked Miss Freer to undertake these duties and to begin the investigation in the absence of Taylor, who was pre-occupied with a family bereavement at the beginning of 1897.

Miss Freer, after having engaged a staff of servants in Edinburgh, took up residence at Ballechin on 3 February, accompanied by her friend, Miss Constance Moore, a daughter of the Rev Daniel Moore, Prebendary of St. Paul's, and Chaplain to Queen Victoria.

Thick snow lay on the ground. The gloomy house looked forbidding. Inside, wrote Miss Freer in her Journal: "It felt like a vault, having been empty for months. None of the stores ordered had arrived. We had no linen, knives, plate, wine, food and very little fuel or oil." After dining off bread and milk and a tin of meat which they bought in Logierait, they went to bed. "The room was so cold that we had to cover our faces, and we had no bed linen."

The two friends slept from exhaustion, for they had had a busy and tiring day in Edinburgh, but they were awoken at three in the morning by loud clanging noises echoing through the house. At 4.30 they heard sounds of voices. None of these sounds could be accounted for in the morning.

The house was paralysingly cold and they spent some days thawing out the icy rooms, and trying to make the place comfortable. "It will soon be very pleasant," wrote Miss Freer optimistically, "and only needs living in, but it feels like a vault."

The next night they heard a phenomenon which was repeatedly experienced during the investigation—the sound of someone reading aloud in the manner of a priest "saying his office".

The devotion and determination of these Victorian psychic investigators is something to be marvelled at. Their energy and patience were inexhaustible. Not only was Lord Bute willing to pay a substantial sum of money to maintain a large house-party for the sole purpose of a ghost-hunt, but his assistants and collaborators freely gave their time and were prepared to face possible dangers and considerable discomfort in pursuit of what they considered to be psychic knowledge. The lady ghost-hunters of that romantic age were no less intrepid than the men, and showed a toughness and tenacity which gives the lie to the legend of the frailty of Victorian womanhood.

They took their experiments and investigations at Ballechin in deadly earnest. They kept records and times of the observed phenomena, listed as "visual", "tactile" and "audile". They tried to reproduce the various noises by normal means, nearly always without success. They continually changed bedrooms so that a variety of reports could be collated on the noises heard in the different rooms.

They had a staff of servants to minister to their needs. Below stairs the ghost-hunting of the various lady and gentleman guests was the subject of some derision, except by those servants who had themselves been frightened by paranormal phenomena. In particular was the continual change-round of bedrooms the subject of ribald comment in the servants' quarters, with jokes of a predictable nature.

A detailed account of the investigation was collated into one of the most curious ghost books on record entitled *The Alleged Haunting of B—— House*. This was a joint report by Miss Freer and Lord Bute, and it followed an acrimonious dispute over the whole affair with the Steuart family, with the result that nearly all the proper names, including that of the house itself, were suppressed. This book, now something of a collector's piece, was published in 1899 by George Redway of London, and is the main source of information on the haunting.

Miss Freer herself saw apparitions of nuns on the snow near the frozen burn several times. On the first occasion it was a solitary nun weeping in a way Miss Freer described as "passionate and unrestrained". Other times there were two nuns, one on her knees weeping while the other was trying to reason with her in a low voice.

These nuns were naturally related to the time of John Steuart when Ballechin Cottage was used as a nuns' retreat, although the weeping nun was thought to be Major Steuart's sister, Isabella, who it will be remembered had entered a convent where she died in 1880.

Psychic experiments in automatic writing were made with an apparatus known as a Ouija board, and messages were reported from "intelligences" giving their names as Ishbel and Marghearad (Gaelic forms of Isabel and Margaret). In reply to questions as to what could be done which would be of use or interest, the writers were told to go at dusk and in silence to the glen near the burn— the place where Miss Freer had seen the weeping nun and her companion.

It seemed that the haunting was centred around three sets of circumstances. Firstly, the nuns. What sin or sadness caused Isabella to weep so desolately in the snow-covered glen? With this was obviously connected the sound of the priest chanting, and later the appearance of a spectral crucifix. Secondly, there was the mysterious death of Major Steuart's young housekeeper, Sarah, which apparently made him limp eternally around the bed upon which she died—not in the servants' quarters, but in the best bedroom in the house, and ever since haunted. Thirdly, there was the Major's beloved black spaniel, into whose body this strange old man wished to enter after death, and which was shot remorselessly with all the other dogs in a vain attempt by the family to prevent this happening.

Animal ghosts have been reported before, but none is better attested than this case. It will be recalled that Mrs John Steuart felt the phantom dog brush up against her while in the Major's study shortly after the old man's death in 1876, and during the next twenty years a number of people reported the pattering of the feet of invisible dogs, sounds as of wagged tails striking on doors and wainscots, and frequently the noise was heard as of a dog blundering up against a door.

A Pomeranian aptly named Spooks shared with Miss Freer the most frightening and unnerving of all these canine experiences. The dog slept on Miss Freer's bed, and in the middle of the night of 4 May, 1897, Miss Freer was woken by the animal uttering terrified whimpers. Lighting her candle Miss Freer saw Spooks staring in terror at the table beside the bed. Following the animal's gaze, Miss Freer saw a pair of black paws, and nothing else, resting upon the table. "It gave me a sickening sensation," she said.

The party had servant trouble, of course. Some of the maids were terrified of the noises in the house and left. The cook didn't believe in ghosts, but thought the house "very queer" and the mysterious noises made her feel uncomfortable. She told Miss Freer that Ballechin was famous all over the countryside for being haunted, and that there was a story that a priest had been murdered by the wife of a former owner. This was supposed to have happened about the time of the Reformation.

Even the most sceptical of the maids shared in the strange experiences of the other inhabitants of the house. Lizzie, the kitchen-maid. who had been greatly lacking in respect for her betters in the way she ridiculed the ghost-hunting ladies from the south, had the frightening experience of having her bedclothes torn off her by invisible hands, after which she spent half the night screaming. Carter, the upper house-maid, woke up one dawn to see plainly standing beside her bed half of the figure of a woman in a grey shawl. The woman had no legs. Her body ended at the waist and was suspended in the air. The petrified maid hid shivering under the bedclothes till morning when she fled from Ballechin never to return.

When Miss Freer and Lord Bute published *The Alleged Haunting of B—— House*, they clothed their book in such a cloud of anonymity that it made no impact at all. Few people knew what "B——House" was, despite the curious slip on page 82 where Ballechin is accidentally printed in full. The silly squabble in *The Times* had been long forgotten, and to call it an "alleged" haunting was to belittle the book, for it was obvious that its authors did not regard it as an alleged haunting.

Thus the Ballechin haunting never acquired anything like the fame of Borley, though it well deserved to. The similarities between the two hauntings are remarkable. In particular a former owner of each house was morbidly interested in ghosts and vowed that he would come back and haunt after his death. And in each case—if we are to believe the evidence—he did.

Ballechin House finally went out of the Steuarts' possession. In 1932 it was bought by a Mr R. Wemyss Honeyman, who still (1965) owns the estate. In later years the house was uninhabited— at least by denizens of this world. Its end came in 1963 when it was demolished.

The Amherst Mystery

A strolling player, in the world of the nineteenth-century theatre, might see and experience many strange things. But Walter Hubbell, "an actor by profession, being duly sworn before a Notary Public in New York" in the year 1888, gave testimony of having been concerned with some even stranger events than are usual in his profession.

In 1879, he told his hearers, he had been acting with a strolling company in Amherst, Nova Scotia. They were based there for some little time, their repertory was familiar and needed no further rehearsal; Mr Hubbell found himself with some leisure time to fill in. His was a lively, enquiring mind, with a keen curiosity about the fashionable cult of Spiritualism, which had swept over America. Everywhere mediums had sprung up, and Walter Hubbell had given himself much satisfaction proving some of their "phenomena" to be fraudulent. Now, in Amherst, he heard of a conspicuously haunted house, and determined to investigate it.

The house, at first sight, did not appear particularly ghostly. It was a pleasant detached cottage, with a pretty garden, in it lived the Teed family—Daniel Teed, a highly respectable and respected foreman in a shoe factory, his wife, as "good a woman as ever lived", according to her neighbours, their baby, little Willie, and Mrs Teed's two sisters, Jennie and Esther—both pretty girls, but Esther particularly attractive with her large dark-lashed grey eyes, tiny hands and feet, and frank, charming expression. John Teed, Daniel's brother, also lived in the somewhat crowded house.

The trouble had begun one night. Jennie, who shared a bed with Esther, had been suddenly awakened by her sister leaping out of bed with a scream, and a cry of: "A mouse! there's a mouse in bed with us!" Search revealed no trace of any mouse, and the sisters went back to sleep.

Next night, also in the girls' bedroom, violent rustling noises were heard in a green band-box which stood on the floor. After a few minutes, to the sisters' alarm, the band-box rose a foot in the air of its own volition, and went up and down several times. When it had returned to its normal position Esther screwed up her courage and opened it. But it was quite empty.

Next night an even more alarming thing happened. Esther, who had gone to bed feeling unwell, found herself to be swelling up, as if from some dreadful disease, until her body was almost twice its usual size. When her family rushed in, summoned by the cries of her and her sister, they were further alarmed by loud peals of thunder—or what sounded like thunder—which suddenly peeled out, under a bright evening sky without a cloud in it.

Esther's swelling subsided, but next day she was still unwell, and could only eat "a small piece of bread and butter, and a large green pickle". Four nights later, all the bed-clothes covering her and Jennie flew off as if ripped away by invisible hands, and came to rest in a corner of the room. Once more the Teeds rushed in to investigate, and found the uncovered body of Esther "fearfully swollen", even more so than before. Her sister replaced the bed-clothes, but they instantly flew off again, and the pillow struck John Teed a smart blow in the face. "I've had enough of this!" he declared, and left the room without waiting for further manifestations. But the rest of the family bravely remained, and seated themselves all round the bed, holding down the struggling bedclothes with the weight of their bodies. Again the mysterious peals of thunder sounded, in the midst of which Esther suddenly fell peacefully asleep, the bedclothes settled down, and the family tiptoed away.

The local doctor, Dr Carritte, was summoned next day to examine Esther. While he was doing so, the bolster beneath her head launched itself at him, struck him a violent blow on the head, and then soared back into place under Esther's. The doctor staggered to a chair, overcome with shock; and while he sat there, nerving himself to continue his examination of the girl, he heard a metallic scratching noise coming from the wall behind him. Turning to see what it was, he found on the wall the sentence:

"Esther Cox! You are mine to kill."

This was the first of many pieces of writing, all of a threatening character, which "came out of the air and fell at our feet", the family testified. While the mystified doctor was examining the writing on the wall, bits of plaster fell from the ceiling and began to whirl about the room, while the peals of thunder renewed themselves. Terrified, Dr Carritte left.

It says something for his courage that he returned next day. This time, as he bent over his patient, a hail of potatoes from an invisible source flew at him and sent him reeling across the room. More prepared for trouble than on the previous day, the intrepid doctor produced from his bag a bottle of sedative mixture and administered some to Esther (we are not told whether he took one himself). The medicine, however quietening its effects on the girl, had no influence on the manifestations—loud pounding noises were heard from the ceiling, and continued until the doctor had left the room.

Now the clergy began to take an interest in the case—which they somewhat oddly attributed not to the supernatural, but to electricity, a discovery of which America had become conscious—commercial electric lighting had been in use for about three years, and electric trams and street cars for about one. But general knowledge of the powers of electricity was not wide. The reverend gentlemen's curiosity seems to have been keen, for they visited the Teed house for months, and were only driven away when poor Esther fell ill with diphtheria. On recovering, she went to recuperate at the house of some friends in Sackville, New Brunswick. Her departure brought peace to the Teed home; nor did any haunting trouble the house at Sackville while she was in it. But once she was back in Amherst, the nuisance broke out again with redoubled force. "I'll burn your house down!" cried a voice—and a rain of lighted matches fell from the ceiling, to be promptly extinguished by the family, who by now were prepared for almost anything.

But having begun to play with fire, the ghost could not leave it alone. His next trick was to set Mrs Teed's ample skirts on fire. She was more frightened than hurt, and the subsequent fires started about the house did little actual damage. However, the heads of the Amherst fire-brigade heard of the incidents, and suspected that an arsonist—probably Esther—was at work. Threats were uttered against her—the righteous Dr Nathan Tupper suggested that she should be flogged, as a way of driving out the evil. Her brother-in-law promptly removed her for safety to the house of a Mr White. But the ghost (now known as Bob, by which name he signed some of his communications) had got really expert at fire-raising, and continued his larks in Esther's absence. A piece of iron placed on the girl's lap "became too hot to be handled with comfort" and then flew away like a ponderous bird.

At this point the inquisitive and sceptical Walter Hubbell came on the scene. He spent days with the Teeds, and very much to his own surprise could not find any of the evidences of fraud he had expected. Was Esther, then, a genuine medium? "There's money in this!" thought the astute young man, reared as he was in show business. He decided to become impresario to Esther, exhibiting her on a platform while he delivered a lecture and "Bob" obliged with manifestations.

But his idea was doomed to failure. The exhibition took place, but the only objects to fly through the air were those hurled at Mr Hubbell by the spectators, and the only loud noises were their hisses and boos. Bob had failed to oblige, as is the way of ghosts when called on to perform tricks. Back to Amherst came poor Esther from her unsuccessful tour. Mr Hubbell, still determined to find out more about Bob, moved in with the patient Teeds, and had ample evidence of the reality of the hauntings. In Esther's absence from the house, his own umbrella and a large carving knife threw themselves at him furiously, and only his natural agility saved him from serious injury. As he was getting his breath back, a huge armchair moved ponderously out of its corner and charged at him like a bull. "To say that I was awed would indeed seem an inadequate expression of my feelings," commented Mr Hubbell with restraint.

The ghost's next trick was really unkind. Three times was little George Cox, Esther's brother, undressed in public by invisible hands, to his great distress. Then Bob returned to his favourite pastime of fire-raising. Walter Hubbell's own words are the best account of his reactions to this.

"This was my first experience with Bob, the demon, as a fire-fiend; and I say, candidly, that until I had had that experience I never fully realized what an awful calamity it was to have an invisible monster, somewhere within the atmosphere, going from place to place about the house, gathering up old newspapers into a bundle and hiding it in the basket of soiled linen or in a closet, then go and steal matches out of the match-box in the kitchen or some-body's pocket, as he did out of mine; and after kindling a fire in the bundle, tell Esther that he had started a fire, but would not tell where; or perhaps not tell her at all, in which case the first intimation we would have was the smell of the smoke pouring through the house, and then the most intense excitement, everybody running with buckets of water. I say it was the most truly awful calamity that could possibly befall any family, infidel or Christian, that could be conceived in the mind of man or ghost. And how much more terrible did it seem in this little cottage, where all were strict members of church, prayed, sang hymns, and read the Bible. Poor Mrs Teed!"

One member alone of the family had never been the object of Bob's malice. This was the cat, a sedate character who had reacted with calm acceptance to all the terrifying things that had been happening in her home. One day Walter Hubbell, looking down at her plump form comfortably couched on the hearthrug, observed: "At least *she*'s never been tormented." At this, the cat was instantly lifted five feet high in the air, suspended for a moment, and then dropped on the shoulders of the screaming Esther. "I never saw any cat more frightened," said Walter Hubbell later. "She ran out into the front yard, where she remained for the balance of the day."

Now the versatile Bob turned his attention to music. The Reverend R. A. Temple, minister at the Teeds' church, called to hold a meeting of prayer and exorcism—his own recipe, using slips of paper inscribed with a verse from the Prophet Habakkuk: "For the vision is yet for an appointed time, but at the end it shall speak, and not lie." The ghost retaliated not by speaking, as requested, but by loud and raucous trumpet-playing. This it kept up until Mr Temple rushed from the house; and, pleased with its own performance, continued to play afterwards until the wretched Teeds were almost deafened. The proceedings concluded with a sort of firework display of lighted matches.

Things had gone too far. Daniel Teed was only the tenant of the cottage; its owner was a Mr Bliss, who heartily disliked the way his property was being treated. He insisted that Esther leave at once. It seemed hard to part her from her family, but on the whole, they agreed, it was the best thing to do. Esther removed to the house of a Mr Van Amburgh, and Bob's demonstrations instantly ceased.

Only once did he break out again. Esther was accused of setting fire to a barn, in which she happened to be when it broke into flames. Now that the hauntings were fading from the public memory, she was arrested for simple incendiarism, and sentenced to four months' imprisonment. But those who remembered all too vividly the works of Bob pleaded for her, and she was soon released.

Like so many other young girls who have been the centre of supernatural happenings, when she married, as she soon did, all

FIFTY GREAT GHOST STORIES

the horrors ceased. She became a normal young matron, and faded from history.

And what of Mr Hubbell? It is not recorded that he entirely gave up his hobby of psychic research, but he certainly did not bring to it his former sceptical attitude. It would be satisfying to know that one of his roles was that of the Ghost in *Hamlet*.

Glamis, the Haunted Castle

Glamis Castle, the Forfarshire seat of the Earls of Strathmore, home of the present Queen Mother and birthplace of Princess Margaret, has had for many years the reputation of being "the most haunted house in Britain". Its outward appearance certainly does much to further this claim, with its high cluster of ancient-looking towers and turrets, in stone that is grim and almost frowning, apparently grey with age and heavy with the weight of time. Inside, too, many of the gloomy rooms, long stone-flagged corridors and cold echoing vaults, with walls which are in places fifteen feet thick, all combine to give an overpowering air of massive antiquity and eeriness—though there are some very charming suites of rooms and pleasant apartments also.

Built on the basic traditional pattern of a strong central tower surrounded by a fortified courtyard, Glamis lies in a valley about twenty miles north of Dundee. It is overlooked by Hunter's Hill, traditionally the location of the assassination of King Malcolm II of Scotland in 1034. The castle itself was at one time reputed to be the place where Macbeth, Thane of Glamis, murdered King Duncan in 1040; and a sword and a shirt of mail, both supposedly belonging to Macbeth, are on view in one of the rooms.

But no part of the building can actually be dated much earlier than about the end of the fourteenth century, and in fact only the central tower itself can definitely be ascribed to that period. Later additions, in deliberately feudal styles of architecture, are responsible for much of the "atmosphere"; over the years and the centuries, successive owners have pulled down, rebuilt or added on different parts of Glamis, until now it is difficult to tell where the real ends and the imitation begins. There was extensive reconstruction, for instance, in the seventeenth century; new wings and passages were added, wide stone fireplaces were constructed, and the Great Hall on the third floor was constructed. But since that time many of these alterations have in their turn been altered again, or replaced with others, so that now it is not even certain which parts are "genuine" seventeenth-century building, and which merely imitations of it.

The site itself, however, is an ancient one which had been fortified and held for many centuries by the early Kings of Scotland. It was given by Robert II (grandson of Robert the Bruce) to his son-in-law Sir John Lyon when he made him his Great Chamberlain in 1372. Sir John began extensive building there, though presumably a ruined castle already stood on the site, but he was not able to complete the work, being mortally wounded in a duel in 1383.

His son, who became the first Lord Glamis, lived to finish his father's work, and he died a natural death in 1445, being one of the few members of the family who succeeded in living-out the whole course of his life peacefully and quietly. But *his* son, the second Lord Glamis, more than made up for his father's respectability: he was a notorious drunkard and gambler, known to all as "The Wicked Laird" and, because of his thick whiskers and long hair, also as "Earl Beardie". There is a portrait of him at Abbotsford, and he it was —as we shall see—who in time became a traditional bogeyman for Scottish children, his name being corrupted to "Earl Patie" by the Forfarshire peasantry.

But with none of these persons or events can Glamis Castle really definitely be associated, however. Written historical records are inadequate until nearly a hundred years later, when John, sixth Lord of Glamis, was living there with his young wife Janet Douglas, who was famous throughout Scotland for her dark beauty. He was living there, that is, until he was discovered one morning lying on the stone floor of an inner apartment, having died suddenly while eating a meal alone. His wife was charged with having poisoned him, but the evidence against her being insufficient, her trial was abandoned.

Six years afterwards, however, she was again on trial for her life, charged this time with plotting to murder no less a person than James V of Scotland, and also with being a witch. Her servants were bribed to give false evidence, and her young son was tortured until he agreed to assist the prosecution by committing perjury against his mother. The beautiful Janet Douglas was found guilty, and was burned to death on Castle Hill in Edinburgh in 1537 "without any substanciall ground", according to Henry VIII's representative in his report from Scotland to his King.

The son's estates were annexed, and he was imprisoned. But after three years he was released, and after the death of James V his estates and possessions were restored to him and he became the seventh Baron Glamis. His son, another John like his father, also like him continued the family tradition of being involved in violence and misfortune, meeting his death at an early age in a street brawl with a number of the Lindsays, the hereditary family enemies of the Lyons.

By the time Patrick Lyon succeeded to the estates in 1660, Glamis lay almost deserted, badly neglected and poorly furnished, and the family's standing and fortune was at its lowest ebb. But Patrick was a proud, determined and methodical man. By what one of his contemporaries described as "a course of self-denial"—by which he meant refraining from the sort of riotous living, drinking, brawling and heavy gambling which most of his ancestors had indulged in— in a period of thirty years he succeeded in restoring both the castle and his family's fortune.

A man of great integrity and honour, Patrick was made the first Earl of Strathmore and he became a Privy Councillor in 1682, loyally serving James II of England until that monarch fled from the country on the arrival of William of Orange in 1688. There is good reason to believe that Patrick was deeply implicated in Jacobite plotting for the restoration of the Old Pretender, but two years later he eventually took an oath of loyalty to William.

Perhaps as a precaution for his own safety during these times, Patrick ordered many structural alterations to Glamis, chiefly to create a number of secret chambers within its walls. But methodically he kept a "Book of Record" of all the work which he had done, and this was discovered and published by the Scottish Historical Society in 1890.

In it can be read such entries as: "June 24, 1684. Agried with the four masones in Glammiss the digging down from the floor of the litil pantry off the lobbis a closet designed within the charterhouse there." Another entry on 25 July of the same year indicates that the work was being made more elaborate: "I did add to the work before mentioned of a closet in my charterhouse, severall things of a considerable trouble, as the digging thorrow passages from the new work to the old, and thorrow that closet againe, so that I now have the access off one floor from the east quarter of the house to the west syde."

Patrick died in 1695, and once again tragedies began to occur regularly in the Lyon family. Patrick's son, the next in succession, died fighting at Sherrifmuir in the abortive Jacobite rising of 1715. His brother Charles then became Earl of Strathmore, and he was a lrue upholder of the Lyon family addiction to gambling. He was killed at the gaming tables in a fight in 1728. According to local tegend he was losing heavily in this game and to try to end his constant succession of losses persisted in betting on, staking all his possessions one by one until eventually he lost Glamis Castle itself to his opponent, who was one of the hereditary family enemies, the Lindsays. Incensed at this final indignity, Charles leaped to his feet, drew his sword and accused his opponent of cheating. In the fight that followed, he was run-through and died.

But this is yet another legend. Records show that he was in fact killed by a man called James Carnegie of Finhaven. The fight may well have been caused by an accusation of cheating, but as the estates and the castle have remained in the hands of the Lyons, the story of their being lost one by one must be only a fiction.

In the eighteenth century Glamis had a widespread reputation as a haunted building, full of secret chambers containing terrible secrets. Sir Walter Scott arranged to spend a night there so that he could experience its atmosphere for himself, and perhaps use it in one of his historical novels. He wrote afterwards that he found it a deserted and barely-furnished place, with suits of medieval armour standing in lines along its corridors. He was given a room which had a four-poster bed with tartan hangings, and he wrote "I must own that when the door was shut I began to consider myself as too far from the living and somewhat too near the dead". But to his disappointment he neither saw nor heard any evidence of ghosts or hauntings.

Numerous other people since Scott claim to have done so, however, and are prepared to swear that they have seen the gigantic figure of the bearded "Earl Patie" roaming the corridors of the castle. He is perhaps looking for someone to play cards with, since the original legend concerning him naturally features gambling. It was described by a ghost-story writer at the beginning of this century like this:

"Many many years ago, when gentlemen got regularly drunk at dinner-time and had to be carried to bed by their servants, there reigned at Glamis one 'Patie', known to all as 'The Wild Lord of

Glamis'. He was notoriously good at all the vices, but his favourite was that of gambling, and he would play even with the servants and the stable hands. One dark and stormy November Sunday night he called for the cards and, drinking heavily, demanded that someone should play with him. But no one would, not even any of the servants, as it was of course the Sabbath.

"In desperation Patie at last sent for the family's Chaplain, and demanded a game of him. But the cleric refused, forbidding all in the castle to desecrate the Sabbath with such things as cards, which he described in forthright tones as 'the deevil's bricks'. Finally Patie swore a terrible oath, and went grumbling upstairs to his room, saying he would play with the Deevil himself then.

"He had not been long in his room when a loud knocking at the door of it was heard, followed by a deep voice calling out and asking if a gambling partner was still required. 'Yes,' roared Patie, 'Enter, whoever you are, in the foul fiend's name!' A tall dark stranger, muffled in a long black coat and with a huge black hat, strode in and sat down at once at a table, swinging the door to behind him with a bang.

"The terrified servants who had crept upstairs and along the corridor to listen could hear within the most violent oaths and curses from both the players as the game got faster and more furious. Patie lost game after game, until finally he had nothing left to play with, and offered to sign a bond for anything the stranger should wish, so long as the game could continue.

"Greatly daring, the old family butler put his eye to the keyhole, so that he might spy what was going on within the room. But no sooner had he done so than there was a blinding flash of light and he fell backwards, rolling in agony on the floor, with a bright yellow circle round his eye. The door flung open, and Patie strode out furiously cursing the servants for spying on him—but when he turned to re-enter the room to continue his game, he saw that his opponent had disappeared, taking with him the signed bond—which was, of course, for Patie's soul.

"Pale and afraid, Patie knew then that the other gambler had truly been the Devil himself. The game had broken-up, he said, when suddenly and without turning round to look at the door behind him, the fiend had called-out 'Smite that eye'—and no sooner had he done so than a flash of lightning had crackled across the room and hit the keyhole into which the unfortunate butler had been peering.

"Patie lived on for another five years after this incident, but after his death every Sabbath night in November his ghost returned to the room to play again with his opponent the Devil, and try and win back his soul. Shouts and curses and strange noises could plainly be heard by any who were brave enough to stay and listen nearby, until at last, so great was the annual disturbance that the incumbent Lord of Glamis many years ago had the passage leading to the room bricked up, since when Patie and his gambling companion have been seen and heard no more."

*　　*　　*　　*　　*

If Glamis depended only on this folk-tale for its reputation of "most haunted house in Britain" it would never have achieved such status, for the legend of "Earl Patie" is little more than a traditional mock-horror bed-time story for Scottish children, intended presumably to deter them from excessive card-playing, particularly on the Sabbath—and perhaps also from keyhole peeping.

But guide-books to the place are emphatic and unanimous in their constant reference to other and more real terrors, connected with the castle—nearly all of which spring from rumours of a hidden chamber within its walls, reputed to contain a terrible Strathmore-family secret. This secret is traditionally known only to three people—the possessor of the castle, his heir, and his factor (steward). "Why the factor should be one of the three", says one popular guide-book, "is a question which has always excited the Caledonian mind."

"There is an impenetrable mystery at Glamis," asserts another, "and the legend of Earl Beardie will not account for all the things which have been seen and heard there. All that is known, beyond all possible doubt, is that the secret of Glamis—whatever it is—is revealed to the heir to the estates on the evening before his twenty-first birthday: and though successive heirs, when they were young men, have made light of the mystery, after they came of age and the secret has been revealed to them, they have obviously found it so truly dreadful that they have never thereafter talked about it."

The rumours have of course inspired many guesses, both at the location of the secret chamber and at what exactly it does contain. By some it is said to have been the scene of Patie's gambling with the Devil and that he is condemned to stay there at play until Judgment Day: others are sure that the beautiful Janet Douglas still lives on, because she was a witch, and is now confined there, hideously old of course but quite indestructible. Some say that the Lyon family are cursed with an immortal vampire who was born into the succession hundreds of years ago, and has to be kept hidden for ever; and others again, that the secret chamber actually contains a pile of mouldering skeletons, all that now remains of sixteen members of the Ogilvy family who once sought refuge in the castle in the seventeenth century, and were treacherously kept prisoner there by their host and eventually starved to death.

Wild though these rumours are and always have been, they are persistent enough and long-lasting enough to indicate that there really is (or was, in fairly recent times) a genuine secret concerning Glamis. According to Lord Halifax, the Earl of Strathmore whom he himself knew personally became, after his twenty-first birthday, "a changed man, silent and moody and never smiling. And his own son, when his turn came to be initiated into the family secret, absolutely refused to be enlightened because he could constantly see the effect of it on his father".

The resident Earl of Strathmore in 1870 is quoted as having said to his wife: "I have been into the secret chamber, and I have learned what the secret is—and if you wish to please me, never mention the matter to me again. I can only say that if you could guess the nature of the secret, you would go down on your knees and thank God it was not yours."

But it seems Lady Strathmore, her curiosity aroused, persisted in her inquiries and approached the other person who knew the secret, the Earl's factor—who was described by Lord Halifax as a shrewd, hard-headed Scotsman, not given to exaggeration or gossip. He replied that it was fortunate she did not know the secret, and then looking earnestly at her went on very gravely: "If your Ladyship did know it, I assure you you would not be a happy woman.'

By 1880 a contributor to *All the Year Round*, the magazine which had in its early days been edited by Charles Dickens, wrote that a workman who had "recently" been carrying out some structural alterations to Glamis had on one occasion inadvertently driven his crowbar through what he thought was solid brickwork, and had discovered a large cavity on the other side of it. There being no one about to supervise him, he had enlarged the hole and climbed through, finding himself in a secret corridor. He had gone along to the end of this, and found a locked door; then, frightened at his own boldness, he had returned and gone to the foreman of the work, telling him what he had done. The Earl, who was in London at the time, had been hastily summoned back to Glamis by the factor. The workman had been given a large sum of money, as an inducement to him and his family to emigrate to Australia, which presumably he had done, as he had never been heard of since.

At that period many strange sights and noises were reported by good authority: the wife of a former Archbishop of York, when she stayed at Glamis, said that she had seen a huge bearded man dozing in a chair before the fire in her room, and as she watched him he had groaned softly and slowly faded away. A Provost of Perth had seen this same figure too, and that of a lady dressed all in white, gliding silently about the corridors in the middle of the night. There were "strange, weird and unearthly sounds", said another lady, who reported being awakened one night by the feel of a beard brushing her face; and others had been disturbed by nocturnal crashes and bangs, usually at about four o'clock in the morning.

That inveterate and itinerant Boswell of the minor aristocracy, Augustus Hare, had stayed at the castle: and he noted in his diary that the Earl seemed to have a look of perpetual sadness. He had also, said Hare, built on a whole extra wing of the castle for children and servants to sleep in, because so many frightening things happened in the older parts of it in the night.

In 1908 a writer in *Notes and Queries*—by no means given to publishing mere sensationalism or idle gossip—referred to the current story "that in the castle of Glamis there is a secret chamber, in which is confined a monster who is the rightful heir to the titles and property, but is so unpresentable that it is necessary to keep him perpetually out of sight". And in 1925 another writer referred to the castle and "its inviolable secret, which is no nearer solution to-day than it was hundreds of years ago".

That there has been a mystery connected with Glamis Castle and the Earls of Strathmore there can be little doubt: and many o those who made guesses at what it really was were not as far from the truth as might have been supposed. The subject has recently attracted the attention of the contemporary writer and historian Paul Bloomfield, and after lengthy and most careful research he has now produced what may probably be regarded as the definitive solution of it. He reveals a story of a family haunted, not by a ghost, but by a living being who in their own eyes at least had brought shame upon them. To help to conceal it they used the traditions and legends concerning Glamis which were ready at hand, and encouraged inquirers to believe them: before long the family secret had become inextricably confused with old rumours, and what was current and real had taken-on the guise of a centuries-old mystery.

The painstakingly precise piecing-together of the painful and now long-passed family secret by Paul Bloomfield reads at times like a detective-story, and the interested reader who wishes to study it at length is referred to his *Red Blood and Royal* (1965). Briefly, the story is this:

Bloomfield discovered in an early edition of Cockayne's *Complete Peerage* that in October, 1821, the first-born son (and consequently the heir) of the then Earl of Strathmore was recorded as having died within a month of his birth. He was in fact born severely deformed, probably mongoloid, and it was not thought that he would live for very long. When in the following year another son, Thomas George, was born, he was therefore registered and regarded as the family heir.

On the death of his father, Thomas became the twelfth Earl of Strathmore: but it was then revealed to him that he had in fact an elder brother *who was still alive*, but who was kept out of sight because of his physical and mental deformities. Thomas himself died at the age of forty-three, in 1865, childless: and the title and the estates then passed to his younger brother Claude, who was already married and had five sons.

On and on lived the first-born son of the eleventh earl; year after year fed and looked-after and excluded both from public view and from the position of Lord of Glamis, which in truth he could neither have filled nor even understood. It is he, Bloomfield suggests, who was the occupant of the "secret chamber", and the constant and unnerving problem which he was to his family came in time to be believed as a "centuries-old mystery" rather than the result of a well-meaning miscalculation about his likely age of death.

He remained alive probably until he was over fifty years old, during which time the succession fell in turn upon three men, each of whom had to be told who the rightful heir really was, and what he was. When he did eventually die, which Bloomfield deduces to have been some time in the 1870s, the next heir could then "absolutely refuse" to be initiated into the family secret—because there was no longer any need for the "mystery" to be perpetuated. The myths and legends had served their purpose at Glamis.

The "crashes and bangs in the night" which many guests have reported? Probably the old-fashioned mechanism of the central clock, whose weights rise and fall noisily within the central tower. And the bearded figure of "Earl Patie", and the white lady? Well . . . there is no doubt that many people have seen ghosts in many places; and certainly Glamis Castle, both by tradition and by appearance, would be a fine place for them. . . .

The Horror at No. 50 Berkeley Square

In 1890, the Society for Psychical Research organized an inquiry among the citizens of London to try to discover how many of them had had experience of ghosts and hauntings. Questionnaires were sent to seventeen thousand selected at random. Of these 15,316 replied that they had not had any such experience, while 1,684 replied that they had. This figure represents some ten per cent, and is certainly high; at the same time, however, it is not disproportionate for a city so old as London and so rich in its history of violence, strange events and ancient buildings.

At that time, in the 1890s, when Berkeley Square was in the hey-day of its elegance, No. 50 was one of the most famous of all London's haunted houses. Sightseers from other parts of London, and even visitors from the country, seeking a thrill which would cost them nothing, found their way to the Square and stood before the house, imagining what it might be like to submit to the experience of an encounter with the Nameless Horror.

The house itself served to heighten the chill spasms of cold which coursed down the spines of even the least imaginative as they stood gazing at it. It had been empty for many years, and its Georgian façade was pocked with every evidence of general decay. Window-panes were broken, and those that were not were covered with grime. Through some less opaque than the rest, curtains could be seen hanging tipsily from cock-eyed rods, their tatters moved by interior currents of air. The paint of the window-frames clung precariously here and there in flakes; the brick-work was shadowed with the dark grease-dirt of the capital's soot-laden atmosphere. The area, leading to the basement, was a rubbish dump for torn and dis-coloured scraps of paper, bottles and the carcase of a cat. Even the house-agents' To Let sign contributed to the general dilapidation, for it hung crazily from its tilting post.

All this was bad enough, but the elegance of the rest of the houses surrounding the dignified railed-in garden of the Square accentuated No. 50's eccentricity, and added to the awesomeness of its super-natural tenant. Its identification as the Nameless Horror was, in itself, enough to provoke a response in anyone who recognized the existence of the supernatural; and it was an apt name, for, on the evidence of those who at one time or another claimed to have been in its presence, it had no human shape, nor any recognizable animal form. It seems to have been a presence rather than a ghostly object, though the horror expressed in the eyes and features of those who had challenged it and lost, indicated that it did at times make itself visible.

Before the house achieved its evil reputation it had resembled any of the others in Berkeley Square. But this conformist period did not last long. Its strange non-conformity descended upon it after it had been vacated by a tenant of the late eighteenth century, a Mr Du Pré, of Wilton Park, and was attributed to the fact that Du Pré had confined in its attics an insane brother, whose madness made him so violent that no one could approach him. He even had to be fed through a slot in the door.

Whether this unhappy man's restless spirit was the Horror or not it is difficult to say. For the room which the Horror haunted was not in the attics, but a bedroom on the second floor.

Rumours naturally tend to enlarge the reputation of a house so haunted; and it was certainly rumour on which the author of an article in the now defunct society magazine *Mayfair* relied when he wrote in 1888: "The house in Berkeley Square contains at least one room of which the atmosphere is supernaturally fatal to mind and body alike ... The very party walls of the house, when touched, are found saturated with electric horror. It is uninhabited, save by an elderly man and woman, who act as care-takers; but even these have no access to the room. That is kept locked, the key being in the hands of a mysterious and seemingly nameless person, who comes to the house once every six months, locks up the elderly couple in the basement, and then unlocks the room and occupies himself in it for hours."

Rumour also provided alternatives to the Nameless Horror. One was that the haunting was by a child in a Scots plaid who is said to have been frightened to death in her nursery and afterwards wandered about the house wringing her hands and sobbing. Another purported that the ghost was of a man who had gone mad in an upper room waiting for a message which never came. (This is close enough to be a variation of Mr Du Pré's mad brother.) Yet another stated that the spectre was a young girl who threw herself from a top-floor window to escape the sexual importunings of a satyr-guardian who was also her uncle. She rarely came into the house, but fluttered outside a window like a bird, tapping on the panes, begging for entrance. None of these ghosts, however, has ever been authenticated.

This is not true of the Nameless Horror, who was vouched for by no less a person than Lord Lyttleton, member of that family whose experiences of the supernatural give them a valid claim to the title of being "the most haunted family in England". Lord Lyttleton demanded to be allowed to spend the night in the room, and when permission was granted, armed himself with two blunderbusses loaded with buckshot and silver sixpences. The latter, taking the place of silver bullets, were to protect him against any machination of witchcraft and the Powers of Darkness. He reported next morning that something had come into the room and leapt through the air at him. Fortunately he had been able to fire one of his blunderbusses at it, and it had fallen like a plummeting pheasant and then suddenly disappeared. Asked to describe what it was that had entered the room, he could not.

Even the Horror is differently described in two newspaper reports of the early nineteenth century. One maintained that it was the ghost of a man with extremely horrible features, white and flaccid, pierced by an enormous round mouth. (This has affinities with Mr Du Pré's brother.) The other report described it as a strange creature with many legs or tentacles, and declared that it was no ghost but a reptile of darkness which periodically emerged from the sewers of Berkeley Square. If this were so, it is odd that it haunted no other house in the Square—only No. 50.

Besides the Lord Lyttleton already mentioned, there are two authenticated accounts of encounters with the Horror. One is of a gentleman who refused to be deterred by the reputed fate of earlier victims and insisted on passing the night in the Ghost Room; the other is of two seamen of her Majesty's Navy who emulated the gentleman in all ignorance, one of whom afterwards gave a full account of his experiences to the Metropolitan Police.

Sir Robert Warboys, seventh baronet, was the first to challenge the Horror. He was a young man, just turned thirty. His patrimony was such that he could afford to live in fine style, while his tastes, though lavish, were well controlled, so that there was never any possibility of his becoming bankrupt, as so many of his class contemporaries, often much wealthier than he, became within a few years of inheriting.

His seat was at Bracknell, in Berkshire. It was a large Queen Anne country-house, yet not so large that it was a drain on his resources. It was beautifully appointed and furnished, the mirror of the impeccable taste of the wife of the third baronet who had built the house. His servants and his tenants admired, loved and respected him.

His fortune and his establishment alone made him an extremely eligible bachelor in the eyes of those mothers of nubile daughters senior to him in rank, at least up to and including Viscountesses. His striking good looks, virile deportment and sporting prowess made him even more eligible in the eyes of the daughters themselves. Even those mothers and daughters who knew of the presence at Warboys Hall of a darkly handsome manservant, and who had heard faint whispers that the relationship between master and man was not quite an orthodox one, did not deter them, just as it did not deter the servants and tenants from respecting, loving and admiring their master or from being on terms of cordial friendship with his personal servant, for the young men comported themselves with the utmost discretion.

When Sir Robert visited London he stayed at White's or Boodle's. He was always in Town for the season, and made two or three other visits of a week or two's duration at other times of the year as the whim took him or necessity drew him. Though most of his fellow clubmen were aware of the reason for his disinclination towards matrimony, only the most unreasonably bigoted found it necessary to boycott his company on this account. In fact, the majority of those who came into contact with him, whether knowledgeable or ignorant, found him a pleasant companion. His prowess as an expert shot and a hard rider to hounds, together with his patronage of the race-courses and the prize-ring, far outweighed his alleged secret sporting with the valet. In short, he was regarded as an honourable gentleman, a pleasant acquaintance and a good master.

Sir Robert was also a practical man. Warboys Hall was an eminently practical place. It had been built in the middle of a field— since converted into an English park—on ground that had no history beyond a brief and indirect mention in Domesday. The house had no holes and corners which might provoke the invention of legends, and its former owners had died peaceably in their beds. No apparitions, no mysterious tappings and nothing at all that could have a claim to the supernatural had any attachment to the mansion.

Brought up in such surroundings it was not surprising that there should be "no nonsense" about Sir Robert, and this being so that when the conversation in White's smoke-room turned, one day, upon the haunted houses of London, he should feel constrained to pooh-pooh the existence of ghosts. He did it in such a way, however, that the believers felt they must convince him of the mistakenness of his views.

They soon discovered that he was not easily swayed, and it was when they were trying to find some argument that might at least make him reconsider his stand, that the then owner of No. 50 Berkeley Square came into the room.

"Here's a man you can't refute!" exclaimed Lord Cholmondeley.

"Oh," said Sir Robert, "and why not?"

"Because he has a ghost in his house—50 Berkeley Square. You must have heard of it!"

"I fear not, my lord," Sir Robert confessed.

"Benson," Lord Cholmondeley called to the newcomer. "The very man we wanted to see. We're trying to convince Warboys, here, of the existence of ghosts, apparitions and the like. Tell him about yours. He must be convinced then."

Benson looked at the company seriously.

"I hope your lordship will not press me," he said. "We prefer not to talk about it."

"What! You have one of the most famous ghosts in all London living with you, and you prefer not to talk about it?" Lord Cholmondeley expostulated. "Come man!"

"Perhaps it's because Mr Benson doesn't really believe in it himself," Sir Robert remarked.

Again there was a brief silence as they all looked at Benson to see whether he would respond to the challenge.

"We believe in it," he said at last.

"Have you ever seen it?" asked Warboys, who seemed to be intrigued now by Benson's patent reluctance.

"No, we have not," he was told.

"Then you've heard it, perhaps?"

"No."

"Then why . . . ?"

"Because, Sir Robert, the records are too well authenticated to leave any room for doubt."

Lord Cholmondeley brought his hand down heavily against his thigh.

"Now you've gone so far, man, surely you can tell him in outline at all events," he said to Benson. "Warboys is the most sceptical fellow in this matter that I've ever encountered. You obviously believe in the supernatural, as all the rest of us do. You have a duty to convert him, if only for his own sake."

So Benson gave way to the pressure of the company, and once having begun overcame his reluctance and made a full recital of the Horror, much of which was new even to the well-informed among his audience.

When he had finished, Lord Cholmondeley turned to Sir Robert. "There, Warboys," he said. "Changed your mind now?"

Sir Robert shook his head.

"I'm afraid not, my lord," he said. "My whole reason rejects the concept of ghosts and apparitions. Those who claim to have seen them have allowed themselves to be swayed by irrational concepts and, since they are predisposed, have placed themselves outside the control of reason. In such a state imagination can easily run riot. No, my lord, I do not believe that any practical man who sets store by reason has ever seen a ghost. As proof, you have only to look at Mr Benson, there, to see that he is an utterly rational man, despite what he has told us. He has lived at 50 Berkeley Square some ten years, he has said, and neither he nor any of his family or household have seen or heard the Horror."

"But he told us," remarked another of the group, "that he has kept the room shut up all the time he has inhabited the house. That's why he has not seen it."

Sir Robert laughed.

"My dear fellow, if ghosts are as active as you say they are, it presupposes that they have personalities of some sort," he said. "This one in Berkeley Square by all accounts has a most unpleasant personality. We all know that unpleasant personalities are people who force their attentions upon those with whom they come into contact. I submit that your—er—Horror would demand an audience, and if It were deprived of an audience, as you say, sir, It has been these ten years, It would have made Itself known in other ways. Ergo, since It has not done so, It does not exist.

"This is pure surmise, Warboys," Cholmondeley suggested.

"No more surmise, my lord, than your contention that the Horror exists."

Before any other voice could be added to the argument, a young man who, so far, had not spoken was heard to say: "Sir Robert, you're a sporting sort of fellow. Why not volunteer to spend a night in Mr Benson's haunted room; then we should all know."

"I could not possibly permit it, Sir Dougall!" Benson exclaimed firmly before Warboys could reply.

"I don't see that you would have any responsibility, sir," the young Scots baronet maintained. "Sir Robert is fully adult. If he is prepared of his own free will, without the slightest coercion, to challenge your Horror, the responsibility is entirely his."

"But . . ." began Benson.

"Young Forster's right, you know, Benson," Lord Cholmondeley said. "I'm sure that not a single one of us here, including Warboys, would hold you in the slightest degree responsible. What do you say, Warboys?"

"Certainly not, my lord."

"What do you say to Forster's suggestion?"

"I'm willing to take up his gage, my lord," Warboys smiled. "And what's more, I'm prepared to wager a hundred guineas to fifty with anyone here that I shall emerge from the room in the morning entirely unscathed. I undertake to hand over the whole of my winnings to—well let's say, since I am myself an orphan, to the Foundling Hospital."

"Well said!" exclaimed Cholmondeley. "Now Benson . . ."

"I still don't like it, my lord," Benson replied.

"Supposing all of us here come to your house on the night arranged and share the responsibility with you?" a Colonel Raynes suggested.

"That's an excellent idea," Cholmondeley agreed.

"I'm quite prepared to take any means to safeguard myself that you care to name, Mr Benson," Warboys said.

Benson looked round the company and gave a short laugh.

"I'll agree that Sir Robert has not been coerced in the slightest degree," he smiled. "But I shall always maintain, gentlemen, that I have been submitted to the most strenuous coercion from all present."

"Then you agree, Benson?" the Colonel asked.

"On condition that Sir Robert arms himself and that he rings for assistance immediately he feels he needs it," Benson said. "Further, that all of us shall stay on watch all night."

"Well, Warboys?"

Sir Robert bowed. "Of course. But I am quite certain my weapon will be unused next morning and no bells will ring."

"Right," said Cholmondeley. "Forster, be good enough to ring for the secretary to bring the betting book."

"There, gentlemen," objected Benson, "I must ask you to humour me. In my opinion this is not a suitable wager to be recorded in this or any other betting book. By the same token, Sir Robert, I hope you will excuse me from not responding to your wager."

This was agreed, the gentlemen merely stating their stakes. When all had done so, Warboys stood to win three hundred and fifty guineas, or lose seven hundred.

So it was all arranged. The gentlemen present were to dine at 50 Berkeley Square at nine o'clock three evenings from now. Next day, Benson sent his wife and children, their governess and nurse down to the country. When Mrs Benson pressed him for the reason, her husband adamantly refused, asking her to bear with him and he might explain later.

When the company met at the appointed time, an impartial observer would have noticed at once that not one of the gentlemen present was in normal control of his nerves. They talked more loudly with a bonhomie which they would have considered far from *comme il faut* either in their own drawing-room or in the club smoking-room. One or two had clearly attempted to fortify themselves beforehand, but nevertheless accepted the before-dinner drink which Benson offered them.

They raised their glasses to Sir Robert.

"We trust," said Lord Cholmondeley, "that it won't be too scarifying an experience for you."

"I am obliged, my lord, gentlemen," Warboys replied smiling, but again the observant would have noticed that his smile was fainter than usual, an uncertain flicker around his lips.

"Are you still as sceptical as you were, Sir Robert?" Sir Dougall Forster asked him.

"I would like to say yes. Indeed, I will say yes," Warboys told him. "On the other hand, I must admit that I am not quite so inwardly calm as I should expect to be. But that is the result of your treatment of the affair, gentlemen. I suggest that I would have to be unusually insensitive not to be affected by the excitement you are so kindly trying to hide."

"Look here, Sir Robert," Benson said, "if you would like to withdraw, I am quite certain that none of us would hold you to your undertaking. Am I not right, gentlemen?"

"Certainly," Cholmondeley agreed. "None of us would think the worse of you, Warboys."

"Come, Sir Robert," Benson went on. "Withdraw, I beg you. Let's turn the dinner into a celebration of discretion's superiority over valour, eh?"

Warboys shook his head.

"I am sorry, sir," he said. "If I withdrew I would never again take any pride in my self-respect. Please do not press me, gentlemen. I have armed myself, as you required. My pistol is in its case in the hall. You may load it for me, before I retire."

"Very well," Benson said. "We will press you no further, Sir Robert. But I would request one thing of you. Indeed, I think that as your host, I dare insist upon it."

"And that is, sir?" Warboys asked.

"That you will give your solemn promise that should anything happen and you should feel you need assistance, you will not hesitate to ring. My butler has rewired the bell so that it will ring here."

He pointed to the wall above one of the drawing-room doors.

"That is the bell there," he said. "We can be with you in two minutes of your ringing. You will promise that for my peace of mind, will you not?"

Warboys nodded. "Yes, sir, I will do that. But I will ask you something in return. If I need assistance—which I am convinced I shall not—I will ring twice. If I ring once, ignore it, since I may do so from sheer nerves, for I will confess to you again, gentlemen, that I am experiencing an internal excitement which I did not at all expect to do. Do you agree, sir?"

"Yes, I agree," Benson told him.

At that moment the butler announced dinner. Though Benson suggested that for the duration of the meal they should make no reference to what was to come, most of them seemed to find it difficult, if not impossible, to keep their thoughts, at least, free. The result was that the conversation was cast in an entirely artificial mould, which increased every guest's discomfort. Benson had gone to great pains in devising the menu, and his cook had excelled herself in its preparation. It ought to have inspired wit and brilliant talk; instead there settled over the dining-table an atmosphere that one can imagine attending a wake of Irish mutes.

Benson, at all events, was relieved when the port had gone round the second time and he could suggest the adjournment to the drawing-room. Here Warboys declined coffee and presently announced that he would be glad if his host would show him his room.

"I suggest we all go up," Cholmondeley said.

So they all trooped up to the second floor and were shown into the room which was now open for the first time in ten years at least. They saw a dark room, furnished with heavy furniture. A large four-poster bed faced the two windows which overlooked Berkeley Square; it filled at least one-quarter of the floor-space. Much of the rest of the latter was taken up with heavy mahogany chests and presses, two or three chairs and various small tables. Two lamps burned on commodes one on either side of the bed.

Going to the bed, Benson turned to Warboys and said, "Here is the bell-pull, Sir Robert. It works with great ease."

He gave it a vigorous pull, and in the silence the faint ringing of the bell in the drawing-room on the floor below could be heard.

"As you saw," Benson went on, "since the drawing-room is on the first floor, we have only one flight of stairs to mount and we shall be with you."

"Let me remind you," said Warboys, "not to disturb yourselves if I only ring once."

"Right," Cholmondeley muttered. "Well, let us leave him to it, gentlemen. Good-night, Sir Robert."

Left to himself, Warboys removed his coat, cravat and shoes and lay down on the bed, outside the covers, for the fire, which now glowed in the grate, had warmed the room. Beside his right hand he placed the pistol cocked; beside his left hand he arranged the tasselled end of the bell-pull. He did not expect to sleep, so he propped himself up on the pillows and prepared to watch out the night.

When the gentlemen returned to the drawing-room, the ormulo clock on the mantelpiece indicated twenty minutes past eleven.

"What shall we do?" Lord Cholmondeley asked. "Shall we organize ourselves into watches or what?"

"There is little need for that, I think, my lord," Benson remarked. "I for one shall not sleep, and in any case, if we do drop off, the bell is loud enough to waken the soundest sleeper. Though I pray God we never hear it."

"Amen," said Cholmondeley. "I confess this is a wager I shall be happy to lose."

So the company settled themselves, and sank into a drowsy silence. The hands of the clock on the mantelpiece approached midnight, and presently its silver chimes sprinkled themselves on the breathing room. Half-way through, they were joined by the more, masculine bass of the grandfather clock on the landing, and the last of these was still vibrating in the air when the bell above the drawing-room door pealed shortly.

The men sat up, their half-stupor shaken off, their gaze fixed upon the bell.

Benson had started for the door, but Lord Cholmondeley reminded him of their undertaking. "He must ring again, Benson."

The last word was stifled by a second violent peal, so violent that the bell seemed on the point of jerking off its spring.

Benson was first through the door, with the others hard on his heels. Taking the stairs two at a time, he was half-way up when a shot rang out. Seconds later he flung open the door of the room.

Sir Robert Warboys was sprawled half on the bed, his head near the floor, his legs agape on the covers. In his left hand he grasped the bell-pull which had come away from its spring; on the floor by his out-flung right hand lay his pistol.

Benson knelt on one knee, placed his hands beneath the shoulders and raised the body on to the bed. It was only now, as the light from one of the lamps fell on to the face, that the onlookers drew in their breath, and young Sir Dougall Forster let out a cry.

"My God!" he exclaimed. "For God's sake cover him!"

For Sir Robert's eyes stared at them and his lips, drawn tightly back over his teeth, revealed the latter tightly clenched as though he were suffering an epileptic fit. But it was the ineffable terror, the stark dread, in the dead eyes that almost unmanned them.

"Is he dead?" Lord Cholmondeley asked in almost a whisper.

"Quite dead," Benson replied.

"How? Did he shoot himself?"

"No, my lord, it is no suicide."

"For God's sake cover him!" Sir Dougall urged again.

Benson drew a cover about the lifeless body and over the face.

"Let us go down, gentlemen," he said. "It is my fault. I should never have permitted it. It was like this with the rest."

"But what can it have been that struck such terror into him? Colonel Raynes asked, speaking more to himself than to the company.

"God knows!" Benson replied. "No one has ever seen It and lived."

The death of Sir Robert Warboys preyed so much upon Benson's conscience that within a few months he decided to vacate 50 Berkeley Square. It was now that the house entered upon its long tenantless period. For more than forty years it stood, gradually becoming more and more derelict, and it was shortly before the end of this time that the two sailors came upon it.

The frigate *Penelope* returned to Portsmouth, from a year or more's cruise in the West Indies, at the beginning of Christmas week, 1887, and after making their vessel ship-shape, the crew were paid off and given two weeks' shore leave. Among the ship's company were two young seamen, who decided that rather than slake their various thirsts in the tap-rooms and stews of Pompey they would make for the greater excitement of the metropolis.

They reached London the day before Christmas Eve, planning to spend twenty-four hours in carousal before they parted to join their families in Halstead, in Essex, and Reading, respectively, for the festivities. Unfortunately their recent deprivations had been so protracted that they lost all count of time.

They also lost all count of their money. So when at last they realized it was Christmas Eve they discovered, too, that they had no money to get them home.

Earlier in the day it had begun to snow and though it was no longer doing so, it was freezing hard.

"I'm not walking home in this," Edward Blunden said. "It'll get colder during the night. Besides, it may be possible to get a lift in a carriage tomorrow, at least part of the way. What are you going to do, Bob?"

"I'm of the same mind as you, Ted," Robert Martin answered. "We'll find somewhere to lie up for the night and see what the Christmas spirit turns up for us tomorrow. Let's start looking for shelter before we freeze to death."

It was as Martin said this that they turned into Berkeley Square.

"Well, we shan't find anything hereabouts," said Blunden.

"You never know, Ted," Martin remarked. "We may see some skivvy in an area who'll take pity on two poor waifs and offer to share with them the warmth of her attic."

"And pigs may fly, Bob!" Blunden retorted. "Let's make for Euston. At least we'll have a roof over our heads there."

"Why tramp all the way to Euston when there's an empty house at hand?" Martin asked, coming to a stop before No. 50 Berkeley Square, whose TO LET sign reeled askew on its pole, insecurely tied to the area railings.

They backed to the edge of the pavement and looked up at the dark house.

"Can't be anyone living there," said Martin. "Look at those broken windows."

"You may be right at that," his companion agreed. "Do you think we can get in?"

"Let's try the area."

So they made their careful way down the weed-overgrown steps. The door to the basement was closed securely, but a nearby window was hanging loose from its hinges. Without a word, Martin climbed through, followed by Blunden.

Martin pulled a stub of tallow candle from a pocket and lit it. Surveying the shambles in what had been the kitchen where Mr Benson's cook had prepared the dinner on the evening of Sir Robert Warboy's death, the two seamen were for a time speechless. Then Blunden said in an involuntary whisper: "No one's lived here for years. Let's see what the rest of the place is like."

Cautiously, the flickering candle casting the fantastic shadows about them, they mounted the stairs to the main hall. The dining-room, which led from the hall, was empty. In a far corner a dark object scuttled, its shadow thrown on to the wall momentarily monstrous.

"Rat! remarked Martin.

"Looked more like a sheep," Blunden said. "Look, it's gnawed away all the boards in that corner. What a hole!"

"We shan't freeze, anyhow, Martin pointed out. "There's plenty of wood for a fire. Come on, let's see if there's anything more inviting upstairs."

As they mounted the main staircase, the stairs seemed to register their objections at being trodden upon after so long a period, in shrieks of pain that went billowing up the well of the stairway, until they died away in the high distance.

"Eerie," remarked Blunden laconically.

"You're right," his companion agreed. "Have you got another stub of candle handy, Ted. This stub's nearly done."

"For God's sake, don't let it go out, Blunden pleaded, fumbling in his pocket and producing a length of candle. When this had been lit, they continued with their exploration of the house.

All the rooms they entered had the same dank atmosphere, the same air of forbidding dilapidation.

"The place hasn't been lived in for years," Martin remarked. 'I wonder why? Because this is what they call a desirable residential London square."

"Maybe the owners died leaving no one to follow," Blunden suggested.

"But whoever looked after things would have to try to get what he could for it. Besides, you saw the To Let board down there. Someone's obviously trying to sell it."

"Yes, that's right. But it stumps me.

"Me, too."

While they had been talking they had mounted to the second floor, and having looked into the room at the back of the house they came to that overlooking the square. As soon as they crossed the threshold, both together gave an exclamation of surprise.

"This is the place for us!" Martin almost shouted. "Carpets on the floor, chairs, even a bed!"

"I don't like it," Blunden replied. "Let's go, Bob."

"Are you out of your mind?" Martin exclaimed. "I'll go down and get some of those rotten floor-boards and we can light a fire. We'll be as snug as bugs."

"I'd rather go to Euston," Blunden persisted.

"In heaven's name why?"

"Well, look. The rest of the house is empty, but this room's fully furnished, Why?"

"That's as may be," Martin said. "But you can see for yourself that no one's been in this room for years, even if it is furnished. Perhaps who ever lived here didn't like this furniture and it's to be sold with the house. Or perhaps he was moving to a smaller place, and the furniture was too big for it. Look at the size of that bed! It'd take four with comfort. . . . Come on, Ted, be reasonable."

By degrees, Martin wore down his friend's resistance, and presently a fire was burning in the hearth, before which the two sailors gratefully warmed themselves, while they ate the scraps of food which they had carried in their packs for just such an emergency.

"I told you we'd be snug here," Martin remarked. "And we are! You're glad we stayed now, Ted?"

"I suppose so," Blunden replied, though obviously not fully at ease.

"Well, I'm for bed!" Martin declared, throwing an armful of wood on to the fire. "What about you?"

"You go to sleep if you want," Blunden said. "I'll sit here for a bit."

Martin looked at his companion, his bewilderment showing plainly on his face.

"What is the matter with you, Ted?" he asked.

"I don't know, honest, Bob," Blunden replied. "But this place has a funny feeling. It's still giving me the shivers a bit."

"I don't feel it. You're imagining things. Come and sleep a bit, like I said. You won't get far on the road to Reading in the morning if you stay up all night. Tell you what, we'll leave a candle burning, if that'll help."

So once again Blunden allowed his friend to persuade him, and with a candle stuck in a bed of its own tallow on top of one of the commodes at the side of the bed, they lay down, and were presently both asleep.

The next thing that Martin knew was being roughly wakened by Blunden.

"What's up?" he asked. But though Blunden's lips worked, no sound came from them. With an obvious effort he raised a trembling arm and pointed across the room to the door.

The fire was still flickering in the grate; the candle on the commode made one or two grotesque shadows dance on the opposite walls. But apart from these, the room appeared just as it was when Martin had last seen it.

Puzzled, Martin asked again, "What's up, Bob? What's the matter?"

At last Blunden found his speech.

"Listen!" he said in a harsh whisper.

Martin listened intently. At first he could hear nothing. Then a sound reached him. Curious padding footsteps were mounting the stairs. They came slowly, with a long pause between each; but after each pause the next sound was undeniably nearer to the landing. Then they were on the landing itself.

"It'll be someone like us," Martin said quietly. "Someone looking for shelter. A tramp, maybe, who's seen the light from the fire. Hey, you outside? he called out. "We're in here!"

Again they listened, and heard the slithering steps approaching the door. Then slowly the door began to open, and as it reached half-way suddenly "something" glided quickly through the opening into the room.

Blunden let out a yell, as together they leapt out of bed. For a second or two they looked at the intruder, then Blunden, spotting a curtain rail propped up by the wall near one of the windows, made a dash for it. It was a false move, for whatever it was placed itself between the bed and the door, effectively barring escape from the room.

The shadow from one of the bed-posts fell across it, half obscuring it, so that neither man could make out its exact form. All they could see were two outstretched hands which looked like talons.

It stood for a moment like that, then gradually it began to edge its way forward towards Blunden, who let out a shriek and raised the curtain-rod over his shoulder, prepared to strike.

At the sound of the sailor's yell, the Horror began to move more quickly, its feet making scratching sounds on the well-worn carpet. In doing so it left the door unguarded, and seeing his opportunity Martin leapt across the room, and tumbling rather than leaping down the two long flights of stairs he reached the front-door.

He said afterwards that he could not remember pulling back the rusted bolts which securely closed the door, but soon he was running along the square calling for help. As he reached the corner of the side-street by which he and his companion had entered the square only two or three hours earlier, he collided full tilt into a policeman on his beat.

"For God's sake!" he implored. "Come quickly!" and then collapsed, half-fainting at the policeman's feet. As the policeman bent over him there came the sound of crashing glass, followed by a series of cries, then silence.

He raised Martin to his feet and demanded, "What've you been up to then?"

"For God's sake, come quickly!" Martin repeated. "My pal . . . and seizing the policeman's arm he dragged him into the square and to No. 50.

Seeing the open front-door, the policeman exclaimed, "My God, you haven't been in there!"

"Yes. We were sheltering there, upstairs in the room with the bed," Martin told him. "My pal's being attacked up there. Please . . ."

"He was being attacked, you mean," the policeman said half to himself as he flashed his dark-lantern down into the area.

Martin looked down the lantern's beam, and on the flag-stones of the area saw the motionless body of Blunden sprawled on its back. But it was not the grotesque attitude of the limbs of his friend which caused Martin to collapse fainting once more against the rails. The look of indescribable terror in Edward Blunden's staring eyes was to trouble him in nightmares for the rest of his life.

The Bird of Lincoln's Inn

In January, 1901, four years after the Diamond Jubilee celebrations which marked the sixtieth year of her reign, Queen Victoria died at the age of eighty-two at Osborne House in the Isle of Wight. There the following day her sixty-year-old son Edward heard himself at last proclaimed King of England. His Accession Speech to the Privy Council—which he composed himself and delivered without any reference to notes—announced his determination to be a constitutional sovereign in the strictest sense of the word, and during the next session of Parliament which he opened the following month he took only one additional title—"King of The British Dominions Beyond The Seas".

After descriptions of the great State funeral of Victoria, and news and comment about the accession of Edward, who though he had now succeeded to the throne had yet to be crowned, contemporary newspaper readers then for a few months at that time had a quiet and unexciting period, with little to inspire or alarm them, or even merely to hold their interest.

During the first weeks of May, 1901, readers of the London *Daily Mail*, for instance, were chiefly concerned, like nearly everyone else in England, with the dull and apparently interminable accounts of the war in one of the "King's Dominions Beyond The Seas", South Africa. By then it had dragged on for over two years: though of course it was invariably presented in the Press as increasingly successful. Bloemfontein, Johannesburg and Pretoria had all been captured; and after long sieges both Ladysmith and Mafeking had been re-

lieved, and the war was in fact as good as over. But though their
defeat was obvious to English newspaper readers the obstinate
Dutch settlers, or "Boers" as they were called, refused to recognize it.
They continued determined guerilla-resistance under their newly-
appointed Commander-in-Chief Louis Botha (who was eventually
to become the first Prime Minister of the Union of South Africa).

"Botha's March—Boer Move East With Five Guns—Another
Raid On Cape Colony" were the headlines to one report from the
Daily Mail's War Correspondent in South Africa at that time: a
young man named Edgar Wallace, who in later years was to earn
world-wide fame as a prolific writer of detective stories and thrillers.
An article by him on "How The War Stands To-day" gave, said the
introductory paragraphs for it written in London, "a most interesting
statement as to the condition of the Army, of a very reassuring
character. It will be read with gratification."

Elsewhere in the same paper's pages was a report of an interview
with the young Member of Parliament for Oldham, Mr Winston
Churchill, who had returned the year before from South Africa
where he had been held captive for a short period by the enemy.
He stated that any rumours that the Boers had deliberately allowed
him to escape were completely false, and a story to this effect by
the Chief of the Transvaal Secret Police "was a lie from beginning
to end. Not only did the Boers make no arrangements for my
escape", went on Mr Chirchill in the interview with the *Mail*'s
Lobby Correspondent at the House of Commons, "but they made
every effort to effect my recapture. The whole suggestion is just the
kind of desperate lying which one has learned to expect on any side
of any controversy connected with South Africa."

From the continent there was news of a different kind. "Paris,
Wednesday. The ingenuity of Monsieur Lepine, the Paris Prefect
of Police, has no limits. After the *cycling agents* he has now inaugu-
rated the *automobile police*. Their function is to chase the "chauffeurs"
who persist in exceeding the legal pace. Hitherto offending motor
men were watched and pursued by the *cycling agents*, but in the
chase between the bicycle and the motor-car the policeman was
bound to get left. But it has been remarked that the policeman will
exceed the regulation pace himself—and so who is going to look
after him?"

The paper's Correspondence Column was constantly agitated
by a lengthy controversy on a subject which aroused fierce
passions—the question of whether or not women should smoke in
public. "Why will not a salutary fashion set in", asked one liberal-

minded writer, "permitting all women who so desire to smoke openly and in public without the stigma of being declared 'fast', outrageous, or 'bad form'? The life lived nowadays is so fast that women, no less than men, frequently much more than men, require a mild narcotic."

Next day a stern answer came from another correspondent. "Any scientific medical man or woman," he proclaimed, "who has studied the subject of nicotine knows that it is not very hurtful to the male, but acts quite in a different manner on the female." Any claim to "scientific" objectivity that the writer may have had then disappeared. "And Heaven forbid," he went on magisterially, "that ladies should smoke in the streets; for we already have too many degenerate hoydens."

But by far the strangest item of "news" which appeared in the *Daily Mail* of this period was a story which has since become famous, and has frequently been told and retold, and often with a great deal of imaginative embellishment. It first appeared in print on Thursday, 16 May, 1901, under the headlines "A London Ghost— Inexplicable Happenings In Old Chambers".

"The following story", it began, "is contributed by a Correspondent of the *Daily Mail* on whom every reliance can be placed. It seems inexplicable, but perhaps a solution of the apparent mystery may suggest itself to some ingenious reader. It is very easy to laugh at a ghost story, but here is one which, laughable or not, actually happened on the night between Saturday, 11 May, and Sunday, 12 May" (that is, five days before the report appeared), "in a house in a square, in one of the Inns within a stone's throw of the Law Courts."

The writer then attempted to define his own position: "A personal explanation is inevitable in a thing of this sort", he said. "But I will make it as short as possible. I am not a believer in ghosts, neither am I a disbeliever. I am no spiritualist, nor am I a sceptic. I simply don't know. But I *am* curious."

He then went on to describe the situation into which his curiosity had led him. "A rather well-known man of letters, a personal friend, took chambers about eighteen months ago in the said Inn, of which he is not a member. It was an old house, early Georgian probably, and consisted mainly of sets of lawyers' chambers. His rooms—three sitting rooms and a bedroom—were the only rooms in the building inhabited at night, save for the caretaker who lived in the basement.

"The writing-man's rooms were on the third floor, and shut-off from the rest of the house by a short staircase and a solid door. He paid an unusually low rent, and explained this by admitting that there must be something queer about the rooms, as there had been seven or eight tenants in two years. They had one and all left in a hurry, and the agents were anxious to let at almost any rent.

"My friend filled-up most of the wall space with books, read, wrote, and mused during most of the day and part of the night, and he admitted to me in his more confidential moments that 'things happened' there. He did not specify exactly what occurred, but after a time he became nervous and fidgety. Last month he left the chambers rather suddenly, declaring he could stand it no longer. He cleared away all his belongings, and once more the rooms were empty.

"With another friend who is of much the same temperament as myself, I arranged an all-night sitting in these rooms where 'things happened'. Two chairs and a table were absolutely the only furniture left in the place. We unlocked the front door a little before midnight on Saturday last, locked it behind us, and turned on the electric light. We were alone in the house.

"After mounting the stairs from the outer door, there was a smallish room through which we passed into the principal apartment. This had a fireplace on the north wall and two doors in the south wall, through one of which was the entrance from the stairs. The other door was that of another small room which had no means of communication, so that there was no connection between the two small rooms save through the large room.

"We searched the place thoroughly, closed and locked the windows, and pulled down the registers of the three fireplaces. There was absolutely no possibility of anyone being hidden anywhere in the rooms. There were no cupboards, no recesses, no dark corners and no sliding panels. Even a black beetle could not have escaped unnoticed.

"The walls were entirely naked, there were no blinds or curtains. On the floor of the two smaller rooms we spread powdered chalk, such as is used for polishing dancing floors. This was to trace anybody or anything that might come or go.

'We had been warned that nothing happened in a room in which folks were watching. The doors leading to the little rooms were closed, and we sat in the big room and waited. We were both very wide awake, entirely calm, self-possessed and sober, expectant and receptive, and in no way excited or nervous. It was then about a quarter past midnight.

"We talked in ordinary terms, told each other tales, exchanged experiences, for we had both travelled a good deal; and curiously enough discovered we had a mutual friend whom we had never mentioned before, although we had known each other for years. I only mention these trivialities in order to imply that so far as I am able to judge we were in quite an ordinary frame of mind. We did not deem it necessary to feel each other's pulses or take one another's temperatures, but I am convinced that having done so we should have found ourselves to be entirely normal.

"At seventeen minutes to one, the door opposite to us on the right leading to the little room to which there was no communication save through the room in which we were sitting, unlatched itself and opened slowly to its full width. The electric light was on in all the rooms. The click of the turning of the door handle was very audible. We waited expectantly. Nothing happened.

"At four minutes to one precisely, the same thing occurred to the door on the left. Both doors were now standing wide open. We had been silent for a few seconds, watching the doors. Then we spoke.

" 'This is unusual,' said I.

" 'Yes,' said the other man. 'Let's see if there's any resistance.'

"We both rose, crossed the room and, expecting something, found nothing. The doors closed in the usual way, without opposition or resistance.

" 'Draught of course,' was our comment, and we sat down again. But we knew there was no possibility of draught, because everything was tightly shut. While the two doors had stood open we had both noticed that there was no mark on the sprinkled chalk.

"We talked again, but there was a tension, a restraint, which we had not felt before. I cannot explain it, but it was there. Longish silences ensued, and I am sure we were both wide awake.

"At 1.32—my watch was on the table with a pencil and sli p o paper on which I noted the times—the right-hand door opened again, exactly as before. The latch clicked, the brass handle turned, and slowly the door swung back to its full width. There was no jar or recoil when it became fully open. The opening process lasted about eleven seconds. At 1.37 the left-hand door opened as before, and both doors stood wide. We did not rise, but looked on and waited.

"At 1.40 both doors closed simultaneously of their own accord, swinging slowly and gently to within about eight inches of the lock, when they slammed with a slight jar; and both latches clicked

loudly, the one a fraction of a second later than the other. Between
1.45 and 1.55 this happened twice again, but the opening and closing
were in no case simultaneous. There were thus four unaided openings
and three closings. (The first time we had closed them ourselves.)

"The last openings took place at 2.7 and 2.9, and we both noticed
marks on the chalk in the two little rooms. We sprang up and went
to the doorways.

"The marks were clearly defined birds' footprints in the middle
of the floor, three in the left-hand room and five in the right-hand
room. The marks were identical, and exactly $2\frac{3}{4}$ inches in size. We
are neither of us ornithologists, but we compared them to the
footprints of a bird about the size of a turkey. There were three toes
and a short spur behind. The footprints converged diagonally
towards the doors of the big room, and each one was clearly and
sharply defined, with no blurring of outline or drag of any sort.

"This broke up our sitting. We raised our voices to normal pitch,
measured the footprints and made a sketch of them, lighted our
pipes and sat down in the big room. Nothing more happened: the
doors remained open, and the footprints clearly visible. It was just
half-past two.

"We waited till half-past three, discussing things we knew nothing
about. Then we went home, locking the outer door behind us and
dropping the key in an envelope into the letter-box of the house
agent's office nearby. On the Embankment we were greeted by an
exquisite opal and mother-of-pearl sunrise.

"I have stated here exactly what happened, in a bald matter-of-
fact narrative. I explain nothing, I understand nothing. I am not
convinced nor converted nor contentious. I have simply recorded
facts. And the curious thing about it is that my curiosity has not
been cured."

*　　*　　*　　*　　*

Not surprisingly the story when it was first printed excited
considerable comment. The next day the *Daily Mail* reported that
many letters had been received "from people anxious to investigate
the story set forth at length yesterday". But the report continued,
obviously with the intention of deterring crowds of would-be
ghost-seekers: "On referring the matter to our correspondent we
learn that, at any rate for the present, it is not possible either to
repeat the experiment or to give publicity to the address of the
chambers."

But more serious investigators also had their interest aroused.

Mr E. T. Bennett, the Secretary of the Incorporated Society for Psychical Research, was enthusiastic about the story and told a *Daily Mail* reporter that it was going to be considered at the next meeting of his Society's committee. "The worst of these stories", he said, "is that as a rule when investigation is proposed their authors cannot substantiate them, and the stories themselves will not bear any inquiry. This particular story, however, seems to be told with sincerity and in a commonsense manner that is unusual in such cases. Therefore it becomes really interesting. One of the objects of my Society is to carefully enquire into alleged phenomena apparently inexplicable by known laws of nature, commonly referred by spiritualists to the agency of extra-human intelligence. This seems to me to be such a case, and I shall certainly bring it before the members of the Society."

But the results of his Society's inquiries were not published in the *Daily Mail*. Nor is there much reference to them in the Society's minutes or annually-published *Proceedings*, from which it may be concluded that little concrete or conclusive information was discovered to substantiate the story. Occasional references in the *Proceedings* through the years suggest what conclusions were reached. The writer of the article was seen, at some unspecified time and place, by Mr Pidding of the Society for Psychical Research, and told him "he and his friend had no anticipation that night as to what they might discover"—a statement which conveys more by what it omits to mention than by what it actually says.

Five years after the alleged occurrence, in 1906, another reference in the *Proceedings* sounds, in passing, a note of doubt about "the value of the story of the bird in the *Daily Mail*"; and the last reference to it of all, in 1913, is even more sceptical: "If reliance is to be placed on the statement of the writer in the *Daily Mail* it is a point on which judgment may be reserved.

Yet the story itself, unlike many ghosts, refuses to disappear, and over the years it has gradually gained credence as something which really happened. At different times and by different writers it has been described as "A story than which there is none more strange, more eerie or more macabre"; "One of the major mysteries of the ghost-hunter's world"; "One of the most ghastly authenticated hauntings of all time"; and "The terrible true story of the Bird Elemental."

As most popular writers of ghost-stories use one another as sources rather than go to the trouble of checking back to primary accounts, their stories show little variation apart from a few improvements in what might be called the "mise-en-scène". In one well-known version the two men are described as "sitting at a green baize table in a room blindingly lit by electric light, while the floor and walls shone with a ghastly whiteness", and on the table were "a bottle of whisky, a syphon of soda, a packet of sandwiches and a pack of cards". In another, the occurrence was described as "inopinate and inexplicable" and before the marks appeared in the chalk on the floor the watchers allegedly heard "scribbling noises at the windows".

No one has yet explained the significance of an apparently-invisible turkey, the point of the whole story, or what conclusions are meant to be drawn from it. That it is as one writer described it "One of the major mysteries of the ghost-hunter's world" is certainly true, for the whole story certainly has numerous mysterious elements.

Perhaps the major one is why the writer of it was not identified to readers of the *Daily Mail*—particularly as it was in fact that paper's own News Editor, Ralph D. Blumenfeld; and the friend he claimed to have been with him was Max Pemberton, at that time Editor of *Cassell's Magazine*, later a director of Northcliffe newspapers, who was knighted in 1928. Two such responsible and experienced journalists could have done much to substantiate the story by putting their names to it. Yet Pemberton never even referred to it in any of his own writings, and Blumenfeld concealed his own connection for many years.

When he did finally admit authorship, well over twenty years afterwards, he was adamant that the story as he had written it was true in every detail. "I've heard a lot of ghost stories in my life," he said to a friend who questioned him about it. "And I've sent a lot of reporters out on assignments to haunted houses. I don't believe in ghosts one way or the other—but I do know that this thing happened. We both heard what we heard, felt what we felt, and saw what we saw—but don't ask me for an explanation."

He was willing too to be a little more specific about the actual location of the house, being prepared to say that it was "actually in Lincoln's Inn". But he could—or would—give no more details than that: and anyway, he said, it would be impossible to find as the house had been pulled down after the First World War, and another building had been erected on its site. "No hauntings have been noticed there in the new building", he added.

In re-telling the story, he claimed that he had taken a twenty-four-hour lease of the chambers at the time of the incident, in an attempt to discover what happened there. He had himself ordered all the furniture to be taken out, and the rooms stripped quite bare in preparation for the experiment. Apparently he was overlooking the fact, when he said this, that in the original printed version of the story which he wrote at the time, the occupant of the chambers had supposedly left, clearing away all his belongings and leaving the rooms empty. . . .

What really happened "in a house in a square in one of the Inns within a stone's throw of the Law Courts" during the night between May 11th. and 12th., 1901, it is now impossible to tell, and no really serious evidence as to the veracity of Blumenfeld's story can ever be produced.

But as a tail-piece to this story of an invisible bird there is one little curious and minor coincidence. On the night of 11 May, 1901, in Cambridge, over fifty miles away from London, and knowing nothing of what was going on in Lincoln's Inn, a medium named Mrs Verrall was sitting in the dark doing what she called her "automatic writing"—holding a pencil on a sheet of paper and allowing it to be moved about by any "spirit" which wished to use this method of communication. As usual she felt the pencil moving rapidly; and as usual she went to bed without looking at what had been written.

The following morning, when she looked at the paper, she thought it meaningless; there was a very roughly scrawled drawing and underneath it some words in Latin. "I showed the script to my husband next day", she said. "We could make nothing of it, and were much amused at the drawing of what we often referred to in the next four days as 'the cokyoly bird.' It was certainly a very strange-looking creature, rather like a child's drawing of a turkey: and underneath it was carefully written "Calx pedibus inhaerens difficultatem superavit". Which, roughly translated, means "Chalk sticking to the feet has got over the difficulty".

She kept the paper, and dated it. Four days later she read in the *Daily Mail* the account of what had happened in the chambers near the Law Courts.

Writing about the incident twelve years later in a paper for the Psychical Research Society, she described it simply as "a minor demonstration of precognition"—for by that time none of her fellow-members of the Society was prepared to accept, without reservation, the still-anonymous account in the *Daily Mail*. "But at least it shows that I was told what was going to appear in the peper", said Mrs Verrall—and it was left at that.

The Ghosts of Versailles

Marie-Antoinette was a figure of romance and tragedy. Legends have gathered around her. Ever since her death on the scaffold on 16 October, 1793, her ghost has haunted Europe both figuratively and literally.

In 1816 her daughter, who never forgave France, saw her mother's last letter written in the condemned cell and kept secretly by Robespierre, who knew what its value would be. It was yellow, stained and blurred with tears. ("Never seek to avenge our deaths. . . . Oh God, how heartbreaking it is to leave my poor dear Children for ever!") By then Marie-Antoinette was already back to haunt Versailles, where on a memorable day in October, 1789, a breathless page ran to her with a letter warning her that the Paris mob was upon Versailles.

This particular day, said by tradition to be 5 October, became the centre of the most famous and most widely accepted of the world's ghost stories. But long before two English maiden ladies paid their celebrated visit to the Petit Trianon in August, 1901, the story of the haunting of the place by Marie-Antoinette had been told at Versailles. It was said that on a certain day in August not only does Marie-Antoinette appear in the gardens of the Petit Trianon, but also her courtiers are there to re-live that afternoon in the unforgotten past—perhaps the very last day of the *ancien régime*.

1789 had been a year of disaster for Marie-Antoinette. Her eldest son died, and so did her brother. She was blamed for being responsible for France's bankruptcy, which was the immediate cause of the Revolution. On 14 July in that memorable year, the revolutionaries of Paris captured the Bastille and razed it to the ground, and on 5 October the mob marched on Versailles, the royal family were removed to Paris, and the long idyll of Versailles was over for ever.

On that last afternoon before the days of terror when the mob arrived at Versailles, Marie-Antoinette had sat sketching in her own private garden called the Petit Trianon. It was a pleasant October afternoon. The leaves were on the ground. The Queen, depressed by her thoughts about the bad times in which she lived, and the disturbances which had even affected the sacred precincts of the royal palace itself, sought the company of a girl called Marion, who was the daughter of a gardener, and who had lived in the grounds all her life.

Marie-Antoinette then returned moodily to her sketching in her favourite grotto. A feeling of gloom, of terrible foreboding, came upon her, and again she called to Marion, but instead she was surprised to see in front of her a page from the palace, all breathless after running, a letter in his hand, fear in his eyes.

The letter was from the Minister at the palace telling her that the Paris mob was approaching Versailles, that the situation was urgent and that she should return to the palace with all speed. The Queen at first proposed to return to the palace by foot, walking by a short cut through the trees, but the page dissuaded her by impressing on her the danger of the approaching situation, and begged her to go to the château in the Trianon while he went for her carriage. The page ran to the château to order it to readiness. She followed him there more sedately.

This story was apparently told by the girl Marion to Julie Lavergne, who lived at Versailles from 1838 until 1844, and who included it in a volume of reminiscences of the *ancien régime* she compiled, entitled *Légendes de Trianon*. Marion had married a man named Charpentier who was appointed head-gardener at Versailles by Napoleon in 1805, a position he held for many years, and his son after him, and so Marion would have been accessible to Julie Lavergne when she was gathering material for her book at Versailles during the eighteen-thirties and forties. The story of that afternoon at the Petit Trianon on 5 October, 1789, is therefore considered to have a good foundation of truth.

In 1901 two English ladies walked right into this scene in the past. They were Miss Anne Moberly and Miss Eleanor Jourdain, who were successive Principals of St Hugh's College, Oxford. They were women of education and some standing.

Anne Moberly was born in 1846. Her father was Headmaster of Winchester College and later Bishop of Salisbury. She lived in a cultured, donnish society. All her brothers were scholars, and though she received no formal education she eagerly acquired both culture and learning and developed a facile pen. After her father's death, she was in 1886 appointed Principal of St Hugh's and had in her charge the first Victorian girls who dared to invade the man's world and become undergraduates. The University made her an honorary M.A.

Eleanor Jourdain was born in 1863, the daughter of a Derbyshire vicar. A brilliant, ambitious girl, she went to Lady Margaret Hall, Oxford, and got an honours degree in Modern History. She was an M.A. of Oxford and a Doctor of the University of Paris, and she specialized in French literature. She became headmistress of a large girls' school at Watford, and upon the resignation of Miss Moberly in 1915 she was appointed to succeed her as Principal of St Hugh's. Since 1901 the two women had been close friends, for in that year Miss Jourdain had been appointed Vice-Principal to Miss Moberly.

In 1900 Miss Jourdain acquired a flat in Paris, which, in partnership with a Mlle Ménégoz, she ran as a small finishing school for her English pupils at her school at Watford. During the holidays she used this flat as a very useful *pied-à-terre* in Paris. Here Miss Jourdain was staying with Miss Moberly in the August of 1901, when the suggestion of Miss Jourdain becoming Vice-Principal of St Hugh's was under discussion.

On 10 August the two friends went on their famous trip to Versailles. Neither had been there before. Although both of them were teachers and lecturers, they professed that they did not have an intimate knowledge either of the French Revolution, or of the history of the palace of Versailles, or of the topography of its grounds, considerably altered since the days of Marie-Antoinette. Miss Jourdain confessed that in August, 1901, her ignorance of Versailles and its significance was extreme, and Miss Moberly said she had a limited knowledge of French history, though her brother had once written a poem on Marie-Antoinette which had won the Newdigate Prize in 1867. It was usual for people to feel very strongly about the fate of Marie-Antoinette in those days and certainly the Misses Jourdain and Moberly were no exceptions.

At Versailles they walked through the rooms and galleries of the great palace and then Miss Moberly suggested that they went to the

Petit Trianon in view presumably of her youthful feeling for Marie-Antoinette, for, although the Petit Trianon was constructed by Louis XV for the enjoyment of Madame du Barry and Madame de Pompadour, the place has always been associated with Marie-Antoinette.

And so, armed with a Baedeker map, they set off. It was warm and cloudy, with a flower-sweet wind blowing across the gardens into their faces as they walked. They reached the Grand Trianon, and passing it on their left, continued in the direction of the Petit Trianon.

Their subsequent wanderings in the place have long been the subject of discussion, but the best, and indeed only, description of their famous adventure is their own, put down in two separate accounts, written by each of them, and published under the modest and appropriate title *An Adventure* by several famous publishing houses in a number of various editions. The edition used here is that published by Faber and Faber in 1931.

Beyond the Grand Trianon was a broad green drive which led, according to their map, to the Petit Trianon, but Miss Jourdain espied an attractive-looking path which had been cut into the rising ground, and at her suggestion they went along it. They passed some farm buildings, at a window of which Miss Moberly saw a woman shaking a white cloth.

According to Miss Jourdain's observation, these farm buildings were deserted and she noticed agricultural implements, among which was a plough, lying about. Miss Jourdain found the impression of this place "saddening", while her companion was surprised that the French-speaking Miss Jourdain did not ask the way from the woman at the window. But apparently Miss Jourdain did not see her.

They were now in the middle of their joint dream, their hallucination, their ghost world, call it what you will, and they walked forward with a strange and steadily deepening feeling of depression and unreality enveloping them. This feeling of melancholy and dejection, which was very intense and which they both shared, was one of the most interesting aspects of their strange adventure in the past, for they themselves had no reason to feel in this way.

They next encountered two men in greenish uniforms with three-cornered hats. They were obviously gardeners and were working with a wheel-barrow, and, says Miss Moberly, "a pointed spade". They asked them the way and the men directed them straight on.

It is worth noting at this point that gardeners at the Trianon in

1901 did not wear uniforms of that kind, and there had been no plough in the gardens since the days of Louis XVI. These and other strange facts the two ladies discovered later.

As they stood talking to the gardeners, who replied to them in a "casual and mechanical way", Miss Jourdain observed a cottage, detached and well built, in the doorway of which a woman and a girl were standing. Miss Jourdain paid particular attention to their unusual mode of dress. Both wore white kerchiefs tucked into the bodice. The dress of the girl reached down to her ankles, although she seemed to be no more than thirteen or fourteen. The woman was in the act of handing a jug to the girl. Their clothes were quite different to the style of 1901. Only Miss Jourdain saw this particular little tableau from the past.

They continued towards a wood, beneath which was a circular garden kiosk, rather like a small bandstand, in which a man was sitting. This man, seen by both women, wore a heavy black cloak and a slouch hat. His face somehow filled them both with fear and unease. He was marked by smallpox, his complexion dark and his expression, said Miss Jourdain, evil. Although he turned to look at them, his eyes were somehow unseeing. He looked through them.

This strange feeling of unreality and unnaturalness was felt acutely by both women. The scene itself had an eerie, lifeless, other-worldly appearance—"like a wood worked in tapestry", as Miss Moberly put it. "There were no effects of light and shade," she said, "and no wind stirred the trees. It was all intensely still." As for the man sitting in the kiosk, Miss Moberly found his appearance repulsive. His odious expression gave her a "moment of genuine alarm". She asked Miss Jourdain which was the way and, as neither of them wished to approach the dark-visaged man in the cloak, they were a little relieved to hear someone behind them, running towards them in breathless haste.

Turning, they found themselves face to face with a man who, though they heard him running up towards them, appeared suddenly and unaccountably beside them, as though he had passed through the nearby wall of rock.

"Distinctly a gentleman," wrote Miss Moberly. He was dark-eyed, handsome, with crisp, curling black hair beneath a large sombrero hat. His good-looking face was red with the exertion of running. He wore buckled shoes and a dark cloak thrown across him, the end outflung with the speed of his running.

"*Mesdames, mesdames,*" he exclaimed excitedly, "*il ne faut pas passer par là. Par ici—cherchez la maison!*"

Miss Moberly said that he might have said "madame", not "mesdames", and Miss Jourdain, the French scholar, said that he pronounced "faut" as though it was "fout". According to Miss Moberly he said a great deal more which she was unable to follow. But they gathered that he desired them to go to the right and not to the left.

He then ran on with what they described as a peculiar and curious smile. Where he went they did not know, and were not prepared to admit that he vanished. But suddenly he was just not there, although they could still hear the sound of his running, a sound which Moberly said was close by them.

And so they continued and walked over a small rustic bridge which crossed a little ravine. A tiny waterfall trickled from the bank above, so close to them that they could have touched it as they passed over the bridge. Across the bridge the path went under trees towards the English garden in front of the Petit Trianon, which Miss Moberly described as a "square, solidly built small country house".

On the terrace in front of the house Miss Moberly saw a lady in a shady white hat sitting sketching. The lady's light summer dress was arranged on her shoulders "in handkerchief fashion". It was long-waisted, full-skirted, though the skirt occurred to Miss Moberly to be rather short (by 1901 standards), and showed too much leg. She wore a pale green fichu. Miss Moberly thought her appearance was unusual and old-fashioned, although, she said, people were wearing fichu bodices that summer.

Miss Moberly said that the lady looked up as they passed by. She had a pretty face, though she was not young. "It did not attract me," said Miss Moberly, who said she felt annoyed at her being there, for she took her at first to be a tourist. She was of course describing the feelings she experienced at the time, when she did not suspect who the lady might have been. If she had known, her reaction would certainly have been very different.

Miss Jourdain did not see the sketching lady, in the same way that Miss Moberly did not see the woman and the girl in the cottage doorway. To her the place was deserted, but she remembered drawing her skirt away, as though someone were near her, and then wondering why she had done so.

They went on to the terrace, with Miss Moberly feeling that she was walking in a dream—"the stillness and oppressiveness were so unnatural". As they crossed the terrace she once more noticed the sketching lady, this time her back view. At the corner of the terrace they saw a second house, a door of which opened and a young man came out. He slammed the door behind him and then turned to them saying he would show them the way into the house. He took them to an entrance in the front drive.

Miss Moberly said that this man had the "jaunty manner of a footman, but no livery", and he seemed to be mockingly amused at their appearance. The feeling of dreariness and depression was very marked at this point.

In the front entrance of the Petit Trianon they came upon a French wedding party, a very gay affair, in which the two English maiden ladies joined, and, although they did not disclose the extent of their gaiety upon this nuptial occasion, Miss Moberly said she found it very interesting, and that they "felt quite lively again".

Afterwards they took a carriage back to the Hôtel des Réservoirs in Versailles, where they had tea. They did not mention the events of the afternoon until a week later, when Miss Moberly said to Miss Jourdain: "Do you think that the Petit Trianon is haunted?" "Yes, I do," replied Miss Jourdain.

When they began to discuss their visit to the Petit Trianon, they both realized the strangeness of their experience. Why had not Miss Jourdain seen the lady who was sketching? It seemed inconceivable to both of them that she had not done so. Why did they both experience the same feeling of inexplicable depression beginning at exactly the same point in their walk—a fact which they both concealed from each other at the time? How to explain the mystery of the running man, who though he was out of their sight seemed to be running by their side?

Their strange adventure haunted them for years, and during that time they conducted intensive research in order to solve the mystery. First of all they deposited on record in the Bodleian Library their two independent accounts of what had happened, with the result that they were later able to establish a convincing case for the genuineness of their experience.

They found out that the woods, the bridge, the ravine, the cascade and the kiosk no longer existed, though they had been there in the days of Marie-Antoinette. The door in the Petit Trianon through which the young man had come had been blocked up for nearly a hundred years. Long-forgotten maps were discovered which bore out the accuracy of their description of Versailles as it was in Marie-Antoinette's days.

When they returned to the same place again, everything was different. They could find no trace of the paths they had taken. The Petit Trianon itself had a different aspect. The trees and the grass where the lady sat sketching had gone. It was all totally different to the atmosphere of "silent mystery by which we had been so oppressed".

As a result of their researches, they came to the conclusion that the dark-visaged man at the kiosk was the Comte de Vaudreuil, a Creole who had suffered from smallpox and who was one of Marie-Antoinette's friends. The running man they placed as the messenger who had come to warn the Queen of the approach of the Paris mob. They had now read Julie Lavergne's *Légendes de Trianon*, and the story of this incident as told by the gardener's daughter, Marion—called Marianne by Lavergne. Marion would have been about fourteen in 1789, and Miss Moberly and Miss Jourdain thought that she was the girl seen in the cottage doorway by Miss Jourdain.

It was after they had had their Versailles adventure that they heard the legend about Marie-Antoinette and her ghostly retinue regularly haunting the Petit Trianon on a certain August day.

A number of people had seen these Versailles ghosts, and came forward to substantiate the story of Miss Moberly and Miss Jourdain, in particular a Versailles couple and their artist son who lived in a flat overlooking the grounds of the old palace, and who had seen Marie-Antoinette several times sitting at her sketching by the Petit Trianon. They too had observed the topographical details as they existed in 1789. They too had encountered a man in eighteenth-century costume with a three-cornered hat.

This was no ordinary ghost story, and neither Miss Jourdain nor Miss Moberly thought of it as such. They put forward an interesting explanation.

It will be remembered that the incidents which triggered off the haunting took place on 5 October, 1789, but the date of the adventure at Versailles was 10 August, 1901. The legend was that Marie-Antoinette always appeared at the Petit Trianon in August. It was on 10 August, 1792, that the Tuileries was sacked and the doomed royal family took refuge in the Hall of Assembly and later the Temple.

The Moberly-Jourdain theory was that when Marie-Antoinette sat in the Hall of Assembly during those agonizing hours, she cast her mind back to her last afternoon at Trianon, when the messenger arrived with the news of the approach of the Paris mob. So intense had been her emotion at recalling this scene, that it had been projected into the minds of people who in later times were in the spot where it had taken place. Miss Jourdain and Miss Moberly believed that they had entered into this act of Marie-Antoinette's memory through their being at the Petit Trianon on that particular day.

The intense bitterness and sadness of the Queen's thoughts would explain the depression which fell upon Miss Moberly and Miss Jourdain as they entered into the "act of memory" one hundred and nine years later. It would explain also their fear of the Comte de Vaudreuil, for Marie-Antoinette considered him responsible for much of her suffering.

The "running" man who begged them not to walk through the gardens but to go to the house would have addressed them as "madame", not as "mesdames", as Miss Moberly thought he had done, for in the scene they were the Queen, and not themselves. It would also account for his pronunciation of the word "faut" as though it was "fout", which was apparently the Austrian way of speaking French, and Marie-Antoinette had surrounded herself with servants and courtiers from her own country.

Such was the theory of time-travelling telepathy which they put forward to account for their adventure at Versailles, and the years of research they spent confirmed in their minds that they were right.

Miss Moberly and Miss Jourdain hesitated to present their strange adventure as a ghost story. In their opinion no well-educated person would think it could be explained by calling it one. They had many critics, particularly among the intellectual ladies of their acquaintance, who received the story of the haunting at the Trianon with somewhat wounding scepticism and put forward ingenious explanations in attempts to discredit it.

But although they received short shrift from their own sex, their story was taken seriously by such prominent men as Professor C. E. M. Joad and J. W. Dunne, who regarded it as one of the best-established ghost stories on record.

A Bargain with a Ghost

Is it possible for ghosts to live amicably with humans? A psychic practitioner and palmist, well known internationally many years ago as Cheiro, claimed to have had this unique relationship in a haunted house he rented in the centre of London before the First World War.

He was Count Louis Hamon, and his pseudonym Cheiro was derived from the Greek "cheir", the hand. It was pronounced the same as Cairo.

Count Hamon's remarkable story solved a murder mystery of eighteenth-century London, and told a strange and sad love story which continued after life on the astral plane, though earthbound to a room in an old Georgian house in Central London.

Hamon in his account of the incident declined to identify the house for the curious reason that he believed he would be liable to be sued for heavy damages by its owners on account of "damage to the reputation of property" under an old English law. He stated that he had lodged documentary proof with the editor of the London Publishing Company. Any such documentation of this kind, however, was almost certainly lost in the 1940 Blitz on London which obliterated the records as well as the stocks of so many publishing houses in the city.

Hamon came across the house by chance and was greatly attracted by its air of old-world charm, standing back as it did from the busy thoroughfare which had grown up around it, and from which it was half hidden by trees.

The Count was a man who had travelled a great deal, and he had decided to settle down in London for a while. This, he thought, was just the house for him. Although there was no indication that the place was available either to be bought or rented, he went up to the front door, through a quaint overgrown garden where a little fountain splashed placidly as it had done for the past two centuries. He pulled the iron chain of an ancient bell.

The door was opened by an elderly man who was deaf and Hamon had some difficulty in making him understand that he was looking for a house, and had heard that this one might be to let. The old gentleman was telling him that he had made a mistake when his wife appeared in the hall.

She told a different story. The old house was full of strange noises, particularly knocks on the woodwork, and no servant would stay. Her husband was deaf and did not hear the noises. The house was getting more than they could manage and she had it in her mind to try and let it, as the noises had been getting on her nerves.

Her frankness about the noises impressed Count Hamon, who reckoned that he was not afraid of such things. The house intrigued and attracted him immensely with its unusually shaped rooms, its age-black oak beams and panelling, its Tudor fireplaces and mullion windows. He learned that the house was owned by the old man who had inherited it from an eccentric and aged uncle less than a year previously.

"Do you think the place is haunted?" asked Hamon.

The lady of the house would not commit herself. It was sufficient that she had warned the prospective tenant about the strange noises, which were certainly not her imagination, for every servant she had employed had heard them and had refused to stay.

"What about the eccentric uncle?" asked Hamon.

She could not tell him much about this mysterious character, except that he had lived there alone with an ancient butler and they inhabited only the front part of the house. The back rooms had been shut up and were never allowed to be used.

Despite this somewhat ominous introduction to the house of his dreams, Count Hamon took a lease upon it, and acquired the key two weeks later. He decided to have the place redecorated and restored to something like its ancient style, before he moved in.

As he walked around the empty silent house, planning the redecoration, he came into one room which had a strange effect upon him and seemed to defeat any attempt to fit it into his plans for the house. This room was in the oldest part of the building, was below the level of the hall on the half-landing leading down to the basement. The decorator who was doing the work was equally at a loss, and so Hamon decided to lock the room and leave it untouched.

The work proceeded smoothly, and as soon as two rooms were completed Hamon fitted them up for himself and his secretary, and moved in. He did not engage any servants and he arranged that they should have their meals out. His secretary was a Yorkshireman named Perkins, a stolid, down-to-earth man older than the Count.

Among the improvements Hamon had installed in the house was electric light, which had the effect of dispersing some of the more mysterious shadows in the place. On their first night he and Perkins got back from the evening meal about ten, made sure that all the doors and windows were properly fastened, extinguished all the lights and retired to their respective rooms.

Hamon read for a while, then switched off his light and settled down to go to sleep. The house was quiet, with the sound of the London traffic a distant lullaby. He lay there for a while, then suddenly sat up with a start.

Downstairs there was a distant noise of the opening and shutting of a door. This was followed by heavy footsteps sounding on the uncarpeted floors. The footsteps came upstairs and became louder and louder as they approached his door.

By now Louis Hamon was bolt upright in his bed, his heart hammering. He was afraid to switch on his light for fear the gleam under the door would attract the intruder, whoever he might be. He heard the staircase squeak on the loose tread he had particularly noted that evening as he came up to bed.

The footsteps stopped right outside his door. At first he was convinced that the intruder was human, despite the stories the old lady had told him. He got out of bed, picked up the heavy poker from the fire-grate and stood there waiting.

Instead of the door bursting open as he expected, there was a sudden, sharp rat-a-tat, tat, *tat-tat* on the door, the last two knocks coming with almost bone-breaking force on the centre panel of the door.

For some reason this knocking banished the thought from his mind that the intruder was human. He switched on his electric light and went over to the door, some awful fear clutching at his very bowels. But whatever it was, he was determined to face it. All his life he had dabbled in psychic matters, and he had learned to respect and to dread the unknown. But he knew that whatever agency was here in this house, there was no escaping it, once that grim knocking had been made upon his door.

Pulling back the bolts, he opened the door wide. A dark and empty landing faced him.

He stood there breathing hard and staring into the darkness, words beginning to form on his trembling lips. As if to answer him before he had spoken, the reply came in a way which froze his very blood.

Upon the open door right beside his head came that awful knocking once more—as clear and sharp as though hammered out by knuckles made of bone without flesh.

He jumped back and slammed the door with a crash that echoed and re-echoed through the empty old house. Hastily shooting the bolt home, he returned to his bed and waited, quaking with fear.

But nothing more happened that night, and with the courage which daylight and the rebirth of another day in the city brings he scoffed at his fears of the night. After all, he was a psychic observer. There was really no need to be afraid of such things. Anyway, it was more likely that he imagined the whole thing, that it was perhaps a dream prompted by the stories the old lady had told him about this house.

If he had thought that his experience had been some kind of hallucination, this idea was banished from his mind by a talk he had with Perkins at breakfast-time. He too had heard the noises in the night—the footsteps and those nerve-racking rat-a-tats.

"I'm damned if I'll stop in this house another night, sir. I was scared, I don't mind confessing."

Hamon was surprised. Perkins was a man of affairs, level headed, honest, and had had considerable experience of the world.

"What are we going to do about it?" he asked.

Perkins suggested giving up the lease on the grounds that the house was not habitable, and getting the owners to return what money had been spent on it, under threat of legal proceedings if need be. But when Hamon explained to him that the lady concerned had warned him about the strange noises before he took the house, and that anyway he liked the place and had no intention of leaving it, Perkins agreed to stop.

The following night both men spent the hours of darkness seated in armchairs before the fire in Count Hamon's room. They had armed themselves with coffee and sandwiches and stout pokers besides, this latter precaution upon Perkins's insistence, for the master of the house had little faith in pokers being of any defence against whatever was troubling the house at night.

Once more they heard the footsteps followed by the sharp rat-a-tat-tat upon the door. This was followed by the sound of a click—the unmistakable noise of an electric light being switched on.

"That's no ghost!" exclaimed Perkins, unbolting the door and pulling it open.

The landing was flooded with light. But there was no one there. They stood listening. The house was enveloped in the silence as of death. They could see that the lights were on in the hall. They had distinctly remembered turning them off. Both men descended the stairs, their pokers gripped firmly in their hands.

"Can't be a ghost with all these lights," muttered Perkins to reassure himself.

When they reached the hall every lamp was on. To their left the dining-room door was wide open and the room was in darkness. Beside the door they could plainly see the three brass switches controlling the three lights in the room, and as they watched the switches were turned on one by one before their eyes, filling the room with light.

They stepped inside, expecting that someone was playing a trick. But the dining-room, ablaze with light, was empty. It was not possible that anyone was concealed there, or that the lights could have been pulled on by means of wires or strings.

As they were making sure of this, a strange hollow laugh sounded so close to them that it could only have been made by someone in the room. And yet there was no one there. The laugh sounded again, more sinister, mocking them and terrifying them.

They turned and fled to Hamon's room, without bothering to turn the lights out. They were found all turned on, even down in the basement, when the workmen arrived in the morning, after Hamon and his secretary had spent the rest of the hours of darkness sitting shivering by the dying fire and wondering what strange and unpredictable force they were up against in this old house.

They were determined not to give in. Perkins produced a terrier the following night, on the principle that if there was anything human about the ghost, the dog would be certain to smell him out. Hamon was quite agreeable to the scheme for he knew from experience that dogs showed more terror than humans when encountering the supernatural.

Taking the dog with them, they made a tour of the house before they retired, locking all the doors and windows and seeing that all the lights were switched off.

They arrived at the door of the small room on the half-landing leading down to the basement which the decorators had so far not touched and which Hamon kept locked.

He unlocked the door and went in, striking a match, as there was no electric light in there. Perkins came in after him, calling the dog to follow.

But the dog refused to go inside the room. He lay crouching outside, whining, his hair standing up on end in terror, like bristles. Hamon himself, with his extra-psychic perception, felt something of what the dog felt. It was an extremely uncomfortable feeling. Locking the room, they left it and went upstairs, followed by the dog still trembling and whining.

"Well, what do you think of that, Perkins?" asked Hamon.

Perkins did not reply, but poured two cups of coffee with an expression on his face which was a sufficient commentary on the situation.

The only footsteps they heard in the house that night were those of the policeman on the beat, who came knocking on their door in very unghostly fashion, wanting to know what was going on in the house. He had tried the back door, found it locked securely, and then he heard the sound of the bolts being drawn back and the door was opened before his eyes. He went inside to find the place ablaze with lights, but empty.

Count Hamon had some difficulty in assuring the policeman of his bona fides, the house being mostly unfurnished and still in the hands of the decorators. It was useless trying to explain what was really going on—even if he knew himself. The constable searched the house from top to bottom, including the small room on the half-landing into which the dog once more flatly refused to go, crouching down in terror, trembling from nose to tail.

The policeman ponderously made notes, said he would have to hand in a full report on the affair, and finally he left.

Hamon heard no more from the police, and the strange thing was that after that for some weeks he heard no more from the ghost. But he did not believe that the visit of a humble London bobby had deterred any supernatural agency there might have been in the house.

The decorations were completed and Count Hamon took up residence in the house officially. Among his early visitors was the dramatist Henry Hamilton, who had a strangely interesting story to tell him.

He told Hamon that he knew about the house being haunted, as some friends of his had once lived in it, and had had to leave because of the strange noises and knockings. He said that he himself had got in touch with the ghost in that very room and received a message from it. This he had written down and placed in a sealed envelope which he handed to his host, suggesting that he should also attempt to do the same thing and then compare the two messages.

Hamon promised to do so, though he heard no knocks for some weeks, until the night he had a party of friends to dinner. They sat around the fire in the drawing-room, having coffee and brandy after the meal.

Their conversation was suddenly interrupted by a series of sharp knocks on a crystal bowl. The knocks were so persistent that Hamon, believing that the ghost was trying to get through with some message, took out a pencil and writing pad and addressed the unknown entity telling it that he proposed to call out the letters of the alphabet, and for the ghost to make a knock on the crystal bowl when Hamon reached the requisite letter which would spell out a message.

This arrangement worked well enough and the message came through beginning: "My name is Karl Clint. I lived here about a hundred and twenty years ago." If they went to the empty room in the half-landing, the message said, they would hear more.

The party did so. They lit candles and sat around a small table, and the tapping message laboriously continued, the sounds much stronger than before, being made upon the wall above where the candle burned.

"I am Karl Clint. I own this house. I murdered Arthur Liddel in this room and buried him underneath."

The mortals asked the ghost if there was anything it wanted them to do about it. The reply was that there was nothing they could do. In answer to the question whether the spirit wanted any prayers said, the answer came very firmly in the negative.

Hamon asked if there was any way in which he could help, and the reply was that the ghost wanted to be left alone in his own house. "Why can't people keep away?" he demanded.

At this point the ghost apparently became exasperated, for the candle was suddenly extinguished and there was a loud bang on the door. The company groped their way out, only too glad to escape from the haunted room.

When his friends had gone Hamon opened the sealed envelope which Henry Hamilton had given him and which he had kept locked in his desk. The message which had been received by Hamilton was precisely the same, almost word for word, with the one Hamon had taken down from the ghost in the little room that night.

Hamon then began to make inquiries about the history of the house. He examined the old records of the parish and found that the original part of the old house—that is, the part at the back which included the room on the half landing—had been a farmhouse which was owned by a German named Karl Clint between the years 1740 and 1800. Hamon also found reference to the disappearance of a man named Arthur Liddel who had been associated with Clint and was last seen in his company. Some years later Karl Clint left the neighbourhood and since then the property changed hands many times, and was enlarged by the addition of what was now the front of the house. The farmland itself disappeared and was swallowed up in the expansion of London during the nineteenth century.

Count Hamon gradually built up his menage in the old house, engaging servants, opening up some of the old rooms and installing electric light everywhere, except in the one room which he kept locked.

With this gradual encroachment into the old part of the house, the noises began once more, and Hamon was awakened by the spectral rapping on his bedroom door. Two of his servants who heard the noises, immediately gave notice.

Hamon decided to hold a seance. He had a plan to get to the bottom of the haunting and to come to terms with the ghost if possible. He invited to the house a blind medium named Cecil Husk with whom he had worked before, and who seemed to have the power to make spirits materialize.

The seance was held in the dining room with the blind medium sitting in a circle of Hamon's friends before a table on which was a small lamp with a red shade. All the other lights in the house were extinguished.

Immediately the knocking started—on the ceiling, on the mirror, on the chandelier. Then began the tramp of heavy footsteps, which seemed to come from the unused room on the half-landing.

The footsteps stopped outside the door of the room, and then, says Hamon, a dark shadowy cloud formed inside the room by the door, which grew thicker, more dense and opaque and moved over towards him. Out of this cloud materialized the head and shoulders of a man—a face with a weary hunted look, lonely, and long dead. As the features developed more clearly they could see a close-cropped beard and reddish hair, a teutonic-shaped head. It was the face of a man of about forty-five or fifty.

All the company, except the blind medium who sat before the red lamp deep in his trance, stared in fascination as the lips of the man from the past began to move in an attempt to speak. At first they just opened, and no sound came; and then after what seemed a tremendous effort, the sound of a voice materialized into the room, issuing from the lips, coming first in unintelligible whispers and guttural mutterings.

Only gradually did sense come out, and then suddenly the ghost demanded in a voice that everyone in the room could hear:

"Why are all these people in my house?"

Hamon replied that they were his friends, and they were all there to try to help him. Would he not tell them something about himself?

"I am Karl Clint. I lived here as far as I can make out a hundred and twenty years ago. But time makes no difference to me now. It is people who change. Why have you come to my house?"

"Because I liked your house," replied Hamon. "Perhaps I can help you by living here."

"No one can help me. I want only to be left in peace." The voice was filled with infinite sadness.

"But you are not at peace," Hamon said. "If you were, you would not frighten people as you do."

"I can't get away. Since the night I died, I am here all the time."

Hamon asked Clint to tell them about the murder of Arthur Liddel, and the ghost replied that during his lifetime he was living in this house with a woman named Charlotte whom he loved more than life itself. They were not married, and Liddel took a great fancy to Charlotte, and tried to tempt her to go away with him by offering her money. Liddel was better off than he, Clint, who was a hard-working farmer, and he thought he could buy Charlotte with his money.

"One night he went too far," said the ghost, "and I killed him as I would a mad dog."

Although he knew it was murder, he would not hesitate to do the same thing again if he and Liddel were living. He buried the body in a hole he dug in the floor in the room downstairs. He filled it with quicklime, and cemented it over. So far as he knew the body was still there.

Charlotte helped him to dispose of the body, he said, but she never got over the fear of being found out for the murder. She died a few years later and was buried in the churchyard nearby.

After that Karl Clint returned to his native Germany, but he never knew a moment's happiness. Finally he committed suicide.

"And then—I can't tell you how it came about—but one day I seemed to wake up in the room downstairs and I have been here ever since."

He did not want to leave the house, he said. Why should he? It was the only place he called home—the only place he was ever happy in. It was where he lived with the one woman he ever loved. The only happiness he ever knew, he experienced here in this house. Why should he ever leave it? There was no place for him to go. No release for him, ever.

Besides, there was Charlotte. "She is here with me. We live the old happy days over and over—until Liddel comes. And then I kill him again—over and over again."

Hamon, very much moved by all this, wanted to know whether there was any way in which he could help this unfortunate being from the past. The fact that he had murdered did not make Hamon any the less desirous of helping him. It seemed that his punishment was very long and very grievous.

The ghost wanted only one thing—the room downstairs, where he lived his incomprehensible existence with the shadowy Charlotte. He wanted the room to remain untouched, and for no one ever to enter it after dark. He required only two chairs and a table there. The human occupants could then have the rest of the house to themselves, and the ghost would not trouble them again.

This Hamon promised. That night he placed two chairs and a table in the little room where had taken place that murder long forgotten by everyone except the wretch who had it on his eternal conscience. Hamon locked the door and put the key in his safe.

The ghost troubled him no more. There were no more knockings, no more disturbances. Behind the locked door of Karl Clint's room there was silence and, it seemed, peace. Whatever was going on between the ghostly lovers in that lightless room where they had had their happiness and had committed their crime, no sign or sound of it came to the world outside.

After some years Hamon decided to move to another house in a different part of London. But he did not feel that he could go without letting Karl Clint know what was happening, and at least thanking him for keeping his part of the bargain so faithfully.

So he had another seance. Clint soon materialized once more. Hamon told him what his intentions were, and duly thanked him for keeping faith. Was there anything he could do to help him before other people moved into the house?

To his great surprise, declared Hamon, the ghost asked if he might move with him to his new house, for Hamon was the only person he had ever known who had shown sympathy and understanding.

There was nothing very much Hamon could do about it, and anyway he was not afraid of this particular ghost now. Clint told him that there was a portrait of Charlotte hidden in the panelling of his room, and would he take it with him and hang it in his new house?

Hamon found the picture and when he moved he hung it in his study.

He swears to the truth of this extraordinary ghost story, which he told in a book entitled *True Ghost Stories* and which was published many years ago by the Psychic Book Club.

The Ghostly Cavalry Charge
and The Spectres of Crécy

When, where, and why, does one see a ghost? Ninety-nine people out of a hundred probably never see one at all. Of those who do some clearly imagine that they have seen a ghost. Others may create a wishful vision and convince themselves that they have seen a ghost.

I confess that although I have been interested in ghost stories, local legends and folklore all my life and have sat up until the small hours in thirty to forty of the most haunted houses in Britain, I have only once seen what I am prepared to swear was a ghostly vision.

There was the night when I sat late working on the Bowes-Lyon family papers in the Charter Room of Glamis Castle "the most haunted house in Britain". Lord Strathmore was out to dinner. The butler had gone down to the village. Only the cook and a maid-servant were left in that great, grim, turreted castle of 120 rooms, the oldest inhabited castle in Scotland, the home of the Monster of Glamis, the place in which Macbeth was murdered, the house where Earl Beardie gambled with the devil—and has been seen since by more than one person sitting in a great armchair by the flickering fire. The house of the Tongueless Woman, of Jack the Runner, of the Grey Lady, of blood-stained floorboards and secret chambers. What other house could offer such a field of ghosts on a dark night in winter when the snow fell, wild geese bayed overhead—and the lights suddenly went out. The whole place was plunged in darkness.

I groped my way to Duncan's Hall. I struck a match and saw a prison door yawning open in the wall and a grizzly bear standing guard over it—stuffed. I stumbled down to the Crypt where surely ghosts should walk and into Malcolm's Chamber where the king was murdered and bolted doors opened on their own account.

It was a chance in a million to see, hear or feel the presence of a ghost. Not a thing moved, rustled or showed during that hour of Stygian blackness. Then the lights went up. A snow-storm which had blacked out half Angus had failed to produce a glimmer of a ghost.

There was that night in Craster Tower on the bleak Northumbrian coast where Crasters have dwelt for more than eight hundred years and a Grey Lady walks. My wife and I slept in one room, our small daughter in another just across the landing. At two in the morning she came into our room to say that someone had opened the front door, walked upstairs, come into her bedroom and then crossed the landing and gone into the drawing room—"a woman all in grey".

I spent the next three nights in my daughter's bedroom. At two each morning I woke. I saw nothing, heard nothing and, although I tried hard to imagine it, I felt nothing. The Grey Lady was not for me.

I have met three men and a woman who swear that they have seen Black Shuck, the ghostly dog of East Anglia. I have walked the lonely paths by cliff and breck and fen where Black Shuck runs —and have never seen him. But I have heard the bittern boom on undrained, quaking fens and seen Wills o'the Wisp dance their corpse-candle dance over stinking swamps which beckon men to death. Black Shuck was not there.

I have slept in Blickling Hall, that magnificent Norfolk house, but saw no sign of Anne Boleyn, whose ghost visits her ancestral home, although the man in the next bedroom complained that he was woken twice in the night by uncanny noises. I have waited for the ghost of Thomas Wentworth, "the Great Earl" of Strafford, to walk headless down the staircase at Wentworth Woodhouse and saw not even a mouse. Nonetheless, a footman swore most solemnly that he had seen "Black Tom" walk downstairs with his head underneath his arm.

I have lived and slept many days and nights in a small and enchanting manor house, built in 1421 and the home for two and a half centuries of my father's family, but I saw no sign of the Strangling Ghost, although he terrified a blameless brigadier and frightened a vulgar profiteer out of his wits when they both slept on successive nights in the bedroom called the Justice Room. The legend is that the Strangler only grips by the throat, as they sleep, those who deserve to be hanged from the kingpost beam where they dealt justice in the old days. Perhaps the brigadier was not so blameless after all. Certainly the wife of a dead and gone Royal Academician, who fled screaming from the room one night when her husband was in London, was, as we all knew, no better than she should have been and not half as good as she ought to have been. I saw nothing—which is my alibi.

True, I was once kicked down the oaken stairs at Holme Hall, high in the Derbyshire hills, by the ghost of Bradshaw the Regicide, who signed the death warrant of Charles I. My host swore that it was Bradshaw's ghost who launched the kick. I prefer to think that I slipped on the polished oak as a result of his '45 port.

The explanation, surely, of all these failures to see the appropriate ghost in so many authentic ghost-haunts is that one was not there at the exact moment of time when ghosts are due to appear according to whatever supernatural laws may govern them.

A highly competent scientist, who is also a ghost-hunter with a notable bag of apparitions to his credit, swears to me that ghosts only appear on the scenes they choose to haunt at certain fixed periods of time. These periods may, according to his theory, be annual, bi-annual, even centennial. On the other hand, whoever is lucky enough to see the ghost may be one of those rare people of extra-sensory perception to whom the supernatural is more or less an open book.

After all, when we consider that, today, it is possible to transmit pictures from the moon and to televise voices, noises, colours and events round the world in a matter of seconds, it is perhaps not unreasonable to suppose that events of the past and the people who took part in them, have been "photographed on the retina of time" to recur at stated intervals and be seen by the few.

This brings me to my own one authentic vision of the supernatural. I went to France in the First World War shortly before that war ended. Youth, and a bit of luck, saved me from the horrors of trench warfare. When we moved up to the Front Line the Germans were on the run. Dead lay in tens of thousands on the battlefields of Ypres, Mont Kemmel, Vimy Ridge, Messines, Bailleul and Warneton Ridge. Towns and villages had long been battered flat. Outerdem, Meteren, Neuve Eglise, Vlamartinghe, Poperinghe and the rest, in that grey land of the dead, were heaps of rubble.

Here, if anywhere, was surely the place where the dead should walk. I, as a young soldier, daily in charge of drafts of German prisoners, scantily guarded, relying for my escort parties largely on B.2 and C.3 types of infantrymen, had no time to think of ghosts. Each day was a kaleidoscope of dirt, danger, lice and hard slogging.

One afternoon I climbed into the upper floor of a half-ruined barn and gazed out over the grey, rolling sullen fields, pocked with shell-holes, writhing with barbed wire, stinking of the dead. Every tree was a tortured skeleton of itself. The cornfields behind the Line, where the tide of battle had surged back and then retreated, were yellow, sodden, beaten flat by rain, men, tanks and the dead. I thought for a brief moment that this land on which I now gazed had been torn and tortured by wars and armies from Alva to Wellington, from Waterloo to Sedan. That moment of thought raised no ghosts.

A month later the Armistice had been signed. We were in camp on a sodden hillside at Neuve Eglise, a bitter winter ahead.

The guns in Flanders were silent at last. In that final month of the grey winter of 1918 an eerie stillness dwelt on the battlefields of France and Belgium. Dead lay unburied in fields and sodden trenches. Guns and rifles, shells and Mills bombs lay rusting. Warneton Ridge was a wilderness of mud and crawling wire, shell-pocked and lonely as the wind. Mont Kemmel, "The Gibraltar of Northern France", alone with its dead and its torn trees, loomed above the grey plains that have been Europe's cockpit for centuries.

By day carrion crows croaked death-like from shattered trees, travesties of nature whose bare trunks were bullet-scarred and shell-splintered. Moated farms and straggling villages stood ruined, roofless, and gaping-walled—if they stood at all.

By night the winter moon looked on the twisted dead, the cornfields and roofless farms with white dispassion. Frost mantled the trees and whitened the tents where No. 298 Prisoners-of-War Company crouched by the gaunt ruins of Neuve Eglise, the village which was blown to atoms in an hour.

No longer was the night horizon lit by the fantastic spears and flashes of gunfire, the ghostly aurora borealis of the front line, no longer pin-pointed by star-shells or shuddering with the thunder of guns.

In our tents and shacks outside the great barbed-wire cages which prisoned 450 Germans, newly-taken, we, the guards, shivered with cold. In their prison-tents the Germans slept like sardines for warmth's sake. We were new to our prisoners, who, a month before, had been fighting us. The arctic cold smote English and German alike.

So when at the railhead to pick up post and rations I heard by chance words of a great country auberge—an old posting-inn of the eighteenth century—whose stables and ruined rooms were full of abandoned Queen stoves, that perfect little camp-cooker, I determined to impound the lot.

Next day, late in the afternoon, after a morning of sudden thaw, I took Corporal Barr, that minute but unquenchable fighting man, and set off along a rutted road to the east. Flooded fields lay on either side. Rotted crops stained the soil. The smell of dead men, cold and oily, that smell which strikes to the pit of the stomach like the smell of a dead snake, was heavy on the air.

Ahead, in the afternoon sun, the road gleamed with sudden splashes and shields of light where water lay. Two kilometres, near enough three, and we came to the standing archway of the auberge. The yellow walls of what had been a fine old Flemish inn stood windowless, gazing like dead eyes over the fields of the dead. Bullets had sieved its walls. Shells had shattered the roof where rafters and roof-tree stood stark as the ribs of a skeleton.

Under the great arch which had echoed to the clatter of coach-wheels and rung with the guttural cries of Walloon and Flamande farmers, the courtyard, with its mighty midden, showed a four-square array of stables, barns, cart-sheds and coach-houses. Doors sagged on broken hinges and sandbags filled empty windows.

Within were wooden bunks, the black ashes of long-cold fires, rusty dixies and mouldy webbing, mildewed bully and Maconochie tins—and Queen stoves!

We found at least a score—enough to warm our pitiful shacks and spare one or two for the prisoners. I told Corporal Barr to bring a party of prisoners next day and remove the lot.

That dour and unimpressionable little man with the square, short body, the beetling black eyebrows and steady eyes—a soldier among the best of them—said "Aye". He was being loquacious.

Then we started back. It was, maybe, three to three-thirty and far from dark. In the sunset the sky had cleared to a wide band of apple-green fading into pink. Overhead, high clouds caught a sudden ethereal sheen of crimson and flamingo. The heavens were alight above the stricken earth. On our left, fields lay waterlogged and gleaming—lake beyond miniature lake.

On the right a low upland swept up to a torn, fantastic wood of larch and birch. The thin trees were twisted into grotesque shapes by shell blast. It was a Hans Andersen wood of Arthur Rackham trees through whose sun-reddened trunks we could see cloud-masses lit with a Cuyp-like glow.

Suddenly, as we splashed through the sunset pools of that deserted road, German cavalry swept out of the wood. Crouching low over their horses' withers, lance-tops gleaming, red pennons flying, they charged out of that spectral wood—a dozen or more German Uhlans in those queer high-topped hats which they had worn in the dead days of 1914. I saw horses, men, lances, and flickering pennons clear and sharp in the level sun.

And up the slope to meet them galloped French dragoons—brass cuirasses flashing, sabres upswung, heavy horse-tail plumes dancing from huge brass helmets. Fierce-moustached and red-faced, they charged on heavy Flemish chargers to meet that flying posse of grey-faced men who swept down with slender lances on flying horses—the hurricane meeting the winter wind.

Then the vision passed. There was no clash of mounted men—no melée of shivering lance and down-smashing sabre, no sickening unhorsing of men or uprearing of chargers—only empty upland and a thin and ghostly wood, silver in the setting sun. The earth was empty. I felt suddenly cold.

I am no spiritualist, but to the truth of this vision I will swear.

I glanced at Corporal Barr. He looked white and uneasy.

"Did you see anything?" I asked.

"Aye—something mighty queer," said that non-committal little Glasgow baker. "Ssst! look! Wha's that?" he gasped. His rifle bolt clicked back, a cartridge snapped in the breech and the butt leapt to his shoulder. In a gap in the hedge on the left two baleful eyes glared at us from a dim, crouching shape. At the click of the rifle bolt it sprang to its feet—a wolf in shape and size—and loped into a sudden burst of speed.

Two rifles cracked almost as one as the grey beast splashed through the shallow floods. Bullets spurted up sudden fountains as it raced away. Not one touched it. Yet the day before I had killed a running hare with my .303 and Barr could pick a crow off a tree at a hundred yards.

The beast raced belly-low into the sunset, leaving a trail of flying water. Bullet after bullet cracked after it, missed by yards. We were both off our shooting.

No wolf was that half-starved ghoul of a beast, but one of the lost, masterless Alsatian sheepdogs of the dead farmers, pariahs of the battlefield who ravished the flesh of the staring dead.

We reached camp, shaken and oddly shy of talking too much.

Next day, at Neuve Eglise, that skeleton of a village on the spine of the Ravelsberg, I drank a glass or two of vin rouge at the estaminet of the one and only Marie, a kilometre up the road from the Armentières Road *douane*.

I asked her of the wood and the auberge. And Marie, forty-five and peasant-wise, said: "Ah! M'sieu, that wood is sad. It is on the frontier. A wood of dead men. In the wars of Napoleon, in the war of 1870—in this war in 1914—always the cavalry of France and Germany have met and fought by that wood. If you will go beyond the auberge half a kilometre only, you will find a *petite eglise*. There you will see the graves of the cavalry of all these wars. It is true, I tell you."

I went. In the tiny churchyard were the graves. And the headstones told the brief and bloody tales of gallant horsemen in frontier skirmishes which had played prelude to three mighty wars. And since I love a horse and revere a good rider, whether he is a Uhlan or a Gascon under Murat, a turbaned Mahratta or a red-coated fox-hunter, I stood in homage for a frightened minute.

Now that is a true tale. Twenty-six years later I told it in the Second World War to a few men. A Sheffield steel man, Colonel Shepheard, listened intently. I finished on a faint note of defiance—"believe it or not".

"I do believe it,"he said steadily."I saw something of the same sort in the last war!" And he told me this astounding story in a calm, matter-of-fact voice.

During the 1914–18 War, as a staff colonel, he was travelling in a car from Hazebrouck to Wimereux. He had with him a French captain as interpreter and aide. The car passed through various villages, none of outstanding note. He took an idle interest in the flat, poplar-lined fields, the white-washed farms and grubby villages.

At Wimereux they dined and slept. And the colonel dreamed.

"I dreamed, he told me,"that I was travelling the same road again in the same car through the same villages. But with a difference. As we approached one village the car slowed down and stopped. On either side of the road were flat fields.

"Suddenly out of the earth on each side of the road rose up the hooded, cloaked figures of silent men—rank beyond rank. There were thousands of them—all cloaked and hooded like monks. They rose slowly, and every man stared fixedly at me. It was a queer, wistful, sad stare, like a dumb question or a dumb warning.

"Their cloaks were grey, almost luminous, with a fine, silvery bloom on them like moths' wings. I seemed to touch one and it came off on my fingers in a soft dust.

"I can't remember if I got out of the car or just sat and touched the man nearest me. But they stared and stared endlessly, pitifully, with a sadness which went right to my heart.

"Then, slowly, they all sank back into the ground—rank after rank of hooded men sinking into the earth, their eyes fixed on me to the last!"

He shook his shoulders with a half-shiver, half-shudder. I waited.

"Next morning at breakfast," he went on, "I told my French aide of my dream. He listened and suddenly became excited."

"'You know the name of that village near where your car stopped?' he asked.

"'No,' I said, 'What was it?'

"'Crécy!' he said.

"So," said ex-staff Colonel Shepheard, "I had seen in my dream the cloaked and hooded thousands of the archers who died on Crécy field in August, 1346. That," he added simply, "is why I believe your yarn."

And, to cap this tale and that of the ghostly cavalry skirmish at Bailleul, there is the tale of Major S. E. G. Ponder, the Oriental traveller and novelist, who lives at Torquay.

Major Ponder, a Regular gunner, served in the 1914-18 War in a Heavy Battery of the Royal Artillery under a Major Apultree, a red-faced, choleric officer with a sultry blue eye, a scalding flow of language and the kindest heart imaginable. He was, says Ponder, the last man on earth to see a ghost.

On a night in autumn, 1916, on the Aisne, a captain whom he prefers to call "A" and a subaltern whom he calls "B" were ordered to go up the Hessian trench to the most advanced O.P. in order that Captain A should show Lieutenant B the field of fire.

"It was," said Major Ponder, "a macabre O.P., for the parapet and parados were built mainly of the bodies of dead Germans! For some reason the dead did not seem to decompose on the Somme—something in the soil. They simply looked like alabaster—very odd.

"Well, the Boche put down an extra-heavy barrage that night and neither A nor B showed up. I wasn't particularly worried about them as there were several deep dug-outs they could get into.

"Next morning, about six, I was having a mug of tea in the mess— a half-buried Nissen hut—when Apultree appeared in the door. He was dead white and shaking like a leaf.

"'Good Lord, what's the matter,' I said.

" 'I've seen B,' he said queerly.

" 'He's back all right, then?' I said.

" 'No, he's dead!'

" 'What on earth do you mean?' I said.

" 'He suddenly appeared in the door of my dug-out,' said Apultree, 'and I said, "Ah! so you're back to report all right!" '

" 'No,' he said, 'I'm not back to report, sir, only to tell you I was killed last night.'

"And," added Ponder quietly, "he was too. Shell splinter in at the back of his ear and right through his head. Apultree had seen him all right—no doubt about that. I believe every word he said."

The Mystery of Borley

A great deal, far too much in fact, has been written about Borley Rectory. Here was a good haunting which was exploited in the most cynical fashion until it became history's most profitable ghost story. When Borley Rectory was discovered by Harry Price and Fleet Street in 1929, apparently there weren't enough ghosts for these incorrigible publicity hounds, so others had to be invented. Thus poltergeist phenomena were engineered which has caused the cynics to dismiss the whole haunt as the biggest ghost hoax of all time.

The answer is perhaps not as simple as that. The existence of ghosts is not disproved by the discovery of unscrupulous invention of man-made phenomena. Whatever be the truth about Borley Rectory, it remains one of the century's most interesting ghost stories.

Borley is a hamlet in Essex, a few miles from Sudbury. It has an early English church, and according to an unsubstantiated legend, a monastery once stood upon the site of the Rectory. Seven miles away at Bures was a nunnery. The legend goes that in the thirteenth century a young novice at Bures fell in love with a monk at Borley monastery and they eloped. Their fleeing coach was pursued and overtaken by the ecclesiastical authorities and the pair of lovers were brought back to suffer death. The monk was beheaded—some say hanged—and his would-be bride was bricked up alive in her own convent. Since then Borley has been haunted by the headless monk and the nun as well as the phantom coach.

This story has been told locally for generations, despite the fact that the probability is that there was never a monastery at Borley, though it is thought there was a Benedictine priory there.

But the nun herself is not so easy to disprove. She has been seen by a number of witnesses. Dressed in black, with bowed head, she walked in the Rectory garden, her hands clasped in prayer.

Another explanation for the nun's ghost came out of a series of seances during which the story was told of a French nun named Marie Lairre, who came from her convent at Le Havre in the seventeenth century and married Henry Waldegrave, who lived in a house on the site of Borley Rectory, where he strangled her on 17 May, 1667, and buried her body underneath the cellar floor.

The Waldegraves were an influential Roman Catholic family who were patrons of Borley church and owned Borley Manor for some three hundred years. Their splendid tomb can be seen in the church, and there was a legend that their coffins in the crypt under Borley church had been tumbled about much in the same way as those at Christ Church, Barbados.

The Waldegraves fled from England with James II and his court in 1688 during the struggle for the Protestant succession when the Catholic branch of the Stuarts—the Jacobites—was banished for ever. There is a story that one of the Waldegraves, Arabella, became a nun in France, then renounced her vows and returned to England as an agent for the Stuart pretenders. She came to Borley and there she was murdered and has since haunted the place.

Thus we have three stories in explanation of the Borley nun, each one strongly romantic. But the Marie Lairre story appears to be better established, if one can accept the various contacts which have been made with the ghost by means of seances, planchette and wall writings. Marie Lairre's alleged remains were found under the old cellar floor at the Rectory and were given a Christian burial at Liston churchyard in 1945. Masses have been said for her soul at Arundel and Oxford.

Another branch of the Waldegrave family held the patronage of Borley during the eighteenth century, but it was not a sufficiently important living for it to be of any consequence until the end of the century. In the first part of the nineteenth century the living was held by the Herringham family.

Finally came the Bulls, a family of parsons and landowners who acquired Borley in the middle of the century. The Rev. Henry D. E. Bull (born in 1833) became record of Borley in 1862 and the following year he built the famous Rectory.

It was an ugly, rambling, red-bricked building, to which in 1875-76 he added a wing in order to house his innumerable family —he had fourteen children: some reports say seventeen—as well as his large staff of domestics. The rectory had some twenty-five rooms, extensive cellars, about three acres of garden, a cottage and other buildings. It cost about £3,000 to build.

Bull was a sporting parson who wore canonicals only for Sunday morning service. The rest of the time he was in tweeds and usually with a shot-gun. He would even pot at rooks from the Rectory drawing-room on Sundays after church. It didn't look as though the Victorian Sunday hung very heavily at Borley.

The new rector acquired, along with his tasteless house, a well-established ghost, for the nun had been seen for centuries. She walked regularly in the rectory garden.

Henry Bull, far from being put off by his spectral tenant, was fascinated. He did her the honour of erecting a summer-house in his garden opposite the Nun's Walk, which was a long path which skirted the lawn, in order to watch her. There are no records of her walking at night, but always during daylight, particularly at dawn and at dusk.

Henry's son, Harry, also followed the family tradition and was ordained. He became curate to his father, and the two of them would spend hours in the summer-house sitting there, smoking their pipes and watching for the nun which they claimed to have seen a number of times.

It must not be thought that the Bull family were morbidly obsessed with the occult. The opposite impression is created by those who later gave their recollections of those Victorian days at Borley Rectory, where Henry Bull's great tribe of offspring was frequently joined by those of his brothers and sisters whose marriages were equally fruitful.

The Bull family were rich and they entertained well in their great rambling Rectory where the ghosts were all part of the entertainment. The staff, however, were not all amused by the apparitions. In 1886 a nursemaid (later to become Mrs E. Byford) left her post at the Rectory after hearing the ghostly noises. "I only stayed a month," she said in 1929, "the place was so weird."

Not only was the nun seen a number of times by various members of the family and their guests, but also the phantom coach and four would come clattering down the narrow lane beside the Rectory, waking the household and bringing white faces and round eyes to the many bedroom windows to see the celebrated sight, though some claimed they got so used to it that they slept right through it.

As early as 1886 poltergeist activity was reported within the Rectory—stones thrown about, visitors' boots being found unaccountably on top of the wardrobes, tooth glasses sailing across the room. The poltergeists did not, as some people aver, have to await the arrival of Harry Price in 1929. They were, it seems, active at Borley when Price was a mere five years old and could hardly have been held responsible for them.

The Rev. Henry Bull died in his sixtieth year in 1892 and his son succeeded him as rector of Borley. Life continued at the Rectory with the same massive family parties and ghost hunts. Old Henry Bull apparently now joined the company of Borley apparitions and was seen by his son and members of his family, rather, one must think, to their concern, or were they so used to ghosts at Borley that it didn't worry them?

On the evening of 28 July, 1900, the four Misses Bull were returning to the Rectory from a garden party. It was getting dusk and as they were crossing the lawn they all of them saw the nun, dressed in black, head bowed, hands clasped in prayer. Miss Ethel Bull saw the nun on several occasions, and she also saw other apparitions, notably a strange man who stood beside her bed, and once or twice, she said, she felt someone sitting on the side of her bed.

The Rev. Harry Bull, who married in 1911, and not unnaturally took a great interest in ghosts, joined his father in the shades in 1927 and the sixty-five years of the Bull incumbencies at Borley ended. Throughout the whole of Harry Bull's incumbency the Borley ghosts continued their haunt—the nun, the headless monk, and the phantom coach clattering along the road from Sudbury.

Harry Bull died on 9 June, 1927, and Borley Rectory remained empty of human habitation until 2 October, 1928, when the new rector of Borley, the Rev. Guy Eric Smith, and his wife moved in. The Smiths, who had lived in India, came to Borley ignorant of its ghostly reputation.

The Rectory was a shock to them. The great, rabbit-warren of a place was without gas, electricity or main water. The water supply, which had to be pumped from a well, was totally inadequate. Apart from the bad sanitation, the place was in a dilapidated state, with broken pipes and leaking roofs. Grimly cold, the huge house was impossible to heat. In all, a great contrast to the warm gaiety of the place at the height of the Bull days.

In this dark, cold, oppressive Rectory the Smiths found themselves not only up against Victorian housing and sanitation at its worst, but also in the middle of a rather formidable haunt.

Thoroughly alarmed and worried about their parishioners' fear of even entering the haunted Rectory, they wrote to the Editor of the *Daily Mirror* in June, 1929, asking him if he could put them in touch with a psychical research society and telling him of the extraordinary things which were happening in the Rectory—strange lights seen in empty, locked rooms, bells ringing unaccountably, slow dragging footsteps heard in empty rooms. The nun had been seen again, and the phantom coach had swept through the hedge on to the lawn and then vanished.

The *Daily Mirror* put the Smiths in touch with Harry Price, who was already well known for his investigations into psychic phenomena. Price went to Borley Rectory on 12 June. The place was already headline news.

With the arrival of Harry Price the poltergeist phenomena increased in the most marked fashion. Small missiles flew about the Rectory, keys leaped unaccountably from keyholes, ornaments hurled themselves down the stairs.

It seems clear that at this point at least Harry Price had his own reasons for keeping the haunt going, by fair means or otherwise. During one of these noisy and dangerous sessions with the alleged poltergeists, Charles Sutton, a reporter on the *Daily Mail*, was hit on the head by a large pebble. He says he was suspicious of Price and felt his pockets which he found full of brick ends and pebbles. His editor wouldn't unmask Price, on the lawyer's advice, owing to the risk of libel, as there was no other witness, and so the story couldn't be told until after Price's death.

Sutton wasn't the only one who suspected Price of creating additional phenomena in order to boost the Borley sensations. It was obvious that the Rev. and Mrs Smith were suspicious, though they were too polite to say so. After they left the Rectory, they said they had done so because of its broken-down condition, and that they did not believe that the house was haunted by anything else but rats and local superstition. Mrs Smith said later that after the arrival of Harry Price she and her husband were astonished at the sudden onset of phenomena. It is worth noting incidentally that Price was an accomplished conjuror.

A seance was held at the Rectory by Price, in which several people took part—the Smiths, two sisters of the late Rev. Harry Bull and a reporter from the *Daily Mirror*. After unsuccessful attempts, Price later reported, they finally got through to the spirit whose footsteps were heard in the Rectory, and the spirit declared itself to be that of Harry Bull. Various private matters were addressed to the spirit by the Misses Bull, and the result of the attempted communication does not seem to have been very successful.

During the Smiths' incumbency at Borley a skull mysteriously appeared in the library cupboard. It was a small skull in perfect condition and said to belong to a young woman.

But according to some villagers the skull was a possession of the Rev. Henry Bull. During the 'nineties, they said, the skull was buried in the churchyard, but such a commotion broke out in the Rectory —knockings and screaming and crashing, and bedclothes being pulled off the beds while their occupants were sleeping—that the thing was hastily dug up and restored to its place in the library. Screaming skulls of course are a fairly common form of haunting.

If the Smiths' incumbency of Borley aroused many questions in people's minds about the haunting, what followed during the next incumbency was strange and remarkable indeed.

The Smiths left the Rectory in July, 1929, finally leaving Borley for Norfolk in April of the following year. The Rectory remained empty for seventeen months, and then in October, 1930, the Rev. Lionel A. Foyster, with his young wife Marianne, and baby daughter Adelaide, moved in. Foyster was a cousin of the Misses Bull, daughters of the Rev. Henry Bull, who were patrons of the living.

Immediately upon their arrival the haunting began at an even greater intensity. The phenomena were now mainly poltergeist. Objects were moved, bottles, stones and other missiles were thrown about the Rectory, doors were mysteriously locked and unlocked, bells rang unaccountably, furniture was overturned, messages appeared on the walls. Apart from this there were footsteps, strange odours, apparitions, as well as a tremendous noise.

The Borley ghosts seemed somehow attracted towards Mrs Foyster, a young and vital woman, and the phenomena which took place were observed not only by her husband, but by several independent witnesses, some of them people of standing.

Strange footsteps were heard about the house on the day that the Foysters moved into the Rectory, and a voice was heard calling "Marianne, dear". No one was ever able to trace the voice, or anyone who could have made the sound of the footsteps. For a short period Harry Bull made a spectral appearance in his old Rectory, being seen on the staircase in a dressing-gown carrying a scroll of paper.

After a lull in this ghostly activity, the poltergeists then got to work, particularly in the kitchen, where jugs and crockery were moved about, often disappearing for days. Bells jangled although all the wires had been disconnected. Hymn-books suddenly appeared in the oven, and articles of all description began to hurl themselves about the Rectory, propelled apparently by no human agency. During this poltergeistic bombardment, Mrs Foyster was hit and hurt several times.

Foyster himself made a diary of these phenomenal happenings. At a later stage Price, seeing what enormous interest there was in what was happening at Borley Rectory, turned the whole thing into a very profitable publicity stunt.

The truth of this strange story of ghosts and humans will probably never be known. It cannot be said that Harry Price, who died in 1948, emerges with much credit from the affair.

In 1931 a series of messages addressed to "Marianne" appeared on the walls of the Rectory. They were all appeals directed presumably to Mrs Foyster—"Marianne, please get help", "Marianne, lights, Mass, prayers". They were written in a childish hand, and seemed to have a Roman Catholic flavour, and the impression was created of some poor soul in the nether world wanting the prayers, the Mass and incense of those in this world. These messages were investigated by a number of interested people, and several theories were put forward to explain them. One of these was that Mrs Foyster was a polter-geist-focus, and this of course could explain a great number of things.

The Foysters left Borley in October, 1935, as Mr Foyster had to give up the living owing to his persistent ill-health. The ecclesiastical authorities, owing to Borley Rectory's somewhat infamous reputa-tion, decided to sell the place and provide other accommodation for the Borley incumbents.

It was not an easy place to sell. Price offered to rent it for a year, and he entered into a tenancy beginning in May, 1937, He didn't intend to live there. He wanted to carry on his psychic experiments. To this end he advertised in *The Times* for investigators who were prepared to go to Borley and make scientific observations of the phenomena.

A number of ladies and gentlemen of integrity and sincerity joined in Harry Price's great ghost-hunt, which attracted enormous attention and was featured both in the Press and on the BBC. Among those camping out in the cold spooky rooms of the near-derelict Rectory was the famous Professor C. E. M. Joad, who is reported to have seen pencil markings appear on a wall.

The spectacular activity of the Foyster period ceased with the departure of Marianne and her invalid husband. During the Price tenancy very little occurred which could not have been contrived by Price himself, and indeed he is gravely suspected by a number of his associates of artificially creating phenomena.

In 1937 seances were held in the Rectory to try and get in touch with the departed spirits which were troubling the place, and it was from these sessions that Miss Helen Glanville, using a planchette, obtained the story of Marie Lairre, who was murdered by her husband, Henry Waldegrave, in 1667 and her body buried unceremoniously beneath the cellar floor of the old demolished house which once stood on the Rectory site. Marie Lairre's trouble was the fact that she had been buried in unconsecrated ground without any Masses or prayers said for her soul, a matter of grave and eternal importance for a woman who had been a nun in the seventeenth century.

Many other messages were received in various ways from the several restless spirits of Borley, the total effect of which seemed to confuse the issue. One message received in March, 1938, said that the Rectory was to be burnt down that night.

Actually the place was burnt down eleven months later. One supposes that spirits travelling in the infinite pathways of eternity may be forgiven being a year out in their calculations. But destroyed by fire Borley Rectory was, and it happened on the midnight of 27 February, 1939.

There was nothing supernatural about the fire. The Rectory had been bought by Captain W. E. Gregson, in December, 1938, who renamed it Borley Priory, and who was experiencing the usual Borley phenomena of strange noises, furniture tossed about, and waves of incense in some of the rooms. On the night of the fire, while the new owner was sorting out some books, a pile of volumes fell, knocked over a paraffin-lamp and within seconds the room was in flames. Unable to cope with the formidable conflagration which rapidly spread, the alarmed Captain ran to the nearest phone and alerted the Sudbury Fire Brigade. By the time the engines arrived the Rectory was a mass of flames and the roof had fallen in.

The watching crowds saw figures moving in the flames as Borley burnt itself out. The local constable saw two figures, a man and a woman, dressed in cloaks, leaving the Rectory at the height of the fire. He asked Gregson who they might be, but Gregson told him that there was no one on the premises but himself. The constable was certain he had seen them leave the burning building and cross the courtyard.

The villagers also saw these two unearthly strangers leave the Rectory, walking out of the very heart of the flames. They wore cloaks, the villagers said. One was a young girl, the other a "formless figure".

And so Borley was burnt to a shell. The walls and chimneys stood. Inside was blackened, twisted desolation. But it was by no means the end of the story.

The sceptical said that Harry Price saw to that. He certainly kept the story going, and to a large extent kept a monopoly on the Borley news by making his observers sign an agreement not to divulge anything they had seen or heard except to him. He was working on his first book on Borley, which was published in 1940, and which became a best-seller. The interest in Borley continued unabated. At least it took people's minds off the darkest days of the war.

The Borley ghosts apparently had not been driven away by the fire. Mysterious figures were seen among the ruins and at the windows of rooms which now had no floors.

Interest in Borley was enormous. It was considered by many to be the most authenticated haunting in the world. Price's many critics had to keep silent about what they knew or suspected, owing to the law of libel.

During the war Borley was the centre of many a ghost hunt, and a spooky visit there was a popular diversion for occult-minded servicemen of various nationalities. Harry Price, of course, was as busy as ever, propagating the legend, lecturing, broadcasting, writing another book about it.

The gutted building, however, was in a dangerous state. It had been greatly damaged by gales and it was finally decided to pull the ruins down.

Seances were still being held at which contact was claimed to have been made with the mysterious nun, Marie Lairre, and at one of these Marie Lairre revealed the place where her bones were to be found. In August, 1943, Price supervised digging in the cellar of the ruined Rectory and some human bones were found which were claimed to be the remains of Marie Lairre. In 1945 these remains were given a Christian burial in Liston churchyard by the Rev. A. C. Henning, and it has since been assumed that her unquiet spirit is finally at rest.

But what of the other Borley spirits? According to reports, the Borley site has continued to be haunted. The haunting has survived the death of Harry Price (in 1948), which event was immediately followed by a series of accusations against him by people who no longer had the libel law to fear and who said the whole haunt was a hoax.

There is little doubt that Price faked some of the Borley phenomena, but it still remains one of the most interesting ghost stories of all time. When the dust of controversy dies down, it will no doubt emerge as one of the strangest and most formidable haunts on record.

The Ghostly Trapper of Labrador

In 1959 Lord Beaverbrook suggested that I might like to go on a tour of exploration throughout the "barrens", muskegs, trackless forests and scattered outposts of Newfoundland and thence into the far north of Labrador where no English or American writer had been before. The suggestion was that I should write a book covering the long history of Newfoundland, Britain's oldest colony, of which Labrador is a political part, together with a survey of the economic resources and future of those vast and bitter lands where winter reigns for most of the year, the silence can be felt and men are scarce.

It is the land of the giant, shambling moose, of herds of caribou moving like prehistoric shadows against blue-green lichened rocks, of the bear and the wolf and the dancing spearpoints of the Midnight Sun.

There followed an intensive tour of Newfoundland, by plane, truck, canoe, log raft and on my flat feet.

It is odd, but true, that the hairy-chested, iron-fisted men of the frozen north hate walking. Trappers and hunters walk. The rest go on wheels where wheels can go.

Once on a three-mile walk out of St John's, Newfoundland, with Brigadier Michael Wardell, Beaverbrook's right-hand man in the Maritime Provinces of Canada, we were passed by a Cadillac. The driver turned and looked at us curiously.

We reached the point of our three-mile stroll, Signal Hill, where Marconi received the first transatlantic wireless message from

Poldhu in Cornwall in 1903. We stood on the hill where history had been made, gazing out across the Atlantic for a few minutes. Then we turned and started striding back on our Sunday morning constitutional. A mile along the road the Cadillac drew up alongside.

"Say, you guys wanna lift?"

"No, thanks," we replied.

"Gee, you wakkin' all the way back?"

"Sure," I said. "We like walking."

"Jesus, you must be Limeys." And he drove off.

Not, you see, the sort of country, one would have thought, to believe in ghosts. They believe in newsprint, iron ore, pulp mills, salmon and the dollar.

Yet, a week later, a world away out of this world, they told me what is surely the strangest modern ghost tale of this century, whilst we were sitting round the stove in an Atwell Arctic hut, on the bleak shore of Wabush Lake, in the wilderness of Labrador. Three days later I heard an echo of the same tale from Ashuanipi Joe, my Red Indian guide, away up at Mile 274, in the heart of the birdless forest. Wolf and bear country. A week later I heard it from Magistrate Corbett at Goose Bay.

Finally, when we got back to St John's, the 400-year-old capital of Newfoundland, Mr Leo English, the Curator of the Museum, an erudite, scholarly man, confirmed the story.

We were a pioneering party on that day of autumn sun and lonely wind, on the edge of Wabush Lake. Five of us: Mr W. J. Keogh, Minister of Mines, Fred Gover, Secretary of Mines, my friend Gordon Pushie, Director of Economic Development for Newfoundland, my wife, and myself—guests of the Premier of Newfoundland, the Rt Hon Joseph Smallwood.

A land of bleak, unending, grey-green wilderness—of long lakes and utter silences. This is Labrador. Arctic winds blowing over an earth that even in the brief, hot summer is frozen, hard as iron, to a hundred feet or more below the surface.

This is the land where "Smoker" and his white ghost team run. Irving Penny, a trapper, can tell the tale.

One day of blinding snow, Irving was driving his ten-dog team over the bleak Partridge Hills, hauling a heavy komatik (sledge) through slushy snow. The sou'-east wind blinded him. His eyelids almost stuck together. He "mushed" on, cursing, hoping for a snow-bank to burrow into for the night.

Suddenly he heard, faintly, in the blizzard, the sound of another dog-team. The heavy figure of a man, dressed all in white furs, loomed out of the swirling snow. He was driving a team of fourteen pure-white huskies, pushing on into the teeth of the blizzard with utter confidence. Irving yelled at him. The man did not even turn his head. Irving followed him.

Half an hour later the winter huts of the fishermen of Frenchmen's Island loomed up in the swirling snow-mist. The white team ahead passed the first house, disappeared behind the second one. Irving, pretty well done in, pulled up at the first house, rapped on the door.

The fisherman who opened the door welcomed him in. Every man's front door is open to you in Newfoundland and Labrador, where they still speak, not with the nasal twang of North America, but with the soft West Country accent of their Bristol ancestors. They use the antique words and phrases of Somerset moors and marshes, the rolling hills of Gloucestershire.

Irving put up his team for the night, and when he had settled down in front of the fire, said to his host: "Who was the feller in white who came in, in front of me?"

"No one came in—not a soul," his host replied.

So Penny told him his tale of the all-white trapper with the all-white team who had guided him to safety. The fisherman laughed shortly.

"That was 'Smoker'. He brought you here. He always turns up when it blows a blizzard. Saving his soul—*and* it needed it."

The story began in 1910, when a trapper named Esau Gillingham, a Newfoundlander, crossed over the Straits of Belle Isle into Labrador, and put down a few lines of traps. They did not pay too well. But Esau soon got to know every fisherman, Red Indian, Eskimo and trapper along the coast from Battle Harbour and Black Bear River in the south way up to Nain in the Fraser River country. Some say that he even travelled as far north as Cape Chidley, where the ice-flows of Ungava Bay meet the cold tides of the Atlantic Arctic.

In those lonely settlements life was, and still is, as hard as nails. If you cannot shoot, fish, or trap, you starve. The coastal steamers, few and far between, and the Grenfell Mission are—or were, before the coming of aircraft—the sole links with the outer world. We were lucky. We had ex-Canadian Premier Mackenzie-King's own big plane with the two finest bush pilots in the north, plus a little red Beaver float-plane to hop from lake to lake. But when Esau Gillingham hit the north in 1910, Bleriot was a futurist nightmare buzzing like a bee from France to England.

Hard living demands hard liquor. Rum, in those northern winters, is a godsend. But rum supplies were few, far, and precious. So Esau set up a secret still in a forest of black spruce and there, until his death, he brewed a hellish concoction from spruce cones, sugar, and yeast. Sheer deadly moonshine. The Labrador trappers called it "smoke". Hence Esau's nickname.

Moonshining paid better than trapping. So in summer Smoker sailed his boat from cove to cove selling his poison. In winter he travelled with a big keg of it strapped to his komatik. The stuff did its worst.

Some who drank it went mad. Others beat their wives, smashed up their miserable homes. Some died of exposure when they collapsed dead drunk in the snow. So the Mounties took a hand. They caught up with Smoker, smashed his keg, and clapped him into gaol in St. John's. Twelve months of hard labour and penitence. When he came out he swore: "They'll never see me inside there again."

Back to Labrador went Smoker—with a plan. For months he trapped—with one object only. He wanted white skins. One by one he caught three dozen ermine, a couple of white fox, and made himself an all-over suit of pure white skins. At the same time he collected every white huskie he could beg, borrow, or steal. He built a white komatik and lashed a white-painted keg to it. Then he started up business in "smoke" once again.

Year after year the white team with the white-clad figure cracking his whip yelling them on, "mushed" from settlement to settlement, from log cabin to Eskimo igloo. Poison was abroad in the land once more. Time and again the Mounties tried to catch him. But the white figure with the white team melted into the white silences.

Then an informer split on him. "Smoker's still is in a spruce-belt near Brazil's Pinch", he told them.

The police rounded up Smoker. They took him to a wood.

"We know your still's in there," the sergeant said. "Now lead us to it. We'll shove you in gaol for the rest of your life, if you don't."

"My still's in there, O.K.," Smoker replied. "Go right in, boys, and find it." A policeman started to walk towards the trees. Smoker grabbed him, said quietly: "Son!—there's fifty bear-traps scattered around that still. Mind where you put your feet."

Since a bear-trap can break a man's leg, the police thought better of it. They had to let Smoker go, for lack of evidence. They never caught him again.

Things went from bad to worse. More of his customers went mad.

One or two went blind. Then Smoker kidnapped a woman, strapped her to his komatik, and took her off to his log hut, out in the forest where the timber wolf slinks like a grey ghost, and the black bear dwells. Weeks later he sent her home. She was raving. Apart from this ravishment he had three Eskimo wives. Meanwhile, not a white dog was safe on the coast. Smoker stole them all.

In the end he took to drinking his own rot-gut. He killed an Indian, strangling him with his bare hands, in berserk rage. What few mothers there were on that cold coast of winds and loneliness, terrified their children with the threat that "Smoker'll get you if you're naughty".

Finally, he went back to Newfoundland. There, in 1940, he fell off a fish-platform, near the Gander River—one of those spindly "flakes" on which they dry the cod—and broke his back. Three days later he died in agony, repentant. With his last breath he gasped:

"Lordy, Lordy, God! I don't want to go to Hell. Let me drive my dogs along the coast to the end of Time. I'll make up for all the bad I've done."

So if you turn up in Labrador one day when the snow drives like the white breath of death, and the Hamilton Falls, higher by far than Niagara, shout their hoarse thunder over the lonely wastes—remember Smoker. He may show you the way to go home.

The Sceptic's Tale

All right! I will allow you your triumph, all you believers in ghosts. I will make my admission right away. I used to be a sceptic about ghosts, but I am a sceptic no longer. I hardly could be, not since I went to Cullen. I know *you* won't scoff. Scientists may. Let them. I am a journalist. I work with facts. And the fact is that, at Cullen House, Banffshire, on the night of 8 August, 1964, I heard the footsteps and felt the presence of a man who died in 1770.

By a strange irony, it was my total disbelief in ghosts that led me to have this experience. It all began when I went to interview Tom. Tom is a clairvoyant. When he told me about his work, it was hard for me to understand; when he added that he could detect and identify ghosts, my disbelief must have been very apparent. He asked me point-blank whether I believed in the supernatural. I shot back a blunt "No".

"Come with me to Scotland," Tom replied. "And I will prove to you that ghosts exist."

Who could resist such a challenge? Not I—especially when Tom told me that Cullen House is one of the most romantic and splendid of Scotland's castles and that its owner, Lady Seafield, is the most generous of hostesses. So I accepted—on two conditions. Tom was not to tell me the ghost story. And he was not to say which part of Cullen was haunted. That way, my imagination would have no chance to act up.

We flew to Aberdeen on 8 August: Tom, myself, and Alan, a Fleet Street columnist who had long wanted to see Tom "at work" with ghosts, and thought he might get a story. Alan was, if anything, even more sceptical than I. As we drove through the rich farmlands Tom told us ghost stories about the castles we passed. Green Ladies, Curses, Warnings of Death . . . we heard the lot. In the bright sunshine they sounded preposterously melodramatic. If we had known that in some fifteen hours' time we were to be gripped by the same forces at which we laughed . . . But how could we? It was inconceivable.

However, when we arrived at Cullen even Alan had to agree that it was, at least, the perfect setting for a ghost-story. Long before we reached the village great thunderheads had built up in the sky; by the time we turned in at the gates everything was still. We caught a glimpse of the sea, heaving beneath a smooth, oily swell; then we were in the drowned gloom of a wood, the bare trunks of the trees twisting their way upwards as if to the surface of water. A turning suddenly brought us right into the courtyard of the house, a huge, fortress-like pile of granite blocks, heraldic beasts, gargoyles, coats-of-arms, all crowned by a jumble of towers, turrets, mossy slates and sly little windows, rearing up against a background of inky sky. When the engine was switched off a tremendous quietness fell about the place, broken only by thunder muttering round the distant hills, and the roar of the burn, foaming over the rocks at the base of the crag on which the castle is perched.

It was all gloriously appropriate, the Gothic castle of fiction come to life. But the interior gave quite another impression; all was light, white, beauty and taste. Paintings and tapestry, china and glass; huge rooms, airy windows; everything had clearly been modernized in the eighteenth century and again, discreetly, in modern times. No ghost, said Alan and I to each other, smugly, would stand a chance in such a civilized setting.

Tom's room was on one of the main bedroom corridors; when Alan and I were led on and up I thought we would find that we were in deliberately spooky rooms; I expected slit windows, fourposters, black oak furniture. But although we were in the oldest part of the house, and somewhat isolated from the others, no one could call our rooms atmospheric. Alan's—the Pulpit Room—was at the head of the spiral staircase; small and white, with plain, "good" furniture. Mine—the Church Room—was around the corner. It was three times the size of Alan's but no more ghostly, with its modern twin beds, enormous windows and thick carpeting; the archers' turrets in the corners had even been converted into walk-in cupboards. Opposite the door was a bathroom; the passage continued only a few yards before stopping at a low little door in the wall. I mention these details to show that there was absolutely nothing to stimulate the imagination.

There were a number of people staying in the house. All knew Cullen well; all knew why we three were there. Yet no one referred to the ghost. I never had the impression that the subject was being avoided; rather that it was not of sufficient interest to be mentioned. By tea-time I doubted whether Tom's challenge would be met. And when, at dinner, I asked a cousin of Lady Seafield's whether Alan and I were in the haunted part of the house and received a direct and faintly amused negative, I was sure nothing would happen.

We went to bed around 11.30. The thunder had long since ceased; now the moon glimmered through a light sea-mist that coiled past the windows. When I leaned out, the air felt cool and fresh, and I could hear the slight noises of night-birds. When I closed the curtains and shut my door the whole tower was lapped in utter silence. I was glad. I was dog-tired from our 6 a.m. start, and expected to go to sleep almost at once.

But I did not. The more I tried to relax the more tense I became. The bed was exceedingly comfortable; there was nothing to keep me awake. And yet I felt exactly as I used to feel when on night patrol in the army; all my animal senses were tuned up to their fullest extent. I could not imagine why, until I realized that the atmosphere in the room was changing. Very slowly, so slowly as to be almost imperceptible, I felt a growing thickness, an increasing oppression, as if the afternoon's thunderstorm was gathering again in the room. As it grew stronger I felt the symptoms of fever; my body alternated between heat and icy shivers; I had difficulty in breathing evenly; my heart pounded; I felt a vague illogical distress.

It was a ridiculous situation. Here was I, a man of thirty-six, who did not believe in the supernatural, sleeping in the part of the house I had been assured was not haunted, with another man only a few yards away—but acting like a child afraid of the dark, staring now at the faintly moonlit windows, now at the long cheval glass glimmering in the corner. And listening. Straining my ears. But for what? Nothing. . . .

I must have lain there for an hour and a half before I heard the footsteps. For a second my heart bounded. But the sounds were so faint and far away that I thought, after listening for so long, that my hearing was playing tricks with me. Then it was unmistakable. They were footsteps. And they were coming up the stairs. The footfalls were uneven; every now and then they stumbled. But they were not in the least furtive; I could distinctly hear the scrape of leather on stone. I felt no fear—until I thought of something that made my flesh crawl. I heard feet on stone. *But the stairs were thickly carpeted.*

One cannot remember degrees of emotion, but I think my fear at that moment was the worst fear I have ever felt; worse than fear in the army, worse than fear at sea—and that can be bad. I had never known that one could be literally "scared stiff". Now I did. I was rigid. I felt I must have light, but I had to make a vast muscular effort, as well as that of will, to switch on the bed-side lamp. In fictional ghost-stories light usually defeats the supernatural. I can only tell you that in this case it made no difference whatsoever. In the second before switching on the lamp I thought: "I shall see familiar objects; ordinary, everyday things; my clothes on the chair; my shaving gear; luggage; books. And they will dispel this terror". They did not.

I remember, too, thinking that I only had to get up, open the door, and see who it was. I am not ashamed to admit that I simply could not do this.

The footsteps stumbled round the corner of the passage and stopped outside my door. My bed was only four or five feet from the door; I propped myself up on one elbow and stared at the handle, terrified that it might turn. A cold sweat trickled down my chest. For a second the handle seemed to tremble, and I felt my scalp tighten and the hair on my neck rise like a dog's hackles. Then the footsteps retreated. I do not know where they went. I think my fear was so intense that it confused my mind for a moment. In any case, they died away.

I am sure no one will be surprised to hear that I did not sleep much for the rest of that night. I hoped that the atmosphere of the room would die down after the footsteps ceased, and return to normal; but it remained hot and turbulent until dawn. I did, of course, doze off. But I awoke several times, with a violent start, as if someone was in the room.

True ghost-stories never seem to parallel fiction. In a story the haunted guest enters the breakfast-room haggard or furious, and either receives or demands an explanation. End of story. I did no such thing, for the simple reason that in daylight I felt a fool. I did ask Alan, casually, whether he had gone downstairs for anything in the night, but he said no. I also asked whether he had slept well; he said he had. As for telling Tom anything . . . it was unthinkable.

Someone *could* have come upstairs; the room *could* have been hot. I had proof of nothing.

That night there was a large dinner-party, and we did not get to bed until the small hours. I did not look forward to returning to the Church Room, but I was, by now, very tired and consequently, I suppose, more relaxed. I did not hear the footsteps again, but the atmosphere was as thick and as ominous as the previous night and, as before, I slept fitfully. However, this I put down to nervous expectancy.

The following morning Tom took us to meet the Ritchies, Lady Seafield's factor and his wife. Mrs Ritchie is an expert on the history of Cullen House and has, in fact, written the visitors' guide-book. I asked her how my room and Alan's received their names. She was in the middle of a fascinating account of clandestine services held on our staircase during Jacobite days when she looked at me with a quizzical expression and said: "And might I ask why you're so interested in those rooms?"

"Because we are sleeping in them," I told her.

Mrs Ritchie gasped. "Have you been all right?" she asked.

I suspected the truth in that moment, but I was still hesitant as I told my tale. When I finished, and before anyone else could say anything, Alan broke in.

"But this is fantastic," he exclaimed. "I haven't heard the footsteps, but I have felt exactly the same atmosphere as you describe. In fact," he admitted. "I have spent two of the most disturbed and frightening nights of my life."

Tom exploded with laughter. "Wonderful!" he crowed. "I asked for you to be put in those rooms, but I never really thought you would hear the ghost."

Alan and I turned to Mrs Ritchie.

"Why, yes," she said. "That is the haunted part of the house."

Then she told us the story.

Soon after Bonnie Prince Charlie's final defeat, Cullen was inherited by James, 6th Earl of Findlater (the title has since died out) and 3rd Earl of Seafield. James was known as "the Mad Earl". One gathers he was not permanently insane, but periodically he would be seized by some kind of fit, during which he became violent. As he always knew when a seizure was coming on he would lock himself into the library and drop the key out of the window. When he had recovered, his factor, who was also his closest friend, would let him out.

One day—3 November, 1770, to be precise—the factor returned

too soon. When the Earl came round he found that he had murdered his friend. Horror-stricken, the distracted man rushed from the room, stumbled up the tower staircase just outside, and went into the attics—the attics that lie past our rooms. There he cut his throat.

So much for the story? What of the hauntings? Mrs Ritchie herself had had no experiences, beyond "uncomfortable feelings" in the library. However, both she and Tom promised us all the corroborative evidence we needed back at the house.

Walking back through the soft sea mist Alan and I discovered that our experiences tallied exactly. But we were still not prepared to concede the point to the triumphant Tom, until we had heard what Lady Seafield and her relatives had to say. And we would both sleep in my room that night.

Most of our resolution to hold out was immediately shattered. When Tom told our hostess and fellow-guests of our experiences no one looked in the least surprised, least of all Lady Seafield, who looked up from carving ham and said in her usual quiet way: "I am so sorry. Would you like other rooms? She might have been apologizing for uncomfortable beds.

Over lunch almost everyone had a tale to tell. Lord Strathspey, Lady Seafield's cousin, a bluff soldier with an immensely distinguished record, admitted: "I wouldn't sleep in those rooms for a thousand pounds. My wife and I usually stay in the room below, and any number of times I've heard the most frightful racket coming from up there when I know the rooms are empty. Footsteps on the stairs and someone tramping about." He went on to tell us that only two months before another relative was so disturbed in the Church Room that he had rushed downstairs at 3 a.m. and refused ever to sleep there again.

Lady Seafield's son told us that as a child, long before he had heard the ghost story, he had always been "terrified" of the library; after lunch, Lady Seafield herself said that although she had never actually seen the ghost she had "felt his presence" many, many times, especially when she was a child.

"I knew nothing about the ghost," she said. "But I always hated the library and that staircase. My fear became so bad that my mother, who was also worried by strange stories told her by other guests, had the whole area exorcized. She didn't tell me, of course, but I can remember her sending me and a cousin up to the library afterwards and, for the first time, we weren't frightened".

Apparently, however, the exorcism was effective for only about thirty years. In 1943 Mrs Yeats, now a guide, then a maid in the house, nearly witnessed a re-enactment of the tragedy. One afternoon, when the family was away, she went into the library to dust. To her astonishment she saw an old gentleman sitting in one of the big armchairs.

"I can see him as vividly today as when I first saw him," she told us. "I got the impression he was a kindly person. He was smiling and watching someone who was seated at the desk. I never looked to see who that person was, but I noticed him out of the corner of my eye. The atmosphere in the room was very strained; although the old gentleman was smiling he looked ill at ease, almost fearful.

Imagining that the two men were staying in the house Mrs Yeats apologized and retired. In a bedroom only a few yards away she found the head housemaid, who told her categorically that there was no one staying in the house. Mrs Yeats insisted that she come and see the two men. The other woman agreed; but when they re-entered the library the room was empty.

Tom thinks (and most people agree with him) that Mrs Yeats—the last person in the world to imagine such a thing—saw the ghost of the murdered factor. The shadowy figure at the desk would have been the Mad Earl.

Alan and I had only one more task ahead of us—to visit the attics. Before it got dark we went through the little door beyond my room, up a steep, narrow, spiral stair, and found ourselves right under the slates. The outer room was unremarkable; there were a few pictures and some odds and ends of furniture stacked neatly around the walls. Nor, at first glance, was there anything remarkable about the inner room—until we saw the huge irregular stain, a great blotch, roughly a yard square. It looked just as though someone had spilt oil on the rough pine floor. Later, in London, I asked a doctor what an old bloodstain on soft wood would look like. Without a moment's hesitation he said "Oil".

After such a sensational day Alan and I were so convinced that our last night at Cullen would be anticlimactic that we decided not to share my room after all. However, no sooner was I alone than the atmosphere closed in with such speed and force as to seem positively menacing, and I was plucking up courage to summon my neighbour when a sheepish Alan appeared to ask whether he could move in after all. The Pulpit Room, he said, was insupportable.

Around 2 a.m. I heard the footsteps approaching, exactly as on the first night. As they reached the door I switched on the light. Alan awoke with a start, just in time to hear the footsteps retreating.

As before, we were both awakened constantly, once by a tremendous crash from somewhere overhead. At 5 a.m., when Tom came to call us, we capitulated.

On the plane back to London we talked of nothing else. *How* can one hear the footsteps of a man who died nearly two hundred years ago? *Why* should one feel, even share, his emotional instability and despair?

Tom could not tell us; he only had a theory.

"Just because we die it doesn't mean that we change our way of life in a hurry," he said. "The Earl is tied to Cullen; he comes back with the same agitation and agony of mind in his present existence, whatever that is, that he had when he was alive".

We listened, and nodded, and said that he was probably right. After all, who were we to disagree? We were sceptics no longer.

Brighton Ghosts

Brighton has more character, more history and more architectural beauty than any seaside town in Britain. Among its manifold attractions is the fact that it is renowned for its ghosts—if one can list ghosts as attractions.

Although there are no really ancient buildings in Brighton, it nevertheless has some unique features which are not to be found elsewhere. There is, for instance the Lanes, a network of narrow alley-ways and twittens situated right in the centre of the town, and which represent the old paths which once separated the various gardens or parcels of land.

In the Lanes are to be found all manner of quaint little shops selling antiques, bric-à-brac, second-hand books, old silverware and china. Victoriana and Brightoniana. Antiquarians and seekers of the unusual find the Lanes a happy hunting ground. The late Queen Mary was frequently to be seen in the narrow, drowsy passageways of this oasis in busy Brighton.

Though the district has been largely rebuilt within the last century or so, there are many very old houses, and some of the buildings were built into part of the ancient Priory of St Bartholomew, the old walls of which with their characteristic flint buttresses can be seen in the cellars of some of these quaint houses. Beneath others are to be found ancient pillars, gothic arches, and the massive oak timberings of medieval times.

Various ghosts are reported to have been seen in the Lanes, the most persistent and most famous of which is the grey nun who haunts the alley-ways at twilight. This nun is distinguishable from all other nuns by the fact that if you peer underneath the dark cavity of her hood, you will find that there is no face there at all. Such human inquisitiveness causes the nun to glide quickly towards the Old Friends Meeting House where she walks through an archway which has been bricked up for more than a century.

Her story is linked with the Chapel and Priory of St Bartholomew which was built shortly after 1120 and destroyed, together with the whole town, during a naval attack upon Brighthelmstone by the French fleet in 1514. During the twelfth century the Priory, which was only a small one and dependent on the Priory of St Pancras, Lewes, was guarded by a detachment of soldiers against the depredations of the bands of robbers who roamed the Sussex countryside.

The girl—no one knows her name—was a novice in a religious institution not far away, beautiful of course by tradition, and she fell in love with one of the soldiers who guarded St Bartholomew's. The two eloped and were chased by soldiers. The novice and her lover, who put up a valiant fight, were finally overcome and brought back to face the rough justice of the time—the traditional punishment of being bricked up alive together within the walls of St Bartholomew's.

This is a familiar story. There are countless legends of eloping nuns being walled up alive with their lovers; but it must be remembered that countless girls in those days were forced into convents without their having any desire to pursue the way of life prescribed by these institutions, and the savage punishment of being walled up alive for the crime, not so much of unchastity, but of getting married, was not uncommon in those days. Though a dreadful death, it was convenient for the ecclesiastical authorities, for it did not actually involve them in the shedding of blood; and as the wretches slowly starved to death, the good Abbot and his monks could pray for their souls on the other side of the brickwork.

This unfortunate nun has for the last eight hundred years haunted the scene of her miserable incarceration and death. But why the nun only? Why has not the soldier joined his mistress in the haunting? The reason is that by tradition the nun had committed the far greater sin, and has probably damned her immortal soul for all eternity, poor thing.

Brighton really came into its own when the Prince Regent, later George IV, settled there and built his fantastic Pavilion. He was followed by his Court and society, for whom the many rows of splendid Regency houses, now the glory of Brighton, were built.

Prinny himself is said to haunt the underground passageway which connects the Royal Pavilion with the Dome, though not many have seen him. Martha Gunn, the famous bathing woman, is said to haunt the Pavilion kitchens which she frequented during her lifetime.

Queen Victoria quickly abandoned Brighton as a royal residence as it was far too vulgar and public for her tastes. She sold her uncle's Pavilion, ghosts and all, to the town for £50,000, which has turned out to be an excellent investment, for, restored in all its splendour. this unique building is now one of the showplaces of England.

Despite Victoria's frown, Brighton greatly prospered during her long reign, for the curious but probably human reason that it was one of the few places in her realm where Victorianism did not take a firm foothold. Brighton always remained raffish and gay.

But many aspects of the grinding puritanism which was one of the characteristics of nineteenth-century life took root in Brighton, as was only to be expected. The harsh poor laws and the unfeeling treatment of unmarried mothers caused untold suffering and unhappiness all over the country. In consequence of this, a particularly interesting haunting resulted in Finsbury Road, which is in early-Victorian Brighton, on the slopes of the steep hill which rises on the eastern side of the Old Steyne valley. The building concerned had once been a workhouse, and then later became a Church Army Home for Fallen Women.

In 1952 this building was taken over by Mr and Mrs B. B. Funnell, who own a furniture-making business, Bevan Funnell Limited. Mr Funnell at the time was a member of Hove Borough Council, and became Mayor of Hove in 1960. He was also a Special Constable, and both he and his wife are practical, matter-of-fact business people. The truth of their story is indisputable, and there is no question of their imagining the strange and ghostly things they experienced in this building.

As soon as they took over the place and moved in with their staff and equipment, strange things began to happen. Although the building was locked up carefully every night, as all business premises are, the constable on the beat continually found the doors all unlocked and Mr Funnell had to return to lock up again. So frequently did this happen that Mr Funnell and the police were convinced that intruders were getting into the place, although there was no evidence that this was so, and nothing had been stolen.

The matter was investigated by Brighton CID, who went there one night with Mr Funnell to find the place unlocked, after all the doors had been previously locked most carefully in the presence of several persons when the staff left earlier that evening.

Upon entering the building both Mr Funnell and the police officers heard footsteps plainly on the upper floor. It was the sound of people running about and talking.

The police, confident of arresting these troublesome intruders at last, ran up the stairs. The noises and the footsteps were coming from a large room in the upper storey. The police officers flung the door of the room open.

Instantly the sounds ceased as if they had been cut off by a switch. There was no human being in that room, and the whole building was now wrapped in utter silence. Puzzled, the police made a thorough search of the building, but found no one and could find no cause for the strange and quite unmistakable sounds of people talking and walking about which both they and Mr Funnell had heard very plainly.

Baffled, the police left. Someone, they said, must be playing some kind of trick.

But trick or no, the noises continued and increased, and soon began to be heard in the daytime. The staff became a little unnerved by the ghostly footsteps tramping about on the floor above them. They often went up to the floor above to try and locate the sounds, or surprise the intruders, but, like the police, whenever they opened the door of this haunted room they were greeted by an unnerving silence.

Once one of the workmen saw a ghostly woman in black standing in the workshop. At first he thought it was a customer, and turned to Mr Funnell to comment to him upon the fact, but when he looked again at the woman she had vanished. A thorough search failed to find any such woman in the building.

The Funnels and their staff were now convinced that they were in a haunted building and they began to make inquiries about its history and found out that it had been a workhouse and then a Home for Fallen Women. Unmarried females unfortunate enough to have children were treated harshly in Victorian times, and institutions for their "rehabilitation and salvation" were run practically on penal lines.

This Finsbury Road building was a gloomy place and it had seen much tragedy and unhappiness. "You could feel the misery in the very walls," Mrs Funnell said.

In the centre of the building was a small room they used as an office. Across the passage was a cloakroom and lavatory.

One day in this passage they were assailed by a strong perfume. This was no ordinary perfume and it was smelt by everybody. Mrs Funnell described it as a perfume such as she had never smelt before. It was a heavy, musky smell, almost like incense. But it was by no means an ecclesiastical smell. It was peculiarly feminine and sensuous—a woman's scent, quite unforgettable.

Sometimes this extraordinary perfume would seem to blow in waves through the building. They could discover no reason, no origin for it. Nothing that was used in the workshop could produce such a smell.

Spectral smells of this kind are not uncommon. They were noted at Borley Rectory (in pre-Price days) and also at Hinton Ampner.

One day a heavy knitted cardigan in black wool appeared mysteriously in the cloakroom. It was hanging on a peg and was deeply impregnated with this strange perfume. No one owned it. It had been left there by no one. A day or two later it vanished as mysteriously as it had come, and was never seen again.

The pet dog belonging to Mr and Mrs Funnell was on one occasion found shut in one of the upstairs rooms by a heavy sliding door which could not have been accidentally closed by the dog itself. There was no one on the premises who could have closed the door.

It is true that that little mystery as well as the problem of the black knitted cardigan impregnated with the mysterious perfume, could have had a natural explanation; and in fact the Funnells suspected for a long time that they were being subjected to tricks played upon them by a person or persons who had some interest in getting them to leave the building.

But even supposing this were so, some of the things that happened completely baffled explanation.

The eerie business of Mrs Funnell's typewriter set all their nerves on edge. This typewriter was in the little office across the corridor from the cloakroom. Mrs Funnell at that time did all the office work connected with the firm's business and was the only one on the premises who used the typewriter. Upon a number of occasions this typewriter would be heard typing fast and furiously when no one was in the room. When the door was opened the noise of typing instantly stopped. No one was ever able to explain this mystery.

As was to be expected, the Funnells had plenty of trouble with their staff over the haunting. Many were frankly scared off straight away. Others laughed at the idea of ghosts being there, but soon changed their minds. Others stuck it out of loyalty to the firm, or a reluctance to believe in such supernatural nonsense—in particular one woman who at first was plump, jolly and looked the picture of health. After a while the atmosphere in the factory at Finsbury Road played upon her nerves and health to such an extent that she was a changed person. She lost weight, became worried and unhappy. It was as though the weird feeling of misery which was in the very walls of the building had in some way become transferred to her.

In 1953, a year after the Funnells took the building, some local spiritualists held a seance there in an attempt to get in touch with the troubled spirits, often a way by which a haunting can be ended.

Mrs Funnell attended this seance, during which the ghost was apparently contacted by the medium, a man, who asked it why it was troubled. The reply came through in a girl's voice, speaking in an uneducated Sussex accent.

"Matron is cruel to me. I am desperately unhappy. I've tried to be good, but I can't." She sounded a miserable, weeping thing, said Mrs Funnell.

The Funnels were sceptical about this seance. After all, it was well known that the place had been a home for unmarried mothers in Victorian times, and it was easy to imagine that it had been a house of desperate unhappiness and harsh, even pitiless, discipline.

Nevertheless, a strange thing happened immediately after the seance had finished. As soon as the spiritualists had left, there was a tremendous noise of people running about the building, of doors banging, people calling, of pounding footsteps.

And then suddenly there was silence.

This silence lasted uninterruptedly until the Sunday before the Christmas of 1954, when Mr Funnell went to the office in the building by himself to catch up with a rush of work. By now the ghosts had been almost forgotten, and the strange, unaccountable events of the past couple of years had completely gone out of his mind which at that moment was concerned only with the urgency of coping with the rush of Christmas business.

He went into the little office where his wife's typewriter had been heard unaccountably typing in her absence. It was a bright sunny morning and there were no shadows or reflections in the little room which was half-flooded with December sunshine as he opened the door.

He got the shock of his life.

As he entered the room he heard something drop, and he turned to look at the sloping desk which ran along the wall to the corner of the room. In this corner, which was perfectly light and without any shadows, he saw a dark grey shape upon the desk. The shape was half-hooded and in some strange way incomplete. It was a shape without a great deal of form, though it seemed to have density and substance. It would appear that when Mr Funnell came into the room it was in the act of materialization, and it was materializing on the desk, resting upon it.

Mr Funnell said that this thing seemed to emanate a strange and deadly power, which filled him with an overwhelming fear. The effect upon him was devastating. He fled.

When he arrived home he was ashen, and his wife said that he looked almost like one dead himself.

Mr Funnell was so shaken by his experience that he told the story to the Vicar of his Church, who arranged an exorcism. What took place at the exorcism was not revealed, but the exorcist, a Sussex man, claimed to have been able to make contact easily with this troubled spirit and was able to give it such comfort as was necessary to prevent its further activities in Finsbury Place.

Whether one can believe this or not, the Funnells were not troubled any more by this particular ghost. They presently left the building which was pulled down, flats being erected in its place. But strange noises are still reported from the part of the flats approximating the position where the little office and cloakroom were.

The feeling of malignancy, directed towards him, as opposed to his own natural fear, which was reported by Mr Funnell, raises interesting questions. He described it specifically as a feeling of hate towards him. Some would say it was an evil spirit "from the bottomless pit of hell" and this would explain the sensation he felt. On the other hand the exorcist apparently did not come into contact with any malignant spirit of this kind. There may have been more than one spirit there, of course. Judging by the uproar sometimes heard in the place there must have been a whole flock of ghosts disturbing the building.

There are some who think that the dead are envious of the living, hating them because they possess flesh and blood they no longer have, and desires and lusts they can no longer satisfy. This is a very old idea and is embodied in the primeval Cult of the Dead, which held that the young in particular resent death and return to the place of their demise in order to torment and terrify the living.

Equally terrifying and somewhat more grisly was the experience some years ago of a Brighton antiquarian. He had heard that there was a hoard of old books in the basement of a junk shop near the junction of Upper Rock Gardens and Edward Street, a part of Brighton which was built in the early years of the nineteenth century.

He found the books stored in what had been the old kitchen and which was now disused—a musty, desolate place which did not boast an electric light. His attention was particularly drawn to an alcove in which was a great stone sink shaped like an ancient sarcophagus. Above the alcove was an archway of small, blood-red bricks set in a curious zig-zag pattern. The place had a strange, eerie atmosphere, and had it not been for the very promising collection of old books which were stored there he would not have cared to stay. It was getting towards evening, and the owner of the junk shop said that he never remained in the place after dark, and gave him the keys, telling him to look through the books at his leisure and lock the place up when he went.

Arming himself with a couple of candles, a flask of coffee and some sandwiches, the antiquarian settled down in the gloomy basement and began to browse through the fascinating books he found there, oblivious at first of the silence which was deep, oppressive and unearthly.

After a while a feeling of macabre chill began to creep over him. The place had an atmosphere of evil as well as coldness which made him feel afraid and uneasy. Suddenly the books lost all interest for him and he could not shake off the feeling that he was not alone in that silent, candle-lit basement kitchen, with its great coffin-like sink, and that someone—or indeed something—was there also, watching him.

He stood up suddenly and looked towards the archway, and to his terror he saw a naked woman standing beside that dreadful sink. The woman was fat, almost shapeless, and his terror was caused by the fact that she had the face of someone long dead, with eyeless sockets and cheeks falling in with decay. But her limbs, he said, were swollen and blotched. It was an appalling and ghastly sight.

The spectre seemed to hover there beside the great sink, the eyeless sockets appearing to be fixed upon him.

"Who are you? What do you want?" stammered the terrified antiquarian.

If he expected a reply—and ghosts sometimes do reply, though it is said they have to be spoken to first before they can speak themselves—he was disappointed. The ghost just stood there, or rather hovered, before his eyes.

He had a book in his hand and he suddenly flung it at the apparition. It went straight through her and hit the archway behind. Then slowly the thing disappeared.

Gathering his belongings, the antiquarian left in a hurry, no longer interested in the fascinating old books.

He had arranged to leave the keys with a woman who lived in the upper part of the tall old house.

"Good gracious me, sir!" she exclaimed when he knocked on her door. "Have you been down there in that dungeon? You look as pale as a ghost. Me—I wouldn't go down there for all the money in the world. The old boy had no right to let you—not after dark."

The antiquarian asked what it was down there that was so frightening, not revealing what he himself had seen, and the woman told him that the basement had been haunted for the past half-century or so, and that she herself had once met the ghost on the old cellar stairs, and the thing had gone right through her, leaving her in a state of shivers for weeks afterwards and bringing back her rheumatism and arthritis in the most painful fashion.

It transpired that about sixty years previously a man had murdered his wife in that kitchen and had dismembered her body in that great old sink, with the object of burying the remains underneath the stone floor of the kitchen. Fortunately the law caught up with him before he could complete his odious work.

A Mayoress of Brighton, as well as a Mayoress of Hove, was involved with a Brighton ghost. This was Mrs Anne Johnson, wife of Major A. J. M. Johnson, T.D., who was Mayor of Brighton in 1960–61. Shortly after the last war Mrs Johnson was living in a flat in Prestonville Road.

Every night as she got into bed she noticed a curious sensation that somebody else was sitting on the end of the bed, although no one else was in the room. After a while, the invisible presence vanished. She got used to her nightly unseen visitor, although she did not stay in that particular flat for long. After she had vacated the place, a retired member of the Brighton Police Force told her that it was at that flat and in that very room that a man had murdered his wife. Mrs Johnson is not a psychic type of woman and has never had such experiences either before or since.

A curious haunting took place at the turn of the century in Whitchurch House, one of those large detached residences which face Brighton's Preston Park on the main road coming into the town, and it was told many years later by a woman who had been a housemaid there at the time, now a Mrs M. E. Holland of Woodingdean, Brighton.

Whitchurch House stood in its own grounds and had its own stables and coachhouse. Leading off the dining-room was a small room called the den, which had french windows opening on to the lawn. Mrs Holland's duties included cleaning the den, which she did at six-thirty every morning.

At this hour precisely every morning these french windows slowly opened and slowly shut again. At first Mrs Holland thought it was the wind, or that it was a trick by one of the other maids. But there was no wind and there were no other maids about.

What was really strange was the fact that when the doors opened they were securely locked and bolted, and so they were after they had closed again.

This happened regularly every morning at half-past six. The puzzled Mrs Holland regarded the phenomenon with great curiosity. She tried to stop them while they were being opened in this peculiar manner, but was unable to, for they were being moved by an irresistible force. Once she opened the doors herself before half-past six, but they immediately shut themselves and waited until the appointed time.

On each occasion when the doors opened themselves in this mysterious way, cold air came into the den, regardless of whether it was cold outside or not.

Becoming frightened, Mrs Holland told the master of the house, who at first laughed at her, but then got up early one morning and witnessed the phenomenon himself. Visibly shaken, he sold up and left the house immediately, leaving the mystery unsolved.

This is the kind of ghost story which surely no one could possibly have invented.

INDEX

Acknowledgements

The editor and publishers express their acknowledgements to Geoffrey Bles, Ltd., and the Executors of the late Lord Halifax for permission to condense from *Lord Halifax's Ghost Book*, and to Rider and Co. for permission to condense from *Ghosts with a Purpose* by Elliott O'Donnell.